Paul Verhaeghen

Omega Minor

Dalkey Archive Press
CHAMPAIGN • LONDON

Originally published in Dutch as *Omega Minor* by
Meulenhoff | Manteau (2004)
Copyright © 2004 Meulenhoff | Manteau en Paul Verhaeghen
Translation copyright © 2007 by Paul Verhaeghen

First English Translation, 2007

Library of Congress Cataloging-in-Publication Data

Verhaeghen, Paul.
[Omega minor. English]
Omega minor / Paul Verhaeghen.
p. cm.
ISBN-13: 978-1-56478-477-3 (alk. paper)
ISBN-10: 1-56478-477-0 (alk. paper)
I. Title.
PT6466.32.E663O5413 2004
833'.914--dc22
2007025354

The translation of this book was funded by the Flemish Literature Fund
(Vlaams Fonds voor de Letteren—www.fondsvoordeletteren.be)

Partially funded by grants from the National Endowment for the Arts,
a federal agency, the Illinois Arts Council, a state agency,
and by the University of Illinois, Urbana-Champaign

www.dalkeyarchive.com

• This translation is for Shelley, who is always there •

Omega Minor

Pour ma part, je dirai que tous les livres sur la vie pèsent moins qu'une vie d'homme. Mais, direz-vous : quelle vie? quel homme? La réponse est : n'importe lesquels. Dieu seul juge ses créatures en termes absolus. Nous ne possédons pas ce pouvoir. Elles ont toutes les mêmes droits. Leur existence relève du même mystère.

(As far as I am concerned, I would say that all books on life carry less weight than the life of a single human being. You may ask: what life?, what human being? The answer is: it does not matter. Only G*d judges his creatures in absolute terms. That power is not ours. All G*d's creatures have the same rights. Their existence is rooted in a shared mystery.)

• Elie Wiesel •

Ich gedenke nicht. Ich bin hier, mehr weiß ich nicht, mehr kann ich nicht tun. Mein Kahn ist ohne Steuer, er fährt mit dem Wind, der in den untersten Regionen des Todes bläst.

(I have no intentions. I am here, that is all I know. There is nothing more that I can do. My boat has lost its helm, it rides on the wind which blows in the nether regions of death.)

• Franz Kafka •

OPHELIA, UPON DROWNING
(A Form of Prelude)

Im Anfang war die Tat—In the Beginning was the Act.

And this is what concludes that act, that serpentine pas-de-deux so skillfully performed against the satin backdrop of the blackest night: A lightning bolt hurls upward in a blinding curve of pristine white, the laws of gravity suspended for a quarter-second. There is a scream of triumph as the gushing garland—that string of boundless energy—spouts into the springtime air: With a dull thud the alabaster blob flops on a silken belly, tan and taut and humid with moonlight, and in the panting silence after the victory cry the room echoes with the silent howl of half a billion mouths that never were: 23-chromosome cells thrash their tiny tails in terror on the bare and barren skin. An illicit hand sends another power surge through his penis, fiercer still than the first—then a compassionate tongue descends, its trembling tip dipping into the basin of his navel: For an instant, a sticky thread of pearls connects the woman with the Center of his Being, then she swallows—*she drinks my seed*, he thinks, *she WANTS my seed*, and the thought makes his heart swell, not with love but with misplaced pride—and then her lips slide full over his lingam and the last fruits of her labor slither down her shiny throat. And while the man's mouth is still screaming in triumph, the gametic hordes yell out in *Todesangst*, for their worst nightmare has come true: In the woman's churning stomach the cell membranes break open, the molecules dissolve, and the strands of code unwind, and naked lies the blueprint, the secret of who Goldfarb is—the nucleic acids adenine, cytosine, guanine, and thymine swirl around in irreparable chaos, their alchemy forever lost. Here lies a man, exulting over the demise of a world population.

In the Beginning—*beresheet*—was the Act.

And the Act was sterile. Though that didn't make it less pleasant. Or less meaningful. It was mystical, maybe, or even magical, that act—and certainly maniacal.

"Cigarette?"

It did not occur to Goldfarb to ask the question: "Was it as good for you, ma'm, as it so clearly was for me?" Goldfarb did not need verbal affirmation. Goldfarb observes the cosmos. In Goldfarb's presence, a woman's body never lies. Goldfarb's women are always satisfied. Right?

"Cigarette?"

Our mind has the technology. Let us unlock the permanence of memory and use it to our advantage.

Let's rewind time, let's force the clock to swallow its own digits. We'll choose a starting point and we'll take it—slowly—from there. Remember. It is springtime. Even though there's still a dusting of snow on the ground, the daffodils outside the *Gästehaus* wave their heavy crowns in the golden light of the lamp that hangs above the entrance. Memory's trickery rewinds the time. The young woman removes her lips from her lover's cock, a narrow thread of pearly liquid flows from her mouth onto his belly, and then that stream suddenly jumps back into his bloated glans. Watch how it swells; observe her teasing the creamy harvest back down into his balls—isn't it so much more exciting to watch in slow motion? Let us release the clock again: Behold the purple head that sways so swiftly on its heavy stalk; see how it glistens with her spit and juices; watch the little crater at the top spit out its zigzag line—out shoots the slime, the whirling weathervane, the drunken comet that climbs past the stars: In the moist cloud chamber of Donatella's room a signal lights up in silvery white, an almost perfect circle described by the tumbling ribbon of spunk, an acrobatic snake snapping at—but missing—its own tail: an ancient Greek symbol, the letter Omega, capitalized—Ω.

•

Im Anfang . . .

Not every act ends with those deadly acids.

For instance.

On April 1st 1964, my father had one hell of a surprise in store for the woman who would soon become my mother. In a hotel hallway in Paris (Yes, a hallway, not a room. "Hotel Falstaff, or something like that? Or Hotel Parnasse? What was the name again, poochie-bear?" My dad mumbles an answer from behind his newspaper. He always mumbles. He hasn't even heard the question; he has given up listening to my mother a long time ago), he had let the shriveled walnuts in his scrotum take full possession of his brains: A meager load of burning hurt shot up into my mother's plumbing—that final squirt from which, nine months later, your narrator would so reluctantly be born. They'd been going at it the whole night long, my mother and my father, they'd been chewing and clawing at each other for hours, in wild abandon, in the utter nakedness only a one-night stand with a perfect stranger in a foreign land can provide, and the only reason I was conceived by one of those terminally exhausted swimmers, from those very last drops squeezed out of his aching balls, and not by a more strapping fellow from a previous batch, was that the six-pack of condoms that my dad had so gallantly purchased at the all-night pharmacy was all used up, and that my mother, convulsing in her umpteenth orgasm of the night ("I am not keeping track, *chérie*, I'm not an accountant," she had said, and the private joke was that he in fact *was* an accountant on a business trip for his bosses, the firm of Ofer and Dunn-Witt, importers/exporters—mostly export tonight, one might say), dizzy from the booze and the excess of raw sex, had just seconds before thrown away the towel supposed to cover her nakedness while she and her lover were on their way to the shower. She had her hand firmly planted around the root of his penis, and she had begged Mr. Andermans to please-please-*please* do it to her one more time, please baby: more, more, *more!*, and my dad had obliged, for we all know that under such circumstances—a woman's hand around his cock—a man cannot refuse.

More, she had said.

Gimme more.

More!

More! More! MORE!

It does not bode well. What good could come from this? What good could come from the lonely last spermatozoon left after a night of terminally heavy drinking and total physical exhaustion?

Case in point: What came from that final tired cell was me.

•

14

My father is an amateur poet. Here is one of his haikus:

First five syllables.
Next line seven syllables.
And then back to five.

This poem dates from his self-declared iconoclastic period (around 1978).

There was a time, or so my mother tells me, that I worshipped the man. That I learned his poems by heart. They were not easy to find. He only managed to get them published in small mimeographed magazines, the cheap ink stained your fingers as you touched the page, so that the very act of reading destroyed the text. I have been told that as a child I recited his poems out loud before I went to bed. The rhythms lulled me to sleep and the turgid metaphors invaded my dreams, dreams full of shifting sands and winding walls and winds sweeping over moonlit plains and angels soaring over the landscape, carried away on mysterious winds—that sort of thing. More than once I woke up screaming at the top of my lungs, batting at imaginary gulls that were screeching around my head.

I would have preferred to imagine that I had been conceived in a spontaneous display of pure beauty. My mother and father as ballet dancers caught in a smooth, nimble mating dance; his magnificently gleaming lingam sliding effortlessly in and out of her luscious yoni, glistening with the glow of an eternal love that transcended everything. And then things went seriously wrong between the two of them; something happened that set them against each other for the rest of their mortal existence.

That something, I imagined, was me. If not for me, my parents would have lived a long and happy life filled with heavenly fucks in foreign beds on countless business trips. But we know how it went, in those days: You knocked up a woman, you got married, and then you turned prematurely bald. It was all my fault.

For the remainder of her life, my mother would attribute the state of uncharacteristic lewdness in which I was conceived to the bottle of champagne my dad had brought up to the room—the alcohol, she claims, had clouded her judgment. Consequently, she kept warning me against the disastrous side effects of this particular beverage. "The bubbles go straight to your head, my dear," she told me, time after time. "The fumes fill your brain; they chase every possible thought away until all that's left is empty buoyancy." This would start her on one of her ever longer, ever more formulaic litanies of reproaches, and those tirades in turn left my father so dejected that with each repetition he would withdraw deeper and deeper into his lonely misery. I never knew why he didn't simply stop her; why he didn't tell his wife what he should have told her years before, the words that would have saved his marriage, namely that it hadn't been the bubbly alcohol that had driven him to her, not the giddy sensation of having a live oyster slide down his throat for the very first time, not just the loneliness of the hotel room that had lured him into the bar and finally into her arms—no, he had really fallen for *her*, instantly, in the blink of an eye—the blink of *her* eye—he had fallen in love with *her*. It wasn't the alcohol that had so terminally intoxicated him, but her eyes and the way she had smiled at him across the hotel bar. It was as if she had been waiting for him all her life; for him and him alone rose the scent of Chanel from her cleavage in such a sultry whisper. She had put a spell on him. But when the barrage of reproaches started, he somehow never worked up the courage to tell her; the courage to tell her that he loved her. He did the decent thing: He married her and forgot that he had once loved her. She checked out the next morning, leaving nothing but the scent of Chanel on his sheets and on his raw dick. A soon as she found out she was pregnant, she called him at his company. When he showed up on her doorstep an hour later, with flowers in his hands and lips eager to kiss her, she smacked him across the face with the thorny end of the bouquet and dragged him to the town hall. I was conceived in sin, okay, nothing you can do about that, but she was making damn sure I wouldn't be born out of wedlock.

Maybe my dad just refused to save his love. Maybe he felt the need to suffer; maybe he felt he needed to atone for those few hours of uncharacteristic abandon. For once in his life he had thrown caution to the wind, and it was only fair that he should bear the consequences of his thoughtlessness. His advice to me echoed my mom's. "Think hard, my dear boy"—such were his words—"Think before you act."

My father was a dreamer—read his windy poems if you don't believe me. Dreamers rarely accomplish great things. His hotel stint was his only act of heroism; the only time he made a dream of his into reality. He suffered for it. Hence his advice: "Think hard, my boy. Think before you act." Later I learned there were other things he regretted. His idiot brother, for instance, who died a horrible death in a faraway land. Yet another boy who didn't think hard enough before he acted.

Of course I have no brothers or sisters. My parents thought so mercilessly hard before they acted that they never even had sex again, I suspect. Of course I had a lonely childhood. I looked for solace in books and I found it. I couldn't find love at home, so I adopted it from literature.

As a child, I thought it was my fault. Later, I *knew* it was my fault. Without me, my father would have never seen my mother again. The sheer fact of my existence transformed their one night of mindless bliss into a marriage-long dark night of the soul. By the time I started working on my dissertation (*Mood-Dependent*

Memory and Overshadowing: A Study in Episodic Priming) and was finally making a living, courtesy of the National Fund for Scientific Research, their divorce was final and the marriage undone.

It has been said that the male of the species gets imprinted with the memory of the victorious spermatozoon. We are forever looking for a way out of a dark labyrinth. But me, I stumble through my small apartment and crash into chairs that stand where they have always stood. I have been told that I was named after my father's brother. It looks like I did not inherit his wanderer's spirit.

The hotel story! Imagine the confusion of the young prepubescent boy who asks his mother in all the perversity of prehormonal naïveté how exactly he came into being, and then gets to hear *that story*. For a long time, my confusion bordered dangerously on desperation.

Fortunately, my parents spared me the most intimate details. But as soon as I reached puberty—did I mention I read way too many books?—my imagination, usually my ally, my solace, and my anchor, unhelpfully filled in the particulars. My mind projected in front of me, in vivid color, the loud and lewd events in that hotel hallway. I saw him kneeling behind her, his hands digging into her hips, his flesh pounding hard into hers. Then again I imagined how she lay nailed beneath him, her hands clutching her wet, tangled hair in some sort of Victorian despair, her head rhythmically banging against the floor, her mouth wide open, her buttocks red and raw, her pupils turned upwards in the rolling waves of ecstatic oblivion.

I read way too much. I stole this image of ecstasy out of a book, from the reproduction of a painting, *Ophelia, Upon Drowning*—W. G. Simmonds, 1910. Indeed, I allowed myself to compare the aftermath of the vulgar act that led to my conception to the aftermath of Ophelia's final, ultimate act of love—that is, to the ultimate exhaustion, the final kenosis, the fatal tragedy of a great, unnecessary, self-inflicted death. The white dress billowing under the drowned woman's shoulders looks like the open, lifeless wing of an enormous angel.

•

No surprise in this novel's opening. If you read a story set in Potsdam and Berlin, you should expect a fair amount of spying, no? I admit that I witnessed the aforementioned act, my stinging eye glued to the keyhole of Donatella's room. The hot air dries my tears quickly, although it's no comfort to know that all that heat has been generated by the ardent, gymnastic, and apparently never-ending lovemaking that said eye has been witnessing.

My father and mother in their hallway—quite a number of eyes must have been spying on the exposed beauty of their intertwining bodies, with a gleam of disapproval or a hint of lust or mirth. Or jealousy perhaps.

The hallway is cold, the naked concrete hurts my knees. Mefista runs circles around me, then she gets impatient. She head-butts my thighs and presses her head against Donatella's door. Her movements make the door knock against its frame. The sound returns me to my senses. It's a familiar sound for those who live here—the hallway is drafty, the door locks are worn; every time somebody opens a door all other doors in the hallway start to rattle—but it's still probably safer for me to retreat. Mefista thinks so too. She places one paw on my knee and scratches me with apparent gusto. The claws pierce through the heavy cotton of my jeans; she knows that this short, sharp pain will get my attention. I lift her off the floor and the compact heat of her small body, the softness of her fur, her little purring engine warm my heart. She generously rubs the scent of her eye glands into my T-shirt. We cross the hallway to my room. Time to go to bed.

I'm really not to blame for this bout of voyeurism. It's not my habit to spy on my neighbors. Blame the kitty. I let her out around six, and she came back home around midnight, crying her usual two-note *me-ow* underneath my window. The cry was just loud enough to climb up the wall and penetrate the thin glass behind which I was working—not on a scientific article, but on my damn book. I ran downstairs as soon as I heard her. She was sitting right in front of the door, her white neck stretched proudly towards me, a freshly picked daffodil between her teeth. Mefista brings me a present every night. I fear her gifts. Sometimes it's a small animal from the woods: a little dead bird wet with cat spit, or a field mouse still quivering. Sometimes she leads me to a small puddle of vomit that glistens with tiny white bones. Once she deposited a balled-up piece of paper with hastily scribbled equations at my feet. Another time she proudly displayed—where did she get it?—a used condom. And although I'm scared of what Mefista brings, I invariably lavish praise on her and stroke her little chin. Then she follows me inside and runs up the concrete stairs, two, three steps at a time. When she gets to the landing she waits for me and then she pushes open the door of our room, happy to be home. Don't laugh, but I do think that this is love, the kind of love I learned about in my childhood books. I share my milk with her and I shake pellets of cat food into a bowl; in return, she brings me the spoils of her foraging trips and the sweet warmth of her nearness.

We had just gotten to the top of the stairs, that evening in March, Mefista's flower sticking from the neck of my T-shirt, its golden trumpet tickling my throat, when I heard those rutting sounds coming from my neighbor's room. My heart sank instantly.

Had I peeked around the corner when I went down to pick up Mefista, I might have noticed a paint-splattered ladder rising out of the bushes, propped right under a second-story window. If Mefista would have finished her tour of duty just an hour earlier, I might have observed an older gentleman scaling that ladder on the soft leather soles of a pair of fashionable black Salamander moccasins, goose grass and thorns stuck in his pant cuffs—a man with short white hair, his footwork swift and firm, the gleam of conquest in his eyes and a panther's smile on his lips, slipping inside with the assured grace of someone who had performed this particular trick a thousand times before. I would have recognized that man at once: He was one of the heroes of my childhood, the man who wrote all those popular books on dumbed-down astronomy. The man's reputation had by now sunk far from its original zenith; he was like one of those red giants he used to write about, slowly turning into a white dwarf. And yet he was apparently still scaling the heavens, on the way to his very own red-haired angel waiting for him behind the open window, ready to receive him in her slender arms and loving womb.

•

Why him? Why Goldfarb? The question kept me awake all night, while Mefista dreamt of all kinds of tasty morsels, sniffing and licking her lips and twitching her legs in anticipation. In my distress, I didn't realize that I was asking the wrong question. The real question was: why me? The lighting in the room had been sparse. Why had it been arranged so that I could get such a good look? Why had Donatella positioned herself so that I might witness every little detail through her keyhole? And why had she launched their noisy endgame at the precise moment when I arrived at the top of the stairs? Donatella was well aware of Mefista's habits; she must have heard me go down to open the front door, she must have heard Mefista's cry of triumph when she ran upstairs. It had all been a bit *too much*—Donatella's screams had sounded a little too spectacular, her body contorted just so, the timing a tad too convenient. Donatella's passion must have been staged, and not just for the benefit of her lover—the intent must have been to communicate something to *me*. But whatever it was that Donatella was trying to tell me, I didn't get it. I fell into the classical Hollywood trap: I was concentrating so hard on the protagonists that I neglected to pay attention to the plot and the subtext. I stored the image and the soundtrack in my memory, I retained the superficial features of the scene, but I had no clue as to the underlying Truth.

Did I say I stored the image? Stored is too weak a word. The episode got *branded* into my mind. Painfully so. Inescapably so.

Over the next few days, the memory of the event kept popping randomly into my head with cold precision and painful persistence. But something was wrong with that memory. In my mind's eye, it were indeed Goldfarb and Donatella's bodies that I saw hotly fused like flames in a furnace, but the faces bobbing on top of those bodies were not theirs—the faces I saw were my mom and dad's, as immortalized in their wedding photograph. If only my parents had concluded their lovemaking the same way Goldfarb and Donatella did, life would have been different. You would have never heard of me or my misery.

For all their falsehood, those images tortured me relentlessly. They forced themselves upon me when I shut off my computer screen at the end of the day; they awaited me in the kitchen when I came to get some butter from the fridge; they popped up when I turned on the shower. Like legendary monsters, they surfaced and resurfaced from the cool dark lakes of my memory, polluting the fresh waters of my conscious mind with their slimy scales. There they were, inflicting themselves on me even as I was fighting the howling wind and the punishing rain on my way to the *Komplex I–Neues Palais* bus stop, on my way to see the man who was waiting for me in Berlin with his stack of stories—even on that noble quest, those images intruded.

Ever since those mischievous Viennese twins, the Jew and the Christian Hindu, concocted their theories, it is impossible to consider Eros without invoking the image of Thanatos as well. Behold the dark cloud of smoke that rises from the torch in his hand. Do we not shudder to see the shadow of the butterfly he clutches in his other hand, the grotesquely flickering patterns on the walls of our cave?

So, yes: Those memories pumped cruel blood through my heart and utterly shameful blood into my sex, and so I needed some distraction, and therefore it was with great zeal that I threw myself—not yet purified by Fire—into the continued writing of The Great Book.

We all make our mistakes, small or big.

But enough about me.

How are *you* doing?

PART ONE

TAMAS

ב

THE NAME

The first thing I noticed was that the birds were no longer silent.

That sentence started everything.

The letters are staring back at me, in blue ink on a white page in DIN A4 format—the good old *Deutsche Industrienorm*. The words themselves originated in my associative cortex, conjured up in 40 Hz impulses after a few milliseconds of careful weighing in the anterior structures of my frontal lobes. The connotations of those words, their full impact and their broader context, are all still implicit, available only to those neural networks. My memory is a conspiracy on the point of being uncovered. My neurons are slyly stretching their dendrites; they cautiously lift their tentacles, scribbling their graffiti, unreadable for now, on the inside of the bone box.

Here comes sentence number two. And there goes number three. Etcetera. I watch in shock and disbelief; with utter revulsion I observe the insidious alchemy that covers the page with glyphs:

> *A tree rises.*
> *Oh—pure transcendence.*
> *On a branch a dove sits.*
> *White as a blank piece of paper.*
> *She coos.*

Those sentences are deadly, even though they seem to be breathing freedom—even though they must *mean* freedom.

One lonely dove cooing? G*d, my head is exploding with a true orgy of sound—from the fields, from the woods, from what must be the heavens themselves the multitudes descend, all bearing down on that poor tree, a thousand birds of a thousand feathers, each of them singing their own song, different from all the others, each of them fighting to drown out the others. No longer silent? All hell breaks loose in that tree: chirping, peeping, chattering, squeaking, cheeping, chipping, tweeting, twittering, warbling, all at ear-splitting volume. The naked tree has become a tree of Babel: all possible bird species gathered on its branches, each one showcasing its most personal gimmick, its highest notes, its most magnificent trills—and all that mingling beauty quickly turns to harsh cacophony.

This is not according to plan. The price you pay for survival is anesthesia. Every camp survivor I've ever met confirms this. It's the simplest truth about survival. You have to live your life under a bell jar. You have to keep the lid firmly on your memories. It's best that way.

No, I'm not doing too well, right now. I'm staring at the blank space at the bottom of the page and I fear the words that will appear. I fear the Auschwitz that they will summon.

Outside the window, the world rages—a twilight zone of glass and concrete. Rain falls solemnly. The buildings are so colorlessly gray that they vanish in the drizzle. This city is condemned to live in an eternal fog, in an everlasting in-between season that dares not speak its name. No wonder that the local myths of immortality, the Wagnerian dramas that draw the masses to the opera houses, are so sluggish and top-heavy. Their strength lies in muscular power, in heroic courage and mysterious anonymity; they have nothing in common with the sheer madness of the Greek heart. If Orpheus had been German he would have entered the underworld with a drawn sword instead of a lyre with broken strings. I can hear them bragging and brawling out on the street, those would-be Lohengrins, even though I live twenty stories high. The flat rectangles of cheap GDR-brand glass can't stop that stampede of acoustics—they yell and bark, they flex their muscles, they open their throats wide and shake their swollen tongues; they pound their heads frantically to the broken beat of the savage songs that explode out of the deeply moronic boom boxes they carry on their shoulders: melodies shouted, never sung, in perplexing languages. Cheap, worthless concrete! Twenty stories high I live, and I can still hear the subway train entering the subway station one block east from here, balancing high on rails that converge in an illusory vanishing point far beyond the horizon. It's as if the sound waves get stuck in the air bubbles in the cement (it was mixed too carelessly, too fast), and get released only slowly, bit by bit—what I'm hearing now might as well be reaching me from a distant past, with no use for the present; it has nothing to do with the oppressive, relentless *now* that teems outside.

It has its advantages, this dissonance of the outside world. For instance, the birds do keep quiet in this city, shouted down by the surges of white noise that the blond beasts pump through their territory. No cooing pigeon, no croaking magpie can imagine winning the struggle against this unfathomable display of libido, those incomprehensible cries of electric lust under a sky dripping with gray. So the birds hide their beaks in their sorry coats of feathers and—as politely requested—they shut the fuck up.

My room is littered with books. An hour or so ago, I was looking for stories that told of a solace no longer granted by the outside world. But I dropped the books with a sharp cry of disappointment when I realized they held nothing that could comfort me. Now they clutter the floor in insufferable chaos, the type of chaos from which nothing ever gets born. They're piled high on the carpet and on the tables and on the seats of chairs, leaning drunkenly against each other, their margins packed with edgy, scratchy scribbles, their priceless leather bindings stained with ink and coffee and powdered with the ashes of fine cigars—it is my opinion that certain books can only be fully understood through the slightly intoxicating haze of pure Cuban tobacco.

Here is a lesson learned from books. G*d created the world out of thirty-two secret paths of wisdom. Ten digits and twenty-two letters were all He needed. Out of the ten digits—the Sephirot—He created the abstract entities. Out of combinations of the twenty-two letters He created reality. After this act of creation was completed, each of the new beings took their prescribed place in the three concentric strata of the cosmos: the world, time, and the human body. Moral of the story: The universe—all that is, and all that happens—is a Book, written in Digits and Letters.

And here is another old Jewish story. Two Talmudic scholars, Hanani and Hoshayah, met twice a week to study the Books. They labored for years; they were trying to crack the code; they wanted to imitate G*d's act of creation. Then finally they were successful. Out of the correct combination of letters they crafted a live three-year old calf. And here is an old Jewish lesson: After achieving this triumph, they took a big knife and led the calf to the grilling iron and relished in its flesh.

It's late in the game. G*d's no longer in the business of creating. And when I look around me, can I still find rabbis that take the trouble to actually *read?* *Ach!* Reading is always in vain. That too is old Jewish wisdom. In the Babylonian

Talmud, the first page of each treatise is missing, to remind the reader that no matter how far he has advanced in his studies he has not even arrived at the first page yet.

Books. Franz Kafka, yet another Jew, earned his living by day in the *Arbeiter-Unfall-Versicherings-Anstalt* of the kingdom of Bohemia, juggling digits and numbers in a boring office job in the insurance trade. By night he lived among letters and wrote the most bizarre stories. On his deathbed, Herr Kafka asked his friend Max Brod to burn these writings. The scholars assume that Kafka meant to imply that he was not worthy. (And Max Brod was, thank G*d, a treacherous friend.) But how can we be so certain that this was indeed the case? Maybe all Kafka was trying to tell us was that every story is ultimately unfinished—that it is really the reader who spins the tale. The text as such does not exist—it is nothing more than mental space in the mind of the reader. Every library is like the library of Alexandria, doomed to burn. Every piece of theater is a failed attempt to recreate one of Aeschylos's eighty-three lost plays. Livy's masterpiece has forever disappeared, and nobody will ever read Aristotle's essay on laughter. Nine days before his death, Nikolai Gogol shoved the second part of *Dead Souls* into his fireplace. The flame, oh yes, the trusty flame is the fate of most writing. Would it be so terribly strange to presume that Kafka knew very well that Brod would not destroy his manuscripts, but instead would try to get them published? Sometimes, the threat alone suffices. But if Max Brod had really thrown everything into the fire, Kafka might have been even more famous than he is now.

Good. Here they are then, my books, their dust jackets torn, piled high in jumbled stacks. From time to time, there is one that makes its escape and slides down to the ground with a dull thud. In its disorder, this mob of books is itself like a radically postmodern novel that carries within itself the flame of its own destruction, a shabby crowd of stories that resolutely and tastelessly refuse to solidify into a purposeful whole, much to the dismay of the bourgeois reader. I hope somebody has the good taste to throw them all away.

The Lord G*d ordered John of Patmos to eat the Book. It was honey on my tongue, wrote John, but it sat bitter in my belly.

I open the encyclopedia. I become John and I force myself to eat the pages that contain images of soporific, analgesic, poisonous plants. The pages indeed sit heavy in my stomach.

In spite of everything, I keep listening to the sounds from the outside world, the feverish sounds of an early evening in the weekend. And I also turn to my inner world and there I conjure up what I saw with my very own two eyes half a century ago—a world adrift, a world in which murder was no longer a crime but a duty. My library, spread out over my apartment, over shelves, armoires, tables, chairs, and floor, is testimony to humankind's wrestling with that past; these books all struggle with those specters of long ago: They wage war with the reality of Century XX. How can words fight the masses of men in uniforms of brown and gray and black; how can they battle those mourning bands of red and white in which the poisonous Aryan spider has sunk it jet-black claws? Century XX. Suddenly the world turns the color of night, the color of blood, and the color of the blinding light of an all-consuming explosion.

The struggle of Text against World. The World wins.

There were rabbinic scholars in the camps who tried to divine YHVH'S intentions by placing the forearms of prisoners together and reading the number combinations formed by the combined tattoos. YHVH: just another four-letter word used as a dam against the four-pointed cartwheel. We want to understand. We *need* to understand. An academic cottage industry has emerged based on that most noble of human endeavors, namely to understand precisely *this*—this monstrous genocide, this senseless but massively successful mass slaughter. Well, *Herrn Professoren*, have we made any progress yet?

G*tt mit uns—G*d be with us. I don't think so. G*d is G*d, He has no human traits. What kind of explanation could there be? Was the Supreme Being perchance taking a nap? Did He set us up for some sort of perverse ordeal? Was this a punishment of sorts? Here is what I think: I think the twentieth century was just not Hashem's. It wasn't the time for orderly signs. I maintain in all sincerity that there is nothing to understand here. Keep on walking. What is, is. Humans are human. Big deal.

Not exactly an edifying conclusion. This is, after all, the century of the illusion of knowledge. We firmly believe that the world in which we live is ultimately comprehensible. Yet the only reason why we hold on to this absurd notion is that little flesh machine lodged inside our skulls; it's hooked on meaning and cohesion. Something clicks between the synchronicity waves of our neuronal fields and certain harmonic structures in our perception. That is all. The world is an illusion.

The lesson of this past century must surely be that reality is beyond our understanding, that behavior is irrational, and that the world is governed by the most brutal chaos. But that's not what we have learned. On the contrary. We can't sustain our attentions for very long, and so we have shrunk the Ten, the Twenty-Two, to just One. Everything has its origin, or so we suppose, in One Single Moment, the moment of the Big Bang. And we go on to claim that this is all there is, that everything logically follows from that point: The universe expands and then it freezes over and everything dies in the stiffening cold. One shot is all we get: One shot is all the universe gets.

My memory, so cruelly cracked open by that one sentence that appeared out of quasi-nowhere on a piece of paper, is not just my own—it is the memory of a people.

(*Numbers 33:55*. Over and over. And over. And over.)

The first thing I noticed was that the birds were no longer silent.

I crumple the piece of paper as quickly as I can; I don't want the words to escape and slip through the cracks in the window—I don't want them to get out into the world. A sentence like this should simply not exist. It certainly shouldn't be allowed outside. I shred the page into ribbons and then I shred the ribbons into confetti—I want to make sure that nobody will ever, ever read this. What good could words like these do? What good is another set of deep and righteous memoirs, ready to be excerpted in the glossy Sunday supplements, a subject for whispered conversations at elegant cocktail parties? Life's lifeblood is change. He who is not continuously reinventing himself is dying. He who wants to live needs to get away from himself. If you truly want change, it is your duty to forget.

My memory is the axe that broke the frozen sea inside me—or inside us. I leave it up to you, dear reader, to decide who I mean when I say "us." Maybe you are part of that group, or maybe you're not? Too late for rescue, the ice is broken and the waves are crashing over me. The deadly salt is seeping into my mouth, upsetting the sodium-potassium balance of my central nervous system, and it strangles the very core of my existence—it's the final round in my fight against entropy, and down I go. I swallow, I spit, I—I, I can't stand it any longer.

On the new page that somehow appears under my hand, new words get written, all by themselves, much bleaker than the words I just destroyed, and far less poetic.

As if every sparrow that ever landed on the barbed wire skewered itself to death on the rusty thorns; as if the last robin had scorched itself black in the smokestacks; as if the mere presence of the soldiers in the watchtowers made the starlings turn back.

I have seen rubble before. I have stood knee-high in it; I have seen the flattened world from a man's height, and I know the vertigo it gives you. It makes you shiver; it makes you want to hide from death in half-destroyed hallways. The rubble I am surveying now is the rubble of my own life, and it is I who wrecked it. Is there anyone who survived Auschwitz and had a happy life? Our fate was worse than death. We were given irreparability. Did I really witness how adult men were crushed against brick walls by ridiculously polished black cars? Until they bled to death? Did I see with my own two eyes how fat rats jumped out of piles of human cadavers, freshly harvested intestines trailing from their jaws?

This is too much. Too much for words, too much for my poor old mind packed with books and stories, loaded with theories. The shock of it, time and again. The shock of being alive. To rise, day after day, morning after morning, from the deepest depth of sleep, to wake up with that inescapable sense of dread. All of fifty years. Eighteen thousand nights, and always the same dream, always the same nightmare riding my wheezing chest, foaming at the mouth.

To be alive.

Or else to stop the dreaming.

To have the courage to move forward. To unleash sleep's more radical brother, the fellow with the bare bones, that ill-bred sibling with his hot-headed dog—I don't need a ferry to get me across, sir, I'd rather swim, I can sink and drown very well on my own, thank you, I'll let the undertow carry me to the other side, don't you worry, I'm used to it, I do it every night in my dreams—I swim, I sink, I drown.

Yes, I do need something stronger than sleep. I lower the blinds. The blackout is complete, the last little bit of meager sunlight still out there is safely locked out. The air I breathe is the same air that is always circulating in this room; it reeks of the Big War. Nothing but walls in this house, and each wall has its very own perfectly rectangular hole that leads to another set of walls, each equipped with its very own exactly identical framed hole, that again leads to another set of identical walls.

Once I was a phantom, astonished at the mere existence of sunlight. I used to live in a big flat country without shadows. Light reflected off the river; during the few days of summer it hurt your eyes.

A train journey brought me to this city. Then there was another train journey. The hinges of the cattle wagons screeched, deadbolts squealed. Who among the hierarchy of angels would have heard me, if I cried out? Who would hear me now?

I get up; I limp to the wall. I switch off the lights. I have to hold on to the doorframe or I'll fall. The room is filled with a sudden silence. That means that I must have shouted. The doorframe, my hand—they're covered in blood. I drag my palm over my face and the glass shards of the medicine bottle cut my skin. I must have squeezed it until it broke.

Half an hour ago I took a pill. I swallowed it with some water. Swallow. Pill. Water. Swallow. Pill. Water. Swallow. Pill, pill, water. Swallow. Pill after pill after pill, until my throat hurt. I swallowed the poison, the small-flowered herb of my release.

The world turns liquid. My face becomes what it was before I was born. *Alles will schweben*—well, everything supposedly pines to fly, but I, I want to fall; I want to fall to, no, I want to fall *into* the earth.

I finally found my courage—the courage to forever hold my peace.

What?

What?

There is a clattering outside, somebody is rattling my doorknob, and then there's the sound of breaking wood, and the door is roughly lifted off its hinges. Light flows in from the hallway, fluorescent light—crushing, exploding, cold, sharp, stinging, hard as steel—and in the harshness of the light I spot a silhouette. It sways—I can't see too well, I, I . . . and a sound as if of large wings and . . .

•

In the ambulance that races through the majestic avenues of the Fourth-and-a-Half Reich, he lies gasping for breath under an oxygen mask. His skin feels like ice, his heart pounds erratically. His eyes are wide open, but they cannot see. Someone pulls the wallet out of his back pocket, looking for identification.

What is his name? The Red Cross volunteer had given him the ledger, and a pen. Then she put her hand on his head and ran her fingers through what remained of his hair. Here he was, a survivor fresh from the camps, witness to all the cruelties humans visit on humans, and the lady treated him as if he was a mere child. He defied her, he decided to write his name formally, preceding it with "Mister." So he started writing, with a flourish: "De Heer." Then he faltered. He stared at the words. There was such an enormous disparity between the calmly grown-up man implied by these words, and the harsh, forced growing-up he had been subjected to. Tears came into his eyes and under the lady's tender touch he felt himself shrinking. No longer even a late adolescent, he dwindled further and further, until he was seven years old again, and then smaller that that, and smaller still. His hand refused to cooperate (a bundle of dead branches, wrapped in dead moss), and then he sank beyond the age at which he had learned how to read, and right in front of his eyes the scribbles he had made blurred, became empty, devoid of all meaning. What did his name matter? Though he shouldn't forget that he was now the very last carrier of that name. He looked at the page. "De Heer." He pushed the book away and the lady, endlessly patient, took it in her slender hands, and she took the pen too. She didn't speak German and she didn't speak Dutch, or any other language that he could understand, and so she mistook his non-name for a name and she asked him, a motherly sound in the back of her throat, her eyebrows frowning, her hand wandering through the stubble of his skull, what his first name might be.

He thought about this for a while. A brand new name. That would be good. The forgetting could start right here. He would become a new man.

What name should he choose from the long list of possibilities?

Moshe, Bram, Mordechai, Isha, Ezra, Benjamin? Joshua maybe—G*d saves? The camp had been an excellent education in the higher forms of humor: irony, sarcasm. But why would he want to be branded as a Jew? He had burned his yellow star. He was officially disinfected. He needed a nice Christian name. Something like Hendrik. Johannes maybe. Petrus?

An orderly opens his wallet. For a second, he blinks at the foreignness of the spelling. Then he solemnly intones, for the benefit of his colleague who is filling out the forms: "*Name des Patienten: Jozef De Heer.*"

Jozef, the silent carpenter. Father of the false Messiah. The last Jew, before those pale, murdering Christians imposed their dominion upon the world, before they started acting out their curious obsession with funeral pyres. Yuseph.

Jozef was the perfect name. There was that other Jozef in the camps. The blond angel of Auschwitz, the angel of death who handed out candy to the gypsy children and then led them by the hand to the gas chambers, an imperturbable smile on his lips.

Jozef was a good name. He would be strong, this Jozef De Heer, this new man that he had just invented. Jozef De Heer, a man who would never cry.

•

The Jozef De Heer who was carried into the hospital was not in a state of shock. Rather, he was in a state of complete indifference, truly an old man, a compact bundle of passive resistance, a massive pain in the ass. He would not move. He would not speak. He was a monument, an obstacle, a stumbling block. He sat upright on his stretcher, hands folded across his chest, suffering—cliché of clichés —the pain of being human, the same pain that he had wanted to inflict upon the entire world, less than a few hours ago.

The taste in his mouth turned bitter when he realized he was no longer a survivor.

ג

THE OBSCENITY TRILOGY

"Bloody fuck'n' Krauts."

Danny's facial hair is truly monumental—an impressively frazzled beard and the mane of a lion. It is good to be equipped with a natural filtering device when eating at the Potsdam student restaurant, the Mensa. Thick banks of cigarette smoke float majestically through the long hall. It's hard to see your plate through the smog, and that's probably for the best. Danny shouts it out—he doesn't care if anybody hears. This is his last day here, and he'll *bloody fuck'n'* tell it like it is. Minuscule particles of *Bratwurst* shoot out of his mouth, and the little balls of fat slide over the tabletop as if it were a newly polished skating rink. They fly over the edge and land squarely in my lap. Thank you, Danny.

I had passed on the sausage, although it was the *plat du jour.* The meat—if that was what it was—had been floating in a pool of what looked like pus: Fluorescent bubbles the size of cat's eyes were bobbing in the liquid. I made the understandable mistake—it being my first Friday here—to nod my head in the direction of *der Pizza.* Nobody stopped me, although everybody in the room must have known that Friday's pizza was not a food item but a search engine, topped with the mercilessly burnt memories of every item that had been on the past week's menu (*Putengeschnetzeltes, Brathering mit Zwiebelringen, Szegediner Gulash, Gyrospfanne, Hähnchenhaxen, Frikadelle "Fleischermeister,"* and who knows what these things are anyway?). If you look deep enough into the crust, you might even find remains of last week's pizza. A multilayered Troy, minus the buried treasure.

architecture of gloom. Much like Frederick the Great's architects had built him a mount of romantic ruins to look at from his bedroom window, so did socialism in its former glory impress upon its citizens its particular vision of the collapse of history. Sure, close to the palace the proud villas of the courtiers of Frederick's time are still standing, but safety nets have been spread between the garden walls to catch the crumbling facades, and the balconies are supported by makeshift wooden beams. People here walk about in long trailing coats the color of stones. They look both somber and skittish, as if they rarely spend time outdoors. Even their bodies look gray, and I shudder when I think how dead their souls might be under those gigantic winter coats.

A paved road lead us past Frederick's gardens. Tall wooden crates stood stiffly upright like misplaced vertical coffins. These are the winter cloaks for the imperial statue collection: The combination of winter wetness and hellish cold would make the marble crack if it were exposed to the elements. The packaging will be removed in the spring. That's around the time when my stay here will be over. Why didn't I come here late in May, or during the summer, instead of during winter's long endgame?

We took a turn and arrived on campus. Poles sported yellowing placards that announced now defunct departments of the communist vocational school that was housed here not too long ago. For every arrow pointing at something innocent—the "Music Education Department," for instance—there's one leading off to a more mysterious spot—what is the *Sektion ML*? Some of the inscriptions are quite threatening: This one shows the way to the *Betriebskampfgruppe*, the "Work Combat Unit." According to a disintegrating poster, students here were more than eager to be "firmly joined with the working class, prompted and guided by the militant ardor and the collective wisdom of the Marxist-Leninist party, elevating the youth of our country in the spirit of the worldview and the morals of the working class to become highly educated citizens, in imitation of the combat-filled life of Karl Liebknecht." Imitation, that's what it says—they wanted the students to imitate the martyr, not just to take him as an example; they wanted to fill their pupils' heads with the desire to be shot down by riffraff in a dark lane in the Tiergarten, and then rot forevermore in the putrid waters of the river Spree. Fortunately, the students of 1995 seem to have a brighter outlook on life. I spotted quite a few very Western blue jeans and here and there even an anorak in canary yellow or fire engine red, and even the odd piece of white clothing: white ski coats, white boots, white tennis shoes, white pants, all the more remarkable given that the campus appears to be built on top of a great many varieties of mud, and paved roads here are rare.

Danny steered the car onto a donkey track in the frozen grass that grows between two particularly depressing buildings, and we ended up in a modest grave-yard for Wartburgs and Ladas and Trabants. This turned out to be the parking lot for *Haus Eins*, House One, where I would be living for the next three months. A last rasping of the two-stroke engine was our salute.

Four rusty and alarmingly bent iron columns carried a small concrete roof spanning the entrance. There were crumbs of concrete on the welcome mat. "You would have thought they knew how to mix concrete in the GDR, no? Well, all the good stuff went into that Big Concrete Fence around Berlin, my friend. Don't lean too hard against the walls, will ya?"

A new coating of light green paint had been applied to the hallway, but I could still see the dusty outlines of a few large square frames from which Comrade Ho-necker must have eyed the visitors, an earnest look in his eyes, ready for battle and inspiring courage in all and sundry. Such courage is needed, for instance, to walk up the stairs—the concrete steps don't look all that solid to me. The railing looks like it was flown over from a chalet in Bavaria, the wood painted in a glossy bourgeois white. The plants in the lobby show a remarkable combination of wild proliferation and exhausted shabbiness, as if they had been recruited from a nurs-ing home. Four plastic chairs nearby make a sitting area that doesn't contradict this impression.

Seemingly without effort, Danny lifted my suitcase onto a narrow bed. There were two in the room. That night I would be sharing the room with Danny—the guesthouse was booked full. But what a view from the window! I could see the emperor's old horse stables, now reconfigured into classrooms, and behind that a majestic colonnade, and behind the colonnade a dome of green and black that rises out of an enormous pink brick candy box; it points straight to the heavens. That must be the *Neues Palais*, Frederick's New Palace. Voltaire visited there; it was where Johann Sebastian Bach improvised his *Musical Offering* for the emperor; and it was the place where Wilhelm I had the bright idea to start off the century with World War I.

"You probably want to take a shower."

The shower room confused me. It's huge, for one thing, more a ballroom than a bathroom. It's tiled in gray from floor to ceiling. There are no stalls, just open space with wonderful acoustics, no doubt. The rows of tiles look like the stubby rotting teeth of a panhandler, the grout is cracked and crumbling. I count ten showerheads (everyone on this floor could bathe together), though I wasn't sure that I believed they would spout hot water. This university has a history, as Danny told me on the way down. They used to train security officers here. I turn on one of the faucets, and what comes out is—but how could it be otherwise?—clear, warm, night. The minuscule matters of the mind, the elementary cognitive processes. Try explaining that at a party. Nobody cares. And why would they? It isn't the slightest bit of help to anyone. And that's exactly what makes it perfect for us: It is rarified science. A person can't be asking themselves the Big Questions in life all the time. You need something minor to get you through the day.

I do memory. (That's what we call it in psychology. We "do" memory. Or attention. Or persuasion. Or food attitudes. Whatever it is we do.) "Sure," is what my friends said. "Potsdam. It's obvious, isn't it? Such an old town, centuries old! And Berlin: Berlin is a city built on memory!" I nod pretend-enthusiastically. It takes too much trouble to explain. Cognitive psychology is a beautiful, never-ending enterprise. To lose yourself in the details of the mind, in phenomena that last for only a few milliseconds and then dissolve into the great melting pot of consciousness without leaving a trace, it's like trying to guess the number and function of the cogs of a tiny machine encased in a steel box that has been welded shut, just by shaking it. There's a warning sticker on the outside of the mind: *Warranty void if opened. No user-serviceable parts inside.* Yes, this is the life! This is the real deal; it's like getting a chemistry set for Christmas, but someone forgot to include the instructions.

Danny doesn't run off to the kitchen at parties. He's prepared. He comes with his own small arsenal of stories.

His favorite anecdote is the one about the pigeons. Everybody who's ever worked in a pigeon lab knows that his animals get drunk with joy when they see their caretaker walk into the room, but that the other students' pigeons couldn't care less. Danny and one of his graduate student buddies at the lab at Adelaide, Will "Work For" Foode, were going to prove once and for all and scientifically that pigeons do indeed recognize their caretakers. Graduate students will do anything to postpone writing their dissertations; Danny's real work of course was concerned with subitizing in pigeons. The Skinner boxes in the lab—smooth prisons of plywood, painted black on the inside—were equipped with two Plexiglas keys, small transparent levers. When a pigeon pecked the correct key, a lamp lights up and a food pellet rolls into the cage. Pigeons have tiny pigeons brains and those brains are used almost exclusively for the fine art of foraging. They are hungry all the time, and always game for food. If they want to get a complete meal out of their session in the box, the pigeons have to be very alert. As a consequence, they keep peering out of their little window with keen anticipation, eagerly examining their world—a computer screen, that is—for anything that could possibly lead to a food delivery. For the who-is-Danny-and-who-is-Will experiment, Will and

Danny removed the computer monitor. Instead, the two men presented themselves as stimuli, jumping in front of the window in random order. The pigeons can hear the rattling of the dice (Will is even, Danny is obviously odd), but they have no idea what that sound is. Maybe it's a fresh bag of pellets being emptied in the chute? Yum!

A head appears at the window.

It's Will!

Head disappears.

A peck.

Another head.

It's Danny!

Head goes away.

Head reappears.

Let's try another peck.

Again.

Will!

Peck. On the Will key.

Pellet.

Yum!

And Will again!

Peck. On the Danny key.

No pellet.

Danny!

Peck.

Danny!

Danny!

Peck.

Will!

Will!

Peck, peck, peck.

Will!

Danny!

Danny!

Danny!

Danny stubs out his cigarette. "But there's a problem. Danny's a skinny-ass guy with a beard, but so is Will. The pigeons get confused. They're not very successful. They get hungry. They get grumpy. Peck-peck-peck! But after a while they do learn. If you keep this game up for an hour or so, the pigeons finally start answering with stopped subsidizing us. *Fuck'n' bloody administration types*! And what can you do with a lab full of jobless pigeons? There was a suggestion, not a serious suggestion, mind you, to slaughter the animals and have our Moroccan research fellow cook us a nice *bastiya*. Phyllo dough, almonds, puree of apricots, cinnamon. Add tender pigeon meat. No, we were going to set the pigeons free, of course.

"So, there we all go, on a sunny afternoon late in summer, in procession, with tears in our eyes, and we carry our birds in improvised cages to the park to release them there. The pigeons are cooing nervously; they scrape their little claws against the plastic bottoms of borrowed parrot cages and the cardboard of shoeboxes; they beat their wings against the walls of perforated paper bags and Chinese take-out Styrofoam; they stick their little beaks out of improvised air holes in extra-large Tupperware containers. In the park we form a circle in the grass as requested by our resident *feng shui* expert, and then we throw the lids off the containers. Take to the air, dear friends! Go, fly into the golden sunlight, free, free at last!

"But that isn't what happens. We have to shake the cages, we have to turn the boxes upside down. Some of the birds immediately scramble back into captivity; we have to wrestle them out of the cages and onto the grass. None of the expected shrieks of joy, no happy flapping of pigeon wings in the limitless sky. They all huddle together on the lawn, scared shitless, pecking their feathers and trying to find purchase with their stumpy feet in the loose gravel and the damp earth. Their little heads are rotating like antennas, and what are they looking for? Us, of course. Us they trust, we're the guys and gals who offer them food and scratch their heads, and so suddenly they all decide to run towards us, beaks wide open, cluck-clucking away. I swear to G*d, the wild pigeons in the trees are rolling off their branches with laughter. And so there we are, flapping our arms like windmills, showing our pigeons how it's done. Fly, dear friends, don't be scared, go on, fly! And so there they are, taken aback, staring at us with big dumb pigeon eyes—you can see them thinking: What the hell? So we run directly at them, thinking we can maybe scare them into flight, but even that doesn't work—like a nervous flock of gray mini-sheep they fan out over the lawn, but they don't spread their wings. Only when Will gets a little toy pistol out of his pocket and starts shooting in the air do they take off, with a mighty whoosh, all at the same time.

"It's an incredible moment, those dry pops and the smell of gun powder and actually *feeling* the pigeons finally lift off, like a single cloud, like a small reverse tornado, an explosion of wings in the sunset, a momentary eclipse of the sun—and then it's all over, they settle in the lime trees, nervous and visibly confused. And then gray feathers start whirling down from the sky—the wild pigeons, the mob that owns the park, are ganging up on the newcomers, and they engage in some seriously vigorous pecking and a group rape ensues on a massive scale. Pigeons don't scream, right? Is that what you think? Pigeons can't scream? Well, let me tell you, we sprinted out of that park as fast as we could, covering our ears with our hands, and none of us ever set foot in the place again.

"See? Another nice example of how classical conditioning actually works in daily life. Will Foode 'For Thought' later became a true cognitivist. He studied extrasensory perception. He shaved cats and glued electrodes on their skulls. Then he went to a soundproof room at the other end of the hallway and tortured their kittens. Let's see if that leads to a spike in mommy's brainwaves.

"*Seey-eh-dhere*?" Danny nods his head in the direction of a strawberry blond, paper-thin young woman with a wild head full of tangled curls. All she has on her tray is an apple. "*She's fuck'n' eye-tell-yun!*" The apparition, cloaked in mist, holds my attention for a second. For some reason, fucking Italian sounds better than fucking German.

"When you go to Berlin, you'll see all that modern anti-pigeon weaponry," says Danny. "Spikes on the beams in the subway stations, barbed wire on the roofs of historic buildings. What is a pigeon to do in Berlin? With no place to rest, they fly around aimlessly; they sail through the monuments of public transportation; they float over historic sandstone and postmodern concrete, forced into perpetual motion. After a few days, they fall dead on the ground, killed by exhaustion. At least they provide work to a few sanitation workers who would otherwise be jobless."

Danny has finished his meal. All of a sudden, we have nothing more to say to each other. We feel our way out of the Mensa. We dump the remains of our lunch— some potatoes and sauerkraut for Danny, half of *der Pizza* for me—neatly into the garbage trough and put our tray carefully on the rattling conveyor-belt. *Raus*!

We walk past the *Communs* towards *Haus Zwei*, Building Two, where the psychology department has its home. The visibility outside is not much better than that inside the restaurant. The two stone lions in front of the library—one is called *Patienz*, the other *Tatkraft*—look a bit feeble and quite on edge. Our bodies leave a trail of condensation bubbles in the over saturated air; the cigarette smoke slowly evaporates from our clothes. The smoke is warmer than the surrounding air and it rises into the sky, a burnt offering for the Teutonic g*ds of this nebulous place, in the shape of two misty men. A black poodle, nose to the ground, visibly lost, tries frantically to pick up the scent of his master.

Believe it or not, but the sun makes a valiant attempt to break through the mist, though this is clearly an impossible feat in the humidity of early February. Nature, shrouded in veils, does not easily tolerate mere mortals to contemplate her in her naked state. The pounding of the hammers of the renovation crew working on the roof of the *Communs* sounds muffled. Slow, prehistoric percussion. The blue and yellow light of the welding torches sparkles through the dull ribbons of haze that hide the day from view. The new Germany—*Enhanced Formula!*—is being built here. On one of the two-hundred-year-old walls, a number has been spray painted in fluorescent green, in a big, round, elegant hand; the number is 117. Further down the road, I see the same number repeated on another wall. Danny's stride is rather more graceful and determined than it was before lunch. Most likely he is already quietly dreaming of California girls, and *fuck'n'*.

"What if," Danny proposes when we're about to enter the building, "What if we posted ourselves at the door of the student hall and whenever a wisp of fog passed by we would open the door and wave it inside? It would get darker and darker inside and lighter and lighter outside. Let's assume we keep this up for ten thousand years, until all trace of humidity has disappeared from the Berlin air. The mist would be forever gone, and the sun would always be shining. Wouldn't that be a tremendously good deed, something humanity would be eternally grateful for?"

"The world would have become a barren, hot desert," I reply, "and the walls of the student hall would crack under the pressure, if they hadn't long since crumbled from mold and moisture."

It is better to leave the world as it is. The smartest thing to do is to travel the globe, looking for the place that suits us best. This place here doesn't agree with me, it seems. The town feels so despondent, so nauseatingly misty. I want clarity; I want a wider horizon of thought; I want to see a real city—I want to see the mythical Berlin. Tomorrow I'll go and buy a monthly pass from the Berlin transit authority, the BVG. I'll hop on the first train available and ride into the big city—a local migration. Away from the dampness of the grass—pavement and asphalt is what I crave, oceans of sandstone and steel and concrete and glass.

T

SHABBAT (I)

The traveler arriving in Berlin receives a metal token from a policeman posted at the exit of the railway station. The number on the token indicates the number of a cab. The visitor can opt for a motor vehicle ("*Auto*"), a horse cab ("*Droschke*"), or a luggage cab ("*Gepäckdroschke*"). Fare for the Auto option is 70 pfennig for the first 400 yards, plus 10 pfennig for every additional 200 yards. When his destination is close to the station, the traveler may choose to walk and have his luggage delivered by the Berlin Parcel Delivery Company (*Berliner Paketfahrtgesellschaft*). This company has agencies conveniently located at every major station. Yet another option is to utilize the electrified City Rail, or *Stadtbahn*, best known as the S-Bahn. One can transfer to the S-Bahn system at any major railway station.

Our train came from the west; our point of arrival was the Lehrter Bahnhof. We decided to leave our luggage in the capable hands of the BPG and we took the S-Bahn to Bahnhof Zoologischer Garten—the natives simply call it "Zoo." As its name indicates, this station is located right next to the city zoo. Amsterdam's urban music is the screeching mockery of sea gulls; Berlin presented us with a more exotic serenade: the thundering roar of hippos, the high cries of cassowaries, and the mighty trumpets of Indian elephants. Father led us through the Hardenbergstraße. Amsterdam will always be an overgrown village devoid of any elegance or style. This new city—we would soon call it home—has grace and flair; the people who live here do not walk, they are on parade. Although we arrived on a work day—a Friday, if memory serves me well—the streets were teeming with dense masses of extremely well-dressed people.

On our way to our new home, Father pointed out the Romanische Café. Mother looked doubtful. "That's the place where you think you can get a gig?" It looked too big. Too posh. "Their clientele is all artists," said my father. "Writers, musicians, actors—folks with a taste for good music and good musicianship. They'll gladly pay a buck or two to hear me play. And maybe they can help me land a real job." "Yeah. Right," is what my mother said. She said it in Dutch—"*Dat zal wel.*"

The apartment used to belong to one of my father's friends, a sculptor. This man was apparently a better analyst of the political climate than my parents were. He had booked a one-way passage on a steamship to New York, and so he needed cash. He was slick too—while he advised my parents in the strongest possible terms against trying their luck in Berlin, he also managed to talk them into handing him an amazing sum of money to take over his mortgage. The apartment was spacious and located right in the heart of the town—opposite the upscale department store KaDeWe and close to Wittenbergplatz, one of the more important subway hubs. And also in walking distance of the Romanische.

True, it was expensive, but as any real estate broker will tell you: location, baby, location, location.

•

My G*d, the sun is going down. The dark sludge of the dusk liberates G*d's creatures from their labors, and I, and I alone, am getting ready for my struggle with memory. The nightly spasms in my legs may be over, probably forever, and still I can't sleep—worse, I *may* not, I am not allowed to fall asleep. A flesh-and-blood angel has saved my life and she led me to this place, a hospital, improbably called La Charité. There must be a reason for all this. Am I then to ignore the call? Should I keep my story to myself? Can someone like me, who does not believe in coincidence, remain silent after such divine intervention? I have to share my story. All right then, I will be a blind Homeric bard; in the darkness and the silence of the Shabbat night I will sing my song.

Whoever can hear it, let him write it down.

Tonight is Shabbat night. What shall I sing? Deuteronomy, chapter 28, verses 64-67, in psalmody. A Kaddish, another Kaddish, who knows how many of those I've sung in my lifetime? A song written by none other than Moses himself, a song for all those comrades, all those fellow travelers who never got a proper funeral, who never had any sons of their own.

If the story needs to be told, let it be told true to nature. Let me tell you how it really was. We are pawns, nothing more than pawns pushed across the board of life by an invisible Hand. From time to time, that Hand will lift one of us from the board. He will weigh the cold wood in His Palm, and then He will cast it aside, just like that, and throw it on the pile with all the other useless pieces, a wobbly stack of withered souls, many many more than the four times four who populate the eight times eight. So what if a few unfortunate pieces roll off the pile onto the dirty floor and join the balled-up papers, the cookie crumbs, the empty soda cans? Once they were kings or queens or knights or bishops, respectable dignitaries with a solid reputation; now they're lying there in the filth, just a bunch of stiff wooden marionettes. So what? Is there any reason to think He even cares?

Tell us what happened, Mr. De Heer, and be honest. Tell us how the pieces once moved smoothly over the squares, tell us what those moves looked like, but do not pretend that you can discern a pattern. Only the Master Himself knows the rules, and even He does not always play a flawless game.

Deuteronomy. The ancient Greek name of the book means "copy," "duplicate." A double Kaddish? A Kaddish sung for the dead, but also one sung in my name, the name of a living being?

•

He was standing on a large dark boulevard; he clutched his briefcase to his chest. The ice-cold spray of the surf splashed across the cobblestones; the waves were pounding—the ocean was showing off its power, wild and raw. What a strange idea to organize a conference on high-energy physics in Bath at this time of year. He stood at the railing and watched the sea rage. Then he got bored. It's the same old song; it's been going on for centuries: The ocean charges at the shoreline, foam at its mouth, and the beach wards off these attacks with casual flair. The ocean never gives up, and neither does the beach. If only they had held the conference on Corfu, it would have given the conference-goers the opportunity to reenact a few of those merry Greek myths. No use in having some graduate student play Naked Venus on this here shore—if anyone wants to get born out of Bath's autumnal waters, they'd better put on a wetsuit, don some jackboots and an oil-skin coat, and wear a thick Laplandic sweater underneath it all.

Astonishingly, one tent was still up on the promenade. It was bulging in the wind, a hot-air balloon ready to take off. Goldfarb looked at it skeptically, but then his companion pushed him inside before he could voice his protest.

Goldfarb was tired. Jetlag had accompanied him all the way from California, and the day had been filled with boring repetitive scientific announcements and the usual schmoozing with colleagues who did their best to feign some moderate enthusiasm for Goldfarb's latest paper. His jaw hurt from all the fake smiling. Boring chats during coffee breaks, boring chats during lunch, boring chats at the urinal. So Goldfarb was happy to sink into the fortune-teller's pile of cushions and watch the walls of striped cloth billow in the wind. Earlier, an inexplicable fear had been gnawing at this heart; now a cruel peace descended upon him. The young woman next to him, her hip so deftly touching his, her hand poised oh so delightfully on his thigh, must have told him her name—at conferences like this, all the young graduate students and postdocs were very determined to introduce themselves to the master, enunciating their names carefully and slowly, possibly even spelling out their surnames. Occupying a spot in Goldfarb's field of attention, even for the shortest while, was a priceless commodity, and some students would go to great lengths to get noticed. By that reasoning, this young woman must have told him her name, but he had long since forgotten what it was. During the afternoon tea break in a little wooden conference pavilion that was shaking in the stiff breeze, she had walked up to him and simply by holding his eyes and placing her hand on his upper arm, she had provoked in him the familiar conferential hard-on. The titillating accent in her low alto helped with the magic. He had been looking for that boner all day, getting a little worried when it failed to appear—are you getting old, Goldfarb?—and so her intervention had been most welcome. They decided to "escape the crowd." To "get some fresh air." To go out "to get a drink." Whatever the exact phrase they had used, here they were, in a freezing tent that seemed ready to fly away on the wings of the storm, Goldfarb and the student, and the rising glow in his belly, well, it felt quite pleasant. She was leaning against him, talking away a mile a minute, deeply absorbed in conversation with the black-haired faux gypsy seated opposite. The woman had some fake Indian name ("Mahadurga!"), spelled out on the backdrop in big fat rhinestone letters. It was all just a bunch of baloney, of course. The woman was dressed in a painfully colorful and obviously counterfeit sari straight from Carnaby Street, and her eyes were wide with coke, or was it belladonna? A crystal ball was sitting in the exact geometric center of the triangle formed by the professor, the student, and the fortune-teller, waiting patiently for all the hullabaloo to be over.

The cryptonymous girl apparently had a vast knowledge of matters esoteric. The unstoppable flow of her Gallic accent and the false intimacy of touching a stranger in a sparsely lighted tent made Goldfarb's half-hearted erection spring to full attention again. French women are so wonderfully verbal. Their international reputation for gastronomic refinement and erotic know-how is largely based on the simple truth that the only way to ever get a Frenchman (male or female) to shut up is to fill up their mouths. And even then their jaws and saliva glands just keep on munching away. Decidedly erotic. Although Goldfarb himself was bearer of the dreaded accent in which every "w" sound becomes a "v" and every "r" sounds disagreeably throaty, he avoided German students like the plague, and not just for moral reasons. He had managed to overcome his ethical revulsion on a few occasions, but he hadn't found those situations pleasurable. They'd just lay there, those German students, passive as a buffet spread in a cheap hotel in the Harz Mountains. Their pink bodies had reminded him of slabs of headcheese in jelly and flabby slices of obscenely undercooked roast beef. For days after, he couldn't shake the impression that his cock was reeking of pickled onions from a jar.

The Frenchwoman requested that a Fortune be told.

Not her fortune. His. (She took his hand firmly in hers.)

Mahadurga! directed her glance at Goldfarb (one of her eyes was brown, the other an uncanny blue, clear as a baby's but hidden behind a milky veil—probably some trick with colored contact lenses). She spoke in blank verse. She was good, Goldfarb had to admit that. She got a good flow going, slow and sticky, but there was some sting in her words as well:

> *Swollen with the craft of self-deceit,*
> *Wax wings rise beyond their reach,*
> *And melting heavens plot his fall,*
> *Because he, the devil's pupil,*
> *Stuffed with golden gifts of learning,*
> *Has committed damn'd necromancy.*

"Whoa, easy now!" thinks Goldfarb. Lady, this hits a little close to home.

The woman at his side starts giggling. She too knows what the poem is about. All those graduate students, they all know what his reputation is really based on. His so-called big secret. Everybody at the conference knows it and maybe the gypsy woman knows it as well; after all, these folks probably read newspapers too. Why would the student care about his future, or, for that matter, hers? She knows all she needs to know about their joint future: In a short while, the professor will dip his honey stick into her honey pot, and upon the satisfactory conclusion of this vanishing act, the Nobel Prize winner's gratitude will know no bounds. The only magic the woman is interested in is the magic of his letter of recommendation.

Oh, wait. There's more.

Nothing is sweeter to him than witchcraft,
He prefers it over the greatest bliss,
Such is the man seated in this chamber.

The student gets a little impatient. She has a question.

"What about his love life?"

Mahadurga! intensifies her gaze on Goldfarb. He finds himself in a staring contest of sorts, and it looks like he's losing. Well, it must not be all that difficult to read him after all. He grins the grin of those who know not love. Mahadurga! shifts her strategy accordingly and resorts to prose.

"I see some pretty fierce lovemaking," she says, and she coughs and winks at him. "In the near future. With some smoking-hot brunette."

The graduate student shakes her yellow locks. She is annoyed. "*Impossible*! It *must* be a blond! Are you certain?"

The fortune-teller grins at her, the same wide grin that lit up Goldfarb's face just moments ago. She leans over and places her hand at the student's ear and mock-whispers: "Not everything is what it seems, honey." The presumed blond claps her hands in delight. "*Mais non! Comment saviez-vous?*" A mock-gold tooth flashes at Goldfarb.

When they step outside, the *Herr Professor* pretends that he is somewhat unwell and out of spirits. "It was very stuffy inside, wasn't it? Would you mind—I think I'd better lie down for a minute. Is it okay if I pick you up in an hour or so? In the lobby of the hotel? Thank you! You are so wonderful! Why don't you go shopping or something? Here's some cash. I'll see you in an hour. Have fun!"

He watches the woman round the corner, his eyes glued to her swaying hips. Then he turns around and walks back into the tent. No pretenses this time: His grin is that of a carnivore.

Without saying a word, the fortune-teller takes off her wig. Her hair is indeed a very dark brown. She takes Goldfarb by the hand and leads him behind the curtain. A short but vigorous percussive concerto ensues (the band of bells around her head starts ringing first; the pleasing alto of her arm bracelets chime in a little later; next the dull rhythmic clunking of the belt of coins around her hips; finally joined in joyful harmony by the jingling of her anklets ringing from high up in the air), and then everything turns pleasantly, pleasantly quiet. Quiet and restful. And then it's suddenly time to get going, to get up from the comfortable pile of cushions and to crawl through the back of the tent until he finds a circular opening. The many constellations wink at him, and as he walks the boulevard, he feels twenty pounds lighter. Goldfarb doesn't realize that there's a perfectly logical reason for that feeling: He's left his briefcase in the tent. For a moment, he contemplates the starry sky, then he puts his hands deep inside the pockets of his coat. With long firm strides he heads back to the hotel, to finally get it on in earnest with the Française.

It isn't clear why Goldfarb, currently snoring comfortably under his warm eiderdown blanket in his expensive penthouse in the Tiergarten district, dreams about precisely this short erotic episode, and not any other. There's really no shortage of such episodes in his biography. There must be a deeper reason. Dreams are portals to the shadowy palaces of the mind. The guard grants you passage, but there's no guarantee that he will ever let you leave again. Every dream is therefore precious and unique. You dream for a reason. Or is that just an old Jew's tale?

·

And may we reveal to you what Donatella is dreaming about? It is *un sogno fortissimo*. Donatella is dreaming of pyramids with eyes. Not the pyramid printed on the green dollar, not the *novo ordo seclorum*. Her pyramid looks like a scientific diagram. The eyes, threefold, have inscriptions where their pupils should be, reading O_{CDM}, S_{CDM}, and Λ_{CDM}. The words OPEN, FLAT, and CLOSED move about tentatively, as if trying to find their proper place in the figure, and on the sides the symbols Ω_m, Ω_k, and Ω_Λ shake with enthusiasm. In the dream, these trilingual inscriptions swarm over the cosmic triangle, circling each other in a complicated dance, ever-slowing, searching for a stable equilibrium. When the symbols finally find their slots, they vibrate ever so slightly, hovering around the error minimum of the three-dimensional maximum-likelihood function that underlies their existence. As soon as this happens a graph lights up, each of its curves a lifeline thrown at a drowning man. One of the lines rises to a first peak, then a lower second peak, then a still lower third peak (this line is labeled O_{CDM}). The lines S_{CDM} and Λ_{CDM} each have five peaks—the CMB-temperature anisotropy as a function of the multipole l (the abscissa is an angular scale of π/l radials, expressed in logarithmic coordinates ranging from zero to about 10^3). A smile breaks out on Donatella's sleeping face—yes, this is exactly what she had been looking for, all those years!

Donatella typically remembers little or nothing of her dreams. The dream she is dreaming now will have evaporated by morning, the values of the parameters and the peaks in the functions lost with her sleep. Although they would fit so

ter how deep the surgeons have burrowed inside the gray/white/pink matter of the brain, they haven't gotten a glimpse of the soul yet. The article mentions that after you die, your body suddenly loses sixty grams. Sixty grams? Two ounces? That's the weight of the soul? Ridiculous! If this estimate is true, I feel deep compassion for the astral homunculus in each of us. He or she makes up less than a part in one thousand of our total body weight. The human soul must feel very oppressed indeed by that big fat sluggish lump of flesh.

I put my hands in my pockets and I continue on my way. As planned, the horn of a Volkswagen Jetta starts blaring about a hundred feet behind my back.

•

Well, dear reader, did you check the Deuteronomy quote?

I bet you didn't, so here it is. (Glad to be of service.)

And the LORD shall scatter thee among all people, from the one end of the earth even unto the other; and there thou shalt serve other g*ds, which neither thou nor thy fathers have known, even wood and stone.

And among these nations shalt thou find no ease, neither shall the sole of thy foot have rest: But the LORD shall give thee there a trembling heart, and failing of eyes, and sorrow of mind:

And thy life shall hang in doubt before thee; and thou shalt fear day and night, and shalt have none assurance of thy life:

In the morning thou shalt say, Would G*d it were even! and at even thou shalt say, Would G*d it were morning! for the fear of thine heart wherewith thou shalt fear, and for the sight of thine eyes which thou shalt see.

Thus spoke the Lord.

For the sight of thine eyes.

ח

HEY-HEY, WE'RE THE NAZIS!

Hugo wakes up slowly. A train thunders past, uncomfortably close to his ear. His cheeks are caressed by a smooth tree root—pale, naked, damp fingers that feel their way through the hollow, resounding room, imperceptibly slowly, hunting for solid ground.

The sound and fury of the trains have long ago stopped bothering him. Hugo can hardly remember the heady days when they were living in the squat and he used to get tickled awake by the sunshine hitting his nose. Sunshine. That was a long time ago. A ray of light piercing through a bullet hole in a window of steel-mesh-reinforced milky glass—how did that feel again, the sun stinging his nostrils?

In the reddish orange glow of the heating spiral that so valiantly fails to heat up their corner of the universe, two pairs of black boots stand on the naked concrete. The laces are almost fluorescent bony white. They were placed there very neatly, heel to heel, the limp shafts leaning against each other in a tipsy military salute. (Let's count, shall we?—this is *one*.) Hugo scratches his skull, the blond stubble (hail to hydrogen peroxide!) feels stiff under his fingers. (*Two*.) Two white T-shirts lie carefully folded on the chair next to the mattress. (*Three*.) The music that comes from the next room—if one can call it a room, the immense space of the station has been roughly subdivided with walls improvised with cinderblocks—should be pounding and arousing, but the volume is kept quite low; the disciples do not dare to disturb the Leader's sleep. (*Four*. And *five*.)

Hugo rolls over. He presses his chest against Nebula's back and his groin against her sweet little tush. The sensitive nerve endings at the tip of his prick register the shallow relief of the small tattoo at the inside of her thigh. (That makes *six*.) When he first met her, she wore her hair with long side-swept bangs in front, but short in the back and sides. When she was working, the hair would get in her eyes; she would blow it away or flick her head back impatiently. These gestures used to fill Hugo with an unnamable tenderness and a dull yearning. Now she's growing it out. Too many women wear their hair in a Hitler-hairdo this winter, she pointed out. A lot of them even bought the riding boots to match. "I want to be special, Hugo. I'm not like everybody else," Nebula had pleaded, and Hugo had allowed her to break the unspoken rules. Because she was right. She was not like everybody else. (Are we going back to *five*?) Hugo takes a strand of Nebula's hair between his lips; his hand slides down her belly until it touches the tiny Hitler mustache on her pubic mound. The way she feels down there, the warm welcome of her slit—it sends him to *seven*th heaven. Nebula pretends to be asleep, but her spine shivers ever so slightly. Hugo snuggles deeper into the sleeping bag and licks her skin, so magnificently bronzed (the coins they steal out of the *Videoarkaden* serve Nebula well in the self-service tanning salons), until his lips hit the folds of her pussy and Nebula starts purring. Who says that skinheads are only capable of hatred?

·

Count the signs.

The December 3, 1991 issue of the popular tabloid *Bild* provides a handy guide.

Has your child suddenly decided to get a buzz cut?

Did he or she buy a bomber jacket in either army-green or black, and has the collection of blue denim jackets in the closet gone completely forgotten?

Is he or she requesting strange alterations to the aforementioned new acquisition? For instance, did s/he ask you to sew an Iron Cross patch on the sleeves, or a spread eagle on its back?

Are your tender offspring's delicate feet now exclusively shod in steel-tipped and white-laced Doc Martens-brand boots, even though only six months ago you spent half a month's salary to buy her/him a pair of just the right type of Nikes? Do those Nikes, despite having finally acquired the perfect patina, stay in the closet, looking so expensive and a tad forlorn?

From now on, is the only acceptable color for T-shirts white? Do they have to sport slogans in the mother tongue?

Has your child's record collection been expanded to include albums by *Störkraft* (for example their album *Dreckig, Kahl und Hundsgemein*—"Filthy, Bald and Mean as a Dog") and *Noie Werte*, or other bands that consider skulls and swastikas the pinnacle of cover art?

Is his/her new favorite catchphrase "*Oi! Oi! Oi!*"? Is your son goose-stepping through the house, barking out songs that go something like this: *Seht ihr unsere Fahnen, hört ihr unsere Lieder / Dieser Staat geht unter und das Reich kommt wieder*—"Listen to our songs, behold our flags / The new Germany goes under and *das Reich* comes back"—or like this: *Adolf Hitler, unser Führer / Adolf Hitler, unser Held / Adolf Hitler war der Größte Revolutionär der Welt*—"Adolf Hitler, hero and leader quite contrary / Adolf Hitler, the world's greatest revolutionary"?

Is your child only interested in the evening news when it shows images of immigrants, especially when the story is about North Africans being beaten up, or their houses going up in flames?

Have posters of pop stars and rock musicians been replaced by authentic copies of World War II posters?

Does your child keep a baseball bat in his or her room, even though the corresponding balls are nowhere to be found, and neither can a rulebook be discovered, nor any other type of equipment or for that matter enthusiasm for this decidedly un-German sport?

Did your child cancel her/his subscription to *Bravo*, and does s/he keep copies of *Frontal, Der Kampftrinker,* or *Yah—Skin Reports* on the bedside table?

Has he or she started going out late at night more often, and is there a new circle of friends, and does your child prefer the subtle mispronunciation *Froind* over the regular *Freund?*

Has your child developed an unexpected passion for the martial arts?

•

Deep in Hugo's wallet there's a newspaper clipping with a photograph, hidden behind a counterfeit thirty-day railway/subway pass—the card is there purely for show, since no subway cop in his right mind will ask a skinhead for his transit pass. As if hiding the clipping isn't enough, Hugo has also folded it up three times. The picture dates from the riots at the Eisenhüttenstadt refugee center, back in 1991. It shows a sturdy woman, one of those German *Muttis* of the efficient short-haired GDR variety. The woman is dressed in a cheap striped jogging suit and shown in left profile; the photographer has lit her silhouette dramatically against the nighttime sky. Her right leg leans forward; her left leg is bent slightly backward. She holds her hands stretched out horizontally, palms down. This is an excellent starting position for a fiery tango. Her dancing partner is a head or two taller than she is, but it's clear that the woman is leading this dance—his body is bent backwards, as in recoil, his hands the feeble forelimbs of a T-Rex. If the woman in this picture

well aware of the burden of our calling; we stumble under the weight of what remains to be done. After such an onslaught on the senses, you need time to readjust to reality. You need to hold your head high in the cool nighttime air; you need to shake the long trance out of your aching skull. Without a word, then, Hugo and Liebenfels walk to the car, to the petite Lada that stands out among the BMWs, the Mercedeses, and all those other twelve-cylinder monsters.

They do not need words.

Liebenfels takes the long way home. The direct way would be to head east from Bismarckstraße onto the big avenue that leads through the woods, past the Große Stern, the circular square where the gilded statue of the G*ddess of Victory watches over the city with her spear and her wreath and her wings and her crown of flames and the eagle on her head; under the arches of the Brandenburg Gate onto the Unter den Linden boulevard, and then over the Castle Bridge, past the cathedral and the Altes Museum, continuing past City Hall and the Neptune fountain to Alexanderplatz and then straight on to Lichtenberg. Instead of heading east, however, Liebenfels turns south through the streets surrounding Nollendorfplatz, where men are walking arm in arm with other men and women french-kiss other women under street lights for all to see, and then the car turns into the Kreuzberg district.

It's midnight, but Oranienstraße is packed. It's quite the assortment of people. Young German men with long manes and creative configurations of facial hair have their arms wrapped around almond-skinned women with men's haircuts. Small groups of Turkish boys strut about as if they own the street, their arms around each other or around Moroccan women with paisley head scarves or around long-haired blonds with hair buns held in place with chopsticks or around Asian women with golden highlights in their black hair; some even walk around with combinations of the above. Middle-aged potbellied men stumble around in studded leather jackets, emitting drunken hiccups. Fourteen-year-old punks with acne scars roller blade through the crowd with ghetto blasters on their shoulders; they shout happy obscenities over the blaring hip-hop music—without missing a beat, they make split-second decisions about whether to steal the next passerby's wallet or merely cop a feel.

Hugo's education is apparently not over.

Liebenfels pulls into a parking spot.

"Open your window."

Hugo does as he is told.

The sounds and smells of the street fill the car. The smell of pita and shawarma, falafel and fried chicken, *Currywurst* and mayonnaise and clove cigarettes. High-pitched Algerian *raï* music blasts from a crowded bar; the massive beat of a *synths'n'samples* track bounces from a club at the other side of the street; in less than a minute the crisscross fireworks of at least thirteen different languages bursts into the car. What blasphemy! Hugo's ears are still echoing with trumpets and timpani; his belly still smarts from the sonic assault of pure Aryan power; his eyes still sting from the dust kicked up by the destruction of the Rhineland castles—and now he has to endure *this*. Liebenfels and he, freshly initiated in the purest expression of the German soul, are surrounded by gallivanting North Africans, their gaze both shifty and proud, conversing in an agitated and incomprehensible, guttural code.

This is the spot that Liebenfels has chosen to address Hugo, with urgency and full of concern, a father educating his son. Liebenfels will speak of Germany, here in the heart of Kreuzberg—his sermon from the Lada.

Germany! How can one speak of Germany, here, in the middle of one of the largest Turkish enclaves on earth—here in Kreuzberg, after Istanbul the largest Turkish city in the world? Is this a place to speak of Germany?

Apparently it is.

Because the best moment to talk about love is when one realizes that love might be lost.

Liebenfels starts by pointing out the window. His sweeping arm embraces the street and the city, perhaps the world. "Look around you, Hugo." Hugo looks around. It is confusing indeed. Here, in the middle of Berlin, live tribes of people who are so obviously different from the Germans, and somehow they seem to think that this difference is not a cause for concern, but a reason to celebrate. Liebenfels seems to be waiting for some kind of reaction. "They are . . . different," Hugo offers. Liebenfels snorts. "Indeed, my friend. Different. Very different. Look closer. Do you see anyone you like? Someone you would want to be friends with? No? Really? You don't? Look closer. Still nobody that looks sympathetic? See? So what do we have in common with this . . . this . . . riffraff? This scum? What use are these people, Hugo? What good do they do, this jobless rabble, these slackers pompously parading right in front of us? Vermin—that's what they are. Vermin too lazy to learn the language, and they're breeding like rabbits too. How do they make ends meet, Hugo? They live off our welfare system, Hugo, they live off *our* social security. Each and every one of them, Hugo, each of these monkeys—their rent gets paid and there is food on their table, but it is we who pay for all this, Hugo, you and I.

"Please don't get me wrong.

"I have nothing against Turks.

"But I can't help it.

"I am a German nationalist.

"I simply have to stand up for my people's right, for our right to maintain our identity. This is a right that I hold sacred. I grant every people on earth that right. I do not believe in the superiority of our race over the other races. I sincerely believe that cultural diversity is one of the great natural resources of humanity. And that is why I resist the multicultural project. It fuses us all, Hugo. It makes us indistinguishable. It dilutes who we are and it waters down what is good in us, what is good in them. All this so-called equality, my friend—it just means *massification*, and massification is what the people in Bonn want. We should all be the same, in their mind, we should all be bland, all copies of each other, all our personality drained away. See where it leads us, Hugo, all this affirmative action. It leads to laziness and lasciviousness, it leads to . . . nowhere. Could you imagine, even for a moment, the Lohengrin overture sounding from one of these windows?

"National socialism, my friend, is not an ideology of hatred. Let me repeat that. We are not hatemongers. Nobody can live by hate. No, on the contrary. We live by *love*, Hugo. We live to love, and we love with a love that is deep and pure. This love fills us and it fulfills us, Hugo. The love for our country, for our language, for our culture. We love Mozart, Hugo. We *made* Mozart—our culture did. And Goethe, and Schiller. And of course Wagner. Do we not love all the small rituals of daily life? All those small things that make a German a German? We do not need falafels, we do not need dill pickles. Why should we have to listen to this barbarian Berber music, why should our youth be smoking marihuana, why should we tolerate the homosexual lifestyle, what good is this colony of apes, this gang of *Alis*, this pack of Turks? German culture, Hugo, is Christian. Muslims, believe me, do not belong in this country."

During Liebenfels's monologue, a small group of men has gathered around the car. None of them says a word, but a cool, naked menace emanates from the small crowd. Hugo does not feel safe—they are two men in a small tin box in the middle of enemy territory. Liebenfels gestures that maybe it might be better to roll up the window again.

"See how far things have gone? We are not welcome here—in our own town, in our own country! How can this be allowed—we are unwelcome in what once was the capital of the Reich? That is impossible, isn't it? Impossible!"

Liebenfels turns the key in the ignition. The engine sputters. The men let them through. Hugo stares straight ahead. Big drops of sweat have gathered on his brow.

•

Liebenfels navigates them safely through the labyrinth of small streets, finally turning onto Mehringdamm. With a quick sideways glance, he assesses Hugo's state of mind.

His false beard and his white wig and his glued-on eyebrows may give him an imperturbable air, but internally Liebenfels is grinning. Hugo passed the test. This boy is excellent raw material. Exactly the type of man Liebenfels can use. Put a man like Hugo behind the barricades, in the company of his band of brothers, and he will be the bravest of the brave. When he and his men walk the streets, they do not walk, they prowl. But left alone, he will be afraid. Afraid that he has been abandoned. Eager to win back your love. Such people are useful. They do not think independently. They think they are leaders, but they are not; they are followers, without even bothering to try to find out exactly what or who it is that they are loyal to. Rebels without qualities. Ready to fight at the drop of a hat, fight for whatever ideal is momentarily comprehensible. They are like Wagnerian fairy tale characters roaming the woods, always talking to themselves, always miserable, on the lookout for a pot of gold. They aren't clever enough to realize that even the biggest pot of gold is totally useless when you're all by yourself, deep in the woods.

Liebenfels doesn't care about ideals. Ideals are cold abstractions. No ideology is worth dying for. Liebenfels has lived too long and has experienced too much to still believe in anything. Ideals are simply means for mobilization. What counts is the movement—the stream, the swing of things. Everything flows; nothing is permanent. Hugo is too young to understand the fundamental truth about the human condition, namely that we are nothing but tools, blind slaves of hacked memes. We are parasites of ideas that flow on the Zeitgeist, ideas that do not care who or what we are, as long as they can use us for recombination and thereby guarantee their own survival. That is why Liebenfels likes men like Hugo so much. Make them members of a group, give them a goal, and off they go, and before long their goal-related velocity will be too high for them to stand still and ponder. Grab these guys by the shoulders, point them in the right direction and convince them that what they are looking at is the coolest thing on earth and they are yours—and the easiest idea to employ in this service is the age-old variation on the "me-myself-and-I"—the idea of a well-delineated "us" that is in danger.

Liebenfels firmly believes in chaos theory. Somewhere in the Nile Delta, a butterfly starts its day by flapping its wings. The small turbulences in the air get amplified, the weather turns, and eventually a storm will hit Berlin. Chaos is a good thing. It is a precondition for the new. And it is Liebenfels's lifeblood. Wait and see what the butterfly's wings will bring about—Liebenfels just loves unpredictability. This is where teacher and student complement each other. Liebenfels is a traveling salesman dealing in chaos, and Hugo, sweetly ignorant hotheaded Hugo, is his supplier. Hugo is the artfully fluttering butterfly, and he is caught in Liebenfels's net.

Liebenfels pulls up the car at the abandoned factory. He goes for the final push. "Just an hour ago, Hugo, in the theater, did you not feel it? When the applause erupted, did you not feel this new beginning, this opening of the gates—did you not sense that the opera house had become a portal, the promise of a surprising and overwhelming new world? Wagner is a tamer of g*ds, he forces them into incarnation. Frightened actors are hoisted in chain mail and Wagner makes them—freely, bravely, magically!—speak the words of g*ds. Hugo, my friend, we too must wear such armor. We too must go into the world, and fight the good fight of the g*ds. But we have to be careful. Very careful. I know you, Hugo, I know you and I understand you better than you understand yourself. Have you never considered an act of desperation of such tremendous proportions that the world would notice? Hang fifty pounds of dynamite from your belt and blow yourself up on the fifth floor of KaDeWe? We all have to go down one day, after all, don't we, and why then not go down in an act of admirable violence, a gesture of supreme anarchy? I understand the temptation, my friend. I understand it all too well. Be patient, Hugo. Be patient. The day will come, the day of the grand ceremony, the day of your big bang, the hour of violence that will end all violence forever. That day, however, is not today. Today is the day of small, precise gestures; today is the day of minor resistance. We push our pins in the elephant's skin until the elephant has had enough. And then, when the animal finally starts moving, maybe when it breaks into a trot, that's when we will go all out, that's when we will release the nest of hornets, and we will shoot it straight at his big fat dangling sack of balls."

Hugo nods his head. He understands. He understands his mission perfectly well: He is a soldier for the homeland.

"Here." Liebenfels takes Hugo's arm and slides an envelope in the inside pocket of Hugo's jacket. The envelope feels fat and full. "Here, my brave warrior. A nice stack of cash. A set of instructions. Take them and read, and do as directed. For Germany, Hugo! For town and country! Take care, my dearest friend!"

•

The Kreuzberg trip was not Hugo's first encounter with what the folks on television call "the Turkish community in Berlin." His first bodily encounter with Turks was also the first time he met Nebula. It was also Hugo's first street fight in Berlin.

Where do Hugo's men come from? Hugo himself doesn't know. He walks the streets of the workers' neighborhoods. Like puppies, they find him and they follow him home. Without exception, these young men are all political refugees from the former deep East. Is there some hint of nest scent around Hugo? Do they recognize him as one of them, or rather as one who once was what they are now: a man so thin and lost to anger that he is nothing more than an edgy shadow? Hugo doesn't know. He never asks them why they follow him to the factory halls. What true master wants to know exactly what his disciples see in him?

It helps with recruiting that Hugo is almost six foot six, and so blond as to be almost white. It's hard to miss him. Tallness often gets mistaken for leadership ability, just like Hugo's silence often gets mistaken for profundity. They follow him, and that's all he needs to know. They move into the squat and drag in heaps of hairy blankets and stacks of cardboard boxes filled with shoplifted shaving supplies and stolen Walkmans. For food, they pilfer potatoes and leeks and bread and tomatoes off the fruit carts in the streets of Wedding. They form a nice group of codependent primates. Like good Japanese monks, they shave each others' skulls every other Wednesday.

Human groups can reach critical mass. You can walk the streets with a bunch of friends and nobody takes notice. But there is a point at which a group of friends parading down the sidewalk with their arms wrapped around each others' shoulders suddenly becomes a mob, a posse, a pack of wolves.

One fine Saturday, Hugo's posse is walking around the toothy church stump near KaDeWe, that bizarre city beacon that is too ugly and artificial to carry any real meaning—it's just a target for tourist cameras and therefore a good spot for illegal fast food stands and men selling synthetic scarves and Nepalese jewelry out of velvet-lined suitcases. Honestly, Hugo and his friends aren't looking for trouble. Not at all. Their intention is not to be a menace to the general public. They're just doing what everybody else does around the Gedächtniskirche: They hang out, they bore themselves to tears, they stroll along the streets everybody else is strolling along, around the condemned buildings by Zoo Station, past the Vietnamese and Chinese mini-marts and the improvised currency exchange booths manned by furtive, curt Ukrainians, where the canned moans from the illicit porno theaters drown out the bad imitation hip-hop from the pirated CD stores. This is the neighborhood where the glitter of the Ku'damm shopping district gets a little scratchy and dirty under the nails. Dented tour busses with Polish license plates are parked tipsily half across the sidewalks; their passengers are out in the streets, filling their plastic shopping bags with discount versions of the German dream—six-packs of undrinkable lager, tins of salmon that tastes of nothing but salt, aerosol cans of

inaudible farts while staring expressionless at the steel doors. Let's light a lighter and stick one arm up to the elbow into a mailbox. Adolescent escapades. Snot and earwax as lubricants of the revolution. Be vigilant. Train yourself. Maybe, once in a while, beat up an innocent bystander.

•

A messenger delivers a package from Liebenfels. It contains cotton patches to sew on their jackets: a wide armband in red with a white circle and inside the circle the black silhouette of a dancing Hindu g*d, clearly on the other side of the law. There are also stickers in the package, with the same image. And a small stack of stencils, so they can quickly spray-paint the symbol on the walls of the city. A Hindu g*d? Dancing? What the fuck?

The cell phone rings.

"Hindus are the original Aryans, Hugo. Behold Shiva. He is dancing on a dwarf. The Aryan trampling the subhuman underfoot. Behold Shiva, he is dancing in a ring of fire. The fire from which the new world is born."

"Why me?" asks Hugo. "Mr. Liebenfels, sir, why me?"

A click near his ear, and then the busy tone.

•

Nebula is a free spirit. She likes to roam the city, but she never tells Hugo where she is going. She comes and goes. She is a cat. Her hair tangled, she rounds the corner of the tunnel, meowing for her lover. Hugo lets her go. It's worth it. Her meow when she comes back, it turns him on so much.

•

Most of us think that the streets are what constitutes a city. Hugo has a different opinion. The underground is his Walhalla, the hero's lair of his grubby gang. The trains are the luminous carriages of the g*ds, the poorly oiled metal doors of the cars the screeching gates to the dark world where they reign. "What are we doing here?" Hugo's men ask their leader. "Why do we have to live here, in darkness and cold, in icy drafts and that shrill racket, between these shaky walls of merciless concrete?"

Hugo tells them a story. "We are spies of the NSDAP, Hitler's party. In 1945, we went underground—literally. For half a century, we've hidden in the boundless system of tunnels that interconnects the city, the *Netzwerk Lebensraum* for which no maps exist. We keep a tradition alive, my friends. One day, we will erupt from our subterranean existence. On that day, we shall possess the world, in a flash."

Over the past few months, the cell phone has been ringing less and less frequently. The instructions have become less precise. Liebenfels is happy. "From here on in, you are on your own, Hugo. Don't ask. Do what you have to do," says the voice over the telephone. "Just wait. There will be one more phone call. Wait, and be ready."

"What if I make a mistake?"

Liebenfels answers: "You will know quickly enough when you've made a mistake."

•

Nebula walks into the big room. She yawns. The room is a mess. Four ashtrays filled to the brim; seven beer bottles, all beheaded; one half-empty bottle of vodka, wobbly with sloshing liquid; a dozen crushed CD jewel boxes, the shards strewn like sullied diamonds on the concrete; a tabloid newspaper that someone's probably crapped on; colorful wrappers of cheap candy bars; cellophane bags of Aldi potato chips. A boom box burps up rhythmic ska music at medium volume—somebody must have set the alarm at the wrong time—but the men wrapped in their sleeping bags are all still snoring. Their subterranean existence among the trains combined with their exhausting life at the surface makes them just about impossible to wake up. Nebula's gaze drifts over the sleeping bags. Viewed from the corner of her eye, the men look like monstrous insects drying in their egg sacks, each in his own stage of decomposition and hopelessness. These are Hugo's men. His mates, and therefore—shudder, Nebula, shudder!—transitively, also hers.

Along the wall that separates the ghost station from the working subway tracks she can spy the only sign of order in the room: a neat stack of black plastic boxes, each the size of a hardcover book, each marked with a number in white lacquer paint. This is Nebula's masterpiece in progress.

Consider this: What is likely to happen if you keep a dozen or so men, and of late also a few women—Nebula's presence has made some of the men restless—more or less captive in a more or less limited space? They need a hobby, a safety valve, right? Sure, from time to time they venture outside and release some of the pent-up testosterone at the expense of some easy victim, but you can't do that too often or you'll get the cops looking for you. They all wear that little symbol, their tiny circular g*d. The sign is not just their pride, it is also their brand. It makes them identifiable. Therefore, they have to be careful; they can't let themselves stand out too much. This was a very clever move on Liebenfels's part. And it is also very good for Nebula, the filmmaker. All that pent-up energy needs to be released, somehow.

The filmmaker. It doesn't matter whether he or she makes documentaries, or whether she or he is interested in fiction—the filmmaker is the perennial observer. S/he is the person that gives you the creeps on the bus with that stare—the stare that sees everything, but is too cold to communicate anything about its bearer. The artist (the filmmaker, the writer, the painter, the sculptor, the director, the actor, the photographer) is a repulsive character. Artists always claim to be interested in honesty and authenticity, but they will kill authenticity in an instant and mount it on a pedestal, all in the name of art. They are taxidermists of the truth; they prefer the beauty of a murdered innocence over the living variety. They stare at you when they think you're not paying attention; the goal is to study you in that rare moment when you're completely yourself, when you think no one is watching you. You'll never catch them red-handed, but you can see their pupils darting away when you look up from your coffee; you can see their shifting gaze in the park; you can hear them step away from underneath your bedroom window. All artists are in love with themselves—for precisely this reason: They can observe themselves, their varying moods, their very own bodily sensations, all day long. After all those years of living in close quarters with yourself, you can't help it; you simply have to start loving the smell of your very own belly-button lint.

They crawled away into one of the tunnels, Bøk and his lover Linde. They took Nebula's camera and a tripod with them.

It's so human. Some people affirm their existence by writing poetry. Some people want to capture their own image, and what better image to capture than the one you yourself can never see, the exact moment when you lose yourself: the blazing flame of ecstasy, the moment of falling, of rushing, of singing? And then someone else will accidentally put the tape in the VCR, because Bøk made the honest drunken mistake of taping over the cassette that contains the street fight. Soon, the whole gang gathers round the television screen, hooting and howling at the antics onscreen.

Nebula, no less than Bøk and Linde gifted with an artist's soul, sees things differently than the rest of the troops. In the midst of the men's joy about so much *cinema vérité*, she remains silent. Watching, being *allowed* to watch the love exchanged between B. and L.—all the endearing and awkward moments of their lovemaking—it awakens something inside her. No, she does not join the gang in its mirth. Rather, she quietly walks over to the despondent pair and she puts her arms around the both of them. Under the touch of Nebula's cool dry palms the blush on their cheeks and the glow on their necks cool down. She whispers in Linde's ear: "Freedom from the imperative of mimetic desire and the straightjacket of narrative structure, freedom to take the radical dive into a reflective, self-conscious meditation about the *Dasein* rather than to undergo the conditions of the *Dasein* itself—that and nothing else is signified by Mr. Bøk's eager yet tentative leap into Ms. Linde's expansive-endemic vagina."

Linde giggles. She has never heard such nonsense before. She wriggles her shoulders. Not to break free, but to better feel the firmness of Nebula's grasp. Nebula pinches back. She leans over and looks the both of them earnestly and invitingly in the eyes.

"Shall we?" Nebula asks.

And while the rest of the gang is busy chatting—analyzing and criticizing the finer points of the choreography, offering their interpretations of those passages that were literally dark—Nebula shoulders the camera and disappears into the labyrinth of tunnels, playful and paratactical, with her two new best friends.

•

"This is odd, sweetie-pie."

"Trust me," answers Nebula. "It serves a higher purpose. And you're not missing out on anything in the sex department, are you honey?"

"No," says Hugo. "I am not missing out on anything. Come to think of it, I do see the higher purpose. And of course, honey-bunny, I trust you." Nebula, he reminds himself over and over again, is a free spirit. No, he keeps reminding himself, he is not missing out on anything. There is a higher purpose. Hugo repeats it, like a mantra. There is a higher purpose. I trust her. Higher purpose. Trust.

People in love do the darnedest things.

•

The first part of the number on the cover indicates the content; the second part is the customer ID. If you're making tapes like these, you might just as well earn a buck or two by selling them. All big enterprises—communism, for instance, or gigantic capitalist joint ventures, and above all love—sooner or later have to perish. The small shadowy businesses, however, the ones that serve small needs, never go broke. There will always be a need for bread and beer and gossip. Likewise, there will always be a need for all the rich varieties of prostitution and for the liberating honesty of homemade pornography. You don't need to be a genius to understand that. And just as there is no substitute for bread, there is no substitute for porn. The grimy close-ups, the grungy decors, the gritty determination of the actors to reach their climax no matter what it takes, these things have to be seen first-hand; they can't be conjured up in the darkroom of consciousness, not even with the most detailed of scripts or the most articulate sequence of still photographs. Watching those poorly lit images shot with a single cheap camera, often including the director-cameraman's live commentary, is so much more than watching. It is meta-watching. One embeds oneself in many layers of reality, many layers of reference and of convention. One watches somebody watch. It is a transcendent experience, dangerously close to the sublime.

Porn is a drug. Drugs have commercial value. In Germany, you cannot buy porn tapes discreetly. The lonesome wife who feels the urge to try out a vibrating dildo or the unfulfilled husband who longs to merge with a plastic *Kunstvagina*— these people have mail order catalogues at their disposal. But whoever wants to possess images of the sexual act, and a fortiori moving images, is legally required to get face to face with a certified salesperson. He therefore has to get out of the house and into the shopping districts, running the risk that his neighbor or his neighbor's teenage daughter or, worse, his boss will see him enter or leave the specialty store. This creates the need for a different, handier, and much more tactful distribution system.

A young woman and a young man enter into a joyful biblical acquaintanceship. Both are wearing nipple piercings. The friction created by their movements generates static electricity, which in turn makes beautifully crackling sparks fly between the two performers. Nebula films this fortuitous event with a Sony-1000 camera on loan from the film academy. She is working on her thesis; at least, that's what she told her advisor. Nebula is not simply pointing the camera at some folks fucking. She has an aesthetic theory. For instance, she often keeps the space purposely dark, with only a few candles in the foreground. When she processes the images at her computer in the *Hochschule*, she digitally enhances the brightness. It makes the images grainy and it cools down the color palette; it gives the whole film an excitingly illegal look. Two interconnected video recorders supply the masses with copies.

The public wants *cinéma verité*? Bøk tells Nebula how on Sunday afternoons his dad used to get so drunk and bored and pissed off that the only thing that gave him any joy would be to carve his son's skin with a knife. Small cuts, superficial wounds that left no scars. (He might have been drunk, but he still knew what he was doing.) Nebula tapes the conversation, and then she and Linde get out the razor blades, and Linde laps at the blood that seeps from the cuts. Here Nebula makes an exception: She turns on the bright lights—the drops have to glisten like rubies. Or they get their inspiration from the professional literature on the subject, for instance a book that Linde recently stole from Kiepert, *A Hand in the Bush: The Fine Art of Vaginal Fisting*. Nebula even films the journey through the tunnels to the place of debauchery. She glues a microphone to her breastbone; this adds some heavy bronchial action to the soundtrack, like the breathing of a serial killer in a horror movie. If the live sound doesn't get captured well, she does the post-synchronization sound effects herself in her editing booth at the Uni, way past midnight. The sounds of fucking, she has discovered, can easily be imitated by rhythmically beating a stalk of celery on a raw slab of filet mignon. Sometimes Nebula takes on the role of director more explicitly. From behind the camera, she mouths words for her performers to repeat, words that sound remarkably dated and pompous coming out of the lips of the pale maggots that her actors are. At the same time, they are strangely arousing. She gives them directions with such confidence that it seems as if she reads from a script she knows by heart. She uses naked walls of concrete as her background, or rusty beds in bunkers that have gone unused for half a century—yes, in the Berlin underground, everything is connected to everything else. Or she choreographs semi-acrobatic moves on narrow stairwells with corroded iron bars for rails. Some of the tunnels contain spectacular murals, images of life-size SS-men lifting other SS-men on horizontal black shields, for instance, or gigantic black bats with ominous eagles resting on their open wings. She asks her performers to lean against this painted coldness while penetrated, their arms wide in crucifixion. Or she asks her actresses to jerk off the men and spray the wall with their semen, thus destroying the frescoes shot by shot. She keeps returning to this mural, until the whole painting has been erased.

Nebula never shows the latter type of tape to anybody; if she keeps the footage, she keeps it in a secret location. The other tapes are for sale. It's not particularly difficult to sell them. Put a tape in the cotton shopping bag of a young man that looks like he could use some action. Attach a note: *More to come!*, with a little drawing at the bottom, a caricature of a little dancing g*d. Repeat this scenario. It is the tried and true technique of every drug pusher: free samples. In less than two weeks, the Shiva-boys get little return notes stuffed in their pockets with special requests and the specification of a drop-off location. *U1, on Thursday, the train that stops at Wittenbergplatz at 6:13 P.M. I will be in the first compartment, a* *white carnation in my breast pocket. In the back pocket of my jeans you will find a hundred deutschmark bill; please drop the cassette in my open briefcase without attracting any attention.*

•

Time for the men to wake up. They yawn. A few scratch their balls, until they realize that the boss's wife is there, and then they stop, even though Nebula has filmed their family jewels six times or more, and in stark close-up. Nebula likes the eager tension that radiates off these men: the casual concentration with which they bite their nails to the quick, the unnecessary fierceness with which they turn the wheels of their disposable Bic lighters, the hunger with which they smoke their cigarettes until the butts burn their lips. They are her very own endearingly clumsy, surly pyromaniacs.

It was obvious they had never taken a good look at themselves in the mirror, Hugo and his men, when they called themselves the best men in the nation. Oh no, says Hugo when she broaches the subject, that's the wrong way to look at it. All of them, himself included, were merely humble instruments in the hands of a higher power, a power that they have no control over, but that nevertheless claws its way through the world, stirring up trouble. Then what about the invisible man you so admire, what about Liebenfels?

"Liebenfels too is just a cog in the system."

She looks around, she watches the men scurry out of their sleeping bags. She picks up her camera. Those bald boys all look exactly the same in their pale skins and crusty underwear. And even after they get dressed, they still all look the same. A set of identical duodecuplets. Can Hugo tell them apart? Nebula hardly can. But their uniformity is not all that surprising after all. As a soldier, you are nothing. Absolutely nothing. You are the empty vessel of an alchemist, an instrument that only acquires meaning when it is being used. Nothing remains of you. You will become the Work. Your name, your body, your personality will dissolve. You will be released from all responsibility, from all of your duties as an intelligent human being. Nothing will remain and you shall be nothing. For No-Thing is what you are: less than a worm. Bow down to the Higher Power. Sing it, sing it loud and proud, when you're marching through the streets, sing your creed, sing of your master, sing of your g*d: *Deutschland, Deutschland über alles!*

•

What a shock for her and Hugo to receive that package from Liebenfels, with that symbol designed especially for their brigade. Because that first night, under the glow of a single candle, Hugo's wild teeth had bitten through the elastic band of her panties, and by doing so he had uncovered, high up her inner thigh, a minuscule tattoo, smaller than a one-mark piece, yet very detailed: a sharp ring of flames and in the center of the ring a dancing figure, a cobra wrapped around its torso. Out of the hair of that figure flows the Great Life-Bearing River and in one of his many hands he holds the Drum that beats the Big Bang of Creation. One of the other hands carries a flame of the Fire that will consume the World. A third hand is raised vertically, in a gesture of Do-Not-Fear. One foot is firmly planted upon the demon Apasmara Purusha, the other is lifted in Dancing Freedom. Hugo's gaze travels upward, to Nebula's eyes. His eyebrows are frowned questioningly.

"Do not fear," says Nebula.

"Shiva is a g*d, Hugo. A Hindu g*d. The g*d of movement, the Lord of the Dance. Worship him, my sweetheart. Make him your totem! Make Shiva dance, honey mine." And that is exactly what Hugo did. He made Shiva dance, and he made Nebula dance, that night and the night after that and the one after that and the next; Shiva dancing under Hugo's hands and Hugo's tongue and Hugo's cock and Hugo's reverential breath.

Who can explain attraction?

Bøk offers her a mug of coffee. The liquid warms her stomach. She puts her hand on her belly, making a conscious effort not to let that hand slide down to the sweet spot where her memory of Hugo, now sleeping again, spreads its own delicious warmth.

She has to face it. She has become one of them. She dresses just like them: boots, straight-legged jeans, black jacket. She eats the fatty foods they eat, she drinks their cheap coffee, she guzzles their efficient beer. (Loving their music is still asking a bit too much.) She gets a rubber band out of her pocket and ties her long hair into a ponytail. Otherwise, it will fall over the camera lens. She looks around, to see if anyone is interested in taping a short segment.

Could this be true, has she started to fall for Hugo? Has she begun to love her damned existence underground?

words that remain, a lingering gaze fondly remembered by a loved one, maybe a few mixed-up genes that then go on to mix it up themselves. You can't hope for a more permanent future in this sublunary existence.

We cross the Glienicke Bridge. This used to be the border crossing between East and West, the place were spies were exchanged while the mine-infested waters of the Havel River flowed beneath. The GDR called this the Bridge of Unity. In the hills on our right—Danny behaves like a regular tour guide now—we see the fake medieval towers of Park Babelsberg. Somewhere in those hills, Studio Babelsberg is hiding. "That's where the movies were born, my friend," explains Danny, "*The Blue Angel* and *Metropolis*, man. Marlene Dietrich and Helena Guna, picture that. *The Golem* and *Doctor Caligari*. The great expressionists, man. Can you imagine the parties they must have thrown up there? Like, continuously? "Hey, what the hell, dude, we invented a new language of film, let's celebrate!" "

It's no more than a glimpse, then we're already entering the outskirts of the city.

The first few miles we drive through are mainly forest, then there are rows and rows of stylish villas, then a tangle of boulevards and low-rise apartment buildings in tints of brown and ochre. While we drove through Potsdam, it looked like we were going at a pretty good speed, but here in Berlin the two-stroke engine buys us no more than a snail's pace. Sleek, gleaming monsters of expensive metal dash past us, and the drivers of these luxury vehicles hardly even turn their steering wheels—they would get further out of the way for a bicyclist. The city impresses upon us the relentless necessity of tempo, the rush of straight lanes, the sharp tang of flashing glass—we must be on one of the main axes leading to the shameless heart of this turbulent metropolis. It feels like making a triumphant entry—like an ancient European monarch—I open up the window and breathe in the gasses, I let my hair flap against my forehead until Danny starts cursing and asks me to bloody well keep the *fuck'n' bloody* window closed because his *fuck'n'* balls are *bloody* well freezing off.

The departure hall at Zoo Station resonates with the insistent barking of scruffy dogs. They are tied to their masters, comatose bums who rest their heads on the hard steps of the stairs. They snore with their drunken mouths wide open, their breathing rattles. The fluorescent light—partially there to guide us to the shops, partially there for security reasons—hurts my eyes. I climb to the S-Bahn platform upstairs. Behind the wall of glass rises the snaggletoothed church that has become the emblem of West Berlin. The new tower next to it, octagonal, and very seventies in its ugliness, is lit up from the inside; it casts a bluish glow in the bluish dusk. Under the black steel-and-glass dome of the station, panicky pigeons flap about wildly, frantically overcompensating for their waning muscle power with the erratic mood swings of their wings.

Danny recommended that I take the eastbound train. He promised me a spectacular view of the old city. The *Siegessaüle*, the white palace of the President, the burnt-out corpse of the Reichstag, the Brandenburg Gate. I was planning on delivering myself into the hands of the city, on being a tourist, utterly and completely. I would go strolling on Unter den Linden, maybe drink a cup of coffee with *Schlag* in one of the *Konditoreien*, and then walk over from Bebelplatz to Gendarmenmarkt to greet Schiller's statue. I would probably have dinner in the basement restaurant at the Brecht Museum, where they serve the playwright's favorite dishes, the recipes taken from his wife's handwritten cookbooks.

We all know that life is governed by coincidences. We pretend there is a plot and self-determination, but in reality we know all too well that coincidence is the true order of things. The moment when the stream of coincidences stops, that is the moment to pay close attention and watch your step. When coincidences stop, reality stops offering alternatives. This is the moment when the indefinable it will strike.

I ride the S-Bahn and I press my tired head against the cool glass of the window. The heat is going full blast—squat perforated cylinders hang under the seats, patient as bombs in their bays, hot as hell. They are painted in a vile color of brown that does not exist in nature—no autumn leaf, no piece of bark, no spot of rust, no natural turd has this color. Someone must have taken a big empty oil barrel and emptied all the leftover paint from the GDR in it—such is the color of these contraptions. The blast of heat bites you in the calves and ankles. The passengers all rest their heads against the windows or lean against the partitions. The doorknobs are levers in the shape of stirrups.

This subway, like any other subway, is a vanishing machine. It makes the individual invisible. Each of us stares through the window, trying to catch our neighbors' reflection in it, and we all must be thinking of something, but if you would ask us what it was we were thinking about, we wouldn't be able to tell you—so fleeting are our thoughts. Even what's inside our heads isn't really there. Where then do we store our hidden world?

The world, here and now. Wessi-studs with artfully torn jeans, bulky plastic bags of the Gap or Banana Republic at their feet, are busy rolling a joint, just to have something to do; they talk loudly into their cell phones, setting up an appointment at the tanning salon. The masses dressed in many hues of navy heading home after an honest day's work. There is a boy with his arm in a sling. It is calm in our compartment, but it is the calm at the edge of hysteria that can often be felt when the dusk creeps up on you. And it's Friday evening: The whores are heading towards their *Strich* on Alexanderplatz or the Oranienburgerstraße, wearing short jackets of shiny PVC and high boots of patent leather. They lean far back on the benches, G-strings freely visible under their micro skirts. This is their last moment of rest before a long night of hard work and they let the heat crawl up their legs, all the way to the crotch. Outside in the raw evening air, girls that-can-be-had-for-free-if-you-play-your-cards-right are running around, so thin they're flirting with invisibility; slipover dresses in black spandex flutter like moth wings around their thighs. They take big steps, their hips sway broadly; they give every impression of being headed somewhere. They sport the bony knees and heavy lace-up boots necessary to keep the city underfoot. Their legs are bare, the cold notwithstanding. They look like cheerleaders for anarchy; just what the doctor ordered for the lonely man's heart. The cold vibrating glass against my temples feels refreshing.

I look out the window. I see the same graffiti on the Berlin walls as on the Potsdam campus; the numbers I can discern are 117, 116, 115, sometimes a 119 or 120. They appear to be painted in a thick impasto. Maybe somebody is working on a countdown on such a large scale that he can't possibly keep all numbers up to date?

I catch part of a conversation. A man and a woman.

She: "Do you have any siblings?"

He: "A brother."

She: "Younger or older?"

He: "Younger. And uglier. Fatter too."

Another fragment, in Berlin accent: "*Füf en Wessi is er janz in Ordnung.*" It takes me a while to translate, I only know a bit of standard German. "For a Westerner, he's okay." There are many layers of meaning to that sentence.

The apartment buildings and churches of the Moabit district bathe in the last natural light of the day, a necropolis with silver windows and weathervanes that groan in the icy wind. I catch glimpses of the River Spree, gentle, tame and *orderlich*, yet its black waters seem to still be rippling with the memories of the deaths of Rosa Luxemburg and Karl Liebknecht, thrown into these waters in 1919. The Spree's inky surface mirrors the fraying edges of the palaces of the bourgeoisie and the billboards of the New Reich. The last remnants of the mist have disappeared, the clouds are shredded into ribbons, and the sun is setting in a dusk gathered out of a few last gasoline-soaked rags of indigo and some crimson-fingered dirty flames. In between the Tiergarten and Bellevue Stations, I catch a glimpse of the campy guardian angel of the city, proudly displayed on top of her two-hundred foot column at the Große Stern, holding up her wreath of laurels and her iron cross. She sends out her blessings in a glow forged partially from her own gold, partially from the last rays of the setting sun. Alone and sovereign, she spreads her wings over the park, ready to take off and crash. Far behind her, I can make out the silhouette of the *Fernhsehturm*, the tower of East German television, an enormous globe covered in blunt spikes of stainless steel, hoisted a thousand feet in the air on an impossibly slender stalk of concrete. In the dying light from the west, two rows of the globe's facets light up, one horizontal, one vertical, meeting in the sun's focal point, a broad cross of sparks, a crypto-Christian evening blessing over town and country, courtesy of the communist architects. And then *they* make their entrance, through the harmonica doors that connect the compartments; *they* enter my rattling wooden cage and just in time too: under the sign of the Eastern Cross, with the final rays of the sun fading: the perfect time for the Angels of Dusk to enter the stage. On their shoulders they carry, like the blasé movie stars that they are, tape machines that blare some pumping walk-on music. Their heavy, lazy steps make their earrings sway; their backpacks are full of mysteriously bumpy objects, like the burlap sacks of thieves in an old silent movie. The bristle on their skulls stands upright; it makes them look like irate boars with yellowed teeth. One of them sucks on a bottle with an amber-colored fluid—it could be beer, it could be urine, the man's facial expression is compatible with either hypothesis. The second man has a Star of David painted on the soles of his boots; that way he can trample the state of Israel with every step. The third one bares a calculated grin of horse-like magnanimity. They are speeding in, and their paths lead them right in front of the boy with his arm in a sling. Soundless voices orbit the four (the victim, his attackers)—the unspoken thoughts of everybody in the compartment. I hear disgust and revulsion in those voices, but also a threatening undertone of approval, and here and there some silent applause. The boy looks Asian. A heavy backpack slides off the shoulder of one of the skinheads, by accident of course; it hits the boy's arm, also by coincidence; then it lands heavy as a bag of lead in the boy's crotch. His scream of pain is the only sound in the compartment. Riding becomes gliding, the landscape is frozen, the passengers' stares stiffen to a strained hollowness.

Almost the only sound.

You need a precipitating event; you need *something*. It needs not be a spark in a gunpowder keg—sometimes a simple drum roll may suffice.

Here is one.

I make two sounds.

First.

I click my tongue against my soft palate. Twice. Tsk-tsk.

Second.

I make a muffled sound of protest.

I say: "*Hey!*"

That's all that is needed.

Tsk-tsk.

Hey!

The squeaky wheel in an otherwise perfectly oiled machine. For a brief moment, the clockwork halts, and then, suddenly, it returns to motion, faster and more powerful, to make up for the lost three seconds. Three seconds are all that is needed for me to become as entangled in the history of this city as a bat in the elaborate hairdo of an opera soprano.

•

According to Daniel C. Dennett (*Consciousness Explained*), human beings are purely virtual representatives of themselves. Our goals and intentions all derive from the simple and unplanned fact that organic molecules that can create copies of themselves stand a better chance at survival than those who cannot. Our bodies are complicated machines, serving only one goal: to facilitate the act of copying. Evolution and development have altered our brains in such a way that they have become capable of faking self-representation so convincingly that they themselves fall for the scam. Consider, for instance, one trivial mystery of the brain, namely the remarkable split between its two halves (one half specializes in language and time, the other in space): It is a split that we never experience. Consider the deep miracle of eclectic synchronization, the 40 Hz quantum impulse of consciousness that rides on the waves of asynchronous brain activity: What we "are" amounts to nothing more than a ghostly apocalyptic rider on a nonexistent and yet very real horse. Consciousness is a theater in which we can see only perfectly predetermined or long-transpired acts, and yet we have the illusion of a freedom of improvisation unmatched by any jazz musician. Our brains are the authors of our lives. We are merely the actors.

Another way to put this is: Often we act first, and only after we have acted do we think.

There is something wrong with the man who approaches me. His stubble is too blond, the color of his eyes too azure, his step too Wotanish, and he is also too tall—he fits this role way too well. Steel caps at the tips of his shiny, newly polished boots. What can I do? I get out of my seat. And just like in schoolyard fights, all those years ago, I stand speechless and I let the other party make the first move. Bad idea. Every street fighter knows: He who gives up the initiative has already half-lost.

It is a ballet, a series of acrobatic moves that are all the more exciting to watch because the soloist is performing them in the deadening grip of a leather jacket and rough workman's cotton, with clanging chains around his waist and his ten toes imprisoned in heavy-heeled, firmly-laced mid-calf boots. A valiant *terre-à-terre en avant* with a balled white-knuckled fist hidden behind his back, a gliding *pas du chat* that forces his dance partner to reply with a *demi plié* and a *fendu*, followed by the inevitable *glissade en arrière* on the upbeat.

Good.

We've got a rhythm going.

His hand goes in the pockets of his jacket and his palm now holds a fair amount of pfennigs and thalers, his fist effectively becoming a cold sledgehammer at the end of a perfectly outstretched arm.

We dance.

His arms go in orbit. The coins catch some of the last golden light of the sun.

He: *coup du pied.*

I: *en l'air*, followed by a convincing *couru.*

He: *en face.*

I: *en terre.*

He: *fouetté.*

I: a less than brilliantly performed *échappé sauté.*

And now the guy is jumping right at me, squealing like a bat: *battement!*; *battement tendu!*; *battement frappé!!*; *grand battement!!!*

I: *en croix.* A foot beneath my ribs and I get turned over on my side.

A simple dance, lasting all of ten seconds, with hardly any contact made between our bodies—it's enough to get me on the floor in the fetal position, clutching my stomach, clutching my balls.

Then he takes a step back. He calls his two mates. They get down on their haunches and eye me curiously, engineers convening around some device with an odd mechanical problem, little kids gathering around a June bug, ready to tear its legs off one by one. "Still nostalgic for the gas, huh, after all these years?" What is

And then and there, on the platform of gray and dirty pavement, my head suddenly fills with the immutability of midnight. (The vision: My maimed fingers cramped around the trigger of a phantom rifle, an atrocious cold seeping through my bones. I am flat on my belly, inside my skull my brain feels like ice, I feel the weight of a woolen coat, I hear screaming and gunshots and the whistling of bullets and their dull impact on human tissue. I crawl deep into my sensory organs. I become touch, I taste the elasticity of my skin, the beating of my arteries, I feel the blisters of gooseflesh, the deep resistance of tensing muscle, the deep obstinacy of bone. I become tongue, licking at wounds and slime. And I become smell, sniffing and snorting the metallic scent of my own blood, the spiciness of gunpowder, the stench of fresh shit; and I become ear, all ear: the moaning, the idle threats, the cursing, the pleading, the begging, the panting, the wheezing. And then my eyes are pulled wide open, and the sudden movements and distortions of the images make me drunk: the lightning flashes and the sudden purple darkness of the blow smacks me down—oh, and I see more, I see far away, behind my closed eyelids the future blooms. I stand in a city of ruins, and I see small horses and a sword. Wordlessly, my mouth is screaming. I spit my breath into a scarf, I smell the rancid stench of my teeth, my adrenal gland is pumping, my heart muscle is stressed to the point of collapsing. My hands do their mechanical dance: I load the gun, I pull the trigger, I wait for the dull ache of the recoil against my shoulder, I reload. Somebody is yelling in German, somebody yells back in a West Flemish accent, and my head is empty, my hands are doing all the work, completely independent of me, loading, firing, recoil, loading, firing, recoil. My eyes are glazing over, I cannot see beyond the flame at the end of my rifle, but from that wall of white a deadly rain keeps coming down. Pharmacist, give me something to sweeten my memory!)

(I hear a voice, calling my name. Paul? Paul?)

•

The day I walked out of the oven's mouth, naked as a Frankensteinian creation—that was the day my life snapped in two. I witnessed both my life's end and its beginning.

This morning, a young nurse stopped by—it is hard to disguise age in your voice. He proposed to shave me. But I can't see him. How can I trust somebody enough to allow him to drag a razor blade across my throat when I can't see him?

There is the pain behind my eyes. Morphine might help, but they do not give me morphine. German doctors know no mercy. They have bad teeth, they carry their hair long and unwashed, and they visibly long for a cigarette break all day long. They aren't scientists, but poets in disguise; they have a bottle of absinthe hidden in their desk for the wee hours of the night. Poets, and this is well known, only have mercy on themselves.

I cannot sleep. There are too many noises in the hallway, and my blindness has sharpened my hearing. Leather slippers shuffle down the hall, rubber wheelchair tires screech, and there is the desperate dry scratching of cheap lighters operated by men with bandaged hands, to no avail.

The things that go on in and around a hospital, in between dusk and dawn. Ambulances sail to the emergency exit with their sirens turned off, suddenly all business-like and serious. Rusty-sounding trucks deliver the carcasses of cows and pigs and sheep and horses, each animal neatly cut into quarters, their frozen state a bad pun on rigor mortis. Around sunrise, last night's dead are exported through the same doors; a line of long black limousines is waiting, humming quietly. The dark is now so real to me that it is almost a substance. It touches me, it embraces me, and yet it also travels right through me. The feeling of mystery that darkness brings can only come from darkness itself.

My self-inflicted blindness is, I have been told, temporary. The first thing I will see will probably be the television set, so strategically and conveniently positioned in the corner of the room opposite my bed. The trusted gizmo will smile at me like an old familiar friend. I keep the set off, so that I will be greeted by my own shape on the empty screen, elongated and grossly blown-up around the middle. I will see myself as a tiny body with a swollen head—a distortion much closer to the truth than the reality is.

"*Hallo*," says a feeble voice. The next weakling is being wheeled into the room—my room—on a bed of sterilized steel. What could this guy's problem be? Drank too much and lost control over the wheel? A bad acid trip? A major case of constipation?

"*Loop heen*," I threaten him, in Dutch, as I threaten everybody who has dared to intrude in my personal space. I deserve my privacy; I almost paid for it with my life. I've also found that such curses are more effective in my mother tongue than in German. I somehow sound more convincing in Dutch.

The guy says: "*Pardon?*"

I reply with a snide remark: "*Ben je doof?*"

And he answers, in Dutch: "Yes, I am. I am deaf. And you speak Dutch!"

•

I wish I could tell you the following story (says the man with the sour breath), namely that I walked up the stairs at Kiepert, carrying the new edition of the *Thousand and-One Nights* under my arm, in my mind joining Scheherazade and her little sister in the bed of the Shah, and in my senile half-blindness I didn't see the open window—and I cut myself badly by my eyebrows. The wound started festering and gave me fever dreams. The dreams were so bad I worried I was going crazy. And that's how I ended up here. But it would all be lies.

I would like it, however (the man with the sour breath continues), if you would visit me at home, after this ordeal is over, after I'm released from this crypt. Then you could read to me. My terminally depressed chambermaid would let you in and you would wait for me in the antechamber, seated on a delicate Louis-Quinze chair. I would enter, my soft hand extended in greeting. "So, dear Paul from Leuven," I would say, "Thou descendest from the terrible heights of rigorous scholarship to read a decrepit man a book?" And I would propose the following, "Shall we perhaps read Sholem Aleichem this afternoon?" And of course we'll read Sholem Aleichem; it wasn't really a question. The words will be spoken in your voice, but my lips will move along to the sound.

•

Deep in my palms I carry the shards of my glasses, ground to diamond dust under the soles of my attackers. My ear is swollen, red, fleshy, wide open. A protective perforated plastic shell in robin's egg blue covers it, held in place by a ribbon of gauze wrapped around my head. Of the two options—screaming loudly from afar, or sitting on the edge of my bed and talking directly into the auricle—he chose the latter. Maybe the mesh in the bandage—he touched it with hesitant fingers and I was fully prepared to sink my teeth into his hand if necessary—reminded him of the ears of a priest, sitting behind the punctured particle board of a confessional?

Daylight filters through the blinds. The night is over. Maybe it's raining outside, I don't know. The light diffuses softly over the ceiling: woolly, bland, and innocent. I lie on my back in a bed in a small cell, above me there are hundreds more of these identical cells. The roof is too far away for us to hear the rain beating down—if there is rain. The cell above me, like my cell and all the others, has a balcony. The rain can't get at the window; there would be no telltale ticking of raindrops. I can't go to the window and check, either—I'm too dulled by the haze of painkillers. Dust particles float through the room, dancing and turning in the horizontal rays that pierce through the white blinds, a whirling ballet of chaos in this orderly abbey of surgeons and white harried angels. One good thing is that the ministers avoid our room, because it contains an atheist and a Jew.

"I'd love to come visit you. I'd love to read to you." The tone of honesty in my voice takes me by surprise.

•

"So what was it?" he asks. "Reckless drunkenness, etcetera?"

I tell him the story.

He laughs. "Who do you think you are, Flemish boy? A member of the Kami-kaze School of Political Naiveté? Don't you recognize provocation when you see it? Did your mother never teach you to mind your own business?" He spits while he talks, he's a sputtering man—little drops hang from the web around my ear.

"You're from Belgium? I remember Brussels well. I remember the stench of urine in that town. In every alley, in every vestibule of every abandoned building, the homeless, the drunks, the students, the hasty bourgeois all piss to their heart's content. It seeps into the sandstone, and when the moisture evaporates in the summer sun the urea crystals stink the place up. Berlin is different. A much more volatile town. This city carries its smells in the clouds. The smell of lignite and of two-stroke engines in the East, carbon dioxide in the West. And then the stench of history itself. Berlin is a funeral pyre. Books have been burned here, and people too. And ideologies—all thrown into the fire. Berlin is a city that has knowledge of the death of G*d. You can smell it in the air."

I don't know what to say. I hear his breathing at my ear.

His voice gets smaller. Meek. Sentimental. "Are you sure you would want to visit me, Paul?"

"I'm sure."

He grabs my hand. "That's very sweet of you," he says. He's switched to the polite form of "you," I notice. The teasing is over. "You'll really read to me?"

I nod. "Or you could tell me your story," I propose. "A lifetime in this city—you must have stories to tell." He withdraws his hand. It's not a gesture of rejection. He does it absentmindedly, just reclaiming a lost body part. Maybe he needs to concentrate his whole being, regain his strength by getting himself together, literally, as separate from the rest of the world as possible. He considers the question. "My story," he says, savoring the words slowly.

"Your story."

"My story is . . . a long story."

into my bloodstream, circulating freely throughout my body, finally lodging itself forever in my liver."

"There were rabbinic scholars in the camps," he continues, "Who tried to divine the Lord's intentions by placing the arms of random prisoners together. They were cabbalists, looking for patterns in the number combinations, for signs of a divine providence. Kind of odd, isn't it, young man? Assuming that Hashem had a hand in those horrors, in that terrible suffering?"

•

I hobble outside in the first chaste sparks of morning, a reluctant apprentice-demon on newly acquired hoofs, in borrowed clothes. The clothes of a dead man, probably, his family never bothered to pick them up. De Heer's words still resonate in my ears, burning themselves into the loops of my hippocampus: "Paul. Paul? Look? I am staying, Paul. I'm not going anywhere."

Two worlds are ringing through my ears at once. There's the pain, the very real pain of crackled cartilage and a squashed earlobe—the hammer hitting the anvil. And then there's the pain, no less real, of a story, hardly started yet but with a familiar ending. I have his address in my wallet, and I gave him the phone number of the Potsdam *Gästehaus*. "*Sei gesundt*," he told me when I went over to his bed to say goodbye—be healthy. He said it with a glimmer in his eye. Oh, he'll see, he adds, eventually he will see and he's been told by one of those poet-doctors that it won't even take all that long.

"I'll come and visit you," I promise him.

"Thank you," he replies.

I hobble through the street, looking for a subway entrance. It has been said: "The traveler arriving in Berlin receives a metal token . . ."

•

On this Monday morning in the *Gästehaus*, just like on any other morning of the working week, the cleaning ladies, joyless creatures in amorphous housecoats of third-class vinyl, scurry from room to room, doing indefinable and bad smelling things to the furniture and the floor coverings. In the kitchen, I bump into the Italian woman. Of course. Where else would she be staying then at the *Gästehaus*?

I am wearing my new glasses, bought on my walk from the hospital to the station. I saw them in the window of an antique store near Friedrichstraße Station, almost identical to the model I had been wearing on the day of the attack, but much more refined, the lenses almost round but not quite; the frame is real horn, the arms made of fine gold. The shop assistant didn't need to wrap them, they fitted my prescription exactly.

I went to the kitchen because I wanted to get some butter for the ebony-colored bread I had just bought at the corner shop. (The shop is called *Kaufen-und-Verschnaufen*, shop-and-catch-your-breath, quite an impressive piece of Dadaist poetry.) I carry the loaf under my arm, loosely wrapped in thin white paper. The kitchen is narrow. The woman is in the way.

"My name is Donatella," she says.

"And mine is Paul."

"I know," she says. Apple peels are snowing on a piece of newspaper; she's slicing some fruit for a late breakfast. She turns the paper over. A short article is circled in red. I see my name. An assault by right-wing extremists, etcetera, a young man who came to the aid of a foreigner was the victim of a cowardly attack, etcetera. The article makes it sound much more heroic than it was. A police officer had appeared at my bedside on Sunday; he asked a few questions and made me sign some forms. And now my story made the *Tagesspiegel*, ten lines or so right next to a story about an old man who died in his flat and was discovered long after, his body eaten by rats.

"Tshu left this here. We're proud of you."

"Thank you," I say. It's not clear if she's serious. There's something in her look, something that scares me, because I can't place it. She could be making fun of me; yes, it's quite possible that she's making fun of me.

"Tshu? Is that the guy who I 'came to the aid of'?"

"Zhu," she says. "Z-H-U. Zhu is the Chinese guy who lives opposite the kitchen. No, it wasn't Zhu. A friend of a friend of a friend, or something like that. He had heard about it, and he saw the story in the paper this morning. Every morning, he buys the *Tagesspiegel* to practice his German. He has very good memory, he remembered your name from the list next to the doorbell."

That's German efficiency for you: I've been living here for less than a week, and someone already put my name on a list next to the front door. Everything in the world is in its place. I try irony. "You're proud of me, and now you're using the newspaper to collect garbage?"

"It's the only piece of paper that was available, honey."

Donatella keeps on peeling the fruit. I feel a hunger pang coming up. I also feel awkward and uncertain, and for some reason impatient. And then there's the pain—the pain makes me grumpy.

"Excuse me," I say, "Can I get by you?"

"Oh," says Donatella. The easiest thing to do would be for her to just step out of the kitchen for the time it would take me to get to the fridge. Instead, she twists her hips just so, leaving me hardly any room to slide past her. I keep my butt to the wall, my dead man's jeans graze the paint. "You can touch me if you want," she says, teasingly, and for a second it looks like she might stick out her buttocks and pin me against the wall.

I smile politely. "I just wanted to get some butter."

In a half-empty jam jar with Donatella's name on it, an early (or is it late?) fly is rolling around lazily. I get my tub of margarine and some cheese.

"Would you like an apple?" she asks when I'm halfway out the door. She presents the fruit on her outstretched hand. "We better be friends, no? The house is so small, and the walls are far from soundproof. Soon we'll know everything there is to know about each other."

I look at the piece of fruit. It's intensely green, with frosted red cheeks. Is this an offering to the ridiculous hero? She must know, this woman with that apple on her extended hand, she must know what really happened in the subway, that it was plain stupidity and not courage. I didn't come to anybody's aid. I extend my own hand and for one solitary moment we stand between parallel mirrors, endlessly reflecting one another. Then both mirrors fall to pieces, and I take her gift. I polish the apple with my sweater until it blushes, then I put it back on my own outstretched hand. "Only if you take the first bite," I say.

She takes the apple and she bites. A big, deep, impressive, ravenous bite. The hard flesh of the fruit snaps; juice runs down her chin. She looks at me with a hint of malice in her eyes. Donatella chews and chomps, her purple tongue curls around the cream-colored flesh of the apple, then her throat swallows hard. I take a puny bite on the other side of the piece of fruit. She spits a pit into the sink. "So," says Donatella. "I do particle physics and cosmology. And what does the dapper pugilist do when he's not gallantly saving our defenseless Chinese brethren's narrow asses?"

And I, I do nothing. Not right away, anyhow. Right now, I just stand there, not knowing what to say. The apple turns brown and spongy while I look at it, urging it to supply me with a clever riposte. "Psychology," I finally squeak. "I'm a psychologist." Donatella shakes her hair back, her tongue shamelessly searching her molars for any last shreds of apple flesh, and she keeps her eyes locked onto mine, totally expressionless, except for that gleam that I can't place. I recognize that look. Physics is a respectable science. Everybody loves physicists. They talk about worlds that are palpable and totally strange at the same time—so strange that nobody can understand them, including the physicists who came up with those worlds in the first place. The person who doesn't tremble before the theories of quantum physics or the idea of super symmetry has not fully understood these theories. But what is there to love about psychologists? Yes, I recognize that stare all too well. My shoulders droop, the pain in my chest suddenly becomes unbearable. I have nothing more to say. We keep staring at each other. She breaks the silence. "Psychologist. I knew it. Always the observer."

"Huh," is all that I can muster. I want to leave. An incomprehensible sadness has taken hold of me; I need to lie down. "I think I'm going back to my room," I say. "The pain," I add.

"Right. Yes. Sure, the pain."

"See ya."

"You forgot your bread." She hands me the package. I grimace—my ribs really hurt now, even the light burden of my lunch feels too heavy to carry. The way she puts her hand on my sleeve, the way she holds my gaze—as if she's not afraid to get to know me, and not afraid to let me get to know her. As if other people were really worth the trouble of getting to know. "I'll see you too," she says. Emphatically.

Maybe I'm imagining things, but the door opposite the kitchen seems to sway, as if somebody has been spying on us through the crack. I throw myself on my bed. I fall asleep almost immediately, my mouth still filled with half-chewed apple pulp.

PART TWO

RAJAS

ד

EXILE

What does it take to become a Nobel Prize winner? How do you make a Nobel Prize winner out of a simple boy?

It helps to be Jewish, apparently. Almost one quarter of all Nobel Prize winners of the twentieth century are Jews. Literature: Bergson, Singer, Pasternak, Agnon. Economics: Friedman, Simon. Medicine: almost every year since 1964 a Jewish winner. Peace: Kissinger (*Kissinger*? He got the Nobel Peace Prize?), Wiesel, Begin, Peres, Rabin. (It helps to live in a permanent war zone.) Chemistry: Prigogine, Haber. Take my own field, physics. Einstein, of course, first and foremost. Rabi, Feynman, Lederman, Gell-Mann.

And I, Goldfarb, the preeminent guardian of the secrets of the world's most remote past, the End Times turned inside out. I am Earth's foremost authority on the Absolute Beginning, the Nanosecond Zero from which all else originates. All. The Everything. That is what I have tried to grasp: the Everything. Don't give me that look. It is possible. I'm not saying it's easy, but it is possible. All you have to do is reverse your thinking. Time has no intrinsic direction; the flow of time is just a clever illusion. Reverse your thinking, and you will be aiming straight for the Source. The present does not only give birth to the future, it also carries the past in itself, all of it. The Everything is utterly predictable. It is fixed, and that means that it is already here. I listen for the faint echoes of that first second, hidden so far away in the mists of time. I listen for the grating of dust between the stars, and from those minuscule frictions I deduct the future as well as the past. Once we have the missing element in our hands, that one missing piece of information, we will know everything. Everything.

No, I have never been a humble man. I am a seer. A true clairvoyant. That must have been the meaning of the dream I had on Friday night, the dream that rose up from such remote memories. I am a true fortune-teller: I can share the cushions and the bed with the best of the wandering gypsies. With one important difference, namely that my predictions are fantastically more precise than theirs, even though I, unlike for instance the lady in Bath, do not have a hand in the future I am projecting. We all run around like crazy on this little planet and we pretend that our wrigglings are of some consequence, but in the proper scope of things our deeds are microscopic and of no consequence at all. Whatever humans do, the cosmos remains what it always was. Outside, in the vast realm of space where almost everything that exists is situated, we do not count at all.

How many Jews are there? Not more than fourteen million. A quarter of a percent of the world population. Five-and-a-half million of those live in the United States. Two percent of the US population. Thirty-six percent of American Nobel Prize winners are Jewish. Do the math. Those numbers never sounded all that astounding to me. They merely reflect the greater laws of the universe: Everything is an echo of some past, the inevitable expansion of some point zero, and at the end of the day everything returns to that same singularity. So many of the Jewish physicists who won the Prize were German or Hungarian or Austrian refugees. Hunted by the Nazis, they fled across the ocean, and then they were all gathered in that magical place, the place where all the applicable knowledge of twentieth-century physics converged, where all those brilliant minds gathered, forcing the young science of physics into adulthood and thereby bringing on the inevitable disenchantment that comes with adult status. The flat-topped mountain range of New Mexico was the place where we finally got a glimpse of the core mystery of matter.

In exile, in diaspora, and then gathered again—such experiences make a person think, they make you wonder, they get you to write. I was part of that diaspora, part of that exile. I was a member of that band of apprentice-magicians; we were the first humans to make fire, fire from almost Nothing, fire from the innermost layer of the smallest observable unit of matter. I did not choose to be an exile. All of us had been forced to emigrate, and somehow all of us had drifted towards this wild and unforgiving place. What does the exile do? The exile looks over his shoulder, he wants a glimpse of what lies behind him, he wants to return to the place he came from. But you can never return. While you were gone, everything has changed.

I know that for a fact, since now I live again in the town where I was born, Berlin. I have no memories of this city. I was a small child when I made the passage, holding tightly onto my mother's hand.

•

The exile stands up straight, breathing through a narrow tube of silver.

Her body, heavy with drying plaster, hangs in a groaning harness of leather, metal tubes, and chains. The sculptor paces nervously around this scaffolding. He is merely an overseer now: Will it all proceed as planned? She has her arms raised symmetrically; they intertwine like the necks of two swans mating, or two snakes engaged in a bitter battle of strangulation—it isn't clear to her what exactly the artist envisioned, but she sure knows his vision hurts like hell.

She had undressed in front of him. Sterling Calder himself had bathed her feet and applied the glossy balm to her soles and the spaces between her toes. While his assistant shaved her armpits and her pubes, he sat on a chair watching, nervously smoking a cigarette. He paced up an down the room while the assistant hid Margarete's golden hair under a wig of rubber and covered her sex with a flexible cup of latex, and he shuddered when his muse's body was rubbed with the required mixture of lard and oil. He watched her nipples harden in the cold, or perhaps it was the assistant's rough rubbing that caused her flesh to bloom.

She had struck the pose. She had forced her body to obey his vision. Which one of us is the true artist?, the sculptor wonders as he circles the scaffolding, his hands in his hair. He already sees the radiating crown of stars around her head. Handcuffs are locked on her wrists, the chain between the cuffs gets attached to a heavy hook. For one interminable moment, the sculptor grabs his inspiration by the slippery hips, then his assistant rolls the concrete ball that will become the World under the model's feet. Calder's Star Maiden staggers. He stabilizes her, digging hard in her flesh with his fingers; the impressions will be visible bruises for weeks.

The buckets with plaster stand at the ready. Calder and his assistant take up their positions. They start at her feet and they apply layer after layer in a hurried silence; they build their way up with quick precision. The sculptor fills the space between the model's calves; he spreads the slurry between her thighs; his fingers glide into the cleft of her buttocks. Under his hands, against the warmth of her body, the mass tightens to a hard white gloss. Supple becomes hard; his vision of flesh begets a frozen star.

After he has covered Margarete's mons, Calder calls in the workmen. Together they slide the tower of hoops closer to the dripping figure; they attach girdles of leather around the drying star and push a set of heavy support beams against her stiffening lower body. Margarete in bondage. Imprisoned, unable to move. From high up, a worker pours plaster over the rubber cap that covers the moon-pale ghost's head. With the utmost haste and great concentration, Calder splashes thin layers of plaster against her neck. Margarete closes her eyes. He stops her ears with cotton wool. He brushes an extra layer of grease around her eyelids—they flutter briefly. He takes a deep breath. This is the critical moment. Resolutely, he plasters his muse shut.

•

This. Is. Your. Mother?

There were guys who had a framed picture of their mother on their nightstand. With a practiced flick of the wrist they turned the portrait facedown when the point of no return arrived. There were guys who kept copies of Italian alabaster nudes on their desk or posters of pink Flemish oils on their wall, all in the name of art. There was one resourceful student who had designed an ingenious system of pulleys and levers, so that he could switch at will between two reproductions of Goya's work—one of the clothed Maya, one of the naked version—all from the privacy and comfort of his mattress. But *this* boy's taste in art—well-well, that was something else.

Hannah was always decidedly generous with the charms of her body—she liked the lights on, for instance, to give her man the pleasure to scrutinize her nakedness in all its fulsome glory—but this witness to the proceedings was somehow disturbing. The figure on the nightstand, molded in bronze and not too small either, depicted a woman bearing a torch, the tip of which, held high above her head, ended in a frozen flame of frosted glass. Balanced on one toe, the woman seemed ready to thrust herself forward, perhaps into her lover's arms, or else into battle, or possibly into some dark ravine. And she was stark naked too, except for a piece of cloth draped rather complicatedly around her chest—one bronze hand held it up, for this scarf, or whatever it was, was subject to some heavy frontal storm winds, and therefore did not conceal the woman's form at all; on the contrary, the makeshift garment hugged her body so closely that it had the effect of accentuating her more than mere nakedness could—her nipples, her bellybutton, her pubis were all clearly delineated and sculpted with clear enthusiasm. To top it all off, Hannah had just learned that this clever piece of half-sublimated lust in Goldfarb's dorm room was modeled after a life cast of Goldfarb's mother.

This then is her competition. (For a second, Hannah Sidis becomes Hannah Freud.) "Don't you think this is maybe, you know, just a little bit odd?" Goldfarb shrugs. "It's my mother," he explains. (Woman, what do you want of me?) "Exactly. She. Is. Your. Mother! Don't you think that this is a problem?" Goldfarb shrugs

again. That's how he is, Goldfarb-the-student. He just floats along, he drifts wherever life takes him, and he gladly accepts whatever life throws his way. There's
nothing strange about having an artiste for a mother, is there? He's so used to the
lamp sculpture that he doesn't really see the problem—he doesn't even understand
how it could be a problem. He thinks for a moment. "Maybe we could, uh, turn her
around?" he proposes. All his life, as long as he can remember, he had fallen asleep
with this lamp at his side, safe in the glow of Mother's torch, secure under her half-
ecstatic and encouraging gaze. He extends his hand and rotates the sculpture a full
180 degrees. Hannah watches and immediately realizes that turning the lamp over
is not exactly going to solve the problem. The sculpted cloth that did such a poor
job at covering the front of the figure has left its backside completely bare. The
curves of the model's derrière are disturbingly well-polished, and her lower back
presents the viewer with that definitive hallmark of true beauty: two symmetrical
dimples, one on either side of a thrillingly curved spine, so soft, so eminently kissable, so breathtakingly pretty that they must have been molded from Aphrodite's
body itself.

Goldfarb, in the meantime, is not too happy himself. He does not like this
turn of events. He hasn't seen Hannah for a week, and this caused him an alarming amount of pain. He'd been looking for her all over campus in the last few days,
all in vain, and then he ran into her by accident near Houghton Library, a place
neither of them had ever visited before. He hesitated, because he didn't know how
he should greet her after this long absence (has she been avoiding him?), but there
was no need to worry—Hannah had come running, her face lit up with such unmistakable joy that Goldfarb experienced an instantaneous hot flash. They had
started kissing right then and there, to hell with scandal, and she had followed him
straight to his dorm, her arms wrapped tightly around his waist.

Two young lovers (if that is what they are, or will become) on a narrow bed
(*mit einer Lampe*), in their underwear (*Sie pflückt eine Sternblume und zupft die
Blätter ab, eins nach dem anderen*), and by the looks of it both rather ready to commit a certain act (*Sie fängt an zu singen*) that, if they were ever found out, would
cause them to be banished from Harvard/Radcliffe immediately.

Goldfarb is quite certain that his three friends have their ears pressed against
his door—there's that telltale scratching sound: Whenever one of them moves, the
frame of his glasses scrapes against the wood.

Hannah had asked him, in jest, who this woman might be who was holding
her torch so high over the goings-on in his bed—she must be the g*ddess of love,
right?—and for some reason he had provided her with the requested information,
and that had led to his present predicament. That Goldfarb unveiled the identity

of the lamp's model was unusual in and of itself. He is not what you would call a forthcoming person. For instance, neither Ted, nor Saville, nor Jake were in on this particular piece of Goldfarb lore. He has known Hannah for only a brief time, and already she's coaxed all his secrets out of him. And Hannah . . . Well, at this time, Goldfarb is too much focused on his own irritation, too wrapped-up in the blur of lust that he fails to notice that, conceivably for the very first time in her life, the practiced predator seems a tad uncertain. But, then again, even if Goldfarb noticed Hannah's uncertainty, he would have attributed it to something he certainly had an abundance of: lack of experience.

Hannah, why don't you just close your eyes and get on with it? There is no reason to worry. There is no way bronze—even of such faultless form and patina— can ever compete with living flesh; there is no way stilled perfection can compete with the suppleness of real-life limbs and the agility of a clever mind. Don't you remember that nobody in the world has ever been able to resist the warmth of your smile, especially in circumstances like these, when you (*das letzte Blatt ausrupfend, mit holder Freude*) drop your petticoat and panties on the simple hardwood floor next to the simple boy's hard bed?

•

Margarete Gottlob is, as always, ready for her close-up. This is perhaps the most important role of her life. Her neck is wet with her favorite perfume, her remarkable face caked white with powder. The perfume was acquired illegally: She stole it out of the medicine cabinet of a Parisian woman with a passion for gambling. While the wife made her extended forays into the ship's casino, the husband pursued some passions of his own. As the man languished utterly sated on the bed, lazily smoking a raspy Gitane, Margarete had poured some of his wife's perfume into a flask, a relic from her own husband, the brandy long evaporated. The face powder came out of the jar that was briefly made famous by the *New York Times*.

Margarete rehearses her lines. The English words taste foul on her tongue, an awful new language that requires such totally novel movements of mouth and lips, and such peculiar grimaces that she already knows she will never master it completely.

She had been practicing the whole trip long. She was thoroughly prepared. In her imagination, the Statue of Liberty, Eiffel's frivolous version of the New World, rose behind her in the speckled mirror, and her lips shaped themselves around the lines of text that she thought would have the largest effect on the immigration officer at Ellis Island. When she rehearsed, she did not restrict her imagination to sounds and vision; she also dwelled on smells, for instance the purported bad breath of the women around her, the moldy fragrance of their overcoats—the long humid storage aboard the ship taking its toll—the raw potato reek of their armpits, and obviously the stench of fear and insecurity itself. How much more attractive would she be than these unwashed masses, especially when she wore the pilfered perfume. Margarete was strong; she knew she could transcend all fear. If you can fool a Nazi, how hard would it be to persuade an American civil servant? She would lay out her arguments carefully: her career so far, but also her nonverbal means of persuasion par excellence: her fatal beauty, part nature and a good deal nurture. She might even use the ultimate emotional prop: her irresistibly pathetic little boy. With his big blue eyes, that eternal frown in his brow, and his stare permanently fixed on the floor, he seemed to sag under the weight of his own shoulders, as if he alone carried all the suffering of the Old World. His irritating refusal to look anyone in the eye was often mistaken for a touching timidity, and his paleness seemed to cry out "Where-oh-where is my daddy?". What horrors those eyes must have seen!—that's what their Dutch and French and English shipmates thought. The ladies fed him biscuits and tiny chocolates, and little Gottlob accepted those offerings with inaudible mutterings of half-thanks, and then he disappeared, much faster than etiquette prescribed. Margarete knew better. There was no reason to pity her son—he simply lived in a world of his own, a platonic heaven in which the stars (how clear the sky, by the way, on the ocean: how mighty the stars at night!) were replaced by numbers, in ever-changing patterns; he observed them with the inner eye that he had inherited from his father, grasping their beauty in fractal dimensions, in some idiosyncratic, mathematical language.

•

The shell is blindingly white and cool on the outside, but inside it is dark, hot, and suffocating. No matter how often she's gone through this process, the model always has to suppress a mounting sense of panic when the army of assistants approaches her. The shell is rigid and inflexible, it does not give; its shape is determined at the moment the plaster hits her rib cage. If the sculptor and his crew catch her at the moment of exhalation, when her lungs are depleted, she will hardly be able to take in any new air—no matter how hard she sucks at the silver tube, the plaster remains unyielding. Deep shallow breaths and hyperventilation result—a panic attack inside the mold is something she wouldn't wish on her worst enemy. (Herr Hitler maybe excepted.) The model has learned to expand her lungs to the fullest when the sweating platoon comes hither with their buckets full of sludge. She arches her back and sucks herself full of air. The consequence is that she will be ever the gentleman, took his Ariadne on the beach at the island of Naxos, and around midnight he left her there and took his boat back to Athens. Nothing you can do about that. Human males are not so good at this fidelity thing. Neither are the G*ds.

•

"I saw your picture in the paper," says the waiter as soon as they walk into the diner. He hangs around at their table to schmooze and rests the knuckles of his hand nonchalantly on the tabletop while he offers them his take on the weather and the political situation in Europe. Margarete comes here quite often. The coffee is cheap, the sandwiches are edible. On the bulletin board next to the kitchen, Margarete sees her picture, all stretched out in tiny dots, and a newspaper headline: "Model escapes Nazi Germany thanks to powder jar." Are there really waiters or cooks who read the *New York Times*? One of the Hispanic ladies in a hair net winks at her from behind the blue smoke of the deep fryer—is she an admirer of Calder's work? All this she has to endure because of Alan's insistence that she talks to a journalist looking for a good story—probably somebody he owed a favor.

"Inconceivable in the old homeland, isn't it?" says her lunch companion, a director she urgently needed to talk to, again according to Alan. "A waiter chatting with the customers at Kranzler? No way! Everybody is truly equal in America. No servility, no presumptions. Equal opportunities." He rolls a cigarette on the Formica tabletop and stops talking to seal the paper with his spit. "Shocking, of course. Liberating, but shocking." It's always a good sign when a director lights a cigarette. Nicotine jumpstarts the brain, this has been scientifically proven. That's why so many writers and actors smoke; that's why Margarete smokes. When a director is willing to use his brain, that's a very good sign. And when, after exhaling the first blast of smoke, he exclaims a curt "*Okay!*," that is a very good sign indeed. Heywood leans in closer, but he keeps the column of smoke away from Margarete; an old reflex of Berlin courtesy. He used to work as an assistant for UFA, the film company in Babelsberg; she still vaguely remembers the young Polish man who chewed his gum so religiously while pulling cables and carrying lenses; he was always blabbing away, always full of flights of fancy. His name was Hiacynt, back then. He wanted to go to Hollywood. Well, he made it about halfway, to New York. They speak English together. He's a Jewish boy from Warsaw—the German language has too many negative connotations to him now, he says. "Forgive me my political sensitivities," he mock-begs her, and she forgives him. She too has her political sensitivities.

Alan is Margarete's agent. Him too she knew in Berlin, as the young playboy

Alexander Provitz; he emigrated five years ago. Now he does casting on Broadway. Casting—the word conjures up images of Calder's workshop. Ugh.

Contrary to the experiences of these two gentlemen, Margarete's move to New York had been in no way the fulfillment of a dream, no gold rush, no new exotic world of unlimited possibilities. Margarete's passage was an escape; she made it just in time. A pity, actually, that all her rehearsing in the cabin had been completely unnecessary, a complete waste of time. She hadn't expected it, but the whole immigration procedure had been a joke. She didn't even land on Ellis Island; the formalities had taken place in a small office in some New Jersey harbor. They didn't ask for her story; she never had to perform her close-up with the trembling lips; her little son needn't have stared so despondently at the floor tiles. The officer had simply looked at her passport and read the document called affidavit, that piece of paper that reassured the authorities that somebody—Alexander—would be waiting for her in the States and pledged to support her financially. The officer had stamped her passport and had given her a work permit, to be used as an ID card as well. Only after leaving the building did she notice that the man had made a mistake. He had changed her name from Gottlob (so clearly calligraphed on her passport, in beautiful gothic script) to Goldfarb. She wanted to go back immediately. Alexander advised her against it. "Start a new life, Grete. Your new name is good omen. Goldfarb—Tinseltown, don't you see the connection?" In the Holland Tunnel, Alan casually showed her the tiles that indicate the border between the state of New Jersey and the state of New York. Margarete's very last border crossing before she disappeared forever into the big city. If she had batted an eye, she would have missed it. She felt strangely disappointed, almost cheated. This was the richest, most powerful nation on earth, and you could enter it just like that? Lazy laxness, unforgivable shoddiness, inappropriate joviality—what other certain signs of the approaching apocalypse would she have to endure here?

·

Exiles have so much to complain about. What is there to live for, in the belly of this leviathan of a town? The pamphlets, the hastily improvised cabaret performances, the quick glimpses of some Old World celebrity or other—that's all the excitement they have. The old poets keep reworking their old thoughts, keen and incisive, about racial prejudice (by which they mean: goyim versus Jews, not white versus black, what would German poets care about Negroes?), or they write odes to the loves of their lives, forever lost (they had conveniently forgotten to buy them a ticket for the ocean liner), or they write bitter essays about joblessness (although to realize that the lightshow playing across the curtains might not in fact be a hallucination caused by alcohol but the reflection of something very fiery and very real taking place outside. With trepidation he walked over to the window and peered through the crack in the curtains. He stood transfixed for a moment or two; then he called the minister of propaganda. Goebbels listened for a few seconds to Putzi's tall tale and then he hung up. *Der Reichstag brennt*, what a bad joke. Hitler was a little more suspicious, and he gave the minister the humiliating order to immediately get Putzi back on the phone. "And no more bad jokes, Putzi!" Hanfstängl had just enough self-control to tell Goebbels that if the *Herr Minister* didn't $#%#!! believe him, he could damn well ride his fancy #@%& car downtown and see it for himself with his own two @$#%&! eyes. The sound of the receiver smacking down on the telephone set was wonderfully satisfying. Putzi opened the curtains wide and unbolted the window: Fire and heat and the smell of burning wood filled the room. It made him cough. Or was that the flu?

Göring himself was already at the scene of the crime, and the glow of the flames amplified the glow of cocaine in his brain. The field marshal was terribly elated. He paraded up and down the sidewalk in front of the building in a camel hair coat hung with an impressive collection of mostly invented medals, and he enacted a hilarious parody of despair. Göring loved the opera, he adored the theater. He wasn't afraid of grand gestures. As soon as he had arrived at the scene, he had barked his first order: "Save the tapestries!"—those gobelins had been his personal raided property. Oohs and aahs emanated from the crowd when the colossal dome collapsed in a fury of glass and copper. The flames rose high above the gigantic fountains of water that the fireboats in the Spree were aiming so ineffectually at the building. In the meantime, a bewildered Dutch stucco-worker had been found wandering inside the burning labyrinth; he was now being interrogated at the Gestapo headquarters in the Prinz-Albrecht-Straße. The man didn't have much to say; he was just regurgitating some ill-founded Marxist-Leninist slogans; he also consistently asserted that he had acted alone. The authorities didn't need a confession from Van der Lubbe's to draw their own conclusions. When Herr Hitler stepped outside Goebbel's house on the Reichskanzlerplatz he briefly watched the reflection of the flames on the low-hanging clouds. After taking a whiff of the evening air he formulated his conspiracy theory. "Glad we got rid of the old barracks," Goebbels thought he heard the boss mutter, but it's possible that he misheard over the loud stammer of the engine of the service car that was waiting for them.

What was the truth? There was a rumor that SA-troops had been spotted in the underground walkway between the palace and the Reichstag earlier that evening. Was Hitler really as surprised as he let on? How authentic were Göring's dramatic statements ("This is the beginning of the Communist revolution! We must not wait one minute longer! Every communist must be strung up!")? Whatever really happened that night, the empty shell of the parliament building was still smoldering when SA-soldiers descended on the town like hawks. Four thousand members of the communist and socialist parties were taken from their beds and rounded up "for interrogation." The jails on Alexanderplatz and in Tegel quickly filled up, even when they were putting sixty men in a cell. The interrogations involved more than questioning; if any of the brownshirts felt that the information being provided left something to be desired, eyeballs were pulled out of their sockets, jawbones were smashed with rifle butts, noses were broken, fingernails pulled out with pincers, or penises dipped in acid. There was the infamous left-handed SA giant who brought his own whip, made of hippo leather; he always ended his performance with a biting double lash, left and right across his victims' face, leaving them forever marked with a sinister red X. When the jails started overflowing, the detainees—their numbers grew exponentially in the coming days and weeks—were packed in the basements or the courtyards of apartment buildings in Friedrichstraße, Rosinestraße, Kastanienallee, or in the Gladenecksche Villa in the Köpenick district; they even stacked them in the Universum exhibition hall in the Tiergarten. There was an SA-squad that forced their prisoners to lie down flat on the ground; they killed them then by dancing a crushing dance of death on top of their rib cages. The abandoned water tower on Knaackstraße was filled to the brim with communists. Detainees were dragged outside in the freezing cold to sing nursery rhymes for their captors. They were forced to dance barefoot in heavy oversized army boots until their feet were bleeding; then the SA-men urinated on their heads and threw buckets of ice water over the fresh wounds in their soles. Detainees were coerced into whipping their fellow inmates and then they were beaten up with sticks because they were such treacherous cowards—a crash course in National Socialism. There was one communist cell, eight young men, who were simply bricked up in the basement of the building where they held their meetings—a terrifying, hopeless time capsule of a grave.

In other words, violence reigned, and it was freely expressed in all its explosive force. The SA had a town full of accomplices. Screams can only blossom in silence. Friedrichstraße, Rosinestraße—these streets lie in the very heart of the city. The nighthawks who roamed from jazz club to beer cellar must have heard the cries of pain. They chose to remain deaf. So many of the windows of the wealthy on General-Pape-Straße overlooked the headquarters of the SA *Feldpolizei*. The inhabitants closed their shutters. The small farmers in Oranienburg pulled weeds and planted their leeks and beans for next summer within hearing distance of an overflowing concentration camp.

We are all born blind, right? Blind and free of sin.

What was Margarete's crime? A triple curse hung over her: She was Jewish, she was a socialist, she was an intellectual—just like everybody else who ever sat at Brecht's table at the Romanische, just like everybody else, or so she thought, who had ever stopped to wonder about the ways of the world. But her real crime was being an actress, possessing a body and having a voice, and sharing these with the world. Her crime was to be lit by the sulfur lamps of Babelsberg while she spoke somebody else's words. To be recognized on the streets as the woman who played supporting roles in so many masterpieces of the cinema of the left. Her most famous films included *A Trollop's Tragedy* and *Mother Krausens's Journey into Bliss*. Mother Krausens's journey consisted of opening the gas main in the artificial proletarian apartment built especially for her in the Babelsberg studio and then lighting a cigarette. Since the Nazis came into power, such a final journey was not a far-fetched scenario. So many of Margarete's friends carried capsules of cyanide sewed into the lining of their coats.

Margarete did not care for that option. A faraway, uncertain paradise held no attraction for her; she needed a more tangible haven.

A temporary escape. A short trip abroad, a vacation at her sister's place in Prague, and after the storm had passed, maybe in three or four months, she would go back home. How long can such madness reign, after all? A temporary farewell. Until her husband—he was a member of the *Kommunistische Partei Deutschlands*—returned from prison and called for her. (Margarete's husband was not one of her crimes. More one of her mistakes. But she couldn't leave him—he was the ostensible father of her child and held a mildly impressive position among the UFA top brass. Margarete hoped it was her talent and not his position and his feelings of guilt that had landed her all those glamor-*proletarienne* roles.) Anyway, a short breather. Getting away from it all. Just some time to recover.

•

"What kind of things do you do? You do bowling? You do bowling roles, or you only do non-bowling?" Margarete shakes off her thoughts. Bowling? The master filmmaker from Warsaw, the man who used to dream out loud about making Alpine mountain-climbing movies for the Americans—set in the Rocky Mountains, obviously—this man is preparing a movie about a beer-hall game? Margarete doesn't need to think too hard. She might look mighty fine in her booth in the diner, but this is the only

good dress she has left, and it's wearing out. And she's sick and tired of having to scrub that creepy white stuff out of the folds of her skin every g*ddamn night; sick and tired of rubbing smelly petroleum jelly all over her body every miserable night before going to bed. The plaster makes her skin rough to the touch, it makes her eyes tingle. And then there's the pain, always the pain, the pain of twisted, bruised muscles, the pain of ribs being squashed and breasts being crushed. No, Margarete has never visited a bowling alley. The queen of German proletarians was never one to indulge in simple blue-collar pleasures.

"How much does it pay?" The director laughs. It is a warm, agreeable, throaty laugh. "You're a fast learner, ma'am," he says. He leans even closer towards her. "More is always better isn't it? If you're willing to bowl on camera, I think I can get you a good clean five hundred. For a single day's work!" He puts his hand on top of hers. Black curly hair sprouts from the back. It is a gesture of encouragement, and she responds. With the index finger of her other hand, she quietly strokes his wedding band. In her own imagination, Margarete Gottlob, ex-supporting actress at the UFA Film Studios, has grown into a true world-famous-in-Germany film star, and now she has to make a decision. Her first role in an American movie. Maybe it's not the part she had been dreaming of—she never saw herself as a middle-class hausfrau in a beer hall—but immigrants should be happy with whatever job they can get. (Bark, you dachshund! Here's a biscuit!) And the money—that kind of money would pay the rent for a long time. She swallows her pride. "Count me in. Count me in for bowling!"

"And dye your hair blond, will ya? Very blond, as blond as you can get it—hair as white as snow, hair as white as Chancellor Hitler's ass, that's what I want to see!"

•

What did you say? Oh. The powder jar?

I'm so sorry.

A rather trivial story, actually.

A bit of an anticlimax, not unlike Margarete's whole life.

The goyim behaved as if nothing was happening. Everything was hunky-dory, life a bowl of ripe round cherries. As if all of a sudden, in front of their very own eyes, the raging bull of history hadn't just been unleashed, breaking clear through the fences, bright red blood gushing from his shoulders. In that atmosphere of furtive violence and massive self-deception, the Nazi government announced new elections, less than a week after the fire that proved to be the big bang of the swastika.

Posters appeared in the streets depicting, from left to right, as in a natural progression, the heads of Frederick the Great, Bismarck, Hindenburg, and finally Hitler, a historically inevitable series of ever-greater statesmen. The implication of their similarities—what had been conquered by the king and beaten into shape by the chancellor and defended by the field marshal would now be united forever by the humble former corporal—lulled the moderate-conservative factions to political sleep. There was hardly any opposition. Across the Reich, the Nazis got forty-four percent of the vote, thirty-seven percent in Berlin. After the landslide election, the parliament reconvened in an emergency meeting in the somewhat surreal décor of the Kroll opera house. Short-tempered SS-men in black uniforms guarded the doorway with hungry and irascible German shepherds at their side, and they refused entrance to any of the representatives who were likely to vote against the emergency law. The Horst Wessel song ("The street free for the brown battalions / The street free for the Storm Troopers / Millions, full of hope, look up at the swastika / The day breaks for freedom and for bread") resounded in the streets at night. By day, the German nation was a unified band of brothers.

Nobody knew where the father of her son might be found. On March 31st, the day before the official boycott of Jewish stores, Margarete took the train, her little son at her hand. Fifty deutschmarks was all the money an emigrant was allowed. Certainly not enough to survive three or four months in one of the more expensive capitals of Europe. Margarete hid a thousand-mark bill in a glass jar that she filled to the brim with face powder. In those days, every lady carried her supply of face powder, nothing suspicious about that. Margarete's container was made of glass. It was easy to see from the outside what it was: a powder jar, no further inquiry necessary. And it was very unlikely that police officers would stick their hands in a jar full of perfumed talc. In an overnight bag, she packed some underwear and just a few of her favorite clothes, a set of handkerchiefs, some toiletries and an innocent romance novel. Just the kind of stuff a lady on her way to visit her family in the East would have in her suitcase. What else could she have packed? The undeveloped roll of pictures that friends of her husband had given her, containing, they said, images of the maimed and tortured bodies of fellow party members? A copy of notarized eyewitness testimonies that the party had collected? Of course not—way too dangerous. She burned that stuff in the fireplace. She had a son to look after. But even if she hadn't, risking her life over her husband's politics did not exactly appeal to her.

They had a whole compartment to themselves. They didn't speak. Margarete's eyes were scanning the pages of her book, but she wasn't able to concentrate. The little one was looking out the window. Maybe he missed his dad. Or maybe he was counting the poles of the power lines and correlating this data with the ticking of his new watch; maybe he was calculating their average escape velocity.

They were arrested in Dresden.

Nazis stormed the train and forced their way into the compartments. They rounded up whoever looked suspicious. Margarete had her passport with her: that alone was enough to raise suspicion. The police pressed all of them into delivery trucks. Actually, the police weren't so bad—it were the SA-troops that kicked everyone who looked Jewish, beating them with their short truncheons. One older gent was forced to load his heavy suitcases onto the truck all by himself. When it was obvious that this was putting such a strain on his frail body that he was close to a heart attack, a police officer silently pushed the SA-man aside and heaved the suitcasesonto the truck himself, with averted face. Margarete considered the cyanide capsule in her handbag, a goodbye present from Käte. Would there be enough for the little one as well? On their way to the headquarters of the police and the SA, the former headquarters of the communist worker's union, now appropriated by the government, she thought of her husband and his political friends. The police refused to give them a reason for their arrest. This was merely routine, they said, a pure formality, ma'am, a simple administrative procedure. They were in essence free to go, but locked up in a large room. They could stretch out on the couches or the thick carpets in the rare moments when they were not being harassed ("Take a good look around you, you communist pigs," was the snide comment of one of the SA-officers. "This is how the corrupt representatives of the working class really lived!"). Policemen accompanied them to the toilets. Five times they examined Margarete's handbag and her suitcase; five times Nazi hands frisked her body and her son's; five times they fingered the all-important jar while Margarete applied all her acting talent to looking as disinterested as she could. They didn't find anything incriminating on her, those soldiers. The interrogations continued over the next day. The suitcases of the travelers were heaped in a formless pile in the hallway, badly locked, their contents bulging.

Late in the evening of that second day, they were released. Just like that. And as there was no apparent reason for their arrest, they were not given a reason why they were being released. No reasons were necessary, of course: Everything was in order. The police did retain their passports. A broadly smiling officer explained that whoever had a clear conscience could reclaim their documents in the police station of their town of residence. It all felt like an April Fool's Day joke that had gotten a little out of hand. Most of the travelers boarded the first train that would get them out of Dresden. Not Margarete. She was too tired. There was a hotel directly opposite the police station, and she booked a room there—she was just too exhausted to look elsewhere. They ate their *Abendbrot* in the dining hall. Margarete took a bottle of wine upstairs and fell into a bottomless sleep.

The decision to stay in town turned out to have been fortuitous. She had the habit of reading the newspaper at breakfast. This habit saved her life. The Sunday paper reproduced the newest edict from Berlin—all travel to foreign countries was from now on strictly limited. Only new passports handed out by the Nazi authorities and with the right type of stamp were valid for travel abroad. An exception was made for those travelers who were already underway.

Margarete decided to postpone her visit to the museum to see Raphael's Sistine Madonna. She had everything and nothing to lose. How could she ever get her passport back in Berlin, let alone get a new one? She drew a hot bath and took extra care with her makeup. She combed a fashionable part in the little one's wet hair. On the sidewalk in front of the hotel she did the deep breathing exercises she always did before walking into the limelight, and then she crossed the street. The guard at the door recognized her from the day before and greeted her with a rude sneer: "And what does the Jewish pig want *now*?" Margarete, totally immersed in her role, lifted her chin and with blazing eyes and in a curt official tone she demanded to be led to the responsible officer, im-me-di-a-te-ly. The guard was too flabbergasted to refuse. Inwardly, Margarete thanked G*d for the automated responses of the German civil servant, and she followed the man closely. When he opened a door, she quickly slipped in behind him. Some mid-rank officer was soaking his feet in a tin tub. The man was visibly embarrassed—Margarete was by now behaving quite like a lady of the higher castes—but she offered him her sweetest smile and a flutter of her hand.

"I know how these things go, Herr Doktor," she said. "My husband is a civil servant just like you, and Sunday shifts are long and lonely. One would rather be home, with one's wife and children, *nicht wahr*?" The officer nodded. He dried his feet and put on his socks and boots. "I was on my way to Prague, Herr Doktor, for a brief vacation. Well, you know how busy the life of a *Beamtenfrau* is—going to receptions with your husband, organizing dinner parties. I need a breather. If I have to go back all the way to Berlin and then back to Prague, nothing would be left of my vacation." Again she smiled, and she spread her hands out in front of her. "And my little son! He was so much looking forward to seeing his cousins! Well, you know how children are!" She took the newspaper out of her bag. "Here is a decree by Adolf Hitler. You see? Here, it says that travel is permitted to those who started their journey before yesterday. Would you, could you, might you be so good as to check whether it would be possible at all to hand me back my passport?" This was the carefully planned coup de grace. Who other than a bona fide traveler would voluntarily enter the bowels of the repression machine and make reference to one of Hitler's orders? Nobody had recognized her in Dresden—very few policemen are fans of Brechtian socialist drama. If anybody had, she wouldn't have been released, yesterday.

"I'll see what I can do, ma'am," said the officer, "but I'm afraid that the passports have been mailed to Berlin already."

Long live the occasional glitch in the bureaucracy, thinks Margarete when he returns, less than three minutes later, waving her passport in the air with a triumphant smile, as if this were his personal victory. A sisterly kiss on the cheek is what he gets for his troubles. It makes him blush.

They take the early afternoon train. This time all the compartments are full, but still nobody speaks, and nobody looks their fellow travelers in the eyes. When the train crosses the border, a collective sigh of relief goes through the train. They are all refugees. They all made it, barely, and right on time.

•

But oh, the humiliation. The model Kismet—just recently reborn as the movie actress Lene Lavli—spends evening after evening in a smoky hall in the Bowery, trying to get a handle on those heavy Brunswick balls, running around like a vulgar housemaid, beads of sweat collecting on her skin. She tries to inhabit the role, according to the principles put forward by that new-fangled American-Russian acting method that's all the rage now. Oh! So many terrible misses, and then one time the humiliation of slipping on the floor and falling flat on her face: the slow process of acquiring a new skill, of practicing until your fingers turn blue and your legs cramp up. But she persists, and finally, lo and behold, the evening comes when she can at last send the wooden ball elegantly down the maple chute, hitting the king pin and his whole entourage in one stylish sweep. Not bad for a girl, not bad at all, and a dashing figure she cuts too, declare the guys who sit behind the long bar counter in the back of the hall, chewing gum and shooting the breeze, and by way of respectful salute they raise their brown bottles of Budweiser in her direction. Every now and then, the young boy Goldfarb will meet one of the cuter members of this gang at the breakfast table. "What's your name, buddy?" the guy asks, and his still un-pomaded hair falls into his eyes. "Goldfarb," mumbles the sulky preadolescent, and he continues to work his way through his bowl of cornflakes without saying a word. He does not avert his gaze from his mother's lover—oh yes, he can manage eye contact very well, if that suits his plans—and he answers all the guy's cordial questions with silence and slow mastication. It is a most refined performance, and his mother is thankful for it. American men misunderstand her easy favor, they all want to go steady; they've hardly left her bed before they start dreaming of having a family. Goldfarb's behavior is very helpful in keeping the beaux at bay. With their square jaws and their boisterous good nature, these American lovers have a hard time dealing with sullenness and gloom and rejection, especially if it comes from the lady's peevish son. It'll never work out, they think, and they never again attempt to seduce the powder-white queen of the bowling alley. Those hopeless *Amerikaner*, scared of a sluggish kid.

·

But no, then *this* humiliation! The director had looked strangely at the canvas bag she dragged to the set and stranger still when she showed him its contents—a big black heavy ball. She explained that she didn't have the money to have one made to measure, but that she had been able to buy one off the bowling alley—it was an almost perfect fit. "Boh-ling?" he asks, and he laughs. "No, not boh-ling, dah-ling! Bah-ling is what I said. Bah-ling!" An immigrant who hasn't understood the accent of another immigrant. There's a world of difference, she learns quickly enough, between bowling and balling. What an eccentric mountaineering movie is being filmed here! What peculiar mounts, what dizzying descents! She'll be able to laugh about this later, she's sure, but right now, she's much closer to tears. If only it had been an ordinary stag film, the filmstock as dirty as the subject matter, with bad focus and everything either over- or underexposed. But no, Mister Yablomi needs to behave like G*d's gift to the world of the blue movie. He's an artist. An auteur. He hired a bunch of makeup artists off Broadway and there are girls running around with tissue boxes, performing a procedure called fluffing, and there's even a hairdresser hired especially to cut and shape and blow-dry Margarete's pubic hair, while somebody else is—heaven forbid!—powdering her butt.

She'll be able to laugh about this later, yes she will. Immigrants have such a misguided sense of pride. Grin and bear it. Don't let on that your own stupidity got you into trouble. Instead of hitting Yablomi in the face and leaving the premises in well-justified anger, foregoing her five-hundred dollars, she does what she's paid to do—she lies naked under the unforgiving lights, trying hard not to listen to the director giving instructions to his crew of male "actors." She understands why she had to be whitish blond for this role: the color of her hair, the whiteness of her body, it all contrasts so nicely with the black satin sheets. She doesn't have to do anything, he says, please don't move, the customers don't like it. And in a characteristic display of insensitivity regarding her past he adds: Just pretend you're a statue, dearie, a statue of alabaster. Would she survive it if a waiter in a coffee shop ever walked up to her and mentioned with a crooked grin that he saw her in a movie in the backroom of a dirty bookstore on West 26th—a legendary performance, and with such beautifully sinister close-ups? Margarete bites her lip and this makes the director cry with joy: It makes her lips puff up, they're so much fuller and redder, what a gorgeous effect, just hold that pose, will you, honey? She wants to scream but, well, yes, later she'll be able to laugh about this, she promises herself, really, and are there actually people who go see these movies? And the people who do, do they ever watch the actresses' faces? She rakes her hand through her hair, so that it falls into her eyes. She's lucky: Heywood just loves it. And the tear that rolls out of the corner of her eyes? This too fits his artistic vision magnificently!

●

And Daedalus, tired of Crete and his long exile, longs for the land of his birth. The king and the sea block his way, but he says to himself: Minos, you may rule over the island and the ocean, but we shall go by air—for you do not possess the sky. (A few quail feathers, remnants of the royal supper, lie in the gutter. Let us mount those on a frame of wood; let these become our wings.) For you do not possess the sky!

●

How do you reconstruct a past that is not, in effect, your own? I was a puppet, thinks Goldfarb. A prop. I became an émigré because my mother was one. I am only a half-Jew, I could have stayed in Germany. Or with my aunt in Prague. I don't know if I should be grateful or not that I was dragged from Berlin to the far-off coasts of the New World, to that harbor town that seems to be populated exclusively by washed-up refugees from Germany or Russia or Hungary, by expats from China and exiles from the deepest forests of Africa. People who landed here unwillingly, disowned by their homeland, like the Jews, or that were simply taken, like the Africans. This New World is no more new than the Old World is old. What it was I helped bring to fruition in that remote corner of that new country—this too was new and old at the same time. And the story of our invention, our crime and its lack of punishment—that story could just as well have been biblical.

See where it got me, my winding life. I live in a penthouse in the Tiergarten. A very German apartment, quintessentially Berlinesque. The building hardly registers on the outside, but inside my flat is unashamedly gaudy. Gigantic black-and-white abstract paintings in the living room, a rooftop garden in Japanese teak with a miniature pond inhabited by giant koi, walls covered in antique books and a choice collection of classical music next to the stereo. I had nothing to do with the interior decorating or the taste in books or music: I left it just as it was when I bought it from an American businessman on the move. He cared as little for these luxury items as I do—he just cared about appearances. The place must have been done by one of those postmodern architects that you can pick up on every street corner these days. My apartment is worth a couple of million deutschmarks, and yet you might not even notice it: there's a furniture store on the ground floor of the building, and the entrance to the apartments is hidden behind a door of frosted glass—bulletproof and shatterproof of course, with even the security cameras carefully hidden from view. Exactly the kind of place I would have lived in, I guess, if I had stayed in Germany and gotten my degree under Heisenberg, for instance, and had become the *Direktor* of one of the Max-Planck-Institutes. The Tiergarten, that's the park where my mother used to play as a child. This is the city where she went shopping as a young mother, me in the baby carriage or, later, walking next to her and holding her hand. I don't remember anything about it, I remember nothing at all of our flight—not the train ride, not the interrogation in Dresden, not the ocean passage. All those things have been excised from my memory. Maybe it didn't even register at the time, maybe I didn't even realize what was happening. I was very much absorbed in my own world, then.

How much time do people really spend looking through windows? The brightly lit G*ddess on her column of granite two hundred feet above the ground is staring directly into my eyes. She guards my penthouse without so much as a hint of a smile, and she raises that wreath of hers as if she preparing to crown me with it—not because of my past, but because of what I will soon accomplish. My reflection in that window: a trim man in his seventies, dressed in an expensive black turtleneck sweater and black corduroy pants, freshly shaven, with horn-rimmed glasses and powerful jutting jaws, ready to spend another night all by himself. I have adapted well to this city. I seem fit and in shape, yes, perhaps even sexy in my aura of self-confidence and money and my flattering Italian clothes, but how much time do I still have left, and can one ever fully repair the damage one has done?

Good. Enough of the wretched present. Let's give imagination free rein once more.

•

The queen, frazzled, her cheeks red with excitement and exhaustion and embarrassment, staggers out of the cow, humiliated to the core, her desire for sex forever ruined.

The procession of dwarves comes and goes. Their chisels hammer the plaster like the beaks of woodpeckers. Kismet lies in ruins on the floor of the workshop, the fragments of her body's negative artfully arranged according to the laws of anatomy.

Lovingly, Daedalus straps his son into a suit of feathers.

Goldfarb ejaculates in vigorous spurts in and around Hannah's mouth and it doesn't stop, it just keeps coming and coming, and she does her best to swallow, but she can't keep up, and then she suddenly erupts in a fit of squeals and hiccups and giggles.

Kismet/Lavli sits at the kitchen table. She writes and writes. It's late in the evening; the cigarette smoke floats like a bank of fog through the room. The money is spread out like a deck of cards in front of her. It will pay this month's rent, and the next, and so on. Tomorrow is the second day of shooting; there's always a second day, no matter what directors say. But the movie isn't on her mind at all: She is completely focused on the play that she is working on. Heywood's movie gave her the inspiration. If she has to humiliate herself so, why not write about it? It is a courageous piece of drama, a mixture of myth and memoir, and over the course of her writing it the events of the day will find their way into the manuscript, much in the same way the residue of the day finds its way into her dreams. In the quiet of the night she writes the title of the play on the cover of the folder. The work will keep her occupied for the better part of a decade. She writes the title in her mother tongue, in big deafening letters—in between these covers lives, ready to explode, the book *PanzerFaust*!

•

The phone rings. Who could be calling me at this hour? I put the receiver to my ear and I press the speak button, but I say nothing. There's no response. I hear white noise, nothing but white noise. Wrong number? Bad reception? And then, right when I'm ready to lay down the handset, a voice in my ear, a woman's voice, soft and vulnerable and at the same time utterly final: "Professor?"

I wait a few seconds before answering. I take a deep breath. I consider my options. I watch my reflection in the window, I watch the golden G*ddess, I watch the reflection of my face coincide with hers. I consider my options, but maybe not long enough. There's precious little time to think. I open my mouth. I lick my lips. I cough.

"Yes?" is what I say. "Yes? Hello?"

THE STORY OF THE TWO SLAPS IN THE FACE
AND THE TIDES OF THE WORLD

"Are you recording all of this faithfully, Mr. Andermans?"

De Heer was released from the hospital just a few days after I was, a full seven days after being admitted. I sit in his living room, in one of his armchairs. De Heer called me. That the call reached me was no mean feat, as I probably should have realized when I gave him my number. There is only one phone in the Gästehaus, a relic from the days of Bakelite, an almost religious artifact preserved under its own little peaked hood in the ground-floor lobby. On the rare occasions when the phone does ring, nobody is much inclined to run to that little chapel. More often than not, it's a wrong number, or else the caller is looking for one of the other housemates, and then you have to go through the trouble of running up the stairs and locating that housemate. On top of that, one of the cleaning ladies—the one who wears her hair in short curls, thick and blond as butter cream—is constantly using it during the daytime. Seated on an upside-down tin bucket, she yaps away for hours on end, entertaining her many relatives in Karl-Marx-Stadt with amusing stories of her latest surgery or the rising price of gasoline. Undoubtedly, she considers this an act of insurgency, a serious subversion that somewhere down the line will do irrevocable financial damage to the recently re-established university of Potsdam that has so disappointingly aligned itself with the neo-capitalist political forces of the new Germany.

It was this lady, then, who came to tell me that there was a phone call. I was still in bed, using the pain in my bones, slowly ebbing away yet ever-present, as the excuse for my own subversive decision to not show up at my office. I never asked De Heer how often he had "called on me," as he termed it, before he finally reached me. He sounded urgent and exasperated enough on the phone: "My soul, dear Paul—my soul! After I awoke, it knocked at the gates of life, begging for an ear, burning for a voice. My soul, dear Paul, it screamed for you!" Although his words gave out a lot of pathos, his inflections were too sincere to be sarcastic, and so I rushed to his apartment, my heart thumping as though it was a romantic rendezvous. (Though the fact that I had to take the S-Bahn to get there didn't help with keeping my heart rate low.)

"Mr. De Heer," I had told him over the phone, remembering my promise to read to him, "It will be hard for me to be your voice. I do not read Hebrew or Yiddish, my German is stilted, and nobody's ever written anything in Dutch that can stand the test of being read out loud." (As you can see, De Heer's particular linguistic quirks were already contaminating me.)

"There is no need for you to read to me, young friend. Before too long, I will be able to do that myself. Just today, I was able to distinguish red from blue. Soon, I will regain the full faculties of sight, as foretold by my doctors." I told him how happy I was for him, happy that he was doing so well.

"So, do you want me to listen? Will you tell me the rest of your story?"

So, yes, indeed, that was what he wanted. He wants me to listen to the story of his life. More than that, he wants me to write it down. The German language, he says, is too fraught with bad memories to be used for memoirs, and his Dutch has become too fragile. He asked me to buy a tape recorder, but I told him I'd rather take notes. I assured him that I'm good at taking dictation. "No pen is that fast," he objected. "I have my laptop with me," I said. "I just finished my dissertation, so I'm well-practiced. I type extremely fast. The machine hums quietly, and you'll hardly hear the keys, it'll sound like a mouse is tiptoeing through the room, it won't disturb you at all. In the evening, I'll edit my transcription, and you can correct it the next time I come visit you."

A few seconds of dead air in the receiver. "I like mice," he said.

I sit opposite him. His gaze is still half-dead and his lips are black from the charcoal pills he takes to absorb the quinine. There's no chambermaid, of course, and neither is there a waiting room. But there is this living room, much more a library than a living room, an enormous library, occupying three of the four walls, and even from my chair I can see that the shelves contain many interesting old spines. They are all arranged neatly; he must have an orderly mind.

Well, yes then, let's get the story started! De Heer crosses his legs. He closes his eyes and licks his lips.

"This," De Heer says, "is the Story of the Two Slaps in the Face and the Tides of the World."

•

THE STORY OF THE FIRST SLAP IN THE FACE

I am eight years old. Underneath my window the world is changing. Changing forever.

It is the middle of the night. I am woken up by the louder-than-usual hubbub and clamor of the streets, and by a physical sense of mass in motion—indescribable but real, a rowdy wave of gravity traveling through the street, beckoning me, dragging me out of bed, forcing me to my feet. I open the curtains. Below, I see a giant dragon shaking his fiery scales, a sneaky mile-long serpent with jewel-studded armor and a hundred-thousand throats, and into those flaming throats a golden drink is being poured, a drink for g*ds, and from those flaming throats a song is coming forth, a song for g*ds, sung with an urgency that is unmistakable, although I cannot make out the words.

I am no stranger to political parades. I have seen so many in my young life. Every time one passes through our street, Mother pulls me away from the window. When we encounter one when we're outside, she takes me by the hand and leads me into a side street. None of those precautions are necessary; I am not the least bit fascinated by those endless rows of rough-hewn men and their ridiculous goose-stepping. Conversely, those men pay no attention to a little tyke like me. But tonight is different, I feel it, I feel it in my gut, tonight is completely different. This is not the usual procession of butchers' sons and postal employees, four abreast, mighty proud but also ill at ease in their borrowed costumes. They do their best to look threatening, but underneath all their bravura—these are my father's words—you could sniff out the petty hesitation frequently displayed by common thieves.

No, tonight the crowd is undeniably different. There is no order here, no order either new or old; what's being flaunted is religious abandon and divinely inspired disarray—a force of nature has been unleashed, so say the masses, chaotic and unstoppable: Behold that twisting river, the stream of gold and fire, thousands upon thousands of men, many more men than I have ever seen together in my life, many more men than have ever marched through the streets of this city or any city in the world, this is the largest parade of all time, an endless flow of human lava. It is impossible to keep track of any individual face, so turbulent is the crowd, just like it is impossible to keep track of a single snowflake in a storm, but

I can catch some glimpses. I see men with poorly shaved cheeks, clutching tin mugs in their hands; I see men whose gaze floats upwards, ever upwards, in the grips of some religious ecstasy; I see men with bloodshot eyes that flicker around nervously, scanning the crowd of spectators; and all these men are singing, a thousand uvula vibrate freely in the cold night air, a song sung in twenty different keys, and twenty different tempos too, but it is all the same song—*Deutschland, Deutschland, Über Alles!*—and so enormous is the mass of people that echoes blend with echoes and my skull rings with the harmonics of the multiple versions, the volume swelling and shrinking in unpredictable waves, the words and the music pursuing each other in a futile mating dance. There is the white and pink of eyes and flesh, the pale lightning of a suddenly revealed pair of fangs, and whenever a set of those furtive pupils catches my eye I shudder—but why should I? Why should I be afraid? I am a little boy in maroon pajamas, watching out his bedroom window with mouth wide open, giddy with excitement: What's wrong with that?

My bedroom is the only room in the whole street, it seems, that still has its windows shut. Also the only room that is still dark, since the demonic flickering on the bedroom ceiling of our neighbors across the street is probably just the re-flection of the torches carried by the marchers. Yes, I am quite sure of it now: Only real flames throw such capricious half-shadows and such freakish reflections; only real flames can give the glasses of the citizens hanging out of their windows such an urgent glow of historical fever. From the open windows, neighbors throw scraps of paper onto the marchers in imitation of the triumphal ticker-tape parades in faraway America, and whenever a piece of paper hits a torch, it lights up and flares upwards, spiraling and dancing like a firefly. Little mortal that I am, breathless behind the window glass, I read the dragon's fire signals, and even though I never knew I had the decoder, I understand what's being said: The signals' meaning is humming in my gut.

Come.

Come!

I must have misread the signs of my body. No, I'm not afraid. Excited is what I am, aroused. *Come*, the mass of people intones. *Come, come with us.* Small as I am I climb onto the marble windowsill and press my forehead against the irregular sheet of glass, and cold as death it presses back, and the room is cold too, while everything outside looks so warm, so magical, so—alive!

Come. Come with us. Dance. Dance with us. What am I doing here, locked inside this chilly room? I want to be with *them*, I want to be outside with the celebrating masses. What and why they are celebrating I do not understand, but it all seems so happily out of control, so utterly different from what the four walls

accident. One is saved by an angel who then disappears, the other is left to his fate. I was saved because I thrashed around in my agony. If Herr Eberhardt had also made a lot of noise, he might still be alive today."

"Mr. De Heer," I say, to get us back on track, "what about the Story of the Second Slap in the Face?"

•

THE STORY OF THE SECOND SLAP IN THE FACE

Each and every day, the glorious dream of National Socialism moves one day closer to its full realization. An important step in the realization of the ideal is the elimination of the enemy from within.

Plop!

Something hits the back of my head. The outside of this object (the thing that causes it to go *plop*) is soft and yielding; its core (that what hits my skull with its plucky "!") is hard and painful. The hit stings, just like a magpie's beak must sting when it goes a-pecking on a young rabbit's skull.

A second projectile hits its target, this one more vicious than the first, more nauseating in its stickiness, more biting in its sting. I have no time to think, I just keep going, reciting the poem loud and proud, the way the principal told me to. "Like a general addressing his troops," he had said, "That is the way to speak, young man. Pull in your belly, proudly pump up your chest!," and so I stand, my chest puffed up, filling my lungs to the brim with pure German air, air that when pushed through my vocal chords becomes the words of the poet, the words I so diligently learned by heart:

> *Was dich auch bedrohe, ein heil'ge Lohe*
> *Bringt dir Sonnenkraft.*

> (Whatever threatens to conspire,
> You burn like the sun with holy fire.)

They're getting serious now. The trickle of projectiles has turned into hail, and the freshly starched front of my brand new bright white shirt gets covered in brand new bright red stains. The missiles lash my ears, they splash with tiny wet sounds on the lapels of the black jacket my mother bought just yesterday at Hermann

Thiel's. For a moment, they cling to the fabric, then they slide downwards—my formal clothes are dripping in dark saturated red. The missiles are cherry stones, hastily chewed in my classmates' oily spit, then quickly loaded into the leather triangles of their slingshots. This then is the result of all those hours they spent practicing their aim on tin cans and milk bottles? Already a few brave hearts approach to spit the pits in fat parabolas directly out of their mouths. The stones curve through the air, shedding dribbling halos of slime, and suddenly my heart stands still in my breast. I can no longer breathe, it seems as if time itself has come to a grinding halt, and then, in the stopping of the clock (birds hang motionless in the air, their wings broad smears of charcoal against a stark blue sky; the cherry stones hang motionless, suspended from the heavens on silken threads, the side of the pits that point at me sharply defined, their backsides blurry and smudged, and thus I can calculate the trajectory of each of the projectiles; even though they are immobile one can easily trace a vector from their multiple origins—some Aryan boy's purple mouth, some black leather patch—to their singular destination—me: my ears, my forehead, my nose, my chin, my hair and even—some folks are quite malicious—my crotch. If this fermata would have allowed for a breeze, I might have seen the stones swaying lazily on their strings, circumscribing the confidence interval of their trajectories) I see Harald, his face contorted with hate. Hate? *Hate?* Harald? We always used to play marbles together. Why would Harald hate me? Behind the phalanx of boys there are the girls. I see Stella for instance, and although the girls are not chewing on cherries, there is definitely something guilty about their demeanor—they have their hands folded across their mouths and their knees pressed tightly together. It is abundantly clear: They are giggling out loud, they are having fun at my expense, and they giggle so hard that they have to make a conscious effort not to pee in their panties. Quite a few of them, I see when I circle around the group, are hiding brown paper bags behind their backs, stained with crimson fruit juice, and although time has come to a secure halt, I blush; my face turns a luscious red that spreads all the way to the roots of my blond hair, and although the sands of time stand safely petrified, the cherry juice still dribbles down my face and onto my new clothes. From the corner of my eye I see one of the playground guardians approaching with a mighty war horse's trot, Herr Puttkammer no doubt, and I hardly have the time to return safely to my body before time starts rushing forward again—I continue my motion, I sink to my knees, plumes of dirt rise up around me, and though I tremble with shame and fear, I am also grateful for the good teacher's intervention, though that feeling ends abruptly, very abruptly, when I get lifted off the ground by a slap in the face, an uppercut delivered with the back of the hand, and Herr Puttkammer grabs my ear to hoist me up.

He cannot get any purchase, his fingers slip on the slick cherry juice, but I know what is expected of me and I rise to my feet obediently, shaky and dizzy, close to crying, not from pain or humiliation, but out of pure anger. Snot drips out of my nose and runs over my already terminally soiled shirt. I hardly feel that nose, it has been blasted numb, and the girls laugh out loud now—Stella for one is laughing so hard she holds her tummy with both her hands—and then another hot slap makes my cheek tingle and another, and Puttkammer is yelling, rattling on and on like a mechanical toy that has been wound too tightly, but the slap has literally deafened me and I cannot understand him—but why do I need to hear the words? I get his drift, even without hearing what he has to say.

I understand. All of this is my fault and my fault only. Such German words, extolling German virtues, should come out of German mouths only. I—the Jew!—am polluting the clean German air with the slime of my Jewish lungs, and the noble words of the poet Hoffman von Fallersleben should never be tainted by my un-Aryan diction.

The poem is titled "*Kämpfe, blute!*"—Fight and Bleed. I would find this ironic if my sense of irony had not been erased instantly, replaced by an icy cold rage and a white-hot hatred both. I decide to aggravate my sin by rendering the words of the poem forever unusable: Despite the raucous bellowing of my classmates I reprise the whole performance *da capo* and I hammer the stupid words into their callous heads with all the brute force I possess; even under Herr Puttkammer's barrage of blows, I do not desist. He then tries to drag me off the battlefield, but where can he grab me without staining his suit? Finally he lunges clumsily for my feet and topples me over, and he drags me by my ankle to the place of detention. I keep on reciting, I won't give up, even when my shoulder blades bounce off the smoothed cobblestones of the playground, and I find some meager comfort in the thought that Mr. Puttkammer is now a sweaty beast of burden, a common ass, and that I am the plow in the field, sowing for the harvest (but what bloody harvest this will be!). This thought emboldens me and I raise my voice and greatly exaggerate my gestures—I want to do the poem justice, I want to make the poet's intent crystal clear.

Kämpfe, blute, werbe; siege oder sterbe,
(I roar under the elm trees)
Deutsch bin ich ins Mark.
(—Fight and bleed, campaign; be victorious or die,
German to the core am I)

There is some scattered applause, sarcastic no doubt, but I am not done yet. I skip the next two sentences—this is a repeat performance after all, and time is running out—and I end with the final three lines, giving it all I've got:

Laß dich nimmer knechten,
Laß dich nie entrechten,
G*tt gibt den Gerechten wahre Heldenkraft!

(Never be servile,
Your rights are yours, don't cower,
G*d grants the righteous man true hero's power!)

Although I try to make it sound as commanding as possible, it comes out a tad syncopated—Puttkammer drags me down the three steps to the dungeon and the back of my head hits each of them in turn. When the door is finally banged shut behind me, a roaring applause echoes off the brick façade, and I am free to interpret its meaning: Are they applauding the successful conclusion of my arrest or the strength and courage of my acting performance?

•

The principal sighs. The principal is good at that; his sighs are wonderfully expressive. It must be one of the major requirements of his job, to turn his palms to the sky and let out short and plaintive sighs, discreetly implying that there is a higher authority—he leaves it tactfully unnamed—that we all have to yield to. It is not our fault, sir, ma'am, his sigh communicates, and that brute fact alone absolves the principal from having to spell things out. It's the Law, sir, ma'am; it's the Internal Rules of Conduct, maybe it's even the Moral-Law-Inside-Us. In my case, the appeal is even more vague. Dear lady, the principal's sigh implies, what else can I do but give in, repulsed though I may be, to the ultimate law—the Law of the Jungle? If Mother would insist, he likely would call it outside pressure, and while pleading for forgiveness, he would invoke rationality—isn't it in your son's best interest, even if just for his personal safety, to withdraw? I squirm in my seat, in my badly damaged suit, in my ragged shirt and torn shoes. I am perfectly ready to make the observation that the all-against-one is not a particularly refined way to boost your argument, but I have been told to keep my mouth shut and I take such prohibitions seriously, at least when they come from my mother.

the way home, maybe we could get a *Mohrenkopf,* a Moor's Head, my favorite pastry—maybe at the Café Kranzler, Mama, pretty please?

•

De Heer has long stopped talking, but I'm still typing—I'm slower than I expected, or maybe he's a fast talker. Still, I didn't miss a word.

When I look up from the screen, De Heer is mumbling inaudibly. Is he lost in prayer, or is he maybe rehearsing the next installment, or is he searching his memory for the taste of the comfort pastry of his first big defeat in the New German Empire, the cake dough filled with yellow custard, speckled with black vanilla?

"You were all alone," I say when my fingers have finally caught up to his words. "And you wanted so much to be a part of it all. The march—you felt left out. The recitation—you were deprived of your rights, and you wanted to show off."

"I was very young," De Heer says. "Very young." His lips move again, but no sound comes out. Then: "But I quickly gave up the urge to be part of what was happening—although every human being feels that urge. This was not budding wisdom on my part, or precocious historical insight. I gave up because I was forced to."

•

When we arrived here, Berlin was the most amazing city in the world. Even I, a small child, got drunk on the fabled *Berliner Luft,* the Berlin air—it poured down the canyons between the tall stone office colossi; it fermented in the half-dark of the *Filmpalasten;* it clouded up the theaters and the *Kaffeehäuser.* Within walking distance of our house I counted more than a handful of those coffee shops: Café Trump, Café Stefanie, the Romanische Café—on a good day, you could see *le tout Berlin* there, the whole Berlin art scene: Kokoschka, Döblin, Brecht, Lenya, Weil, Tucholsky, Nußbaum, Pritzel, Grosz, etcetera—and then there's Café Wien, and let's not forget Café Kempinski and the wonderful Schicksaal, and the most famous of all *Konditoreien,* Café Kranzler. Kranzler was the place my father used to take me on Sunday mornings. He would study the breakfast menu for a full fifteen minutes, in complete silence, as if the right choice of pastry was a matter of life or death—is *Baumküchen* rolled in chocolate an acceptable choice so early in the morning, or should we order something else and take some *Baumküchen* home for later, for afternoon tea? Further down the room, a young woman smokes a cigarette. She is dressed in a silk cream-colored men's suit and wears a gold-rimmed monocle; her short hair is slicked back in a pomaded wave; it is rumored that when she had her long hair cut her barber fashioned a whip out of the locks for her to flog her mistresses with. She and I, we both breathe in the same Berlin air. That same air sinks exhausted into the big rental barracks where people are piled on top of each other, six or seven stories high; it dissolves in a salvo of coughs in the fumes of the *Lastkraftwagen*; it coolly wafts around the delicate decadence of the foodstuffs on the top floor of the *Kaufhaus des Westens*; it gets sucked into the lungs of the passengers on the overcrowded trams and busses— it knows no distinctions of class or status; it comforts the wage slaves in their impeccable gabardine suits as well as the workers in their grubby blues; it unites us all like brothers and sisters on our travels to the point beyond the horizon where our materialism will no longer be dialectic, but will be forever transcended. The city air makes us all drunk; it turns us into clever bullfighters in the arena of life, toreadors who know how to evade the roaring mechanical carriages with a mere sway of the hips, crossing a thousand streets without stepping even once into the foaming puddles of fresh horse piss or the steaming heaps of dung. Whereto did I ride on those late Sunday mornings, seated high on my father's shoulders, my belly filled with Kranzler pastries, nauseous from all the sugar and the rocking and rolling and the thrilling thinness of the heady air so high above the ground? I rode on the vibrations of the Berlin air to an open-air concert on the Königsplatz or to the stillness of the Altes Museum, where the air congeals majestically around even the most frivolous of friezes and draws mirrored spaces around the breathless marble youth—the expression on the faces of those nude ox-herders and bellowing ocean g*ds, those nymphic nerds and stark-naked love-struck idiots echoing exactly the emotions of the plump citizens who lazily slide their hands down their cool hard marble butts: a mildly dazzled ecstasy, colored by slight amazement at finding oneself exactly here, in this precise spot on this precise crossroads of the world. Life's winds blew us all together in this city, and *Stadtluft macht frei*, that is well known—city air sets free. Berlin is the fastest city in the world, and in these feisty 1920s there was nothing that could faze us. My father used to say, "If I stuck a bouquet of flowers in my ass and did a hand stand against a shop window on Ku'damm, nobody would notice. ("Must be some publicity stunt or something.") If I ran around naked, yelling 'I believe in the Eternal Feminine!', nobody would interrupt their routine for even a second. ("Probably a new cult or something.") If I shouted: 'In ten years' time, this government will have killed six million people!' nobody would be shocked. ("Probably a Dadaist performance or something.")"

At the same time, the city always felt temporary to me—fake. Even the sturdiest of buildings seemed to be in flux, the streets an ever-changing backdrop for whatever opera performance its citizens are putting on—a city that turns ever faster pirouettes around its own navel. Berlin does not have the self-assuredness of Paris, a city that has always existed and behaves accordingly, with slow grace. Berlin is like an insecure adolescent girl, always running after the newest trends— jazz (pronounced: *yahdz*), nude reviews, expressionism, whatever the flavor of the day is—and that makes it feel like a pastiche of a metropolis rather than a city with a mind of its own. The city doesn't reach upward, like those American towns that rise from the rocks; it squats close to the ground because the sand on which it is built can barely support its weight—no building is more than seven or eight stories high. The long rows of uniform structures gives the city the atmosphere of an army camp, a garrison in which somebody has also planted a few cathedrals and some academies and a brothel here and there, and some concert halls and row upon row of brightly lit shop windows, and expensive penthouses inhabited by an incomprehensibly large contingent of nouveaux-riche who throw champagne parties on the roofs and aim big blobs of saliva at the wide open mouths of the proletarian masses who look up to them in amazement. Something is wrong with this picture, of course; something is festering in those jobless masses, but the yeasty heat of that revolutionary process does not rise to the penthouses, and from so high up one cannot hear the footsteps of the underpaid and overworked converging on the factories, all marching to the same beat, the rhythm of a herd of cows being led to the slaughterhouse long before the sun is up.

What was the composition of that fabled Berlin air? It was a most dangerous mixture: one part blind magnificence and one part hopeless naïveté. Both parts of that cocktail are extremely volatile, a fact that the intellectual elite of this town is all too happy to ignore. Not much is needed to change a city forever.

•

Father had met my mother during summer school at the Sweelinck Conservatory. She sang, and how! Because of her, he stayed a little longer in Amsterdam. In the end, he stayed for seven years, seven years that were as fat as could be, and some-time during that period I was born. And then Father had had enough of the weak tea of the Dutch and their tiresome flat beer—he heard Berlin calling once again, the city marinated in the spirit of Weimar. The people in Berlin are gay, gay, gay!, he sang for me, and their farts foam like the finest chocolate mousse! He lifted me onto his shoulders and in a fit of jolliness, I transformed my little anus into a roll-ing trumpet and rattled my father's ears with a cosmopolitan fart that made the Damrak ring with laughter. The girls in Berlin, Father said, walk on their toes like

Siamese cats, and they carry their heads high on their elegant necks like pretty accessories that serve no practical purpose.

•

Once we moved in, the city started changing drastically. When my father had moved to Amsterdam, Josephine Baker was still a superstar in Berlin. Philosophers wrote essays about her—she was "the exact midpoint between jungle and skyscraper"; they considered her "forcefully stylish," and attending one of her performances made us all feel "ultramodern and ultra primitive." Now that gal with her lacquered Aztec hairdo and her *Jazzmusik der Nigger* got on everybody's nerves after less than ten seconds of banana skirt wiggling. The rightwing satirical magazine *Rumpelstilchen* advised the owner of the *Theater des Westens* to "stop stirring the brown puddle." The black Venus was forced to retreat back across her ocean, and my parents wondered whether it was still considered fashionable to go see that new young dancer from the Indies in the Wintergarten, what was her name again, Mata Hari? This city was very different from the open-minded town of my father's memories, and he found the change horrendous. Communism had been his first intellectual love, and Berlin communism had always come with a healthy dose of tolerance. Equal opportunity for all, a fair distribution of wealth, the abolishment of all class differences—such ideas should captivate the mind of any twenty-year-old. Einstein played the violin at one of the first party meetings my father attended, and the grand physicist occasionally visited us at home. Now, the actors in the theater were no longer g*ds; even their best dramatic performances were overshadowed by those of that new amateur actor—only the world itself was a large enough stage for him—and after dusk, or so we were told by the weekly newsreel at the movie theater, he set up his telescope and peered at worlds beyond the solar system, filled with greed and longing. Nothing could stop this man's megalomania.

At first we only heard his voice; it came to us through the radio. The man was good, it needs to be said. It was difficult, no, it was *impossible* not to listen to him. Once you listened, it became impossible not to fall for the beautiful rhetorical tricks he kept up his plain soldier's sleeves: After a slow, apparently tentative start that made the audience prick up their ears (here speaks a man who lost his way in a strange town, is there anybody here to help him in his predicament?), the orator finds his voice, and he no longer hesitates, no, he starts building rock-hard certitudes, he conjures them out of thin air, he rides a wave of ever-rising truths, and then he strategically interrupts this mellifluous ride with consciously unmelodic, biting diction, thus recapturing our attention, and this leads very quickly to a high plateau of constant staccato fire, only the cadence counts, and no more than a few words are still understandable, and then he explodes in a rage of hysteria that cannot be ascribed to anything else than honest evangelical zeal ('*ra-ra-ra-RÜCKSI-CHTSLOS!!!-ra-ra-ra-ra-NICHT-VERSAGEN!!!-ra-ra-ra-GERECHTIGKEIT!!!*"), and just when we realize that we cannot take this any longer, the speaker descends from his high horse and slides back into our midst, humming his melodies in a ringing rubato-cum-ralentando—emphasizing the main aspects of the message ("Struggle! Rebirth! Fatherland!"), and what else can we do but believe him. On the silver screens of the movie palaces we see for ourselves how his live performances are enhanced by the beauty of his gestures; he has such beautiful fingers, they twirl like moths in the concentrated spotlight, and when he finally reaches his climax, in an ecstatic culmination of rapid ejaculations ("*Kampf! Wiedererhebung! Vaterland!*"), his shoulders stoop and his head drops unexpectedly, as if the executioner has cut it off and here it is, his ultimate sacrifice, rolling straight into the nation's lap.

"I! Cannot! Detach myself! From the faith! I have! In our People! I! Cannot! Shake! This! Belief! That this once great nation! Shall rise again! The! New! German! Empire! Of greatness! And *honor*! And *strength*! And GLORY! And JUS! TICE!" The audience jump out of their seats, applauding wildly, and from a thousand mouths sounds a univocal: "AMEN!"

Oh, to behold these affecting images right before the main feature, in which a nonchalant hedonist actress breaks a bowl of raw eggs over the poor head of the cackling Herr Professor who had the impudent audacity to love her—the carefully contrasted image of a man who does not allow anything to divert him from his path, a leader who will never be submissive, who will never love a mere mortal. In his knee-high boots, the former corporal rides a surprisingly high horse, but he can also metamorphose effortlessly from a tough would-be world leader into an affable man, gracefully kissing the hands of the giggling farmer's wives who throw themselves in front of his automobile's wheels. These ladies are flushing with health and familial bliss and their crush on the Führer may seem innocent, but according to my father, with his sense of history, it's just the same old story: Women are easily seduced by warriors, and once they force their men into this role, the latter have no option but to go to war, all in the name of love, the lace panties of their stout Dulcineas stretched between the horns of their helmets. But Our Leader has his soft side too. He can be a friendly uncle who hands out chocolate to the mountain children from the safety of his car. On top of that, he is also a simple man of the People, exchanging firm handshakes with farm boys and factory workers. "*Herr*

Führer, here is my grandchild!," and for an unthinkable moment his feverish palm rests on the forehead of a lucky random toddler and the eyes of the moviegoers fill with tears.

For the millions who supported him he was a flashing meteor lighting up the darkest sky, flaring up right in front of their astonished eyes. The fulfillment of a mysterious desire, a miracle of enlightenment and belief in a world prone to skepticism and despair. Many Germans apparently had been waiting for a savior to rescue them from their dreary and sadly oppressive sublunary existence. They had been yearning for somebody to look up to with eyes moist with faith, a truly great leader who expressed and then fulfilled the People's desires on a never before encountered scale. His political program did not matter; his was a cult of personality. Teenage girls put his portrait on their bedroom walls. There was no quibbling over the relative attractiveness of Hermann or Heinrich, it was Adolf and Adolf alone, except that no one ever used that name. His first name was *Herr*. Herr Hitler. And because the leader had the heart of their girls, he also had the ear of the young men who were vying for those girls' hearts. Whenever Hitler was in town, the sidewalk in front of Hotel Adlon became an embarrassing display of frothing female desire. Not an edifying spectacle: the ladies were fierce and terrifyingly explicit, going from girlish adoration with glazed-over eyes to complete emotional release in an instant. Windows might break at any moment, doors could be forced open—this was a love that would do everything to conquer its object, this was a love that would tear out its own heart. But who were they falling in love with? Hitler's image was carefully managed. Look carefully at those pictures from the early 1930s—the young would-be-ruler, uncomfortable in his expensive suit, subliminally telling us that he is not one of your usual politicians: His slender body longs for the glory of a soldier's uniform, his authenticity doesn't fit in well with the starched cravats and the faux friendliness of the Berlin politico.

Listening to this man's voice—his voice, not his words—became a handy antidote to any accidental overdose of thought. For those who learned his speeches by heart, the world became a more hospitable place, even though they didn't understand much of what was really being said—or so they claimed, fifteen years later. So many of them were able to cite the Leader word by word, every calculated hesitation intact, every crack in his voice remembered. Each of the orchestrated mistakes in his speeches was a subtle indication that he was not playing a role—their idol was really putting his all into those speeches. Everyone in the nation acquired a deep intimacy with his image, with every inflection of his voice and with each permutation of his facial expression—the man was inescapable. He was truly a g*d, omnipresent.

What did my parents see? After all, they had grown up with and in the theater—they could spot a phony from a mile away. They saw a preposterous man stepping out of a luxury Mercedes sedan—with his raincoat the color of clay, his riding boots, his leather jodhpurs and matching horse whip, and his grayish skin, he looked more like a bragging Chicago gangster on a mountain vacation than the future president of the Great German Nation. An incorrigible loner, my mother surmised, one of these men who make every woman who comes near them deeply unhappy, a man who has studied well a script labeled "fatherly", but with a mounting feeling of nausea—a small-minded man, aloof, repressed, and repressive. A city dweller who lives out a country idyll with daily pastoral walks to a local teahouse, but he only walks downhill; when he's done, an automobile is dispatched to the village below to ferry him back up the mountain. My parents saw cool calculation, no veracity at all, and a chilly contempt for his fellow human beings. Bizarrely stylized performances, governed by laws as impenetrable as those of Noh theater. The carefully planned vagueness in his discourse makes the promise of a faraway Utopia, when the nation will be liberated from the yoke of Versailles, appear plausible, but only because the murderous path to that far-off land is described in the most general terms, with crippled metaphors and cheap allusions. His idea of the good life is to sit endlessly around the lunch table, sucking up sweet pastries and boring his lunch companions to death with his endless monologues about the firm loyalty of sheepdogs and his one experience with mustard gas near Ypres; a few operettas are projected on a hastily improvised movie screen during dessert, and then he goes back to another of his mind-numbing monologues—a dog's devotion, the perils of poison gas. The newspapers carry the news: The Führer has had another pleasantmidday meal! Will away that pathetic little mustache of the petty Austrian civil servant, my father says, and nothing remains of that face, nothing but pastiness. My father, home from another blistering evening at the Romanische, swears that none other than the great satirist Tucholsky had jumped on one of the tables and declared that he would never ever write about the Nazis again—there is after all a limit even to satire!

Why does nobody else see this? The rumor on the street is that the cultural riches of the past have come to life again, and that it is speaking to us again; new things can be learned, startlingly different from the worn-out trivialities of the familiar. There is a Teacher among us. It is permissible, again, to think. Who cares that this man once lived in a poorhouse: Money and education mean nothing, just look at his wonderful, wonderful hands!

"I advance with the certainty of a sleepwalker along the path laid out for me by Providence," says the future helmsman.

Applause!

Protected by the half darkness in the theater, my father grumbles. "Sleep-walker—damn right, buddy! Stupid airhead! Fucking *Phantast!*" Somebody a few rows behind us bites back: "*Die Schnauze!*"—shut your trap!

The newsreel shows images from Nuremberg. A quarter-million brownshirts have gathered in the Zeppelin Field to hear the man speak. Searchlights point straight up through the night, parallel columns in a cathedral of light, and one of these days those searchlights will find their mark at the focal point where the parallels touch: the G*d of Israel, once unattainably high in His heaven, now caught on a spear point of Nazi photons, His retinas burned like any old rabbit sitting hypnotized, watching helplessly as the silhouettes of His attackers draw nearer, burlap sack in hand. Once the blindness lifts, He will behold, at the head of the pack, the Ruler of the German People, that minuscule self-declared Messiah, a mere fleck of paint on the podium, a four-limbed insect that sends mechanically distorted screams into the skies. He is a gnat, a newt, a monsterkin less than a thumb tall, and yet every movement of his torso, every twist of his eyebrows is clearly visible, every sweep of his index finger, every lash of his fist is neatly distinguishable. Everything he does gets magnified, even the anger with which his balled left fist hammers his right-hand palm, and every gesture gets imprinted too on the flickering brain of the Almighty. People are swooning, literally fainting with joy over this creature's senseless shrieks, and this in Nuremberg, the city of Master Singers!

A man in the theater shouts back: "*Die Schnauze!*" How could we—I mean, people like my mother and my father, socialist intellectuals, profoundly in tune with the working class—how could we not have seen this coming, how could we not have seen how badly things were going in Berlin, how could we have missed this eerie correlation between the blossoming of the arts and the success of the riots? We held our discussion evenings and our civilized palavers and it escaped us completely that the Berlin masses were drowning in poverty. The workers eat the exhausted meat of retired horses and drink lung soup, sixty pfennig a pint. Walk through town and look up at the menagerie of concrete angels on the once-fashionable townhouses on Nollendorfplatz: Their rotting cement flesh snows over the rusty balconies and pigeon shit leaks down their little cherub butts. The U-Bahn trains on their tracks high above the street keep everybody up all night, the insomniac whores in their army boots spit at the bourgeoisie from under their umbrellas. The Nazis have noticed this, they understand that discontent is brewing, and they noticed this because this is where they live, this is their turf; the communist leaders live in the Mitte or the Tiergarten or in villas in the expensive wooded areas of town and on the weekends they go to the government quarter to march in never-ending processions—if only they had strayed from their course and looked the reality of the city right in the eye. Gangs of violent youth cluster together on Wittenbergplatz, yelling *"Deutschland erwache!"*—Germany wake up! Is there anybody in this city who still dares to stand in the middle of the street and intone a chorus à la *"Life is a cabaret, old chum?"*

The newspapers print brief stories about irregularities in the streets, unexpected, arbitrary attacks—knives suddenly appearing under the noses of midnight revelers; bullets fired through ads for frivolous nightclubs; street gangs with the rubber caps of beer bottles wrapped around the buttons of their stark white shirts beating up random bystanders with brass knuckles or a broken stein; there are even reports of poodles being shot dead in the streets, purportedly for being sissy French dogs. Fifteen seconds of wild terror, and then it's over. But are those stories true? Nobody ever sees anything—this is a big city, and crime is a statistic as long as one never experiences the violence firsthand.

The citizens of Berlin, the history books declare, chuckled at the Nazis. They made boys-will-be-boys jokes. They didn't like Hitler's lieutenants: One was an overly ornate Mardi Gras pig, the second an empty vat of slick and deadly charm, the third an overripe plum with a mustache and monocle, hardly able to sustain the weight of the countless decorations he has awarded himself. This band of riffraff would govern the nation? A morphinomaniac bon vivant? A failed novelist? A sadistic pederast? There was a joke that made the round of all the pubs. "What does the ideal Aryan look like?" "Blond as Hitler," was the answer. "Tall as Goebbels." "Slender and muscular as Goering." If the leaders of the party had only looked the part, if they had only conformed to the blond, Nordic ideal that they propagated, things might have ended differently. Now, the internal discrepancy absolved the citizens from the duty to take them seriously. "The circus is in town!" the Berliners had yelled, only a few months earlier. "Look at that! They let the clowns run free in the streets!" Thus the Nazi party began its unstoppable advance: as a bunch of harmless, pathetic imbeciles. If you wanted to draw a caricature of each of those bigwig politicians, people said in the cafés, all you had to do was draw a lifelike portrait. Well, okay, that Hitler guy, he was something else. He was a *man*, you know. But things had changed since then. These days the clowns in Hitler's entourage were carrying whips: The comic-strip characters had turned into lion tamers, and before anybody realized what was happening, they had donned evening wear and a top hat—masters of ceremony, and the ceremony was about to begin.

I have one simple question: if the whole of Berlin was chuckling, where did the hundreds of thousand who marched in those parades come from?

Talleyrand once wrote: "He who has not lived in the years before the revolution cannot know what the sweetness of living is." I see it differently. Cursed, I say, be the man who has to live through somebody else's revolution. For a while the arts and the riots blossomed together. Then the arts succumbed, and quiet, state-sponsored riots took over. After only a few days of the new regime, Kurfürstendamm turned into the world stage of dark propaganda. The fabric stores and jewelers had signs in the window: "*Deutsche, verteidigt Euch gegen die jüdische Greuelpropaganda, kauft nur bei Deutschen!*" Helpful as always, the sign included an English translation, for the foreign clientele: "Germans, defend yourselves against the Jewish atrocity propaganda, buy only at German shops!" Men of the *Sturmabteilung* stood guard in front of these stores, and sinister four-legged spiders danced on blood-red bands tied around their sleeves. On April Fool's Day 1933, the windows of Café Kempinski are kicked in and a gang of looters goes after the customers with billy clubs. Signs appear by the doorbells of Jewish doctors: "Attention: Jewish! Entrance unlawful!" Students plunder the Berlin Museum for Sexual Sciences and they load their spoils in moving vans of the Pagel Company, never to be seen again. (Let's hope that the students did put the collection of nude pictures and sex toys to good use.) The new brown stain spreads all over town like an oil slick—tough, sticky, inflammable. The Nazis understand very well how important the street is to win the political battle. You need to control the slogans and caricatures that are displayed in windows; you need to spread the kind of jokes that people can tell in bars ("Do you know the one about the Jew who . . ."). The world of meanings, of interpretations, of whispered secrets, all the half-truths of society, all the ideas that only dare emerge during drunken nights—whoever has possession over those memes has the masses by the balls.

That first slap in the face, the one I received from my mother, was justified. But this collective slap in the face, where did that one come from? The noise of the street, the humming that had once lulled me to sleep, no longer sounded reassuring. The buzz used to be fluid and tuneful and as happily predictable as a Schubert sonata; now the murmurings of the boulevard sounded like a much grimmer music—a march of shattering brass by day, a pompous funeral procession by night. A city's appearance is made out of chameleon skin; it's easy to change. A spark strikes an old dusty parliament building and the whole town goes up in flames.

I had also deserved that second slap in the face—at least from the point of view of Herr Puttkammer, card-carrying member of the NSDAP since May of 1931. When blackshirts dream, they dream of black sheep—of race defilers, of parliamentarians, of Marxists, of democrats, of capitalists, of freemasons, of bourgeois, of internationalists, of Bolsheviks, of intellectuals, of homosexuals, of abortionists, of ultramontanists, of rationalists, of Dadaists—all distinctions dissolve in the sulfuric acid of the official dream of a world that gleams with the right kind of beauty. The unexamined life is glorified—theirs is a world without the physical whims of the quantum, without the hidden space-time dimension of general relativity, without the grotesqueries of Grosz and the weirdness of a song like "Yes, We Have No Bananas." All that goes wrong in Germany is the result of a conspiracy of international Zionism, never mind the contradiction that, according to the Nazis, the Jews are secretly running international capitalism and at the same time spreading the poison of the Marxist doctrine. Maybe they were just jealous, those Über-Aryans? The moneychangers in their grubby backrooms, the owners of small pawnshops, the bricklayers, the men carving dreidls in humble huts under the shadow of the synagogue had suddenly turned into doctors, pharmacists, bankers, composers, fur traders, and terrifyingly successful alchemists. Niels Bohr, Sergei Eisenstein, Arthur Rubinstein, Amedeo Mondigliani, Max Liebermann, Camille Pisarro, Alfred Döblin, Arthur Schnitzler, Friedrich Holländer, Ernst Lubitsch, Peter Lorre, Fritz Lang, Marc Chagall, Boris Pasternak, Rosa Luxemburg, Jascha Heifetz, Vladimir Horowitz, Kurt Weill, Herbert Marcuse, Erich Fromm, Leon Trotsky, Kurt Tucholsky, Albert Einstein, Karl Marx, Sigmund Freud, Marcel Proust, Franz Kafka, Gustav Mahler, Arnold Schoenberg—yes, we Jews, as a people, had hugely disappointed the Führer. Let us invoke those names, the names of the men and women whose work has been banned; let us invoke their names as a litany, and may the sound of their names rise like incense, and may the scent wake our blind G*d out of His ruminations. Those men and women forged Modern Times with their own bare hands, in the glow of a ferocious fire. Fire, dear friends, lest we forget: FIRE! And *that* is what the Nazis want to kill. They are not killing a people, they are killing a way of looking life in the face. They are not after a religion, what they want is to turn back modernity, get rid of rationality and its twin brother uncertainty. The Nazis are not eradicating an ethnicity; they are doing away with the realization that all truth has been lost, that all humans from now on need to find their own path and go their own way.

If Goebbels and Hitler had asked the Berliners to take a good look and to examine the pernicious influence of the Jew in their own life, they would never have made it this far. They were smarter than that: They had a rhetoric of sores and bruises, of pestilence and pus, of exploitation and of games with scorpions, and this helped to unleash some very powerful emotions. And emotion is, always and everywhere, the true motor of revolution.

•

On April 7, 1933, the Law for the Restoration of Professional Civil Servanthood comes into effect. Jews are no longer allowed to work for the state. That implies that Jewish musicians can no longer teach at the conservatories or play in the state orchestras or the opera. Father, who had just landed a good job at the Staatsoper thanks to his friends from the Romanische, gets fired. Mother, who sings in the Opera choir, likewise loses her job.

"*Die Schnauze!*" yells a man in the theater. Nobody seems to disagree with him. On the contrary. Two weeks before the *Berufsverbot* comes into effect, Bruno Walter is locked out of the Philharmoniker. From behind the stage door he can hear the hastily recruited Richard Strauss direct the *Berliner Philharmoniker* in his stead, to great acclaim. Hitler was only two weeks into power when the *Zeitschrift für Musik* accused Otto Klemperer of bastardizing Wagner with his version of Tannhäuser. Mahler? Mahler is a senile old fart who piles up gigantic blueprints of unpalatable harmonics with hysterical twists—at best his music yields a few entertaining details, and the geezer's old-testament-like zeal might make you smile with pity. All Mozart operas that have a libretto written by the Jew Da Ponte are Aryanized.

The only music-related income my parents can still get in a town that has for all intents and purposes become *Judenrein*—clean of Jews—is money from private lessons. If they still wanted to play in an ensemble, they would have to become registered members of the *Kulturbund Deutscher Juden*, but they were too stubborn to even consider this option. And because no Aryan wants to be seen crossing the threshold of a Jewish home, our music room falls silent. My parents travel all over town to visit their pupils, those few members of the well-off middle class that are courageous enough to let a Jew enter their house. My father carries his violin in an oversized briefcase.

But even that soon becomes unsafe. The street has become the private territory of dilettantish petty criminals with the most meager of motives: They're pissed off. These men, my father says, have faces of raw flesh and hands that are all too accustomed to strangling poultry and small mammals, brutes with the smell of the Reichstag fire still smoldering in their coats. The G*d of Scattered Trash himself, the chicken farmer Himmler, must have educated them.

Besides, one after the other, my parents' pupils tell us, after much head-scratching and throat-clearing—this drives my mother crazy: Don't do that!, she wants to shout, you'll hurt your vocal cords!—that maybe, you understand, possibly, well, it might just be better if you no longer, well, and, *ach*, the times, you know? The times don't really call for chamber music, do they?

•

Why do we stay? My parents' answer is simple. Why should we leave, why should we flee like thieves in the night? "This is our country," my father reminds me. "Look it up in your family tree," he says. "Our family has been living here for centuries. We have made ourselves useful and loved for many generations." And thinking of the dykes of my mother's Dutch youth, he adds: "The tide always turns." He is right. "Germany is Germany," my father also says. "What is happening now is not German. There were never pogroms in Germany, and there never will be—in Poland, yes, sure, and in Russia. But not in our Germany!"

"There is always work," my mother says—she is the determined one in the family. They have so few students now that we can no longer support ourselves through their lessons. "Look at the people in the street. They are getting thinner and thinner. They have become ghosts of themselves. They are slowly disappearing. I can make good money by taking in their clothes." Mother, who was always so proud of her body, who so liked to accentuate her finely chiseled face with fiery reds and charcoal blacks—Mother throws all her makeup in the garbage. Someone in the subway had called her a whore and a traitor; with the nation under attack, we should follow the Leader and abandon all frivolity. One thing she tells us she will never do: She will never wear her hair in pigtails on top of her head, and never grow the wide hips that are so fashionable among our German neighbors.

"I can go and play in cafés and restaurants," my father proposes. "People always want to have some fun," he says. But while my mother sounds convinced, my father's voice is scratchy with dread and uncertainty. It is unlikely that he will be able to spread much joy, in his state.

•

It was a good thing that I did not return to that school. The new curriculum ("What are the three things that give in abundance?" "The land, the sea, the Reich!"—ah!, the old belief that you can rewire the mind by repeating the same simple messages over and over again!), the oppressive rows of desks and chairs bolted to the floor, the desktop slanting downwards (you couldn't even sleep with your head on your hands; you slithered to the floor to a rude awakening), the teachers high and far away on a podium—none of these things were particularly appealing. The worst was that whenever a teacher entered the classroom you were supposed to jump out of your chair in a spontaneous demonstration of respect. After the slap in the face delivered by Puttkammer and the principal's cowardly retreat, it was impossible for me to feel any respect for my purebred teachers. But civil disobedience and passive resistance is not in our blood. We are Jews, true, but we are Germans first and foremost. When we go biking in the Grunewald we do not stray from the indicated paths.

A cousin of mine did stay on in that school. Then a few of his classmates dragged him to a *Stürmerkästchen*—a display case for the SA propaganda maga-zine—and forced him to read the whole issue out loud while providing them with precise, anatomically detailed descriptions of what was shown in the pictures: a half-naked innocent German maiden molested by a band of vile Jews. When they found my cousin's descriptions lacking in pornographic zeal, they hit and kicked him until he discovered a lyrical vein deep inside himself he did not know he pos-sessed. From his lips welled up a fount of a depravity that deeply disturbed and distressed him. During music lessons, the children still sang the "Lorelei," the art song with words written by Heinrich Heine, but the score now stated that the lyri-cist was "unknown." A simple change in the power structure, and a great Jewish writer suddenly ceases to exist.

I did not miss the old school. There was little that I still had in common with my former classmates. The few of them that I visited from time to time—for some, the mere fact of my shadow falling on a sandbox made the whole playground un-clean—had a portrait of Hitler on the wall, fitting nicely along the family pictures and the scary plaster-white man on the wooden cross. There was a difference, of course: The Führer's defiant mien made it very clear that he was not going to be anybody's grandfather and that crucifixion was out of the question. Even my most tolerant and well-meaning classmates said their goodbyes by extending their arm and intoning a cheerful and sonorous and completely unironic "*Heil Hitler!*"

If I had recited von Fallersleben's poem at commencement, I would have re-ceived the prize package that all other star pupils received, a package containing among other things an attractive leather-bound copy of *Mein Kampf* and an equally appealing special edition of Rosenberg's *The Myth of The Twentieth Cen-tury*. These books would have taught me a lot of interesting and surprising facts about my race. The school could have had them sent to my house, but the principal wisely assumed that this would be a waste of precious postage.

•

De Heer adjusts his posture. We are seated in armchairs positioned at a ninety-degree angle—the arrangement preferred by clinical psychologists and counselors (my host picked the configuration)—and during his whole monologue he had been staring straight ahead, his gaze passing in front of me. Now De Heer bends forwards and turns his spotlights on me—looking me straight in the eyes.

"Beautiful, pink, healthy Lutheran boys, Paul. Their Book of Books teaches that only he who is without sin should cast the first stone. And one has to humbly turn the other cheek when one has been slapped. Who was the child among the Christian boys who hit me first, and in the back of my head—who was that squeaky-clean coward? His aim was true. Somebody must have been preparing for that moment quite a long time—practicing his aim, and carefully refraining from sin."

He sinks back into his old position. "That is the Lutheran boys' so-called New Testament. Who, may I ask, has inherited from it? Who are the true heirs of that meek, sweet Jesus, and who has taken it upon himself to play the role of the vengeful G*d of the Torah, the jealous G*d who is so easily offended?"

•

I come home, my lips still stained with black chocolate icing, a splotch of golden pudding adorning my cheek and an overlooked streak of cherry juice remaining on my face, and I find the doors of the big bookcase in the living room wide open. Books and folders are spread all over the floor, knee-high in places, and Father sits at the center of the pile, his collar open, his sleeves rolled up to his elbows; he takes a break in the middle of his cruel and radical revision of our bookshelves. He is not capable of speaking. Mother goes to sit down next to him, her blue skirt spread wide under her like a pool under a nymph, and she takes turns caressing the book covers and my father's spindly arms.

"Certainly not Stefan Zweig?" he asks, despair in his voice.

Yes, Zweig, my mother says without making a sound.

"What about Remarque? Döblin? And the brothers Mann? And *Kästner*?"— my favorite book, *Emil und die Detektive*, lies on the floor, thrown off the shelf in haste, its corners bumped, its cover torn—"And the Mendelssohn scores? Egon Erwin Kisch's pamphlets? And Freud? And Marx? Tucholsky too? Tucholsky too. Flaubert? Proust? Proust, of course. *Les Temps Perdus!*"

It seems that Germans are allowed to keep almost no books, except the One, the One that describes the struggle. That is the Book. From now on, all personal quests into the roots of the world, and all free research into the limits of morality will be illegal pursuits. What are we to do with the books that need to be discarded? Giving them away would just displace the problem. We can't just throw them out either; that big stack of paper in the trash room would attract attention—what if one of our brand-new patriotic neighbors started sniffing through the garbage cans and traced the forbidden works back to their origin?

We could burn them. The weather has turned. It is rather chilly out; a slow drizzle darkens the sky. One could light a fire without raising suspicion. My mother takes her place at the hearth; my father, in his shirtsleeves, labors by the sweat of his brow—a scene that would certainly please any National Socialist. We could burn the books. See how assimilated we are? Righteous Jews so respect the name of G*d that they do not dare pronounce it or write it down without at least censoring the vowels, and they never throw away even the smallest slip of paper for fear it might carry the Lord's name and that they thereby are destroying a piece of YHVH Himself. In the Jewish archive in Cairo *everything* gets saved: marriage contracts, love poems, bookseller's catalogues, everything, including shopping lists. In the shtetl, in the eastern lands, every synagogue has a big wooden vat in the back where the faithful deposit their old books and newspapers. The vat is emptied from time to time but the paper is stored indefinitely in the temple's basement. Jews love books, they thrive on words. Read all those old Jewish stories from the Talmud and the kabala and the folktales from Poland and Russia: Long-lost books reappear in hidden caves, letters rise up from the page, names are etched into foreheads. The correct pronunciation of a word can make the difference between heaven and hell. Burning a book means more than giving up a part of one's possessions: it means selling one's soul to an evil spirit. Today our bookcase will go up in flames, today we are selling our soul to the demon Hitler.

Father has a Heine book in his hands. He opens it and reads out loud. "*This was merely foreplay. Where they burn books, they will end in burning human beings.* Here," says Father. "Look at an open book with your eyes level with the table-top—feel free to kneel—what you see is an angel, its wings spread wide, ready to fly. Each book is an angel that takes you, naïve Argonaut, on a journey. (And just remember, not every angel is benevolent). A book is a membership card to a secret society—a society of minds, with manifold interpretations and moods and intentions. You enter that society, the book's lines imprint on your retina, and your brain will never be the same. Every book is ready to burst wide open. Here! Take this one. Open it up. What does it say? *In the beginning* . . . This book is bursting, I tell you! Ready to burst open! Burst! Burst!"

In the beginning . . . Here they come, the *schwankende Gestalten*, we observe them with sad and troubled eyes. Mother is ripping pages out of a communist treatise, it will make good kindling. I carry the books to the fireplace in the small stacks that fit my small arms. I walk carefully, because I love those books. I do not want to hurt them unnecessarily. Their death has to be short and merciful and I want to make their final journey soft and light. I want to carry them to their final resting place, to their ultimate transformation, so softly that the clueless heroes and heroines between the cardboard covers do not feel anything at all. This also spares, I hope, the overblown yet fragile egos of the authors whose pictures grace the back covers.

It is not an easy task, burning books. And I don't just mean emotionally, though it is gruesome watching even a lifeless object get punished for something it did not do. And I don't just mean theoretically, either—even though burning vessels of ideas is certainly a powerful gesture. I mean it in the most practical sense: Paper, cardboard, and glue are harder to destroy than one would think. You have to break the books' spines, you have to dismantle them before committing them to the flames. Is it blasphemy to say that this is also true for humans? But when the fire has finally caught on, it cannot be contained. If self-reproduction is the main characteristic of life, then fire is a living thing. When the theory of the proletarian revolution starts attacking degenerate prose, when a tongue of fire greedily licks a page until that page grows its own eager tongue, a cycle starts that will only come to an end when all books in the world are gone. From the fire, black butterflies leap into the chimney, each butterfly carrying a fragment, a word or a part of a sentence or maybe just a single letter, a charred cipher that once might have meant the world to whoever wrote it, to whoever read it. Words precious to us, to Father, Mother, or myself. Words that gave direction to our life. As so often my father's hand hesitates—whenever he recognizes a text as a dear old friend with whom he does not want to part, he starts trembling—and I, the little one, have to pull the book out of his hands. Destruction has to be blind; you can never look your victim in the eye. I tear at the pages until they loosen under my fingers like a cancer patient's hair.

We stand in front of the bookcases. Our faces are aglow, our arms ache, our palms are rubbed raw. Our eyes glisten with the heat. Behind our sweaty backs the fire is a twisting, ever-transforming circle of hell in which grim red heathen g*ds are dancing. The bookcases are still far from empty. What is left is legal to read, or at least not expressly forbidden: how can one forbid a German to read his Goethe, to browse through his Schiller? Up until this moment, I have kept my mouth shut. But now I speak.

"Burn them!" I demand. "Throw them all in the fire. All of them. German books. German!"

"Burn them all?" I have never seen my father so despondent. "Should I hate all of this, then?" The sweep of his arm includes tens of thousands of pages. Stories of beauty, stories of love, stories of betrayal—the stark condensate of human existence. He points at the tens of thousands of pages of musical scores, full of passion and emotion.

"Should I hate what is dear to me? Do I have to feel contempt for Mozart or for Schubert? What about Bach?"

"I cannot do it," my father says. "If I did that, I would have become just like them."

The musical scores he can keep. But with regard to literature, I am relentless. All words go into the fire, for all words are in excess—even the opera librettos, even the *Singspiele*—let them transform into little black butterflies, let them end their lives as rough pellets of ash. The scores fit in a suitcase. The suitcase goes under the bed. Then my father chops up the bookcases. Not the way I would have done it, in angry splinters. My father has little rage left inside him; his gestures are simple and efficient; he chops the cases into even pieces that will fit nicely into the fireplace. After he has checked whether the hallway is empty, we—he and I—carry the wood in armloads to the inner courtyard. As I mentioned, the weather has turned. We will probably make somebody very happy with this extra bit of high-quality wood. Old oak, nicely cut—good firewood that will burn long and give off lots of heat. One should always help one's neighbors when one can.

•

"Now then, Paul," says De Heer after one of his characteristic silences, and he says it with a surprisingly firm voice, "wouldn't this be the perfect moment for a short walk?" When we leave the building, he pulls a flat box out of the pocket of his sports jacket, and from this he produces a surprisingly fashionable pair of sunglasses. The lenses proudly reflect the stars and the *Spittelkolonnaden* and a few bats that circle around the monument, plus a few owls and a crazy, crazy moon.

•

When I come home, a little note is stuck under my door. In English. "*Shall I cook for you tonight?*" It is signed -a. It takes me a while before I realize who that is. Well, the last letter of your name is as good as the first to sign with. In Donatella's case, the last letter is even better than the first, because it occurs twice in her name ("-a-a"). A strange piercing pang shoots through my heart. I would have loved to share her food, I would have loved to spend the evening with her, but it's probably

allowed to dream, isn't he? A mind can wander? But if you're feeling at all scandalized by this confession, rest assured that there's hardly any reason to: Grüneberg's dreams are extraordinarily chaste. He dreams of mountain hikes in the Swabische Alp; he dreams of a little hotel with home-style cooking and an open fire in the dining room; he dreams of sitting in on a clumsy recital by an unknown local pianist in the town hall—perhaps the man will play a modest set of Mozart sonatas for them. Does Monika like Mozart? In his daydreams, Grüneberg drifts as far away as possible, far away from everybody who knows the two of them, to a place where nobody could conceivably notice their ethnic differences, where nobody would be bothered by their love. And while he dreams away, he fulfills the mechanical duties of a shop owner: He checks the stock, he refolds the shirts, he straightens the line of moccasins, he rearranges the men's ties, he cleans the display cases with his breath and the sleeve of his shirt.

He is in the back room, getting out the books, when he hears noise in the shop. Not *again*, he thinks. In the summer, the good-for-nothings had painted slogans on his windows. It had been quite a pain to scrape the glass clean. Fortunately, nobody had protested while he did this—for all he knew, the government now had a law that prohibited the removal of smutty, anti-Semitic graffiti—but nobody had offered any help either. Not even Monika. She had ducked underneath his ladder to enter the store and she had blushed. Had she been ashamed to work for him, a Jew?

Grüneberg steps into the main room, maybe a bit more briskly than he should. Never let on that you're upset—it only makes matters worse.

A man stands in the doorway.

"We're closed," says Grüneberg. Ouch. That sounded pretty harsh, and much more angry than was probably wise—why should he offend a customer who just happened to come late? But Grüneberg needs his quiet time; he needs his peace. Why don't people understand that, that even somebody like Karl Israel needs his peace and quiet time?

The man is in uniform. So many people walk around in uniform these days. This observation fills Grüneberg with a mild surprise, as though he is realizing this only now, for the first time, after five long years of Nazi rule. How had the man been able to get in? The door had been locked, hadn't it?

Watch the man's hand. That hand is swaying slowly by his side, dragged down by a heavy weight. A polished bat of maple wood lies in that hand; it gleams in the yellow light that flows in freely through the wide open door. A silver aureole of crushed glass is pooled around the man's feet.

But so late in the evening! In June, the brownshirts had done their window-smashing during daytime, and they had passed him by—apart from the graffiti from a few weeks before, his store had been spared. A good omen, Grüneberg had thought. By coincidence, Monika had taken that 16th of June off, and she was visiting the jewelry store when ten young men in Hitler-Jugend uniforms broke through the windows, waving carving knives in the air—the official Hitler-Jugend dagger must have been too precious to soil with Jewish blood. They screamed that the Sudenten-Germans needed space (should they be given lodgings in the Jewish stores, then?), and then they proceeded to slide rows of golden rings over their slender boy's fingers, briskly lining the pockets of their uniforms with watches and pearl necklaces. It took just a few minutes; then they hopped out the window again. A boyish prank, Grüneberg had thought, an *expensive* prank, but still a prank. Monika thought otherwise. She had been very upset and she had run to Karl's store to see if everything was okay there. Upset and relieved at the same time, she had—for a brief, all too brief second—put her head on Karl Israel's shoulder. For a brief, all too brief moment, Karl Israel had intoned a soothing nah-*nah*! in her ear, and he had whispered "Hey, girl, it's not that bad," while his open hand circled her back. This was what a concerned older uncle was supposed to do, nobody could mistake this for the touch of a would-be lover. It had made Karl Israel happy nonetheless, this short communion of body and ear, much more bodily contact than he could ever reasonably have expected to share with his Monika, the way the world was these days. And now one of those boyish pranksters had materialized right in front of Karl's own two eyes.

The intruder advances two or three steps; he peers at the shaken merchant's face. He slides more than he walks, he is a snake on supple boots of leather. He stops right in front of Grüneberg. The bat rolls on the floor, the man has simply released it. Then he reaches for Grüneberg's temples, with a mother's tenderness. With both hands, he relieves the storeowner of his glasses; he sticks them in his own breast pocket. The man is blond, but in a strange and hazy way; his eyes are the icy blue color of a summer lake; his mouth has a melancholic quality, with a grin of almost-compassion at its corners—here is a man who looks at another man intently, a predator assessing the fear that lies behind the eyes of his prey. It's not hard to understand what is going on here. Here are a man and his bat, and it is late at night.

The man speaks softly. Karl Israel has to strain to understand him.

"Assaults have to be chaotic and amateurish, Herr Grüneberg, and somewhat random. Right? Do you understand? Do you agree, Herr Grüneberg?"

That is what the man says. It almost sounds like an apology. Then he spits out the word. The word that serves as the signal.

"*Jude!*"

All flesh is grass. We are all straw dogs, about to be thrown into the sacrificial fire. Lilies of the fields wither in the heat of summer, birds fall exhausted from the sky, the carp freezes in December's ice; even a young man's bones are brittle. Such is life. A troupe, a horde, a full wolf pack invades the store. The slivers of glass in their soles tear up the carpet. Their bats and clubs sing the songs of the ages—they whistle and they wheeze and then they splinter whatever they touch, in rhythm. The blond giant, behind him now, throws his arms around Grüneberg and presses the merchant's back against his chest; he forces Grüneberg's sagging chin up with his hand: Watch this, don't miss this, you have to see this part!

Revenge for Paris! With a great crashing sound the shelves come down. The mob rips the coat racks out off the wall and puts them to good use: They smash the windows with the long poles. The diamond dust of freshly crushed glass covers the gold tie bars and the inlaid tie tacks. One of the men lowers his pants and takes a dump in each and every one of the shoes on the table, methodically working his way through the whole row of *Preiswerte Modelle*. The rest quickly grab whatever they can; they throw the stuff into a small truck that is conveniently parked in front of the store. Coats, a few handful of cufflinks, ties, jewelry—yes, even the soiled shoes are hastily loaded into the van. When they are almost done, they drag Grüneberg to the street. Somebody hoists him up, and a woman hands him a torch. Grüneberg shakes his head. She insists. "*Doch!*" she says, and again she presents him with the flame, while another member of the gang kicks him carefully in the shins. "Fire means liberation," the leader whispers in his ear, "A brand new start. What do you say? To start all over again, with a perfectly clean slate—isn't that what we all long for, Mr. Grüneberg?" The woman moves the flame back and forth in front of his face, almost scorching his beard in the process. With her free hand she unexpectedly grabs him by the balls. And squeezes. No! He shakes his head, he doesn't want to do this. Snot pours out of his nose. "*Doch*," she says. "*Doch!*" And with her knee she kicks him hard in the groin. Grüneberg doubles over. Two men fold his hands around the torch. Then they throw their victim, flames and all, into the store. The dry carpet—g*d only knows how often it has been cleaned with g*d knows what kind of inflammable chemicals—ignites with a mighty sucking sound. Grüneberg has just enough energy to crawl to the exit, coughing, retching, crying, while the last of the jolly looters jump over him on their way out.

Grüneberg's left cheek rests against the cold cobblestones, his right cheek basks in the heat of the fire. He remains motionless. He has no choice; he is simply too exhausted, too dog-tired to move. He doesn't know if he is even capable of move-ment. Despite being without his glasses, despite the salty tears lashing at his eyes, he is aware of everything that happens around him. Women run through the street with baby carriages that contain no babies, shawls bound in front of their mouths; all kinds of treasure are piled up high in the rolling cradles.

In the glow of the fire, the blond man dusts himself off, with perfect poise. Orangey-red accents and deep blue shadows flicker over his tranquil face. He takes one last look at Grüneberg. It is no more than a brief glance in passing, the glances we give drunkards who sleep off their booze in the street. This reminds the man of something. His hands slide into his breast pocket. Yes, the glasses have survived. He puts them on his nose, those tiny Jew spectacles made of horn and gold. They look good on him and he doesn't squint: He and Grüneberg must have the same prescription. The last thing the clothes salesman thinks—and how sad this is, how guilty does he feel that he isn't ready or able, in that hour of dire need, to devote at least a fleeting thought to the fair Monika—is that the man's uniform fits his body like a glove. Magnificent tailoring. Grüneberg suspects a Jewish hand. Then the pain and sheer terror knock him out.

A neighbor drags the merchant's limp body further up the street. That is the only reason Grüneberg survives. Then another neighbor calls the police: A Jew is disturbing the peace; he's lying right in the middle of the street, obstructing traffic! They come to get him, the cops. After that, Karl Israel curses his life.

•

There's a scratching at the door—a cat coming home from its long night of wandering, afraid to wake up the neighbors. But the voice is human, though barely so: It sounds raw and hoarse, gruff and urgent. Through the mail slot, the voice whispers my mother's name, over and over, like a mantra, like a password. We don't recognize the voice. Go away, my mother says. Who are you? And then finally the voice falls silent—we are paralyzed with terror, Mother and I—and four fingers appear in the mail slot, the nails crushed and torn, clotted blood at the edges. One of these fingers has a ring of squashed flesh where a band of gold used to sit. The hand is naked as the dawn, four fingers we recognize immediately. Mother gasps for air and opens the door for the ghost who's come in from the tatters of the night. She opens the door for her broken husband.

•

Fire licks the wooden windowpanes; a layer of powdered glass covers the cobblestones like a crust of early frost. Far away in Paris, a German diplomat has died. The smoking gun lies at the feet of a startled and speechless Jew, Hermann

("Herschel") Grynszpan. The Germans know perfectly well how to avenge that murder. Two hundred and fifty synagogues go up in flames, seven thousand five hundred stores are looted, a hundred people—no, a hundred Jews—are killed in cold blood, and three thousand five hundred people—no, three thousand five hundred Jews—end up in jail. It appears that Grynszpan had a lot of accomplices. Finally the mask has been ripped off the worldwide Jewish conspiracy! How can the diplomat's murder be an isolated incident? It must be part of well-orchestrated campaign with roots in either Jerusalem or Brooklyn or maybe both. Grynszpan is hardly eighteen. Once again, the international Jewish conspiracy has exploited a naïve and innocent youth.

This is the official version. Grynszpan wanted to take revenge for the deportation of his family from Hanover to Poland. In the early morning of November 7th, he walks into the embassy and requests an interview with ambassador Welczeck. Instead, he gets to meet Ernst vom Rath, a low-ranking diplomat. Grynszpan assumes that the man standing in front of him is Welczeck and he shoots the hapless civil servant in the guts. The man is carried to the hospital. For two days, vom Rath is stuck between life and death. The newspaper headlines go into overdrive. Every hour, the radio transmits a news bulletin with the latest reports from the two doctors that minister to vom Rath. Hitler had them flown in from Berlin—one of his own personal physicians is among them. Then, on November 9th, at half past five in the afternoon, right on the anniversary of Hitler's first attempt at a coup d'état, vom Rath finally succumbs to his wounds, the first victim in the war that international Jewry is waging against the Third Reich.

What is the truth? Grynszpan is a confused young man in a sloppy raincoat with a furtive glance and a cigarette glued permanently to the corner of his mouth. He is a James Dean *avant la lettre*, a boyish man who made the heart of every *Parisienne* who ever crossed him in the street go giddy-up. He could have made a woman melt with just a wink of his eye, if only he wanted to. *Quod non.* Grynszpan bought the revolver in *À la Fine Lame*, in the Rue du Faubourg Saint-Martin. It cost 245 francs. He loaded it in the restroom of the bar *Tout Va Bien*, a place he frequented often; it was the bar where he met vom Rath. A gay bar. The irony that the embassy is very close to the Solferino Métro station does not escape young Grynszpan. He rings the doorbell at half-past nine. The embassy isn't open to the public yet. The wife of the concierge—maybe she recognizes him from earlier visits?—lets him in. He tells her he needs to show "the secretary" an important document. She ushers him into a waiting room. The secretary of the secretary, Herr Nagorka, enters the waiting room. No, Grynszpan needs to hand over the document in person; he has a personal communication to make as well. The secretary will surely understand, just tell him Herr Grynszpan is here. Vom Rath asks Nagorka to let Grynszpan in—no, there is no need for him to sign in. A few minutes later, a shot is heard.

It's easy to guess the reason. The secretary has had *les relations les plus intimes* with his petite Jewish murderer—a double cardinal sin against the laws of the Reich. In 1937, vom Rath returned to Germany from his post in Calcutta with an intestinal problem. In Berlin, he is treated at the roentgen institute of Prof. Dr. Halberstaedter and Dr. Tugendreich. The therapy is short-wave radiation, the usual cure for intestinal infection with gonorrhea. Both of the doctors are Jewish; going to Jewish doctors is vom Rath's way of trying to keep his condition quiet. Most probably, the cure was not completely effective. Rectal gonorrhea is very contagious. Vom Rath almost certainly infected Grynszpan: He signed the Jew's death warrant with a shot of his sperm. This, then, is the extent of the conspiracy of world Jewry: The Nazi pig that the Jewish doctors tried to save is killed off by another poor Jew with nothing to lose. Perhaps Grynszpan did his lover a favor. A mercy killing. Dying quickly from a bullet wound in the gut—isn't that preferable to the slow rot of intestinal infection?

When night falls over Berlin, men in brown uniforms pour into the streets; they stop every car with a driver that looks Jewish. In boundless empathy with their dying compatriot in Paris, they smash the car's headlights. In a dizzying display of solidarity with the poor innocent diplomat they kick in the windshield. Then, in a further immensely affectionate gesture of unity with the unfortunate secretary, they open the driver's door and punch him full in the mouth, brass knuckles hidden underneath their rough gloves. With infinite tenderness, they push the Jew's head backwards until he screams with his mouth wide open and with the tip of their billy clubs they rake his dirty Jewish teeth out of his filthy Jewish mouth, all to the greater glory of the fine diplomat vom Rath, until the Allee is littered with teeth and blood.

•

These are turbulent times. Not every heart can bear it. With increasing frequency we find ourselves at the cemetery, in front of a gaping family grave. The entrance of the Jewish cemetery at Weissensee sports a ridiculous enameled plate:

ACHTUNG! Friedhofsbesucher! Es is verboten, an der Strassenkreuzung Lothringenstrasse-Berliner Allee am Strassenbahnkörper entlang zur Insel der Strassenbahnhaltestelle zu gehen. Haltet in Eurem eigenen Interesse Verkehrsdisziplin. Geht an der Ecke geradlinig über die Strasse auf den gegenüberliegende Bürgersteig.—Jüdische Gemeinde zu Berlin e.V. Friedhofs-Verwaltung.

Those Jews, why do they always have to use so many words? Summarized: If you want to take the tram back home, don't walk along the tram tracks in the middle of the street, even though that is the shortest way, but first cross the street to the other side, walk sixty feet to the right and then cross the street again. The Berlin traffic police have laid a little ambush at the cemetery; they write out tickets to whoever breaks the law, even when there's no tram in sight. Of course, they only stop people who are returning from the cemetery. That way they're certain that they are arresting Jews. The Jewish Question is after all solved through strictly legal means. A traffic violation ticket is 150 reichsmarks. If by accident the cops catch an Aryan, his ticket will cost only one. On the 18th of September 1938, the newsletter of the Jewish Congregation publishes a handy guide to the traffic rules for pedestrians, urging all members to adhere strictly to them. In particular, we are told that crossing the street is only allowed when the light is green, and that one needs to wait a short while when the light moves from red to yellow.

One fine October morning, my father went out to buy some tobacco. The street was as empty as can be, and so he ignored the traffic light. They kept him at the police station for over five hours. They took down his name. He was now on the list. He was officially an asocial element.

·

"My husband is not at home," Mother said. It was true: He had gone out, his camouflaged violin case under his arm. Life goes on, whatever happened to that guy in Paris. Could we afford to lose the money if he skipped an evening's work at the bar? "Don't go," Mother had said. She had begged him. "Walking the streets, now that that man has died? Are you out of your mind? Didn't Goebbels just declare in his radio address that the soul of the people is boiling with rage?"

Now she was glad he hadn't listened. The two men at the door do not believe her; they have to see for themselves. With their broad shoulders and their long overcoats they push Mother aside.

"What is behind this door?" That's the kitchen. One of the men turns on the light. The kitchen is neat and clean. Mother loves neatness. The men open the cupboards, even though there isn't enough room in any of them to hide an adult male. One of them is clearly eying the dinnerware.

"And here?"

"The living room."

"You live well." Mockery in their voices. And threat. Your living situation can change at any time, it says. A silver Shabbat candle disappears under a coat flap.

That's probably not following the rulebook, but is Mother in a position to complain?

They walk up the stairs. "That's the bedroom."

"Are you sure he isn't in bed?" One of the officers pulls out his gun and aims it playfully at the messy heap of blankets. "*Pang!*" he sings, but he doesn't shoot, nor does he go nearer to inspect. He is King Solomon. Mother's reaction tells him all he needs to know.

"And this?"

"That's the little one's room. Let him sleep. Please."

The men enter my room with lots of noise, letting in the harsh light. I wake up with a jolt and I scream at their silhouettes in the door—the sheer bulk of their shoulders, the broad rim of their hats: There is no escape possible. One of the men pulls the bedspread off me, the other opens the doors of the armoire and rummages through the drawers, while number one, satisfied that I am not sharing my blankets with Father, now pokes his nightstick under the bed.

They go back to the hallway. They tear through the empty guest room. The bathroom echoes as in a spy movie. Now they walk down the stairs, the clicking of their heels fading slowly. They whisper at each other, there's some fluttering of paper. They're probably checking us off the list, looking up the next address.

"Nothing, just like I told you. See?" Mother does her best to make it sound neutral, without any hint of triumph or relief.

"When your husband gets back home, will you tell him to report at the police station? As soon as possible, yes? Tomorrow morning. At the crack of dawn!"

They are on their way out, they are already at the front door, when Father sticks his key in the keyhole.

•

My mother holds my father's battered head in her lap. She strokes his face, tears roll down her cheeks. If Father had only come home half an hour later, at his usual time, instead of cutting his performance short because he was worried about us; if only he hadn't come home early to make sure that we were safe. "Don't you worry about us," my mother says. "Don't ever worry about us. We will be okay." What she means is: It's every man for himself now. Father cannot even help himself. Like her, he cries and cries and cries.

•

I can't stand it at home. I have to get on my bike.

The Schöneberg district is empty this morning. The streets are drenched in a dreamy De Chirico *sfumato*. Neither man nor beast is visible, but a tangible Presence lurks; today's dawn is blood-fingered. Closer to Ku'damm the streets grow more restless, the sidewalks are alive with the sweeping of big brooms. A couple of men hunt for cigarettes and dirty magazines in the smoking remnants of a tobacco shop. Stores are being boarded up by old men with shaky hammers; nine-inch nails stick out of their worried mouths. Defiled and decapitated mannequins lean out of broken shop windows. A man complains of a terrible injustice to an empathetic circle of onlookers—apparently his shop had been looted even though he is not Jewish. I race through the streets—riding slowly seems like a provocation, even though nobody ever pays attention to a kid like me. A big pillar of smoke rises out of the gold domes of the Fasanenstraβe synagogue. A group of people has gathered in front of the temple; they dance and cheer and shout anti-Semitic slogans. Yes, the crowd is right. This temple does not belong here, its onion-shaped domes are so round and heavenly that they have no place in a city of gray that has its teeth permanently bared. Later in the morning those copulas will collapse, like so many others in the Reich, dreams of a heaven on earth, carelessly broken. A fire truck is parked in front of the synagogue, but the firemen only keep the neighboring houses wet, they don't care about G*d's House.

I have seen enough. I have to get to school. And if there was any doubt left: After this night, none of us still considers himself to be German.

•

I reread the text; I recite it out loud for De Heer to correct. Two hundred and fifty synagogues, seven thousand five hundred stores, one hundred Jews dead, three thousand five hundred Jews arrested. "The big picture," says De Heer, head in hands. "The big picture. Just what I was trying to avoid."

"The present is all I can handle," he adds. "The present with its minor inconveniences, with the small pains of living as an obsolete citizen—a retired ex-GDR-man in a Western land. Plus, whenever you make a broad sweep like that, you reduce the events to history. The little chaotic doings of human beings, what makes life life, they get lost in translation; you push people into categories, you make them exemplars of a species. I have no need for the past and its statistics, no, no need whatsoever. But still. The chain that tugs at my throat—and for once the roles are reversed, dog leads man here, Cerberus himself is yanking at the other end of the leash—is the chain of cause and effect, the rattling links of karma and samsara—indeed, the rationality of the European languages deserts us here and only Sanskrit can come to the rescue. The bitter haggling with despair and loss and exhaustion and despondency, the endless negotiations with guilt and blame, it can only be spoken of in a dead, a very dead tongue."

•

Even as a young child I heard so many stories. In June there had been a first flurry of arrests—the police went after the most stringently asocial elements on their lists, even though these were often men that had done the regime no more harm than my father had: A traffic violation or a frank comment within earshot of the wrong person was all that was needed to land them in jail.

I had my hiding spot on the landing, behind the balusters, and from there I listened in on the late-night conversations in the living room. I wasn't allowed downstairs when we had certain guests, old acquaintances not seen for a long time, invariably showing up much thinner than I remembered them. Whenever one of these rang our doorbell, my parents sent me to my bedroom. Fifteen minutes later, I took up my position in my shadowy corner to listen breathlessly to the stories told by these shaggy half-strangers. Sometimes the storyteller would take a break and climb up the stairs to go the bathroom. He would pass me on the way and look at me with dead eyes, saying nothing. In the bathroom, he would take his sweet time, peeing loudly and splashing water over his face, and then he would simply be silent for what seemed like an hour. Never did one of the storytellers tell me to go to bed; never did they tell my parents I was sitting there. Maybe they didn't care. Or maybe they didn't consider me a child anymore, but a miniature adult who could decide for himself what it was he wanted to hear—we all grew up so terribly fast in those days. Or else they assumed that hearing these stories might further my education in the school of life. What I found strangest of all, even then, was that those stories did not provoke any anger in me, nor did they lead to sadness or compassion or even fear—I observed it all coolly. I was ashamed of that observation, since one should always react to such horrors with the proper emotion. I tried to practice compassion by imagining that all this had happened to Father and not to some distant acquaintance, some geezer who once played the cello in our salon. I couldn't. The stories never came alive, they remained paper-thin, maybe because the storytellers themselves were as white and blank as notebook pages. Or maybe I should blame the attack with the cherry pits? Maybe those sharp little shocks had chased the ability to empathize out of my skull? I hadn't felt any fear during that attack, or only briefly, and maybe it was that, the fact that I had only felt anger—

that most volatile, most cold, most egotistical of all emotions—had severed the connection between my brain and my heart, forever killing all kindness inside me. Or had I internalized my father's stance, his state of mind on the night of the cherry harvest? How stoically he had destroyed his library, his most prized possession after his violin. There had been pain in his heart, but not agony. A few matches and a few well-planned strokes with his axe and it was all over. And then he offered the wood to our neighbors. And never ever talked about it again.

Father once told me a story. It came out of one of those burned books. A story from old Japan. (We all carry loads of books inside. Maybe that was it. Maybe he didn't mourn his lost books because he had kept them in his soul.)

A powerful samurai visits a frail monk. He is on a quest. He wants to know the secrets of the universe. He bows deep in front of the venerable master and then he raises his voice, a voice that thunders, the voice of a man who is used to being obeyed.

"Monk, teach me the secrets of heaven and hell!"

The fragile old man looks up at the towering warrior. An expression of pure contempt contorts his face. "The secret of heaven and hell? Why should I tell *you*? I cannot teach you anything. You're hopeless. You're rough. And filthy. You stink. You're a slob. Your sword is rusty. Your clothes are smelly rags. You bring nothing but shame to the samurai class. Go away! I can't stand to be in the same room with you! Shoo-shoo! Away with you!"

The samurai fumes with anger. He has never been so furious in his life, he sees red, a deep blush spreads over his face, and he pulls his sword—gleaming, spotless—and raises it high above his head, ready to cleave the monk's skull in two with one mighty, clean blow.

"That," says the monk quietly (and quickly), "You see: *That* is hell."

The samurai does not know what to say. He is speechless. The compassion of the monk, who risked his life to teach him the secret of hell! Slowly he lowers his sword. He drowns in gratitude; his heart is filled with joy.

"And this, you see," says the monk in the same whispering voice. "This is heaven."

But last night it had been Father's turn.

•

The Gestapo officers speak of their prisoners in the past tense. Their truck belongs to a moving company. It has no windows. It's difficult to guess how many men sit inside, their chins resting on their bony knees, but every time the truck wobbles high on its suspension—a truckload of Jews is much lighter than a truckload of furniture—Father's narrow shoulders bump into the man to the right of him, and then into the man to his left. The sway of the wagon makes Father feel so tired, so deadly tired, and he wipes his eyes to clear away the veil of inebriation that has lately become such an integral part of his evenings. It has been a long time since he was been invited to one of the better salons or played in the well-lit coffee houses of civilized amusement. These days he makes the rounds of the seedy bars in the neighborhood in Charlottenburg called Charlottengrad. The owners are former officers of the Russian army, coarse exiles pockmarked with dueling scars; the customers are cheap strippers and professional wrestlers and cynical retired sea captains looking for somebody to hustle. The kind of bar that has a *taroteuse* in residence; the kind of bar where nobody cares that the sands of Time have eroded my father's playing from its old majestic jubilation to a tragic rasp. As long as the vodka and the Natashas keep flowing, life is good. The customers speak all dialects of Russian, Romanian, and Polish, and on occasion you might even hear Yiddish, and there's always a few paperback novels lying around, their covers depicting helpless maidens, bare breasts scored with teeth marks. Even German soldiers—shockingly young, children almost—come here, attracted by the aura of decadence. They raise their glasses to the solidarity of nations and they shout clumsy obscenities at the waitress in their thick Swabian or Rhinelandish accents. Every other day, one or another shady fatso comes up to Father during his break and starts a conversation about that oversized violin case. "I bet you can fit a lot of stuff in there, mister! Why don't you work for me, man—walk around Ku'damm with that fiddle briefcase of yours, just hiss *Zsssigaren! Zsssssssigaretten!*, and when a passerby answers you with a snort you hand him one of these little packages and you get twenty marks in return. It's pure aspirin, man, diluted with washing powder, you don't run the slightest risk with the authorities." Every other day my father considers the offer, but then he also considers the broken nose a customer might give him, a customer whose thirst for anesthesia has been insufficiently quenched by inhaling a mixture of aspirin and detergent, and he politely declines the offer. Then he buys the cocaine pusher a pilsner, which was what the man was after all along. By closing time—it always falls over the bar like an unexpected and most unwelcome thunderstorm—alliances are made: Who will support whom on the dangerous way back home? No matter how much vodka the customers have poured into my father, he always ends up safely between his very own sheets, even though he often can't remember how exactly he got home and who had taken care of him. That's the way it goes, the disenfranchised look out for each other; the more able bar-goers search the drunkard's pockets until they find his official ID, and then they deliver the man home safe and sound, and good as new.

From time to time the truck makes a stop. The big doors open and a new load of terrified people find a spot on the floor. The inside of the truck is bathed in the darkest night imaginable. When it's completely full and the smell of sweat and the prickly heat of fear threatens to overpower them all, the car finally picks up speed. They drive a long distance and then they arrive at their final destination. The driver kills the engine, but the passengers continue to shudder. When the doors open, they realize where they are: at the police headquarters on Alexanderplatz.

The man right in front of Father wears nothing but his pajamas underneath his winter coat. "Nice crisp blue," the officers mock. They frisk him; one officer sticks his hands down the man's pants, checking for weapons. They find nothing, of course. "You have a nice round belly, you Jew. Enjoying our fine German nation's food a little bit too much, aren't we?" The prisoner keeps silent. "Open your mouth!" The officer sees a false tooth glimmer in the back of the prisoner's mouth. "It smells like gold in here. Gold and garlic. You smell. You pig."

They take my father's watch. It goes into a cardboard box. There are four of such boxes on the table. *Pocket watches—gold and gilded. Pocket watches—silver. Wristwatches—gold and gilded. Wristwatches—silver.* "You will get it back next time." Father signs a receipt. "Why next time?" (And why would there be a next time?) The man sneers. "We are stretched to our administrative limits." Father nods. He understands this, yes; this whole operation must take a lot of work, a lot of organization. So much preparation! Next time is fine. Of course. I'm looking forward to meeting you again.

"Kneel." They are pushed into a room, ten, fifteen men at a time, a big waiting room with chairs lined up against the wall. Father recognizes a few of the detainees. They aren't close friends or real acquaintances, just people he sees from time to time in the bars or coffee houses. People that have heard him play—he notes a gleam of recognition in a few eyes. The men kneel because they have been ordered to.

"Crawl!" The men crawl through the room to the opposite wall where another set of officers are waiting for them, one for each prisoner. Father reminds himself that these people are good civil servants, they are just doing their job; they are merely following the rules; they go strictly by the book.

"Lie down! Arms outstretched!" All my father can see of his personal police officer are the tips of his shoes. Also the cuffs of his pants—dust has gathered there, and mud from the streets. The shoes have seen better times, they look neglected, the leather is cracked. The shoes creak whenever the man shifts his weight. The heels are hardly a hand's width away from my father's fingers—ominously close. Paper rustles.

"Violinist, huh?" The voice comes from high above. "Are you right-handed?" Father nods, inasmuch as one can nod when one lies prostrate on the floor, helpless and vulnerable. The police officer wiggles his toes. One of the shoe tips rises. It taps a rhythm. The tip touches the ground a millimeter away from my father's left hand, the hand he needs to shape his notes. A Masonic rhythm. The rhythm stops. The man places the shoe tip lightly on top of Father's fingers. My father starts sweating. Then the man applies some force. Just when the weight of the shoe becomes unbearable, the man removes his foot. It is too easy. Too cliché. The executioner loathes his smooth, effective routines, much like the teacher ends up being horrified by the slickness of his own easy jokes, much like the violinist hates the fluttering passages that sound virtuosic and stir up the audience precisely because of their lack of substance.

When the detainees get up again, they brush the dirt off their clothes. The particles whirl through the room; slowly they descend to the floor, ready to receive the next batch of prisoners.

There's no end to the surprises the architecture of the police headquarters has to offer the prisoners. They are lined up in a long hallway. A guard walks slowly up and down, smoking an eternal cigarette. He has a machine gun at his hip. One after the other, the detainees disappear into one of the small rooms that line the corridor. Time becomes honey, sticky and sweet; this is the time before the interrogation, the last moments of presumed innocence. Two uniformed policeman drag a man out of one the interrogation rooms, his pants are soaked in blood from crotch to knee. Then finally my father's turn has come.

What immediately catches his attention, because he does not expect it, is the presence of a young woman in the room, a young woman in a neat, dull dress suit. When the guards bring him in, she is looking out the window, visibly bored. A handful of stars and a cloud sailing through the moonlit sky is all there is to see. A lonely chair stands in the exact center of the room. With a big sigh, the woman puts a fresh, smooth piece of paper in the typewriter.

Then my father's interrogator enters the room, his step buoyant, and three boys dart in behind him, stumbling endearingly, likely new recruits in training. It is the man with the worn-out shoes, the man who didn't think it necessary to crush my father's fingers. He gestures with his hand. Please, sit down. Dust twirls through this room too; dust and dust, always dust. My father closes his eyes. The back of the chair feels sticky against his jacket. These then will be the instruments of his terror: a wooden table, a typewriter, a chair sticky with blood, a reading lamp, and a secretary in a neat gleaming polyester suit, batting her eyes.

They get down to business; suddenly they have no time to lose. Names is what they want, and dates and places. They want the code words of the organization he belongs to. Father cannot believe it. One fine autumn morning he crosses the street while the light is yellow, and that makes him a member of the organized resistance? Really, the impatient jaywalking of a man in urgent need of nicotine is considered an infallible sign of a revolutionary, conspiring mind? They yell at him. Why does the prisoner refuse to give names and dates and places? Well, he can't reveal any secrets he doesn't posses, can he? Don't they understand? No, this interrogation turns out to be most unsatisfactory for all parties involved. And how long can one keep answering such stupid questions with the patient smile of somebody who just recovered from a long illness?

The interviewer gets irritated. It's all going way too slowly. He asks Father to stand up. Short rubber clubs appear in the hands of the apprentice sorcerers. Although Father tries to protect his face with his hands and elbows, he quickly loses three teeth. They take a quick break. One of the guards silently hands my father a glass of water to rinse his mouth. After the break, it turns out that Father is no longer capable of sitting. He spends the rest of his interrogation lying facedown on the floor. The three young men are informed of the fun fact that Father is a professional musician. These three are still at he beginning of their careers; they have less aversion to clichés. So they take the wedding band off his finger and stomp lustily on his left hand, crushing the brittle bones to a bloody pulp.

Pain is a good teacher. Father now mentions a name. Of a friend that has emigrated long ago, a friend who safely made it to Cuba, and then the name of another emigrant, and another one. The interrogator keeps his head tilted; he is terribly disappointed with this much predictability. Father's battered brain goes into free-association mode—maybe he mentions the name of somebody who is still in the country. Maybe. In any case, the interrogator nods curtly to the secretary, who finally starts typing. A list, we may assume, containing the names Father is dictating. She makes short runs with her fingers and then she uses her thumb to return the carriage to its starting position. After each name a bell sounds from the black steel casing of the machine. The rattling of the machine wakes my father out of his trance, out of his gushing mantra of useless names. He stutters, he hesitates, and then he stops. The interrogator nods again, and the young woman rolls the paper out of the Olivetti. She steps out of the room. The four men light their cigarettes and smoke in silence, without so much as a glance in Father's direction. When the secretary returns, a stamp and a signature have been added to the piece of paper. That was what they were waiting for. Father is escorted outside, and while he passes his interrogator, the man briefly rests his hand on Father's shoulder and presses the raw flesh.

At the first sign of dawn the men are released. They stumble onto the square, men in slippers and nightgowns and pajamas and crinkled city suits and bloody shirts, men without watches, men without any ties to time, men that do not dare look each other in the eyes. "Next time"—these words echo in each of the men's heads. A woman passes by, she has a dachshund on a leash; she spits at their feet. A child is crying. It sounds like the engine of a car starting up. The cab driver looks at Father and says, in his fat Berlin accent: "*Hast wohl Neesebluten jehabt, wa?*" Yes, says Father, I had a most ferocious nosebleed indeed.

This is all our own fault. We do not learn our lesson. We must be punished; how else will we learn? Left to our own devices, all we do is disturb the peace. In the aftermath of the pogrom—which we only have ourselves to blame for—all companies are forcibly Aryanized. All Jewish department stores change owners, and often also their names, because even Jewish names are unclean. Leonard Tietz AG becomes Kaufhof; the department store chain of Hermann Tietz becomes Hertie; Alsberg remains Alsberg, but the public is informed that its management is now guided by purely Aryan reason; Karstadt likewise does not change its name, but has a brand spanking new Board. Big banners announce things like: *Kaufhaus Max Cohn is now in Aryan hands! New name! You'll buy better at Ahrend!* On the Havel river, in the surreal light of early morning, a ship floats by, a slogan painted on its side: *Buying from Jews is stealing the People's property.*

•

This is unusual. It is way past eight o'clock, but our teacher isn't there. We're excited, of course, but we don't use the time as we normally would—we don't cover the blackboard in bad caricatures of Doktor Wollheim or Frau Rosenthal, we don't sketch crude and uncertain depictions of the external organs of the human reproductive system just to make the girls squirm in their seats. We don't even throw blackboard erasers at each other, although we generally like doing this when unsupervised: It gives us all the look of powdered actors in some happy *comme-*

dia-dell'arte production. This morning we swap stories. I tell about my breathless biking tour, but I keep my mouth shut—that much I've learned—about the bitter hurt at home, about what happened to my father. The school is close to the Tiergarten and the kids who came by S-Bahn have all, like me, seen the pillar of foul smoke rising from the central dome of the Fasanenstraße synagogue. So many of us had celebrated their Bar Mitzvahs in that temple.

Then Doktor Wollheim stumbles into the classroom. His face is grayer than usual, and the smell of cigarette smoke, coffee, and anxiety that always accompanies him is stronger than ever. When he speaks, he does not look at us, but his gaze wanders to the windows, as if he expects the Nazi hordes to march through the gates at any minute. Which is exactly what he *does* expect. "Go home, dear children!" is what he says. Wait a minute! Did he, the earnest mathematician, just call us *liebe*? "Don't hang around, children, don't dawdle, don't loiter—go straight home, do you hear me, straight home. Right away. Your parents need to know that you are safe. Don't go in a group, don't do anything that can attract attention. Please, go straight home! Go now!" And even though none of us—including Doktor Wollheim himself—is *Ostjude*, Doktor Wollheim adds a Yiddish blessing to his exhortation: "*Sei gesundt.*" We did not know, and how could we have known, that this would be our very last day at school; that our school, and all other Jewish schools in Berlin, never would reopen.

•

"Come on," says David Zwingermann, always the ringleader. "Three is not a group."

"Come on," says Horst. "Or are you scared? *Feige, Feige!*"

So we ride our bikes down Ku'damm. We want to see what's going on. And I want to delay my homecoming. David is strong and daring, which makes him dangerous company on a day like today. With his tan skin, his long, elegantly crooked nose, his wavy hair combed backwards with a mass of pomade, with his fast smile and that twinkle in his eyes, he looks so Jewish, and I'm ashamed that I even dare contemplate this. Horst is smaller, with less generous lips, but today I notice for the first time that Horst is also recognizably Jewish.

We hear crowd noise from a side street. It is the Markgraf-Albrecht-Straße, and in front of the Friedenstempel—the Temple of Peace—a mob has gathered: Nazis in full regalia and onlookers in more sober attire. The firemen lean against their trucks; they roll their cigarettes calmly. "Hey you!" someone yells in our direction, and I'm paralyzed with fear.

"Oh, shut up!" David yells back and he sticks out his tongue.

"The back entrance," he whispers. This is his synagogue, he knows how to get into the classrooms, he knows the way that leads to the great hall. David and Horst, tough David and skinny Horst, jump off their bicycles and slide through the back door. The hall is full of smoke. The benches have been hacked to splinters, but the Shrine has heavy wooden doors that are hard to kick in. In their blind need to destroy, the looters didn't stop to think that one could simply open the doors with a key, the key that unbelievably enough is sticking right out of the keyhole. David and Horst open the doors—the Torah scrolls are still there. They pile the texts high on their arms; they take as many as they can, and then they race out the main entrance, two little kids—the smoky corridor behind them is suddenly too scary.

What beast comes running out of the synagogue? The crowd hesitates, and when they see the boys, they part out of instinctive respect for so much chutzpah—they let David and Horst and their cargo through. Then they realize their mistake and run after them. But it's too late: David has already flagged down a cab and it tears away from the curb (cabbies! Praise G*d for the ever-defiant cabbie!) just as the mob catches up with them.

This is a bit much for me. I stand petrified. I have three bikes in my hand. What should I do? I drop Horst and David's bikes and jump on mine, pedaling away as fast as I can.

·

De Heer goes to one of the bookcases and feels his way through the spines until he finds what he's looking for. He opens the book at a page marked with a piece of paper and shows me the picture: a dark space, probably a basement, packed with goods wrapped in burlap. The tea merchant with his bristly mustache eyes the camera through thick lenses. He seems very much aware of the gravity of the moment. Next to him stands Horst Löwenstein, tight-lipped, and behind these two stands David, grinning broadly. In front of them, on the table, there is an impressive stack of scrolls, sixteen, seventeen, twenty? They're hard to count. "No, just twelve," says De Heer. "Each Torah scroll has two handles." "Of course," I say. "How stupid of me."

De Heer's fingers wander over the photograph. "This is where I missed my rendezvous with history," he says. "The chairman of the *Gemeinde* got David on the next children's transport to England; they bumped him up on the list. That could have been me, had I been a little more daring. Horst didn't join David, his permit to leave the country was delayed on a formality. He was never able to leave—Horst was killed in Riga, in late 1941."

"Did those scrolls ever get used again?" I ask.

"They returned to Berlin after the war. Later that day, a rabbi, Rabbi Max Nussbaum, saved another of the scrolls, a smaller one, and smuggled it outside in his coat. He took it with him when he emigrated to America. It's now in the shrine of the temple where he used to teach, in Hollywood."

Hollywood! "Isn't it remarkable," I say, "How the Nazis were so methodical and precise in the plundering and destruction of stores, knowing exactly how to hurt the owners in the worst way, stealing their wares or else rendering them useless, and running off with the cash register, but that they lost all their panache when it came to the temples? They only touched the real taboos, the things that would truly hurt the congregation, from afar. Setting fires and chopping down furniture, of course they were good at that, but they stayed away from the core—they left the shrines themselves alone."

"That was pure ignorance," De Heer opines. He sighs. He is less pleased with my questions about the world than I am with his. "Shops, department stores—that the Nazis knew. But when they got to a holy place, they were out of their element; they had no idea what they were doing. And don't forget: Torah scrolls are easily desecrated. One broken letter and they're no longer kosher. No, those scrolls could never have served again. The Nazis had desecrated them even without touching them—empty souvenirs from a terrible time, that's all they are."

"But did the Nazis know? Maybe they were afraid? Maybe they realized that smearing your excrement over G*d-given books isn't a good idea? Let the fire do the job while you stand a good distance away?"

"Maybe," says De Heer. "Maybe."

•

"What happened to Grüneberg?" I ask.

"Uncle Karl, my father's father's brother? I never knew him well. He always had been a distant man, a somewhat wooden character, a man who kept his mood carefully hidden behind the smart suits he got from his own elegant boutique. After his stay at the Sachsenhausen camp he shrunk down to a sagging skeleton of steel wire, loosely draped with ill-fitting but expensive clothes. Not a man a child like me would talk to.

"Have you ever visited Sachsenhausen, Paul—the former concentration camp in Oranienburg, less than half an hour by train from the Mitte? The majority of the detainees from that night of broken glass ended up there. It wasn't an innocent playground. People died in Sachsenhausen, even in 1938—from typhus, from dehydration, from sheer stress. The family of the deceased would receive notice that their beloved father/brother/uncle/son had suffered severe heart failure. In the sickbay at Sachsenhausen, in the little office that the doctors shared, a human skull is on display, its jaws pried open. Go see, it's still there. This is not like Frederick the Great who kept the skull of his favorite dog on his worktable. This is not like the Tibetan monks who drink milk from the stripped and boiled skull of one of their brethren, a symbol of the transitory nature of life and a sweet memento of a friend who has passed on to Nirvana. No, the Sachsenhausen skull bears no name, it keeps no memory alive. This skull doesn't symbolize life and remembrance, it symbolizes death and death alone. One or the other handy surgeon converted it into a lampshade, you see; an electrical cord runs through a bullet hole in the back of the head and light streams from the nostrils, the eye sockets, the mouth. The man whose brains lived inside this bone box didn't get the chance to deliver any famous last words, nor was he allowed to cast one last long look upon his loved ones. There was, most likely, no reason for his death—they shot a bullet through his occipital cortex and that was that. He died because he was Jewish and some other schmuck had a gun. You can just hear the young intern marvel. "Whoa, doesn't that look cool? The bullet hole is dead center! Can you put an electrical cord through there? Yeah! Awesome!"

•

In the evenings, my father, the violinist with the crushed fingers, wrings his hands just like hamsters do their claws in their all-too-tiny cages. My mother, the singer with the broken voice, grows ever more quiet, a sad lovebird contemplating her great loss. When evening falls, the only sound in our house is my father's hand wringing, dry flesh rasping over dry flesh, and my mother's ominous silence. Only now do I realize how slow the poison did its work. It wasn't really a question of my father's sojourn in the bowels of the Alex complex; it was the slow gnawing away of a full five years of oppression. Only a few years ago, my mother would have dealt with a crisis like this by throwing a party, draping herself over the polished lid of the piano, breathtakingly outfitted in one of her low-cut glitter dresses, and carried away by the vibrations in the sound box of mahogany beneath her, she would coo and croon for our guests—*"Es liegt in der Luft"* or *"Wenn ich mir was wünschen dürfte"* or *"Eine kleine Sehnsucht"*—while my father shone like a tango fiddler possessed by a thousand demons and threw in a devilishly fast waltz or a presumably eighteenth-century *plaisir d'amour* improvised on the spot. In those long-gone days of happiness, I—seated on the landing behind the baluster, well-camouflaged in my striped pajamas—would on occasion catch rare glimpses of parties of a more intimate nature, after all the guests had gone home. I couldn't see the piano very well, but there was Mother's favorite dress on the wooden floor, empty and glowing like a puddle of moonlight ("*Oh Mond!*"), and there was the pinkish whiteness of the soles of her feet sticking out over the keyboard while they both, Mother and Father, quietly sang "*Wenn zwei sich lieben*" in a sonorous yet breathy a cappella. The piano resonated with love, and even though I only half-understood what was happening, I too was incomprehensibly happy. But now the appetite for singing had left my parents, and their appetite for dancing was gone too, and the piano stood so terribly alone in the corner of the room, its voice muffled by a thick layer of dust. In its tangible sadness, the instrument looked like a casket for a angel buried sideways. My parents' lovemaking became less and less frequent, and when they did congregate, it sounded more and more like crying. A man who loves his wife with bleeding fingertips—I can tell you: It makes the saddest sound.

•

"Here," says De Heer. "An example of smart Jewish resistance."

He flips through a folder thick with clippings, peering through a magnifying glass until he finds the photocopy.

It's an announcement for the screening of the movie *Chicago*. The movie, it says, will be shown in the Jewish Culture Club, December 30th, 1938. This is the description of the movie:

> *A city goes up in flames and the firefighters are looking on without interfering. The lines have been laid, the hoses are ready, but nobody makes a move. The men are waiting for an order, but no order is forthcoming. Only when the city has been burned to the ground and ash and ruins are all that remains, does the order come. The fire trucks ride back to their stations. An ugly fairy tale? An evil story concocted by some madman? No. This is the historic truth. And it happened in Hollywood.*

"Nobody went to see the movie," says De Heer. "Literally nobody. There was not a single man, woman, or child who wanted to see that spectacle."

•

There's a sound my teacup makes when I put it back on the saucer, a hollow ringing sound. It gives me the shivers.

"By saving the Torah scrolls, David saved himself," I surmise.

"And Horst would have died even if he hadn't participated in that rash act," De Heer adds. "And my father didn't want to name names; they forced him to. If he had remained silent, maybe two or three more people might have been saved—but more likely his silence would have served no purpose whatever. There were others who talked too. And by the end of the war, almost every Berlin Jew had been rounded up anyway."

"And your father's Uncle Karl's only crime were his dreams of Monika, and the ones who arrested him didn't have the slightest idea about that. The dead can't be blamed."

"Why then," says De Heer, somber, as somber as can be, "Why then did I survive?"

"There's no reason. You just got lucky."

This upsets De Heer. "Lucky? Lucky? Who can claim that I got lucky? Fifty years of bad dreams caught in the memory machines of this city? I curse every day of my life, young man, because I have never been able to live my life to the fullest. Do you call that lucky? Do you?"

"No," I say. Sheepishly.

"Go away, you scum," says Jozef De Heer, and he throws one of his slippers at my head. It hits me too. "Take your computer and go. Go away. Go, just go! Out with you, out, out!"

·

Again there are these murmurings behind Donatella's door. When I walk into my room I find not one, but two notes singed "-a." "I guess not then," says the topmost note. A sad smiley underscores the words (is that called a weepey?): a fast curl of ink, two vertical stripes for eyes and a downward hook for a mouth. The other note, from the deeper archeological layer, contains the following message: "How about tonight?," and that note sports a real smiley, the round head colored in with a sunny yellow fluorescent marker; a little red tongue hangs playfully askew out of the smiling mouth.

I turn the notes over. Donatella recycles. The two notes were written on the two halves of the same piece of paper, folded widthwise and separated with a letter opener or some such object, leaving a slightly serrated edge. The newly joined page contains a healthy amount of incomprehensible differential equations and a few lines of text that are equally mysterious to me, something about rolling scalar fields, Drell-Yan cross sections, and nonsingular four-potentials.

How sweet that Donatella thinks of me, and what a pity that her last note shows that she has given up, at least for the evening. I could have used some company after that story and after De Heer's outburst of half-sincere anger. I stare at the numbers and the symbols on the page, at the unfathomable words. Donatella knows what she's doing. She keeps—I think—the whole world in her hands. And I, I study memory, but when I run into memory in real life, I have no idea how to deal with it. I brush my teeth and walk to the icy cave where the toilets are. Still that murmuring behind her door. I'm so forgetful tonight that once I return to my room, I brush my teeth a second time.

ר

TONGUE

The kitchen is alive with the music of domestic happiness. Eggs are being beaten, milk splashes in a bowl of flour.

Every time I see Donatella, she has fruit in her hands. I watch her as she puts a knife into a peach's shallow groove, ever so carefully—and then she cuts. Colorless blood seeps from the wound; she licks it up. It strikes me that the ultimate fruit of Donatella's labor—of her meticulous preparation of the peaches, of her careful mixing of the butter with the flour, of her delicate puncturing of the egg yolks' thin membrane—is Donatella herself: This is what she's made of, these molecules will be absorbed into the basic protein chains that shape her body and her mind. It's trivial, but true: You are what you eat. This evening, then, Donatella will be sweet as cake and so worthy of love.

"Good morning," I say from the doorway, as her long fingers plunge in the dough and the tip of her tongue emerges from her mouth.

It's been a while since I last saw her. I had forgotten how much I like the frizzy halo of her hair, that tangled thorny bush with its fiery glow, and how much I adore the decisiveness of her gestures; I love her energy, her taunts, her earnestness; I admire the unbridled vigor with which she attacks the mountain of dough. I love the chaos that's visible around her—she is deliciously askew, with that barrage of combs and clasps and pins that keep her hair piled on top of her head. I love how her forehead and her nose and her cheeks are wild with freckles; I love the pallor of her face underneath that layer of golden dust; her eyes are as inky blue as Delft earthenware. She is a Ming vase: A dynasty of fragility shines through her features; her mouth is a mysterious pale crack in a vessel of perplexing bone china. She is everything: There's fire in her hair and an ocean in her eyes.

I cough. She looks up, as if only now aware of my presence.

"Good morning, Paul. You came to get some butter?"

"What a great idea to get a head start on cooking." I say. "I'll be home tonight."

Donatella cocks her head and squeezes one eye shut. "You don't really think I'm going to cook for you again, do you? And throw away half the food?"

"You should only give up after three rejections. And, for the record, I never rejected your invitations. I just wasn't home when you asked me."

"I know exactly what's going on, mister. Sneaking out of the house early in the afternoon. Coming back way past midnight. You have a little sweetheart in town."

I laugh out loud. "No. Not exactly."

"This cake is for my boss. Tomorrow's his birthday."

I do my best to look disappointed. Which is not too difficult. I *am* disappointed. The raw dough smells wonderful and Donatella—well, she smells wonderful too. A pin slips out of her hair and a curl falls over her eyes; she blows it away impatiently. I have this urge to put my arms around her. *You can touch me if you want.* Did she mean it? And if so, does the invitation still stand?

"My boss Goldfarb. Do you know him? He wrote all those popular science books for boys? The star books?"

I nod. *A Star is Born. The Preposterous Universe.* I read those books as a child— much more than that: I devoured them. I tell her so. "And his books made you want to become an astronomer?"

"Uh-uh. His books brought me here. Working with your childhood idol—does it get any better than that?"

"Working with a Nobel prize winner," I correct her.

"That too, yes."

"And wasn't he also involved in . . . ?"

"Yes, he was."

"And he's here? In Potsdam?"

"Indeed."

She goes on working the dough. Donatella is thorough. The tendons on the back of her hand stretch and release, the veins pulse blue with effort. "But if you want . . . There are some eggs left, and some flour. Enough to make pasta for two. I have some basil in the fridge, I think, and pine nuts, and some parmesan. *Tagliatelle con pesto* tonight. Would that entice you?"

"Yes," I say. "That would entice me. That would definitely entice me. I would love to have dinner with you. Should I take care of the wine?"

"Okay," she says, and she rakes her dough-smeared hand through her hair.

Then she realizes what she's done. "G*d, now I have to take a shower again!"

I nod my head and disappear.

•

A mind forever alone, traveling the uncharted seas of thought. That was how Gold-farb, in the fall of 1942, saw himself, and saw his future. He would live a simple life as an eternal student, and then change finally into a tweed-clad professor at some small liberal arts college surrounded by two hundred miles of cornfield; books and paper and scribbles on blackboards would be his biotope; slide rules would stick out of his pockets. A simple existence, be it riddled with complex thought.

The future, as always, had other plans in store. Harvard Square was waiting for him, and even though Goldfarb didn't know it yet, the Hill wasn't far behind—the Hill, codename LA, but a very different LA than the one Heywood and Alexander and with them the whole Upper East Side were dreaming of. This LA was populated with a singular breed of Angels—the fallen kind. Los Alamos, a town of barracks, a slum for the scientific elite, hastily erected on top of a chilly plateau; thousands of Jews and white boys elevated high above the scorched valley homes of the Indians and mestizos of New Mexico. A chilly town, yes, but also a town of burning faith. A town nobody had yet heard of, officially; a town so tiny that it fit in a post office box—a city that wasn't much more than a number: PO Box 1663, Santa Fe.

Harvard burst wide open. Open like a sore. Burst by history itself, cracked open by war. The army had taken over Eliot House and Kirkland House; it had invaded the Sigma Alpha Epsilon fraternity and taken possession of the larger parts of Leverett and Winthrop Halls. Bunk beds were installed to increase the dorms' capacities. The baseball field was renamed Soldier's Field; in the morning students worked their sweaty way through elaborate jungle gyms while their book bags waited patiently for them, leaning against the fence. The Art History department added *Fine Arts IX* to the curriculum (a class on camouflage, strangely labeled "protective hiding"); somebody offered a class on the economic aspects of war; there were crash courses in the Japanese language and Russian; navigation and nautical astronomy and calisthenics were suddenly the cool classes to take; on the open squares, you could see grown-ups throwing medicine balls at each other. Chaplains-in-training crawled grimly through the muddy banks along the Charles. Football players rehearsed their most vicious tackles on sandbags that bore a silk-screened picture of Herr Hitler. Clarions sounded intricate tattoos over Harvard Yard. Chancellor Conant donated his residence to the Navy, moving with his wife (eternally described as charming, because there was nothing else to say about her) to humbler quarters off-campus. John Connolly, supervisor of the Yard, removed tennis-playing citizens from the grass with a trembling hand—soldiers needed the space to march, you see. Last year in June, during commencement weekend, honorary degrees were bestowed upon Winston Churchill and H. L. Stimson, Secretary of War, and also on Frank Knox, Secretary of the Navy—at the conclusion of the ceremony the Harvard Band played a deafening rendition of *Onward, Christian Soldiers*.

Harvard also made a different type of contribution to the war effort. In the labs of the Chemistry department, two young assistant professors succeeded in synthesizing quinine (the poison that fifty years later would almost kill Jozef De Heer); in the laboratory for chemical warfare at the Medical School, Bartlett was researching how to shut down certain neuronal pathways in the malaria mosquito; and elsewhere in the same building, people were working on techniques to extract albumin, gamma globulin, thrombosis, and fibrin from blood plasma—long queues of pasty, pale-nosed students lined up to get pricked by the needle. Fieser's team played with fire; he brewed a slow fuel in his lab called naphthenic palmitic acid. Botanists compiled a compendium of Polynesian plants both edible and poisonous; B. F. Skinner strapped his pigeons in faux cockpit chairs and made them peck at pictures of submerged submarines and enemy ships; in the sound-proof room of Beranek's lab the ears of helpless, screaming would-be wireless operators were bombarded with hundreds of decibels of white noise pumped past twenty-thousand cement wedges. (During his student days, Beranek had been a drummer in the Harvard Band.) And why were those trucks parked in front of the physics buildings: What was it that workers were carrying away in crates, so cautiously that it had to raise suspicion? Were they really shipping Hickman's brand-new cyclotron, all eighty-five tons of it, to St. Louis, where it would be used for medical research? Of course not: Goldfarb would later come eye to eye with the wretched machine on the Hill, where it shook arrogantly and incessantly on its weak foundation of concrete, noisily challenging the current state of natural affairs. And, perhaps most amazingly of all, somewhere in that multitude of buildings at Harvard, somebody was building a brain in a box, a brain that was fifty-one feet long and ten feet tall, an Automatic Sequence Controlled Calculator made up of five-hundred miles of wires and two million connections, regulated by 1,467 ten-pole switches and about 3,500 relays (nobody knew the exact count). The machine, called Mark I (for it was clear that more of the monsters would be following soon), rattled its cage of steel tubes like a some angry mythological beast, ready to burst out into the world and take over. Its makers kept the ASCC a strict secret, not just for military reasons, but also to avoid trouble with their fellow Harvard professors and graduate assistants, who would be hard-pressed to admit that one day this powerful apparatus, this offensive blend of art and technology, might exceed their own brainpower. After all, Harvard men consider themselves, and rightfully so, to be the pinnacle of what the planet has to offer in terms of raw cognition—they could have easily matched Mark I's dizzying speed at ballistic computations if only they hadn't been so caught up in their own, more creative work. Each and every one of them was convinced that if ever a war could be won through sheer intellectual power, it would be this war, with its advanced weapons technology, with its new-fangled methods for radar detection and radar evasion (and the detection of radar evasion), and with its need for ever advancing developments in cryptology—they, the men of Harvard, would be the ones to do the job and crack the Nazis' spine. Almost in passing, the Harvard scientists collected a quite immodest number of Nobel Prizes—around the time when the committee in Stockholm readied itself to announce this year's winners, some of the more ambitious graduate students sported lapel pins boldly stating *Not Yet*.

Many of the students cultivated strange habits in the hope that their affected lunacies would be mistaken for creative madness. After all, mathematics purifies the spirit; it lifts its practitioners high above the rules of normal human behavior. Goldfarb, for instance, took to lying flat on his back whenever he could, by preference at the most unpredictable moments, wherever he happened to be struck by inspiration—on a park bench, on the grass, on a dining-room table, on the floor of a graduate student's office, or even on the pool table in the common room in Lowell—his exalted gaze would drift upwards and he would mumble algebraic formulas or meditate out loud on one of those obscure theorems that govern the solution of differential equations. He prided himself on his finely tuned performance; he carefully balanced himself on the border between psychotic behavior and the appearance of total absorption in the sacred discipline of mathematics: not crazy but merely eccentric; noticeably bizarre but not really too repulsive. It didn't bother anybody, and nobody paid much attention to it, except when his behavior obstructed their pool game. But even that was considered a challenge rather than a real difficulty: For a mathematician, playing a game of pool around the prostrate Goldfarb was an odd, but ultimately solvable problem.

To wrap himself in a second layer of eccentricity, Goldfarb took to writing, unaware of the connection-at-a-distance he was thus establishing with his mother. He wrote short stories drenched in the kind of mysterious symbolism and dreamy mysticism that one associates with the end of adolescence; the stories' protagonists wore tweed and flannel and overdosed on tobacco while staring out of dirty windows to the rainy fields beyond. They were the sort of backwards self-portrait of desperation often produced by people with a great surplus of brains as well as a great shortage of life experience.

Harvard, in the meantime, was emptying out. Every month, fifty or so lower-division students disappeared, off to faraway fronts. Every morning, fewer and fewer of the higher-division students showed up at the breakfast table. And professors were disappearing too. By the end of 1943, around the time that Goldfarb himself would join the ranks of the vanished, only eight of the original forty-four pre-war physics professors were still in Cambridge. The rest had been replaced by young bucks with exotic accents and a certain furtiveness in their eyes. Harvard, that nexus of learning, was no longer an ivory tower; it had become a fortress of khaki. All its money went to the military and to war-related scientific research. There were no funds left for decent food, for instance: The Faculty Club served horsemeat to its diners.

It was obvious what battlefields the undergraduates were sent to, but where did the professors go? Goldfarb didn't have a clue, but he was soon to find out. He did not, as we would have expected, earn this ticket to the Hill through the miracle of his intellect; he won it through the tempestuousness of his heart.

•

The first thing he noticed was her legs—long, tanned, and naked, a nice and muscular contrast with her bone-white bobby socks. Those legs disappeared most elegantly under a tartan skirt in the glorious club colors of Radcliffe College, ending halfway down her thighs. Wild and greedy legs that kicked and flew in every direction, that desperately wanted to free themselves from the tame embrace of the listless lindy hop rattled off by the jaded band. She was the only person on the dance floor who seemed to be having a genuinely good time; she danced with such a fervor as if Roosevelt himself had ordered her to liven up this dullest of student balls, and thus contribute to the morale of our troops and our glorious victory over the Nazi hordes.

Goldfarb was there with his friends from Lowell House. They were sitting in a corner of the room, deeply entrenched in a discussion over a matter of life and death, namely the game-theoretical aspects of blackjack and whether or not it was possible to cheat the bank using purely mathematical principles. The discussion had, of course, nothing to do with the party itself—the party was a teary affair for a bunch of society brothers (new money) who would be shipped to the European front tomorrow morning, straight from the seminar rooms of the business school.

The boys wanted to celebrate their incorporation into the Allied Army in grand style; apparently they also wanted to board the train with one hell of a hangover, or, as one of them was just now telling one of his many girlfriendettes in a display of faux blaséness: "*Aprés nous le deluge* and all that rot." In the background, his mother nodded approvingly—all those French classes at the most exclusive boarding school in the country had clearly paid off: Soon her over abundantly sophisticated sons would be awarded a priceless degree from Hah-vuhd. An expensive party it was too, smack in the middle of the maple floor of the center basketball court in the Indoor Athletic Building. None of the four friends in the corner knew the brothers in question, but the IAB was located right next to Lowell, and free soft drinks and food ("And women!," Ted had exclaimed. "Free women!") are always a good thing. The foursome didn't have much experience with women, but they did like music, however poorly performed. After 11 P.M., the Crimson Network switched from music and talk radio to messages in Morse code. The aim was to train the students in decoding. That floating beat hijacked the brainwaves— it was hard to think with that enervating beeping sounding from the speaker. "If only they would transmit the complete works of Henry Miller," Ted sighed. "That would increase my motivation to learn by at least a factor of ten-squared." Miller was Ted's favorite writer and his only source of knowledge about women. But the foursome's gamble worked out well: The moneyed siblings knew so many people on campus that each of them thought the other had invited that raggedy mob of Arts and Sciences students, or maybe they assumed that they indeed knew at least one the four friends—the brothers did look as though they had the ambition to become America's first set of twin senators, and they had worked themselves into the good graces of so many people that it was impossible for them to keep track of all their acquaintances. Ted, Saville, Jake, and Goldfarb all agreed that the Army had made the right decision in picking their hosts as cannon fodder.

Women! Of course Harvard didn't admit female students, but there was Radcliffe College, where young ladies were taught by Harvard professors. Now that the number of instructors had dwindled dangerously, a select group of more mature "Cliffehangers" had been admitted into Harvard's smaller auditoria. "She, for instance," Saville pointed out, "is in my class—well, van Vleck's class—in quantum mechanics." That one there, the one with the legs. And by way of a greeting, Saville toasted her with his Shirley Temple. She didn't interrupt her dancing for so much as a nanosecond, but she waved at the boys, or so it seemed, with the sparkling white rubber soles of her flat shoes, thereby drawing even more attention to those marvelous legs. For one long agonizing moment, the four boys each independently considered the possibility that the development of an ultimate probability theory for casino-goers might be just an idle pastime—so powerful was her presence. In fact, all the young men in the room were following her every move, every circle she spun, each complex figure her feet beat on the floor, and even those few boys who didn't have their eyes glued on her knew exactly where she is on the dance floor at all times—so potent was her trail of pheromones. The nostrils of the men in the hall, *all* men, quivered in unison, and that is no exaggeration.

"Oh my!" Ted moaned. "See that sugar bowl do the tootsie roll!"

"And she's heading our way!"

"Holy shit-a-mango!"

"You are, well, you must be the dreamer." It sounds cool and businesslike. He's still figuring out how to fit his hand in the hollow above her hips when she's already spinning in quick circles of quasi-Brownian motion on the hardwood floor. This is mere fact checking on her part, the confirmation of an old diagnosis. It comes as a shock to Goldfarb. He never thinks too much about himself, and he's never seriously considered the possibility that stories might be circulating about him. He's not a good dancer, and this partner in particular is too fast and too unpredictable for his taste and level of skill.

"Goldfarb," he croaks, as if the mere mention of his name is both an explanation and an excuse for his clumsy behavior.

"Goldfarb? Is that a last name or a Christian name?"

"It's a Jewish name," Goldfarb replies, with slight irritation. (He can't help himself.) "Isn't it enough? How many Goldfarbs do you know?" (How many are there? How many rebaptized unbaptized Gottlobs could there be in the world? Two, probably, just two in the whole of the United States of America—Goldfarb and his *Mutti*.)

"My name is Hannah."

"A palindrome!" Goldfarb exclaims, delighted by the mathematical regularity.

"It gets better, Goldfarb. My full name is Hannah Sidis. A double palindrome. Here I am, Mr. One-Name Goldfarb. Hannah Sidis, I'll be your double palindrome for the evening." She puts some extra sway in her hips. Goldfarb perspires. She's so totally hell-bent on having a good time.

"Quantum mechanics?"

"Nuclear physics. The force field inside the atom. Electromagnetic forces? The weak and the strong nuclear force? The glue that holds all matter together? I work with, or under"—she giggles—"van Vleck."

"Shouldn't you be at Princeton? Working with Einstein, for instance?"

"Einstein doesn't teach, silly. The Institute for Advanced Studies doesn't take students—those high priests of science don't talk to ordinary people, they only converse with the *Herrg*tt* himself—the latest bulletin from on high categorically denies all rumors of Him throwing dice. And Princeton doesn't accept female students. They think our brains are weak, or something like that." She snorts depreciatively. "What about you?"

"Literature and mathematics. Short stories and Hilbert spaces, number theory, diophantic equations."

"And why aren't you at Princeton, Mister-Goldfarb-with-no-Christian-name? Professor Birkhoff here must be one of the most anti-Semitic mathematicians in human history. None of those brilliant refugees from your homeland has ever been able to get tenure here, and rumor has it that he had Wiener removed from the school—chased him straight to the other side of town, to MIT. Oh, and you're editor of the *Hasty Pudding*? Don't look so surprised, do you really think I'd dance with any old freshman? You have to be worthy of me. I'm well informed, Mr. Goldfarb. Physics is an empirical science, as opposed to your dull theoretical mathematics and the futile speculations of literature. What are you working on right now?"

"An extension of Bertrand's theorem—that there is always a prime number between n^2 and $(n + 1)^2$. It seems simple, but nobody's ever been able to prove it."

"Is this going through your head? I mean, like, right now? Are you working on it even as we dance?"

"No," says Goldfarb truthfully. "This moment, Hannah, does not leave room for speculation—this moment does not need proof."

"Sil-ly!" exclaims Hannah and she hits him on the shoulder with a limp hand. "You're a writer alright—I read your stories. I like their, uh"—here she pretends to look for the right term, and the terms to choose from are apparently floating close to the ceiling—"dramatic nihilism, and their, uh . . . stylistic apathy. They fit well with the curvature of your spine—you look like you're carrying the weight of the world, man!"

This is the way conversations at Harvard go, everybody always tries to get the upper hand, since witty repartee is considered the hallmark of a truly bright mind.

From the other side of the hall one of the brothers watches the conversation between Hannah and Goldfarb intently. His eyes are squeezed half-shut and an angry expression darkens his face—he probably took a few acting classes. He is too Bostonian to intervene directly, but as soon as the music stops, even before Goldfarb withdraws his hand from Hannah's back, he storms the dance floor and grabs her by the arm, with that little excess of force that men think says "I love you," and then he sweeps her madly across the floor in a furious foxtrot of prerogative.

The rest of the evening is a blur. Somebody managed to empty a bottle of brandy in the big old punchbowl, but it isn't really the alcohol that makes Goldfarb dizzy. He doesn't dare watch the dancers for fear of seeing Hannah happy in somebody else's arms. And he doesn't dare walk back home alone, for fear of assault. The brother who claimed Hannah might have a knife; he might well be hiding a gun underneath that natty sports jacket. Men who are about to leave for the front sometimes acquire a totally new perspective on the relative importance of life, death, sex, and mutilation. On top of that, all their calculations on paper napkins and even the quick simulation study with a real deck of cards had led the group of friends to the final conclusion—unanticipated yet uncontested—that there is after all an untraceable element of chance in blackjack, and this had made them all feel inexplicably blue.

But then, just as the evening wears out, there is this unexpected tap on his shoulder.

"Would you be a dear and get my coat for me?"

It makes Goldfarb jump; he almost knocks over his chair. Hannah is so close that small bubbles of her warm spit have landed on his cheek. He stares at her, eyes wide. He puts his hand on his heart in the generic European gesture of terror, amazement, and worship.

"Here, silly," she says—his miserable shuffling and his rickety conversation, had those been the way to her heart?—and she disappears in the direction of the restrooms. A warm chip of metal burns his hand: A number is etched in it. She's made up her mind then; she knows what she thinks about him. Goldfarb's fate is sealed; all he has to do now is to fight his way to the coat check, search his pockets for a quarter, and wait for her at the door, her purple woolen poncho slung casually over his arm. When she approaches, he holds the coat open for her and while he wraps her in it from behind, he can't help but look down into her blouse (had she opened an extra button while she was in the restroom, just for the occasion?) and drink in the sight of what look like little pomegranates, blessed and downy, resting adorably in a little nest of white fluff.

"Like what you see?" she asks. It's too late to back out now: Goldfarb has been given a part to play, and play it he will. He removes the imaginary cigarette from the corner of his boyish mouth, he steps back from the imaginary rainy window of his adolescence, and he stores his cynicism away. He quickly reduces his event horizon to the here and now. Wordlessly he nods.

"Ha!" she says, and with Goldfarb still behind her, she steps back, thereby pinning the lucky boy against the wall. She has long legs indeed, Hannah does, and Goldfarb instinctively bows his head over her swan's neck and her half naked shoulder. His dry lips graze the fragrant flesh of her cheek. (Why is his mouth dry? Where did all the saliva go?) At the same time Hannah turns her head just so, and therefore his mouth—it is an accident, only an accident!—meets her moist lips, freshly painted and touched up in the girl's room. "Hmm," she says, tasting his fear and his desire, and she arches her back, further pressing the warm world of her buttocks against his bony hips. What is Hannah doing? This is no longer an accident. She sways her hips, she grinds him into the wall. Then, all of a sudden, it is over—she walks to the exit, her pace brisk and happy, and Goldfarb closes his eyes and casts down his eyes, and off he goes, running after wild Hannah, into the muddy square.

•

"Shouldn't you be going home with *him*." It was meant as a question, but in his excitement he has regressed to his full flat German accent, thereby neglecting the question mark at the end of the sentence. They walk along the path that crosses the Yard, no longer the romantic narrow lane that makes you want to hold on to each other, but a newly constructed concrete walkway designed so that the ROTC students have room to march four abreast. Three feet of dead air separate the two soon-to-be lovers. Goldfarb likes the Cambridge evenings, the mild, humid climate of a university campus in the Northeast. You go to a dance party, rain drizzles down, and when you go back outside, the air reeks of ozone and earthworms— heaven and earth connected.

"Him?" she says, and her whole body rises on the sarcastic punctuation mark. "—I'm done with him. Not much use fucking a future corpse, is there?"

Goldfarb winces. Ladies aren't supposed to use the f-word.

"We are all future corpses," he says.

"So what else is new." She rolls her eyes.

"No," she adds, "he was already long dead, that guy. Even if he comes back— have you noticed how little life there is in him? For once the band pulls it off and really starts to swing and the man dances as woodenly as the new flagpole at Hollis. I'm telling you, he's as mechanical as the voices that give marching orders over Harvard Square. He's a wind-up toy, Goldfarb. I wind his spring and I release the key and there he goes, boing-boing, doing the predictable little things he's supposed to do. Useful, yes, but boring."

"Why . . ."

"A girl has to have some fun, no? Do you want to stand in line in Standish Hall every g*ddamn day at seven sharp to get some spotty mush thrown on your plate? Wouldn't you rather drive through New England in a bright red MG convertible, the warm wind of the Indian summer in your hair, sipping a vintage Château Latour on a hilltop in a forest, preferably from each other's belly buttons?" (Goldfarb shudders at the thought.) "But then you run into reality. That boy's g*ddamn dream is to retire to the Caribbean and run a g*ddamn donkey farm." (It's Hannah's turn to shudder.) "Listen," she says. She stops walking. She puts her hand on his underarm. Somewhere deep in Goldfarb's body the priorities of his bloodstream start shifting. "When I first came here, I was a gawky girl from one of the big East Coast culture factories. I fell for him, okay? But I've some growing up. It's about time"—she sends him a sidelong glance—"to swap that slithery, worldly wisdom for some real old-worldly charm."

Goldfarb never thought of himself as charming, but if he looks at himself through her eyes, well, maybe. Goldfarb knows how to open a door for a lady, he wears his sports jackets with a certain nonchalance, and if you look closely you might be able to see a hint of the madness of Heine, for instance in the tenacity of the lock of hair that keeps tumbling over his forehead or in his endearing clumsiness on the dance floor; and then there's that remarkable habit of his to think while lying flat on his back, and there are his published stories. All that could be construed as charm. This confuses him further. So many unexpected revelations about himself—what a singular evening!

"*And* I need you," she concludes. They arrived in front of Holden Chapel. Even at this late hour, squirrels are running over the telegraph wires, keeping their balance with clever whippings of their long tails. It's the time of year when they get into a panic and gather as many chestnuts and dried berries as they can. Not all of them are good at their balancing act—soft thuds can be heard when one of them has to ditch his catch to save his life. "I have this idea for a story. And you're editor at the *Hasty Pudding*. Maybe we can do business?"

"Come on," she says when she spies his pained expression. She holds out her hand and runs up the stairs, two at a time. Goldfarb is powerless, he simply has to follow her. Hannah is fast and agile, but she allows him to catch up with her at the top of the stairs.

"A story of love," she continues. "Bodily love. The conventional morals of our day dictate that young people like us shouldn't copulate freely. Well, there are more and safer ways to make love." Hannah has his attention, as she cannot fail but notice. "The object of my article is a thorough investigation of the oral technique." Goldfarb's face turns beet red. She has her hand on the small of his back. And that hand slides down. "It's all a metaphor, of course. *She* is as seductive as any ideology; *he* is as hard as any fact. Well, let us see what yields in the end: theory or reality." She stops to gauge his reaction. "And because I understand, *Herr* Editor, that you do not carelessly publish work by an unknown, I am ready to offer you a synopsis of my story. Right here," she says, "right now." Her breath whistles in his ear canal, her hands circle over his belly, a few fingers sneak through the opening of his shirt and touch bare skin. Goldfarb forgets everything—he forgets his humiliation (she needs the editor, na?), he forgets where they are—at the top of the stairs leading to the chapel, right on Harvard Yard. He feels so rash, so courageous, (and so drunk and so disappointed with life), that he simply grabs her by the shoulders and kisses her full on the mouth, as if he were the hero of his own story. For the first time in his life, Goldfarb feels female lips yield under his, and deep in the warm cave of her mouth he tastes her tongue, and all of that feels *good*. Then Hannah plants one hand on his chest and pushes him away. He stumbles, his back grazes a Dorian column.

"Every story has a message, a set of ideas and emotions to convey. Every story has a subject, a style, an aesthetic. Every story is composed of this trinity, as well as a series of two-way highways that connect its diverse aspects. And every story is alive. I keep it clean, in my story," she adds. "How can the metaphor sink in if we get too literal? A girl licks a boy's hand. Juice runs down her chin." Is he listening? His head turns purple like a bruise, then white as a skull. "Give me your hand. Come on, Goldfarb. Give me your hand!" And she reaches for his wrist and lifts it, and then he opens his palm for her—his hand feels so naked, so vulnerable, so newly peeled. She gets down on her knees, at the doors to G*d's house, the double palindrome Hannah Sidis. She gets down on her knees, but not to pray. She takes his index finger in her mouth, she looks him straight in the eye, and sucks. Around them hazelnuts and pinecones crash to the ground; the squirrels rub their eyes to make sure they're really seeing what they're seeing. Hannah sucks each of Goldfarb's fingers long and hard and with a cleverness of tongue and mouth that makes him squeak. And when he can't contain himself any longer, she opens his zipper. This latter phase is over quickly, and when she scrambles back to her feet, careful not to soil that remarkable skirt of hers, she quickly kisses Goldfarb on his forehead, leaving a gleaming print of her goodbye in cherry red lipstick, and then she plants a sweet-and-salty kiss right in the middle of his astonished face—he half expects that applause will sound behind their backs, but no: In this cataclysmic night, the two of them and the restless rodents are the only schemers awake.

All this, she promises, is only a rough draft. With his permission and consent she will refine the text. Make it an essay that is truly worthy of the *Pudding's* pages. Who knows, maybe she could make it a little more daring or explicit? These are modern times after all, true? And, don't you forget it Goldfarb, there is poetry in the slow goodbye of two woozy lovers, an aftermath that fits Hannah's narrative neatly, and there are certain narrative possibilities in the story of a boy who believes (correctly or incorrectly) that he has been transformed into a man, who throws his arms around the shoulders of his woman and walks her to the door of her dorm. They both have their eyes turned to the moon and stars, and although they both, the boy, the girl, are scientists, and know perfectly well that what they see is a light-years old trick of the light, he reads the twinkling of the stars as mirrors of the condition of his heart. (We don't have any insight into Hannah's musings, but we can safely assume that the events of the evening have indirectly touched upon her clitoral enervation. After all, Hannah gets off, as her nineties sisters would say, on power trips, an affliction that she will transmit to her lover with the speedy assurance of a viral infection.)

A warm hand around a shoulder, a small hand in the back pocket of some corduroys, and then she runs up the stairs, to her room. Yes, she knows Goldfarb well, even though they only just met. She's read his stories, she knows the unfulfilled desires that lurk underneath the smug exterior of this Harvard man, his yearning to answer the big questions—"Who am I?," "Where will I go?," "What and where and why is the center of the world?"—and she also knows that until this very moment, until the final moment of this night, this night that ends with her running up the stairs, he had simply been neglecting himself, letting the world around him grow in importance to the point that he had forgotten to ask himself those questions. The act of love (or whatever it was) they shared had finally freed Goldfarb to look around, for the very first time, and to see. To see, for instance, the majestic chaos of the universe, the incomprehensible servitude of the All to the laws of chaos and randomness; to feel the last stolen warmth of late summer; to experience the precarious balance between humanity's need for oxygen and the production of that breath of life by the trees in the very lanes that they had walked through just a minute before. It is all Hannah's doing. Tonight Goldfarb has discovered that there is no determinism, that the endless procession of suitors in the countless apartments of his youth was no mistake, but his mother's hedonistic exploration of the limits of practical reason, her choice to drift and float and let life take its course; and when he has fully absorbed this revelation (the way things are, and his place in the midst of this whirling, this *real* life), only then can the Harvard man inside him straighten his back, confident that he knows the way home, in harmony with himself and his surroundings, because from now on he can understand that peace implies turmoil, and turmoil peace, and that it all means—in the end—that he can wave a wholehearted goodbye to the vague specter that appears briefly behind one of the darkened windows on Harvard Yard.

There's no fucking G*d, thinks Goldfarb as he descends the stairs on his way to his own dorm—I am the one who determines what happens. I and nobody else am the g*d of my life.

In other words: Hannah had spread a spoonful of hot butter on Goldfarb's toasted soul and devoured it in two or three eager bites—as if said soul was a frozen breakfast waffle. Which, in a sense, it truly is.

•

The day after this incident is also the day of the add and drop deadline. Goldfarb rushes to the Registrar's office and switches his major from a double major English-mathematics to a single major in physics. And he signs up for a class in guerilla training, where he will learn how to survive when parachuted behind enemy lines. And now that his spine has been straightened by love he feels that he can safely take a few boxing classes, and he beats up quite a few innocent sophomores under the apt guidance of coach Henry Lamar.

•

Something else happens as well. Around the end of that infamous night, close to sunrise, Goldfarb wakes up, half-aware of a dream in which Miss Sidis had played an all too predictable role. Equally unsurprising is that this half-awareness makes him reach for his swollen member, which in turn leads to a powerful instant ejaculation. Then the unexpected thing happens. While the half-guilty ripples of his orgasm slowly ebb away, the blackboard of his mind, emptied for a second or two, gets covered with rapid scribbles, and although it takes Goldfarb a while to understand what it is he's reading on that slate (as if his mind has no connection to any other part of him), once it becomes clear, the implications are momentous: This is the solution to the problem he had been working on, the extension of Bertrand's theorem. He writes down the solution as fast as he can—he always sleeps with his notebook next to him, just in case. As soon as he finishes writing, he slips back into a bottomless sleep, completely exhausted by the force of his orgasm and the vigorous bout of pure math. And although he has officially withdrawn from his class in number theory, he offers his solution, typed out neatly, to his professor. It causes some consternation in the department. It will become Goldfarb's first publication. Maybe it is typical for his freshman naiveté that for a brief time he toys with the idea of including the divine Hannah as co-author.

•

While I break the eggs for our *pasta à deux*, Donatella tells me of the world's slow cold death.

This is the way her story goes:

What is the universe made of?

"Easy," I say. "All matter consists of protons, neutrons, and electrons."

"I know you read Goldfarb's children's books. The universe is a circus of meteors and moons and comets and dust clouds and millions of stars, and it's all made out of those three building blocks, each running circles around the others. Gravitational fields group some of that stuff together into nebulas and star systems and super systems and each of those groupings contains countless flaming suns and planets and clouds of gas and garbage dumps of ice and stardust. Well, there's more to that universe than this simple philosophy can explain, Mr. Andermans."

She clarifies. We can estimate the mass of all the visible matter—that is, all matter that radiates or reflects light and therefore shows up in our telescopes. We can also estimate the total mass in the universe. For instance, from the speed at which star systems revolve, we can calculate their total mass; then we simply estimate the number of star systems and we know how much mass there is in the universe. Or we can look through our telescopes again and tabulate the distortions caused by gravitational fields. Again, this method allows us to calculate the total mass—gravity is, after all, a side effect of mass. No matter the method, the conclusion turns out to be nothing short of astounding: What we can see is no more than ten percent of all that there is.

That is an amazing conclusion indeed.

I counter: "But there must be a tremendous amount of free-floating matter, dust perhaps, maybe the remnants of the novas of dying stars, and there are black holes—isn't that an explanation?"

Donatella clarifies why my explanation doesn't work. Even our most generous estimate of the amount of free-ranging stardust falls quite short of our estimate of the amount of missing matter. The way things are now, it looks as if more than eighty percent of the total mass in the universe is missing in action. And there is another piece of the puzzle missing. That piece is the alarming value of one of the fundamental parameters of the universe. The parameter Omega, otherwise known as the cosmological constant. Einstein discovered it—he needed it in his equations as a correction factor. Later in life he disowned it as the biggest piece of nonsense he ever cooked up. He was wrong: Omega is a parameter that is very much needed to describe the universe, and Omega is the biggest riddle of them all. Omega is the parameter that tells us what will happen to the universe, what will happen to us, and there is something seriously wrong with the value of that parameter.

I'm hooked.

"What's wrong with Omega?"

"All measurements of Omega point to the conclusion that Omega must be close to one."

"Why is that strange?"

It's strange because Omega is not a stable parameter. If Omega had shown only the slightest deviation from the number one at the beginning of time, its value would now be either infinitesimally small or infinitely large. Given that Omega is so close to one, it must be exactly equal to one. Let's take a step back, Donatella says. What is Omega? Omega is the parameter that describes the future of the universe. If Omega is greater than one, then the universe is open, and it will forever expand. If Omega is less than one, then the universe is closed and after an initial period of expansion, a period we are still living in, gravity will bring it all together, and all that is will implode into a single point, a gigantic black hole, and when the pressure becomes too high maybe another Big Bang will result. We can measure Omega by looking at the red shift of the stars and star systems that surround us—they inform us of the rate at which the universe expands. We can also estimate Omega from variations in the background radiation. The whole universe is still bathing in the cold glow of the Big Bang. That glow carries information about the beginning of time; every corner, every volume of space has its frozen memory of that earliest second. And both methods yield the same answer: Omega is almost equal to one.

"So what happens," I ask, "if Omega is exactly equal to one?"

"Then the universe is flat, in perfect equilibrium between expansion and contraction. It will keep on expanding forever, but the expansion tends towards an asymptote—it slows down until it becomes too small to be observable. At that point, the universe will have become flat—that is, static. Then, much later, all fuel in the stars will have been consumed. Then the universe will become very cold. Cold and, for all intents and purposes, dead."

A dead universe? This is interesting. This is large-scale detective work! Omega, Donatella tells me, turns out to be tied to the total amount of mass in the universe. Our best estimate of Omega confirms our observations: A big chunk of mass is definitely missing.

What can the missing mass be? Donatella explains that there are basically two theories. Some physicists claim that the missing mass is hidden in big lumps of mass, brown dwarves for instance, or the super massive black holes we call quasars. They have named these objects MACHOS, massive compact halo objects. But that's not the explanation Donatella prefers—Goldfarb has put his money on MACHOS, but Donatella is trying to convince him to change his mind.

"Change it to what?"

The alternative hypothesis is the existence of WIMPS, weakly interacting massive particles, leftovers from the Big Bang. In one version of the theory they cruise at impossible speeds through space-time; in another they are cold and slow. WIMPS are something else. They are not made out of protons, neutrons, and electrons. They might be neutrinos, particles so tiny and fast that they shoot right through matter as we know it—millions of these things pass through your body at any given second, Paul, and you feel nothing.

So this is what Donatella's research is about: the origin of dark matter, the mass that is needed to close the universe. How exciting it must be to do research like that! As if your own personal effort, your very own dissertation could seal the fate of the world: a cold grave or a hot death. As if knowledge itself created reality. What a bed to lie in!

"How sad." I say. "If Omega equals one, and you find the missing mass, then there will be no End Time and no salvation? Not even the comfort of an eternal recurrence? Everything just . . . dies? And that's that?"

"Well," says Donatella. "It's not all that bad. This universe is, after all, a place where almost everything is already dead, and where those things that are capable of life—all beings sentient or insentient—are dead most of the time anyway, except for those brief, glorious moments when they're not. With a little luck, a human being lives for about eighty years or so. The universe itself is fourteen billion years old. That puts things in perspective, doesn't it?"

"And when can we expect that final curtain?"

"Never. There is no end. It goes on; it goes on forever. But when the molecular structure of mass finally breaks apart, yes, maybe that will be a form of death. Rest assured: we won't be around when that happens."

During our conversation housemates walk in and out of the kitchen. I get to see the people that I only knew as invisible, sound-emitting ghosts who shuffle to the bathroom. I meet the mysterious Zhu, who is mysterious indeed: His German is incomprehensible, and so is his English. There's an American whose name I forget as soon as hear it. Mike or Bob or Dave or Matt or something along those lines. He only impresses by the whiteness of his teeth and the circumference of his biceps. He studies Goethe, but when I ask him why Potsdam is such an ideal spot to study Goethe, he can't come up with an answer. There are also a few Germans studying modern history, and I understand their motivation to spend some time here much better. There's a Vietnamese guy who studies political science, and Potsdam is a nice place to sample both communist and capitalist ideologies. Donatella knows each of them by name, and happily introduces them to me. I am afraid she'll invite one of them to join us for dinner, but she doesn't.

What a pity it isn't summer yet; we could have sat on the bench in front of the house and watched the stars, like new lovers are wont to do, our heads resting on each others' shoulders—she could have shown me a quasar or two, or the empty spot where a brown dwarf is hiding; we could have let ourselves be bombarded by neutrinos.

Instead we eat at the small kitchen table. The pasta is amazing; so is the fresh pesto.

"Donatella, do you believe that—?"

"I do not."

"But you didn't let me finish my sentence!"

"I don't believe in anything."

"And that's hard for me to believe."

"Okay. I believe. I believe you believe that I believe in something. Are you happy now? And what do I believe in, according to you?"

Even before we're born, the number of connections in our brain is larger than the sum total of all the stars in the universe—we will never be able to fully fathom the mind. Not ours, not any one else's. Donatella was born in Venice. Does that explain anything? Does that explain her fascination with the parameter Omega? The sinking city, the sadness of centuries packed underneath the dulling gold of its basilica's domes while the shadows of seraphim glide by, ever fading; a city destroyed by its very admirers—their exhaust fumes and their abundant weight on the streets hasten its demise.

I ask her how we can still find particles that have been created in the Big Bang. My naïve idea is that these things must have either escaped far, far away, or else they must have been destroyed. Unlikely, I learn. Particles are quite eternal, unless they interact with each other, and then anything can happen that our theories allow. (There's also a thing called proton decay, but we shouldn't concern ourselves with that.) If you want to look at those early particles, you can do one of two things, Donatella explains patiently. Either you look back in time by examining cosmic radiation, or else you recreate the circumstances of the time surrounding the Big Bang—you can build a particle accelerator or you can generate gigantic explosions that come close to the energy state of the universe in the first few seconds. Donatella opted for the first possibility. "I look back in time. I install electric cloud chambers in the city. Don't forget that when we look at the sky, we aren't looking up but down, down into a gaping grave, a pit of immeasurable dimensions and an immeasurable but sinister beauty."

"A pit into which we'll all disappear if we don't grab hold of something," I add. "For instance, each other." Donatella ignores my comment.

"I'm hunting for a rare particle," she says, "so rare that nobody has ever observed it. Maybe it only exists in theory. It's called the magnetic monopole. It isn't very popular in the hunt for dark matter."

"What is a magnetic monopole?"

"Magnets are peculiar objects. They always have two poles, north and south. You can't cut a magnet in two to isolate the poles. When you cut a magnet in two, you get two new bipolar magnets, each with a north pole and a south pole. The reason for this is that the electrons in magnets all spin around the same axis. A magnetic monopole can only exist as an elementary particle, that is, an indivisible particle, a particle that has one of its poles on the inside and the other on the outside. This isn't as odd as it sounds. Dirac predicted the existence of this particle in 1931; its existence is a logical corollary of Maxwell's electromagnetic theory. In 1974, 't Hooft and Polyakov demonstrated that the Grand Unified Theory likewise necessitates the existence of the magnetic monopole. Whenever a semi-simple non-abelian norm group is broken and leaves a residual subgroup, monopoles will be produced as topologically stable solutions to the theory."

My eyes are glazing over. "Well," she explains, "it all comes down to the fact that the monopole is a real WIMP, with an emphasis on the W and the M; the monopole is so massive—the size of an average amoeba—that it cannot interact with any other particle. It's simply too big to be subjected to the tiny force fields that the other known particles emit. Therefore, if the monopole exists, it must still be out there; lots of them must be traveling throughout the universe."

"If the thing is so massive, why haven't we found it yet?"

The answer is that we haven't been looking very hard. It should actually be very simple to catch a monopole: You build a detector and you wait. The detector is as simple as can be. Take two niobium wires, bend them into circular loops, place one loop behind the other, and encapsulate them in a superconducting magnetic field. This is standard technology. A detector like that is mobile; just add a strong battery and some transmission gear to the loops. When a monopole flies through the loops, it will generate a small electric current. One loop suffices to register the event, but when the event occurs quasi-simultaneously in the two loops, you have more certainty. "And that's that," concludes Donatella. "All I do is build these loops and hide them somewhere safe, and then I wait. More loops give you a higher probability of observing a passing monopole, of course. I have one on my desk in my office and there's one on the roof of the physics building. Both are connected to a computer that records the data night and day. We're going to build more. If possible, we're going spread them all around town—all across Potsdam and Berlin. Unfortunately, they're expensive; we need a lot of money. Goldfarb," she adds, "likes a little drama. He wants to install the detectors in well-known locations. There is no reason to do so, expect that it sounds good to say that the monopole was detected, say, on top of the Brandenburg Gate. It certainly sounds much better than 'my postdoc's office.' The loops blend in nicely with all those wreaths and other circular structures on classical monuments."

I'm very envious of Donatella, even more than I already was. What is it that I do again? I fool around with people's minds, and I have precious little to show for it. Donatella on the other hand is working on a small, portable cosmogony. You can wax lyrical about this monopole thing. The residue of a bygone time that will never return, a dinosaur that somehow survived but has so far escaped detection; a unity that should be a duality, but isn't; the ultimate metaphor for loneliness—but I know that physicists rarely have the time to get lyrical. The monopole may not even exist, but if it does, then that particle from the earliest beginning will also be a messenger from the end of time.

"My G*d," I say, "Once more, this town will make history!"

The food is gone, the bottle—I walked all the way to Brandenburger Straße to get it—is empty. "Do you want some tea?" Donatella asks. At the sink, she pours herbs and berries in a beaten-up tea egg. Rosehip, chamomile, orange peel, hibiscus. The kitchen turns into a garden, a garden of earthly delights. Pick your flowers, Donatella is the gardener.

"What happens if you don't catch the monopole?" I ask. The night is passing; after midnight such questions are allowed.

"Life goes on," says Donatella. "Nothing lost and nothing gained. I'll move on to the next job, with a recommendation letter from Goldfarb in my pocket." She sighs. "But you're asking the wrong question. You should ask: What happens if I do find the monopole?"

"Yes, what happens then?"

Donatella takes a sip of her tea.

"Nobel Prize," she says. "The monopole wouldn't only be the missing matter that we've been looking for for so long, it would also be the first direct indication that the Grand Unified Theory works."

"Wow," I say. What else is there to say?

"Well," she says. "Fat chance, of course."

She finishes her tea. And she mentions that. She says, "I finished my tea."

It's a signal. I finish mine in one big gulp.

"Shall I make us another pot?" I ask.

"Probably not. I have to get up early in the morning."

"To solve the mysteries of the universe."

"Who knows."

We put the mugs in the sink.

"I'll do the dishes after breakfast," she says.

"No, let me do them."

"Whoever's up first can do the dishes."

"It's a deal."

We fall silent. It is an electric silence.

"Well, I had a good time."

"So did I."

"Shall I walk you to your door?"

She laughs. "Sure."

We walk those twenty feet together. She opens the door to her room. For one exquisite moment, I have no idea what will happen. A broad gap opens in one of those dimensions of time that's usually all folded up, infinitesimally small. Then space-time closes in on itself again; the moment collapses. What Donatella says is, "Okay. Well, I think I'll go to bed."

"Right. You have to get up early in the morning."

"Thank you. I had a really good time. You babble so nicely."

Babble? I babble? Is it her English? What does she mean?

"You sound like modern poetry to me. You know. All abstract." Behind her I can see the unmade bed, so temptingly empty. So cool. So inviting. A dull desire spreads through my loins.

Then somewhere in that room a phone starts beeping. A sharp electronic sound, not to be denied.

"Maybe I should take that."

"Yeah," I say meekly, "Maybe you should."

She slides inside and closes the door.

She didn't even say goodnight. I didn't even have the time to wish her sweet dreams. For a second, I just stay where I am. Behind the door, I can hear the familiar murmuring.

She builds electric cloud chambers.

Cloud chambers! What marvelous associations this invokes: blue skies, a summer afternoon, flat on my back in the grass, bumblebees and butterflies and clouds floating by, a dog barking in the distance, the forget-me-nots miniature mirrors of the big blue beyond, and at my left ear a turtle is tearing off a big fat dandelion leaf. Cloud chambers, wind tunnels, the whole earthly atmosphere in a box. Electric, the whiplash of lightning, the smell of ozone after the storm. I will dream of her; of course I will dream of her. I am innocent, completely innocent, one is not responsible for one's dreams. She rolls in the last foam of the surf, on some spotless empty beach at the Adriatic Sea, her legs spread wide. She spins and turns, the waves hit her between her thighs and the only thing she wears is a man's undershirt, way too big for her slender frame.

Cloud chambers she builds, and she didn't even say goodnight.

STELLA (BY STARLIGHT)

I'm woken up by a dull thud against the windowpane and a scratching at the glass. When I open up the curtains, I find a skinny cat sitting perched on the gray granite of the windowsill. I live on the second floor, the window is a full twelve feet above the ground, but there she is, meowing and licking her paws. Her brown coat is tigered like that of a forest cat, with a golden gleam underneath; her throat is pearly white. I'm still half asleep. I respond mechanically—knock and the window shall be opened. It's chilly outside, I get instant goose bumps; the cat jumps in with a happy growl. A nimble leap lands her on the table, and she parks her bony ass on top of my papers. After wrapping her tail around her hind legs, she eyes her savior with intent, her head cocked just so.

Then she opens her mouth to speak. I must be dreaming this. The windowsill is twelve feet above the ground; how could a live cat make that jump?

This is what the cat says, while she hypnotizes me with those deep green eyes of hers: "Ruff, brflff, ruff—rrrrr!" And then—after she's said what she had to say—she jumps off the desk and walks to the door, tail straight up.

A young man quickly puts on his pants and a T-shirt and jacket, and then the both of them, man and cat, walk down the stairs and into the front garden. Right next to the entrance, in the dewy grass, a tiny, wet baby bird is crying its lungs out. In February? The world has gone mad—it's way too early in the year for building nests.

This is what sweet, sleep drunk Paul thinks: a baby bird, fallen out of its nest. The cat noticed and came to get help, she wanted to save the little thing. How cute! I get on my knees and I scoop up the screeching nestling; I wrap my fingers loosely around the panting ball of down. The little beak hammers away at my thumb, drawing tiny drops of blood. I get up; I look for the nest. There it is, not too high in the tree. I deposit my tiny cargo in the bed of feathers and branches. How sweet, a cat that comes to the rescue of an embryonic bird!

Then I hear a rhythmic coughing behind me. The cat has her body close to the ground, her shoulders are pumping—in one gulp she vomits up a half-digested mush of minuscule feathers, half-cracked bones and carelessly chewed chunks of dark young flesh. She retreats as she spits all of this out, laying an elongated trail at my feet, a half-circular mess of red and white, an abstract-expressionist painting of a grimacing mouth with menacingly broken teeth.

"I see you met Mefista," says Donatella. She wears a breathlessly tight pair of jeans; she must be on her way, I guess, to the lab. I watch the cat walk away solemnly, her glorious asshole swallowed by the bushes.

"Your cat?"

"She's a stray. Offer her some milk, and she'll be yours forever. Don't feel privileged. She'll take up with anybody. Well, off I go."

"Thanks again for last night!" I call out after her.

"Yeah yeah," she says. "Whatever. You're welcome!"

"Wraahrrr!" cries Mefista as she runs out of the bushes. She attacks Donatella's ankles. When Donatella just keeps on walking, Mefista returns to the house and starts scratching at the front door.

Milk, okay, cat, I can do that.

•

Frau Silbereysen was old and frail and slightly confused. The day she came to live with us she wore a long black woolen coat, shiny with use. It was hemmed with soggy, sulky otter fur. She wore a wine-red dress underneath; long ago, when she might have been pretty and the dress a tight fit, she was probably quite a sight to behold, but when I first met her the dress looked as obscene as pantyhose rolled down around ankles, as ugly as the sagging skin on an elephant's behind. A plump little pillbox astrakhan hat sat atop her head in an attempt to crown it all; it had recently been attacked by a medium-sized family of eager moths. From underneath the hat, a shock of snow white hair protruded, stiff and shiny like meringue and looking equally brittle. A tiny little suitcase stood at Frau Silbereysen's feet. Her boots were Austrian, perky ankle-high lace-up affairs with two-inch heels and pointy toes—the favorite shoes of waitresses at the upscale *Konditoreien*, because it makes them look professional and domineering at the same time. Behind Frau

Silbereysen, the boots had left the ski trail of a midget in the thin layer of fresh snow. Frau Silbereysen was still panting from her ten-foot walk.

The taxi driver honked his horn long and hard. He clearly wanted to get rid of her as soon as possible.

Mother sent me downstairs. I ran as fast as I could and so was a little out of breath myself when I came to face our new tenant. My hair had fallen over my eyes.

Frau Silbereysen stared at me in grave silence; misgivings were clearly building. Her eyes traveled up and down my gangly body as though she were frisking me for weapons. I wasn't sure what exactly she saw: A whitish veil hung over her pupils, the cloudiness of cataracts and years of enthusiastic crying jags.

The engine of the cab was idling; the driver was waiting for his money.

"Have fun with your grandma," he said sarcastically after I had emptied my pockets.

I offered Frau Silbereysen my arm.

"Shall we?"

She examined the different doorbells, her nose almost touching the brass plates. "*Meine Güte*," she said when it became clear that we were living on the third floor.

Her suitcase was suspiciously heavy. And it clattered. She waited in the hallway while I carried her luggage upstairs. She looked a little lost. I pretended that the leather monster was filled with feathers—I had my adolescent pride. I was pretty sure that the watery gleam in Frau Silbereysen's eyes was at least partially due to the bottles that made her case heavy as lead. As I walked upstairs, the suitcase rang over and over again, like a temple bell.

She was eying the ceiling with its decoration of sweet, slightly panicky-looking plaster cherubs when I returned. She held out her hand, as if she wanted to lure one of the angels down to graze from her empty palm. (Though angels don't eat— they feed on air.) If she had had a ladder and her limbs had been more nimble, I'm certain she would have climbed up and tested the little cherub buttocks for firmness. When she saw me, she extended her arms.

"Carry me upstairs, you big strong boy! Take me in your arms, you mighty Berlin bear!" Words that every adolescent boy longs to hear, but not from a character like this.

"*Meine Güte*," she repeated when we arrived at the apartment. She disentangled herself from me, much more slowly than she could have, and pinched my biceps approvingly in the process. "*Was für ein starker Bube bist du!*" She offered me her hat and gestured that I should hang it on the coat rack, no, higher up, yes, there, at the very top. Then her coat, to be placed one hook below the hat. The four otter eyes stared at me peevishly; the furs smelled like they had spent the last couple of nights in the gutter. Frau Silbereysen kept her dress on, although for a second she seemed to hesitate on that account.

She clapped her hands and made amazed little oh-sounds when I showed her her room. My-my, what a *beautiful* room! As if she hadn't inspected the house with her son a week before. She lifted her tired eyes to the ceiling, visibly disappointed that it wasn't teeming with nude winged toddlers. Before she retreated, she had a message for me.

"One day, you will make a girl very happy," said Frau Silbereysen, and she puckered her lips and planted a sticky kiss in my neck, which was the highest part of my body she was able to reach while standing on her toes. I shuddered. "*Ja-ja,*" she cackled, worldly-wise, and she giggled as if my frisson had been of pleasure.

Of course Mother had told her that we lived on the third floor, and she had seen the apartment for herself, no? She was just a little forgetful—that's all.

"Excuse me, young man," she said, as if I wasn't in a hurry to leave, "I think I will unpack my suitcase now, thank-you-very-*much.*"

·

The dress never came out of her closet again. Frau Silbereysen's hat remained forever perched at the very top of the coat rack. Her coat ended its lonely, smelly existence in our living room. Under her bed, her shoes exuded their competent lewdness in vain. Frau Silbereysen never ever left the apartment. Day in day out, she wore the same fiercely floral housecoat, with buttons all the way down the front. Every morning and at least a few times during the day, my mother had to check whether all the buttons were still fastened. Frau Silbereysen helped with the cooking, or so she claimed—my mother never saw any real evidence of her assistance, except that Frau Silbereysen warmed herself at the stove and told a million stories, all about things that had transpired in the previous century. She did enjoy helping to open of bottles of wine or beer, and for somebody so slow and fragile she was remarkably good at downing half the contents of these bottles when she thought nobody was watching. From time to time, an empty bottle of more potent stuff showed up in the garbage can.

Frau Silbereysen turned out to be especially forgetful at the end of the month, when the rent was due. After a few days went by, Mother politely asked her for the money, and Frau Silbereysen hit herself on the forehead. "*Natürlich!*" she exclaimed. "*Entschuldigung!*" And she went off to her room. When she reemerged a half hour later her eyes looked a lot livelier than when she left, but she still didn't have any money in hand. This scene repeated itself a few more times. And it repeated itself the next month too. Father, who like Frau Silbereysen needed his own daily ration of forgetfulness, started keeping a watchful eye on the family's supply of spirits.

Then Frau Silbereysen died, at the beginning of springtime, after only three months with us. Just like that. We found her in bed, staring at the ceiling with an expression of intense disappointment on her face. She simply died, I think, when she ran out of schnapps. She never did pay rent.

That was my mother's first attempt at making some extra money. I for one was glad we were rid of this lodger: I no longer needed to lock the bathroom and hang a towel in front of the keyhole—necessary precautions, for Frau Silbereysen had taken a keen interest in me. I could go to bed now without worrying that Frau Silbereysen would barge in during one of her frequent nightly outings. Once she climbed into my bed while I was in it, thinking, she explained afterwards with what seemed to be genuine embarrassment, that it was her own room.

•

We had moved. Maybe there's a few Freudians out there who'd want to read this as the sublimated expression of a desire to take flight—they are free to psychoanalyze our motives, but the truth is much simpler. Only a few months after the night when glass covered the streets like frost, we could no longer keep up with the mortgage payments on the apartment at Tauentzienstraße. Also, my father worried more and more about the neighbors; there were too many things they had seen and heard in those last, wild few years. We had had so many visitors at Tauentzien, so many friends that were now *persona non grata*: communists whose prior election for public office had made them into traitors in the Nazi's eyes; composers who turned out to have been utterly degenerate for at least twenty years (how could that have escaped our notice?); classically trained violinists who were simply Jewish. Just like my father up until the November pogrom, many of the latter had been making the rounds at the bars, willing to play for whatever money landed in their hats (some of them went as far as to glue on a faux mustache and don a fez and play the bouzouki in cheap Greek restaurants).

The *coup de grâce* for our sojourn at Tauentzien had come when one evening —we were still at dinner—someone slipped a leaflet under our front door. It was a single-page brochure, replete with the usual topoi, the sort of breathless expletives that fit conveniently on a shop window or a front door; the text peppered with a bunch of exclamation points. ("The Jew is our misfortune!" "Don't buy at Jewish stores!" "*Juden raus!*" "Jews are vermin!" "Every Jew is a pig!" "Jews smell!") It wasn't the first time we'd received a pamphlet like this. But up until that evening, they had always been delivered in the mailbox outside, and it was often obvious that every other resident of the building had received the same smudgy flyer. As soon as the piece of paper slid into the wall opposite the door, we fell silent. Mother put her arms around Father's shrinking shoulders—a gesture of public affection that had become more and more rare in those days of retreat.

What did this mean? Did the presence of the pamphlet indicate that the brown-shirts weren't aware that Jews lived here, and therefore that we were safe? Or did it mean, on the contrary, that someone was singling us out, trying to either scare us away or hurt us by provoking a reaction? The only way to find out would be to ask our neighbors if they had received the same pamphlet. But that was impossible. It would brand us, if not as Jews, than at the very least as people who were upset by the official and most holy teachings of the regime. After all, those screeds were now so common that most people didn't even notice them anymore. The flyer ended up in the trashcan, on top of the potato peels.

But after an hour of pacing through the apartment, my father went to retrieve the smelly piece of paper. He straightened it out and read it carefully, and then he read it again, and then a third time, and a fourth time. Then he hid his head behind his hands. Maybe he had been hoping that the repeated reading would reveal that it was all meant ironically. It didn't and it wasn't. Mother could no longer bear it. She kneeled next to her husband and put her hands over his. And she cried. "We need to leave," she said through her tears. It wasn't clear whether she meant leave this apartment, or leave Berlin, leave Germany, leave the continent. The further away the better, probably. And she cursed through her teeth: "*Fluch sei der Hoffnung! Fluch dem Glauben—und Fluch vor allen der Geduld!*"—Yes: What use is hope, or trust? And damned, damned be patience!

Father took his hands from his face. His palms were wet with tears. "Yes, my dear," he said. "We shall leave."

The first step was to find a new and cheaper apartment. This proved not to be too difficult. In those days of migration and brutality, lots of apartments registered as Jewish were vacant. Ours was cheap because it had a history—it hadn't belonged to émigrés. The previous renter had jumped off the Castle Bridge. Many a Jew had stood on that bridge in the dead of night, the dome of the Evangelical Cathedral rising behind him, and then jumped, their coattails fluttering behind them like the wings of a swooping bat. When they touched the surface of the slimy river the wool of their coat sucked up the water and turned the garment into a cape of lead that dragged them to the bottom. The mud gently but firmly held them by their feet, and a different, blacker, more merciful night set in, a night thick with the compassion the city above had forgotten. My uncle Karl Israel Grüneberg was one of those who opted for this kind of way out. The police found his body in a bobbing boat on the Wannsee Lake. A bottle of brandy and a bottle of sleeping pills had been his final travel companions; both were empty by the time the police got to him. I heard stories whispered in the nighttime of people who sold all their possessions (Persian carpets, silverware) to buy a few bottles of Veronal on the black market, opting to end their misery by taking an overdose of barbiturates. It's a mystery: Some people survive no matter what, while others let the tragedies of life pull the cover of darkness over their head. To this day, I do not know which of these fates is the cruelest. We visited the cemetery, we put our stones on uncle Karl's grave, and when crossing the street we took great care to abide by the traffic rules.

There were days when my father bit the mouthpiece of his pipe so hard that he needed to make a trip to the tobacco store for a new one.

•

Now we live on the inner side of a huge *Mietkazerne* in Friedrichshain, one of the enormous housing projects. It's a gray and desolate neighborhood. Even the buildings look angry; they squat in the streets like sumo wrestlers furiously pushing and tugging at one another. Only the inner courtyards have small trapdoors to the heavens. Children play in these courtyards and turn them into happy killing grounds for toy cars, bikes, doll carriages, and rubber balls. Their excited voices ring up the walls. I watch those joyful creatures from my window, nostalgic for the times that had so clearly passed, the times when I would have been allowed to join in, and afraid about the times-to-be and what they might bring. Even in the courtyards there are loudspeakers, originally intended to broadcast the German victories during the 1936 Olympic Games. Occasionally, these loudspeakers burst into life, playing rousing military marches or spitting out some news bulletin or transmitting speeches with a sonic background of white noise and phonographic scratches. The Führer informs us over these loudspeakers how much he regrets our lack of living space—our *Lebensraum*—and how it saddens him that no other country feels compelled to give up theirs, especially now that so many people of German descent lived in deep oppression in the eastern countries. When the first blasts of music sound from the speakers, the children interrupt their play, but only for a short while: During the speeches themselves they resume their games. Nobody is listening, but doesn't psychology teach us that such things seep in, that maybe they even influence the mind more strongly than what is processed with our full attention?

Each of the children playing in the courtyard was born after 1933. How peculiar to hear this distorted blaring as your first, maybe even your only voice of authority. Being born a German in Germany in the 1930s: From the cradle on the heavens try to persuade you that you are of superior stock, that you are the subject of injustice and have rightful grievances in this world. Your body and your soul belong to the Reich. With his first cry, the newborn child becomes not a citizen, but a subject. Berlin has turned into a northern Sparta. The state prescribes power gymnastics for every young woman or man, and icy nude baths in the nocturnal lakes of folksy mysticism. Even in those rare moments of unstructured playtime in the courtyard, the state takes away the children's childhood, bombarding them instead with what should have been strictly adult themes—violence, impending war, and the rules of vendetta. The omnipotence of the state, its far-reaching chronic cynicism, the order it makes out of chaos and vice versa, its teaching that form is content and content form and that content is nothing and that nothingness is the norm—all of this (we now know, and how did we not see it then?) will directly lead to the ultimate mechanization, the mechanization of murder, performed with all the banality of ritual slaughter. Adolf Hitler is the zeitgeist of Century XX, and that ghost of the times is not a benevolent angel with downy wings and a snow-white bathrobe—this ghost wears battledress brown as the mud in the trenches festooned with an armband red as freshly harvested arterial blood.

Hitler's simplicity needs no flattery. He is not a dictator, nor an autocrat. He is a Leader—he is connected to his People in an honest bond of mutual loyalty. In his name the dreams and aspirations of the previous generations have been fulfilled. He alone is the man who created the atmosphere that weighs on the city like a damp tropical nightmare: a climate that fosters a desire for real action, a push for purity that cannot be denied much longer. The Germans suddenly notice that strangers are living in their midst, in their towns and in their very houses. Adolf Hitler, their chancellor, their helmsman, will return their land to them, and finally restore the essential and eternal Germany to its rightful owners, the Germans. Despite signs to the contrary, Germany has never changed, it has survived—the Germany that has existed since the beginning of time will live on forever. *Lebensraum*—Hitler tells us it is a matter of life and death.

What is the Jew's place in all of this?

The Jew is a louse. A louse is a half-winged insect that is not capable of flight. The louse possesses powerful hind legs; it crosses the short distance from old host to new host by jumping. The louse is a parasite. It lives by what it finds under its snout, and it gives nothing in return, except a burning itch and a persistent feeling of uncleanliness. Therefore, the louse needs to be eradicated. One can burn a louse, even though this is not easy—lice are small. When they burst into flames, they crackle and dance. This is an amusing sight.

Whether this is political sadism molded into the language of pathology (society is rotten, there is contamination, there are parasites), or pathological sadism molded into the language of politics, who cares? The message is clear: *ausrotten!*—exterminate!

What will they say after the war is over? That wasn't us, those dark Spartans—those were different people, they just looked like us? Or will they say, We never knew? We were misled? We were lemmings, all we did was follow the leader? Following the leader, was that a crime? Are we to blame that when we followed him (he made us feel so happy, so liberated, so *innocent*) he went over that final cliff, the cliff of human decency, and we went down with him?

Personally, I think that no human being should ever forget that there is a world of difference between an act that is permitted and an act that is permissible.

•

Mother earned her money, our money, the money for the family, by working a Singer sewing machine. She had bought the machine with money that came from selling a good part of our furniture—the new apartment was after all much smaller than the old one, and it was practically fully furnished: Our predecessor hadn't taken his earthly goods with him on his final journey. Mother had a good eye for what was elegant. When she saw a dress she liked, in the street or a glossy picture of some *thé dansant* at hotel Eden, she would produce a reasonable imitation and sell it. Sometimes her customers would let her borrow a dress from one of the great designers; she would copy it meticulously. Over time, she taught herself how to simplify the patterns so that she could turn out her approximations of the fashions of the day more quickly. The work paid well. It kept us fed and clothed and it paid the rent, and we could even save a little. But through those relatively prosperous months, my mother stayed thin. Maybe her worries were eating at her; maybe her nerves acted up whenever she had to take the measure of a particularly powerful customer—some were high-ranking party members. Those customers, on the other hand, expanded with their growing political contentedness until the measuring tape hardly fit around their waists. It didn't trouble them in the least to do business with a Jewish seamstress, as long as she did good work and wasn't too expensive. We all have to make our little sacrifices to morality, don't we?

One day Mother was ill and one of her regular customers sent her son—ten, eleven years old?—to our house with a basket of citrus fruit and a jar of honey. It was such a friendly gesture in unfriendly times that Mother almost burst into tears. She made some tea for the boy and she offered him some homemade cookies, but he refused. Mother insisted. For a moment, the child was in a visible panic. Then Mother took one of the cookies and ate it. The boy watched her, his gaze full of mistrust. After a few seconds of icy deliberation, he finally gave in and took a cookie from the jar. Then, after having taken a measly little bite, he asked her in a tiny scared voice if she and her husband really were Jews. My mother's heart sank, and all her joy about the basket of goodness melted away. The child was so young and yet so clearly infected with the prejudices of the day. He could not understand that his mother dealt with these strangers, these creatures from a different part of the animal kingdom. In school, on the street, in the movie theater, and probably at home, he had been well trained in the concepts of racial purity and how valuable German blood is and how inferior the Semitic race. He could not grasp the notion that such monsters really existed, that they lived in his hometown, that they spoke the same language as he did, and that their friendliness was genuine—he feared we had been trying to tempt him into eating poisoned cookies.

Mother not only sewed, she also mended clothes for customers who were less well-off. For ourselves, for instance. As soon as the elbows of a sweater became a little thin, she would remove the sleeves, give them a quarter-turn, attach them again, and we were ready for another winter.

One day, I found a Hitler Youth uniform in the mending basket. This was no big deal. Every Aryan child was de facto member of that organization; before or after meetings, many of the children wore their uniform when they played in the courtyard—brown camouflage on the brown cobblestones. The uniform in the basket looked exactly my size. When Mother left to deliver a dress, I seized the opportunity. As I had suspected, the uniform fit me wonderfully. I ran to the neighborhood movie house and a small miracle happened. Almost every day I walked past the theater to look at the preview pictures in the light boxes outside. Every time the lady from the box office would chase me away—I was the *Juda* from the third floor and my presence alone scared her customers away. This same lady did not recognize me when I came by in the brown uniform, or at least she pretended she didn't. She took my money and let me inside. I don't remember what movie I saw—I hope it was something with Lena Guna in the starring role, Lena was my favorite actress. The problem was that I was unfortunate enough to get into a fight on the way back home, and a completely unnecessary one at that. It started,

I believe, when some neighborhood boy insulted me because I hadn't obtained this or that merit badge—my uniform was blank, the boy to whom it belonged had wisely removed all insignia before he sent it to the seamstress. I couldn't bear being insulted and so I defended my fictitious honor. I lost—I was not as well versed in martial arts nor as muscular as my opponent. During the fight, I managed to tear the elbow (oh, irony!) of the uniform. Mother punished me dearly (for a few days, I wasn't able to sit still in a chair), not because of the extra work or because I had broken a rule or law, but because I had violated the one rule that she really cared about: I had endangered the safety of our family.

Professional salesmen often point at the many qualities of traditional German lace curtains—their beauty, their durability, how pleasantly they diffuse the light, how easy they are to wash—but they fail to mention their core characteristic, namely that they make it possible to look outside without being seen. The windows of Berlin, covered in these translucent curtains, are webs; black widows sit and observe the display case of the city, slowly working their jaws and accumulating their tranquilizing saliva, the phone close at hand and the Gestapo's number on a slip of newspaper glued to the receiver. Even if you weren't directly a prisoner of the Nazis, you always were a prisoner of the hell of suspicion and snitchery those women created. I got lucky. The fight had been spotted, but the uniform had rendered me invisible. Nobody could even conceive of the idea that a Jewish boy would dare steal, much less don, such a sacred garment.

•

More and more often, Father locked himself into the back room where he had installed his headquarters. He couldn't help it. It was his nature—he remained a dreamer. Now that Mother had convinced him that we should leave, he pinned all his hopes on the prospect of emigrating. He did this with the same endearing naiveté that only a few months back had made him dream out loud about the quick collapse of the regime. The Reich would just be a brief time of darkness in between two brightly lit eras, the past of Weimar and the socialist future. Well, now that Mother had convinced him that merely waiting was not an option and that we should confront the darkness, he just assumed that we could easily direct ourselves towards the light—not the light of the future, but the light of some neighboring country from where we could move on to our final destination, wherever that might be. Making plans and working on their realization gave my father new energy. The back room was mostly taken up by our piano, the baby grand that hadn't been played for years. It now served as Father's work desk, and on that table with its slender, feminine legs he spread a map of the world with coffee cups at the four corners to keep it flat. On the map, Germany was a big golden stain; the rest of the world was covered with pins like a voodoo doll, a little colored flag at the end of each pin. The color indicated the status of my father's inquiries. Green flags stood for current applications, black for countries that had turned us down, and yellow flags signified countries that friends had been able to get a visa for. Green and yellow often stood side by side, the reasoning being that where there is room for one, there is room for two. Black next to yellow, however, showed that where there had once been an opening, the door had been closed. Father's fingers caressed the map's surface between the pins; his fingertips read the folds in which our safety was hiding and stroked the ridges into which we might escape our dangerous times.

The Jewish school in the Tiergarten district had taught us a good deal about saying goodbye. Almost every week we gathered in the schoolyard to sing for those who were leaving us. Rain or shine, the big upright piano was wheeled outside and put under the canopy. Doktor Prinzmetal sat down on the velvet bench and bowed his head until his big shock of orange hair flopped over his face, and then he played, his body swaying sadly back and forth in time with the music. He never played something simple, it was always a piece by Händel or Beethoven or Mendelssohn. Something nice for the emigrants to carry with them, said Doktor Prinzmetal, a last memory of German (yes, German!) *Weltschmerz* to hold on to, a little piece of the *Heimat* that could be transplanted to London or New York or Jerusalem, or some place we had never heard of. After the singing, our geography teacher unrolled the linen map of the world and tapped the appropriate country with the rubber tip of his pointer stick. Then he slowly shook his head and wept. We were all crying, even the students we were celebrating, the happy ones who were making their escape: It was as though, still alive, they were attending their own funerals, being buried in unconsecrated earth at that.

Friends of the family—all Jewish, because by then we hardly had any other friends—talked about possible places of refuge. Maybe here, or possibly there . . . "Have you tried Paraguay yet?" A finger strays to the opposite side of the map. "Or Shanghai?" "What about New Zealand? Do they have a quota?" A simple lifting of a shepherd's cane is not longer sufficient to make the waters part. Black is spreading over the map, a plague of rejection crawls over the world. Are these countries full? Do they really think our presence would wreck their society?

"How about America?"

For a while, all conversations in our family revolve around the Three Holy Words. We recite them every evening, like a mantra. The quota, the affidavit, the visa. This is what those three words mean. The quota is the number of refugees that will be allowed inside the country each year. Even paradise apparently gets crowded, and one has to leave a little space for all those baobabs and apple trees and the snakes that are twisted around their trunks. The affidavit is a formal statement made by a family member or a friend in America that stipulates that they will be responsible for the immigrant in case of the immigrant's insolvency. The visa is the stamp that follows from the previous two, much like the Christian Son follows from the Father and the Holy Ghost. Like the Christian Son, the visa dispenses Grace and Entry into Paradise. But those three are not the only things that count. There is also a medical examination by a doctor appointed by the consulate—only healthy people are allowed in. There is also a moral turpitude clause. "It's a good thing that we have stuck together, dear," my mother says—the Americans consider divorce a moral blemish too big to ignore. After lengthy negotiations, my father was able to get a distant family member in the Midwest to sign the affidavit. He took this document to the American Embassy on Hermann-Göring-Straße 21. He was placed on the waitlist, number 51,623. Currently being served was number 38,000. The man behind the counter calculates that at the current tempo, our application will be up in less than two year's time. Hey, be happy! What are two years in a man's life? Two days later, the mailman delivers another form to fill out, as well as the official receipt of our application. At the bottom of the letter there is a notification: *Keine Reisepläne machen! Untersuchung erst nach **vielen** Jahren! Vorschriften sehr streng. Aussichten äußerst gering! Anfragen können mittlerweile leider nicht berücksichtigt werden.*—Do not make any travel plans! Your case will only be examined after **many** years! Rules are very strict. Probability of success is very small! We regret that requests for further information cannot be answered.

Well, that was good to know. My father hired a lawyer—a Jewish lawyer—and paid the man 400 marks to get us a visa for the Dominican Republic. After he pocketed the money, the man simply vanished.

My father had the hardest time with our application for Palestine. This went against his most ingrained beliefs. The path of the sensible, progressive individual does not lead to Palestine, but to Moscow. He used to talk about NaZionism and InterNaZionalism. Then one evening, Mother had another of her long incisive conversations with him—you have to take every chance you can, and think of the little one! After a few hours of waiting in line outside the *Palestina-Amt*, my father finally sat down opposite a Zionist clerk. Did Father support the Zionist cause, the man asked. Always truthful, Father answered that he did not. The man's stare left nothing to the imagination. If you do not support the cause, my dear sir, why would we offer you a spot on an already overcrowded ship to the Promised Land, while so many others who do believe in Zion have to wait? "Is fear of death not a sufficient motive?" Father asked. "The fear that not only I, but with me my wife and child will perish? That we will be destroyed, simply destroyed, just like illegal goods are destroyed at the border, just like damaged machinery is taken apart and left to rust in a graveyard, just like carcasses of mad cows are burnt in the fields?" "We all have our fears," answered the clerk. He averted his eyes and fell silent; he was smart enough not to continue. Continuing would expose his reasoning and his reasoning was as follows: To us, the fear of a faithful Zionist is worth more than the fear of an atheist secular Jew—simply put, some people are more worth saving than others. "So what is it?" fulminated Father at dinner, "What is it that makes these self-declared saints of Meinickestraße so different from the hangmen of the chancellery, so different from the moneygrubbers in Washington? What is that that gives them the right to make such black-and-white distinctions between mere mortals and people of worth?"

There is a rumor that 10,000 marks will buy you an instant visa for Panama. We don't have that kind of money. Besides, there are crackdowns: The Uruguayan consul just got fired by his government for taking bribes in return for fast-tracking the process.

The Jewish Community Center mails out job listings. Somebody in the Fiji Islands needs a male pastry chef; the man has to be unmarried, not younger than 25 and not older than 30. A Central American republic is looking for a man who knows how to sew pelts together. Deep in Manchu China there is need for a Jewish ballet dancer who can double as a choreographer. A South American nation is looking for an unmarried kosher butcher with a penchant for salami sausages. Are you perchance a watchmaker willing to move to Togo? As expected, there was no demand for a violinist with squashed fingers or somebody who knows how to plagiarize Coco Chanel.

Sometimes small cracks appeared in my father's armor of firm convictions. Quite a few friends returned from Palestine. Insect plagues, vermin, the dirt in Haifa, it was all a bit much. In Germany, everything is so much cleaner! Some even returned from squeaky clean England: they missed their friends, they missed the *Konditorei*. Maybe, Father said, we could simply stay? What can they do to us? They're not going to kill us all, right?—Whenever he had such a crisis of faith, my mother would speak to him sternly (think of the little one!) and then he gave it another try.

We also had to find the money to pay the *Reichsfluchtsteuer*, the tax levied on emigration. The official line is that emigration is desertion. Even though you are no longer officially part of it, you are leaving the economic cycle by leaving Germany. This leaves the nation in a financial lurch, and you will need to compensate it for that. Of course, it's really a ransom—we'll let you go, but only if you pay. It's all part of a sinister plan, Father says. The Nazis want to flood the world with poor Jews, restless vagabonds that are a burden to everyone; it is another of their attempts to foster anti-Semitism and rally sympathy for the German plight.

"If only we hadn't burned our antique books. We could have sold them!"

"If you were to try to sell those books, you'd be arrested immediately."

"There's always the black market." My father sounds stubborn and defiant.

"G*d be with us!" My mother turns her eyes to the heavens.

•

That's another unexpected side effect of the times—you turn your eyes to the heavens a lot.

It is said that there are three ways to become a Jew. You can be born a Jew, you can convert to Judaism, or you can become Jewish by decree. The new laws and rules were making the two extremes of the Judaic experience, orthodoxy and secularism, grow closer together. The pressure of the times is creating a strangely hybrid "we."

The faithful among us have stopped following the precepts to the letter. There is no knowing when unexpected visitors might knock at your door, and the neighbors have ears and eyes. So the men shave off their beards and their wives visit the butcher's every other day, buying a nice supply of fresh pork sausages, smoked ham, *Klopse* or pig's feet. And they eat it all too: There simply isn't enough money to make purely symbolic gestures. (Later on, we Jews were forbidden to eat any meat at all. In 1943, a law was signed that stated that the only food Jews were allowed to eat were potatoes, cabbage, and turnips.) What these Jewish neighbors of ours don't realize is that they are still instantly recognizable by their linguistic quirks. All those negations to say "yes," the tendency to answer every question with a counter-question, often taking the form of a complaint. "How are you doing?"—a shrug of the shoulders, and eyes turned famously upwards: "Well, how do you *think* I'm doing?"

Many of us were three-day Jews; we only frequented the synagogue on the three high holy days—the two days of Rosh Hashanah and the one of Yom Kippur—walking to Schul in our best black clothes and wide-rimmed hats. By temperament, my mother is a no-day Jew. She doesn't like religion at all; religion is just not realistic enough. Marxism is an ideology that suits her much better. Her slogan is *"Heute ist heute"*—today is today. But we had nothing left to celebrate. We were by law excluded from all political holidays, all those effusive festivities of the Reich—Mother's Day, Father's Day, the Führer's Birthday, Potsdam Day, Labor

Day, the Day of German Gymnastics. Yes, according to the Nazi ideology, none of us could even feel grateful towards his Mother or Father—after all, his Mother and Father had conceived a little Jew, a common rat with hair that, though it might be blond, did not have the silken sheen of true Nordic flaxen hair. And just like the outside pressure made the orthodox Jews more liberal, we secular Jews were turning more strict. Every Friday evening, Mother lit the candles; on Saturday she refused to do any sewing or mending, and at dinner she often added a plate and a glass for the Prophet, as if every Shabbat was Pesach—just imagine the Prophet showing up and us not being prepared. Father nailed a mezuzah to the doorframe, albeit on the inside and well camouflaged. We now had G*d's name written on the doorpost and we also placed it on our foreheads and arms during prayer, much like I sewed my passport in the lining of my coat as a precaution, much like in the camp the number that was my new name (and may G*d know it!) was tattooed on my arm.

Everywhere, in every time zone, Jews sing their serenades for G*d, whether He's listening or not. Maybe this whole thing started because of a few who stopped singing? The Lord is so lonesome—the Talmud teaches us that He created the world out of loneliness. All the Lord longs for is some decent company. When we withhold that from Him, when we do not continuously stroke His Incomparable Ego by singing for Him under the accompaniment of bleating ram's horns, when we do not regularly whisper in His Ear how Great He is and how Tremendous His Majesty and how full of Compassion He is, the Lord of it All gets insecure and like any other self-doubting drunkard He soon reaches for His Knife.

The total number of precepts in the Jewish religion is 613. These precepts make us into a People. At the same time, they separate us from the rest of the world: The Shabbat laws, the dietary laws, the marriage laws are uniquely ours. A nation is defined by its laws. And now the Nazis, our new g*ds, are adding new paragraphs to the Law, paragraphs that further bind us together and further separate us from our Aryan compatriots. The list of what is allowed and what is prohibited becomes impossibly long, so long it would take another Torah to contain them all, and every new law invariably goes into effect on Shabbat. The list is as absurd as the list in Leviticus. We are no longer allowed to keep ironing irons in our homes. We cannot take our laundry to the cleaner's. In the new German district of Salzburg, Jews are no longer allowed to wear alpine costume, that is (it's all nicely summed up in the decree): no white socks, no dirndl dress, no Lederhosen. Later, during the war, we will be prohibited from keeping pets. We have to hand in our winter clothing; when it gets cold outside, we should simply stay home. No Jews in barbershops. Backpacks *verboten*.

Just think: One émigré stands at the root of all this, says my father, combing through the newly grown beard that hangs full from his chin. My father, once a card-carrying member of the Communist Party, now keeps an inner shtetl—how strange is that? How strange that he has thrown himself into the past of the diaspora, a past that doesn't particularly care for secularized people like him, a past he has little patience for? Yet now he feels compelled to reconnect with it all, and with some urgency. He's even considered returning to the *Palestina Amt*. He is still no Zionist, but he now can understand, he claims, that we Jews share a solidarity-through-fate. And then he starts wavering again, for is what binds us not exactly the irony of our dispersion over the surface of the earth?

That one émigré.

In a courageous act, rejecting the polytheism of his days, Avraham left his home, taking his idea of G*d with him and abandoning his stunned family. He is our Founding Father, son. That is the essence of the Jewish spirit—to be the midwife of the new, to be understood by almost nobody. The spirit of the Road, the spirit of Innovation, the spirit of Apostasy. And is not the essence of Jew-hate the opposite of all that? Fear of the ultimate freedom, the freedom of creation, the cutting of the ties that bind the mind?

Here is an earlier reading of the same story, a reading that my father used to entertain me with long before the times drove him to piety. Monotheism came about because all the g*ds (but One) died. Why did the g*ds die? Well, they died laughing. One of them had started broadcasting to the people below that "There is no g*d but G*d. You are to have no other G*ds but Me," and the other g*ds thought this was such a hilarious statement that they quite simply laughed themselves to death. The g*d who proclaimed this abomination had originally been responsible for the thunder—this job fit his personality well. After a few years, though, he made sure he acquired the job of g*d of war as well. A little later, he took it upon himself to play the role of El, the father of the g*ds of the Canaanites. This guy was quite the jealous g*d, as you can imagine, always ready to start a brawl, even when the other g*ds were rolling over heaven's floor in mirth, calling out: "But isn't that exactly the essence of g*dliness: That there are g*ds, but no G*d?" And that was when this El-guy decided to use capital letters to designate Anything that Pertained to Him.

Every country has its own g*ds, because every cultural community has its own value system. We all have different opinions as to what should be considered virtues and what should be considered vices. These values are projected onto the g*d who fits them best, allowing each human to root for the g*d s/he likes most and to emulate that g*d's behavior as s/he pleases. The ancient Greeks had g*ds with Greek values, well versed in ancient Greek grammar; the Hindu g*ds speak Sanskrit and they have their own favorite brand of mischief. This makes religion fun and useful: You build your value system, you anthropomorphize its varied aspects, you make up a few stories, and *voila*, you now have something to live by and to die for. Like I said: a load of fun. It's not unlike picking a favorite sports team. The divine world is one big salacious soap opera in the sky. But if one of those comedic operatic tenors starts declaring that there is only One G*d, namely Himself, and wrestles all other g*ds to the ground, claiming He is the One Who has the monopoly on moral truth, that's where it all stops being fun and funny. The claim that there is only One G*d kills human creativity; it leaves no room for us to experiment and no way to chose sides and to feel special and divine and different from, yet connected to, all others. We now have only One Football Team. That is unfortunate. The whole work of creation, the whole business of figuring out what it means to be human—what the boundaries of the human condition are and where we fit in—is taken out of our hands and placed into the Hands of the One. That, my father used to say, is one of the deepest paradoxes of existence: The Creator is a fiction, but His creatures are very real.

I, the sullen adolescent, of course preferred this blasphemous view of religion. For a survivor of the Shoah, the only remaining authentic and honest form of theological discourse might after all be the rhetoric of carefully considered sacrilege.

Once the Jews and their descendants—the Muslims, the Christians—accepted monotheism, they were stuck with this G*d of Israel, Remarkable Chap that He is, inordinately keen on using His powers first and foremost to chastise His Own people. The bigger the catastrophe He visits upon us, the more we are impressed with the Lord's power. Every form of adversity is taken as an indication that humanity has somehow failed Him in an unfathomable but meaningful way, that we have broken the covenant. Every good thing that happens to us is in turn is read as a sign of G*d's protection and renewed trust. Luckily, not all creativity is dead. We can still turn these rules around and reinterpret, for example, Jesus's execution as a common criminal as a divine triumph. El's words even contaminate the thinking of self-professed atheists: Marx, for instance, had his dream of an eternity of unadulterated happiness on a quiet and purified planet—is it a coincidence that this was also Zoroaster's dream and that of the community of Qumran?

—Such were the thoughts I was thinking in those days: juvenile and muddled, to say the least.

•

The first time she spoke to me was also the first time she touched me, which was also the first time we truly met, in the stairwell of our house. She was walking up the stairs, her suitcase in hand, and I was going down. I stopped and pressed myself against the wall so that she could pass. She stopped too; I don't know why. That's when she touched me. She brushed away the lock of hair that had fallen over my forehead. And then she spoke. Her words were: "Boy, your hair is getting long. Do you want me to cut it for you?"

Stella, yes, oh yes, please: Cut my hair, caress my forehead, take me in your arms! Stella, Stella, what miraculous, sweet, evil coincidence has brought you here as our new housemate? Before I realize what is happening, I am sitting on a chair in the bathroom, an old sheet wrapped around my shoulders. Stella's fingers comb through my wet hair, scissors clack at my ears, and my poor boy's heart—well, my poor boy's heart thumps madly in my chest.

Stella's arrival in our home coincides with a new phase in my life, initiated by a discovery that—considered in the wider context of the male lifecycle—is so unspectacular that it typically doesn't even merit mention, except that, at this moment of discovery, the event is so sensational that it momentarily unhinges the discoverer's entire world. The young male's firsthand discovery, that is, of an alternative function for that preposterous appendage on his loins. These things happen naturally, of course. To me, it came in a dream, and maybe, just maybe (and I will be the first to admit that I am filled with shame because of this likelihood), maybe Frau Silbereysen's minor molestations were a precipitant factor in my maturation. Maybe her garrulous groping was the magical touch that opened the gates. I am ashamed to admit this, for the woman who introduces the young man to the reality of love should be a sweet siren, and not an old witch.

Our whole collection of books had shrunk down to one volume, namely Van de Velde's book *die Volkommene Ehe*, a book focused on the "physiology" and "technique" of the "ideal marriage." When my parents burned all their books in 1934, the Ideal Marriage had survived the bonfire, not because my Parents were extraordinarily attached to it or because they felt it might come in handy, but simply because it had been overlooked. The book had not been stored in the bookcase but hidden underneath a stack of tablecloths in the sideboard, safe (or so they thought) from a curious boy's eyes; my parents probably had forgotten that they owned a copy of it at all. It had been given the same hiding place in our new home, where I rediscovered it during one of my hunting expeditions for chocolate—an expensive treat my parents occasionally indulged in, and that they likewise did not want to share with me. Rereading the book, the words that were used to describe the multitude of sexual possibilities sounded to my ears like exotic flowers or rare minerals. In my school days I had acquired a taste for foreign languages, despite the scarcity of opportunities to practice. Where in those days would I have been able to hear French? Where in Berlin was living English spoken? I like languages because languages are compliant. Verbs can be inflected, nouns declined. Van de Velde's book contained a new lingo, new tongues so to speak, and I, eager for any kind of education, learned and obligingly inflected and declined. This was hard to do: The color diagrams that were pasted to the pages suggested a complexity that was far beyond my imagination. Neither were the possibilities particularly alluring—they involved organs and bodily products that seemed rather disgusting to me. After finishing the book, however, I possessed an excellent theoretical knowledge of the physical aspects of love, though I didn't truly understand any of it. It was, I guess, like reading a book on butterflies—even after extensive study, you still have no idea what it truly means to have wings and be lighter than a feather and to let a beautiful summer day's breeze carry you all the way to the clouds.

But let us return to the present, where Stella is cutting my hair. She cuts it short on the sides and leaves a modern, charming little tuft on top, a happy cowlick—the hairstyle I wear to this day, because the old fool I am wants to believe it makes me look boyish. While she does this, I experience (it must be her touch or her smell or the closeness of her soft curves, or maybe even the danger of the scissors' bite) the first conscious erection of my boy's life. Fortunately, the old sheet hides this event from view. It would have been hard to hide otherwise: There is no tentativeness in that primal, initial hard-on—this cock-thing clearly knows what it's looking for, and while I'm thrilled, filled with a pleasant form of anxiousness, I also feel rather pained and tense. Meanwhile, the nagging laughter of a few neighborhood boys sounds from the inner courtyard.

Stella is two years older than me. A boy of fourteen and a young woman of sixteen—that's quite a difference. Stella was two classes ahead of me in the German school, and two classes ahead in the Jewish school. Well, let's just say that she was a siren. Not just to me. She was the kind of woman of which Berliners say: *klein, aber oho*—petite, but ooh-la-la. Her hair had just the right shade of buttery yellow. Her smile was mesmerizing. She used both that smile and her blondeness to great effect, and her airy liveliness helped too. She was the stuff of schoolyard legends. She used to bring a copy of *All Quiet on the Western Front* to school; during recess she would read it to her friends. She preferred to sample the steamier passages, laughing out loud when her girlfriends' ears turned red, and the more they begged her to stop, the louder Stella raised her voice and the more salacious her choice of material became. There was also the persistent rumor that Stella earned some extra cash by posing in the *Feige und Strassburger* art academy, in the nude, at 9 marks an hour.

Stella is *that girl*—every high school has a girl like that—the one girl who makes all other girls seem dull and boring. Every boy has a girl like that. She is far away and yet terrifyingly close. He uses his dreams to keep her at bay, and although she is practically begging him to let her become a reality, to be a kissable mouth and a touchable body, the boy deludes himself into believing that this cannot be. The girl, then, that makes a young boy's life sweet and heart wrenching.

When the weather was too rough for biking, Stella and I used to take the same tram home. Separately, of course. I stayed close to her at the tram stop, I circled the halo of jealous and admiring girlfriends that always surrounded her. Sometimes I dared approach her to the point where I could smell her perfume. The fool I was thought that the smell of lily-of-the-valley was the natural scent of her body. I wanted to get close to her, to better hear her laugh, imagining that she released those hearty, full-throated bursts of surprised delight because of something I had said. She never talked to me, not once in all that time, not a word, and I never spoke to her. Aboard the tram, I kept a respectful distance. When her stop approached, I pulled the cord for her and then I took the next tram back—my stop was closer to school than hers.

But now Stella's hands were ruffling through my hair; her scent filled my nostrils, I sensed real sweat underneath the lilies. What must have been an electric wire connected her scissors and her comb to the depths of my being. Something in those depths stirred and then rose to attention.

•

We sit at the dinner table, all four of us. It feels so natural, as if it has always been like this, as if we have been a family for decades. I show off my brand new haircut. I am now a dead ringer for Emil as drawn by Kästner's illustrator, and Pony the parakeet whistles her admiration. Stella remains incomparably Stella, she talks and talks, blabbering on about a thousand things while we mash our potatoes and cut our cow tongue into paper thin slices, and she tells my parents—wowie-zowie!—stories about me. Stories about me! She knows who I am! She *did* notice me, in school!

She reminds us all of a day that I myself had long forgotten. The day our school got Aryanized. Our new school principal delivered his first morning speech; he barked at the assembly like a flea-ridden dog. He spoke of the changes in the curriculum, he spoke of the new order, and then he summoned all non-Aryans to stand up. "Up! Up!" he screamed. "Come on! Up! Up, children. Up!" What a request! All non-Aryans: Rise. There was no reason to comply, everybody's name and race was clearly indicated in their files, and our classmates knew who we were; this was a simple attempt to intimidate us, to set us apart. I was naïve; I was popular with my classmates because I was smart and I could be trusted, and I helped them with their homework. What could happen to me? I felt this pang of misguided reverse pride, and I stood up from my chair, slowly and deliberately. Even better, I climbed on top of my seat, my cheek flushing from the challenge, still stinging perhaps with the memory of my mother's slap of January 30th, filled with the scorching anticipation of what this act would surely bring about: The Jewish kids would heap praise on me, I would be the proud leader of the oppressed, and the Aryan kids would see the silliness of these distinctions. Who knows—maybe Stella might even notice me! I forgot that it is technically impossible to rebel when the authorities order you to rebel. And what I had imagined in that dense romantic head of mine—that a sea of hands would rise, that everybody—Jews and Aryan alike—would jump on the seats of their chairs, that we would for once and for all bring an end to the era of empty slogans—of course failed to materialize. In fact nobody, absolutely *nobody* made the slightest move: Nobody raised their hand, not even the kids who should have—little Seth Horowitz kept his hands in his lap, and so did the Goldbergs, the Cohen sisters didn't stir, and my Stella remained motionless as well. I was standing there, looking down on the other kids, many of whom looked up at me with astonishment rather than pride, and the wind blew around my flushed ears, and I decided to climb down and just sit—and then principal, taken aback by the lack of response, cleared his throat and fiddled with his papers.

This then was the day Stella was telling my parents about, the day that I learned that you don't always need others to make your life a living hell, that each of us is perfectly capable of calling forth her or his own prosecution—the day that would, eventually, lead to the cherry pit incident.

Today, I am proud. Stella remembers me, and she holds my deed—which I never dared confess to my Parents—and myself up as an example of unmitigated courage in the face of vacuous presumptiveness.

But wait a minute. My heart sinks in my chest. This is *not* how Stella tells the story. She does not relate a tale of heroism. On the contrary, she expresses her concern, and I see Mother nodding in agreement and Father looking at me with quiet alarm. I want to speak, but the words are stuck in my throat. I want to tell them, I want to tell the world, that this was no act of stupid stubbornness, no petit-bourgeois rebellion without necessity or consequence. Okay, true, nothing of value came out of this gesture, but how could I have known that it would turn out this way? If the other kids had simply followed my lead, maybe things would have been different? We would have changed the climate at school? Right? I'm right, right? But how can I say things like that when I see them looking at me, all three of them, with that look of grave concern in their eyes, and—oh, comfort!—also a good deal of kindness? I am such an endearing little boy! That perks me up a bit. That little cowlicked tuft on top of my head looks good and I am an endearingly brave little boy—stupid and callow, certainly, but brave nonetheless. My judgment may be weak, my heart is strong—I carry it in the right place, although I might need to learn to be a little less impulsive. "Be careful, my boy," my mother mumbles. My father too is trying to say something, but because he is also chewing a mouthful of boiled potatoes I fail to understand him. Stella takes it upon herself to voice the general consensus in the room: "This boy is such a *sweetie-pie!*" Even Pony agrees; her shrill whistle pierces my eardrums.

•

When all the noise has subsided—the children all in bed, the radios turned off—a quiet cry climbs the wall of the building, a sustained, plaintively wavering note that scratches at my bedroom window—a tomcat pawing at the night with velvet claws. I peer through the crack in the curtains. A young man stands in the courtyard, legs wide, his head strained back on his neck and his gleaming instrument pointed at the stars. Just for him, the moon has broken through the clouds; beams of her pale light bounce off the brass keys and the golden horn. In Stella's bedroom, next to mine, the bedsprings creak. Her door opens. I open mine too, just a crack, just in time to see Stella disappear down the hallway; she holds her shoes in one hand and pinches her cheeks hard with the other. This then is how Stella Sonderlicht goes out for a date, delighting her lover with a joyful but fraudulent blush.

All of a sudden, I feel sticky. I need to cool off. I go to the bathroom. On the makeshift clothesline strung across the room a small battalion of flesh-colored bras is hung out to dry. I open the faucet and splash cold water on my face. I slip into the empty tub. In the glow of the naked light bulb I stare at the strange canopies above my head, these most remarkable parachutes on which the angel Stella has so unexpectedly descended into my life.

•

I dream unquiet dreams. I dream of a poor Jew who walks through the Tiergarten. He mulls over the catalogue of his many sorrows. He gets tired and leans against a tree, a magical tree that immediately grants whoever touches it everything he wishes. The man isn't just tired—he's also very thirsty. When he imagines how nice it would be to have a tall glass of ice-cold water in front of him, the desired glass of water instantaneously materializes in his hand, much to his surprise—big and tall and cold and filled to the brim with the clearest spring water imaginable. The man looks around; he sniffs the liquid and then he gulps it down. He's never felt so refreshed in his life. Then he considers how hungry he is, and a table appears in the grass, sagging under the weight of stacks upon stacks of the most exquisite dishes. This must be my lucky day, the Jew thinks, all my desires are being fulfilled! Well then—I wish myself a beautiful house. The house materializes. Servants would be nice. Servants appear and bow to their master. He wishes himself a beautiful, loving, intelligent bride, and suddenly she is walking towards him (guess who she looks like, in my dream). She kisses her man on the cheek and grabs him by the hand, ready to lead him into the house. "Wait a minute," says the man, "This is ridiculous! This can't be true!" And—*poof!*—right in front of his eyes everything, the table, the house, the servants, the bride, all vanishes into a big puff of smoke. "What did I tell you!" exclaims the man happily, and he walks back to his apartment, mulling over the catalogue of his many sorrows.

•

And this is how Stella Sonderlicht comes back from her date: A car door slams shut, metal against metal, the sound echoes in the street, and two people yell at each other at the top of their lungs—this is clearly a game of whoever is loudest wins. "*Ruhe!*" yells somebody from above and now Stella and her beau interrupt their fight for a joint shouting match with this intolerant neighbor, and when this man, too enraged for words, closes his window with a bang that reverberates through the whole building, they resume their brawl. Stella must be winning, because her lover decides to resort to physical violence: He slaps her so hard in the face that she has to gasp for air and in that second he races back to the car and disappears with a bang and a roar. Stella seems to be shaken, and I shudder with vicarious fury. Through the crack of my door I can see her face as she walks through the front door. It is wet with tears. Then she goes into her room, and I can hear her quiet sobbing through the wall. I rest my back against the doorframe. I am despondent. How can anybody do this to Stella, my Stella? Never will I do anything like this; never will I treat my beloved so badly! Then her door opens again, a ray of pale yellow light sweeps over the hallway carpet. She steps out, in a robe and slippers. She walks straight towards me. My heart is thumping. Now then? Now? Is my Stella finally coming to me? Am I to be the man who will comfort her? I retreat deeper into my room, but she passes me by. Then I hear the door of the back room open—I recognize the particular squeal of its hinges—the room where the map with our escape routes lies bare on top of the piano. As quietly as I can, I follow her. I make myself as small as possible. She has left the door open and I— what's come over me?—I slide in behind her; unseen I slip into the shadows under the piano. With great care, Stella lifts the pile of papers from the piano bench— the brochures from the Community Center, the copies of our visa applications, the ever-growing stack of rejections. She puts them on top of the lid, flattening, no doubt, a multitude of little flags, perhaps tearing the map at its folds, and then she sits down, as if it were the most natural thing in the world to sit behind a piano in the middle of the night. She kicks off her slippers; they land right in front of me. I breathe as lightly as I can.

She lifts the lid off the keyboard. It is well-known that the muse prefers the midnight hour, the dark night of the soul. Of course Stella does not hear me, of course she does not see me—a different spirit has taken possession of her.

Her fingers on the keys. Immobile. Stella is waiting. Peaceful. Composed.

The muse needs to be seduced gently, under a silent curtain of moonlight—she has to enter the regions of the soul unseen, guardedly but resolutely, like a secret lover entering a magic garden.

Stella is willing. Stella is prepared.

A breeze moves through her fingers.

From the folds of silence an arpeggio rises almost inaudibly, a haze of tritones so bare they spread a chill across the room. A cautious foot of brittle alabaster moves to the pedal of flaky gold—the porcelain of white bone, the pastel of pink ligament, the noble blue of her veins. The sound melts in with the surrounding darkness; it evaporates just before the melody becomes recognizable. Is this the serendipity of a sonata dedicated to moonlight, is it a torturously persistent *Gymnopédie*, or does the muse conspire with wood and steel and felt to create a vulnerable requiem? A silent sigh—did it escape from the player's half-open mouth or is it the muse herself penetrating the pianist, uttering the smallest of cries, with small foamy bubbles at the corner of her lips? Or was it a quiver in the listener's throat, a tiny sob that bounced off the piano's sheltering roof?

The listener. A boy. Me.

Stella's robe comes undone.

Stella's heavenly, unreachable breasts breathe my way, pale ghosts of the future, breasts not carved out of granite or marble or printed in gray dots of newspaper ink, but very much alive, drenched in music, with small, light-brown, curious buds at their tips, lovingly gazing my way. Stella may have forgotten the world, she may not be aware of my presence, but her lovely, swelling breasts are definitely there, blossoming before me and mine to behold. For the second time today I answer the call of Stella's fullness, the generous summons of the royal splendor of her body. The music floats through the room, still indefinable, but louder now, like a swallow sailing just a few inches above the quiet waves of a dark lake, yet never disturbing the waters. Stella, the music, and I, we dwell in a world that is completely our own—so disconnected from anything else that exists.

Is that smile, is that oblique tear in the corner of her eye meant for me; is it encouragement and comfort for what she and the music do to me?
Stella spreads her thighs.

A sweet nest of blond silk glistens with a moist sheen of silver; inside that balmy softness a small animal lies sleeping, curled up in feline grace, and now it stirs with a little purr of yearning, and the pianist abandons the bass and slowly, with eyes closed, spreads her left hand over that warm secret creature. A finger dips into the silent slit, a flower blossoms in pinks and purples, and the salty scent of liberation stings my nostrils. What can I do? I simply have to follow her example, I need to take part in Stella's sacrifice—I need to offer myself up to the night, to the muse, to loneliness. I tug down the waistband of my briefs, I expose my pecker to the G*ddess; carefully I put a tender hand around its swollen shaft.

My climax is instantaneous. Deep inside me, deep inside my spinal fluids, deep inside my belly, deep behind my ribs, deep behind my eyes, deep inside my gut, deep inside my burning balls, deep inside the soreness of my loins the world collapses to a single point, a little compact ball of pleasure that pulsates and hums and then explodes in a white-hot, ice-cold bang—I lose control, my head shakes wildly, and I bang my skull against the underside of the piano. The sound box responds with the booming, crashing undertones of a funeral bell—yes, in this mixture of pure joy and dull pain I die, for the very first time I die that death that poets sing of, my cock a geyser of long warm threads, an unstoppable fountain, spraying and spraying and I bite my tongue to not scream like a madman—never have I felt anything like this before, *this cannot be true*, and it goes on and on, it does not stop, and my body shakes and I fall back and my head hits the wall—in warm generous spurts I shoot my sperm straight into Stella's wide-open silk slippers.

"In the Name of G*d! What is *GOING ON HERE!*" My father's presence fills the room, the abrupt overhead blaze of the ceiling light sets the room on fire. Stella screams and clutches her chest—barefoot, her face hidden in her hands, she races through the hallway to her room, her robe fluttering behind her, her tears splattering the floor. I press myself tightly against the wall and—I can't believe my luck—my sleep-drunk Father fails to notice me. He storms out of the room, in hot pursuit of the muse. He stops at Stella's door, the door of the guest room, his hand raised, ready to knock. Then hesitation creeps in—I see the sudden trademark slump come over his shoulders. He thinks better of it. He takes a step back, absent-mindedly closing the door to my room on his way to the master bedroom—let the little one sleep. For a few minutes, I remain where I am, and then I slowly crawl out from under the piano. I push Stella's slippers underneath a cabinet. I feel like I will never be able to walk again; scared and guilty I crawl back to my room on hands and knees.

•

I am back in bed, wearing my briefs and nothing else, flat on my back, the blankets in a heap on the floor. The breath of the world hurts me, and how cruelly my penis swells with the memory of Stella's body; how scared am I that just by touching it, it will start spurting all over again, thereby exhausting my supply of spinal fluids and causing me to die an early death, most cruel but utterly deserved. Thus I am freezing in the cold harshness of the autumnal morning, shaken with the last echoes of my unexpected orgasm and with the pain and frustration of the undeniable demands of this fresh erection, and then, when my cock finally gives up and slumps and my eyes feel heavy and my mind drifts away, an impetuous voice booms through the room, harsh and loud in the chill of the new, dark, merciless day; not just any voice, of course—it is *his* voice, the metallic voice of the G*d of the Germans, unmistakable, passionate, strong, brash, brazen. The whole building shudders to life. Curtains are pushed aside, windows thrown open to welcome the voice in. It repeats a single statement, that voice, the same statement over and over, until there is no doubt as to what it means. *Seit fünf Uhr fünfundvierzig wird zurückgeschossen* . . . The voice is a machine gun, every word hits like a bullet. *Seit! Fünf! Uhr! Wird!*

This is the moment we have been waiting for. Hitler has declared war. Thunderous applause rocks the *Mietkazerne*, people dance, screams of joy shake the walls of our flat. The eastern continent lies like a limp virgin in the arms of the German G*d Mars. She started this—we are merely shooting back, as of 5:45 this morning.

We, Mother, Father, and I—we are trapped.

And Stella is nowhere to be found.

•

The world is changing. In the wedding pictures in the photographers' shop windows the grooms no longer wear tuxedos; the wedding fashion of the day is full uniform with medals so well-polished that they shoot sparks. Newborns are carried into the studios by the basket; pictures for a soldier's wallet, emotional fuel for the short but hard march to the East. We, Jews, are supposed to go the *Gemeinde* and pay 10 pfennig for a piece of fabric to be sewn on our outer clothes. Two overlapping triangles blossom like a flower in a buttercup pasture, and in the center of that star our fate is written, not in the official gothic font, but in a font that is a cheap, mean parody of the Hebrew script—the word that tells us and everybody else who we are, and who we will forever be: No longer are we human, we are Jews: each of us is nothing but a Jew, and that is all people need to know about us. You are just a *Jude*.

Mother and I are assigned a job in the war industry. I make gun barrels for the Mauser-Werke AG; rifling is my job. Mother works on the assembly line of a munitions factory. The sulfur vapors attack her throat; after less than a week, her voice sits permanently low and hoarse. Jews making weapons: It's not just ironic, it also means that the authorities believe us to be so meek that they trust us with a job that offers ideal opportunities for sabotage. What if Mother would miscalculate the amount of gunpowder in the shell, making the grenade explode immediately upon release of the pin; what if I left a welt in the barrel, making the gun blow up in the gunner's face? Don't get me wrong—we do indeed consider being saboteurs, but we decide against it. We have no talent for murder.

Mother remains amazingly cheerful under this ordeal. When she goes off to work she greets the other tram passengers in the Berlin dialect, with a firm and chipper "*Morjn!*" The other passengers groan, they prefer to be left alone, but they always do manage a sleepy "*Morjn!*" in response. The first day we are forced to wear the wretched star, my mother gets cold feet. She steps on the tram, trying her best not to look anybody in the eye, inching her way through the compartment so that she doesn't touch anybody, and she stutters a nervous, tentative, barely audible "*Mor-jn?*"

The passengers all stand up and yell: "*MORJN!*"

"Sit down, girl. There's a seat right here!"

"But I can't. It's forbidden!"

"*Ach Quatsch!* Sit down, *Mensch!* Sit down!"

Ironically, the yellow star makes us invisible. I am quite certain that if one of us would have drawn a knife and demanded somebody's purse, he would have been impossible to recognize thereafter. Even worse, the victim would have no recollection of what had happened—she would have thought she lived a nightmare in broad daylight: being mugged by an invisible man!

The bombings begin around that time. Bombings—they aren't at all what the movies would have you believe: a simple sound and light show. First, there is this rumbling in the distance, a disquiet, like a train approaching from deep underground or the first sign of an upset tummy. Then the humming starts, like a nasty headache, a low buzzing drone inside the skull. Then the feeling is no longer subterranean—the sky suddenly vibrates with heat; it makes your eyes hurt. Then flares light up the night, their glare penetrates even the blackest blackout curtains; and at the end of their parachutes they float down, elegantly swaying and deadly silent: the torches that will show the bombers the way to their target: the town below, with its vulnerable buildings, its citizens exposed.

A split second after the air-raid sirens start screaming, the building comes alive. We hear the muffled stomping of boots in the hallway, the shuffling of slippers, some urgent but hushed whispering—as if making noise, as if merely speaking out loud would betray our position to the enemy. Then the building buckles, hundreds of Lancasters and Flying Fortresses shower their deadly cargo over the defenseless city, incendiary bombs paint crazy sunflowers on the stark black canvas of the night, flowers of unbearable heat, causing terrible shocking pain. The ground beneath our feet retreats in a swell of pain and shakes our terrified bodies to their cores. We lie on the floor, quivering and trembling with the double tremor of our own fear and the cry of the wounded earth. When the impact comes particularly close, the smell of sulfur burns our nostrils and the heat singes our eyelashes. We smell our own flesh burning. In the hallway, cherubs tumble from the ceiling, their wings useless, pulverizing instantly on the tiles.

The others, the Aryans, are down in the basement, but the three of us wait for the end of the rain of fire in the alcove of our apartment; every impact makes the windowpanes bulge in; the blackout curtains seem to catch fire. We should be safely below, but Jews are not allowed to share the main room of the bomb shelter with the other inhabitants. We did go once; we took our place in the little side room reserved for us, small and separated from the main space with crossbeams. It made us look like dangerous animals in a zoo, kept behind bars. We did not like it one bit: We did not like the little kids staring at us with wide open eyes, their hands at the bars of our cage; we did not like their mothers luring them away, not out of compassion for us, but because they thought we might hurt their children—maybe we would lash out with our sharp claws, or poison them with spit from our tongues. After that one experience we stay upstairs in our apartment. This is against the law, though even this has no grounding in concern for our well being. The authorities are simply afraid that Jews might open the curtains and light signals to show the enemy the way. When the alarm sounds, the doorman climbs the stairs and knocks on all doors; he typically spends a lot of time in front of ours, rattling the doorknob and beating the wood with his fist while we keep quiet as a mouse. The doorman must be a good man after all, full of understanding and sympathy, because after a week or two he stops insisting. We prefer the quick and spectacular death, a direct hit from a firebomb thrown by the enemy-that-is-our-friend, a quick and merciful end buried under the burning ceiling; We prefer this to the humiliating stares.

We can imagine other ways to die that are much less merciful. Being transported to the east, for instance, to die at sunrise, naked in a tiled bathroom. We have heard rumors. At a friend's house, Father encounters a man who went underground; he has escaped from a place far east, a work camp named Auschwitz.

"Is it true that they murder Jews over there?"

"It is true. They separate the strong from the weak. The weak disappear, never to be seen or heard of again. The strong work until they in turn become weak and disappear, never to be seen or heard of again."

The man stares off in the distance. Then he speaks again. "I have seen a mother separated from her child. The mother was strong, the child was weak. The child cried for its mother; the mother cried for her child. I saw one of the guards grab the child by its feet and hit it against a wall until the child stopped crying. And then he hit it against the wall again, just to make sure. And again. And again. Until the head of the child had turned into a bloody pulp. When that was done, the mother was transferred to the row of the weak. Never to be seen or heard of again."

"I cannot believe this," Father says. "I . . . cannot . . . believe . . . this."

The man turns his palms upward.

"No," Father says. "I am not saying that you are a liar. I am just stating that I cannot believe this—that is a different thing altogether."

How could we, how could anyone believe that such gruesome things really happen? When reality trumps all imagination, how can we comprehend reality? It cannot be true! Mother objects: Why all these complications, why would they put Jews on trains and transport them hundreds of miles away simply to kill them? It makes no sense. It is economically unsound and it goes against all military logic. All effort should be concentrated on the front. If they want to kill us, why don't they simply kill us here?

One day, the Auschwitz-man vanishes. Did he get arrested? Or was he perhaps indeed an *agent provocateur* of the regime?

We should have tried a vanishing act too; we should have gone underground with our whole family. But we didn't. Going into hiding would have implied that we believed the stories, the rumors, the gossip. We were not ready for that. Was there proof that the man really had been where he claimed to have been? To believe such things makes them real. They say the truth shall set you free. I say: There is nothing that enslaves you more than the truth. Truth makes you lose all your freedom. Accepting the truth implies the end of the dream, the end of hope, the end of the journey. And then, what sense does it make to go into hiding? Sooner or later they will find you anyway. The Gestapo even shows up at funerals, looking for illegal Jews. Would the Gestapo really be so cruel as to round up grieving family members at the edge of an open grave? Yes, of course, they are that cruel. This is the way the Gestapo operates.

And then, after every raid, the silence, a silence as thick and menacing and dizzying as the columns of smoke that rise from the streets.

The grocer's wife asks Mother: "Why do you always do you shopping late at night, when all the good stuff is gone?" Mother shows her the yellow star. She often carries her purse so that the piece of fabric is hidden, even though that is against the law. Jews are not allowed to shop early in the day. "*Mensch*, why don't you come in at the crack of dawn, before we open the shop? Just hide your star. I'll put something aside for you!"

Father does not have to work. Mother succeeded in getting him on a list: Father's hands made him officially disabled. He loves—he loved—to roam the streets at dawn, to roll up his sleeves and pick up a shovel and help clearing the rubble. There is no lack of shovels in Berlin and this work does not require a fine-tuned left hand. G*d knows his help is needed—there is so much rubble. Every morning new houses have turned into red-hot gravel, then the gravel turns into a smoldering heap, and as the nightmare cools down, the day breaks. He didn't have anything else to do. Correction: He didn't have anything better to do. A Jew who shovels rubble for the goyim. O yes, we use that word now. Father still cannot say it with the proper amount of contempt; he still sings it with a sweet tone of compassion. "The goy is as bad off as we are," he says. "Just like us, the goy is a prisoner in this town; he is equally vulnerable." My father will always be a dreamer, forever denying reality.

But there is some truth in what he says. We all share the streets of this city of ever-expanding ruin as equals. Because we all suffer. But Father clearly goes too far when he implies that there is no distinction in the type or color or amount of suffering. That suffering is not just a universal given, but a necessary ingredient of life. That suffering is the glue that binds us all together, Jews and gentiles. That suffering sets us free. That it makes us all human and mild.

Whenever Father leaves the house to help rebuild the city with his bare hands, he wears his special coat, the coat that has the star affixed with just a few pins. As soon as he is far enough away from home, he tears it off and puts it in his pocket. This is dangerous; it can cost him his life. But bombs are equally dangerous. We keep three coats on the rack by the door, one for each of us, coats that have the stars sewn on tightly, in case somebody denounces us and we have to show the police that our insignia are indeed, as the law requires, stitched on securely and permanently.

•

My father finds comfort in the story of the sponge. Press a sponge through a sieve in a bucket of water and you end up with a slushy mess. A sponge is a living organism, a colony of invertebrate animals of the phylum Porifera; the sieve divides the sponge into its smallest constituents, the individual animals of the colony. Wait a while and you will see what panic, loneliness, and sheer determination can do: The little animals start looking for each other, they clump together, and after only a few hours the water will be crystal clear and at the bottom of the bucket you will find a brand new sponge, never seen before.

Every Jew has two angels by his side, my father says. One angel serves to hold his hand over the heart of the pious, egging it on so that it never stops; the other supports the sage's head, so that he may direct his gaze to the Holy One (Blessed is He). But angels are so busy these days; can we reasonably expect two of them to assist every man at all times, one ministering to his heart, the other to his head?

•

The whistling, the hissing, the sizzling of the shells; the dry rasping of my father's hands; my mother's mumbling silence. This is the secret of survival: You have to do it one day at a time. And whatever the circumstances, you say to yourself: This too shall pass.

•

Every evening after work I take the tram from Siemensstadt to Friedrichshain, dulled by exhaustion and the incessant thumping of the machines at Mauser. The day is over, the gray veil of dusk falls mercifully over my shoulders. In the failing light, people take one last look at me; I can feel it. This is not unusual in public transportation, people who scrutinize other people, asking themselves, for instance, what he or she would look like without any clothes on, or where he or she might be going, and also: Is he or she more fortunate than I am, and if so, why? In my case there may be more to the travelers' looks—maybe there's something suspect about the color of my eyes, the shade of my hair, the shape of my left ear? Like Father I no longer wear the star when I am among strangers, but I still know who and what I am. Maybe they know too? Tonight, one passenger in particular pays close attention to me. He is a tall boy in a Hitler Youth uniform decorated with an overabundance of ribbons and pins. He makes his way over to where I'm standing; he moves so slowly through the throng that his movements seem almost seem like an optical illusion, but then suddenly he is right next to me, in my face; I almost gag on the sharp reek of the pomade with which he attempts to cover the stench of his neglected, unwashed hair and the moldy smell of his uniform coat. His face is pointed like that of an Alsatian shepherd dog. He touches my arm. I cringe.

"What's the time?"

I do not want to talk to him, so I show him. I am troubled by his tone of voice: He does not demand or order, but he does not sound courteous or polite either. Here is a man who knows what he wants, and I am his prey. For a brief moment, the boy grabs my wrist. He brings it close to his face, so that he can distinguish the clock face. He nods at me, somehow pleased with himself. When I get off the tram, he does too. I have never seen this boy in our neighborhood before. He makes me nervous. Normally, I use the shadow of the bus shelter as my cover to reattach the star to my coat. I cannot do that tonight—the Hitler boy doesn't leave me alone. I just keep on walking, for once feeling vulnerable because of my lack of insignia.

It is only a short walk from the bus stop to our house. No light shines out of the houses, this is blackout time. It does not bother me; I know the way well, the light of the stars guides me. It is chilly, it is January, I walk as fast as I can. He stays one step behind me, matching his rhythm with mine. When I hesitate, he hesitates; when I speed up, he speeds up too. He is so close that I can hear his breathing, the warm clouds of this exhalation caress the stubble on my shorn neck. I step into a side street. Naturally, he follows me.

"What do you want from me?" I can't bear it any longer. If he's going to arrest me, let it be now, I think absurdly—let it be before the cold and the fear drive me home; let him arrest me and me alone, so that my parents are left alone. This, however, is absurd: Like everybody else, I carry my identification card with me, and it clearly states my address.

"Let me accompany you. The way home is long and dark. You need some protection."

"No, no, thank you. I'll be okay."

"Let me walk you home, you gorgeous boy." I try to wrestle myself free—when did he grab me by the arm? He insists.

"Is this where you live, huh? In this building?" He pushes me into the lobby.

"Yes," I say. I risk the lie. "Yes, this is where I live."

"Take me home with you, little boy. Take me to your little boy's room."

"I can't. My parents." I am panting.

"What's your name?" He's panting too, with an urgency both frightening and laughable. He has his hand around my throat and forces me to look into his eyes; underneath his fingers, my carotid arteries pulse like mad. I say the first German name I can think of, a name that fits the long list of last names on the doorbells— "Helmut" I reply, "Helmut"—and then I stop. Here I am, mere seconds from death, and I just named myself Helmut—"bright soul," pure of heart; a transparent, careless youth. In response to my lie, the boy grabs my hand and pushes it onto his crotch. I am shocked by what I feel—the same swelling that Stella, or the thought of Stella, provokes in me. It is dark and quiet in the lobby, as dark and quiet as the thoughts I send nightly to my beloved. He removes my hand, but holds on firmly to my wrist. Why do I not resist? With one hand, he unbuttons his fly. A long pale dick emerges, a dick that befits his dog's head and dog's stench. With his thumb and index finger he expertly retracts the foreskin, and the self-evidence of that unknown gesture makes me regain my composure.

I offer him my watch. Why? Why not? It is better to give a German boy what he wants. He wanted to know the time. I cannot give him the other thing he wants. For a second, I toy with the idea of taking his dog's dick in my mouth and biting down. But Hitler boys always carry a knife. No, he does not use his weapon to force me. He merely takes the watch, as if it is his due, and then he does press himself against me—like a dog, I think, and it is the only thought I think—and like a dog he humps my leg and then he cries out "Helmut! Helmut!" and he comes all over my pants, in a single generous spurt.

I can file a complaint with the police. They take article § 175 StGB about same-sex relations very seriously. Of course they do. But they also have their opinions about Jews who roam the streets at night without their yellow star. Which of the two crimes would they consider more serious, do you think? And who do you think they would finger as the one who provoked this illicit homosexual encounter?

I am late. I storm into the apartment; the draft makes the flames of the candles in the flower pots that serve as our new Shabbat candleholders flicker. Mother looks at me with a mixture of hope and trepidation; the way she would look at the prophet Elijah if he walked into the room to take his rightful place at the table. There are more than two open places at the table. The prophet and I are not the only ones missing. My father is also not at home. And he is a punctual man. He never stays out past the curfew. The room smells of turnips boiled in wine—the same wine that Mother has poured into the four glasses, a finger for her, two fingers for the men. When the prophet returns to empty his glass, then the time will have come: That will be the hour of the Messiah, and the night will shine like the day, and all mountains will be leveled and all theological disputes will be solved and all questions about law and praxis answered.

Mother bursts into tears.

My father had chosen to interpret the visit around mealtime as a social call. It made him tense and nervous, of course, but still he managed to put on an air of normalcy and decency: "What can I do for you, gentlemen? I think we still have some beer in the closet, and there is the wine, of course. Or would you prefer coffee? We have some real coffee left, saved from before the war, you see? There is some cake . . . *Ersatz* of course. Or would you like . . . ?"

The two police officers had come to arrest him while I was roaming the streets, while a Hitler Youth rubbed his repulsive prick against my leg. That was not the way it was supposed to be. I was supposed to be home. If I had been, I would have been allowed one last look at my father, one last look into those eyes that had long ago forgotten laughter, its corners etched with the grooves of an ever-deepening sorrow. I could have held his hand in a last and brief farewell, that broken hand that had turned increasingly more brittle, increasingly bony-white, the desiccated trophy of some tribe of cannibals. I could have pressed my lips one last time to his, the way I always did before going to bed, without ever thinking of it. A Hitler

Youth boy's pressing need to empty his testicles had robbed me of my last memories of my father.

His traffic violation had put him on the list of *Asozialen*; his disability made him a parasite, useless human waste. Our crime, Mother's and mine, was to continue to live with him, to stand by his side, to love him, while we knew very well that this was all in vain. It did not help him, and it condemned us to death as well. For they will be back, that much we know, Mother and I. They have taken just him, but only because that way Mother can serve as bait: The woman will keep me here for the short period of time they need to walk up the stairs—no need to hurry, because the building has no back exit, the doorman has told them that. I wonder in which of the parked cars they had been waiting, on the lookout for the silhouette of a boy that looked like he was on his way to the weekly Friday evening feast? They had all the time in the world—time for one more cigarette, time for one last sip from the silver flask. Then they would spring into action.

I think of Father. How he returned home on the night of broken glass and smoldering roofs: blooded, torn, and broken. The smell of burning tiles, the smell of burning paper, the stench of burning flesh. I know what I have to do. I have been waiting for this moment. I am ready. Underneath my bed I keep a small suitcase. It contains my Bar Mitzvah suit with quite a lot of money sewn into the lining, a few sets of clean underwear, a toothbrush, ridiculously enough, two or three shirts, a tie, four pair of socks, and, wrapped in those shirts, the one silver candle holder that the Gestapo had not stolen on their first visit. A razor too, a man should never be without a straight razor. Mother has her own suitcase. I take the coat with the star off the rack; the lining rustles discreetly—money here too.

The knock on the door is businesslike, yet surprisingly soft. They know we are in; they know we are awake and waiting for them. We have no choice but to open the door; they know that too. Their faces sport the grin. The universal grin. The grin they have in common with every third-rate crook and every child molester in the world—the grin of the Manila pimp who just talked a tourist into going bareback with the whore who has the worst case, the grin of the contractor who knows he skimped on the cement for the bridge's pillars. The grin of the idiot, the grin of a man who gets fucked up the ass by life itself, night after night, and realizes that payback time has come. The grin of the boy who had no choice but to become the class bully, shunned by all, knowing full well that he is still missing the all-important little piece of the puzzle that could make him a respected or even loved member of society; the grin of the man whose only answer to life's questions is to shrug his shoulders and say "What can I do about it?"—the grin of the moron who knows he's finally found a way to screw the system and that way is to screw you. The grin spreads over both their faces; it spills into the room the way coffee spills from a mug when you just keep on pouring.

There's two of them; one is older, the other younger. They don't need to say anything. I pick up my suitcase and start walking—obediently, my eyes to the ground. Mother follows me with her own suitcase. The older man leads the way. The younger man closes the door behind us. He does not lock it. Why would he? Tomorrow the apartment will be emptied out anyway, our furniture and belongings will be sold or they will be distributed among the Aryan victims of the bombings. It's a short sad parade. All doors remain closed, the hallway empty. Is everybody in the building an accomplice?

I have only one chance.

I know that too.

I firmly grasp the handle of my suitcase and hit the man in front of me hard in the lower back. He tumbles down the stairs. His partner saw this coming and jumps after me, but he trips over the body of his groaning colleague and I strike him with my suitcase in the stomach. Mother screams, I hear her body hitting the stairs. Did she just throw herself at one of the men? Is she trying to help me? I do not look back but race down the stairs—it is more falling than running, I take two, three steps at a time, but I know the stairwell, I am able to slow down right before I break my legs and I sprint through the front door—it is wide open, no doubt to allow the two Gestapo men and their charges easy passage on the way back, and the extra five seconds I do not have to spend opening the door are my salvation. I turn into the street, behind me I hear the dry crack of a pistol, but I hear no bullets whistle by—in the darkness, the man cannot see me, he can only guess at my position.

The veil of my own breath almost suffocates me, sweat drips from my eyebrows and blinds me, the suitcase hits my legs with every step, the pavement is slick with rain. I take a deep breath and throw myself into the labyrinth of streets, slipping in and out of courtyards that I doubt the cops will be familiar with. I do not stop to check whether I am being followed or not; I just run and run. And then—the Lord be praised—the air raid sirens start wailing, and everybody, including the Gestapo, suddenly have other things to worry about. From high above the British rain their Christmas candles of destruction over the city. I roll into the basement of a bombed-out house and throw myself onto the ground, crying and shivering, covering my head with my suitcase and ripping the star from my coat with the other hand. The earth shakes, the world explodes, hungry orange flames lick at the skies, but I am safe. For now.

I cry, tears of regret and sadness and grief, tears of joy and happiness and relief.

I am a free man.

A hunted man, true, but first and foremost a free man.

•

It is part of our ritual to keep silent, Mr. De Heer and I, after he finishes the day's installment. As if we are waiting for somebody who promised to stop by, but didn't. I wish I could tell De Heer how much his story touches me, but I do not find the words.

"Paul, you are my piece of parchment, your buzzing hard disk is my palimpsest. Here, let me give you this. It's a book."

A present! I love presents! And I love books. Books are warm and heavy; all that paper is such good insulation against the onslaughts of the cold world outside. When the last of the layers of wrapping paper falls away (underneath the glossy blue gift paper there is a layer of newspaper with white tissue paper beneath), I find myself holding a book in a Mylar dust jacket, a first edition of *Emil und die Detektive*. Again, words fail me. Is it normal to find such comfort in the world of objects?

•

When I leave the apartment building, I turn around. I let my gaze travel upwards, hunting for the window behind which De Heer must be watching. The façade looks rough like a dog's tongue, three hundred vertical feet of concrete gloom, completely lacking in imagination, stained ochre and sage with mildew. The only thing that distinguishes the individual apartments are how much their curtains have faded, and the many distinct stages of agony their houseplants are enduring. In between the apartment buildings an absurd baroque monument, the Spittel Colonnades, built in faded remembrance of doubtlessly glorious times past, howls silently at the moon. One of its columns bears the impasto of another of those number graffiti things—it is the number 101. I touch the paint. It is wet. I think of the pills that Mr. De Heer took—the preferred escape route in the 1930s—and I stare unblinkingly at the rows upon rows of blind glass eyes on his building. It would have been easier to open the window and take wing, diving for four or five seconds into the ultimate freedom he was so desperately searching for. A breath of void. A gust of g*d. And it would have been over. A man killed, his story lost.

I sniff the polluted air with its unmistakable smell of lignite and cinders, the smell so characteristic of the eastern part of town. I put my hands in the pockets of my coat and start walking. I want to get away from this chemical fog as soon as possible. An old lady with a tiny dog approaches on the sidewalk. She smiles when we pass each other, not out of kindness, but to disarm me, to save her yapping darling from a dirty look or a furtive kick. Life is hard in Berlin. A lonely window with its lonely gray light beckons me to the lonely U-Bahn station. I take the train to Alexanderplatz and then switch to the S-Bahn. At Bahnhof Bellevue the golden angel wishes us all goodnight. The Victory Column shackles her to the earth, but she still spreads her wings and tries to escape. No matter how hard she tries, the earth doesn't give way. One day perhaps she will succeed and carry this whole town with her into the night, high into the darkest darkness, a clandestine nocturnal pilgrimage to the outer ranges of the universe. Berlin will turn into a true Nirvana, the drunkards will be indescribably happy, the sleepers will all dream dreams of such unbearable sweetness that they'll collectively wet their beds, and at dawn the city will alight once more and nobody will have noticed its disappearance. Who knows—maybe this happens every night and we simply don't notice it.

I open the book on the train. A thin strip of metal falls into my lap. Compared to the richness of what's contained on its pages, a book is always way too cheap. But booksellers don't see it that way, and therefore the object needs to be secured. When somebody removes it from the store without paying, the magnet in the strip will short-circuit the security gate, and an alarm will scream out in outrage and sadness over the attempted theft of so much densely packed knowledge.

•

Mefista sees me approaching and stands to attention, her tail waving gaily in the wind. I let her in. When I open the door of my room and she sees the bowl on my table, she lets out her little cry of triumph. I go to the kitchen. Damn, I ran out of milk this morning. I gave Mefista the last drops—I had forgotten. In the freezer I find a box with raspberry ice cream cones. It looks old. Maybe it belonged to a guest who's long since left? After all, who would buy ice cream in the winter? I decide to steal one; ice cream contains milk, doesn't it? Mefista is happy with my decision: When I unwrap the cone, she lets out another one of her happy yelps. I take a bite. It tastes good. I hold it in front of the cat. She licks the ice cream with a pale tongue. Then it's my turn. Then her turn again. We shiver with the delight of the cold raspberries, Mefista the Cat and I. Then I look around, I even go down on my knees and look under the bed, but there's no note tonight, no message from "-a." I turn off the lights and jump under the covers. The cat jumps in too, pressing herself against my side, purring loudly. Within two minutes she falls asleep, with an enthusiasm that exceeds even mine.

ב

G*D'S GLUE

She had vanished in the night. She was still missing in the morning.

Good. Okay. That's reasonable. Not every woman feels the urge to face her lover in the harsh light of morning, or to share an awkward breakfast with him. But then she remains untraceable the whole rest of the day, and the day after that. In fact, she doesn't show up that week at all, nor does she come the next week. He tries to find her; he works hard at it too, running to class after class, hers and also his (in case she goes looking for him), his nose to the ground like a golden retriever. He jogs through every lab in the physics building until men in white coats chase him out the door; he tiptoes through every library that might contain even a morsel of physics knowledge—maybe the age-old parchments in Houghton Library have some snippet of information that touches on quantum mechanics, a snippet that she badly needs to consult? But it's all in vain. There is only one place where she will have to show up, and where he should be able to intercept her, but he's not allowed inside her dormitory—he's male. The girls at the door claim they haven't seen her in ages, but he doesn't believe them. Or, worse, he does believe them and then he tears his hair out in confusion and jealousy.

That she left him once, he can understand. That's the nature of the game: their encounter at the party, the game on the stairs of the chapel, and then her retreat—that's how it works, these are the mores of the day, the rules of modern dating. But then: When he bumped into her unexpectedly the week after, and she initiated him into the full miracle of love, into the miracle of *her* love, making him hers—completely, overwhelmingly, earth-shatteringly hers. How could you follow that up with . . . nothing? Not a glimpse of her, no little note, no phone call, no sign at all. Her joy, her visible joy when she had ran into him at the library, had that been mere playacting? She had linked her arm in his; she had giggled during their hurried, stumbling walk to his room; she had seemed so happy she was almost skipping; she had interrupted their walk a thousand times to cover his face with kisses; and then, under the light of the lamp: her wild fingers in his hair, her firm grip on his cock—had all of that been a lie too? Had she got what she wanted and then got out? She left a stack of papers on his desk; the story she had promised him. She must have carried it in her briefcase all that time between their first and second encounter. G*d, as if the *Hasty Pudding* could even consider publishing that piece.

Goldfarb read the story and his heart turned to stone. There it was. Neatly written down. All of it. Described exactly the way it had happened in real life, including the act that was called fellatio—he had looked it up in the library, he did not remember *fellare* from his Latin vocabulary classes. There are only two possibilities. Either Hannah had memorized everything precisely and then wrote it down exactly as she remembered it—in which case her candidness was a betrayal of their intimacy, turning his feelings into a low *dramma giocoso*. Or else she had had the seduction all planned out according to a prepared script. In that case he had been nothing more than a guinea pig, someone to practice her erotic skills on—fortuitously also the useable editor of a literary magazine. Goldfarb has a hard time deciding which of the two possibilities he finds the more insulting. The side effect being that all this worrying robs him of a good pure anger. Poor Goldfarb, he's the stable boy left in the straw by the baroness, his pants still around his ankles—he should be happy and feel lucky, but he doesn't and he isn't. To add to the confusion, a little voice in his head keeps whispering that she couldn't really be that cruel, that she must know very well that he's thinking these thoughts and that therefore her rudeness must have a deeper meaning. Whatever the case, Hannah remains unfathomable. Under his ruminating gaze, the woman managed to slip away, leaving just the hull of the mystery she had wrapped herself in, as if she was never really there to begin with—her mind games make him drunk and dizzy. And imagine this: Despite the humiliation, his heart and his sex still long for her, each with its own tangible ache. Could it really be that all she wanted was to hurt him?

In his head he replays every second of that night over and over: every touch, every whispered word, every muffled moan, every electrifying lick of her tongue, every gasp of her breath; it's all burnt into his memory. He can't live without her. She is his phantom body, he can still feel her presence; her invisible weight presses down on him at night. Like a limb, she has been cut away from him and Goldfarb suffers, thrashes, and bleeds.

What has he done wrong? Why did she leave him, with no explanation? Had he done wrong by coming in her mouth? Should he have been more of a gentleman, should he have exercised more control? Had he insulted her beyond repair with the gift of his semen? Yes, well, what is the proper sexual etiquette, and how to find out?

The other three musketeers aren't exactly helpful. "Hey, Goldfarb, when will we see her again, that sweet piece of ass of yours?" "Well, what do you think, man, is somebody else licking her pussy right now, do you think?" "Wow, man, maybe you were just too much for her, you know—just too much?" They are unforgivably brutal, crass without restraint, and their ignorance knows no bounds. Geniuses of the mind, but stutterers of the heart.

The cosmic dance they had performed, Goldfarb and his beloved, passionate and mad, as if they were Physics and Metaphysics entwined in a heated mating ritual—had this meant nothing to her? But hadn't he already felt that, hadn't he felt the icy chill of doom while she was still in his arms? (This can't be true; this must be a retrospective memory edit. What boy in his right mind who loses his virginity to such a thrilling creature has time for dour reflection during the intoxicating proceedings?) It was much more likely, given her level of expertise and quick and demanding mind, was that he had simply turned out to be a lousy lover.

Poor Goldfarb. His peace of mind is gone, his soul is heavy and waterlogged.

•

He throws himself into his class work, much like a convert might throw himself into the readings of the holy sutras even after his guru has inexplicably disappeared. The dark mystic night of the soul, his ardent desire to find her, to understand, to recreate her—it drives him to off-campus bars and other girls, but all the nymphs he approaches flee in a panic, scared by his obsessiveness, frightened by the fierce determination of his maneuvers; their intuition tells them that if he were to fuck them, he would go straight through them: His hunt for euphoria is that desperate, that raw, that transparent. Then his mood swings back to gloom. He doesn't shower or comb his hair for days on end, the bouts of madness in which he slumps to the floor, flat on his back, staring motionless at the ceiling are no longer feigned—they have become serious attempts at regaining some sense of equilibrium. His two legs just feel too wobbly to carry his weight. He looks ever more defenseless, pale and sick, a boy wasting away from some terrible internal disease, a boy who could erupt at any moment with either white-hot anger or red-hot tears. He insists on becoming more and more the moody European. He walks the streets of Cambridge with slumped shoulders and from time to time he shrugs those shoulders for no apparent reason, as if shrugging off the whole of creation—it no longer holds any fascination for him. He's likely to stumble over imperceptible bumps in the terrain, as if in the act of walking itself he snubs the earth that carries him. In sum, the rhetoric of his motor behavior rejects human existence as absurd, and that rejection is so self-evident that it does not need verbal clarification.

If Hannah had been Turkistani and he had had her mailing address, he would have sent her a package containing a handful of tea leaves, a blade of grass, a piece of red fruit, a dried apricot, a lump of coal, a flower, a lump of sugar, a river stone, a falcon's feather, and a walnut. I cannot drink tea anymore, without you I am as pale as a withered piece of grass, I think of you and I blush like an apple, my heart burns like coal, you are beautiful like a flower, sweet as sugar, but is your heart made of stone? I would fly, if only I had wings. I am a nut in your hands. Break me open.

But where would he fly, Goldfarb, and where are the strong thighs that can crack his shell? In his sleep he mumbles away, relentless and unintelligible as an alpine brook.

●

His research becomes an ode to his barren love and his vanished lover. What was it she studied? Nuclear physics. The force fields within the atom—the electromagnetic force, the weak and strong nuclear forces. "The glue that holds all matter together," she had said while her fingers drew postcoital circles in his chest hair. Hannah apparently doesn't want him to bond with her. So instead he creates a bond with what fascinates her. He promises himself to read all the library books she has ever requested; to examine the tables of contents of every journals that has ever gone through her hands and to search therein for clues to her disappearance. Maybe she carried her stash of information to exactly this desk, the desk where Goldfarb builds his paper fortress, with narrow slits in between the stacks of books to keep an eye on the aisle, since he doesn't want to miss her potential entrance into the temple of learning. He takes turns staring out the window and reading, and during both activities his hands caress the pages, hoping to harvest a few minuscule molecules of her skin, her hair, her nails. He sniffs the paper, hunting for a few microliters of her sweet, sweet sweat.

Then something remarkable happens. He started reading because he was fascinated by Hannah, but more and more often he finds himself actually concentrating on the reading matter, mulling it over for purely scientific reasons rather than letting it wash over him in an attempt to let the atom's glue mend the erotic fissures in his soul.

The eagerness with which Goldfarb immerses himself into the literature makes his teachers shake their heads. He reads and reads. At the outset, he works his way through the standard works in alphabetical order: Hans Bethe, Niels Bohr, Marie Curie, Paul Dirac, Enrico Fermi, Otto Frisch, Otto Hahn, Werner Heisenberg, Frédéric Joliot, Lise Meitner, Wolfgang Pauli, Emilio Segrè, Edward Teller, Eugene Wigner, paying particular attention to the works of his own mentor, Professor Van Vleck. After a few weeks, he understands the basic frame of reference; he is now able to see through the basic equations. Then he starts working thematically, disentangling the chronological and systematic threads that these scientists spin around each other. Goldfarb is a good student; in his attempts to forget Hannah he is sharpening his scientific mind until it becomes like a scalpel. He's the right age for it too—in the years of boundless intellectual hunger. He devours it all as if it were a detective story. Which it is. He gives up sleep; he lugs a red cardboard notebook around campus that he fills with hasty scribbles. He keeps a small arsenal of pencils in his breast pocket, black, blue, red, and green, deployed according to a self-devised code of urgency. A rainbow of pigment stripes appears on his white shirtfronts, like a klutzy imitation of a general's stripes drawn by a toddler. Each of the pencils has a round eraser at the end, but these go unused. He also carries a pencil sharpener; he leaves an easy-to-follow trail of scented wood shavings all across campus.

Goldfarb's greatest discovery in going through this massive amount of information is not what's written, even though this is astonishing enough, but what is *not* written—the stuff that only appears when you read between the lines. When he goes through the material chronologically, he finds that at first everything works the way it should work in the sciences, with false starts and hesitations and small cries of triumph over small breakthroughs. When the number of established facts increases, new and deeper theories make their appearances. And then something strange happens. A remarkable reticence creeps into the texts, as if the whole field is collectively applying the mental brakes. And then there is a resounding silence. As if all research concerning the atom has vanished from the surface of the earth. This is not the silence of unknowing—this is no map with white spots signifying *terra incognita*, not an emptiness like the emptiness that echoes through Goldfarb's soul (the object of my love has vanished—I can no longer sing of her, where has she gone?). Rather, this silence is the kind of eloquent silence exercised by parents whenever a precarious subject is broached while the children are still around. It is, in other words, the silence of well-aimed censorship.

Well, well. This is intriguing!

•

Here is the story, or rather Goldfarb's reconstruction thereof.

You need a good theoretician to convert a trivial accident into groundbreaking science. In 1896, the French physicist Becquerel notices that a few of the photographic plates he keeps in his drawer have become dark, shrouded in a mysterious veil, even though he had carefully wrapped them in black paper. No, the lightproof covering is still intact. Becquerel goes through the drawer. He finds a half-forgotten jar of uranium salts he inherited from his father, an amateur scientist who was fascinated by the fluorescent properties of uranium. Becquerel's hypothesis is that the uranium produces some sort of radiation, and that this radiation must have shot right through the black paper. He repeats the experiment. His hypothesis turns out to be correct. Becquerel rolls up his sleeves and gets serious. Soon he finds out that uranium emits at least three types of radiation. When you send the mysterious beam through a magnetic field, two streams separate themselves from the main stream, one bowing off to the left, the other to the right. The interpretation is simple: One stream has a positive charge, the other a negative charge, and the third has no charge at all. Twelve years later, after countless experiments in which people like Rutherford bombard gold foil and other exotic materials with radiation to see what gets reflected, the physics community arrives at a theoretical identification. The positive stream, labeled alpha radiation, is made up out of the nuclei of helium atoms. The negative stream consists of much smaller particles which all have the same specific mass and volume. Gamma, the neutral radiation, is something unique and as yet anonymous. (Much later gamma will be identified as a beam of photons, the particles that make up light.) These results allow Rutherford to build his model of the atom: a nucleus, positively charged, with a surrounding cloud of negatively charged particles. The atom turns out to be thinly populated: The nucleus makes up only 10-14 of the atom's volume. This is a revolution: Everything we see and everything we can touch, all the stuff that looks so solid and massive from the outside consists mostly of tiny dots whizzing around in absolutely empty space.

Niels Bohr starts working in Rutherford's laboratory in 1911. He notes that a crucial element in the story is missing. Rutherford's story in fact seems to indicate that matter should not exist. When the electrons are whirring around the nucleus, they undergo the acceleration of their circular trajectory. This makes them lose energy. That energy has to go somewhere, probably radiating outwards; because of this loss of energy the electrons themselves should move closer to the nucleus, in effect describing a downwards spiral—the atom should collapse under its own dynamic. But this is not what we observe in reality—matter is quite stable, and it's been around for quite some time. Bohr finds the answer by applying Planck's theory of the quantum to the atom. Planck's model states that nature's forces are not continuous. Instead, the exchange of energy takes the shape of small packages of a lawfully predetermined size. Sand is a good metaphor for this: It looks fluid, but if you rub it between your hands, you feel the grains. This duality of granularity and fluidity is inherent in all we know. Take light. For the modal observer, light behaves like a wave, but if you look closely, light is made out of particles that you can push, one at a time, through a narrow opening, and you can register the impact of each of the separate particles of light—strange particles, by the way, because the equations teach us that they have neither a mass nor a charge. Einstein and Planck discover the grains of light, and Gilbert Lewis names them photons.

Bohr proposes that the electrons in an atom do not really or symbolically circle around the nucleus, the way the old theories see it, but that they "exist" in a particular "energy state": sharp, well-defined levels of energy, with a clear energy jump from one level to the next. Schrödinger and Dirac write down the equations for this theory. Experiments confirm their predictions. Bohr's model also predicts the known chemical characteristics of the elements: what they will bind with and what happens when they do.

With the introduction of quantum theory, the world becomes uncertain. Newton's world, which is also Rutherford's world, is knowable. It is completely determined. When one knows the world as is it now, and knows it exactly, one can predict with one hundred percent accuracy what the world will look like tomorrow. This type of physics is like playing pool on a cosmic scale. Everything is written down in a giant rulebook. When one knows all the variables—the table, the balls, the queues, the players—there is nothing left to the imagination. In the quantum world, uncertainty rules—Heisenberg for instance showed that it is theoretically impossible to know both the position and the momentum of an atomic particle. The laws of the new physics are those of probability.

This is where it gets interesting, because this is where the omissions start. The theory introduces a new force. The nucleus of the atom consists, as we know, of positively charged particles, called protons. These particles repel each other, and therefore a force is needed to hold them together. This is the "strong nuclear force," the "binding energy" that keeps the nucleus of the atom from falling apart. In 1928, Rutherford discovers that the nucleus also contains neutral particles, the neutrons, typically as many as there are protons, and with about the same mass. One interesting corollary of the theory is that the total mass of an atom will always be smaller than the sum of the mass of its components. Mass and energy are mutually exchangeable, as Einstein has taught us. It follows that a part of the individual energy of the protons and neutrons gets lost when they gather to form an atomic nucleus. The part that gets absorbed is the binding energy, and that energy is negative. This in turn implies that we have to add energy if we want to break up an atomic nucleus—the exact amount depends on the size of the atom. The curve of binding energy is shaped like an inverted letter U, and asymmetrical. Very small and very large atomic nuclei (those with more than fifty protons per nucleus) are easier to break up than the medium-sized ones. Or, that's what the theory dictates. It's already ten years old by the time Goldfarb reads up on it. It's all there, no censorship yet.

Another interesting corollary of the theory is that when the nucleus of a heavy atom splits, positive energy will be released. This is because when a nucleus splits, it will by definition form two or more new nuclei, and each of these will have a lower atomic weight—that is, fewer protons in the nucleus. According to the curve of binding energy, these atoms will have a higher binding energy per particle than the original heavy nucleus. Remember, this energy is negative. In other words, the absolute value of the sum of the binding energies of the result of the breakup is larger than that of the original atom. Therefore, when an atom splits, positive energy will be released.

That's the gist of the theoretical story. (There are subplots too. For instance, Dirac's story about antimatter and Fermi's story about the weak nuclear force, but those are not important to understand Goldfarb's story, or at least not Goldfarb's story about the Bomb.) The theory becomes reality in an unexpected way around Christmas 1938. Fritz Straßman and Otto Hahn capture a strange phenomenon in their lab in Berlin. They shoot low-energy protons at a preparation of uranium nitrate to make radium, 88 protons per nucleus, as predicted by the tabulations of Curie and Savitch. This is not what happens, however. They get barium, 56 protons per nucleus, a tad heavier than half a uranium atom. They send their result to their colleague Lise Meitner in Sweden, and confess their confusion. Meitner is Jewish and has fled Germany.

Meitner has a houseguest, her nephew Otto Frisch. Frisch works in Bohr's lab in Copenhagen. They discuss the remarkable result. Then they realize what is happening. One of Bohr's favorite metaphors for the atom is a drop of water. The nucleus is not a stable ball, it is shapeable and elastic. A drop, Meitner and Frisch realize, is divisible. It can fall apart as smaller drops when it becomes too large. A drop is held together by surface tension. Large drops split when the forces that drive the molecules apart are larger than the surface tension. Isn't it possible then that atomic nuclei break apart when the collected forces of the protons that fight each other become large enough to overpower the strong nuclear force?

This idea strikes them in the middle of one of their walks. Otto lays his skis on the ground; he and Lise sit down on a tree trunk and they do a few quick calculations. They don't have the tables with the exact numbers in their backpacks, but they have a pretty good idea of the forces at play. They end up with an atomic number of about a hundred. When there are more than a hundred protons in a nucleus, the nucleus will spontaneously break apart. This result must be correct. The heaviest element in nature is uranium, with 92 protons in the nucleus. Meitner and Frisch now know why nature has this limit. Everything that is heavier than uranium will simply fall apart of its own accord—the nuclear force is no match for the combined wriggling of so many protons. Uranium itself, an element that lives on the edge, is easy to destabilize. Meitner and Frisch imagine a balloon filled to the breaking point with water. Poke it, however lightly, and the balloon soon becomes a jiggling mass that will waggle out of control, and finally the rubber bursts. When you fire a neutron at a uranium atom, the neutron will be absorbed into the nucleus (Bohr had already demonstrated this in 1936), and when it binds it will give up the energy of its momentum. This will increase the total amount of energy in the nucleus and then: Bang—there goes the atom! There's no reason to suppose that the nucleus will break into two equal parts, it is quite possible in fact that the individual neutrons will break free and get absorbed into other nuclei. In other words, it has all the makings of a chain reaction.

Meitner and Frisch sit down in earnest in Lise's study. Their model predicts that when a nucleus splits, a small part of the mass of the nucleus, about one fifth of the mass of a proton, will be transformed into energy. That may not sound like a lot, but in fact it's a tremendous amount—Meitner calculates that when a uranium atom splits, it will release about 170 million electron volts—much, much more than is released in any known chemical reaction. And this is almost a free ride: The energy released by splitting the atom is about one-hundred-thousand times the energy needed to set the reaction in motion. Frisch retreats into the laboratory and confirms this incredible result experimentally. Hahn and Straβman publish their paper in *Naturwissenschaften* and Meitner and Frisch publish their theoretical model and the experimental confirmation in *Nature*. Both articles appear in January of 1939. Within a year, more than one hundred papers about this subject appear in the scientific journals. (Goldfarb won't read them all, but he does his best to get a fair sampling.)

And then there comes this drum roll of silence. It's abundantly clear where all this is going. One atom breaks up, and then the next one, and the next one, and so on, etcetera, in an exponential series. One becomes two, two becomes, four, four becomes eight, eight becomes sixteen—the energy level multiplies rapidly, reaching previously unheard-of levels. One could forge a new weapon out of this, much more powerful than anything ever witnessed by human eyes—endlessly more deadly than anything ever dreamed up by the intelligent mind. And this information is not classified, all the physics principles are well-known; it's only a matter of filling in the details, a matter of technology and engineering skills. If you could get together maybe twenty or so of the best scientists and a few hundred brilliant engineers you would have the ultimate bomb in hands before you knew it.

It is wartime. The cream of the crop of German physicists, certainly the majority of scientists who have worked on the topic of binding energy and the theory of atomic fission ("fission" is the technical term given to the splicing process) are Jewish, and most of them are probably right here in the States. And the American scientists aren't stupid either. This then is the explanation as to why all these professors vanished. This is what they are doing right now. And that must be where Hannah is: some top-secret place where the ultimate bomb is being built. And the fact that all these scientists, all those physicists, all those chemists and mathematicians are still there—wherever there is—indicates that the weapon is not yet in production, that many barriers still stand between dream and action, that there are practical impediments.

This must be the largest scientific-technological effort of all time. Goldfarb wants to be a part of it. He reads and reads, and in the rare moments when he isn't reading, he thinks, mumbling his unintelligible g*dless prayers into the night.

And then the letter appears in his little pigeonhole of a mailbox, like a flower popping up after a desert rain.

The address is written in a woman's hand. Is this *her* handwriting? The message inside is in German; does Hannah speak German? It is a single sentence: "*Du kommst mir gar nicht aus dem Sinne*," and Goldfarb's heart goes into overdrive ("I can't get you out of my mind"). There's a return address on the envelope (PO Box 1663, Santa Fe), but the message itself is unsigned.

He is an instant believer again.

Next problem: how to respond?

Goldfarb responds with as equally a carefully chosen, equally random, equally distorted quote from Goethe: "*Was ist die Himmelsfreud in deinen Armen?*" ("What are the joys of heaven in your arms?"). It took him a day of searching through Faust to come up with that.

And then, simply to show her how much closer he has grown to her, he adds an equation of his own hand:

$$R_c^2 = (\pi^2 D\tau)/(\nu\text{-}1), \text{ in which } l = 1/n\sigma_t, \text{ and } \sigma_t = [\sigma_f + \int \sigma_s(1\text{-}\cos\theta)d\omega].$$

Her reaction is immediate, considering the distance between Boston and Santa Fe, all the way in New Mexico: "*Wo so ein Köpfchen keinen Ausgang sieht, stellt er sich gleich das Ende vor*" ("Where such a small mind sees no way out, he immediately imagines the end."). And then, probably an afterthought, scribbled at the bottom of the paper: "*Du ehrst auch nicht die heil'gen Sakramente*" ("You do not respect the holy sacraments.").

The equation that Goldfarb had written, ending in that ominous lowercase omega—the last letter of the Greek alphabet, literally the end—is the equation that indicates the diameter of the critical mass of fissionable matter. It will be the climax of his paper for Van Vleck's class.

And right after Hannah's letter an official letter arrives in his mailbox as well, in a plain manila envelope without return address: a request printed on army letterhead, to please report at such-and-such an address in Manhattan, Monday, by preference with a packed suitcase, and (no joke) to please burn this invitation after reading.

Bingo, Goldfarb thinks. My ticket to New Mexico.

It is January 1944, six months before the invasion of Normandy.

•

Nice local color, muses Goldfarb when he gets off the train in the sleepy station of Lamy, New Mexico. It's one of those desert towns with sand-colored houses, half of which are boarded up. In a town like this, people can do one of two things: Either take the next mail coach, no matter where it goes, or else commit suicide as soon as possible. On the dusty platform a real-life cowboy—jeans, boots, Stetson, poorly shaved, ill-tempered—is slowly chewing an obstinate piece of gum. The man disentangles himself from the wall leisurely and he steps forward to greet the two travelers. The Santa Fe Super Chief pushes off from the platform, with its strange mixture of passengers: bespectacled business men in suits and bolo ties and blanket-peddling Navajo Indians sipping from bottles wrapped in brown paper bags. The cowboy is not the messenger boy of the Fred Harvey Hotel where Goldfarb has booked a room, just in case, but a real mathematician, sent to pick up the new batch of bozos and drive them to Santa Fe, or wherever their final destination may be.

"M'ster Newman." He touches his hat. Goldfarb's fellow traveler smiles. Goldfarb had passed him a few times on his way to the restless rest rooms; a squat forty-something immersed in a sci-fi paperback—a different paperback every time.

"Roy," he says. They know each other.

"M'ster Goldfarb?"

"Goldfarb. Indeed."

Silently they walk to the jeep.

"Jesus," says the faux cowboy when he lifts up Goldfarb's suitcase. "What have you got in there, man?"

A lamp in bronze that weighs about twenty pounds, among other things.

One should surround oneself at all times with the most important aspects of one's past.

•

The past is past in Santa Fe. The present and the future await. And history too. At 109 East Palace Avenue they get checked in, or "processed," as the cowboy calls it—like meat gets processed and sealed in a tin can—in a small office rented by the Army Corps of Engineers, hidden behind a Spanish patio and a dirty screen door. When Goldfarb signs in, he can read his fellow traveler's name: John von Neumann. Goldfarb gets an instant hot flash. Von Neumann is the "it" mathematician of the moment, the man who formalized quantum mechanics back in the twenties.

Dorothy hands them their temporary passes and then they get back into the car for a silent hour-long drive. First the Taos highway, then the dry Pojoaque Valley; they cross the Rio Grande by means of the wobbly Otowi Bridge, and then they take a nameless dirt road through rusty, rocky hills. When they start climbing, Goldfarb regrets not having bought a blanket from one of the Navajo vendors on the train. At the top of the Pajarito Plateau (*The Hill*), about 5,400 feet above sea level, they enter Area L, or Project Zia, or Project Y, later better known as the Los Alamos National Laboratory. They pass some old school buildings, a barn, a set of huts, an icehouse, and then they drive through a gate ("*U.S. Government Property.*

DANGER! PELIGRO! *Keep out!*") heavily guarded by military police in battle dress. The number on their passes is duly noted and the documents themselves carefully scrutinized. They drive the last few miles through piñon and juniper bushes while the sun is quickly sinking over the mountains. An umbrella of black smoke hangs over a city painted army-green; the snow is speckled gray with soot.

They get their sleeping quarters assigned. The secretary gives Goldfarb the key to room T-236. "That must be right next to U-235, I suppose?" Goldfarb jokes. "Shit," says the secretary. Nobody in the outside world is supposed to know about purified uranium (235 elements—protons and neutrons—in the nucleus instead of the usual 238), and what it's capable of. She picks up the phone and calls Bacher, the physicist reluctantly responsible for the welcoming program for newcomers. It can wait until morning, he tells her. What's the smartass's name? Okay, let me write that down.

•

The city of Los Alamos is less than a year old. Like every American city, it wasn't built by humans, but by an idea. Here is salt, let us dig. Here is gold, let us sift. Here is food, let us rest for a while (say, a few centuries) and hunt and eat. As far as Los Alamos is concerned, here is remoteness, here is quiet, let us rest for a while (say, a few months) and build an atomic bomb while we're at it.

The barracks had been designed to accommodate 265 people. Initially, Oppenheimer, the scientific supervisor of the project, had estimated that six physicists would suffice. After a while, it became clear they needed a few hundred. And the number of technicians and administrative staff and army personnel likewise grew exponentially too. Four thousand people live here now. The town is a permanent building site. And a new Babylon. T-shirts with mathematical slogans are drying on the clotheslines; nannies joke with each other in the Pueblo-Indian language; the occasional fake cowboy tries out his Texas drawl; and there are whole bands of physicists who have abandoned their English and converse amongst themselves in Hungarian or German. There is the following joke: It was in Los Alamos that Fermi formulated the famous Fermi Paradox: If there are really extraterrestrial civilizations, how come we've never met them? Why haven't they landed here? Why haven't they contacted us? Fermi's answer is that if extraterrestrial civilizations really exist, we simply wouldn't be in any state to realize it. How could we be able to communicate with a civilization that's a few million years ahead of us? How could a Neanderthal man understand a Homo Sapiens? Even the cutest little gray kitten named Zoe has no idea what superior intellect she is dealing with when she scratches up her mistress's nose. Fermi tries to sell this idea to a group of colleagues over lunch. Szilard silently points with his thumb to the table behind them, the table where Von Neumann is eating his grub. "Maybe they've already landed, Enrico. You just know them as Hungarians." Szilard himself, of course, like von Neumann, was a Hungarian Jew.

The Really Great Men live in the old Ranch School buildings. The Slightly Less Great Men live in houses hastily built by the Sundt Construction Company. Goldfarb, a humble student, Much Less Than a Minor Great, and single to boot, is housed in a dormitory, his bed surrounded by very un-soundproof pressed cardboard. The in-between solution is Morganville or McKeeville, towns-within-the-town, located east of Ashley Pond—scientific slums of prefabricated flat-roof buildings with paper-thin walls, tiny kitchenettes, and cubbyhole shower stalls. The M-villers and Sundters refer with more than a little envy to the old school buildings as Bathtub Row. (Bathtub shortage was a consequence of the war effort. Congress had set up new standards for housing to be built during the war; the standard specified showers, no bathtubs. Manufacturers of bathtubs had therefore ceased production. Even if the army wanted them, they could not get them.) The technicians and secretaries and the Indian personnel (there's a natural order to such things) are housed in rusty Quonset huts: gigantic horizontal half-pipes of steel, cold silos, tunnels to nowhere floating on a sea of mud with walkways made of planks leading to the main street. And to the laundromat. It's hard to maneuver around planks with a basket full of laundry. If you misstep, the ever-churning machines will be there waiting.

Because there aren't enough telephones, it makes more sense to just run to the doctor in case of a medical emergency than to call him first. Dr. Barnett has a hard time getting used to the stumbling noises in his living room in the middle of the night, and to the fact that patients can just materialize at his bedside, sighing and moaning like apparitions. One night one of them slips over a rug and lands with his full weight on the piano keyboard, almost adding a few heart attacks to whatever complaint was ailing him.

As far as work is concerned, even from very early on everything was pure improvisation—mystic, revolutionary, humming jazzzzzzzz. There's a library and a librarian, Bob Serber's wife Charlotte, but initially there were no books. When Serber gave a series of lectures in April '43 to start up the technical-scientific part of the project, and needed to calculate what the expected yield of the Gadget would be, expressed in the standard units of TNT tons, he couldn't just refer to the *Handbook of Chemistry and Physics* with its handy tables in the back—no, he had to do the calculations himself, literally on the back of an envelope. (The envelope had contained a Christmas card.) Let's see, 170 x 10^6, the energy in electron volts, times 4.8 x 10^{-10}, the charge of the electron, divided by 300 (a volt is 1/300 of the electrostatic unit of voltage), that makes 2.7 x 10^{-4} erg per nucleus. Dear Gentlemen of the Military, one kilogram of fissionable uranium will yield the equivalent of about 20,000 tons or 20 kilotons of TNT (a "ton" is a short ton here, 2,000 pounds or 907 kg). The word "uranium" is forbidden, of course: They call it 25—that is, the rare, usable isotope U^{235}—the more common isotope U^{238} is referred to as 28, and plutonium-239 is called 49. The code is simple: Natural uranium has the atomic number 92, that is, there are 92 protons in the nucleus, and the atomic weight 238, that is, 238 elements in the nucleus (146 neutrons, 92 protons); plutonium has atomic number 94 and atomic weight 239. The code takes the last digit of the atomic number and adds the last digit of the atomic weight.

The secretary hands Goldfarb a mimeographed copy of Serber's lectures: *The Los Alamos Primer*. The cover is a screaming collection of fresh red stamps, warning the reader that the document is top secret. The copy is numbered. It contains only 24 pages. Goldfarb opens it right in the administrative office. The enormous, preposterous, almost incomprehensible fact that a mere kilogram of metal can be transformed in less than an eyeblink into something that has an explosive force twenty million times more powerful than its equivalent weight in TNT is casually mentioned on the first page, in the third paragraph of the document. It makes Goldfarb mumble. He runs to his dorm cubicle and throws himself flat on his back on his army bunk. He tries to imagine the unimaginable.

He leafs through the document. It was put together in endearing haste; lots of handwritten symbols and quickly erased typos and hand-drawn graphs of fission diameters and detonator mechanisms. Paragraph 21 ("Autocatalytic Methods") offers a picture of what looks like a stiff and angry penis pointing at a primitive vagina with uterus. The uterus this thing is yearning for is called the "active material." It is a sphere of radioactive metal, not quite large enough to form a critical mass—that is, it won't emit enough neutrons to spontaneously start a chain reaction. This sphere is suspended in a hollow shell inside a layer of insulating material. The phallus is the gunlock that contains the missing part of the critical mass. Shoot this rod into the hole, and fire and doom is the result. The mechanism is simple and elegant and it reminds Goldfarb of that other reason for his journey: the girl who reads Goethe in German.

He knocks at his neighbor's stall. "Where does a man go to relax around here?" The man hardly looks up from the scientific journal he is reading. "Bach or Charleston?" "Charleston." Where else would his Hannah be than in the firm grip of the dance floor?

"Try Theater 2," the man says. He looks a this watch. "Hell, I'll take you there myself." He jumps off the bed and extends his hand. "Leon," he introduces himself.

"Goldfarb."

They walk through the late evening. It isn't easy to manage the usual small talk when there's almost nothing you're free to talk about. So, what do you do? *Verboten.* Where did you get your degree? *Taboo.* How long have you been here? *We don't talk about that.* Leon shows Goldfarb the landmarks. The Tech Area, the place where the Gadget is being built, is surrounded by a blinding circle of search-lights. The buildings are sharply delineated in chilly, thin air. It reminds Goldfarb of a film set, *das Wilde Westen* in an expressionist, Hans Janowitz version, gory and improvised. The illusion is enhanced by the group of young men in blue jeans at the entrance, their thumbs hooked behind the loops of their workman's pants, cigarette smoke spiraling around their wide-brimmed hats. Ha, *Mutti* would love it! Leon shows his security badge and is allowed through. Goldfarb's temporary papers raise more suspicion, but eventually he gets in as well.

In Theater 2, feet are stomping to the rhythm of a band of soldiers with straw-colored hair and squinting eyes. A fiddle, a banjo, a bass, a drum kit. The crowd laughs and talks; against the ceiling, an almost solid cloud of nicotine sways in rhythm with the music, though a tad slower, the pale ghost image of parties past. (Tobacco and alcohol and coffee, these are the substances that keep the city on its feet.) A long table at the far end of the wall bows deep under an onslaught of sandwiches and pastries and bottles of beer and bowls with fruit punch. The room is filled with Nobel Prize winners and their wives, and with lonely future Nobel Prize winners. On his way to the table Goldfarb overhears snippets of con-versation. Somebody discusses Planck's lectures and regrets how forgotten they are. Somebody else is talking about the "compilation" that's expected to come in tomorrow from the "Three-Igloo Workshop." A third is trying to get a fourth to agree to a date for Square Dance evening. On the dance floor, the professors waggle, slow and ungainly as bears—they call this dancing.

Of course she's there. He sees her as soon as he steps in. She's the only one who slides over the floor with style and elegance, as if she were wearing roller skates, as if Benny Goodman were playing and not this poor man's orchestra led by Pig Bodine. She dances with such grace and abandon that you could mistake it for the evening of her wedding. Hannah Sidis, Goldfarb's double palindrome, waltzes in the arms, very *much* in the arms, of another man. Goldfarb's eyes sting. It must be the lack of oxygen at this elevation, or maybe it's the pall of tobacco. Then the dance is over and Hannah walks to the edge of the crowd with heaving chest. She grabs her dance partner's hand and pulls him behind her. Apparently, he isn't just some guy she met at the dance; they belong together.

Suddenly a glass of punch appears in Goldfarb's hand, an offering sure to please his G*ddess. Well, then, go to her. He hesitates. During that second of hesitation, she notices him across the room—oh yes, she notices him. Her eyes open wide in happy recognition, with a naturalness that brings him instant delight. But no, she doesn't come running. She casts down her gaze and keeps on talking with her—what? Her boyfriend? Her colleague? Her date? Her lover?—and then she looks at him again, but now her eyes warn him off: "Goldfarb, stay away!" But then, immediately after sending that signal, she winks at him as if they are both part of some hilarious conspiracy. But what would that conspiracy be? The young man at her arm, stub-nosed and unathletic, his hair indifferently cut and carelessly brushed, is obviously a scientist. When he looks away to check out the remaining dancers, Hannah locks her gaze into Goldfarb's and she brings the tips of three fingers together, thumb, index finger, and middle finger, and she kisses the tips of this entwined trinity ever so lightly, and across light years of separation she stares deep into her former lover's eyes—French chefs make this gesture to indicate that the cream sauce is divine, but all Goldfarb sees is the clear and vulgar echo of her *Pudding* story, and all he remembers is how blissfully she used to employ those fingers to wind her secret little engine of joy, what dizzyingly wicked witch's circles she'd performed on her little clitoris, and what dizzying effects that motion caused in the both of them. Now her tongue flickers over the three fingertips, fast and furious, and she wrinkles her nose so naughtily that Goldfarb's face turns a violent pink; he blushes so hard it makes his skull prickle. Is it possible that nobody else in the room noticed the gesture? He has to do something and he has to do it now; he has to go talk to her; he has to touch her, never mind her companion. But all he does is incline his head, a small nod to indicate his respect for her inventiveness. Then Hannah shifts her attention and kisses her dance partner's neck ever so lightly. And then she winks at Goldfarb again. What the fuck is happening here?

She floats over the dance floor with Bad Haircut Boy and Goldfarb watches the man's hands slide down her back. When those hands take a firm and greedy hold of Hannah's derrière, Goldfarb finds his hands clutched into fists inside the pockets of his wide corduroy pants. That man's paws on her buttocks, Hannah's head on that man's shoulder. But then, with every turn, over and over again: those fluttering eyelids, those stealthy, playful glances aimed at Goldfarb from over her partner's shoulders.

She has plenty of hip for her date, but she has eyes only for Goldfarb.

If you find your G*ddess, should you not follow her?

•

In the budding chill of night and with the threat of snow clouds overhead, Goldfarb raises his gaze to the Origin. Between the clouds the stars flicker like distant and trustworthy allies.

The world, as physics teaches us, is mostly darkness. Out of and into this darkness the universe was born. It's the secrecy of this darkness that binds the world together, in uncertain balance with the equally dark and fundamental forces that tear everything apart—nature has decreed in its laws that it will slowly self destruct; matter is contractually obligated to commit suicide. From this darkness too, from this symbiosis of the force that separates us and the force that draws us all together, the human being and the human being's being are born. This darkness likewise is the source of art, of the silent and heroic struggle that results when healing and destruction converge. The canvas of life swirls with Vincent's night visions; from the cross-roads wails the echo of Robert Johnson's slide guitar.

Goldfarb remembers a question he once asked his mother. The universe is said to be endless, with an infinite number of stars. Why then is the night sky not a blinding field of light instead of this dark blanket with pinpoints of silver? His mother did not know the answer. Even worse, she did not understand why her boy considered this to be such an important question. Goldfarb knows the answer now; it's quite simple. The stars are indeed innumerable, and if they all shined at the same time, the night sky would indeed light up white, not black. But stars are like a meadow of fireflies: Not all of them are turned on at the same time, and that is why we see points. The lifetime of a star is measured in millions of years, the lifetime of the universe in billions: A star's life is a mere flicker. And the light of the stars that are farthest away still hasn't reached us. Another way of putting this is to say that the world we observe is necessarily incomplete.

In that darkness then Goldfarb hides in the piñon bushes. Their needles prick his skin wherever they can and he lets his gaze travel downward again, to what is so sinfully illuminated by a small bedroom lamp deep inside a prefab barrack house. Fascinated, Golfarb watches the dark gyrations of a very different, equally unfathomable, equally incandescent, equally cloudy, equally mysterious Origin.

•

The house of Minos is cursed. All the women of Minos's house are possessed by an intemperate erotic passion. Europa, Minos's mother, was abducted by Zeus in the form of a bull, dragged to Crete and a cruel motherhood. Minos's wife fell for yet another bull, and one of his daughters took off with a bull slayer and ended up left alone on a stony beach. And his other daughter, Phaedra, who was married by fate to the returned bull slayer, fell in love with somebody else: Hippolytus. One complicating factor was that he was her stepson. Hippolytus was wont to work out naked in the gymnasium and Phaedra was wont to spy. Dirt cakes into the sweat and oil on Hippolytus's torso, his hair gets tousled, his muscles dance and slide when he throws his hunting spear. His toes kick up the sand of the arena, his hips twist and Phaedra's gaze singles out his yummy butt and the undulating movements of his supple cock. She loved this stud the way her mother loved the bull, with an unruly passion, and just like her mother she knew her love was doomed from the start. The other complicating factor, by the way, was *odisse puellas diceris*—it was whispered that he despised the ladies. Phaedra sent Hippolytus a letter of seduction dictated by none other than Eros himself. Hippolytus spurned her advances. His stepmother got bolder; she stepped into the arena and touched him. Again, he snubbed her. Then she hanged herself. The erotic letter was discovered and the fuming Theseus sentenced his son—that incestuous villain—to death. The G*ddess Artemis appeared to Theseus to tell him the true story, laying bare the ruse of Aphrodite and her son Eros, but it was too late.

In other words, nothing good ever comes from voyeurism.

Goldfarb, quit looking and make your move.

•

"I was afraid you wouldn't come."

"How could I *not* come?"

His voice is rife with sobbing and dizzy with desire—it makes Hannah shiver. But she keeps her eyes tightly shut. Behind the purple veil of her eyelids she imagines herself the way he must observe her—the creaminess of her skin in the soft orange glow of the bedroom lamp, an exact copy of Goldfarb's Calder lamp—and she hopes that he will notice this too, not now but sometime soon, and realize that she spent her few hours of spare time during the recruitment session in New York in the antique shops of lower Manhattan—that this artifact cost her half her life savings. And she hopes that at that time he will take a closer look at the lamp and notice the markings—that he will notice how and where her fingers have polished the patina, and that he will realize how she has been holding on—literally holding on—to the image of the bronze mother and by extension to the son. He will grasp, she hopes, that while she was caressing the flower of her sex, she coaxed out of the cold wishing lamp the very real genie of Goldfarb's deliciously warm cock, obstinate and steadfast as a pillar of bronze. Not now, though—now she wants Goldfarb to have eyes only for her and her radiant nakedness. She wants his gaze to burn her skin, she wants his breath to make her eyelids flutter—she wants him, she wants to see him, she wants to watch him undress with haste and without taking his eyes off her glorious body for even a second, she wants to see his manhood spring to attention, she wants to see the scented drop of sultry oil that glistens at its very tip, an offering for her and her alone, and—above all—she wants to look into those moist, wide eyes of his. She wants to fathom his awe and his disbelief; she wants to drown in the deep joy and blind admiration of his gaze—but no, although she wants to see him so much it makes her stomach ache, she keeps her eyes closed. Her gift to him tonight is the freedom to possess her with his gaze without any shame and unimpeded—but she does feel him watch her, yes she does: His gaze caresses her shoulders, his eyes slide down her torso until they reach the soft curves of her buttocks, his stare hooks on the umber shadows down there, and she shifts her leg ever so slightly, so he can behold the glistening bounty, so he can smell how wet and soft she is, so he can realize how long she has been waiting for him. She has to hold back the urge to reach out and tame the small purring predator in her lap with a few practiced strokes of her slender fingers. Finally he has seen enough: His clothes rustle. Hannah squeezes her eyes even more tightly—tears spray her cheeks when Goldfarb touches the gate of her inner lips, first with probing fingers, then with his prick, so soft and so hard at the same time, so imperative and tender, so raw and not-to-be-denied.

"I'm here," whispers Goldfarb. "Here I am, *Liebling*, here I am."

"Goldfarb." When he has completely vanished inside her, the familiar tidal wave takes over, the unstoppable wave of orgasm—her mouth opens, cries burst from her lips, her forehead hits the mattress, and her ears rings with Goldfarb's own cries, and then she comes and he goes on until he too collapses, delectable dead weight on top of her.

Ah, the things we do for love and time and memory!

•

Hannah knows her classics. She's read Ovid, that very useful third chapter of the *Ars Amatoria*, but even if she hadn't, she would have known how to proceed; she would have known how to drape her body for maximum effect. She did not need

Ovid to understand what an effective yet dangerous force jealousy can be. She did not doubt for one second that Goldfarb had followed her and her date through the streets of Los Alamos. She also knew he wouldn't start a fight. And she was quite certain he had stayed behind in the bushes to watch. Like him, she is a scientist. She knows what scientists do. Scientists observe, they look in from the outside.

And so she left her curtains open and the lights on.

Another thing scientists enjoy is experimental manipulation. That was something she was very good at, manipulating. She offered her date a nightcap. After all, he had some good dirt on the new right hand of that flabby narcissus Teller, that Ulam guy. She sat close to him on the couch, she put her hand over his, she sent him an obvious smile, and she made sure that all of this could be seen clearly from the window. She allowed the man to grope her a little, nothing serious—they kept all their clothes on. G*d, men always go for this shit; a man is so happy with so little. And after they made out for a while, Hannah yawned ostentatiously, this time making sure that the yawn was hidden from the peeping tom in the prickly bushes. She had to get up early in the morning, you know how that goes, we're starting up a new series of experiments. Would you mind if I . . . ? No, no, he understood. Sure? Yeah, sure, no problem. That was so sweet of him! One last kissie-kiss? A hug? The man holds on to her with the desperate, oppressive, clingy hug of a drowning man. For a second she lets him, then she resolutely pushes him away. He doesn't like that, but she knows his type: He is secretly quite pleased that he spent a few moments in her arms, that he made it to second base. He might even be relieved to be sent back to his dorm; he too has to be up early in the morning, and physicists who are thinking their way through a problem don't like being distracted, not even by the joys of sex. She accompanies the man to the door and kisses him on the mouth with apparent delight. When he walks down the path she does her best not to look around for Goldfarb, keeping her gaze fixed on her date's retreating back. As soon as the man has rounded the corner, Hannah steps inside, quite leisurely, and closes the door. No, she does not lock it.

This is the test. She leaves the curtains open, but turns off the overhead lights. She takes the eight steps to her bedroom in the dark. She switches on the lamp next to the bed and leaves the bedroom door open. If Goldfarb is still outside, he must have his eyes glued to the window by now. She undresses. Her blouse slides off her shoulders. The thick woolen skirt slides down her legs. She rolls down her stockings. She unpins her hair. She shakes it loose. She removes all of her underwear. She does it in a businesslike manner, not particularly slowly and not particularly fast. She doesn't give any of this a particularly sensual twist—she's just a working girl getting ready for bed. This is the moment of truth. Either Goldfarb has disappeared into the night, pained or disgusted by jealously, or else he will be at her side *subito*, and then she knows he will be hers forever. It's cold, but Hannah arranges herself artfully on top of her covers, a precious bonbon in a pretty nest of soft, expensive tissue paper. She spreads her hair over the pillow and turns her back to the door. Her sweet, sweet butt, her most delicious sin against the Holy Spirit, offers itself to the gaze of whoever is at the window, and deep in the shadows thrown by the Calder lamp lies the Alpha and Omega, the Beginning and Ending of Goldfarb's world: Hannah's succulent, lily-white cunt.

•

She is the one who breaks the silence. (If it was summer, the cicadas would have sung outside, but now the first snow of the night is falling softly, and the light makes the inside of the room feel like an alembic.)

She turns off the lamp.

"Goldfarb, you know what we're doing here, right?"

Goldfarb sighs.

"Love?" he says, and he surprises himself. Why did he put a question mark on that one-word sentence? "Love is what it is, Hannah, no? Love, right?"

I followed you all the way down here is what he wants to say, and he doesn't mean: the short walk from the dance hall to your house. He means—he doesn't really know what he means anymore. Did he really travel all the way here to Los Alamos because of her, or was he so desperate to get in because it would further his career and satisfy his thirst for knowledge—because this is the place he simply has to be, the place of his calling? Calling: what a strange word for a Jewish boy to use!

Hannah reaches for the dresser. She opens a drawer. She rummages around until she finds what she's looking for.

"No," she says. "I mean: what it is we are doing here, the collective we, all of us in this fake city in the middle of the desert, in the middle of this continent, at the center of this so-called New World—*what it is we are doing*?" Goldfarb nods cautiously. Where is this going? It's possible to describe what it is the scientists are doing, but not in words that are appropriate to two people lying next to each other in bed, naked and satisfied—words like power, war, victory, destruction. Hannah apparently doesn't want to say those words either. She lights a cigarette, not because she needs the nicotine, but because she enjoys watching it write its postcoital arabesques in the air. Hannah glows pink with contentment, even in the snowy light Goldfarb can see that. She hugs her breasts, she hugs herself—she radiates self-satisfaction. He puts his arms around her. Softly he rocks her body. She feels hot to the touch. The bedsprings creak.

Her hands feel under the mattress. She brings out a book, a slender volume.

"Have you read this?" Hannah asks. Even in the dark he can read the bright red letters on the black cover. Goldfarb knows the book, yes—*What is to be Done?*

Of course he's read that book. They have a copy at home—*Mutti* gave him one for his sixteenth birthday ("When such things still make a difference, my boy."). Of course he had read Lenin, Lenin was such an integral part of Goldfarb's family history: His father had been killed because he was a member of the Communist Party, and his mother had been made a victim for acting on her convictions. That's why they fled the country, that's how they landed in the United States. It wasn't something that held the interest of the security officer during his interview in Manhattan for too long, their family history. So many of the immigrating physicists had or used to have communist sympathies, and every enemy of Hitler is a friend of the USA, etcetera. Goldfarb got his security clearance, communist sympathies or not, and off to the Hill he went.

"I read it," he replies curtly. He sees the relevance. The Soviet Revolution is less than thirty years old, the workers' paradise is a beacon for every progressive thinker. Stalin is the only one who had been able to stand his ground against the Nazi violence. France, Holland, Italy, Belgium, Spain: they all had been brought to their knees. Communism is the only surviving bastion against the brown oil spill.

"Do you know what it means?"

Again Goldfarb nods. He knows Lenin's theses, they are self-evident to him. The Party is the vanguard of the Revolution, its elite injects the masses with the correct class consciousness. Property is theft, religion is the opium that placates the masses on demand. The truth can only be conquered with arms.

"What is this, Hannah? Why this sudden need for philosophy in your boudoir?"

"But do you realize what it means now, in the current climate?" She turns over, so that she can look him straight in the eye. She puts her hand on his balls. Under her touch, his testicles feel spongy and vulnerable, yes, *atomic*. Then it's his turn to light a cigarette, shaking.

"It is no philosophy, honey. It is a user's manual."

"A manual?"

"Think. What happens when this"—she lowers her voice to a hoarse whisper—"this . . . thing, this so-called Gadget falls into the wrong hands?"

"What," she adds, with a voice deep as the humming inside a beehive, "What if Hitler learns about this?"

"What," she further adds, with a voice sweet as the honey inside that humming beehive, "What if Heisenberg has already thought everything through, just like you have in your lonely room at Harvard? What if he—just like us—has collected a small army of the brightest minds, all working on the same project?"

"..."

"What, Goldfarb, if Hitler—just like us—is almost ready? What if his scientists finish first? What if he already *has* the bomb?"

"..."

"What if the Depression continues; what if America, like Germany, falls prey to fascism?"

The smoke is rising to the ceiling. The glowing red point of Goldfarb's cigarette is reflected in Hannah's eyes; they too glow with visible heat.

"We cannot deliberately close our eyes" (This is a literal quote from Vladimir Ilyich.) "We need the bomb, Goldfarb. We—not just America, but also the Communist International."

"What am I to you, Hannah?" Goldfarb asks softly. "What am I?" The words get lost in the sound of his cigarette sizzling.

He clears his throat, he raises his voice. "Who are those others? What do they mean to you? The men you dance with, the men you . . . kiss?"

This time she hears him. "Other ones?" she asks. "What other ones? I play a game, my darling. Its name is deceit. I listen and I learn. Amazing how a few glasses of wine and some attention can make any physicist talkative. I let him spend an intoxicating night on my sofa, and he gives up all his secrets. Those man are useful, Goldfarb—nothing less, nothing more. The man you saw me with tonight—a few weeks ago, I showed him your letter; he was the one who got you here. They tell me what they're doing. They brag, they do their best to impress me, they want to show off their importance. I write it all down. Every few months, I report to a courier of the Soviet embassy, in Santa Fe or Albuquerque."

"So—what am I to you? How do I fit in with your plans?"

Goldfarb sounds bitter. Of course he sounds bitter.

"Goldfarb, somebody like you, somebody who can recreate the crucial equation on his own, can never be just a pawn in the game. Tomorrow they will give you, I guarantee it, a white badge—Access All Areas. You are so much smarter than anybody else on this Hill; you already know so much and soon you will know more than all of my informers put together. I no longer need them. They're gone from my mind, Goldfarb. Just like that. Gone! *Poof!* They are nothing to me. What are you to me? Everything!" Fiercely, she blows out a mouthful of smoke. "Can't you tell, Goldfarb? Can't you tell?"

"Why do you trust me? Why are you telling me all this? What if I go to the military police? What if I take your story to Oppenheimer?"

"Then the network will die," Hannah says. "It's as simple as that."

A sob escapes his throat.

"Aw, Goldfarb, please don't cry!"

She puts her hand on his mouth.

"Goldfarb. Yes. I didn't answer your first question. Yes. We go deep, Goldfarb, you and I, don't we go deep? We go deep, much deeper than this, deeper than that . . . that slit in my skin? We're made for each other, don't you think? Aren't we made for each other?"

Goldfarb says nothing. Hannah strokes his hair, his neck, his lips, his ear.

"Stay. In the morning you will forgive me—you *have to* forgive me."

What is to be Done? He should get out of bed. He should get dressed. He should walk back to his dorm and get a good night's sleep in his own bed. But he cannot bring himself to do that. He simply can't. He's too worn out—a day that was way too long, and with such an abundance of emotions. And how could he walk away from those arms, from these riches, from this world of joy and pleasure so totally different from anything else he has previously experienced—how could he take his leave and say farewell to all this, farewell forever?

He is already flat on his back, his favorite position for the work of thoughtful deliberation.

Their breath fills the room with poisonous carbon dioxide.

"I'll think about it," he says.

In response she kisses him softly on the chest.

And then Goldfarb falls asleep. The long journey, the shock of Serber's essay, the greater shock of jealousy, and then the biggest shock of all, those immense peaks of joy and the cataclysm of their lovemaking—it's all too much. Within seconds, his eyelids flutter under the heavy burden of exhaustion.

He mumbles.

His lips move, but no sound rises from his Adam's apple.

He babbles.

Then that stops too.

Goldfarb sleeps, and Hannah, that devilish Hannah watches him closely—long and hard.

•

This shouldn't become a habit, thinks Goldfarb. To reminisce, to open up a bottle of scotch, to get very sad, and then to reach for the phone. Let's not make a habit of this. But that woman, well, she's something else. There's something about her that makes him do things he doesn't want to do: to roam through his memory, to pick up the phone. Oh dear. Okay. Enough self-control for today. He picks up the phone. He hesitates, his finger above the MEMORY button.

Enough! The man reflected in the window, this man dressed in black with deep furrows in his face, the man whose lonely ghostly image converges every night with the image of the golden, youthful G*ddess on the column—that man has suffered enough for one night. That man needs to be cheered up. Right now. Before it's too late.

He presses the button. The LED screen—Siemens has sent him their most expensive model, a prototype not yet officially on the market—shows the alphabetical list of his contacts. He doesn't even have to scroll down. She is on top of his list: his "-a."

מ

DIE PROZEDUR

The first thing we see are her adorable bare feet. Why don't we hold on to that image for a while, why don't we contemplate those miraculous little contraptions made of bones and tendons, why do we not admire those architectural wonders of tensile strength and litheness, why don't we study carefully the beauty of that little propulsion engine in its skin so tight and gleaming? How strikingly do its well-oiled insteps contrast with the pale dull pinewood of the stairs; how delightfully do the marvelous feet transition into the columns of her legs—smooth tanned pillars, slender and perfect as any art nouveau column. Then our gaze travels upwards and slides past the fraying fringes of her loosely-tied bath robe; it ascends to the scarcely hidden peaks and devilish valley of her bosom, and then, higher still, it climbs to the melancholy manna of her lips and, ever upwards, to her eyes, sensually shut, and it finally comes to rest at her noble forehead and her hurried snarl of hair. A few rebellious curls have escaped the tangle of pins; they frame her beautiful face in sweet disarray. She yawns, even though the day is still young—the whole family sits gathered around the midday table, middle-class style, their plates piled high with food that looks scandalously rich in fat and carbohydrates. Their tummies grumble and they are all a tad giggly—they are awaiting their strong son/brother and his young bride—but what business does she have coming down the stairs alone, and in that state! She greets her in-laws absentmindedly, with the smallest nod imaginable. She opens the sideboard (*their* sideboard!), and rummages around until she finds a tray, which she then proceeds to heap with food—she grabs half a loaf of bread from the breakfast table and puts it on the tray after squeezing it impatiently to test its freshness; she piles up slices of ham and cheese, and when she reaches over to steal the butter dish she bumps the corner of the tray hard into Gregor's shoulder.

A short cry of pain hangs in the breakfast room.

She doesn't hear it or heed it. "Ha! Fruit! Just what we need to build up Frankie's strength!" She turns to Frank's mother. "He needs it, you know," she adds. The implication of her words makes her mother-in-law blush. Helena reaches again to the center of the table and brushes her sleeves against her father-in-law's ears; they turn as violently red as his wife's. When she straightens up again, a pyramid of apples, oranges, pears, and *yes we have no* bananas wobbles at the center of the tray.

She's done. She turns around with a swagger and places her gazelle's foot on the bottom stair, but then rethinks her move—quickly she snatches the two bottles of wine from the sideboard. She giggles and coos as she climbs out of sight. A door opens and bangs shut. Then a dull thud: In the shocked silence a single orange comes bouncing down the stairs (tom-tom-*tom*tomtom), rolling right to father's stunned feet. We're now treated to a close-up of Gregor's face; the camera follows his gaze all the way to the closed bedroom door. His pupils contract and expand rhythmically, as if his eyes were the locus of his breathing. We, the audience, understand that soon Helena will leave Frank for his brother—that, as always happens, the desirable woman will trade the pale student for the brave soldier.

This is, after all, the song of ages: The warrior takes his due, the student learns a lesson.

A collective sigh is heard throughout the theater. It's partially a sigh of sadness, provoked by hunger—fresh delicacies like the ones shown on the screen have become *verdammt* scarce over the course of the war; but foremost it's a sigh of lust—we want to see more of that pouting derrière that climbed the stairs so briskly; we hunger for the curves of that woman, so worldly, so inimitably elegant, so feminine and yet so provocatively androgynous in her desire. And in the front row, deep in the purple plush, sits Helena herself, dreamily chewing on one of her thumbs while the hand of her movie father-in-law walks up her thigh.

Whack!

She smacks his fingers with her rolled-up program.

•

A shadow appears in the fog, a ghost backlit by the toxic steam of a street lantern that makes a heroic last stand against darkness. The specter draws nearer, and the long rays of sulfurous light that shoot out behind it—cold fingers of lightning, filaments of a fluorescent web venomous with slime—make it look as if the man came here especially for me, to drag me, reluctant Don Juan, straight to hell.

A man.

A man in uniform.

A black uniform.

Black as the night that surrounds us. Completely, utterly black; a black that sucks the oxygen out of the air; a black that is not a presence, but an absence. A man like a hole, a man negating the possibility of life. On his lapels the perfect blackness is disturbed by a glimpse of silver—the morning star has descended from the heavens, or is it a comet, a lump of dead ice flickering at the horizon?

Black.

Black as the ink used to sign inviolable contracts.

Black as soot. Black as the fallout of scorched dreams.

Black as the back of a mirror.

Black as potting soil, reeking of minerals and manure.

Black as charcoal. Charcoal cleanses, charcoal filters—the air around the man is clean, the air around him is pure.

A uniform in black.

A black uniform.

A uniform as black as mine.

The darkness begets darkness.

A mysterious rune on the band around his arm—a pierced letter V.

The man holds out his hand, and around his fingers dances the glow of the lamp, like the will-o'-the-wisps on the soggy ground of my youth, like Saint Elmo's fire flickering around a mast, like gangrene tightening its grip around a dying heart. He holds out that hand and I almost—almost—let out a scream.

"Come," the man says. "Come. Follow me."

I drop my arms. I did not even realize I had raised them in front of me, but I had—had I wanted to repel the specter?

"And could you please button up your pants?"

I quickly do as requested.

He snaps his fingers. It is as simple as that: An engine revs up, headlights project their soothing cones into the night.

He must be about my age. We have the same rank. Why then do I follow him?

I step into the Mercedes. He closes the velvet curtains, curtains that are, of course, spun of the blackest of black.

•

"You approach me and you ask me, 'What is man? What is life?' With amazement you contemplate the gigantic sun and its light that travels through the icy cold of space to reach our tiny planet 'Earth,' but your gaze does not stop there; on the contrary, you look deeper into space, that ocean of dense fog where new worlds unfold before your eyes. You discover, my dear comrades, you discover the concept of . . . infinity.

"And now your gaze turns to history. You descend into the darkest days of prehistoric times and you ascend to the present, you follow a golden thread of logic, but once you want to go beyond, the thread breaks off and the infinity of space turns into the infinity of time. Space and time show you who you really are, a cosmic dwarf, and all your knowledge brings you nothing. Do this, and you will begin to despair.

"But one thing remains, there is one thing to hold on to: the idea of Man—the cosmic being, the most brilliant among creatures. You embrace all who came before you, you hold in your mind all your present comrades—they share this brief but momentous moment of world history with you. Yes, there is no other way to describe this brief but momentous moment than to use that most incomprehensible of words, the word 'life.'

"Look around you, and you will see that the two billion people on this 'Earth' are divided into two camps, two armed factions, each looking at existence in opposite ways. You will see that there are people like you and me, human beings who stand up with conviction to fight the selfless struggle against earthly filth, human beings who put their faith in an undying 'ideal'—but you will also see that there are human beings who are simply consumed by this earthly life, who live only for the moment. They are not like us, comrades—they despise any form of spiritual aspiration.

"You see, my dear friends, we National Socialists are different.

"We can safely claim that we are the only idealists left in Germany—for this is simply true. Our enemies, the settled bourgeois and the aimless Marxist, are both vulgar materialists. The former defends his unmerited prerogatives, while the latter fights to make all mankind ultimately equal to the former. *Quatsch*! We, comrades, we believe in a historic calling for the German People, and therefore we will fight, today and tomorrow; fight against cronyism and snobbery and the lack of social consciousness of the morally bankrupt German middle class. Likewise we will fight against the class struggle; with passion we will fight against the Internationalists, against the nauseating demagogy of foreign races.

"We are free, my dear friends. We do not judge people on the basis of their bank accounts or the dusty papers of nobility in their coffers, we look at their achievements and their moral character: That is the ethical thrust of our ideal. Don't you see, my comrades, that our movement has protected and saved the Greater German Nation just for you—that we have defended the Fatherland and taken on this historical mission just to preserve our beloved Germanic Peoples, the men and women we so passionately believe in?

"Well then, comrades, the hour of truth is almost here, and courage will not fail us, whatever our personal destinies may be. Quite possibly we will die on the battlefield, but we will die in honor, knowing very well that we have achieved the pinnacle of true goodness, that we have given the most exalted gift anyone can ever give their country: the gift of his life!"

After that invigorating speech our training at the *Junkerschule* in Bad Stolz is over. We are now SS-officers, ready to be shipped off to the front, ready to reap glory. But before we do that, we are marched into town, fifteen miles of goose-stepping straight into the heart of Munich, the city where the National Socialist world revolution began, and we sing until our lungs burst, for we are filled with joy: It's not every day that we get the order to carefully wash the flap between the foreskin and head of our penises—the officers even mock-threaten that they will subject the area to the white glove test! It is a wonderful paradox: Before we shall most likely give our lives, we shall also—and what a lovely paradox it is!—give our *lives*, in a breeding camp of the highest quality. Carefully selected women are anxiously awaiting our carefully selected semen. With joy and the utmost awareness of the gravitas of our mission we march into the city at the first signs of dusk. Against the backdrop of the granite mountains the houses stand blue with cold, and the sharpness of the evening air drives hordes of adolescent girls into the streets. They push their baby carriages with pride, displaying their newborns in heaps of down blankets. The young mothers rule the sidewalks of the city, for they have given living proof of their total servitude to Führer and Fatherland, their unqualified dedication to the propagation of the People: They parade the future generation of soldiers; they carried them in their wombs, they fed with their own warm milk.

Onwards, my friends, onwards and upwards, all of us: Let us quickly bridge the short distance from barracks to bordello!

•

The place is bristling with brilliant brides. On sumptuous sofas, nefarious nymphs display their advanced states of ovulation, nude *à la Nicoise*. There is Something For Everybody: Purposefully fattened Melancholic Madonnas (magnanimous

Roman semi-virgins) present us with nipples proud and red as strawberries and beg us for our cream; bleached Danish *Muschis* play some merry *trompe-la-queue* with gamy gentlemen in monocles while Parisian *poupées* parade their perky asses, peacock feathers sticking out the cracks; licentious ladies from Leipzig perform dizzying duos on the flute while sorrowful orphans from Weimar chew bitter acorns harvested from Goethe's favorite tree; sari-ous Indian idylls flourish while daring Berlin darlings display their round butts to meat inspectors with boldly red-tipped stamps; Japanese man-fodder thrashes about, suspended *koi*-ly from butcher's hooks by intricate Gordian knots, a knife helpfully weaved in at their throats; philosophically inclined felines with kleptocratic claws finger the naked gangly minds of a gaggle of public intellectuals who absentmindedly sip absinthe from the bowls of their own navels; cunts wide and bald as the Mongolian steppe glisten with pink caviar, and in that corner over there Bavarian belugas thrash around in bays of faux lace—there are roses all around and cinnamon, and the soft sour smell of sweat mixes with the steam of holy water that sings in the silver samovar—the kettle has no lid, for it was this silver lid, or so the madam tells me (she must have instantly perceived my literary interests), that Jan Potocki melted down to load his gun with on that fateful November day in 1815 when he took his life. The document I carry, an *SS-Befehl* signed with unusual flourish by our otherwise dour commander, will grant me a Dionysian hour with any member of this feral pack of urban fauna, an hour filled with the most exquisite emptiness, the most notorious nothingness a man could ever wish for—I will become a Nordic heathen, anointed with holy pussy oil, and I will . . .

Oh, the grotesque fingers of the pianist—unthinkingly he smashes out the most offensive melodies against the pink brothel walls, melodies so vulgar and banal that the whole fornicating crowd can't help but hum along; the blazing wind of their pumping nether-cheeks makes the flowers (the one happy note on that otherwise horribly out-of-tune piano) sway rhythmically on top of their absurd stalks. Really, any minute one expects Mickey Mouse to walk in and take over the pianistic duties. I am perplexed by those bouquets of cruelly amputated sex organs, lusting after insects that have long frozen to death, silently screaming for fertilization, and even though the air in the room is literally saturated with seed (have a whiff: the smell is everywhere!), it does not cool the itch of pistils and stamens. Perhaps the flowers are made of artificial silk? So that they fit with the fountains of fake champagne, the heaps of snail's eggs blackened with shoe polish, the piles of cupcakes made out of papier-mâché?

"*Machen sie es ganz schön literarisch, ja?*" Madam (her accent gets more Polish by the minute) employs her expert's eye to pick out for her hesitant customers—your humble servant among them—what it is they really need. Apparently, I hunger for the exotic and the complex: Madam presents me with a Scheherazade. Although this presumed beauty's head and body are hidden underneath an elaborate veil, her ass is bare, quite prettily perfumed and finely powdered, and a stirring in my loins tells me that this is indeed what I was longing for. Daintily the orgiastic oracle sticks out her darling derrière—she has been created in the delicious mold of Himmler's harem: none of the boyish smallness in the hips that has been popularized by Marlene Dietrich or any other of those anorexic movie stars from the Weimar days; no, this precious lady is gifted with the creamy fullness of a farmer's daughter, she is pleasingly plump and tangibly sweet. "You are a literary man, sir," Madam whispers, "And don't you have a literary rule of thumb? Well, then, sir, why don't you apply that ruler of yours to this scrumptious ass!"

I send telepathic messages to this artificial odalisque: Could you, my dear, slowly wag that tail for me? She can, and she does. Could you turn a little to the right, so that the light of the lamp might shine on the moistest of your secrets? So she can and so she does. She even hands me a small kerosene lamp, so that I can conduct a close inspection at my leisure, and moist she is, I see—the holy never-before-glimpsed mysteries shine warm and juicy, they make me drunk and giddy, and I sniff the aroma of that sun-ripened tropical fruit with relish, I inhale the scent of that small succulent animal with nostril-widening delight, and I . . . (Such is my euphoria that metaphors well up without my prompting. A poem is a-brewing and this woman is a blank, unwritten-upon page—and white ink springs so helpfully from the very tip of my ready pen.)

My uniform pants are too tight all of a sudden, and the woman helps me out of my predicament, unbuckling and unbuttoning me with long, slender fingers; she slides my underwear down to my ankles while Madam, always willing to lend a hand, ties a satin bow (a silver cat-bell at one end) around my balls, so that my beloved can safely pull me closer by that most gentle of leashes. When I am almost hers, she puts her lovely lips to my eager ear and moans some Baudelaire. "*Luxe*," she sighs while her happy hands grip my buttocks. "*Calme*," she urges, inspired by the slow insertion of her immodest middle finger. And then she loads her mouth with salacious saliva before intoning a sloppy "*Volupté*" that coincides with a most inspiring internal *touché* of the prostate.

Ach! What? French? She speaks French! Unaccented, seamless, vile, nasty French! I am a Flemish nationalist; French is the language of the oppressor—never-ever will I tolerate being addressed in that language, not now that the German army has liberated Flanders from the yoke of the Francophone, not now that we have finally come home to the Great German Empire! G*d Almighty, what is my

Flemish finger doing in the slimy depths of a Française? This is no high-class stud farm, this is an ordinary brothel! Angrily I abort the incipient copulation and I look around me with new eyes. Truly a disgusting sight! These are my courageous companions? These corny country bumpkins who labor away (all together now!) at their farcical fucks, their assholes exposed to the air, squinting and farting and panting (all together now!), their dimwitted dicks (all together now!) dipping in and out of the comic cunts of their synthesized desires—every heroic thought in their oafish bobbing brains (all together now!) washed away by the cheap ploys of these insipid semen-demons? What is this? A whore for your last supper? A prostitute as panacea? I can't take it any longer! I smack the fraudulent Française's ass and demand my boner back. I hoist my rebellious pants over my stubborn hard-on, and before I know it the cobblestones are ticking away underneath my heels—if paradise is lost, then at least freedom and dignity have been regained!

•

"Eeeeey-mil! *Liebling*!" She sings it in her vibrato, in her warmest baritone, and with every syllable she lures him deeper into the hidden caves of her hormonal opulence. With her left hand around his waist and her right hand at his collarbone, she brushes the full wealth of her breasts against his lapels—and then her right hand shoots up, high above his head, wrist bent, and with a sudden movement of her fingers and a powerful click of her tongue she breaks an imaginary raw egg over his head; virtual yolk drips over his bald spot. The performance is realistic enough to make her costar cringe, but she keeps on smiling sweetly, her eyes fixed on a dark spot behind the onslaught of the magnesium bulbs, and Bannings (good sport!) flashes a quasi-jovial and quasi-believable grin to the audience. He realizes of course that tomorrow the gossip pages will publish not this jolly image, but the one picture in which that shadow of panic flutters over his face, the gray moth of doom circling around the fading lamp of his career. He already knows that in this picture he will have his eyes closed, his nose all wrinkled up, his bottom teeth sunk into his upper lip, and that the hand of Helena Guna, new star at UFA, will be rising above him, above his head, her fingers pressed closely together, so that it looks as if he—the *vieux premier*—is her wooden marionette.

The Swedish Ice Queen, the audience favorite, the volcanic performer, the g*ddamned bitch in many a mountain farmer drama. Scuttlebutt has it that Guna was the direct inspiration for the city of Germania; the city invented by the architectural firm of Hitler & Speer to take the place of Berlin, city of ruins. A Grand Dome would rise at the end of the Great Avenue, the largest structure ever built, and it is whispered that its upwards curvature, its impossible, soaring proportions, built for the express purpose of eliciting a succulent kiss from G*d's own lips, were modeled directly after her, Helena Guna's, breasts. Some even claim that she is Hitler's mistress and that the hand of the Great Leader himself held up her perfect tits for Speer to sketch and that tears of joy streamed over the architect's cheeks as he was drawing the little tip that crowned its apex; some say that the ragged ribs on the sides of that Great Dome symbolize the rabid teeth marks of the Matchless Guide on Guna's beneficent boobs. Those are all lies, nothing but lies—cheap, vile lies.

"You look a bit pale, my dear Emil. Are you so happy to see me that all the blood has drained from your head and gathered elsewhere?"

It is the evening of the premiere of *Liebe an die Himmelstür* ("Love at Heaven's Gates"), her newest movie, in which she finally, and literally, over the course of the film, makes the transformation from being a Bavarian vamp in the Mae West vein to a courageous soldier's wife. Her husband dies at the front, but she keeps his spirit alive and bears his child. The critics love it. This is the movie, they write, in which she finally manages to cast off her usual persona: the cold blonde, the woman with the eternal pout and the painfully beautiful yet empty body that twists and turns every way the director saw fit; she now has, they say, become her own woman, a role model for all German girls to look up to.

Helena's assault on Emil in the harsh glow of the flashbulbs is merely a symptom, a symbol: She is finally a diva, she has officially arrived; she can afford to be shocking and impudent—she sits on top of the world, her skirts lifted, about to take a dump, and the open mouth gaping at her from underneath is Emil's.

"*Chéri,*" he bleats. "You look so different today. How was India?"

"India? India was *wunderbar, mein Schatz.* India: The sun licked me all over with its broad, smooth tongue, Emil. I melted, Emil, I became molten transparency, the glass jar in which a flame for the g*d is held captive. India is India, Emil, the hot breath of the jungle, the emerald sheen of the rice fields. Do you know what rice fields smell like, Emil, do you know what scent they have?"

Emil does not know, and wordlessly he indicates his desire to be instantly released from the bonds of this unbearable ignorance.

"Semen, Emil. Human semen. Your semen, I bet—that's what India smells like."

Goodness: the great actor suddenly blushes as if he were an adolescent. He looks around skittishly, in the hope that nobody has overheard them. She sees this new opening in his defenses, and she exploits it.

"But lonely, Emil! You wouldn't believe it. Those crazy Hindustani, they simply don't do it with white G*ddesses. Not even a quickie, Emil—I was so insulted! I am so *hungry*, Emil—so damn horny! Emil, hunny-bunny," she whispers in his ear, and as soon as she puts her lips to his auricle the haloes of chemical lightning explode around their heads again, *"Heut' Abend lad' ich mir die Liebe ein."* Bannings turns a deeper shade of crimson—tonight, she tells him, she will invite love to her room. She grabs his hand. "Emil, a wonderland by night!"

Helena's words seep like honey into his aching head.

Bannings quickly unfolds the night's program and drapes it over his lap—something rears its ugly head and he does not want that event photographed.

He looks for a clever answer, but the words get stuck in his throat.

All he can do is whinny.

•

They made a movie. *Die Himmelstür.* She sat in his trailer every day. She brought him a morning offering of coffee with a roll spread with marmalade. He read her like a morning paper, she wrapped him in the scent of her perfume, she bathed him in her unspoken promise of more-to-come. She made sure to inquire about his health. If she ever neglected this, he immediately sent his personal assistant to the director and notified the man that Herr Bannings was desperately ill and needed to be transported to La Charité at once. After he had bored her with the interminable list of what ailed him this morning—most of these ailments associated with the use of alcohol or non-medicinal chemical substances—he lit his morning cigarette, the first of an impressive series. He had to be careful, because during the conversation a makeup assistant had built him an imposing beard of highly flammable material. In the middle of this smoking ritual he looked at her in the mirror with a quasi-shy and semi-shrewd expression and mentioned in passing that he had recently noticed that she had stopped loving him. Why did she keep her distance? No, she did love hem, she swore. No, she did not. If she did, why didn't she take him into her arms, for instance—give an old man some comfort, eh? No, she did love him, and to prove that they were going to make a great movie together! By way of armistice he took the cigarette from his lips and offered it to her and she eagerly sucked out whatever smoke still remained, as if his soul, the soul of the movies itself, was hiding in the tobacco. "Come," he said then, like he said every morning, "Let us project our immortal images onto a few more feet of film stock!"

He's at it again, this morning: the Master having his weekly paroxysm. "Why are you having lunch with him? Why do you never go out for lunch with me? What does he have that I don't?"

"He plays opposite me this afternoon, Emil. We have to practice, don't we?"

"You don't need to practice, Leni. You know your part. You know it through and through. Have lunch with me!"

"He is my movie husband, dear Emil. I have to go to lunch with him! You know how I am: I immerse myself in the role."

"Have lunch with your daddy-in-law, you little flirt."

"Wouldn't that be slightly perverse, dear Papa? I take my job seriously—how could my father-in-law and I . . . ? But once the movie is over, well then . . ."

"Kiss me, you beautiful daughter-in-law."

"No, Emil."

"Kiss me, you heartless slut. Kiss me!"

"No!"

And then Emil throws himself to the ground and tears the hair out of his head and the beard from his chin; he rolls over the floor like a man possessed; he clutches his chest with both hands and he kicks and screams until the trailer rocks and shakes and then he starts gasping for air and then the miracle worker Lena has to rush to his aid and lie on top of him and kiss the old lips that taste of tobacco and glue and stale drama, all the while hitting him with her makeup kit whenever his hands threaten to wander into forbidden territory.

•

"*Heut' Abend lad' ich mir die Liebe ein, Emil.*"

Her lips are painted red. Bright red. It looks as if she's just bitten the head off some very small animal.

Bannings turns a deeper shade of crimson.

She grabs his hand.

"Emil, a wonderland by night!"

Helena's words seep like honey into his pounding head.

Bannings unfolds the night's program and drapes it over his lap.

He wants to say something, but his throat is glued shut.

All he can do is whinny.

"And if I'm in the mood, Emil," she coos, "I might even let you watch!"

•

"I understand your disgust, *Herr Untersturmführer*. It is not what was promised to you. The ladies in that establishment merely sell their bodies. Not so here. The women in our house *offer* their bodies, and they offer them to Germany: a different thing altogether!" My colleague, the man in the dim light, the man who saved me from the shame of my flight from the bordello, lights a cigarette, a real cigarette made with real tobacco, and he hands it to me in a brotherly ritual of sharing.

"What better gift to the fatherland than a child? You are of excellent Germanic stock, my friend—if you were not, you would not have become an officer in our elite corps. Look at you: nicely elongated head, small-boned face, well-formed chin, small nose high on the face, soft golden-brown hair with a slight wave, arched forehead, gray eyes, pinkish-white skin—no, no hesitation, comrade. Manly pride, courage and loyalty, those are German virtues. Regret, the misery of sin, the vague promise of the heaven of prayers and psalms—none of that has any place in our world. Is it frivolous when a woman goes to a man to conceive? That woman acts out of a sense of responsibility; she shows personal courage and strength of character. Man and woman are donors—carriers and receivers of the seeds of life. *Herr Untersturmführer*, have you noticed how people often live in the past? I am telling you: The times have changed. It is our duty to think of posterity—it is time for us to become ancestors ourselves. All you have to do is sacrifice an hour of your time and a tenth of an ounce of bodily fluid. Of course we have every reason to think that you will distinguish yourself in a large number of battles, but just like you, we keep in mind that things might go wrong sometime. Therefore, the time is now. And if the fruit of your labors should not be up to par—well, the railroad at the back of the *Heim* goes all the way to Auschwitz."

What is Auschwitz, I want to ask, but I have the impression that my tour guide wouldn't encourage such questions. I ask a more urgent one. "Why me?"

"Because you made a choice, *Herr Untersturmführer*. The right choice. You were not blinded by lust, you were always aware of the True Goal." The man coughs into his hand. "Well. It is a selection process like any other." There's nothing I can say to that, and so we proceed through the hallway in silence. He leads, I follow. We are like monks on their begging rounds. I hear nothing, except a very quiet, thousand-fold sighing in the chill sharp air, like the rustling of a forest in fall.

"Behind that door you will find the kitchen. An invigorating meal awaits you—I hope you're hungry. We serve oatmeal, the ingredient that has worked such wonders for the British ruling class, and salt potatoes with sunflower seeds, and whole wheat bread with castor oil. Do not talk to the women who serve you. Even if you did, you wouldn't understand them. They speak a gruff language of harsh gutturals."

•

No, that was a lie. India had not been *wunderbar* at all. India had been a big mistake. She had realized this as soon as she set foot on the continent, but the blister of festering regret only burst open the moment Yamatsan released his own shoddy teaspoon of fluid inside her with the quick, sly, contemptuous wordlessness that characterized every dealing between them. Everything about that trip had been a mistake. Above all, Yamatsan had been a mistake. The man had not been able to hide his contempt for her, for Helena Guna, the same kind of nonchalant disdain, she thought, that Jews feel for goyim, the same kind of contempt that Germans feel for whoever is not of German stock, with the exception of Leni, the *nordische* guardian of their sophomoric fantasies; she is almost one of them.

She had imagined it very differently, that trip. The Original Aryans along the Big Stream—she had thought they would be like the Asians she had met in the lavish salons of the Thule House in Berlin, the imperturbable Tibetan monks draped in wide saffron-colored robes with that all-encompassing smile that marinated the heart in pure warmth, men like sweet wobbly buttercups that have been soaking up sunshine a whole springtime long. Or maybe she expected them to be like the quiet Indian teachers who sat cross-legged on the couches, their beards stained with tea and herbs, their hair in buns on top of their skulls, a handy handle to lift them up to the heavens. It didn't help that the big windows of that neoclassicist villa looked out over the vast expanse of the Tiergarten, that the air was perfumed with sandalwood incense, that Himmler himself was sitting next to her, his hand in hers, and that he calmly (a calm, quiet Himmler!) explained how the superior race had not stumbled out of the dry dustbowls of the African desert (of course not!), nor out of the sweating huts of the black jungle, nor out of the moist cradle of Mesopotamia; we have been much more blessed than that, we have been sowed from the Roof of the World; the *Forschung- und Lehrgemeinschaft Ahnenerbe* had studied the matter carefully. Leni, think about that, Leni, nothing between Us and the Cosmos but a few miles of thin air and stars, stars, stars! Leni, it is almost as if we came tumbling down directly from the stars! Angels is what we are, Leni, Angels whirling down on a Wheel of fire, a burning Wheel, a Wheel that soon will re-ignite the world—the Wheel, Leni, that is called Swastika, the holy symbol of Aryan superiority! And the monks kept on smiling and the wise men kept mumbling their monologues, and the incense burned, and the Wheel of Timekept rolling through her head, tumbling down from the Himalayas, rolling through the Ganges plain, and then—by way of the Middle East—into Europe, torching and scorching, until hissing and steaming it came to an abrupt halt in the eternal ice of the country of her birth, and Helena Guna, drunk with the thundering chants on the record player and the voice of the powerful man in her ear, saw a vision in

Guna. She holds on tightly to the rail, fighting a mounting panic and the urge to throw up, a chiffon scarf wound tightly around her mouth and nose, an ineffectual barrier against the horrid smells. Yamatsan hands her a tiny clay cup with a wick and some oil, taking good care to touch her fingertips with his. The idea is that she will set this flame on the water and make a wish. (For instance, to conceive a son with a Himalayan Aryan.) When she looks up, the first light of the rising sun glowers over Manikarnika Ghat. Helena has read the guidebooks, but it takes her a second to recognize the place and to remember its *raison d'être*. Piles of wood are carried in; stretchers overflowing with orange blossoms dance soundlessly on the hands of a swarming crowd of untouchable servants; disorderly rows of men dressed in blinding white sit down on their haunches to have their heads shaved, glum and solemn they offer their throats and skulls to the knife of a stranger who spits big gobs of red slime in the dirt. "Eldest sons. They will hold the torch that lights the wood underneath their father's corpse," Yamatsan whispers—no escape possible— in her ear. "One hour later, they will turn over the body; when the full three hours have elapsed, they will crush the skull with wooden mallets, grinding it to a fine powder." And, G*d, a few feet downstream a small army of *dobhi wallahs* are beating laundry against the rocks, making saris bleed their colors all over the hard stones. The Ganges, that filthy, stinking river, apparently cleans everything. "This is Mahashmashana," lectures Yamatsan, "The city founded by Shiva himself." Leni read about that too. This is the Home of the Big Cremation, the place where the g*d of the circle of creation and destruction set foot on the continent for the very first time, the earth shaking under the violence of the never dying flames that accompany him. The place too where the whole of creation will be put down on the day of Pralaya, when the world will fold back on itself. "The world—ah! Pardon the expression!—buggering itself up the arse, Miss Guna, and then being called to life again in that dreadful act of sodomy." Benares is also called Kashi, the city of light, but in Helena's view, Surya, the morning light that is supposedly divine in nature, is unnecessarily harsh and gruesome. It further burns the blooming purple wounds on the ebony flesh of the lepers. They do not know the luxury of shame; from the banks they beg for her compassion and her money; whirling clouds of flies suck the pus out of the sores on their backs. The cursed light weighs down on widows' spines and pushes the shoulders of sons and fathers down to the ground. It loosens the cobras' tongues; it lulls the fat smooth rats to sleep; it dries up the saliva of *Anopheles*, the malaria mosquito; it shows the impudent monkeys the way to savagery and plunder. Over the Ghat floats the indomitable spirit of Maha Kali, the Black Mother of this country, she who adorns herself with a fierce necklace of bloody skulls: she who uses the ash from the pyres for face powder—and with horror

Helena realizes that the red rag she has wound around her face (her guide bought it for her from a street vendor and handed it over to her with a smile) is in fact a shroud. When she looks deep into the devious water, a fermenting baby corpse rises from the bottom, its rib cage cracked open, the heart gone; arms thin as matchsticks reach for her with clawing fingers. Slow sly crocodiles converge on this easy snack, long and pale as the middle finger of the cruel g*dhead with blood foaming at her mouth: The wheel is still turning, the river flows endlessly back on itself, the cogs of the world spin and purr. Leni stands up in the boat and screams, long and hard, the latest but not the last in the long row of Mother Ganga's mad-women, and neither the boatman with his soothing words, nor Yamatsan with his strong arms can calm her down, not even when they put their hands over her mouth. She beats her head from side to side until the kerchief loosens and her long blond locks hiss like serpents at the sun—her piercing cries make the vultures flee from their high towers and the crows from their trees and the boatman, gruff like Charon, rows them back to the shore where an angry mob has gathered, for the foreign lady has disturbed their prayers and their peace, and she jumps out as soon as she can—even before the boat hits the sands she takes off, she hits the dirt running. In her madness she tears the crowd wide open; she rips through them like a bloodied knife, hitting people in the face with her sharp elbows and poking defenseless bellies with her bony knees. She runs and runs and when her sandals slip in the holy mud and the bovine shit, she kicks them off and continues barefoot; she flees as far from the river as she can, and Yamatsan is right behind her, cursing and swearing, and still screaming she races up the stairs to the town, past endless rows of half-naked *sadhus* who press themselves hard against the wall, startled out of their holy slumber, past portly *pandits* who dive after the clay jars of Ganges water she knocked out of their hands, past blessed matrons who quickly gather their children under their skirts. The number of miracles she performs is countless: Crippled beggars sprint away nimble as antelopes; blind mendicants flawlessly choose the best escape route and do not trip even once on their hurried flight; deaf-mute panhandlers erupt in jubilatory curses of deadly precision—and still she runs and runs, through boiling alleys and earsplitting side streets; monkeys hoist themselves up by the tail; snakes drop fearfully into their baskets; mosquitoes rise like poisonous clouds from shaded doorways, and higher and higher still she runs, Yamatsan in hot pur-suit, and slowly he gains on her, and then Helena hits a wall, a real wall, a tall wall of brown brick, and the *chappals* of her pursuers sound dangerously close—the yogis whose money bowls she's overturned, the farmers whose cows are now hic-cupping in shock, the merchants whose tables she pushed down—and then it's Yamatsan's turn to work a miracle: He grabs her by the arm and a breach opens in the wall, and in the magnificent heat a stairwell with a thousand steps shimmers. The Tibetan catches her at the exact moment her legs collapse, and she lets herself be dragged upwards like a fish thrashing on a line, stumbling and falling. She hits her shins, she scrapes her knees, she bruises her hips on the sharp edges of the stairs, tearing her red sari in the process, and then: At the top of the stairs appears a cloud of fragrance and a vague thunder resounds and from that fog a wooden temple emerges, small and pointed. Without pausing or thinking Yamatsan drags her over its doorstep. Coins rain from his pockets and he yells something at the temple servant and then the world turns dark—the heavy temple gates are banged shut, and wordlessly Yamatsan tears off the last shreds of her sari. He throws the thrashing *shiksa* on the altar, ripping off her panties with one hand and with the other pushing the flower garlands from the Shiva lingam inside her mouth. Then he opens his robes and he takes her, then and there, right on the altar. While the masses shout, while the gates threaten to buckle under the blows, the young mountain guide Yamatsan hurriedly takes the international movie star Helena Guna for his bride, soiling his body with her blood, humping her with the broadest grin on his face, ramming her head against the stone phallus, and Helena kicks her legs and feet, she beats down on his bony ass with her heels as hard as she can and then the strangest thing happens—her thighs convulse and her body gets utterly confused, it mistakes the rape for rapture and it climaxes, and she bites down hard on the yellow and orange flowers, half-suffocating in the saffron pollen, and at the moment when her eyes roll up in orgasm, her assailant, her torturer, her guide, her guru crashes down on top of her and in a stream of the most obscene curses he becomes the father of her child, and then he punches her, hard, repeatedly and without mercy, straight on the mouth. When the blows stop and she opens her eyes again, the man is gone.

•

She will not make the trip to the snowy peaks. When the ruckus dies down (Benares is a busy town, there's always something happening, and the crowd soon drifts away, off to a new locus of excitement), the young temple guardian—a child almost— his eyes shyly averted, hands her a stinking blanket that he got who knows where, a blanket as old as the temple itself, and a necklace too. An amulet, something to protect her? Swallowing a mouthful of saliva, she recognizes the image of Shiva, and of course the young priest has a cousin who happens to be a *rickshaw wallah*, and who would be very happy to take her to the Hotel de Paris, deep inside the safety of the Cantonment.

Benares, city of light, city of the wheel, city older than history, older than tradition, older than legend. Whoever dies here reaches *moksha* instantly, finally liberated from the endless cycle of birth and rebirth. But what, or so Helena wonders, happens to those who are conceived here?

•

A quiet rap of cautious knuckles, and already the door opens wide. This is the formal knock—purely formal—of the lord of the mansion. There is no need to wait for an answer; he owns the place and the people in it. In his cashmere robe and soft slippers of camel skin he walks to the bed. In his left hand he holds a flashlight; in the right hand a silver ice bucket with a bottle of champagne and three flute glasses. Silver is the hair on his chest, and silver is the hair on his generous belly, and silver is the rope that ties the garment.

His smile, on the other hand, is pure gold.

He symbolizes the Father. In the heat of the night, he rushes to Mother, but since he is a thief at heart, he delays the moment of release: He makes a quick stop in this room first. He visits just for a minute; his head, his mind are already elsewhere; but he does sit down at the edge of the kids' bed—did he come to tuck us in, will he draw a little cross on our foreheads with a steady but absentminded thumb?

He carries the indelible smell of dreams with him. At first, the man looks vaguely familiar to me in the flickering light of the candles. Then I recognize him, the high forehead, the lightly upturned nose, the low crown of white hair: His image too I have so often seen projected on the screen.

He no longer behaves like a serf. He is clearly a prince.

"So, my darling," he says. "Finally we will be together." And he puts his strong hand on Helena's beautiful, warm hip, the way a hussar lays his hand on the noble side of his horse.

"So, my dear," he says to me, good-naturedly spanking my buttocks with his hand, just like a hunter playfully slaps his favorite Dalmatian.

"How was it, darling?" His smile is generous; he is the lord of the castle sending the remnants of the upstairs feast down to the kitchen maids.

"It was Walhalla, Emil," says Helena. She looks up at him with eyes as honest and open as her pretty pussy; she changes position slightly, so that his manicured fingers can touch her there, at the center of her being. I fight the urge to untie Herr Bannings's robe and put my head against his silver curls, but Helena reads my mind, she opens the robe for me and presents me with the treasure hitherto hidden underneath. I smack my lips and then I pucker them and slide them over Herr Bannings's smooth knob—it glows so beautifully with warm compassion. I slurp and swallow, and it takes less than ten seconds before I am blessed with the rich lather of the actor's kindness, and with a happy radiance Helena and I rub our face in that frothy broth and lap it up. With careful fingertips, I take a few drops of the white elixir and spread them over her quivering pearl; I am rewarded with a kiss.

"Aaaah!"

A long sigh of contentment escapes Emil. He lies flat on his back, my head on his ample stomach and Helena's on his laboring breast, and the both of us exchange lazy kisses over Bannings's belly button, burping sweet semen burps into each others' wet mouths.

"Children! What beautiful exploits I witnessed through the keyhole! What love! What virtuosity! Friends, verily I say unto thee: Nothing beats the erotic enthusiasm of a twenty-year old who has ingested a nice glass of *Spätlese* spiked with a gram of the purest Cuban coke!"

"Deep, deep love . . ." agrees Helena.

"Too bad it will lead to an equally deep amnesia in the morning."

Words without meaning! I get a firm grip on the pen that somebody has slipped into my hand, and on the piece of paper—more a form, methinks—that has inexplicably appeared on Emil's tepid belly, I sign my name while Helena grabs a set of balls in each hand and gently kneads, moaning his name and mine in turn—"Emil! Paul! Paul! Emil!"—and we respond in unison—"Helena! Helena!" It takes her less than half a minute to fully perk us up, and then we both slide inside her, almost simultaneously. Emil is just a fraction faster than I am, and he takes the road less traveled. The weight of the two movie giants bears down on me, their mating calls scorch my ears, the turbulence of their lovemaking slowly squeezes the sweltering air out of my burning lungs, and when we erupt simultaneously, the breath is finally knocked out of me and I . . .

ב

TRICKS

"She got to you good, didn't she?"

"Hi Donatella. Good morning."

Indeed, she'd got to me good. I sit on the bench in front of the house and feed the cat pellets of *Brekkies mit Huhn, Ente & Truthahn*. The little store had a dusty box of the cat food high on a shelf. Two kilos, four and a half pounds: We'll make it through winter.

Every evening Mefista knocks at my window or whines at the front door, I let her in. We share my bed, although I'm not positive the university actually allows pets inside the guesthouse. As long as I don't check the fine print at the bottom of the lease, I won't know for sure if I'm in violation of the code—so I don't check. At the crack of dawn, she wakes me by licking my ear. I scurry to the kitchen and get her a bowl of milk, and then I accompany her outside. And now we've found a pleasant extension of our morning ritual: I take a handful of the food pellets and throw them on the ground, one by one, and she happily snatches them up. She's getting pretty good at catching them on the fly; she's a miniature physicist of the Newtonian persuasion. It's an agreeable pastime for the both of us, and it delays the dreaded moment when I have to go to my office.

I am not working all that hard anymore. I'm not sure if it has something to do with the assault, but people avoid me. Nobody asks me out to lunch at the Mensa anymore, and so I eat in my room in the guesthouse, all alone. During the day I sit behind my computer in the broom closet, or I walk down to the library and read. Sometimes I take a stroll through the park, all the way to the Chinese

Tea House, an absurd little building with life-size gilded bronze replicas of good German citizens in Chinese costume and droopy fake mustaches; or else I walk to the *Drachenhaus*, the former residence of the emperor's vintner. The house resembles a gigantic cream-and-turquoise-colored wedding cake, except that wedding cakes rarely come studded with giant dragon statues. The house is on top of a hill; the exercise feels good. I have a vague idea for an experiment, but I don't write it up. It's not all that difficult to come up with reasons why this or that manipulation wouldn't really work. Experimental psychology is very forgiving in that respect: There's lots of room for doubt, and you can always pick your design apart until nothing remains. I exploit this property fully. In the ever more infrequent conversations I have with my supposed collaborators, I bring up idea after idea, and then I tear each of those apart with clever references to the work of contemporary luminaries like Steve Monsell or Alan Allport or Nachshon Meiran. It makes me look busy and smart, and I don't have to do a thing. The evasions keep my mind occupied, and that is good: I don't want to spend the whole g*ddamn day thinking about Donatella, or De Heer.

What does Mefista do when I'm not there? When breakfast is finished, disappointment flickers in her eyes, and then she sprints to the bushes and I don't see her again until evening. I've never seen her walk around campus, her dapper tail raised high in the wind. Does she maybe only exist in those few hours between sunset and sunrise? Does she fade to invisibility in the sunlight, or does she have other incarnations I'm not aware of?

"And those ice cream cones you're feeding her, buster—those are mine. Two deutschmarks a pop. Come on, pay up!"

We all need somebody to love, and we all need illusions to hold on to, and I combine those two needs in my belief that I love Donatella. I'm not sure if she means it, but I do take out my wallet. She has bags under her eyes, Donatella: she looks tired and dejected. No, she's doing fine, she assures me, everything is going great. "Glad to hear that," I say. She lights a cigarette and says that she should be on her way. "Okay," I say. But she stays where she is, right next to me. We keep silent. We keep silent a lot, Donatella and I, and for long periods of time. After a few puffs, she throws her Marlboro away. The cigarette rolls over the wet grass and I grind it into the ground, extinguishing it for her. I am a hero. I just saved a medium-sized town from a devastating fire, just like that, and Donatella didn't even notice.

From the other side of the street she waves at me, wiggling a handful of fingers. She is less than thirty feet away when a small crowd already forms around her. She tells her friends a story that involves a lot of hand movements. A funny story too— the young men that gather around her bare their teeth and offer her their throats.

Behind their backs, on the wall, a number: 68. I did not grind hard enough, the cigarette is still smoldering. I let it be; this town be damned.

·

"Did you have a good look?"

"Oh yes," lies Marianne.

"And did you feel everything really well?"

"Sure!" says Marianne. This time, she speaks the truth. It still hurts a little. A war wound, in a sense.

"Do you know what I really like?"

"No," says Marianne. And that again is a lie. Magda is very knowledgeable in all matters sexual; she's always telling Marianne what she's thinking, what leaves her cold and what positions *du jour* make her so terribly horny; and she offers advice too: what simple tricks you can use to drive the boys, like, totally crazy! Boys, Magda always says, are simple creatures. Grab 'em by their dicks—that's definitely the best advice any young lass can get! Marianne can practically mouth it along with Magda, she's heard it so many times: "When his balls bounce against your ass, you know, when he lifts your legs up real high and then he sinks real deep inside you. When you feel his nutsack slam against your asshole. You know?" Today Marianne knows, and she's thankful for this newly gained knowledge, not just because this sliver of information connects her more intimately with Magda— now they have really something to talk about, some information to *exchange*—but also because the experience itself was quite worthwhile—though, to be fair, that short little ride hadn't been her favorite moment of the night.

Hard to say which had been her favorite moment. Not any particular moment, maybe—more the general feeling. Warmth, closeness—something like that. Senses overflowing, a wonderful feeling of too much. Very different from what she had expected, listening to Magda's stories. Better, actually, much better than she had expected. The boy's touch hadn't been rough, but tender and cheerful, and Marianne liked it like that, preferring it to the intense rawness Magda liked to glorify. But Christ, the noise that had come from the next room! Her lover had smiled at the racket—she had literally felt his smile against her cheek. She liked him for that. He was no senseless stud: He had taken care to open a line to her heart. She remembers everything, and she cherishes the memories. How he had taken her in his arms, firmly yet softly; how he had leaned in to draw her close; how he had gasped when his, his, well, his *Ding* had touched her thigh; how she in turn had shivered when his mouth found her nipple and when his hand slid urgent and sweet over her belly and under the elastic band of her cotton panties—were they tearing down the house, Magda and her newfound lover?—and how his tongue had teased the little knob of her breast while his fingers played with the little knob of her, well, her, her, *nevermind*, and then her panties were on the ground next to the bed, warm and empty, and then he was inside her. What did she care about his *Hodensack* and what it slammed against? Well, she had to admit that she was curious—she had felt between his thighs and touched something spongy. He had enjoyed that, apparently, her new, her first, her overwhelming man—her touch had goaded him on. Then it had become painful. And so she had placed the palm of her hand flat against his chest to make him stop, and with a confidence she hadn't quite known she possessed, she had turned him onto his back and climbed on top of him, taking his head between her hands and his cock inside her, how should she say this, her, *oh well*. Inside her. Until she came.

That's what had happened.

Magda never knows when to shut up. Magda always blabbers on and on. Marianne doesn't like this. When you share bedroom intimacies they stop being intimacies, right? What counts, right here, right now, is that she has a boyfriend, and that tonight they will see each other again. Right now, that is all she wants to think about. Not talk, think.

"And do you know what else I like?"

"Nuh-uh."

"When he's, like, completely hard and getting ready and he's so excited and then he pulls back the foreskin. You know, when he shows off the little head, all shiny and purple?"

Pulls back the foreskin?

"I prefer doing that myself, actually, but you know how boys are. So damn impatient!"

"Mmmm-hm," says Marianne. Magdalene had obviously forgotten that Marianne's direct knowledge of boys was only a few hours old. Foreskin?

"Don't you think?"

"I don't know." Marianne coughs in her fist. She sips her coffee. "I can't remember." Her lover had been proudly engorged before she even touched him, maybe that had been it? Maybe it retracts automatically? Something like that? "I don't recall any foreskin."

"But you did get a good look at his schlong, right?"

"Yup," says Marianne. She's lying again. When escape was no longer possible, she had taken off her clothes as fast as she could, leaving just her panties, and she had practically run to the bed, hiding deep under the pile of blankets. She had missed the spectacle of his undressing, and when he slid in next to her—naked, she could feel that much—he had quickly licked his fingers and extinguished the wick of the candle between his thumb and index finger—it made the funniest little kissing sound. How sweet, she remembers thinking: He doesn't want me to feel awkward. And then he had taken her in his big strong arms. A man. Her first. Strong arms, gentle arms, and he smelled nice. Gosh, she can't stop thinking about him. Is she behaving like a schoolgirl or what?

The second time around she had screwed up enough courage to put her hand on his sex, exploring its shape and texture with a hesitant finger, testing its resilience with her thumb. He had been hard all that time. Something was leaking out, it made his cock slide nicely through her fist. She still recalls no foreskin. But well, if he's hard? Come to think of it, wasn't that in one of Van de Velde's diagrams—that it retracts?

"What? Does he have a Jew-cock, your boyfriend? Yikes!"

"Stop it! No! Of course not! The army doesn't accept Jews, does it?"

No, the army doesn't accept Jews. Or maybe the guy had an accident, when he was a child or something? What did she know? Or a battle wound, perhaps?

"You didn't let him squirt inside you, I hope?"

"No, of course not. On my stomach."

Near the end, he had wrestled her down and climbed on top of her again. How forceful he had been, right before his climax, like a—ah, here's the word again!—like a man!

"Oh yuck!" says Magda.

"Yeah—yuck!"

They giggle, two grown-up women. They blush.

"What did you do with it?"

"Uh?"

"What did you with his come?"

"None of your business!"

"Did you lick it up?"

"No, ugh, yucky!"

"Yuck!"

A brief pause.

"It doesn't taste too bad, though, does it? Just a bit salty—it makes me really horny, actually."

"I wiped it off. I just wiped it off," says Marianne. With the sheets, she wants to add, but if she does, Magdalene might want to inspect the stains. Or maybe she would want her to go change the linen. Marianne is always the one who ends up

312

doing the laundry. And it isn't true. They had let it dry, that's what they had done, it glued them together while they held each other close. She had liked the scent, it smelled a bit like a forest in the wet of springtime.

Marianne dreams away. "Twice," she says.

"Twice on your tummy?"

"No, on my back the second time."

"Your back, huh? Your ass, you mean!"

They giggle harder. "He must be quite something, that guy of yours."

"Yes he is." Marianne agrees.

"You should have a real good look tonight," Magdalene says. "Nothing like a good look at a schlong to put you in the mood!"

"Yes, I'll take a long hard look tonight." Nasty pun! This provokes more giggles.

"Or do you want to switch?"

"Ooh!" Marianne isn't quite ready for that yet.

Then it's time. She clears the table. They have to go to work. The day after Hitler's birthday is a working day like any other. You never get a break when you work in a hospital. It was already very nice that the head nurse had given them the day off yesterday, to celebrate. And what a celebration it had turned out to be!

•

At dawn, Marianne licked my ear—my left ear—with her cat's tongue, and then she licked the lonely tear that hung from the corner of my eye, and then she breathed words into my ear, words simple and homely, words to the effect that there would be bread on the table and coffee—real coffee—on the stove, and after making this promise, she ran out of the room, barefoot, to go pee and set the table. I lay on my back deep in the warm bed, totally happy. It had been my first time too, the first time I had ever slept with a woman. I was in no hurry to get up, oh no. Stay in bed, Marianne had said, sleep in and rest well, and then have breakfast and why don't you just hang around and read or something until we get back tonight and then—oho!—well: then!

•

Fresh, happy girls. In BDM uniforms. It stands for *Bund Deutsche Mädel*—Association of German Girls. And, Horst said, it also stands for "Baby Do Me." He had spotted the pair immediately. Hot girls, ripe and ready—I bet you all I own that we get laid tonight, *compadre*. Horst was a daredevil in so many aspects of his life, but this beat everything: two girls in dirndls with blond pigtails wound like sugar pretzels on top of their heads: You can't get closer to the National Socialist erotic ideal than those two.

"So what about this?" I object during a bathroom break—Horst and I are side by side at the urinals.

Tall, elegant Horst peers over the partition. "Okay. So you're circumcised. Keep it dark. Put it right inside her. She'll never know. You take the chubby girl, I'll take the short one. That little fatso has never ever done it, believe me. She doesn't know what a real dick should look like. She'll be very happy with that puny little thing of yours!"

"Hey! Hey!"

Horst grinned and buttoned his fly. "I find that little layer of fat on her quite attractive," he said. "You know, the girl has to get it from somewhere. Fat chick: good food. I bet you we'll have a wonderful breakfast!"

And Horst had been right. There were wheat rolls that must have been paid for with medieval doubloons. Real butter too, still smelling of the meadow, and a pot with precious honey. Real coffee, an aroma I hadn't smelled in years, almost better than sex, and the table bathed in blond sunlight. We came, we sat, we ate.

•

This is the first year Hitler's *Geburtstag* is a festive occasion for us as well. We're still alive, which means that we're doing quite well and that the war is going badly. The loudspeakers in the street no longer spew out the word "Stalingrad"; if the battle is mentioned at all it's in whispers on street corners and in bars, with mute, wide-eyed disbelief. The first escapees return from the east—the supposedly fortunate. They're missing arms or legs. Empty sockets where their eyes had been—men no longer capable of tears. Horst and I sit at an outdoor table at Kranzler, the two of us at a table for four, and we watch the procession of the cripples with interest and secret delight.

The first commandment of the fugitive: The crowd is your best hiding place. It's good to be surrounded by a crowd; anonymity breeds happiness. Every passer-by carries something: a shopping bag, a suitcase, a child. Everybody is on their way, going somewhere, or else they're on the run, fleeing from something. The distinction isn't always easy to make. Nobody's interested in the little mysteries, the histories and destinies of the people that cross their way. It's war—life is cheap, existence is perilous. All of us, German and Jew, legal and illegal, walk around with the same goal: to forget. Forget who we once were, forget the dreams we used to have and how cruelly they have been taken away from us. But that does not put us on equal footing. We watch the parade of broken soldiers, the procession of the lame, the blind, and the madmen, and it warms our heart. Unlike my father, I do not believe in compassion with the enemy and neither does Horst. And then those two girls approach, looking for a spot to sit on the café terrace, shielding their eyes from the sun with their hands. They are like Indian brides in a Karl May novel, and we are like highwaymen ready to pounce. Correction: Horst is the highwayman. He gets up and waves at the girls as if he's known them for years, inviting them over at our table—after all, our two empty chairs are the only ones still available.

Will this work? Of course this will work. Berlin is a city full of horny women, their men either dead or far away. Horst and I pretend to be soldiers on temporary leave from the front, the only good reason for able adult males to be in town. This alone, or so Horst tells me, is what will get us laid. Soldiers returning from the battlefield, looking for a balm for their wounds and healing for their souls—what decent Aryan maiden could resist? No, they can't—after a good look at Horst's sleek, muscular frame and his eyes that squint in a smile, Magda decrees they would simply love to join us, and she drags Marianne with her.

The leave story is dangerous, of course: Soldiers love to show off their uniforms. Glamour. Patriotism. That kind of thing. Therefore, Horst starts the conversation by apologizing for the fact that we are not in uniform. "The battles," he says, and he lets his eyes gaze dreamily over the street and shakes his head slightly at the same time. Oh, the horrors he has seen, he doesn't want to talk about it! "Would you believe that before we left we were weak and pudgy young men, law students fattened by all the goodness of this glorious land, provided in such abundance by the Führer—*Sieg heil*? Feel," says Horst, and he flexes his biceps for the smallest of the pair. "Feel those muscles! At the front, we turned from weaklings into men. Our dress uniforms don't fit us any longer, they make us look like scarecrows. It would be a dishonor to wear these uniforms in public!"

"Well, we're not in uniform either," offers the chubby one.

"Ah, so the ladies are contributing to the war effort too? Nurse's aids, the both of you? What an honorable profession, what a rare calling, and what an honor for the wounded to be looked after by the both of you, what a blessing for the injured to have ointments rubbed on their wounds by such beautiful, willowy hands!" Horst's fingers have now become miraculously entwined with those of the little woman's.

"And what a beautiful day today, especially for this time of year!" the chubby one says.

"That must make the Führer so very happy, such wonderful weather on his birthday!" adds Horst.

"*Heil* Hitler!" exclaims the little one, but it sounds automatic. Her mind is already elsewhere. Perhaps under the table, where Horst's feet are working hard.

"A true sign from the heavens!"

And we all lift our cups to toast the Leader.

"*Sieg heil!*"

We eat cake, trying not to think what it might be made of, and drink a bitter beverage of heated oak leaves. The surface of the brown sludge shivers whenever a tank rolls through the street. Cannons are supposed to be boys' toys, or else a clever ploy to crank up the gross national product; they should never be actually used. Now they rattle through the avenue, painted in camouflage, dented and rusty, to honor the Führer on his birthday. Don't they need those things on the battlefield?

An hour later we sit in the movie theater, both with a sweet maiden next to us, and while the newsreel plays, mine grabs my arm. Our fighter planes and their acrobatics in the Arabian skies make a big impression on her. She squeezes me hard during a thirty-second item about our heroic stand in Stalingrad (at least one person in the theater believes this bullshit, then) and she almost screams at a report of a startling and (so says the voice-over) cowardly torpedo attack on the sovereign fleet of our submarines. She revives a little at the images of our Führer, who lets his dog, an elated oversized German shepherd puppy, jump up on him in the manly air of a Bavarian mountain range.

•

The clever illegals, about to get laid, enter a classy villa in the posh neighborhood of Dahlem, in the southwest of the city. In the hallway a tall stuffed bird raises its slender neck, its beak pointing toward the sky with pride. The four of us express some suspicion that this might indeed be a Chinese crane, a bird that promises a thousand years of good fortune (except—though we do not say it aloud—for the original owners of this house).

Dahlem was not yet a suburb in those days, but very much a village, a quaint ceremonial hamlet populated by creaking demig*ds—professors, politicians, and old money. To get here, we took the red U-Bahn line that connects the big department stores with the villas of their rich clientele.

Marianne's dad is a high-ranking officer stationed in Berlin. He has received the high honor to be invited to the Führer's eagle nest in Berchtesgaden for the week—the place we just saw in the newsreel. A whole week for him and his wife to bathe in the glory of the Immortal. Their daughter was not invited. We are welcome, Marianne said with a blush, to stay at their place for a while. Would we be so kind as to grace the two girls' home with our presence? The villa would be an ideal place to rest and prepare for the long trip back to the front. Horst—he had introduced himself to the women as Gerhard—clicks his heels together in a soldierly gesture of honest gratitude.

The rest of the evening is hazy. We drink good wine from a bottomless cellar. Bravely we work our way through an endless supply of ham and well-leavened bread. Under the table knees, feet and hands do their good work. I am getting a little drunk.

"Let's go to the salon, and have our coffee there!"

So there we are, suddenly surrounded by books. Shelves and shelves of books, books from floor to ceiling, and the sight of a small bust of Homer, the seer with the dead gaze, almost sobers me up again. It takes some effort to not start caressing those spines of leather, to not rub my fingers, still dripping with expensive pig fats, over the eyelids of the poet. Instead, my hand circles over Marianne's back and a naughty finger plays with the clasp of her bra. Concentrate on what is supposedly forbidden—the language of flesh—and thereby avoid the real danger, that of words and ideas. We extinguish all lights and open up the curtains. Magdalene likes it that way: The light of the half-moon in the cloudless sky turns her on, she says.

Of course the sirens sound around midnight, but we don't interrupt our kissing. Dahlem is far away from Berlin proper and there's no heavy industry in this part of town. When the sirens sound and the *Flak* batteries heat up, people in Dahlem do not run to their basements, they eat their cake standing at the window and they watch the bombs fall while they go *tsk, tsk, tsk*. And yet, despite this, while we're slowly sinking our teeth in the first of love's heady delights, the house shakes. And then a thundering sound, as if a freight train is passing right by the window, and that feeling of mass, of an enormous, wordless weight in the sky. Without warning the windows bulge inwards, for a moment the glass seems to liquefy and then it splinters, raining sparks and diamonds on the four of us, and how natural this all feels, it is the way of things—this is how time treats glass and a man's heart. The Meissner porcelain rattles on the table, and, G*d, what a commotion in the room: Books dart through the air, their leather covers broken, and they spill all their ancient secrets, the words dance their dance of freedom, and a few particularly sharp phrases even cut our skin. Poetry falls all around us, fleshy and bloody like intestines on the altar of an oracle. I catch one book's title on the fly: *Über die Willensätigkeit und das Denken*, by N. Ach; one of Aesop's fables whizzes by so close I can almost distinguish its moral by the light of the moon. Then flowers of fire bloom in the booming sky and every page is screaming wildly, just like Marianne and Magdalene—the girls dive under the table as if their life depended on it. Laughing (we are used to much worse in the city—pardon, on the battlefield), Horst and I join them. "That the English have chosen precisely this day to bomb us!" Magda exclaims, shaking with indignation, as if it is the most terrible crime of war not to honor this highest of all the Reich's holy days, the Führer's *Geburtstag*.

To be honest, I have really taken a liking to the bombings. When the Brits fly over, the streets are ours. I love to stand underneath an apple tree in this or that courtyard and watch the fiery spectacle. For the fugitive, the nights of the bombings are nights without danger, except of course the minor danger of being hit by a bomb. That is the second commandment of the fugitive, perhaps in a slight contradiction with the first: There is safety in solitude. Nobody is supposed to be on the street during a raid, and Germans just love obeying the law. They stay inside, they huddle closely together in the bomb shelters and leave the streets to us. We, Horst, WLADIMIR, Maruschka, Peterchen and our ever changing cast of guests, we crawl out of the basement and watch the lightshow, the glow cast on the clouds overhead by the burning city, much the way farmers watch a thunderstorm, and we estimate the damage done.

Underneath the table, I kiss my Marianne, and I throw my arms around her generous waist. And while she looks up at me with a mixture of fear and trust, while she looks for shelter in my arms, I spy a physical hunger in the slow turning of her hips, a hunger we all share, as well as the profound loneliness I thought only Jews possessed.

•

This is how I met Horst, the morning after my brazen escape.

I wake up shivering, amazed that I have been able to sleep at all in the bitter cold. Amazed too that I have survived the night—the homeless so often die in their beds of rubble, simply freeze to death; you read it in the newspapers every day. The city is silent. The chilly glow that seeps into the basement from under the aprons of concrete, that sheen of mother-of-pearl—could that be moonlight bouncing off snow? I like snow. It covers the worst grotesqueries of the debris, it transforms the city into a relic of romantic times by laying a blinding veil over the deepest darkness of our souls; it renders the world pure and slow. High above me the stars stab through the night, cold and distant, like little needles; their flickering light is truth, is silence.

Then the silence is ripped to shreds. Next to me, right next to me, I hear a jolting gasp, a grumbling snort—a man snoring with conviction. I scream and the man jerks up out of his sleeping bag, a wild grin on his face. He has a mop of tangled brownish hair; he needs no time to wake up—his gaze is clear, his smile steady and ironic. Well, the Gestapo's methods may be unorthodox, but I doubt the secret police would spend the night next to their victims. The man's hand disappears into the pocket of his jacket and reemerges holding a flask. He unscrews the top and gives the bottle to me. I take the risk. Whatever is inside, it tastes like mold. I cough loudly.

"Do you realize," the man says, "that it is customary, before one enters another man's house, and *a fortiori* before one moves in, that one asks the resident for permission? Even in times like these it might be a good idea to cling to such elementary modes of decorum, wouldn't you agree?"

I just stare at the man. My throat is clenched shut. I have no idea what he reads in my gaze, but in less than a second he's out of the sleeping bag and holding me in his arms. "You know, this is a dangerous place. So many desperate souls roam the city looking for plunder. So many people have hidden their treasures in the corners and cracks of open basements and under precariously balanced beams, and they can be terribly possessive. You really can't spend the night here, you understand? And don't get me started on the dangers of frostbite—especially of the penile variety." His sleeping bag looks warm, excellent camping gear, possibly real eiderdown. My coat is threadbare, not much better than nothing. "Aw man, it'll be all right," says Horst. "Good fortune and chutzpah, that's all a man needs in this life." And then he adds, "Why don't we get us some coffee, and then I'll find you a warmer place to sleep?" He takes a handkerchief out of his pocket. "Blow your nose," he says, "and if you feel like tears why not just get it over with?" I do feel like crying. I get it over with. It's less absurd than it seems, a man crying in another man's arms. There is so much reason to.

•

The books are still on the ground, scattered in random configurations. Thesis and antithesis rise from the open pages. The stories evaporate and cloud my mind. Whoever was the previous owner of this house, the unfortunate Jew who had to leave everything behind, he loved books, and he led a good life. There is the temptation to stay—the food, the booze, the security, Marianne's loving care, the gorgeous warmth of her body. I don't need to look at Horst to know he feels the same way. But we cannot allow ourselves to give in to this temptation. The true survivor

(I lost count; how many commandments are we up to?) makes himself distant. His body and his mind are the only things he possesses, the only things he trusts. The strength of his mind is all that keeps him alive. It's the only thing that counts, the only thing that remains.

Horst makes the rounds. He finds a suitable suitcase in a hallway closet. Not too big, so that it doesn't stand out too much, but big enough to be worth filling up. The stuff he throws in there is small stuff, things that aren't too heavy, and that will either be directly useful or else fetch a nice price on the black market. Jewels of course and all the cash he can find, men's underwear, a few shirts and a pair of pants that should fit—he's an underpaid gigolo supplementing his income. I stay in the library. I prefer to rummage through the books. I find a slender volume in Hebrew printed in tiny letters on dense pages; weird diagrams are scattered throughout the text. It's bound in red leather; it fits nicely in my hand. I also find a brown leather edition of *Nathan der Weise*, Voβ, Leipzig, 1779. The two extremes of the culture that is mine by necessity. I hand them to Horst without saying a word, and he, likewise without saying a word, shoves them in the suitcase, anchoring them between two shirts.

A short cough from the garden.

"There they are," Horst says, relieved and grim at the same time. I look out the window. Three or four meager dogs of indeterminate provenance run around the garden, sniffing the hedges like truffle pigs and digging in the dirt where they smell buried roots or edible bulbs.

Horst is a free spirit. When he's working at home, he buys his lunch in the busy cafés around Savignyplatz; the cheap restaurant-cafés that offer a *plat du jour* or a casserole—fast, cheap food that fills you up nicely. The principle of the crowd works wonders here; the world inside the café is no less a melting pot than the cook's *Eintopf*. If it wasn't me standing in line next to Horst, it would be some girl he'd picked up. Horst always maintains that a man with a girlfriend raises less suspicion than a man alone. A tall strong man alone—what's that man doing here? A deserter perhaps? Men alone are always carefully checked by the police. No, Horst is a brave soldier on his R'n'R trip home, with his girlfriend hanging prettily from his arm. Horst wears an oversized raincoat and a felt hat. He likes to wear his hat with the front lower than the back, the way the Gestapo likes to wear theirs. If someone mistakes him for an agent, that wouldn't be such a bad thing, would it?

In order to finance his first few months of illegality, Horst had sold his parents' Persian carpets. Where were his parents? I knew better than to ask that kind of question. Another rule of survival: Live in the present and forget the past; your soul will be the better for it. Horst went from furnished room to furnished room, staying nowhere longer than a few days, perhaps a week. Sometimes, if he couldn't find a new room quickly enough, he would spend the night with one of his girl-friends, or he would seek shelter in an abandoned basement—which is when I met him. In the wide pockets of his coat he smuggles papers: falsified documents, altered passports, food stamps that look bona fide in the scarce light of winter. He always carries something to eat in those pockets, too: bacon wrapped in butcher's paper, a piece of sausage, a chunk of cheese, food that he has accepted as payment for his stamps or the curls of his calligraphy, or leftover pieces of meat fished out of someone's lunch stew. He shares those morsels with the other vagabonds. Not just us, but also, whenever he feels like it, with the pack of hungry mutts that always follows him around. They respect his size—Horst is tall and imposing; they never attack him but wait until he calls, and then they know they are in for a treat. From time to time it gets to be too much for Horst, and he tries to escape the strays by dashing into the U-Bahn. Even then they somehow seem to pick up his scent, and sooner or later they always come back.

Like now. Time then to break up camp and leave the house where we're so welcome. We do not sneak out, as would have been my inclination; no, we walk out of the front door with confidence, our heads held high, waving courteously to the neighbors: us, the honored guests of the colonel or the brigade general, or whatever Marianne's father may be.

Horst carries the suitcase. In the hallway we say goodbye to the silent scream of the crane. I also bid a silent adieu to my sweet, lovely Marianne. May you fare well, my darling. You gave me all I could have wished for: a night so filled with stars that it blinded us both. A night so filled with dreams it delighted us both. Farewell, Marianne, and may your father rot forever in a damp cold hell underground.

•

The very first day of our friendship, Horst and I walk silently through the snow. We must have been quite the sight to behold: two young men of, let's face it, breath-taking beauty: one tall and broad as an oak tree, the other small but comely. They carry all the sadness of the world on their shoulders; their thoughts drift away with the smoke of their reckless cigarettes.

I feel melancholic. The city is so different now—the streets, strewn with rubble, feel so much narrower. The city hasn't been a paradise for us in many long years, but still I feel evicted. I stumble over my own feet. The tears still sting my eyes. I slip on the ice. Without saying a word, Horst takes my suitcase.

I know. The very first commandment of the fugitive, the rule so essential that it carries no number, the commandment that trumps all others: Thou shalt not trust. But then, is that rule not trumped by the inner rule that teaches us that true human kindness is so rare that any act of gentleness must be cherished?

"Stay," Horst says. Stay I do—I obey him like any common dog; I stand still right in the middle of a deserted boulevard. I realize that I no longer know where I am; I've forgotten this street's name and its location on the city's grid, as if I was dropped in the middle of a labyrinth. What an apt metaphor—no matter where you are in Berlin, you are always at the center of the labyrinth. The city expands forever, it knows no bounds. I feel ill at ease. My gut tells me that standing still is not as good as moving on. But where would I go? For people like me, there's only one legal way out of this labyrinth. It is the way my parents went. It is a way I do not want to go. Commandment number four: Whoever wants to survive needs the will to survive. And that means more than the instinct and determination I have inherited from my mother (where is she now?—I cannot, must not think of that): it also implies the desire for posterity, the historic consciousness that I received from my father (where is Father?—better not to think about it), a deep identification with the continuity of the human species. I want to be faithful to my parents—I cannot give up now.

Horst's eyes travel up and down my body; he examines me from head to toe. My eyes fill, again, with tears. He moves closer until he stands right in front of me. His hands slide along my sides, they brush my hips. This is not the touch of a would-be lover—I am not being seized up for erotic consumption; this is the quick probe of a tailor who assesses size with his fluttering fingers. "You'll do," Horst says. "Come!" Come, he says, and I follow.

•

In the theater (a poster at the entrance proudly announces: "*Maruschka und WLADIMIR treten auf!*"), an arthritic old man shoves wobbly disks under the bent arm of a gramophone. They make their asthmatic rounds under the dullest of needles, and the big horn rustles, hisses, and clicks. Those veils of white noise remind me of the city of my childhood, the nightly *va-et-vient* of cars and trucks muffled by the curtains. Deep beneath that sonic surface I can discern some bastardized jazz, or maybe it's a lonely accordion that squeaks underneath a voice etched in very old glass. With every revolution of the record the tones swell and shrink, as if the music itself determines the ebb and flow of the world.

The small theater is not exactly crowded. I know something about the loneliness of movie theaters in the morning. Whenever I got cabin fever in our small apartment, I would spend the morning in the cinema. A Hitler Youth uniform is no longer needed—any paying customer is welcome now, no questions asked. The lady in the ticket booth spends most of her time clumsily renovating ruined sweaters with rickety knitting needles. It's warm inside, and movies are the stuff dreams are made of. Yet never have I seen so many empty faces, so many people devoid of any desire, as during these morning shows at the *Kino*. These people have nowhere else to go. In return for getting in at matinee prices, they'll watch anything that will help them fall asleep. For many, the ones that have been bombed out, the theater is effectively their home. It's difficult to find peace in the cold of the night under a bush in the park or in some shaky ruins, and even people who still have a house can freeze when there's no money for firewood. The crushed velvet of the chairs is comfortable, and no air-raid sirens will interrupt your sleep: The Brits and the Americans only attack by night. What's showing on the screen? The usual escapist escapades—*Der Demütige und die Sängerin, Keimendes Leben, Metall des Himmels, Die Große Liebe*. These movies should make us dream, but instead they make us sad. The ninety-minute dramas with their predictable happy endings stand in stark contrast with our lives. The people in the theater are—we are—the useless debris of early morning, and we're painfully aware of our uselessness. The fortunate ones, those who have enough money for two seats and a pack of cigarettes, sit and make out with their rented girlfriends in the last row, the bravest among them even attempting an old-fashioned quickie. Their ladies' little cries sound happy and surprised—what seasoned whore would have expected that this old hobo could still get up to such delightful tricks! Their doings make the sleepers shuffle restlessly in their chairs; those who are awake steal the occasional glance, ready to start a jealous chorus of booing if the proceedings get too obviously raucous.

But no, this theater is different. Men—mostly men, hardly a woman in sight—walk, no, they sneak into the room and sit down on the worn-out velvet, but only for a second; they look around like restless cats on the prowl, and then they disappear though a side door marked *TOILETTE*. The door bears the silhouette of a lady in crinoline holding an umbrella. The man who operates the gramophone sighs; his whiskers are 1930s long and yellowed with tobacco. Just like the gramophone he has a horn at his ear; he sifts listlessly through his collection of records, their sleeves all worn down to a uniform gray, and when the laboring gramophone arm finally reaches the end groove, he scoops up the disk with surprising dexterity, already carrying the next assault on our senses on the three fingers of his outstretched left hand. The bottom edge of the curtain is all fringes, half-eaten by rats.

In the short breaks between records, a different layer of white noise manifests itself: the muffled clanging of glasses, blanketed voices briefly raised and then sinking away again, secret mumblings in some hidden place deeper inside the house. There's a spotlight, but the anemic circle it paints on the curtain is yellow with age, dusty, and utterly exhausted—the seedy atmosphere of the theater infects even the photons with a lazy weariness; they're hardly able to pull themselves together long enough to form a coherent beam. Finally the curtain splits for a most pathetic performance: A robotic juggler stands behind a restaurant table and tries to keep some china and silverware in the air but fails miserably, maybe because he's distracted by the odd sounds from the wretched gramophone—the podium is soon covered in broken china. As soon as the man starts bleeding from a deep cut in his nose, he walks away in icy silence. Next up: Can a tinny waltz by Chopin charm a stinky French poodle into performing a dance on its tiny hind legs? The answer is pretty much no.

In the meantime, the only woman in the room, a faux blonde, decides to put on a performance of her own, the kind of performance I remember well from the early-morning movie theater, though I had never been able to witness it from so close up. She sits herself down right next to me and immediately puts her lips to my ear. I am the lead actor, then, in the not-so-original one-act play she has in mind. "Shall I sit in your lap, honey? Give me five reichsmarks and I'll give you tit for tat. You look like you could get it much cheaper in the streets, sweet boy, you might even be able to get it for free, but you also look as if you might not want to, let's say, screw a full-blooded German maiden in broad daylight. Hum?" I blush. Am I that transparent? Do I belong so clearly to the army of the desperate? But even as she's talking to me, a man reaches over from the row behind us and slides his hand into the back of her wide pants, palm upwards, as if sliding his thumb and middle finger into the two holes of a bowling ball, and with his free hand he sticks a couple of banknotes down her blouse. The cocotte coos, but which of the man's two actions provoked the cooing isn't clear. I am intrigued. The world seems different today; today, for some reason, I find the tiresome spectacle of a woman objectifying herself quite fetching—but then Horst snaps his fingers in front of my nose: *This* is what I should be watching, what's happening onstage.

We came to see *him*, apparently, the squat, elderly gent who now steps into the limelight in a shiny smoking jacket that's too wide at the chest and too narrow at the hips. And it's not just we who came to see him: From the ladies' toilets a small herd of men emerges, many more men than you would expect that space to hold, and they all take their place in the theater and they all sit on the edge of their seats. The little man snaps his fingers and a smart top hat suddenly perches on his previously bare head. He takes it off and a bouquet of flowers blooms from within, a springtime miracle in the heart of the Berlin winter. And a long line of scarves. Another finger snap and flames light up in the back of the stage, spelling a name, presumably the magician's: WLADIMIR. I like this. Not spectacular, but quite entertaining.

We get a shy smile as reward for our applause. When the clapping dies down, the magician addresses the lady next to me, freely and openly, and yet with unmistakable charm. He asks her an important question—and I discern a Slavic accent in the civilized inflections of his voice: "Do you like your poultry stuffed, ma'am?" The trollop nods and chuckles—such fine obscenity!

WLADIMIR again snaps his fingers, and this time a dove emerges from his top hat, blinking its little red eyes and flapping its snowy white wings. The flapping is less than enthused, but a dove it is, and as such it is a symbol, of love and peace for instance, and it does ascend to the starry cardboard heaven, and its short flight is greeted by renewed applause—we all know how hard it must be for the poor undernourished creature to take flight.

But no!—"Ah!" cries the magician, and in his hand appears an fearful revolver, and then a *bang!*, and in a whirl of feathers and a spray of blood the animal spirals to the stage, where it lands with a dull thud. The magician kneels to scoop it up—he's quite athletic for his age—and with a thundering "ENJOY!" he throws the carcass at the half-delighted and half-terrified hussy. The power of the shot apparently has plucked the bird, and decapitated it too, and removed its wings. WLADIMIR bows and points at his name in flames, as if he saying, Would you like me to roast the bird for you too, ma'am?

It is a triumph.

That little packet of flesh and bone, real flesh, real bone—the woman keeps turning it over and over in astonishment—looks real fat and real juicy. I don't think this is an illusion. The magician looks out for his people. These are valuable calories; this is a valuable gift. After all, that's why the woman is here; she peddles her ass to keep herself alive. The magician is her social worker—she won't need to take to the streets tomorrow. What does it matter that this is no pigeon but much more likely rat meat? A chubby rat is much better than a stringy pigeon.

If the first part of the performance was all about manifestations, the illusion of the dove and its sad demise made the balance tip in the direction of transformation and the art of disappearance. The bundle of scarves becomes a snake that transforms into a cane with a silver knob, and when the magician's assistant jumps nimbly and light as a feather out of an empty chest and makes the cane disappear into her wide-open throat, the men in the audience hoot and whistle. The flowers multiply to form an unruly winter garden with a fast-growing tree in the middle that sheds its leaves until only a slender stalk remains; the assistant climbs this stalk all the way to the ceiling. WLADIMIR saws through the wood, but the assistant remains hanging in thin air. He throws her a silk kerchief; it grows and grows until it covers her whole body, but when he snaps with his fingers both the kerchief and the assistant's glittering bathing suit fall to the ground, but there is no nudity, for the assistant herself has disappeared too. When the magician answers an urgent knocking from inside the chest, there she is, now decked out in a black man's suit that is so much the spitting image of my own bar mitzvah suit that it makes me reach for my suitcase, and rightly so: With a small scream I note that it has disappeared from among my belongings.

The performance touches me deeply, and I'm not the only one so afflicted—around me I see nothing but fascinated faces. What they reflect is so much more than childish delight in the many disappearances and reappearances, more than amusement at the dogged magic of transformation; this magic appeals to a much more adult belief, namely that all of this could be an exact mirror of our existence. We certainly live in a world where bombs fall from the sky and people get killed for no apparent reason, a world in which friends and family members are dragged away to their undeserved death and young men sit in scruffy theaters with thin suitcases at their feet and tears in their eyes—but why not turn this existence around with a snap of one's fingers, why not simply decide to be different—to be different and *better* than who or what we are now? This is the point WLADIMIR makes with his wordless performance: He tells us all, loud and clear, that survival is possible—if you only transform. I suspect that it is this message that lures the rough men away from whatever business they conduct in the washrooms (a business, as I will learn soon, that is equally based on illusion), to enter the realm of art and artifice.

But it isn't over—or is it? The back door of the theater opens with a bang. A man storms inside, dressed in a long, wide, blood red officer's coat sprinkled with snow, a coat from a distant past, a remnant from a long-forgotten, long-since lost war. The man stomps his boots to get rid of the snow; he is out of breath and his eyes roll dangerously around in his head, his hand shaking with uncontrollable anger—and in that hand a gun flickers, the same revolver that a few minutes before was used to shoot a dove clean out of the sky.

Terrified, I throw myself on the floor, but Horst grabs me by the shoulders and drags me up. This is all part of the show. The crowd stomps and claps. With a nearly imperceptible nod the coated gent acknowledges their enthusiasm, and then he redirects his attention to the spotlight. In an accent identical to that of the magician he shouts his words, booming like an operatic tenor who needs to get heard over Wagner's wildest orchestrations: "WLADIMIR IWANOWITSCH!" he shouts, and the crowd goes wild. "*WLADIMIR IWANOWITSCH!*" he reprises, even louder, and the audience shouts it out with him, word for word, matching the actor's intonation perfectly: "*WLA-DI-MIR! Wo ist mein Weib?*"

The magician shrugs his shoulders—how would I know, sir, where your wife is? Maybe she went to the bathroom and forgot to tell you? Maybe you inadvertently left her on the tram?

"*Mein Weib!*" cries the man.

The magician shrugs. None of my business, your wife.

"I know where she is! In your bedroom, that is where she is—WLADIMIR!" As the dragoon shouts the magician's name, the flaming letters fall to the floor like shooting stars, and the backdrop catches fire and crumbles to the floor also, and against the smoking wall of exposed brick we see the young assistant, now dressed in lacy negligee. Shy and trembling she steps forward into the circle of light and timidly she puts her arm around the magician's waist.

"Nonsense," says WLADIMIR calmly. "Your wife? Where is your wife? I see no wife!" As soon as he throws his cape over the woman, it drops down to the floor, empty—a needless reprisal of one of his very first tricks. The crowd cheers nevertheless and I hear some nicely obscene encouragement. The cuckolded husband wails and stomps his feet, but the stage remains empty, except for the magician. What is there to do? The man raises his revolver. With an ominous click he opens the chamber, and a single bullet rolls out. One eager audience member jumps out of his chair to pick it up and holds it triumphantly into the light.

"Good man!" yells the dragoon, "Tell me: Is WLADIMIR's name engraved on that bullet?" A small throng gathers around the brash mock-officer while the fortunate spectator who caught it raises the bullet as if it were a sacrament, and indeed, the onlookers all mumble that yes, WLADIMIR's name is indeed etched on the bullet, silver on silver. The Russian hands the revolver to the man holding the bullet.

"Good friend, you look like you know your way around a gun. Here. Load it for me, if you would be so kind."

This is Berlin, 1943. Everyone above the age of twelve knows how to handle a gun. The man complies. He even points the gun at the magician—the paleness around WLADIMIR'S nose suddenly looks terribly real—but the Russian grabs the weapon from him before harm is done, and while cries of approval sound, he takes aim himself. I shudder, for this is a gun, and I know my Chekhov. Then a click—the revolver is now cocked—and then dead silence, except for the rheumatic scratch-ing of the gramophone needle in the end groove of *Lohengrin*. The officer closes one eye and concentrates; he bites his mustache with his lower teeth. Then he lets out a sharp cry and pulls the trigger. The white-hot tongue of a small dragon spews from the mouth of the weapon and a loud bang bounces off the walls, impossibly hard, impossibly barbaric. The stench of sulfur is real: It scratches my throat. In the moment when the mob had crowded around the dragoon, the magician has grabbed a ceramic ashtray; he now holds it in front of his chest, quite a ridiculous shield, but then, right after the bang, or maybe at the exact same time the bullet is released, he bites the air, just like a frog snaps at a fly, and his teeth close audibly around a small, hard chunk which he spits into the ashtray and then throws at the front row—the white-hot bullet—and the man who catches the projectile burns his fingers and drops the object on the floor, and someone else catches it, blowing on it while he juggles it from hand to hand, and when it has cooled down enough to be readable he exclaims: It's the same bullet, the magician's name is there, silver on silver! The man passes the projectile along and we all cheer: for a second we hold a miracle in our hands, while the puzzled Russian hands his weapon over for inspection—the barrel is hot and the chamber is empty.

Before we realize it, the curtains come down. There applause feels endless. The master of ceremonies—also the owner of the theater, the famous Herr Rumpel-peterchen himself—has to climb onstage to calm us down: Yes, us, because I too have jumped to my feet, I clap my hands until they are red and raw. Peterchen motions to the men's room, from which WLADIMIR emerges, all gentleman-like and with a smile from ear to ear. He bows and receives the standing ovation with grace and humility, a humility that seems authentic. A man in the third row, the only man still sitting, now stands up too and takes off his coat and hat and a wealth of chestnut brown hair flows over his shoulders—it is the beauty in the negligee, now reunited with her tall Russian. They too bow deeply, and arm in arm they head towards the exit.

WLADIMIR: the only man in this war who can cheat death simply by biting the bullet.

•

There is nothing mysterious about this last appearance of WLADIMIR. In the men's room a door labeled *"PRIVAT!"* (Horst has a key) opens onto a narrow passage that smells of urine and moist stucco, with walls of whitewashed brick. If you follow it, you'll end up backstage. On the walls there are faded posters, dating from the time when this was a more rowdy kind of theater and the English language was still *en vogue*. From the corner of my eyes, I spy an announcement for the highly suspect swing band *Randy Woody and his Orgystra* and a life-size poster for the peroxide blonde girlie combo *Air Up There* (AKA *Foxygen*), as well as advertisements for long-gone strip clubs with American names—*The Burning Bush, Brave Nude World*—another for *Gordon Blue's Red Hot Jazz Show* ("Ladies, he's cookin'!"), escapist travel posters from the *Argo Reisen* agency, expressionist sketches of exotic Berber dancers juggling anointed dildos and morphine needles, and finally a commercial for an outfit (*Broda Dactylographie*) that provides typewriting classes, thereby affirming the cliché that every stripper dreams of a nine-to-five job.

Behind the stage—on the *Bühne* a group of female dancers called the Sisters Heinie are performing a cancan in costumes that (I can smell it from here) could use some dry cleaning—Horst and I meet the trio: WLADIMIR gallantly grabs my hand, and the Russian introduces himself in accentless German as Lech Lecha (a Sudenten-German Pole?), and the assistant, still flushed, performs an enchanting little bow and introduces herself as Maruschka. Her robe falls open and underneath she is happily and pleasingly naked, apart from a pair of simple white cotton panties. Welcome to show business!

The magician does not release my hand, but raises it high above my head, leading me into a slow pirouette while he watches me intently. I understand. Just like Horst, he assesses my body, the narrowness of my hips, the strength of my muscles. Can I glide in and out of suitcases with ease?, can I quickly slide through the half-open stage trapdoor?—this is what WLADIMIR's eyes are assessing, and I realize that Maruschka and I are very much the same size, as testified by the fact that my bar mitzvah suit fits her perfectly. Under the slight pressure of the magician's hands and Lech's and Marushka's gaze my fingers feel light and alive, they have not been damaged too much by the heavy labor in the munitions factory. I get my suit back, neatly presented on a new hanger, as well as my wallet—I didn't even know it was missing.

"Welcome then," says WLADIMIR, and he calls me by name: He looked at my identity card. There are no negotiations. I am not exactly in a position to negotiate. Well, the illegal Jew and the vanishing artist, they complement each other nicely, don't they?

We wait until the sisters are done dancing. They don't draw much of a crowd. Only the whore and her john are still in the theater, and whatever it is they're doing, it prevents them from applauding. When the curtain has dropped, WLAD-

IMIR leads me to the center of the stage. Lech's fingers slide over the wood, quickly locating the trapdoor.

"Abandon all hope?" I say, smiling nervously, but when WLADIMIR puts his hand in mine, I suppress my fears and follow him to my designated hiding place among the earth's secrets. This is completely logical: The only refuge for the hunted is to go underground. And so I descend from the first circle of refugees to the second. And I try not to be misled by the narrowness of the passage.

•

I become WLADIMIR's assistant. In the mornings he teaches me manual dexterity and speed. I am a fast learner. All those years of piano lessons from my mother have made my fingers strong and nimble. (How I miss her, how I miss her encouraging hand on my shoulder, telling me to go on, except when a false note made her cringe so much that she squeezed it until I bruised. Likewise under WLADIMIR's tutelage, no false notes are allowed—every gesture has to be precise, I have to play the cards the way my mother played a prelude by Chopin.)

I would have liked the magician to introduce me to the deepest secrets of his trade, the things that go beyond marking cards and the manipulation of coins, but that would never happen. I was his assistant, he said, and that should be enough. I could watch and I was free to learn whatever I could from my observations, but he would not explicitly teach me anything. He who does not know, cannot betray. This effectively shut me up—it made me think of Father and how one imprudent step onto the pedestrian crossing cost him his life, but only because some over-zealous snitch had seen him make that faux pas. Ignorance is a precious and vastly underrated commodity. You are an assistant, WLADIMIR told me, day after day, not a sorcerer's apprentice. Sorcerer's apprentices meet miserable fates.

Houdini managed to make an elephant vanish, just like that, on the count of three, and he boasted that even the elephant never found out how the trick was done. WLADIMIR tells that story often, and in a rare mood of defiance—there was lots of potato liquor to be had backstage, the same stuff Horst poured into his flask—I countered that that was easy; the real challenge would have been to make the elephant vanish part by part. First the tail goes, then the trunk, then the tusks, until only a colossal gray pig remains on stage, increasingly astonished, increasingly annoyed, and then, only then—*poof!*—sublime nothingness! My flippant comment makes the magician scratch his five o'clock shadow. He immediately starts brooding and he hardly talks for days. A week later I stumble over a set of long conical tubes and tusks made out of tissue paper. In a cage a highly irritable hog, painted a uniform gray, paces back and forth on stilts made out of clay flowerpots.

I too was part of a vanishing act, and although I had my suspicions, I never knew exactly what happened when I walked blindfolded into the collapsible suitcase and a wall started moving under the pressure of my chest—suddenly I found myself in the basement, but I had no memory of walking down or falling through any kind of horizontal trapdoor.

"I dream," WLADIMIR confides, "of an animal so perfect in its camouflage that nobody has ever found it. Nobody knows it exists, it hasn't been written about in any book. Inside the house it might look very much like a chest of drawers or a spool of thread, outside it might look like an old lime tree or a caterpillar on a birch leaf. One can imagine interesting transitions from inside to outside, for instance one in which the unknown animal disguises itself as a cat, comes inside and then remains unfindable. The only way the animal could be observed would be during a transformation."

·

I did not step into the limelight often. I usually worked in the wings. I managed the props, I threw the clay pigeon in the air at the appropriate moment, I hooked Maruschka to her cables and helped her in and out of her costumes (precious moments when my fingers brushed her naked skin). When I did perform I did so in my black suit, with a neat bowler hat on my head and a vertical stripe of soot on my upper lip: a Chaplin.

Maruschka remained WLADIMIR's real assistant, the muse of his many variations on the theme of transformation, but there were evenings when she was not around and nights when she stayed out until dawn and only sneaked back in around breakfast time, blushing on Horst's arm and beaming with a quiet bliss. I did not ask them what was going on. On these evenings, about once every two weeks, I took over Marushka's role. In the basement, I was made up to look like a woman, tight rubber panties pressed me in between my ass cheeks and breasts made out of rice straw were glued over my nipples; I donned a curly red wig, and, depending on the role, I climbed into a glittery dress, a petticoat or (thank G*d!) my own suit. I was good. Quite a few of the audience members mistook the blush of shame on my face for a sign of virgin innocence. I harvested almost as much applause as the genuine article, and once in a while I even received an envelope with a frighteningly frank proposal for a private rendezvous at midnight. It was easy to deal with those: After I had washed off the makeup I had completed the perfect vanishing act. On the evenings when I performed, Maruschka's name got covered with a strip of paper, but that strip remained blank. I had not yet earned my stripes, even though Lech thought that I truly had talent, if not as a magician, then surely as an actor. Or actress.

But that was subbing. The real work, the work for which I was trained, happened upstairs, in the second big room of the theater, the secret basement room adjoining ours.

•

The ladies' room has its own door with a sign that reads "*PRIVAT!*," but this door is never locked. You open it at your own risk. In the dirty light of the single, never-dusted naked bulb it looks like an entrance to hell: A cloud of bluish smoke creeps from under that door into the toilets, as well as a murmuring that sounds almost threatening, as if the door hides a lair of prehistoric beasts. Open it, and the smoke will sting your eyes and make you retch—there is a hint of real black market tobacco, but the main note is worthless ersatz stuff: oak leaves, I have been told, or shredded ivy cut with tattered old rags. Whoever smokes this stuff must be addicted to a deep and consistent pain in his lungs. Your ears will hurt as well, going in. There is the clinking of beer glasses and the rustling of paper, the pounding of fists on tabletops, and a cloud of loud protest always hangs over at least one of the tables—the place is awash in flushed faces: men with hairy wrists and bloody eyes and yellow stains in the armpits of their shirts, the knots of their ties low below their Adam's apples, their breath stale, their voices hoarse from all the yelling for beer, men who are used to letting their fists do the talking. Plaster mermaids hang from the ceiling, and stalactites of snot cover their breasts; they twist their fishtails in a cheap imitation of ecstasy. In a corner, a stuffed bear, undoubtedly there to symbolize the Russian nation, claws at the smoke; a small gaggle of spears is stuck in his pockmarked sides, and the visitors hang their coats and hats from the shafts. A veil of sly snugness hangs over every face in the room. The main business here is not booze or entertainment, but the things that really count: money and sausage, potatoes and coffee. There is a black market in Berlin, but this is a black supermarket. The masses may have preferred cannons to butter, but that still doesn't mean that butter is worthless, and shouldn't be subject to high-price negotiations. You can always find somebody who wants to haggle.

Or wants to gamble. Gambling is much more thrilling than the direct sell: On the black market you can swap x cartons of cigarettes against y pounds of butter, but the temptation to win y pounds of butter with a handful of cards and some good judgment, without having to put x cartons of cigarettes on the table first, is more than most men can resist. Good judgment? The beer is cheap and abundant, and there's plenty of bootleg vodka to go around, and all of this erodes the higher-order thinking processes in no time. The only food Peterchen serves is a thin gray soup, basically a bowl of mist: not exactly the heavy, absorbent food the gambler would need to keep his head cool.

The first evening, Horst and I walk through the room with no specific purpose. We take a seat at this table or the other, we lose a couple of reichsmarks here, win a few there, and Horst shows me the men who populate this tiny universe.

There are a few general types. The men who firmly believe that six turns of bad luck must mean that the seventh will be incredibly lucky. These are easy prey; they will wager all their earthly possessions and still blame Lady Luck and not the cunning of the house. There are overly cautious men who set a firm limit for gains and losses; at the end of the night, they walk home without joy, but also without sorrow. This is a rare breed better left alone; we only work their tables to not raise suspicion. The easiest men to handle are those who do not believe in luck, but only in ability. They do not understand that the choice of cards is not theirs but those of fortune and of the man with the best sleight of hand. Misleading them is so easy that it's almost immoral. Let them enjoy a winning streak first, and then hustle them. It's important to only zero in on them right before closing time, because these swells will always look for another lucky break—they don't know when to stop, and they won't take no for an answer, unless Peterchen closes the joint. And even then, a hasty retreat through the trapdoor might be in order.

There are also a few local characters who don't gamble, but just hang out and try to make a buck. The poet, for example, who goes from table to table begging for a reichsmark—in return he will *not* read you his poems. If you do not pay up immediately, he will recite a first sentence to give you a last chance to buy out. All his poems start with the word "It" ("It was dark . . ." "It rained . . ." "It crept near . . ."). After one of those deep-dark German lines, everybody suddenly finds some spare change in a hitherto hidden pocket. Then there's the woman with the irresistibly sleepy Swabian accent—whatever the topic of conversation is (her favorite is the weather in Berlin), once you get her started, the whole table will be snoring in minutes. Then she and her earplug-wearing accomplice quickly retrieve watches and wallets and other such useless encumbrances from the pockets of her audience. If the customers complain, Peterchen shrugs. Who's ever heard of such a thing—people falling asleep in the middle of a poker game? That should be his fault?

Of course, every bet is on in this place of evil; and not just for money or small potatoes. WLADIMIR points at his shiny, ill-fitting suit.

"This smoking jacket once belonged to Helena Guna, can you believe that? I keep myself thin: I want to be able to go on wearing it. I won it in a poker game. She went home wearing just her shirt. A long shirt, with tails that did cover her shame, but only barely."

I imagine the scene: Helena Guna, object of so many young men's dreams, half-naked in this locale.

"Did you take her home?" I ask. I know the actress's reputation; she's a real man-eater.

"Alas," WLADIMIR answers smartly. "She didn't feel very favorably inclined toward the man who robbed her of this garment, my dear boy. Here. Feel this. Excellent fabric, *na*? Beautiful cut. First-rate Jewish handiwork from the Thirties. No, she wasn't inclined to bet her shirt—I would have happily taken her up on that challenge, I had a full house hidden in my sleeve. I might have even let her win; the moment when she had to put her stakes on table would have been reward enough. Rumpelpeterchen always works with all bets on the table: In case the loser behaves less nobly than he ought one can still gather one's winnings and dart for the door."

Helena Guna! What young man didn't dream of sinking into the warm tide pool of the actress's questionable morals? This fabric then had fit around her waist; these thinning pants had once held the diva's rump?

"Is that a true story?" I ask Maruschka later that evening, down in the spelunk. She shrugs.

"Could be. Who knows, maybe she did visit this gambling palace—she was a wild one after all—and maybe she urgently needed some cash to score some coke . . . but would she have been stupid enough to try to beat a magician at poker, and would she . . .? Anyway, what do you care if it's true?"

•

For a few weeks, WLADIMIR and I practice the business of my new occupation. The Hindu Shuffle, "finger magnetism," thumb nailing cards on the fly, replacing inauspicious cards with more favorable ones—timing is everything here.

I have one question. "Won't they recognize me?" WLADIMIR smiles. The true magician makes his audience see what he wants them to see, and nothing else. All attention is focused on the magician's hands, but only when the magician wants it to be so. Attention is deflected as needed to face or body or prop. The assistant is such a prop, nothing more than a device to divert attention. A captive audience will recognize the hands of the magician out of thousands, but rare indeed are those who can recognize the accomplice's face, unless the accomplice is as beautiful as Maruschka—but even she would not be recognized in the streets if she wore her raincoat and hat. In Maruschka's case, the attention is deflected by the sequined suit and its desirable contents.

"Believe me," says WLADIMIR. "You could stand next to me on the stage for a thousand years, and still nobody would recognize you."

I learn how to make split-second decisions based on instinct alone—a skill quite useful in the business of exploiting others. I learn the fine art of emotional manipulation—not, as people often think, by wiping all trace of feeling from my face, but by showing counterfeit traces. Let hesitation flutter a moment in your eyelids, allow a quick eruption of triumph to play across your forehead, and make sure none of this lasts longer than a fraction of a second—make it look as if the truth just broke through your mask of impassiveness, and your opponent will register neither the emotional signs nor his own interpretation. But he will act accordingly, and that is what counts.

I also learn how to sleep lightly. I keep a knife next to my mattress. I learn to make the distinction between the footsteps of those I know and those of strangers. Like a mother who wakes up instantly at the slightest sigh of her baby, I wake up when strange footsteps approach my bunk, and my fingers clench tightly around the handle of my knife. I have never used that knife; the strange footsteps invariably belong to a new member of our troupe.

And I also learn and understand that the trust placed in me—their trust that I will not betray the cause; that I will hand over all the money I win—is based on strategy. I cannot betray that trust, for this is my last resort. There is nowhere else I can go. If I can find salvation in this world, it is with this group of people.

•

And what an assortment it is, the troupe that lives in the basement! The composition always changes—artists are, like Jews, a nomadic people. A trained seal who beeps *"Deutschland, Deutschland Über Alles"* on car horns lives in a big vat of strong brine. A supposedly Chinese ventriloquist, Mister Rong, enters the stage with his puppet—a naked woman—and sticks his arm inside her all the way to the elbow . . . and that's the most tasteful part of his act: it's all downhill from there.

It is not surprising that, apart from WLADIMIR, we are all much less than mediocre. All male artists of any talent are touring the front and entertaining the troops. Only those who are too old or too ill to make the trip are left, and of course the incompetent, the foreigners, and the non-Aryans. Even among ourselves, we keep mum as to what category we belong to, but it isn't hard to recognize the skittish pupils of the men who shouldn't be here, the painful miracle of day-to-day survival against all odds.

We sleep on straw mattresses. The basement is only reachable through the stage trapdoor. There's also a door in the corner that's bolted from our side. I have been told that it leads to the sewers. At least once a week Maruschka checks whether the bolt still slides in and out easily, and whether the passage is obstructed—not unthinkable after a bombing, and any obstruction could be catastrophic.

There is no vault, just the flat underside of the stage floor a few inches above our heads. The basement is an auditory version of Plato's cave—we can easily guess what happens above: The chairs of dubious construction scrape over the floor, the dove tiptoes back to its cage, dance steps rain from the sisters' feet. We have intimate knowledge of the floorboards that creak and the floorboards that remain silent, indispensable knowledge for the assistant who needs to move quickly and inaudibly behind the magician's screens. During WLADIMIR's act, I listen from below, able to infer where exactly he is in his routine and at which point I need to open the trapdoor to slide into the fabled fake bottom of his treasure chest.

Bats should be hanging from the rafters, and the basement should resound with the rheumatic moans of the ghosts of entertainers past.

"If you had arrived a few months earlier," says WLADIMIR, "you would have shared the room with a smelly tiger on a leash and twenty live pigeons in iron cages." It's not hard to guess what happened to those animals. We are all hungry.

The only creatures that get fat during wartime are the rats. And the ones we share our living space with are not exactly timid. They only shuffle away, and not too eagerly at that, when I come shooting down through the trapdoor at full speed. At night, when we sleep, they sniff our fingers. There's little doubt that when a hand grows cold enough to indicate that its owner has died, the rats will take a bite. We put down traps—the extra calories are welcome—but it doesn't deter the rodents.

We wash ourselves in the toilets with the ice-cold water that comes out of the tap, and we shave by the shaky light of our one bulb. The women cut our hair. We can't go to a regular hairdresser. Hairdressers are gossips by nature, and they have good memories. Every new head inspires a healthy mistrust in them.

Each of us has friends that went missing: parents, daughters, sons, brothers, sisters, lovers, who all vanished one night. They should be at our side, or we at theirs. A strong sense of guilt is brewing here. Why have we been chosen to see the light of another day, and why not our loved ones? What in the karmic chain of existence makes us the ones who got lucky? Don't misunderstand me—we are very well aware that our fortune can change at any moment. We may have seen the morning, we may not see the night. There are rumors, brought to us by the *JMAG*, *Judische Mundfunk AktienGesellschaft*, the Jewish Word-of-Mouth Broadcasting Corporation—that there are traitors, illegals just like us who rat on other illegals. A beautiful young woman addresses you in the street. She's hungry. You take her out for lunch; maybe you hope for a little more than company. She admits that she is an illegal Jewess; you admit to your own status. She gets up from the table and smiles—she has to make a phone call, she will be right back. Five minutes later the handcuffs are on your wrists. Who would have thought that the angel of death could have such a sexy smile?

But we're all one big family now, and I don't just mean our troupe at Rumpel-peterchen's, but all fugitives, all U-boats (as we call ourselves), and we are all like our undisputed leader WLADIMIR: kings of the handcuff, the vanishing act—graduates from life's school of survival.

The dust in that basement: the almost-Nothing that gathers itself in tumbling tufts.

·

We live in the underbelly of the city, this poor city that is shot to pieces. The few times we go outside, we look around with mouths wide open. Houses have been forced to their knees like exhausted gladiators, but still aren't ready to give up—though, oh boy, they sure do sway. Other houses look like pathetic drunk old ladies leaning over the gutter in a wave of nausea. Others look like skittish animals that just came running from the edge of the wood and then froze in stone-cold panic. Some houses are still standing solidly, except that their front walls have been blasted away. They look like enormous doll houses, and I half expect the inhabitants to walk in and continue their daily activities, lighting a pipe, for instance, and reading the newspaper, or stirring a pot of pasta on the stove (the smoke associated with both activities would stay neatly inside, I assume, as if there were a wall of glass), or perhaps to make neat little doll love underneath cute little blankets. On a metal table in one of the rooms I spot a typewriter, the type bars warped by rust, a thorny bush of twisted language screaming to the heavens.

"You will always live in the underbelly of this city," says Horst. By "you" he means us, the people who once thought they were chosen, but now are almost extinct. "Even when you aren't here any more"—"you," by which he means us, the wandering kind—"even then you will continue to live in this city, live in it through your absence. It will rise through the town in vertical columns, loneliness and sadness soaring like negative light into the sky. Your absence will be noted—it will change this town. Concrete and steel will bend and twist in pain. Imagine this city without Jews: all curiosity gone, and the brute inanity of fashion as king."

"What about you?"

"No," says Horst, "there will always be communists. We will return to Berlin, you can bet on that. They'll hear from us again. But for you there is no way back. Imagine this town in peacetime: a city without artists. No more painters of importance, no more sculptors who can whack reality on the head until it bursts with life. No more filmmakers who can show us what it means to be simply human, to be caught up in our day-to-day existence and yet be a hero. No playwrights and no violinists to translate our melancholy into vibrating falsetto, no singers to lure Orpheus from his Hades. Can't you see what Hitler is doing to this town? He steals away its playfulness, he robs it of its humanity. The baroque architecture of Berlin is frozen Bach—Hitler's architecture is a frozen march. He understands better than anyone how much scale matters. The German people are less taken by beauty than by grandiosity. And that much the Nazi regime can offer: grandiosity, in all its massive, imposing, pompous ugliness: showy, overblown citations of Schinkel's humble classicism—the present is now officially better than the past because it's so much bigger. Hitler writes us a schizography in stone, a celebration of empty form. The architect of the cathedral in the Mitte had a mocha gateau in mind, but what was the architect of the chancellery thinking when he gave his building the color of regurgitated liver? Are we already in the belly of the beast? Hitler's palace is decidedly carnivorous, it breaks people's necks, it snaps perfectly straight spines in two. When the war is over, all that will come down faster than you can say denazification."

"'Denazification'? 'When the war is over'? 'Peacetime'? Horst, are you crazy?"

"This can't go on forever, can it?"

•

I know I'm lucky. I could hardly have found a better home; I could hardly be more thoroughly hidden than I am now—deep under the ground, in disguise, and with false papers of the highest quality. There are people, I hear, who hide in the sheds in the public gardens, cold and quiet; they live off roots they dig up with their bare hands. Horst's first underground address was with a woman friend; his hiding place was the couch. It was a big and heavy piece made out of oak; underneath the cushions there was just about enough room for one man. Horst covered the back and front of the sofa with hinged boards that could be bolted from the inside; whenever somebody knocked at the door he quickly disappeared. A bottle of water and a bottle of cough syrup were kept inside so he wouldn't die of dehydration or betray himself by an inadvertent cough. Horst's friend kept her alcohol behind lock and key—drunken men cannot be trusted. When Horst went outside to ply his trade of stamps and paper, she hung a piece of cloth in front of the keyhole. When he came back, he peered through the hole before entering the house; if the piece of cloth was gone, he would know he had to flee immediately. She also kept an old coat on a rack by the door. If the cloth was still there, Horst would carefully lift it with a pencil to check whether her coat was still on the rack. If it wasn't, he would run too, because that would mean she had been arrested. Horst slept inside the sofa. His dog's life ended when the friend replaced his water bottle and found a handkerchief stained with semen. "You could have done that with me," she said. "Don't you see how I long for you? Don't you know I have needs?" Horst had known, all right, and he wouldn't have minded sleeping with her, except that he knew very well that vigilance vanishes once the bedsprings go creaking.

Yes, what's with all that sex in the ruins, in the basements and hiding places—all those bold bodily embraces precisely now, in the saddest of times? For those in Peterchen's colony, it might just have been opportunity. Thanks to the cracks in the stage, we all have intimate knowledge of what's hidden underneath the dancers' skirts; we know what August packs in those ridiculously wide pants of his. We're stacked so close on top of each other that there's little room or time for shame or prudishness. Quite often when I come shooting through the trapdoor during WLADIMIR's act, I end up in the middle of a performance of a radically different kind. One of the clowns, for instance, with only half of his makeup washed off, in the arms of an overweight and absentminded ballerina who has clearly misplaced her panties. They shoo me away, but I can't go back upstairs, because then WLADIMIR'S trick would be ruined. I stay and at first they pout, but then they resume their business while I simply look the other way. The older artists don't even care if they're interrupted during their lovemaking. "What the heck," shrugs the oldest Sister Heinie, "During the Weimar years, I did this on stage all the time, and under bright white lights too." "And don't I still look pretty good?" she asks, threatening to move the oil lamp closer to prove her point.

Maybe sex is just like any other bodily need. The body lives in frustration. It wants to eat, but there isn't enough food; it wants to sleep, but even in the rare bombless nights our anxiety and the rustling rats keep us awake; it wants to be close to a beloved's body, but there's no time for true love's gifts—there is hardly enough time for a travesty of love in its pettiest manifestations. These random copulations must be more an expression of our desire for refuge than of pure lust; more ducking than fucking, as it were.

The wise old Jew from Vienna, the watcher of the coffee grounds of dreams, might offer a deeper explanation. Perhaps he would point at the Janus head of Love and Death. When one half of this monster speaks, the other half has a hard time keeping silent. When the Death-half screams, the Love-half tries to outscream it. This isn't flirting with Death, it is flirting *against* Death. Rage against the dying of the light, and quite loudly too.

Let the music swell, a thick syrupy orchestral sound, fat with violins and chunky with brass, something cinematic, maybe some Copeland or Williams. Something recognizable, hefty: big billowing waves of sound for us to wallow in, a reason to drown. And baby, yeah: Let's misbehave. Let it be a movie in which a man big as a stable door presses a sweltering woman to his heaving chest of granite. "I do not want to sleep alone tonight," she begs. "Please, don't let me go lonesome into that long dark night!" He hugs her closer. Her brittle body, covered with blood and grime, her body—well, it wows him, it intoxicates him. The eruption of their love will be tremendous. And I, in my corner, I twist restlessly on my straw mattress and I listen-in and shake my head.

Another thing: We are illegal. We can be shot and killed on sight. The bare fact of our presence in this town, in this country, sentences us to death. When you have nothing to lose, you don't have the luxury of despair. You turn grim and bitter. You become dangerous. We've all officially entered the realm of the ghosts. We are no-men, no-women; non-entities; pure plasma is what we are. So many of us no longer have any official proof as to who we are; the smartest among us have even forgotten who they once were. We are men and women cloaked with unreality, our bodies move in and out of focus. Maybe that's what makes us drift together. Here today, gone tomorrow. Yes, we will die, but the night before our death we will at least reap a few brief but intense moments of joy. That too should be part of the weekly news bulletin: In the past seven days, five thousand citizens of the Reich have made love for the very last time in their lives. The death threats have their influence. Our gentle hands turn into dirty paws and claws that hook; our tongues become hasty hammers; our hips are roaring engines—all this coarse screwing has less to do with passion than with the manic pursuit of an illusion: that there is a future. Our lovemaking is a vanishing act, a better one than WLADIMIR has ever conjured up.

And I, in my corner, I hide my head under the blankets. I'm just a boy, so should I have to endure such sounds less than three feet away from a warm woman's body (often one that can professionally contort itself in the most agile positions)? I'm too green and shy to lose my virginity in public, and so I am reduced to the sad milking of the dry teat of my sex; I come, but I do not achieve a real release—no tangible relief ensues.

•

One day a miracle happens. Peterchen pastes a new banner on the poster that advertises WLADIMIR and Maruschka, the one in which the magician stares pensively at the onlooker, chin in hand, while his assistant imitates a dying swan in the background. The banner reads *Mit musikalisches Vorspiel*. We now have a musical warm-up act? Many kinds of variety show have bloomed in our theater, but never we've never had a band. Music softens the heart, and a soft heart is the last thing Peterchen wants in his customers—a mild-hearted gambler, imagine that! Why then this combo, with the strange name *Die Ill-Omen-Ati*?

"They're good," Peter grumbles. Payola, guesses Maruschka, and indeed, after each show the bassist walks into the crowd with an upturned hat. Good for them: What they earn must be at least twice as much as what they owe Peterchen—they're good, and the donations are plentiful.

I get quite the shock when I see the *Ill-Omen-Ati* perform for the first time.

Stella!

Or a woman that could be Stella, her waist expanded considerably, her nose pasty, a woman who clearly lives on a diet of too much alcohol and potatoes. The band's pianist announces her as the Greek sensation Mia Kouri.

The I-O-A is six-piece combo in the old, forbidden style. They do variations on Cole Porter and Hoagy Carmichael and pretend to be American—"Timothy 'King' Lear on bass! Chase Manhattan on drums!"—but all of them look decidedly Berlinesque, and the inclusion in their hand-printed prospectus of a prewar review from the travel page of the Sunday *Times* ("They create performances that are invariably provocative and always uninspiring") suggests that the band has not quite mastered English. Their young saxophone player might or might not be Stella's beau—I didn't get a good look at him from up close, the night of Stella's disappearance. He does have the same crown of thinning hair and he lets the stage lights sparkle off his instrument much as Stella's lover made use of the moon, but so many men lose their hair, and don't all saxophonists go through that same schmaltzy spiel to accentuate a long hot note?

Whoever they are, whoever she is, the singer has clearly been beaten up by life. Her hips have that low sway, that permanent state of stoned inebriation that characterizes the vamp. Later, when I found out what she was really all about, I would understand. The prey that escapes the panther to see another animal being ripped apart in its stead experiences the most curious, druggy sensation—the certainty of being chosen, without knowing by whom or what.

I am a mere apprentice in the entertainment business, nothing less, nothing more, but this Mia Kouri woman clearly is (French accent, please) an *artiste*, and she presents herself as such, hanging on to the mic stand as if it were the mast of a ship in a boiling ocean, pressing the microphone to her lips as if she were a cardinal kissing the holy grail—she did after all wear a blood-red dress and a boa of carmine goose feathers. She sings, princess of many tongues, and so reluctantly does she push out the humid svarabhakti vowels that it makes her song—"Let's Stalk About Love"—sound quite convincing. Even though it's crystal clear that she has long since stopped believing in any of this stuff—those lyrics about stardust and love's inevitability; their assertion that somebody's shoulder (and not, for instance, their wallet) is all you really need—it's also clear that she *wants* to believe in it, and that she wants us to believe in it too, with an urgency that transcends words—she may grind the microphone stand slowly, but grind it she does, and those languid circles might get her off after all. Sometimes she forgets whole lines and then her singing turns into a brittle hum. Hoarse little girl, rudderless at the microphone: You are a holy sinner, and all of us in the audience want to either convert you—or pervert you further.

Once upon a time her dress must have fit her like a glove; now her pale breasts spill uncomfortably out of the tight corset. And yet, despite the singer's opulent form, she has the sharp cheekbones of a death's head. Her face is raw, all the fat melted away; the nerve endings bristle in the naked air. The acid of time has etched its course on that face. She's probably on heroin—if you're willing to pay the price, anything can be found in Berlin. (What was the price she paid? More about that later.) Or maybe a gruesome psychosomatic cancer is sucking the juice right out of her? I would never get to know the full truth, but I do know that when she leans into that microphone for her whispered *Sprechgesang* rendition of Porter's "I've Got You Under My Skin," the hair on the back of my neck stands right up—it's so obvious that the obsessive love she professed was not for a man of flesh and blood, but for some far less innocent, far less common, much more deadly *Fremdkörper*

racing through her veins. I can assure you that whatever foreign spirit was possessing her, she wears the corresponding *tristesse* with unmistakable grandeur. Not a
dry eye in the house. Even the sixty-year old pianist shuffles uneasy on his bench,
blinded by tears, and possible additionally hampered by an untamable swelling in
his crotch.

"Hi," she says when we meet in the wings. "Hi. How are you?" Of course it's Stella
hiding underneath all these layers of *Ton de Feinte*, and this (this?) she said was
"her Rolf." And I am, well, an old schoolmate, a few years younger—she stayed with
my parents for a while, such a small world, isn't it? (Yes, that much is true, Stella,
the world is shrinking every day, and it will go on shrinking until there is nothing left.)

That I call her by her real name startles her: such a small but momentous
breach of decorum. I grab Rolf's hand and shake it; I introduce myself as the ever
cheerful, the happily alliterating and doubly iambic Helmut Hinkel. Yes, of course,
Rolf remembers me, even though he's never seen me. Well, he's heard the stories—Stella has told him so much about me! What stories? I wonder, but then I
have to rush to the stage.

It was quite a smart move on Rumpelpeterchen's part to hire Stella and her band.
Stella's voice is covered in thorny calluses, and so are her looks. She grates her
listeners' souls most wonderfully. Her music doesn't soften the heart at all; on the
contrary, it rubs it raw. And so much bare sentiment makes a man thirsty. The
effects are measurable. For at least half an hour after each of her performances,
the alcohol consumption spikes, and the gamblers are noticeably less alert. After
Stella's performance I rush to the den as quickly as I can—now my dexterity and
carefulness can really pay off.

When she introduced me to him, Rolf had his arm around Stella's waist. They were
together. But nobody *had* Stella. Stella belonged to nobody but herself; as such, she
belonged to everybody. I occasionally got a glimpse out of the corner of my eye,
during a quick costume change or a dive in and out of the trapdoor, of a semi-naked
Stella in a hushed embrace with one of our arthritic acrobats or traveling jugglers
or even a starving chorus girl or two, and once even with Horst—unremarkably
dirty deeds done in the half-dark of a dusty corner under the stage. Stella liked
her afternoon trysts brief and to-the-point; she went for the quick fix, the sharp
kick that could lift her over the surface for no more than a second, after which she
could sink twice as heavily into the mire of despair in which she found her art. It
didn't matter to her whether anybody saw her; when she did opt for privacy she

went behind the basement door, and the cries that rose from the sewers suggested intense pain rather than immense joy. People change, of course. But Stella had come quite a distance from being the young woman who one lonely night had played Satie in our backroom.

Now Stella could be mine. And that is precisely why I made no attempt to conquer her. Stella or not and adolescent hormones be damned: I didn't want my first time to be like this—just a fuck, ear to ear, hands over each other's mouths to muffle the moans and only the crucial body parts bared. It would be a terrible disappointment.

I have to be increasingly careful where I put my feet when I slide into the underbelly of the theater. Whatever else Stella puts in her system, cheap *Kartoffelschnapps* is one of her favorite vices. When she's done, she lets the empty bottles slip out of her hands to roll wherever they might. Stella is stranded and posting messages, except that in her stupor she forgets to put her notes inside her bottles. She also takes *Cebion* pills by the handful, the nauseatingly sweet vitamin preparations meant to protect the Aryans from their own vegetable-poor diet. Those pills are probably the only food she eats, or at least the only food she can keep down—more than once I land in a shallow puddle of watery vomit. This can't go on, obviously. After less than two weeks—thirteen days in which she seems to have slept with everybody except Lech, Maruschka, WLADIMIR, and me—she and her band just give up and leave, without a trace.

They are replaced by The Sad Beats, a mock-cool combo who mix moribund mambos with thanatoid tangos and combines washed-up waltzes with fraudulent foxtrots. They play with expressionless faces; hand-rolled cigarettes droop from lethargic lips; and to counter this excess of weariness, their singer, Kick Knave, performs like a man possessed; he mills his arms around and swings the microphone low over the theater seats, thus flirting with both potential audience-decapitation and self-electrocution. He runs laps on the stage as if he wants to shake all arteriosclerosis out of his body in one fell swoop. This guy is on a much more destructive trip than Stella ever was—Stella destroyed herself, but Kick is out to wreck us too. Peterchen fires them after only two evenings—the decibels made his head ache, and their show lures weird-looking young men in from the street. After that no more music, except of course the creaking offerings of the cranky gramophone.

But Stella's presence has its effect. The *Ill-Omen-Ati* packed up the day before Hitler's birthday—less than twenty-four hours later I'm no longer a virgin, and my deflowering has been everything I ever dreamed it would be: soft and tender, urgent and clumsy; with everything, everything, body and soul, bared and together lilting.

●

I am not sure whether WLADIMIR notices anything when I return from that strange journey—the timid, tentative, thrilling journey each of us takes at that age; the journey that at last made Hitler's birthday a day of joy and remembrance for me. I am changed when I return to the basement. There's not just a new sparkle in my eye and a fresh spring in my step, there's also a melancholy that cuts deeper than ever. The voyager who returns home is always lonely. He has been to foreign lands, and now that he's back home, his travels seem more real to him than the land where he was born. He is forced to both mourn the loss of his homeland and be nostalgic for those lost, distant shores. For the very first time, the basement feels claustrophobic to me. Just doing my job requires tremendous effort, and for some reason I lose at poker, and quite a lot of money too.

What makes a great magician or a great con man?—and those terms are almost synonymous, really. You need ten thousand hours and more of lonesome intimate contact with your art—that's one thing—but even more important is your inner light, your inner faith. Magic isn't just a matter of fingers, it's also a matter of an almost aesthetic sensitivity, making your fingers go instinctively where they have to go. Not unlike, I surmise, the self-confidence of a painter who watches an image result from the strokes of his brush—it doesn't have anything to do with him: The image has always been there. It's that confidence, that blind trust in the conspiracy of mind and hand that makes the difference between a truly great magician and the slick hustlers who ply their trade in the streets with upside-down tumblers and loud wagers. True magic is born our of an inner silence, and it happens sometimes literally at the drop of a hat. A magician is like the ideal lover whose hands awaken his mistress's desires before she can even voice them. The downside is that even the smallest of disturbance of the mind's equilibrium will be fatal. In my case, I pay for my distraction in real cash. Somehow, however, WLADIMIR is not upset when he looks inside my wallet at the end of the day and finds it emptier than ever. He smiles while Maruschka comes over and hugs me. She must be an excellent reader of body language—or else Horst has talked to her. Maruschka hugs me, and I hug her back. When I put my hand on her shoulders, she lets out a sharp cry. I move away quickly. She pants and bites her upper lip to keep herself from screaming again.

"Maruschka?"

"It's nothing."

I open her robe, and she does not protest. WLADIMIR watches in silence, outwardly unmoved, but I know that underneath his poker face he must be subliminally releasing the full maelstrom of his feelings upon me. What I see makes me shiver. A deep wound with tattered edges, only recently scabbed over; a wound less than a few days old. A gunshot wound, most likely. Just looking at Marushka's ripped flesh makes me dizzy with anger, and I understand in an instant whom I have really—beyond any doubt, and unconditionally—fallen in love with.

She reads the question in my eyes, but she deflects it.

Do yourself a favor, my boy—never ask me what I do, never ask me what has happened. That is what her eyes are telling me. Her strength makes her even more loveable.

Later that night WLADIMIR takes me apart. No words are necessary, and no words are spoken. We sit in the back of the theater, we listen to the halting gramophone and we watch the awkward goings-on on stage. We finish a bottle of wine between the two of us, red and noble like arterial blood.

●

Horst is an excellent counterfeiter, a true master with wood and knife. He can forge any stamp. With the shell of a hard-boiled egg he rubs the ink until it looks old and dull. The raw materials are important: A blank form works best; recycling works well too (Sara, the official middle name for every Jewess, can be transformed into Gerda almost imperceptibly). The papers of those who die abroad are revoked; sometimes a civil servant forgets to shred them. If you jolt his memory— a hundred mark note often helps—he might remember which drawer he left it in. Another possibility is to acquire an official identity card by showing a certificate of baptism; the pastor of the Swedish Church will enter Jews in his registry when he feels so inclined—churches are always short on cash, they engage in so much charitable work, hefty donations always make the pastor happy. You can also try the post office. They have identity cards that serve no official purpose, except as a certificate that allows you to receive a certified letter. If you happen to lose yours, they have to provide you with a new one. But that takes some time, good sir—the employee looks over your shoulder at the countless people who are in line behind you, so many people who would rather be anywhere else but here; they all have something better to do and they all stare the postal worker in the face with undisguised hatred and contempt. Of course you reward the poor man for his time and for the indignities he suffers day by day, hour by hour, with another of those cool, crisp hundred mark bills. In other words, I'm getting a pretty good idea how my gambling proceeds are being spent.

•

Horst is a hard worker. He often appears at the theater with an exhausted, hang-dog expression on his face—the result of staring too long through the magnifying glass. When that happens, I take him out, that is, if WLADIMIR agrees to let me go. We go to bars where we know he can pick up fresh beauties even with this tired, squinting, red-eyed stare; he pays for his-and-hers drinks with banknotes that I discreetly tucked into his wallet during our subway ride.

We can't help it—the city is a magnet. At night the streets, illuminated by the headlights of taxicabs, still look the same, if you wish away the rubble—theaters empty out on time, candlelight flickers in the windows of restaurants, their customers half-hidden by the vapor trails of their own breath on the glass. Horcher still serves lobster and *foie gras*. Hotel Bristol has its own distillery in the basement; they play Lehar and *Wiener-Blut* waltzes and Horst dances the night away with one of the rich Heidis that frequent the place. At the bus stops, men engage you in ominous conversations that are suspiciously content-free. "It's raining, eh? It's raining, right? Isn't it raining in the most *miserable* way?" Maybe they want to check your accent. The cityscape, with its ever-increasing barrenness, its mounting destruction, is merely a forewarning of the ruin of our inner landscape.

Berlin by night. Girls who know how to wear a dress use the rustling Tiergarten for their private purposes, rare flowers with a blind trust in all that is earthly, *frotteuses extr'ordinaires* who behave as if they own the place. The oily black river looks tame and gleams. A street vendor sells you a bag of tepid and floury *Maultaschen* from underneath his coat with a nod and a wink as if it's the greatest drug on earth. Earthworms slide fat as snakes out of the humid soil of the Lustgarten, seduced by the promise of spring rain. On the steps of the Altes Museum lovers whisper endearments to each other with the most earnest expressions on their faces; they walk slowly and solemnly as if they were at a funeral, and puree of blind, guiltless worms slushes under the soles of their boots. A night bus drives by, and deafening light splatters from its windows.

There has been a new breakthrough in surrealism; the streets are a gallery of dada. We walk past a house and it rains fruit from above. A woman throws apples and lemons out the window, expensive black market produce. The Gestapo is paying her a visit, and she does not want to betray her suppliers. "I am waiting for the moment," Horst muses, "when NSDAP-members will throw themselves from the roofs and burst open on the cobblestones like juicy fruit."

More surrealism. A bomb must have fallen on the zoo. A zebra mare wades through the moonlight on Unter-den-Linden, high on careful legs, shy, long-necked and thin as a giraffe. Her stripes are navy-on-sulfur; her ribs poke through her skin. A man grabs his pistol and takes her down. A small mob tears the flesh off the carcass with bare hands. Whoever eats that diseased animal's meat will die of rot in their guts. (Horst's band of dogs understands this well—they stay safely away.) A flight of holy ibises circles over the city. Holy ibises feast on cadavers; just breathing in the Berlin air is enough to satiate them. A herd of impalas jumps around on Opernplatz; they break their matchstick legs when they slip on the wet stones. We roam through the crowd that gathers around the animals. I apply my newly learned pickpocket skills and empty the wallets of the well-to-do citizens. They deserve it; they just watched Don Giovanni being dragged to a hell of his own making and they enjoyed it. Out of principle, I refuse to steal from the ones who have earned their money honestly, and so I choose only well-tailored gents, and ladies with shiny stones in their ample cleavage. A large proportion of the money I pilfer must come from the Aryanization of Jewish companies or the forced labor of my brothers in faith. I consider it a small form of restitution. A fight breaks out: A worker beats up one of his bosses over possession of an antelope thigh. The police intervene. Shots are fired. Dead bodies, human and animal, are carried away in moving vans.

Berlin, 1943. Our bodies are now fully inoculated with antibodies for imminent death.

•

Late in summer, the Allied forces begin their offensive in earnest. The basement shakes and shudders, beams bend and sag as if invisible giants are using them as a jungle gym. Chalk falls from the walls, and the flakes break into powder on the floor. The dust invades our lungs, we all cough like crazy. Our first direct hit. WLADIMIR sits in a corner, the cage with the one remaining dove between his feet. I suddenly find myself in Maruschka's arms. From the wall that separates us from the gambling den we hear yelling and screaming—panicked customers and the bartenders who try to shout some calm into them. Our hearts are raging; they beat madly against the walls of our coffin of loose soil and fragile wood. Then Peterchen sticks his head through the trapdoor. He brings a tray loaded with huge, shameless pints of beer, the foam in the glasses exactly one nose-length high—and life is good again. The beer rinses the dirt from our stinging throats, it fizzes and inspires us. We toast to our liberators ("Go Tommy go!"), and the clinking of glass against glass is a symphony.

"Let's go upstairs!" As expected, Goya has painted a halo of yellow and orange and red over the city. Above that crown of flames bomber planes drone while the *Flak* batteries do their best to *rat-tat-tat* them down. With every hit, the ground shudders like a beast wounded by spears. I still have my arm around Maruschka. WLADIMIR holds up a wet finger to test the winds; he announces that we are safe from the flames. This then is what you have reaped, Herr Hitler: this whirlwind of lightening and fire, a storm that colors the far horizons of the city red; an unstoppable, unforgettable inferno. We raise our beer mugs and drink to the health of the squadrons of death.

The bombings throw a wide lane of fire from west to east, from Charlottenburg over the Tiergarten all the way to the Mitte—there the planes fan out southwards and set the Tempelhof neighborhood ablaze. The women's prison at the Bessemerstraße takes a direct hit. The prisoners—most of them race defilers—are let out of their cells and assemble in the inner courtyard. The smoke stings their skin; fire and metal rain down from the nearby Opel factory. Whoever tries to escape is driven back into the inferno of the cellblock by brute force. The guards are clearly in a panic. Some cells never get opened.

A purple veil of dirt hangs over the city for a full two days: an extended desert sunrise. People walk around with wet blankets over their shoulders and tears in their eyes. The cadavers in the streets dry out from the heat and shrivel up like giant fetuses. Shoe soles melt on the hot pavement. People hold handkerchiefs in front of their mouth and noses, but the phosphor burns through everything. We see people with horrible blisters on faces already blue and green with bruises. Fire trucks get stuck in the rubble, their sirens sing desperate swan songs—great waves of noise that beat fruitlessly against the crumbled concrete; ambulances zigzag wildly through the streets, looking for a way out of the maze; inside, the wounded are puking their guts out. Hundreds of thousands of people are trying to leave town. The stations can't take them all: the surrounding streets are flooded with people who drag bulging suitcases behind them—all that remains of their belongings.

•

I roam the streets. Alone. Rumpelpeterchen is closed now. Whatever it is that Maruschka and Horst do together, they do it more often. It hurts. I hurt.

The mistakes I make. The city I live in is no longer the city I lived in. A piece has been carved out of my soul, but I walk around as if I still know the streets. One day I go home but I do not end up at our dear near-collapsing theater, but at the front door of our first Berlin home, the house on Tauentzien. There, right next door to the art academy where she once was rumored to work, I meet Stella. She tells me she has been lucky—her house is still standing.

She melts in tears. "Come with me," she says.

The fundamental law of the hunted—do not trust anybody.

A black Mercedes pulls alongside and trails us at a snail's pace. The man in the passenger's seat whistles at blonde Stella. "What do you say, *Süße*, want a ride with us in this veeee-hicle? Huh? We won't interrogate yah, honey—let's just have some fun? Hey? What you say?"

She dismisses them with a casual wave of her hand, as if you can simply wish the Gestapo away. Miracles do happen: The car speeds up.

I can't do it.

"How can I go home with you?" I say. "Isn't that dangerous for you, to take me to your room?" Stella stops to think. Tram 76 sails through the street on its way to Kantstraße. Stella is still thinking. I hear her breathe through her nose, fast and heavy.

"Yes," she finally answers, "way too dangerous." (Her yes is a no.)

I see her board the tram, I see the tram leave, and I stare at the empty tracks, long and hard, until my eyes sting.

I look around me. The skeletons of haughty hotels. The crystal of their shot-down chandeliers glitters in the rubble.

•

Horst is still thin enough to make narrow escapes, but for how long? An officer stops him on the street. He asks Horst for his papers. He decides that he doesn't like Horst's *Kennkarte* picture, ironically the only part of his ID that isn't forged.

"Who in Germany, I ask you, still looks exactly like he did two years ago?"

The agent arrests him. Horst has to go to the station for interrogation. One agent puts his boot in Horst's neck, and while another boot rests on his kidneys, two others brush his ears. A good matador works close to the bull.

"Name?"

"Gerhard Lichtenberg."

"Where do you live, Gerhard Lichtenberg?"

"With the whores on Augsburger Straße."

"Where are your clothes?"

"In a locker at Zoo Station."

"Where's your little ticket?"

"In my wallet."

"There is no luggage ticket in your wallet."

"Well, it was there before you guys took it."

"What does your suitcase look like?"

Horst describes a suitcase that looks like no suitcase in the world.

The officer talks on the phone. Zoo cannot find a suitcase that fits the description.

"Of course not. Whoever stole my ticket has long since left with my suitcase."

They let him go. Horst's forgeries are near perfect, his words are waterproof, and—most importantly—after a thorough check, they find his foreskin intact.

•

The atmosphere in the basement gets grim. There are light bulbs, but Maruschka burns candles. It isn't a sign of thrift or devotion; she does it for fear of a gas leak. If the candles go out, we know we must leave immediately. All our customers are gone, but none of us have left. Where would we go? We eat our way through Peterchen's food supply and drink our way through his remaining kegs. Peterchen's soup gets less and less misty, clearer and clearer, until it's almost pure water now. We become quite adept at catching rats.

And then, one evening, the unthinkable happens. Horst disappears. The theater is alive with rumors. Horst is punctual: He never misses an appointment.

"*You* will have to come with us, then."

It is a simple statement of fact, like a law of nature. But while Maruschka speaks these words, the words that will seal our fate, her eyes fill with tears.

"Where are we going?"

"I cannot tell you."

That makes me all the more eager to follow her. I am an idiot.

•

I wear my black suit and a black shirt. I carry a small backpack with some food and a bottle of water, and a blanket as well. We walk for about a mile until we reach the edge of the woods. The sun begins to set. Not like in the city, where the blue hour of dusk gets drowned in lamplight and the noise of automobiles, and night only falls when the first air raid siren sounds; here, royal-blue ink seeps majestically into the sky from the east and the silence is absolute.

We find the path and walk into the bushes. About a hundred yards inside the forest, we meet the group. Maruschka shines her flashlight over their faces. The twinkle in their eyes is not just the reflection of the light—it's the gleam I know so well from my father. Hope. There must be about twenty of them, people of all ages, even a few children. Some of them look Jewish, long beards and all; others are more difficult to place. It doesn't matter. We are all partners in misfortune. The people stand close together, and not just because the evening air feels brisk and nippy.

We got off the train in Frohnau, even though our ticket stub showed a destination a few stops down the line. A small town with villas and solid churches, prettily silhouetted against a purple sky. A market square with worn-down cobblestones, rusty grass between the edges. Dead leaves cover the square—autumn's first victims. A white tower with decorative battlements protected by blackberry bushes. Not a soul outside. A curtain moves: a draught perhaps, or maybe the shaky hand of an as-yet-inexperienced snitch. In the far distance there's the glow of the city, a flickering fire that reflects off the underside of the feathery clouds.

Maruschka gives us instructions. "Walk carefully. Avoid the path. Do not step on anything that can snap. Make as little noise as possible. Walk in single file. Follow the person in front of you. And not a word!"

A silent procession. Even the children keep silent. You get old fast in the firestorm of war. Maruschka walks in front; I am last in line. A cricket chirps, another cricket answers. That is the only sound. A loaded silence, a silence pregnant with fear. We walk for about thirty minutes; we take many winding paths and encounter many forks in the road. Maruschka makes her decisions without hesitation—she has done this countless times before.

Then she stops. She waves me closer. She whispers, her hand at my ear. I can feel her breath, a light breeze of intimacy.

"I have a premonition," she says. "The night is too quiet. The woods are too silent. We are not alone. Listen, it's not too late for you. Return. Get back to Berlin." I open my mouth, but Maruschka raises her palm and silences me. "Whatever happens, it will happen on the way back, otherwise it would have happened already."

"But . . ."

"Shh!" She puts a finger on my lips. The twenty people watch. We can't wait any longer or they might panic. "I am the leader," she says in my ear. "Do what

I say!" I shake my head. I am not a follower. I will not leave her behind all alone in the woods. She reads my objections and for a moment it looks as if she might rebuke me, as if she would slip her finger from my lips and slap me in the face. Then she nods, softly. She understands me, and she is grateful for my decision. I know she is right. The forest always has a humid hint of mystery, a sweet smell of decay, but not this kind of silence. Shouldn't we at least hear the alarm of the crows when we near their roosts? The silence can only mean that others have gone before us. We continue on our way, because there is nothing else to do. Although we are dead quiet, my new fear hears our collective heartbeat echo through the forest like a kettledrum.

Half an hour later we stop at a clearing. Maruschka throws down her knapsack. A mud road leads to a hut next to a stretch of brand new railroad tracks. Marushka whispers her orders in the ear of the woman behind her, who repeats them to the man behind her and so on, a prayer traveling down the line of the faithful.

They will hide in the woods at the other side of the tracks, hidden from view until a train comes. The train will stop; a man will jump off and tell them what to do, but until that happens they should not be seen. One after the other the people run along the edge of the clearing to the hut and then they disappear in the bushes at the other side of the tracks. Maruschka and I stay where we are, underneath a big old oak tree.

I have no idea who these people are, the people we are helping. That is not necessary. Jewish families, political dissidents, homos, I don't care. These people are unwanted by the regime. They need help, it's as simple as that. I am proud and happy I can contribute.

When the last person has disappeared, leaving behind nothing but silence, Maruschka turns around and signals that I should follow her, and this time I oblige, because I see the usefulness of her technique. If we were to encounter soldiers or police, we can mislead them by running away from the group of twenty while making as much noise as possible.

The plan is simple but powerful. A freight train, on its way to the north of the country, makes an unannounced stop in a lonely forest. A small group of illegals gets onboard. Inside the carriages, they open up furniture crates addressed to the family of a Swedish diplomat. They unload the furniture and carry it deep into the woods. Inside the hut, they keep crates and lead bars; these will help to make up for the weight difference. The lead and human cargo go inside the crates. An accomplice nails the crates shut and applies new seals. The crates and their contents go to the railway station in Lübeck and will be loaded onto a freighter heading for freedom. Somewhere in a forest north of Berlin a dining set (six chairs and an oak table, a nicely sculptured armoire) will slowly turn to wood pulp, and a piano will rust under the bewildered gaze of a few generations of deer—a small price to pay for twenty human lives. The diplomat is paid off with money WLADIMIR and I have stolen from black marketeers. My heart swells: I was always a part of this plan.

This is just a slower and more ambitious application of one of WLADIMIR's usual tricks. A good trick doesn't need to be perfect, it only needs to outsmart its audience. The only way to see through a good trick is after it has been exposed. The hardest part of all this must be the forging of the seals—a quick wax imprint is made and Horst goes to work with rubber and a knife. He only has a few minutes; he does his work inside the hut, a flashlight clenched between his teeth. Tonight Horst isn't here; tonight the containers will be closed with blank seals, and we will have to pray that there won't be a close inspection in Lübeck.

The refugees also benefit from other techniques that Horst has picked up during his life as a fugitive. They each carry a bottle of cough syrup in their coats, and water and bread for two days, and a big bag of waterproof sailing cloth that serves as a makeshift toilet. The men on the train are bribed. This isn't too difficult. The young hotheads are all fighting at the front, and the older gents who work for the railroad don't mind setting law and order aside in return for a nice little bundle of cash.

There is, however, a cash flow problem. Most of the money comes from gambling. Now that the den has closed, our source has dried up. Maybe there was just enough money to pay off the train guards, but not enough to satisfy the Frohnau police. Or maybe the Frohnau police agreed that the money was enough to allow free passage for the twenty refugees, but not enough to let the designers of the plan go free. Or maybe there's an infiltrator from Alexanderplatz in their ranks who insists on putting things in order. Whatever the case, as soon as the train leaves, we retrace our steps, and when we arrive at the edge of the woods, we hear the barking of dogs and the sloshing of boots in mud. And then a battery of lights is turned on, flooding the road with light as bright as the day. Beautiful, clear, cool, pure white light, designed by Hitler's architect and armament minister Speer. The beams cross each other two by two, tracing a horizontal cross over this century ("XX"), icy tentacles that finger the edges of the woods.

Smaller light cones detach themselves from that mother ship, men with flashlights walking into the woods to look for us. Behind us there is a little creek, and behind that, if my nose isn't deceiving me, lies a dunghill. I react quickly. I take Maruschka by the hand and drag her with me to the stinking heap of manure. Before she knows it we are both knee-deep in the stuff. Then we run along the path (she knows the way, in the forests of Frohnau!) and we jump into the creek and wade upstream for a few minutes. Then we climb back out on the opposite bank, and continue our journey. Behind us the dogs bark in angry frustration—the trail of our scent ends at the dung heap, the trail of shit ends at the creek.

Are they going to systematically search the forest? It's possible. We are a network that helps illegals across the border. We must be high on the list of priorities. Far in the distance, we hear barking and cursing, and men who run into the woods, but the sounds seem to be fading. We still see the silver glow of the floodlights, however. They've decided to wait us out—that road is the only way back to civilization.

We can't go back. But it's pitch dark. We also cannot run the risk of blindly wandering through the forest, looking for another way out. We have to hide until morning. We go deeper into the bushes, our arms around each other, holding each other tight. When we are exhausted I spread out the blankets—mine on the forest floor, hers on top of us. Our fingers claw in each other's flesh. It's the tension, the relief of still being alive—for now. I've observed this in the basement so often. Rubble sex signifying the imminent ruin of our lives. Maruschka raises her skirt and unbuttons my fly with hasty fingers and thus I take her, completely dressed; or rather: Thus she takes me, in rabid haste. It's not at all what I wanted, not at all what I imagined. We are beasts in the woods. For Marushka, it's just a way to release the adrenaline, and I can feel that—she gets rid of a cramp by cramping harder; she cleanses her mind by dirtying her body. Never did my semen shoot more coldly out of my body, never with more contempt, never with greater relief—finally rid of me, away from me, inside another. What I feel then, during the brief seconds of our intimacy, is anger, urgency, and scorn. The second woman in my life, the woman I so longed for: She curses and lets out a short cry and that's that. It's over. Not even a kiss. It's over—everything is over.

We fall asleep like that, worn out, glued to each other, without rearranging our clothes. Just a discharge, that's all it means to her. My love is her sleeping pill. My sleep—and I sleep only because I am exhausted, so many thoughts are whirling through my head, all demanding attention—is unquiet. I wake with a jolt whenever she moves, whenever one of her legs kicks away her nightmares, whenever a possessive arm slips around me.

•

And I dream. I dream of Horst. I dream of Horst's escape. No, Horst cannot have been arrested. Horst, my hero, my savior. He must have escaped.

This is how it must have happened:

Horst never lets himself relax. Making his way to the bar of his favorite café on Savignyplatz, his Anneliese or Hannelore or Marlene right behind him, he hears a voice behind calling his name, no, whispering it—quizzical, insinuating. "Horst?"

Who knows him by the name of Horst these days? He took another name, the name printed on his false ID card, safely stowed away in his breast pocket, secured with a safety pin. The Floriane or Helena or Ariadne at his side doesn't react: she knows him as Gerhard. The voice that calls out his name sweet as honey is not that of an old friend. The woman taps him on the shoulder. "Horst? Horsti!" Horst turns and is now eye to eye with the infamous blond Lorelei we have heard so much about—and he knows it.

"You must be mistaken, ma'am." Horst sounds polite and friendly; he's only inwardly tense. Adder eyes, he thinks, she has adder eyes. She hypnotizes. She has *that stare*.

"Come on. Horst," laughs the woman, "No more games!" She strokes one of the gleaming buttons of his coat with the top of her index finger, the button of the pocket that contains his new life, his new life that will end abruptly when he gives even the slightest indication that his real name is indeed Horst, or that he recognizes the woman. A man towers behind her, a tall man who looks like he has never smiled in his life—that must be the legendary Gestapo officer who always accompanies her. Another man in front of Horst wears an SS-uniform. "Gerd, what's going on?" whines Brünhilde or Charlotte or Liesl-Marie. She weighs heavily on Horst's arm, and the soldier is amused.

"You must be mistaken, lady," repeats Gerd/Horst, ever polite. The soldier's calm gaze assures Horst that he still has a few seconds left. SS-men are trained to recognize the enemy, and they are extremely mistrustful. But Horst is no Jew: he's tall and athletic; he moves with confidence, the world revolves around him. His body language expresses that this is a simple mistake, and the eyes of the siren fly back and forth between Horst's open innocence and the equally open disinterest of the SS-man. The only one who doesn't buy it is the Gestapo officer. But he is positioned right behind the *Greifer*, and he is still considering whether or not he can pull his pistol in a crowded restaurant and start shooting. He hesitates. Just for a second. But that is just enough time for Horst to push away Lieselotte's or Emma's or Jutta's arm and to straighten his shoulders and spread his elbows and dive into the crowd like a battering-ram—glasswork breaks, people curse, a woman screams when a plateful of hot stew lands in her lap, and high above it all floats Horst's own Indian cry. This cry more than anything else makes people scoot out of the way—this man is a wild raging boar!—and in a rain of glass Horst flashes straight through the window. He lands on the grass and rolls onto his back, and behind him he hears the heavy breathing of his massive pursuer, and—it is karma—here are his dogs to rescue him, the pack of bald strays sniffing about the front garden, waiting for Horst to return with something to eat. Well, HERE HE IS! And while Horst is still rolling over the grass, his hand goes inside his coat pocket and he grabs a packet of organ meat; he tosses it in the air, aiming behind him, and—just his luck!—it smacks right in the belly of the Gestapo officer, and then the dogs are upon him and the man starts yelling in a Bavarian accent and Horst/Gerhard runs for his life, stumbling and slipping on the wet grass and then the wet pavement, but then he regains his balance and runs onto Kantstraβe, and jumps on a tram right before the doors closes. He collapses on the back bench, panting heavily.

An older lady on the bench opposite him watches him with suspicion—a strong youngster in a muddied coat. "Young man," she says in a tone of reprimand, "This is a busy street. There is a tram every five minutes. No need to hurry and scare your fellow passengers!" "New in town," pants Horst, and it takes all his strength to keep himself from looking back. "I *see*," says the lady solemnly, and she returns to her *Berliner Morgenpost*. The well-groomed poodle at her side watches Horst intently, its head cocked, as if the noble animal expects something from him. Horst still has a lump of sugar in his pocket. What will he do? Go to Rumpelpeterchen and warn everybody? But maybe the Gestapo would follow him? No, he can't go there—he needs a new address. "Woof!" says the poodle. Horst throws the lump of sugar at it. The dog does a perfect catch and gobbles it down, grinding up the sugar with its perfect row of little teeth.

•

And so I wake up, with that happy dream hanging in front of my mind's eye, filled with a new hope and with the lip-smacking sounds of the ghost dog still in my ears. The sounds, however, are real. Maruschka has my penis in her mouth. I feel nothing. Has the cold numbed my senses? I take Marushka's head between my hands and gently pull her away from me. She smiles.

"I once knew a violinist, my boy, who had the same sad eyes as you, and that same sad sway in his hips. The same kind of scruples too. Like yours they came a day too late." I sit up. I don't believe her. WLADIMIR knows my story. He must have told her about my father.

"I wonder what happened to him," says Maruschka, wiping her lips with her sleeve. "I haven't seen him in years. WLADIMIR and I worked in Café Kuka. He worked there too."

I swallow. I invoke the English, those *dei ex machine* of the early morning. And here they come, exactly on time. From the city we hear the distant wail of sirens, the lights go out, and from the west comes the familiar droning of the airplanes. Except that this time half of the squadron changes course, audibly coming our way. Maruschka's hands dig into my back, and mine into hers. The floodlights that have shone all night over the woods are hastily extinguished. Did the floodlights—did we?—lure the bombers to Frohnau? Never before have I experienced an attack this close without any possibility of shelter. But this is our salvation: The British army is covering our back.

We run and run, in a parody of our flight of last night. We stumble over trees felled by the shockwaves, and we don't even notice that the rain of fire has stopped until we reach the edge of the woods. A hellish vision awaits us there. A factory—it must have been the target for this attack all along—is burning, flames shoot up its halls, an orange glow licks at the clouds. Maruschka seizes the opportunity—this will be our alibi. We run into the compound, hoping that nobody will notice us, praying that nobody will pay any attention to those two strangers who sneak in from the forest. We mingle with the crowd and start working. Maruschka shovels sand in buckets; rugged fellows throw them into the sea of flames. I fight my way into what once must have been the dining hall and drag out people trapped under burning beams; I tear up my shirt to make bandages, I get covered in blood, my own and that of others; the grit of the street, the oil and the chalk bite my wounds. After an hour of hard work we have to give up—our muscles give out, our legs refuse to move. We slump down in the courtyard and use each other for support; we watch the flames have their way. The factory is beyond saving—we know that, we all know that. Together with the workers and like them covered in soot, we stare into the blaze with dread and awe, for some reason stricken by grief. Maruschka gets to her feet slowly and walks over to a police officer—what balls she has!—and explains to him how we lost everything in the fire. She asks for a travel permit to Berlin. The man writes something on a piece of paper. A woman who used to work in the dining hall overhears the conversation and takes us home with her. We protest, but she won't take no for an answer. She insists that we take a bath and after the bath she offers us some freshly laundered clothes, one of her own dresses for Maruschka and a pair of pants and a sweater that belonged to her husband for me. Her husband died on the Eastern Front; she shows us pictures. I look at the man and think: How many Jews did he kill before the Russians got to him? We get a stack of bacon sandwiches for the road.

•

A young woman and an even younger man get off the train at Bahnhof Zoo. They do not need a porter, for they have no luggage. They look like any of the thousand washed-up folks who come to the city every day. She wears an ill-fitting dress of dubious cut. He wears a pair of pants that are way too big—trouble must have emaciated him. Not a trace of urban swagger in their step. It's plain to see that they spent their journey in silence, staring out the window without registering the landscape.

They reach their destination by tram and walk the last mile; the line is interrupted due to the war. Their destination is a grubby factory building, a long wall of brick with a steel door its only entrance. He has a key. He opens the door for her. They look around before they enter. The street is empty. No car with its engine running in neutral, a man behind the wheel and a man in the passenger's seat; no passerby who pays the least attention to them.

Their steps echo in a big empty hall with rows of chairs bolted to the floor, all facing a shallow stage with ragged curtains. The floor between the chairs is dusty— the theater has been abandoned for some time—yet the aisle is clean, polished by many recent comings-and-goings. They climb onstage—he goes first, and then he reaches for her hand. This is mere politeness; there is no tenderness between them, only the deep fatigue of former lovers.

He kneels on the wooden planks and opens a trapdoor. He slides inside. The wide sleeve of his sweater catches on the latch and tears with an mournful sound. She gathers her dress around her legs and follows him down.

The basement floor is covered in straw mattresses. Rats scurry away. She throws herself on a mattress in a corner of the room and looks at him. It is dark, he cannot read her gaze. He picks a mattress as far away from her as possible, brushing rat droppings off the blankets with his bare hands. They lie down, each in their corner. They each listen to the other breathing. Their hearts wants to sigh but their heads tell them to keep quiet. So they both close their eyes. Despite themselves they fall asleep instantly; their bodies prefer shutdown to confrontation.

•

The old instinct kicks in. My hand feels around, but I'm not in my usual spot—there's no knife. Steps sound from the theater. Harsh, anonymous, strange steps. The steady but circling steps of a man who has time and confidence to burn, but is also unsure where to go, because the territory is unfamiliar.

Then suddenly the steps sound loud and close: The man has come onto the stage. Only a thin layer of wood separates us from him now. He stomps the wood to test it for variations in thickness, to see if there are hollows. This is a man who doesn't know that every stage floor is hollow—there are no variations in sound. He scrapes the floor with his soles. Is he looking for an edge? The theater is too old, the floor too worn out for anyone to make out the edges of our trapdoor through the thick soles of their shoes. If the man went down on his knees to feel around with his fingertips, he would find the door in an instant, but he doesn't do that. That is how we know he is Gestapo. Gestapo men never go down on their knees. We have had visits like this before, late at night, early in the morning. That strange inflexibility in the Gestapo officer's character has always left us undiscovered.

All I can see of Maruschka is the whites of her eyes, but that tells me enough. We think the same thing. We do not move, we do not make a sound, but we tense our muscles, ready to run for the door if need be, ready to vanish into the sewer tunnels without end.

Then other steps join in, lighter and more self-assured, steps I somehow recognize but cannot immediately identify. The scratching of nails on the sides of the stage and a light thud: A small person just hoisted himself on the stage. Mouse-steps to the man, then mouse-steps to the exact location of the trapdoor. This person knows what he is doing. A blinding strip of light comes down into the basement: It slides over Maruschka's face and fills her eyes with terror. We both jump up and run to the door to the sewers as fast as we can. I'm the first one there and I push and push and then I throw myself against the wood with all my weight, but the door doesn't budge. Now Maruschka joins me; we both bang against the door as hard as we can—to no avail.

A lithe body jumps effortlessly into the basement.

"The door is cemented shut, *Schatzi*."

Stella!

And even now, now that everything is crystal clear, I can't believe it; even now my first reflex is to go to her, to hug her, to take her into my arms. But behind her the Gestapo officer already forces his way into the basement, pistol in hand, and that grin on his face, that universal grin. Only one man? They must have known we were alone.

"All resistance is futile."

Yes it is. Is it the man who says that, or is it one of the many voices in my head, projected out into the damp space? Stella brings her head closer. Time for a friendly Judas kiss? No, she turns me around and forces my hands behind my back; she clicks handcuffs onto my wrists. What humiliation, to be arrested by her, the woman of my adolescent dreams—it's more than I can bear.

The man now comes to stand before me. He reeks of eau de cologne and his shave is so close it looks as though he finished five minutes ago. His tie is knotted tight, his shoes polished to an zealous shine. He came prepared; he readied himself for this moment as if it were a Saturday night date. With Stella's help, he's managed to uncover an important network of resistance fighters; maybe he even thinks he caught the head honcho.

More steps on the stage, two or three men drag a heavy object over the floor. Stella climbs back upstairs. She sounds bossy and happy but I can't make out the words. The officer raises the pistol and presses it into my temple; I feel a small cold circle burn me. He speaks. With exactly the type of voice, exactly the type of intonation I'd expect from such a man. "Look," he says. "Look, I press the barrel against your forehead, like that, and then I put my hand here, you see? I'm going to fuck you up good and proper, man—but I don't want to get any bone splinters in my face, see?"

Yes, I see. You are a professional.

We are chest to chest. I feel something hard in his chest pocket, and another hard object too, something that presses hard against my hip: The man has an erection. I force myself into the mental space I occupy when I play poker. I cannot deflect a bullet. But the fear, the fear of the bullet, the fear of death, this can be deflected, this I can keep in check. What purpose does anxiety serve? Anxiety paralyzes. Why would I allow myself to be paralyzed? I need to be able to move—fluid, swimming motion. My mind encompasses all space. My mind is as wide as the universe.

It is hard to climb out of the trapdoor with my hands tied behind my back. Two men grab me from beneath, the third one hoists me up from above. They do the same with Maruschka, who protests loudly when one of the men grabs her ass. They laugh at her. Then we are on the floor. A few well-aimed kicks get us back to our feet.

WLADIMIR hangs suspended from a wire, the same wire that makes Maruschka float above the stage. He is dressed in his professional outfit, the smoking jacket he won off Leni Guna. His feet barely touch the ground.

WLADIMIR is there, but his eyes are empty. The same emptiness I have seen all too often in the past few years on all too many faces, the same emptiness that sounded in Stella's crooning, the same emptiness that pervaded Marushka's love-making. An emptiness beyond repair. This man has been through a lot in the past twelve hours; his mind no longer soars, and I shudder to think what would it have taken to break his spirit so.

The Gestapo man puts his hand inside his chest pocket. What comes out is WLADIMIR's revolver. The men cheer, "*Mein Weib! Mein Weib!*" Maruschka's eyes fill with tears. From another pocket the man removes a bullet. He rolls his eyes in mock-amazement. A silver bullet.

"Look here," he says. He holds up the projectile. "Watch carefully. Tell me . . . is WLADIMIR's name engraved in this bullet?" I do not need to look, I know what it is, I've seen it a thousand times—it is Wladimir's bullet. The officer hands the gun to one of his comrades. The man loads it for him. Then he places it again in the officer's big outstretched hand. In the man's paws, his gloved paws, the gun looks like a toy.

I swallow. Loudly, much too loudly. It attracts attention.

"Untie him!" The man points his finger at me.

My eyes grow wide with terror.

"Give him the gun!"

Oh yes, of course, they want to see WLADIMIR's trick. They've heard a lot about it. A grand illusion!

WLADIMIR doesn't look me in the eye. I will be eternally grateful for that.

They hand me the revolver. Someone puts my finger over the trigger, the other man grabs my arm and points the weapon directly at WLADIMIR's heart. The first man cocks the gun. I shake. The grip on my arm intensifies.

I cannot do it, even though I know hat nothing will happen, even though I know that WLADIMIR has rigged the revolver, even though I know that any bullet must somehow be caught in its barrel—I simply cannot do it.

I scream. I have to scream.

"I! Can! Not! Do! It!"

With all my might I push the arm of the officer away. Nobody reacts. Nobody is afraid of a young man with a toy gun in his hands. The silence last a second, two seconds, five seconds.

Stella breaks the silence.

"Oh yes, you can," she says. Her voice is almost flat. Almost. I detect a hint of threat. Or condescension. Or is it hate? Why do you hate me, Stella? Why do you hate all of us? All of us, Jews like you? Now something hysterical creeps into her voice; I fully expect her to hit me, but she doesn't. "It's a trick, isn't it? Nothing but a simple magic trick. Remember? Spare us the drama."

She's right. How right she is. I try the trigger. It gives a little. I take that as a sign that the revolver isn't working the way it's supposed to. A dry click: Another revolver gets cocked. The Gestapo officer has his own gun pointed directly at me. For once, his face is perfectly expressionless. I am grateful for that too.

WLADIMIR groans on the black steel wire. Slowly he swings around; he turns towards me, presenting himself as a wider target. He keeps his head down, his gaze to the floor—eyeing the stage upon which—for which—he has lived.

I understand his signal. Without any further help or encouragement I aim the gun straight at WLADIMIR'S heart—and then I pull the trigger.

A dagger of fire. A bang, a sharp tug at my arm. The mortifying stench of gunpowder.

WLADIMIR convulses. He bites the air in a last desperate desire for oxygen, and a bullet slips from his lips, sticky with saliva.

The trick worked, then!

But no—lower down, where his heart is, something else has come spitting out, a liquid, fiery red, a liquid that pulses, hot and unstoppable.

This is a trick, I think in my despondency—this is a new grand illusion from the great WLADIMIR!, a new special effect!—but then WLADIMIR hangs limp from the piano wire and the wound bleeds more than any capsule of fake blood could reasonably contain.

No.

No!

The magic has gone. Reality has taken over. Reality and its bite. The revolver has worked as advertised—a bang, a gaping hole, and blood over the spot where Helena Guna's heart once used to beat.

And WLADIMIR's.

A different bang now, a dull and heavy bang. The angel that supported my head, the angel that kept me upright through all these ordeals, the angel called forth by my father, that angel finally succumbs to his sadness and collapses on the floor. What can the other angel do, the angel that stands guard in front of my heart? That angel wails in grief and claws at his eyes, and my own heart bursts with grief as well and I start sliding, sliding down into a flaming darkness that knows no bounds.

I slide. If not dead, then certainly mortified.

•

I work away on De Heer's text—this is a long chapter, a long story about appearances and reality and loss and betrayal. Despite its length, I can't put it aside—I work without breaks because it touches me so much. Before I realize it, it's midnight. I hear that single cry underneath my window, that brief meow. Tonight, Mefista isn't going to climb the wall to get to me. So it is I who moves; I go downstairs and open the door for her, for that fairytale changeling WLADIMIR dreamed about.

On my way up I hear those other cries in the hallway—you remember them too, dear reader: They jumpstarted this book. I press my ear against Donatella's door and then I press my eye against the keyhole. I hear what I hear and I see what I see. I see the woman I was falling in love with and her mentor, and I see what they are doing. I see him shoot that whirlwind of semen; I read Donatella's greed in the lapping of her tongue.

It's that kind of night then, yes, the kind of night that packs your heart in ice, the kind of night when love turns out to be betrayal, a night of pain and weeping. I should leave, but I stay where I am, my back against Donatella's door. Why? They are getting dressed. I have to go. Any moment now she could come out to take a shower or to use the toilet. I need to get up, and get up *now*. My body does not comply, however—my body just wants to die, right here, right now.

Mefista's head bores into my hip; her purring brings me back to reality. I get on my feet, although I am barely capable of moving. I feel dizzy, as if I'd just now learned how to walk again after a long illness. There are only six, seven steps to my room, but my knees are shaking and my body trembles. My heart is dead and cold. As soon as I'm inside, I press my back against the door: I need support, something strong and dependable to lean against. Something solid, something that remains. The house is quiet—they are done, Donatella and her professor, they're all done. It's so quiet that I can hear the concrete set, so quiet that I can hear the groans of the windows fighting the cold outside. So quiet that I can hear my own breathing.

I am breathing, I think, with a tinge of regret.

The room is suddenly too small for me. I need air. It's so dark outside that when I open the window, I open the window for night itself—silently, night comes inside, sinister in its cloak of silken black, mysterious in its stillness, and for the longest time I stare it right in the eye, for I recognize it, because this night is no different, no darker or more cruel, than the dark Night that eats at my soul, and it is Night that finally breaks the silence, not with a word, but with a gesture; Night lowers the otter fur and ink-black satin of Night's cloak, until Night stands naked, dressed only in moonlight and a frailty too painful to behold; and then, much to my amazement, I find myself in Night's arms, in the arms of Night, and in Night's firm grip I lose my body.

The cat meows.

I turn my face to Night.

Night, never to be trusted. The stars, those futile companions—too far away, too high up, too cold and strange for life: flickering clumps of dying matter in whose presence we feel obliged to kneel.

Night.

Babies are often born at Night.

I push Night away.

I throw some cold water over my face.

I take the cat in my arms and go stand at the window.

The droplets dry in the biting wind; then Mefista complains about the cold.

We go to bed.

She is asleep. I am not. In my mind I see Donatella and I see Goldfarb. I see the two of them together, and superimposed on that image I see my own misery: tangible, black as soot, bitter as roasted acorns.

How will I be able to sleep?

How will I ever be able to sleep?

DRACHENHAUS

The guillotine—*DZAK!*—comes crashing down.
   Whizzing right past Hannah's ears.
   April 12, 1944.

•

As always, Hannah is right. Goldfarb gets his white badge, Access All Areas, an exceptional honor for somebody so young. Most of his peers wear blue badges, which only allow access to their own building and the general meeting rooms.

Goldfarb had wanted to work in Division T, theoretical physics. Instead, he gets assigned to Division G. Maybe this is Bacher's revenge for Goldfarb's loose-lipped wisecrack during check-in. It could also be an homage to Goldfarb's versatility and ingenuity; Bacher considers him an all-rounder. Division G works on implosion techniques. It requires all the ingenuity Goldfarb possesses; it also turns out to be much more mathematical than he expected.

The world on top of the hill is a little bizarre, a mixture of freedom of scientific expression—no silence here, but heated discussions in agreeable clouds of pipe tobacco—and strategies for secrecy that could have come out of any spy novel for boys. The top scientists, those men and women whose names have been amply publicized in the scientific journals, names that every spy with even the meagerest knowledge of physics would recognize immediately, are to be addressed by pseudonyms only; their real names are never to be mentioned. As if the enemy is among us, roaming through our dining halls and visiting our private parties, a tape recorder at the ready. People like Goldfarb are not important enough to need a nom de plume—people like Goldfarb get a number—but Enrico Fermi, for instance, becomes Mr. Henry Farmer, and Niels Bohr becomes Mr. Nicholas Baker. The "Mr." in their names is another one of the military's ideas. Scientists refer to each other as "Doctor" if they're not on a first-name basis yet; in the context of Los Alamos, this would be a dead giveaway. Moreover, this alternative hierarchy of doctors and professors makes General Groves slightly paranoid; he doesn't really get it. When the scientists keep mum about their work, he gets suspicious; when they try to explain what they're doing, they speak slowly for fear he won't understand, and to his ears it sounds like they're making fun of him. It doesn't matter that the amicable Mr. Baker has the same characteristic Scandinavian mug as Niels Bohr, and that they both have that unmistakable indolent Danish accent—the name change will certainly confuse any infiltrator. Even certain day-to-day words are taboo: If you mentioned "physics" or "chemistry," any outsider could guess what was going on, so every physicist is now labeled an engineer and chemists are called "stinkers." Conversation between two women from the typist pool: "I went into town yesterday and had dinner with a stinker. I really enjoyed it."

Every town has its stories and its legends, the myths and symbols that define it. Romulus and Remus, Jack the Ripper, the bohemians of the Rive Gauche, the lion on the column at the Piazza San Marco, Prague's Kafkaesqueness.

The stories about Los Alamos are still being written; the scientists often try to jumpstart an oral tradition over lunch. A group of physicists with an hour or so of free time isn't much different than a mob of merry schoolboys.

Leon is a good source for these kind of stories. "Look, there goes Dick Feynman. No, over there, yes, there, the guy who looks like he just came in from a breezy walk at the ocean. Yeah, the guy who's fiddling with that bicycle lock. That's him."

The man doesn't look much older than Goldfarb, but rumor has it he's a genius. He holds a doctoral degree from Princeton, where he worked with Wheeler, and he's only twenty-four. His research had something to do with advance waves, backward emissions of light that are received before they are transmitted—time in reverse. It's one of the more eccentric ideas in physics, something only a reckless youth could dream up, but is a logical consequence of the standard theory of electrodynamics. Dr. Feynman can't stand the absurd secrecy regulations , and is quite the practical joker. One day he discovers that a group of workmen from the trailer park are too lazy to walk all the way to the main gate to go home; they've cut a hole in the perimeter fence. Feynman sees the possibilities. He walks out the main gate for a brief stroll, signs out as required and makes sure the gatekeeper remembers him, and then he climbs back inside through the hole in the fence. He repeats this the next day and the day after, until the gatekeeper starts scratching his head. What's up with this guy—he goes out, but never comes back in, but then he comes out again, and again? He calls his commanding officer and the man threatens to put Feynman in jail. Feynman also likes to unlock locks and to stick his nose into stuff that's no business of his—cracking safes is his favorite pastime.

From these and similar anecdotes, Goldfarb gleans that the army is a necessary evil. It protects us, it keeps the Hill and its inhabitants invisible and it pays for the research, but the military men have no idea what the scientists are really doing and what makes them tick.

There are more stories about Dick. He likes to exchange letters with his dad, written in codes made up on the spot—a fun and innocent game, except that it makes the censors nervous. And so father Feynman and son Dick agree to include the code with each of their letters, and the censors agree to throw away the code as soon as they have deciphered the letter. Dick: He's a Marxist of the Groucho school! (And after saying that, you're supposed to shake you head—one has to forgive genius its little eccentricities.)

Other stories. About the time when they had a meeting in the big reading room on the ground floor of the Tech Area (this was way back in the beginning, when everybody still called Oppenheimer "Oppie.") Fifty physicists sit on folding chairs and stare at a blackboard; they do their best to understand what's being said—there's a lot of drilling and hammering going on in the rest of the building— when suddenly a leg bursts through the ceiling, and a stream of Spanish curses descends on the quiet pipe-smoking crowd, so vile it surely would have shocked the hell out of the Lord Himself if He hadn't been so busy listening to Oppie's exposé. After that, the scientists can no longer discuss what they were discussing. The b . . ., for instance, the b . . .—damn, I almost said it myself!—the *thing* is henceforward known as *the gadget*.

And the story of Bo . . . Baker's escape, did you hear that one? In the fall of '43 the Swedish ambassador in Copenhagen has tea with, um, "Nick," and he lets on, quite subtly, that it might be possible for the Nazis to raid the town, and on rather short notice too. "Even professors are leaving the country," the ambassador muses, and he contorts his forehead and nods and winks in the direction of Mrs. Bo . . . Baker—professors are way too absentminded to pick up such subtle hints. The next day the Bakers go hiking and they spend the evening hidden in some garden shed by the seaside; at dusk a fishing boat picks them up and delivers them to the Swedish harbor town of Linhamm. There they take the train to Stockholm. Although Stockholm is a neutral zone, lots of German secret agents are running around town, and the authorities fear they might try to abduct Baker. On October 6th, the physicist Baker, father of the atomic model that made Los Alamos possible, straps on a parachute and climbs aboard a two-engine British Mosquito that carries the diplomatic mail back and forth between London and Stockholm. They put the professor in the cargo load with a set of torches in his pockets. If there's any danger, the pilot will open the loading door and propel his human cargo down, the parachute will unfold and when the scholar reaches solid ground he will indicate his location with these torches. It doesn't go according to plan, however. Baker's big head almost kills him—and that's no joke. The helmet with the built-in intercom system doesn't fit over his skull; he puts it in his lap and misses the order to put on his oxygen mask. When the plane starts climbing in earnest, Baker falls unconscious. The pilot keeps trying to initiate some small talk but never gets any reply, and he finally realizes that something must be wrong. As soon as they've left Norwegian airspace, he dives down, flying low over the ocean and praying that no overzealous German cruiser will track them and hunt them down. When they land in Scotland Bo . . . Baker regains consciousness; he's fine, except that he feels a tiny bit confused.

Or the time when Teller, the head of Division T, drew a list of all possible applications of nuclear weaponry on the blackboard in his office (even at that time, he was already thinking about the hydrogen bomb). He included a column with the means of delivery (*drop on target*, for instance, and *detonate from ground*). The last bomb on Teller's list mentioned *back garden* as its delivery address—this weapon would be so powerful that it could wipe out the entire human population in one go; therefore it didn't matter where it was detonated, and consequently there was no need to transport it.

For a while, there was a persistent rumor that the Hill's own little gadget might be capable of igniting the atmosphere. The rumor started as another brilliant idea from the King of Deconstruction, Edward Teller. When Bethe heard about it, he grabbed pen and paper and quickly calculated that this scenario was impossible, but Oppenheimer was flippant enough to mention the story by way of a joke during a phone call with Compton, the liaison between the Manhattan Project and the National Defense Research Committee. Compton must have retold the story at one party or other and some high-ranking officer with no sense of irony and no knowledge of physics must have picked it up, because somehow a written report of this alarming possibility landed in an official file in Washington. There it's been stuck ever since. Every other month somebody new to DC read a copy of that report and called the Hill in a panic and didn't relent until he got Oppenheimer himself on the phone to explain that, no, this wasn't even a remote possibility—as if Oppenheimer didn't have enough troubles and sleepless nights already.

During their lunch breaks, while chewing ground beef and damp pieces of bread smothered in tame mustard and dripping tomato pulp, the physicists speculate about the stories that future generations will tell about the bomb itself, about the shockwave that will travel around the world, the shockwave they will unleash one day—their moment of (clinking of beer glasses!) *triumph*!

One of the things that's crystal clear to outsiders like Goldfarb is that Americans never really grow up, not even if they are physicists and exceedingly bright. Usually they manage to keep up some semblance of maturity, but deep inside these folks are eight-year-olds stuck in time; they've never given up on the belly-tickling pleasure of coming home with a bloody nose and their knees covered in grass and mud. All they want is to ride a roller coaster forever and shoot their pellet guns at pigeons in the park—North American culture stubbornly maintains that there's something magical about that first taste of life, maintains that immaturity is the most precious commodity of all—highly pleasurable and of a rare sublimity—and that the rest of our earthly journey is mostly a harrowing and sinful fall from grace. In the privacy of their own homes these men secretly sew symbolic parachutes to survive the Fall of Man; they wear clothes in the primary colors usually reserved for traffic signs and eat their fatty foods with wet noses pressed against the windowpane: They don't want to miss even a second of the fascinating ballgame outside. Their hands shake with impatience, their fingers drip with slimy glucose derivatives and faraway cousins of bull-meat, their sneakers are all laced up; so eager to run out and play, if only their hastily chewed sandwich hadn't made them so terribly sluggish and heavy, and if the taste of rising stomach acid didn't sit so unpleasantly in their mouths.

Americans prefer simple stories, the kind of mini-myths that end exactly at the edge of playtime—your wedding day, or the day after Christmas. When it snows, they run outside and drop on their backs; they wave their arms to chisel themselves a neat set of negative wings. Angels of innocence is what they are, their cheeks red and their assholes tingling.

Little wonder then that the folks in the desert work enthusiastically—with *childish* enthusiasm—on a *gadget*, and little wonder that nobody asks any grown-up questions. See them stare into their microscopes, the cream of the nation, their mouths wide open—their Adam's apples quivering with all their appetite for knowledge. It's as if they are forever locked inside a tree house, battling some innocuous daydream demons. Nobody here asks any deep questions. (For instance: what is it that they're really building, and what will it do when unleashed upon the world? What sorrow and death will it sow, and what will it mean for the history of humankind as a whole?) Nobody—except, that is, for Hannah Sidis.

•

Feynman gave the experiment that Hannah and her colleagues are working on its name. He called it chasing the dragon. A better name would have been "tickling the dragon's tail." The experiment itself was Otto Frisch's brainchild.

This is the experiment. Imagine a miniature guillotine, but instead of a blade a bullet of enriched uranium hangs from the wire. This bullet is released. In its fall, it travels through the hollow core of a barely subcritical mass of the same material and emerges from that tunnel a split second later.

Hannah mans the measurement apparatus, a bank of red light-emitting diodes that indicate the radiation levels around the hollow sphere. The purple bullet—if you turn the lights off, you can see the vague glow that surrounds it, an aura of scintillating subatomic particles—exactly completes the critical mass. For that split second, then—the time the bullet travels through the tunnel—all conditions for an atomic explosion are satisfied—this is the closest the scientists can come to an atomic bomb without actually blowing a crater in the Hill.

Frisch got the idea for his House of Dragons purely by coincidence—by his own clumsiness, to be precise. Late one night he was in a playful mood and started fooling around with a bunch of uranium hydride cubes on his desk, building an almost critical pile of the naked material. He called the glowing pile Lady G*diva— she could melt you if you looked at her directly. With a wooden ruler he moved the little building blocks around, pushing them ever closer. Just a little innocuous flirting with danger, as boys are wont to do. But when he leaned in a little too close to inspect his work, the hydrogen atoms in his body reflected the neutrons that radiated from the pile. The unimaginable happened: His little building blocks suddenly shuddered to life, hot and irritable and humming and glowering and growling—the detector diodes around Lady G*diva lit up like a Christmas tree. It lasted only a second: In a lucky reflex, Frisch swept the pile off the table with his bare hands—the little buzzing locusts of the Apocalypse flew everywhere—and so he saved his life and that of everyone else on the Hill. (Or almost everyone else.)

The experiment that they will be conducting today is a more controlled version of that foolish moment. Outside, in Omega Canyon, the world is awake with the scent of wildflowers and pollen and the usual New Mexico Technicolor light.

Inside, everything is focused on the bullet that swings slowly on its steel wire: a tiny ripe plum ready to be shot to the center of the known world by nothing more complicated than the force of gravity. This is the experiment that will determine everything. The measurements will show whether the bomb that so far exists only on paper is really feasible, or whether all their research will end in a whimper.

The bullet is ready. Ready to tickle the Dragon of Atomic Power—though just for a moment, just enough to make the beast open one eye and show us its teeth, just enough to make it click its tongue. The physicists are ready too; ready to see how far that lazy eye will open, how sharp those teeth truly are, how wildly the tail of the beast will whip. Waiting for the monster to click its tongue.

Tsk, tsk, tsk.

As I said before: "All the physics principles are well-known; it's only a matter of filling in the details, a matter of technology and engineering skills."

Hannah works in the theoretical division. She did the calculations for this experiment; she's certain that it will work. As far as she's concerned, the actual experiment is superfluous; it will be a confirmation of what she already knows. But that's why she is here, proud and happy, to read the expected results from the flickering of the diodes. Today she's one of the boys, one of the few female players in the theater of *Knabenphysik*. She has her hands nonchalantly in the pockets of her wide gray overalls, ready to erupt into a big old macho grin—that Hannah, always something special, a woman in overalls!—and eyes the guillotine that will determine the fate of the war.

At the same time, there's another Hannah inside Hannah—a Hannah who keeps an anxious eye on the clock, watching the second hand nudge that sleepy dolt of a minute hand at the end of every revolution. She has a bag of sailcloth hidden under her bed, a gray envelope of army-issue paper inside, and inside the envelope a thin folder—just a couple of pages. Each of those pages contains a few formulas illustrated with rough pencil sketches. It doesn't look like much, but physics is a science that uses paper sparingly—those few pages contain everything Hannah knows, an exhaustive description of her work on the theoretical aspects of critical mass, supplemented with Goldfarb's work on implosion lenses and their joint knowledge about the process used to make uranium-235. From these pages, every physicist in the world could derive everything necessary to build a perfect replica of the Los Alamos bomb, even before the Alamonians themselves have built it.

Didn't I already tell you that Hannah is always right? Indeed, her mind and Goldfarb's put together contain the complete blueprint of the bomb.

How could Goldfarb have refused to cooperate? Goldfarb's ties with this country, these United States of America, are no tighter than those he has with the Union of Socialist Soviet Republics. Let's not forget that the swastika banner flies over his country of birth. The land of his dreams is not the America that is so ill suited to the likes of him and his mother; rather, Goldfarb dreams of Germany— a free, a genuine, a denazified Germany. And he hopes and dreams that this Germany will be a socialist country, a paradise where happy workers and liberated intellectuals freely exchange ideas at the tables of sidewalk cafés; where all will eat their *Sachertorte* in peace and raise a foamy *Schultheiss* brew to each others' health. Goldfarb is not politically naïve; he realizes that after the war is over—soon—the world will need a strong, truly international equilibrium. He will do his best to hasten the end this war, here in Los Alamos, and he will also do his best to make sure that the Soviets share in the secrets of the weapon they are building here. In doing so, he is only serving world peace.

•

The clock keeps on ticking. Everybody in the room knows what happened in Frisch's office; they all know about Lady G*diva's fiery demise. They play it safe. They test the instruments ad nauseam; they check the mechanism over and over, just to be sure. For the thirteenth time, somebody removes the bullet and places a dummy of steel in its stead, just to check one last time that everything is in working order, that the bullet won't get stuck in the hole or emerge from the other end too slowly. And because thirteen is bad luck, they repeat this operation a fourteenth time.

Hannah is ready to go. If things take much longer, she'll miss her rendezvous with Helen, a rendezvous that they set up weeks ago—the Russians are overly cautious; none of their agents stays in New Mexico any longer than is strictly necessary.

•

Goldfarb worked on implosive lenses.

One of the major problems with the construction of the bomb is how to keep the critical mass together in its first few moments—how to keep the explosion nice and tight. After all, as soon as the chain reaction starts, the explosive forces in the material build up fast—the bomb wants nothing more than to blow up instantly, and that would be too soon, because it would cause the critical mass to disperse and the chain reaction to stop. In other words: If they let nature do what nature does, their magnificent bomb will not go off with a bang, but it will sputter and smother itself with a dearth of fuel. Our purpose is to make the most powerful weapon on earth, my friend, not a wet firecracker.

Serber's erotic design of the bullet in the tube will work, but Goldfarb is involved with another potential solution—implosion. The idea is brilliant in its simplicity. The core of the implosion bomb is a perfect sphere that in itself contains enough plutonium-239 to make a critical mass, except that the metal has not been packed densely enough to be critical. All that would be needed to push this bomb over the edge is to squeeze it slightly. Around the core of the thing they build a layer of explosives that will compress the mass and set the deadly chain reaction in motion. Because the pressure is inward, this design ensures that the bomb will stay critical long enough to have its full effect. There is a built-in insurance policy as well: Inside the plutonium core, they implant what they call an initiator, a hazelnut's worth of fresh polonium-210. Polonium degrades with a half-life of 138 days, and during its transformation to lead, polonium emits neutrons. These neutrons will be used to start up the chain reaction. The scientists don't want to run the risk that a bomb made out of a few million dollars' worth of plutonium won't detonate; therefore, they help plutonium's spontaneous emission of neutrons just a little with their polonium injection. The initiator needs to be isolated from the rest of the bomb up until the moment of implosion. In the open air, the alpha radiation of polonium ranges about 38 millimeters, but in a solid metal the neutrons travel less than a tenth of a millimeter before they are absorbed. The polonium inside the bomb is simply wrapped in a few layers of tin foil. When the detonators in the outer layer are activated, the plutonium compresses, thereby pressing the polonium through the foil and mixing its neutrons with the critical mass—about 95 million of those little buggers per second. This means there will be nine or ten of them in the ten-millionth of a second that is the critical period. Not a lot, but enough to make a working bomb. To increase the chances that the foil and the polonium will mix, they make little indentations in the hazelnut; it looks like a miniature golf ball. This irregularity creates enough turbulence to make the foil collapse inward and send its toxic neutrons into the critical mass during that decisive one-tenth of a microsecond. The implosive lenses that Goldfarb is working on are wedges of explosive material packed tightly around the subcritical mass. They serve to ensure that the bomb implodes in its totality—that is, they ensure that the sphere remains perfectly spherical throughout the whole implosion phase. The outer layer of the wedges is thicker than the inner layer, and therefore it burns faster. This makes the shockwave travel symmetrically inward. Or it should:

It turns out to be devilishly difficult to get a perfectly symmetrical shockwave. This is complicated by the fact that the explosion occurs so fast that it's near impossible to measure the degree of symmetry. Goldfarb's subgroup designs the measurement instruments; they test the gamma radiation released by imploding dummy bombs; they chain-link batteries of ionization chambers and then blow them up. It is a never-ending and expensive job of adjusting and fine-tuning, of trial and error, a history of mostly stumbling and sometimes advancing, a matter of keeping your breath and then relaxing it from between clenched teeth.

During the first small-scale test of their bizarre wedges—without fissionable material in the dummy bomb's core of course—Goldfarb sits inside one of the two tanks that serve as mobile bunkers (there was no time to wait for real concrete bunkers to be built), his long body and his legs uncomfortably folded inside the small space. The thing works better than expected, and even gets out of hand: All around them the forest catches fire, tongues of flames lick at the fir trees. The autumnal forest proves not to be wet enough to let the raging fire die by itself. Blissful as a child, Goldfarb watches the golden glow of the raging flames from the small vision slit of the tank. Even through the thick glass he can feel the heat burn his face, and while his comrades panic and throw up like there's no tomorrow—some even try to climb out through the turret—Goldfarb experiences a form of exaltation. Doesn't every true artist ultimately hope to be consumed by his creation, to die in one's own blaze of glory? Goldfarb watches the confusion around him with amazement—did none of these boys ever stop to think that they were building an actual weapon? Something fierce and deadly? Did they not realize that whoever lives by the sword might very well die by it? He carries the stench of soot and adrenaline to Hannah's bed that evening, the reek of his first appointment with death—it's a scent that pleases her, and while they make love, she weeps into the woolly stink of his scorched hair, tears thick with a sacred joy and more than a little heathen delight.

Those twenty-odd pages of sketches and formulas only hint at all the difficulties that have been surmounted, at all the practical problems that have—almost—been resolved.

•

Hannah knows the courier only by her code name, Helen. They met only once, about two months ago, during a forced-cheerful conversation in a coffeehouse in the desert town of Santa Fe. Hannah's earlier contacts with other messengers had been furtive and of little importance. This time she had let the embassy know that something significant was on its way, and they had asked her to cease all further attempts at direct communication and dispatched Helen to Santa Fe for a preliminary conversation. This meeting served two purposes. First, the two women had been introduced to each other, so that Hannah would not hand over the plans to the wrong person, for instance to an undercover agent of the CIA. Second, Hannah and Helen had now been seen together in public, and that defuses things for the secret service. The Americans have their own spies in town, who make sure that the scientists behave as they should and that none of them hang out with any suspect individuals. And so Hannah and Helen spend a nice night on the town together, talking and laughing it up in the coffeehouse, an innocent get-together with a long-time-no-see European cousin. They have fun, Helen and Hannah. They exchange recipes (Hannah is a lazy, indifferent cook), and stories about babies (maybe Helen does have a three-year-old daughter at home, more likely she doesn't) and good addresses for kosher delicatessens in Manhattan (unbelievable as it may sound, Hannah has never even tried pastrami on rye). Who knows, maybe Helen's Russian accent is even authentic.

The code to set the date for the new appointment is of Hannah's own invention. The German quotes she had sent to Goldfarb's dorm had made it past the censors. *Faust* is a long book; most editions have the lines numbered. They will defeat the enemy with poetry: Helen sends Hannah, her *liebe Cousine*, chitchatty letters with a few lines of Goethe's at the top, and Hannah answers likewise.

Warum ein unerklärter Schmerz / Dir alle Lebensregung hemmt?

Here is some context for those lines. Faust, doctor of medicine and religion and of the laws of men, sits restlessly at his writing desk in a vaulted and plausibly chilly gothic room, conversing with his heart. He realizes, the way people do in the middle of their life—and did Goldfarb, worldly-wise through exile and frequent contemplation, not feel the same way? And was this not what Hannah too, in her willingness to flirt with treason in pursuit of her principles, had understood?— that all art and all of science notwithstanding, there is nothing we can truly know: Everything that matters escapes our intellects. The doctor has sought long and burrowed deep. For a while he thought he had found his calling in the practice of alchemy; now even this seems empty to him. His alembics and decanters stand idly on the shelves, gathering dust and dregs and mold. Now the only instrument he trusts is his mind. His study, blackened with smoke, is his only world. And that is what leads him to despair; this is why he sits underneath his vaulted ceiling, speaking that handful of words, the lines that will lead him first to heavenly ecstasy and then to hellish doom.

But Hannah did not choose these lines because of their meaning or implication; She chose them because of the number associated with them. Line number 412, with line number 413 added to make the quote complete. 412, 4/12: Their appointment is set for April 12.

April 12 is today. And the clock keeps on ticking. Could Hannah just disappear in the middle of the experiment to go to Santa Fe without raising suspicion? This is a purely rhetorical question: No, she cannot.

The uranium bullet is being loaded in its harness—finally.

·

It's all a long way from the tree trunk on which Otto Frisch and his cousin Lise Meitner calculated the possibility of fission experiments for the very first time. A long way too from Enrico Fermi's radiation experiments in Rome, eleven years earlier. Fermi had two rooms, each located at the end of a long hallway; he kept the neutron source and the radiation table in one room, the Geiger counter in the other. The separation was necessary to avoid direct contamination of the measurement apparatus by the source. When the material that had been radiated had a particularly short half-life, it was necessary to literally sprint from one room to the other. Fermi boasted that he was the fastest sprinter of them all. To prove this he often held races with his colleague Eduardo Amaldi, and Fermi won more often than he lost. (Fermi was a graceless loser—maybe Amaldi let him win.) One day the Spanish ambassador visited the lab in the hope of meeting the world-famous Fermi ("His Excellence Fermi"), and was almost run over by two wildly sprinting researchers, their white lab coats flapping behind them. He didn't think this was funny at all. In retrospect, this man might have become the first victim of atomic power.

A long way. Today, Hannah realizes, we are nothing less than creators of a new sun. Today we will liberate matter of its fallibility and transform it into its essence: perfect energy.

It is April 12, 1945. The fascist regime is almost down on its knees, the Allied forces are close to Berlin. Why do we still need the bomb? Do none of us even read the newspapers?

·

Now then the bullet comes crashing down, and Hannah can finally smile her toothy smile of triumph. In that brief moment, so brief you would have missed it if you blinked, the bank of detector lights went crazy. The postdocs inform the team that in that tiny instant twenty million watts of energy had been generated, and that this increased the temperature in the hollow core by two degrees Celsius. The explosion, over before it began, produced a net amount of ten thousand million neutrons.

How could Hannah not glow with pride? She had shown the world the heart of matter, naked and palpitating. Today she and her colleagues have seen deeper into the universe's mysteries than she and her roommate, that pathetic refugee, had ever thought possible.

Somebody lets out a short, loud scream—*yay!*—and pumps a fist in the air. That somebody is Hannah.

•

It is April 12, 1945.

The Red Army marches into the heart of Brandenburg; the Russians are almost at the gates of Berlin.

President Roosevelt sits for his portrait in Warm Springs, Georgia, when an artery in his brain bursts. It's as if he has been shot by Frisch's bullet, from the inside out—a bullet with the color of clotted blood. The president dies in the early afternoon.

The British-American Alsos mission, whose job it is to find out the truth about the German atomic project, is on its way to Stassfurt, near Magdeburg. They hurry, because they want to get to the German laboratory before the Russians do.

In Japan it's already April 13. B-29 airplanes are bombing Tokyo. They flatten the Riken Institute, and thus effectively put an end to Yoshio Nishina's hesitant atomic experiments.

It is April 12, 1945.

And it is much later in the day than planned.

Hannah has missed her appointment.

•

Night comes into Faust's room; the moon hides behind the clouds; the lamp almost dies; a column of cold air descends from the ceiling and makes our protagonist shiver. Faust, without knowing what he is doing, opens a moldy book and tries out a spell—he calls forth the Earth Spirit, and when the candle flickers and the Ghost appears in its glow of red, the scholar is shocked at his own creation, and flees—or almost.

•

In Bethe's office Hannah mumbles a quick excuse. She makes up a mother succumbing to cancer, and she makes sure she sounds confused enough to get a weeklong leave out of her charade. It works so well that Bethe volunteers to lend her one of the official cars and drivers to get her to the Santa Fe station. It doesn't take Hannah long to pack her suitcase; she throws on a shapeless beige dress and drapes a nondescript raincoat over her shoulders. Her elegance and the shapeliness of her body is a liability in matters of espionage; she has to come across as earthy and unremarkable. Her plan is to either intercept Helen on the train back to Chicago or else to go to the Soviet embassy herself.

There is a brief moment of panic when the car just ahead of them is stopped at the gate for a thorough check. Hannah Sidis, she of the flexible name, considers herself lucky that she chose to sit in the backseat—so she could "work"—rather than next to the driver. She quickly slides the papers out of their envelope and stuffs them into the tissue box that she takes off the ledge by the back window. She slips the empty envelope underneath the driver's seat. She bows down deep and squeezes her nipples between the nails of her thumb and index finger until tears spring to her eyes, then she sits up again and turns her sad and moist eyes shyly away from the young guardsman.

The blond boy examines her purse and her suitcase. He finds everything in order. He pauses for a moment at her copy of *Faust* but finally declines to declare Goethe an enemy of the state. Hannah in the meantime sniffles and blows her nose in a tissue and blabbers something about her dying mother. Soundlessly (*An der Kreuzung zweier Herzwege steht kein Tempel für Apoll*), the car slides out of the military zone and into the real world.

Is it Roosevelt's death that makes everybody edgy, or has somebody tipped off the military about the imminent transfer of information? The train platform at the Santa Fe station is teeming with plainclothes FBI agents—you can always pick out a plainclothes officer. Two of them enter each compartment; one interrogates the passengers while the other goes through their belongings. They are thorough. Hannah decides to wait until the very last moment. In the station bar she drinks a cup of hot chocolate to steady her nerves, and from this old Indian brew she conjures up the image of a new, third Hannah, a little silly ditzy doll, a country girl on her way to the bright lights of the big city, an innocent gal with an empty head. Then, with less than five minutes to spare before departure, she steps back onto the platform and into the mephitic lights.

She plays her role well. What happened to her *now*? Damn, she lost her train ticket! Other people arrive on time and have their tickets ready in hand; other people have their suitcases packed methodically; but that scatterbrained Hannah rummages through her purse and searches through her coat pockets, she puts the box of tissues on the floor to get down on her knees—she wants to open her suitcase but the zipper is stuck. The train conductor comes running to help her; but, no, it's not in the suitcase either. The people behind her get restless. Hannah's face turns bright red. Then she pushes the box into the hands of the conductor and she sits down on her overstuffed suitcase, somebody helps her to zip it shut (a piece of underwear gets caught in the zipper, but they soon solve that problem), and then she goes through her shoulder bag again. Yes! There it is! How could she have overlooked it? With a broad smile she hands the piece of cardboard to the conductor and rattles off the answers to his questions (destination, purpose of the journey, who packed her suitcase, and so on). Steam whirls around the wheels: the train is ready to depart. Hannah grabs her suitcase and steps onboard. She finds her seat and throws her luggage in the luggage rack. Out of breath, she sinks down into the seat and leans her head against the window. Somebody raps against the glass from the outside: the conductor, with her box of Kleenex. Hannah hits herself on the forehead, opens the window and takes the box from him, mumbling apologies, and slides it on top of her suitcase.

The box with the diagram of the bomb.

Her fellow passengers smile—that sweet girl, she has her head in the clouds!

The wheels spin. Hannah's head bobs against the headrest. Outside, the night rattles past at dizzying speed, the night that leads to Chicago, the place where Fermi unleashed the first chain reaction, a slow and careful dance with blocks of uranium oxide and bars of carbon on the floor of an old gymnasium.

•

Faust, line 430 (April 30th, the day the Führer bites into a poison capsule while simultaneously shooting himself in the head, the day that marks the real end of the war), Goethe's scholar asks himself this question: *Bin ich ein G*tt?*

Am I a g*d? (And if so, which one am I?)

Who on the Hill would have been able to sleep if he had truly weighed the consequences of his Work? Who would *not* have considered himself a g*d, a Shiva dancing the world into being, a YHVH holding It All in His hand, with all the responsibility that this entails? But they do not think. The physicists and chemists, the technicians, the workers, the Indians, the ladies who do the calculations (a human serial computer seated at long tables, efficient and alert)—everybody on the Hill is asleep. It's not the sleep of the just: It's the sleep of the exhausted. They have no time, no glucose left to think about the future of their gadget.

They don't *want* to know, is what Hannah thinks. The greatest minds on the planet collected on a tabletop mountain not much larger than a few football fields—and they *refuse* to think. Is the war too clean-looking, perhaps, considered from so great a height? To stand in the middle of this *rerum concordia discors*, to be so close to the whole miraculous uncertainty of existence, and not to examine, not to enter the debate, not to hate those who muffle the truth—how can it be? It can only be because freethinking is painful. It has consequences. Standing to attention by the heavy, elaborate gates of Death. In a doorman's uniform.

Hannah thinks of Goldfarb. Now that his mission on the Hill has been completed, he's away on the Old Continent, doing something so secret they're hardly allowed to write to each other. She thinks of Goldfarb, her wretched lover, who spent his last weeks here—the implosion project finished, barring a few loose ends—thinking, doing nothing but thinking. Seated on her bed in the half-lotus position he would look through her window—look out over the vastness of the plateau. Then, in the light of the full moon, he would stare intently at the ceiling. He shared his thoughts with her. "Why are we making this bomb?" What a shrill, stupid thought. The answer everybody on the mountain would give you, in an instant, without even having to think about it, would be a booming, "Because we can!"

•

Kismet too has trouble sleeping.

She too is fighting dragons, the dragons of creation and destruction.

Dragons of paper, dragons of smoke. She begins to glimpse the terrible truth behind all art: the writer has no say in her story at all. We may get ideas from how we live with others, we may learn from our loves and conflicts, but poetry only grows from the conflicts within. The writer is a hollow sphere of frosted glass with a troubled voice inside, a voice she does not necessarily recognize, or even claim as her own.

Dragons of paper, going up smoke. Stories never live alone. They grow out of a genealogy—he who wants to storm the heavens can use this tree as a ladder. And she—this particular woman, and the diverse, disposable, magical parts she consists of—has dug hard and long in the ground around this tree, and her work, a mixture of alchemical avant-garde and shamanistic capitalism, has led her to the roots; her prose is fast and fat and hopelessly swollen with the white noise of trivia and bits of homeopathic paranoia; a spectacular vomitography for reviewers—*if* ever it sees the light of day—to sink their baby teeth into: pointed prose, but by necessity ambivalent.

Art, beauty, life. It all amounts to noise in the neurons.

Terrible words. Her book is not an attack on morality—Kismet doesn't even mention morality. Deep in the ruins of her soul she carries the secrets and the fate of Europe, a continent constantly ravaged and raped; this time not by Zeus, but by Thor and Wotan. How does she write? Like a prisoner with secret access to a typewriter, like a desperate voice from death row, like a crazy Johanna banging the cushioned walls of her isolation chamber—the words come, tasteless as ever, excessive and timeless (*spike, stem, stamen, staff; slit, peach, inlet, little heart, le p'tit joujou*), in quick epiphanies of mad exhibitionistic prose—and as often happens, this very rawness and passion stand in the way of art. She may be inventive, but she's also a nag; the sex she hammers into the pages is percussive and repetitive. One has the distinct feeling that when her protagonists clean up their rooms after the sadomasochistic rituals she so exhaustively describes are over, it must take longer and have a deeper emotional impact than the dirty deeds themselves. When she rereads her words, they all seem so déjà vu—"*Kismet eviscerates the most despicable, and at times hilarious, elements of our barbaric culture by draping her imaginary underground world with distantly recognizable hints of our own.*"

What helps, what brings comfort in this nightmare of words is the substance warming in the tin spoon, the brown lumps that melt into the smoke that carries visions of cavities explored and entrails laid bare. Yet this is not the source of her art—all use of language deserts her as soon as the fumes enter her lungs; when her ghostly blue lover takes possession of her and abducts her to a land where pain fades away, where words vanish entirely to make room for an endless collection of film loops with only minor variations in details that never matter and never will. Repetition and aggregation is her only way back, to grab a pen after it all and exorcize it, to write down everything she's seen, in minute and excessive detail, to note every fragment, to ponder every detail, to document every single fissure in her skull—but why hasn't she realized that her inspiration evaporates under such compulsive cataloging, that her impulses get dulled along with them; why doesn't she see that all the wonder particularities of her dream lead to nothing but a muddled and useless ache, that they only get lost in the endless drone of the *Angst* of the world?

To write everything down so meticulously is to write nothing at all.

Kismet scrapes away at her skull and writes and writes, until the opium daze reaches its full force, until her bone box is empty and no flesh remains, and then the pen rolls from her fingers, and her eyes—aflame with the drug—are scorched shut with tears.

•

The lulling rhythm of the train. Hannah's eyes are suddenly open wide.

Midnight. Friday, April 13.

A sudden spasm rises from deep inside her loins, a screeching pain, and electric pulses cut through her flesh—Hannah collapses, she breathes with effort, she bites the air. And then Hannah screams.

And then, unannounced and copious: the *bleeding*.

The screaming.

The bleeding.

The men run out of the compartment; the one woman who remains has her eyes wide open (*oh my G*d!*) and tries to stem the tide of blood with paper from Hannah's tissue box.

ע

THE *PATHOLOGIE*

The next morning she leaves the building with that man. They walk to his car, a long silver BMW with a conspicuously low frame. The car jumps to attention with a cheerful bleep and winking headlights—he must be the one person in East Germany who has one of those keychain gadgets. They walk—the Herr Professor has parked his car on the official parking lot of the Communs, and not in the back of the guesthouse, even though there's plenty of room there and even though Herr Professor grew up in America, where the mere idea of walking a few yards is beyond the pale. The BMW by necessity takes up two parking spots; the spaces in the lot are still Trabant-sized, his full-blooded Bavarian car does not fit.

This is the first time I have a good look at the man without his own nakedness (or Donatella's) distracting me. His silver hair looks expensive, like the fur of an arctic fox. He wears it in a severe Caesar cut; he has the icy blue eyes that fit well with this sort of hair. His face is smooth and tight—here we have a seventy-year-old Californian with a lifelong habit of avoiding the sunlight and anointing himself with costly provitamins and antioxidants. No doubt about it, this man is vain; his dark sweater expresses both a sophisticated taste and a hint of worldly pizzazz. He's the kind of man who loves to make women weak in the knees; when they fall, he catches them in his powerful arms and tames the complex arithmetic of their heartbeat with the rhythm of his hips. It's clear that he has a private gym adjacent to his bedroom; it's equally clear he uses it daily.

When they're almost at the car, Donatella puts her hand around his waist. It's a light and casual, almost innocent gesture, but Goldfarb veers away—this is not how he wants to be seen with her in public. Donatella withdraws her hand much more slowly and deliberately than she could. It can't have lasted more than a few seconds, this guilty yet so unremarkable physical contact—and I feel a fist hitting me in my stomach. I see what love does to them and I feel sick; sick with a love of my own, thwarted and unrequited; it almost makes me run to the sink.

There are multiple truths. There is the truth of those who love and there is the truth of those who do not. The latter fear never again being admitted into that inner circle of glowing, hidden knowledge, and it fills them with a bitter hurt.

I suppress my nausea and I turn my attention back to the couple. He accompanies her to the passenger's side—a true gentleman. Her hand brushes his shoulder. He lets her. He opens the door for her and she gets in. He closes the door. Then he does a quick double take. Muffled expletives sputter from his mouth. He goes down on his knees, right in the middle of a puddle, and strokes the side of the car with an agitated finger. When he gets back up he shrugs a little too ostentatiously; I assume he must be smiling his wolf's smile at the woman in the passenger seat. It must feel wonderful to be wooed in such a vehicle: The doors close with a sigh rather than a slam, and the engine purrs like a big, supple cat. There's a last reflection of the morning light on the broken raindrops on the windshield, and then they're gone, with a roar and an unsubtle spray of mud and a final glimpse of the tainted gold of Donatella's hair.

•

He has his arms wide as he comes towards me—an older Jesus walking the waters; he overflows with parables, his eyes burn with the same tiny holy fire that flickers in the golden tabernacles of all the world's cathedrals.

"Where were we?" he says. "Oh yes, the lion had bitten off Pembroke's foot, and Cassandra had just realized that she knew the mysterious stranger's true identity all along!"

De Heer chuckles. I don't like it when he makes fun of his own story, and he knows I don't like it. Irony trivializes. But I do understand him—some things hit so close to home you need to create some distance.

"Paul," he says, and as always the sound of my name coming from those ancient lips makes my heart tremble—for me, who lay at his side in the hospital, it sounds like a summons from beyond the grave—a call from a man who almost isn't here. "Paul, your life must be pretty boring if you come to these cold halls looking for entertainment."

I protest. "I'm not looking for diversion, Meneer De Heer. I come here to learn."

Of course I am looking for diversion: Last night was some night, and this morning some morning

"Your research must be dull and futile, Paul, if this old lesson sounds new to you. You must have heard it at least a thousand times. Don't pooh-pooh me. One of the skills you acquire as a fugitive is a good nose. You recognize your partners in misfortune. You recognize them a Berlin city block away—as you will learn later in today's story. I in particular recognize those people who like me lack the talent for happiness."

Don't look at me like that, Mr. De Heer. Please.

•

They locked me up. I feigned madness. I babbled, I attacked the furniture, I recited Goethe, I ad-libbed on a line from Rilke. By the time I arrived at the twelfth "Sonnet to Orpheus," they let me go.

That was the plan.

It didn't take long before I realized that I didn't need to pretend. I *was* mad: mad with sorrow, possessed with grief, struck with unbridled remorse. Just because a man asks for his death with a simple nod of his head, just because he presents such a convincing case for his vicarious suicide, doesn't mean he should be obeyed. I shouldn't have listened; I should have fought his execution with all my might, possibly to my own death. Because even though the soul may sink, that same soul—forgive the mixed metaphor—is a phoenix too. The body, however, will never rise again; the death of the body is definitive. Whoever brings about the death of his body destroys his soul with it—therein lies the inexcusability of his sin. My sin.

In other words, my attempts to forget what had happened on that stage made me slip through a trapdoor in my mind into a damp dark basement, a network of underground tunnels with no map and no way out. There I was, running barefoot and on bleeding soles towards that nadir within me, the point where all perspective fades.

I should have palmed the bullet. I know that that was not how the trick was done. Lech was a dapper hussar, a strongman who could move tables and chairs and heavy furniture as though they were pins in a bowling alley, and he was a good friend too—but he was no prestidigitator. I was. I should have palmed the bullet.

WLADIMIR had never revealed the workings of this trick to me. I assume a barrier of some sorts had been installed inside the barrel, a hymen, half-penetrated, that allowed smoke and fire to escape, but trapped the red-hot bullet inside.

Had it been simple bad luck? How often can a bullet, even a bullet made of soft, moldable silver, pound against such a diaphragm until it gives way? But WLADIMIR was always very careful with his props—he folded his scarves until three of them fit into a thimble; he oiled the hinges of treasure chests' fake bottoms nightly; he fed his pigeons out of the palm of his hand. I'm certain that after each performance he must have checked the state of the barrel with a flashlight and a pipe cleaner.

Had WLADIMIR been negligent on purpose? Had he—knowing the end would come soon—risked his life on that stage evening after evening, letting Fate have its choice? His body shook every time Lech produced the revolver from his pocket; had this been more than a well-rehearsed comedy routine? Might the bullet trick have been his daily pull at the Wheel of Fortune?

Or, perhaps, had the Gestapo filed the barrel smooth? In which case, had WLADIMIR been aware of this? I knew nothing about the false bottoms that might have been hidden in the magician's heart; I knew nothing about his love and hate for life; nothing about the relative proportions of the forces of repulsion and attraction in the closed quarters of his mind; nothing of his feelings for Marushka and how deep they went; nothing of what he felt for me, nor indeed if even had any feelings about me one way or the other; nothing of the damage caused in him by the tumor of time growing and growing.

What role had I played, then, on that fateful evening of our arrest? Had I been a remote-controlled perpetrator of suicide, the ultimate naïve volunteer—had my hand in the end been WLADIMIR's? Or had I been part of a larger plan: the man who would grant WLADIMIR his fabled death, a death that would guarantee his place among the legendary magicians of the century? Had WLADIMIR been a gladiator who refuses to die anywhere but in the ring, dressed in the suit of lights that made him famous, hanging from the invisible thread of life he himself had woven out of piano strings? Or had I been an unwitting accomplice of the Gestapo, the passive executioner of WLADIMIR's death sentence? Or, banality of all banalities, had I been nothing more than the final avatar of WLADIMIR's *Schiksal*?

·

"You smell, Jew. You need to be washed."

He puts the washbasin between his feet and forces my head down until my nose touches the water's filthy surface. I hear him clear his throat. A vile glob of phlegm runs to the corner of his mouth and then I feel it dripping down my neck. It coats my skull. The SS-man shaves his face, his foot in my neck, and the soapy foam and the sharp grit of his beard anoint my head, soothing and scratching me at once. Purge me with hyssop, and I shall be clean. Wash me, and I shall be whiter than snow.

The endless tactics and techniques, the predictable stratagems of torture.

Smooth talking. Rough yelling.

I throw my hands in the air.

"Are you my masters, resting among roots?"

They grin the universal grin.

"Do you ever you marvel at the fruit? At its size . . ."

The grin gets broader.

"At the softness of its tender peel?"

They hit me harder.

"Are we truly that fragile, that helpless?"

They want names and addresses; they want points of contact. "Patches and pieces in place of the whole!" They want to know the places where the conspirators gather. I look at them from deep underneath my eyebrows and whisper, "Do we know this, friend, or do we know this not?"

Boots get caked with blood.

"When shall the citadel, high on its peaceful hill, be torn down? Behold the machine, it spins its vengeance—it perverts us, it belittles."

Time is not a circle. Time is a nautilus. Are we traveling on the spiral that leads inward, or on the spiral that take us outside?

The plan was to feign madness. To become a poetic font of verbal diarrhea— I would provide no answers, only questions, always questions. A scientist of poetry, always quizzing life, without certitudes. I would cackle and coo in double-Dutch, I would be mute-and-deaf to everything but the voices that hissed like sidewinders inside my head. I would be strong. I would be a good actor, an impassioned player. The disease was near. I could do it—or so I thought.

But after less than three days the metaphysical questions turned to real anguish. My nonsense lists suddenly acquired content. I had no control over this. I gave birth. My battered flesh became word—it spewed out names and stories and dates, the hours and days of coming and going. It started haltingly, but soon enough the trickle became a steady stream and then a torrent of verbal vomit so furious that the typewriter in all its rattling glory, with all its dapper clattering, could hardly keep up. Oh, the thrashing of the iron whips on the rubber roll; oh, the patient paper stretched so expectantly over the frame of my ruin: I love you—you are so completely in sync with the throbbing rhythm of the horrible ache that pounds in my head!

I am not special. There is nothing unique about me. I am like so many. Doing what so many do, doing what so many did. My father, for instance. My voice gave way to dust. Certainly, some have told the heroic tales of men and women who did not succumb to the pressure—but such men, such women, are rare. I turned out to not be one of them. And how many of those stories are verifiably true, how many come from witnesses rather than the protagonists themselves. It's easy to condemn people like me—but why and where did you get your mandate to denounce me? You yourself haven't felt the boot in your neck; you yourself don't know what it feels like when your fractured ribs poke at your swollen flesh from the inside.

This I know, with absolute certainty: I did not want to talk. I did not want to betray my fellow human beings. But talk I did, although I wanted to remain silent. I opened my mouth and I talked. Only our acts are real. The rest is speculation. Only the man or woman who has lived through all this and is still without sin may cast a stone, and let the stone be small and smooth like the pebbles we Jews carry to the graves of those we love. So many, too many graves. What a mass of graves, what a mass of mass graves. What a pile of guilt; how insurmountable the impossibility of retribution. What a cruel, cruel G*d—He dealt us so little courage.

They know the effect of these interviews on the prisoner's digestive tract. The prisoner's evening meal consists of oatmeal and milk rice; no chewing necessary. It hurts just to lift the spoon. Some merciful soul grabs the martyr's arm and slips in a needle; he fills a vein with jagged kindness and then comes a sugary sleep.

Or did I imagine all of this, in a fever dream of grief?

The darkness inside the Gestapo cellar is different from the darkness in the shabby womb beneath the stage. This darkness is absolute, yet slippery—a darkness that is impossible to endure, a darkness impossible to remember.

Take the light away and the world disappears.

Take the light away and the universe contracts to a blinding ache, full of needle-tipped stars.

I duel with the dark, with those stinging stars in my head, with those imaginary nebulas, those spirals of cosmic violence that wreck my parched synapses.

I fight with what is no longer there.

I have said it so often. Take hope away and life disappears.

The living are a subset of the dead, an exceptionally rare subset. After all this time spent in that cellar—I'm no longer certain if I belong to the living.

Hour after hour, every hour of the day, I see myself: I raise my arm, I hold the gleaming revolver in my hand, I feel the cold metal at my finger as I pull the trigger.

I pull the trigger.

Hour after hour after hour.

The slight resistance of the trigger.

A small flame spurts from a short barrel.

WLADIMIR dies.

The course of events.

WLADIMIR dies.

And dies.

And dies.

Inside me.

In foggy spirals of stars.

I measure the passage of time by the growing length of my beard.

There is no difference between day and night.

They let me lie; I lie alone.

The door opens: they throw me a tin bowl with muck, they empty the bucket of shit. It sloshes against the sides, a liquid stink. Through the open door I hear the persistent barking of dogs.

It repeats. *Da capo*. Filthy Jew, you need to be washed, etcetera.

The same names, the same dates, the same stories.

Again and again and again.

The typewriter hammers nails into my skull; the bell that marks each return sounds ominous and low—tolling to announce a miniature death.

The posthumous blessing of WLADIMIR. What I don't know, I cannot betray. My ignorance is all embracing. That is my salvation. I really know too little. I do not know how and how far out the network branches; I cannot betray anybody of importance.

They batter my battered body further; they beat me and threaten to take my life. All I have to offer them are the names of the men and women in the theater and the story of our trip through the woods. Things they already know.

They decide to go deeper than my skin and flesh.

I cry bitter tears when they threaten to kill my mother.

She's still alive?

A week, a full week, and then they finally decide that I am indeed what I have been claiming to be: A minuscule node in the network. The Zionist conspiracy may span the city and the Reich and, who knows, (the Gestapo suspects) maybe even the world—but in the cesspool of this gigantic organization I am nothing but a tiny turd. This is good: I'm not worth executing. But I am in Berlin illegally, and therefore I must be transported eastward. There's a subtle irony in this decision. The Nazis have rules for everything, even for treating people like me, filthy Jew etcetera and accidental freedom fighter, but even for people like me, Jew and mortal enemy, these rules are not to be broken. My body is wrecked; the rules forbid transport to a labor camp until I have recovered. And so they send me to a hospital, the Jewish hospital, to recover.

·

I wave him away. Go away, I say, go away. My arm feels so heavy I can hardly lift it, so weak are the muscles, so heavy weighs the bone inside. Go away! Leave me alone—let me suffer alone.

He doesn't go away. No, he sits down on the edge of the bed, a squat black insect on the wide white field of pristine linen. I make another vague attempt to wave this new fever dream away. My own dead weight pushes me back down against the mattress. The specter raises an arm. A hand, real and fleshy, pats my knee. A meaty hand, its tendons sunk deep inside a layer of delicious fat.

"*Also.* You are the assistant of the mage. *Na?*" The man's voice is high and shaky. The room smells of camphor and hydrogen; his voice intoxicates like birdsong. I watch his lips move. His teeth gleam yellow, and behind that bulwark of teeth lies a lazy tongue, purple and thick, fat and slow as a springtime slug. It doesn't escape my attention that he—unlike the other men, the men with power over me—uses the polite pronoun *Sie* to address me.

From the breast pocket of his uniform the man removes a cigar and a box of matches. He presses the cigar against my lips. It tastes bitter. He offers me a delicate flame, cupped inside his hands. What else can I do but suck like a baby at the nipple of sotweed? The sharp smoke makes me cough; it fills my mouth and mind with clouds. The inside of my head feels like one of the aromatic particles that float through the room in random patterns, in the spirals of Brownian motion—I am caught in the turbulence of pure improvisation.

This man acts like a magician then. A box of playing cards appears in his hand, a brand-new deck still wrapped in cellophane, the brand made especially for the army, narrower than usual so that they fit nicely in the pocket of a uniform. The man's hat sports a death's-head of dull silver. It doesn't threaten me; it only stares with sad, gauged-out eyes. It does not intimidate; it is merely a memento mori for the officer who glances in the mirror. With his thumbnail the man breaks the seal, impatiently ripping the box open. He bends the cards in preparation for the shuffle. The edges crackles like a cat's fur on a winter night. The sound stirs echoes deep in my soul: The old instinct rears its head. I extend my hands. I want to take possession, right now, of those fifty-two familiar friends.

The man laughs, a hearty laugh from deep inside his throat, exactly the kind of laugh that suits the circumstances: A sickbed visit, and the patient is feeling much better than expected. He fans out the cards: fifty-two identical backsides face the ceiling patiently.

"Pick one! Pick a card!" An accent shimmers through his high-German. Something rural, Pomeranian perhaps? And how sweet the cigar smells! Didn't the Mayas use this herb in their cleansing rituals; didn't they rub the hands and forehead and chest of their dying loved ones with pulverized tobacco to ward off Ah Puch, the g*d of death?

My fingers wander, my fingertips feel the underside of each card. My nerve endings, sharpened by months of practice and the momentary tingle of tobacco, detect little markings—shallow, almost imperceptible depressions near the cards' corners. I can't believe it. This man went through all the trouble of preparing a full set of cards just to impress a petty prisoner? I close my eyes to concentrate better. Smoke drifts in and out of my nostrils; something in my cortex aligns with what I feel: I find that I can read the cards. I know the code. This deck of cards was once prepared by WLADIMIR.

I make my choice and then I open my eyes. I slide the card back into the deck at a random spot.

"Aha! Aha!" The man jumps up from the mattress. He shuffles the cards. I see his lips move. He counts; this is a very transparent trick. One after the other, he throws the cards on the bed; he covers me in two-dimensional snow. In the end, exactly one card remains. He holds it up triumphantly. "It was this one, wasn't it?" His eyes sparkle with the repulsive enthusiasm of the amateur illusionist. "It was, right? Wasn't it? This card? *Nicht war*? Aha! Yes, it has to be this one! Isn't it amaaaayzing?"

He holds up the seven of spades as if it were a holy relic.

Slowly I shake my head.

"No," I say. "That was not my card. *This* was my card." And from the breast pocket of the man's uniform I pluck a card—and when I hand it over I also set it on fire, purely for effect. The man burns his fingers and throws the card to the floor; he tramples it with his big black boots until the fire goes out, then he picks it up. One corner is spared—I had wet it with my fingers.

It is the ace of hearts.

The apprentice sorcerer lets out a cry of joy and he claps his hands. "Oh! Oh! Oh! The ace of hearts!" He puts the scorched miracle inside his pocket.

"You and I, my boy, we will do great things!" he says, and the introduction of the informal *du* into the conversation is not a humiliation, but a crazy offer of friendship.

I smile. Of course I had picked the seven of spades.

•

Well then, let us perform a few more miracles.

A miracle: I walk.

A miracle: I walk out of the hospital.

A miracle: I walk out of the hospital, with an SS-officer's arm around my shoulder.

It's a short walk. Through the garden, onto a gravel path, to a brick building surrounded by barbed wire. The function of the building is carved in the sandstone finial in clean gothic script: *Pathologie*.

I have an SS-officer's arm around my shoulder. This is a miracle regardless of who performs it: someone's arm around my shoulder.

However weak I am, I still have my desire for freedom. I could break free and run for it. The man's grip is firm but not forceful; his hand is small and chubby, his fingers fat and slippery. Even in my present state, weakened by illness, I am a head taller than he is, and I doubt that the man could be faster than me—he's not a true soldier, but a nicely fattened servant of bureaucracy. But there's no escaping the pistol at his hip. Maybe I could steal it? It would be easy to open the holster and press the barrel against his temple. I could yell at the guards that I'll kill their boss if I'm not released instantly, but I also know that before I took even a single step, a hail of bullets would have put their holes in me.

This is the most important lesson I've learned in the past few years: You can never outrun death. One day, death will catch up with each of us: no matter how fast we run, he will pull up alongside, hardly panting. Maybe I would be fast enough to pull the trigger and kill this German miniature potbellied pig before I succumbed to the guards' attack, but what would it matter and what would it change?

My cheeks feel wet in the moist wind, as if Marushka's tears are raining down from the heavens, and I promise her: I will stay alive no matter what. I will never do what WLADIMIR did: I will never choose the moment—the moment will have to find me. I swear it on my dead friends' ghosts.

A final miracle: During that short walk from hospital to mortuary I rise from the dead. My back straightens up, the blaze of fever leaves my body. I turn into a man again. Is it the arm on my shoulder that does it, or is it the friendly deck of cards in my fist? Yes, I am quite certain now: I'm human again.

•

The distance grows. The events slip away. Will these stories survive into a new century, into a new millennium, especially after all of us who survived the Terror will have succumbed to the more banal ravages of life—the slow processes of corrosion and apoptosis, entropy running amok in our cells? There will be a time when our story will need footnotes and endnotes to the footnotes, and that time is not so far away.

Recently, the Roper Organization sampled 993 adults and 506 high-school students, all American, and asked them a few questions. They found that 38 percent of the adults and 53 percent of the students did not know what the term *Holocaust* meant. More than two thirds had no idea how many Jews had perished in that inferno. Almost half of the sample did not recognize the names Treblinka, Dachau, or Auschwitz. The Spartacus College of Judaica asked high-school students in Chicago how they imagined life in the ghetto of Warsaw in 1941. Some typical answers: "Nobody had their own room," "Only black and white television," "No snacks between meals," "No air conditioning," "No more than two pairs of jeans per person."

One out of twenty Americans believes that the Holocaust never happened. Fifteen million Holocaust-deniers in America alone, more than twice the number of people who died in that—apparently—eminently forgettable fire.

•

A miracle. A man dressed in black leads another man across a gravel path, this second man dressed in loose white garments that billow in the wind. The sharp stones cut the white man's bare feet, but he does not feel the pain. His gown blows wide open, it bares his bony ass for all to see, but he does not care.

Where do they go? To a small building labeled *Pathologie*. That is, to the mortuary. The symbolism of reality often surpasses what is acceptable in fiction.

"*Also*," repeats the man in black, and he happily holds up his index finger in the cold air, "You are the assistant of the mage!"

•

He conjures up a room and a queen-sized bed, just for me; the mattress bounces when you sit down on it. Fresh sheets too. Living in the attic room feels pleasantly like being trapped inside the hat of a medieval sorcerer. The rain had kept itself discreetly in the background during our walk; now it beats joyfully against the roof tiles. I am held captive inside the friendly belly, the comfortable rib cage of a familiar beast.

A bowl of meat soup appears on the little table, as well as a big lump of spongy bread. What else does this man keep up his sleeve? Apparently a length of sausage and a pint of beer. He claps his hands and I am clad in a civilian's suit, cut handsomely and fitting my newly trim body exactly—who cares if it's secondhand? When I slip the deck of cards in a pocket, I discover a few coins. They're nicely worn; they slide pleasantly through my fingers. I throw them at my benefactor to pay him for food and lodging, but the coins dissolve in midair. Then they rain from the ceiling lamp onto the mattress. The man counts them; there are six, but when I ask him to recount there are seven, no, five, no, eight coins; the number shifts continuously, though I, the stern fiscal cabbalist, am far away, in the corner of the room, only smiling.

The officer puts his hat upside down on the bedside table. He sits down; thesprings creak in soft protest. He puts his elbows on his knees; his long fingernails scratch his closely cropped skull. "I have had little luck with cards lately," he sighs. I listen. A jingling waterfall of gold coins flows over my fingers. "No luck at all, actually." His smile is so boyish, his teeth so wolfish. I pause for a moment, and then I throw the coins, all eight of them, into the crown of his hat.

"You deserve better, Herr Hauptsturmführer," I say, with emphasis. "Much, much better."

•

This is not the infamous banality of evil. These are not the halls of Mephistopheles. This is not the gaping mouth of Hades. This is the banality of banality. A middle-class card night, trite and ordinary, pleasant in a most unremarkable way. A soldier in plainclothes provokes some passable Schubert from a piano that's plausibly in tune; a charming nurse makes an occasional appearance with a lovely tray of butter cookies; and whenever he thinks the others aren't watching, my savior winks at me through the pungent haze of Cuban cigar smoke. Smiles aplenty. Four civilized people sit around a table and play a civilized game of cards. Not a word is uttered that could offend the lady player. I play with restraint; I allow myself only small capital gains. I am gallant: I deal my partner good hands; I am constructive. The officer is not interested in the modest sums of money that are at stake; he wants to be touched by luck, he wants to feel Madam Fortune caress him with her firm, decisive fingers. That this is all a sham is of no importance—the knowledge that one is cheating is easily removed from one's consciousness. At the end of the day, the only thought that remains is that you have won. I won! I won! I am a child of the g*ds, I am their special favorite!

"Some cake?" Our host interrupts the proceedings. "What would you think of a nice piece of cake, hm? Cake?" He snaps his fingers. "Elli, Elli, bring the cake!"

"But Walter!" The woman claps her hands in delight. The doctor who sits next to her is not her husband. That much is clear from the glances they exchange and from the way she pats his knee whenever he wins a hand, and gathers up the cards with that greedy smirk on his face. The pat is a slight rebuke. The gesture says, Spare yourself, my dear; and save your energy. Save it for later. Save it for me. Save it for us. She may complain that the cards do not favor her, but the truth is that her heart isn't in the game. Love and cards, they don't go well together.

"Walter, dear fellow," says the man. "Is that real butter I smell?"

"And eggs! The aroma of real eggs!" The woman beams, and so does my savior.

"And real coffee, made of freshly roasted, freshly ground beans!"

The glances exchanged between the host and woman—much more is happening at this table than a mere game of poker. The knife cuts a trail through the cake.

"Where does that cake come from, Walter?"

This is a cake like no baker still bakes them, richly soaked in liqueur, plastered with butter cream and spun sugar, its center decorated with a number written in yellow lines of pure sweetness: 33.

"Today," says Walter, and he takes a small stack of plates from Elli's hands, "today is Margot Goerke's birthday. Today, Margot turns thirty-three. This cake—her girlfriends have baked this cake for her. This afternoon at half-past three they delivered the cake to Margot's house." (Did I mention that the lamp above the table has been turned off? That little wax candles burn on top of the cake? That Walter's face, lit from below by this uncertain fire, looks devilish and homely at the same time?)

He hands me a slice—a little boat with a tiny burning mast, adrift in life—and a fork too. He licks the bread knife, and a blob of whipped cream sticks to the gray stubble of his upper lip—he foams amicably at the mouth.

"Only, Margot was not at home. Margot was arrested three days ago. I happened to notice the date of birth on her identity card. Well, well, almost a birthday girl! One of my men was gracious enough to keep an eye on her apartment in case somebody stopped by to mark the happy occasion. He managed to intercept both the girlfriends and the cake."

From the heart of the pastry a glob of cherry jam bleeds slowly onto my plate.

"Maybe we can save a piece for Margot?" proposes the woman. "After all, today is her *Geburtstag!*"

"Aw!" Walter smiles. His disgusting little tongue feels for the cream on his lip. He smacks his lips. He shrugs his shoulders. "That would be hard. Margot is no longer among us. Margot has moved away. She lives in Theresienstadt now."

"What a pity!" The woman sighs. "This is truly . . . a costly cake!"

"Ah well." Walter looks around the table. He looks at Elli. Elli turns the lamp back on. "Why don't you deal us another hand, boy? The night is young, and that cup of coffee has quite invigorated me."

"Don't forget to hand over your money to me, son!"

We stand side by side at the urinal. I admit it, towards the end of the evening I had become a little restless; I had provided myself with a long streak of particularly good luck, and in the silence of my heart I dedicated that streak to Margot and her two friends. Imagine those girlfriends in their clandestine kitchen; imagine the effort it must have taken to find these rare ingredients on the black market; imagine the aroma coming from the oven and the unbearable hunger gnawing at their stomachs (fugitives in Berlin are always hungry). Imagine the temptation to eat the cake or at least steal a little piece of it. No: Let us wait until this afternoon at Margot's place, she will surely want to share the cake with us, and we will share her joy as well: another year gone, another year survived!

Walter shakes the last drops from his dick and puts it back inside. He goes to wash his hands. The barbaric hands from which I had—in a recent past that feels very distant tonight—saved so many people, even though I didn't know I was doing it; the barbaric hands that unflinchingly signed Margot's death sentence and that of so many others; those bureaucratic hands that are so innocent, those the-law-is-on-my-side-who-needs-a-conscience hands glisten with the foam of thick brown soap. He rinses them and rubs them on the towel until they blush with a healthy glow. I wait until Walter has left the restroom. I keep the faucet closed. I want Jewish urine on my hands and Jewish urine on the cards, Jew-piss on the hands of the soldier and Jew-piss on the hands of the doctor and Jew-piss on the hands of the doctor's lover who also wants to be the officer's lover and Jew-piss on everything the officer, the doctor, and the doctor's lover touch with those hands. Whenever their fingers go through their hair, whenever they pick their noses, whenever they insert a pinky in their ear, I watch them cordially and smile at them warmly.

"Goodnight, Herr Doktor. Goodnight, *gnädige* Frau." I politely shake the hands of the pseudo-spouses, and they politely shake mine, even though they know I am a Jew and a prisoner. "Don't take it personally," is what their handshakes say. "We act according to the Führer's ordinances, but we are also human, no?" That is their hidden message. Their kind of people, they make me sick.

•

In my dream I am buried underneath a suffocating net. A sickening smell invades my nostrils, beastly and raw, and the ground underneath my body trembles and shakes. A deep voice hums the orchestral theme form the gypsy choir from *Il Trovatore*, then a female voice takes over and sings the gypsies' theme: "*All'opra, all'opra! Dagli! Martella!*"—she sings it in German: "*An die Arbeit, an die Arbeit! Gebt her! Den Hammer!*"—"*Arbeit!*" shouts the man, "*macht frei!*" and then they both collapse in hysterical laughter—a wolf groans and the earth shudders.

I need air. I throw the blankets off me, and something on top of those blankets, something heavy and plump and hairy and stinky, slides to the floor. I reach out to grab whatever it is and my fingers touch naked flesh, hot and sweaty. I scream, and the sound of my scream wakes me from my nightmare and in a panicky reflex I roll out of bed and grope for my long-lost knife; I end up on the floor in a pool of creaking leather, ratty fur and rustling satin.

A curse crackles high above my head. "*Scheiße!*"

The bed squeaks and footsteps run to the door—the lights are switched on and there stands Rolf, naked as the g*d Pan, his menacing sex fully erect, and above me, in bed, Stella—equally naked—covering herself with the sheet. Rolf draws nearer; he squints to better see me. He whistles between his teeth—look what we've caught here! "I'll be damned if that isn't that clever little magician, the eternally cheerful Helmut!" His hand feels under the blankets for his underpants. He hitches them up; he stuffs his stubborn erection under the waistband; a moist stain appears where the top of his cock touches the cotton.

"And what is dear sweet Helmut doing in our marriage bed, *na?*" Rolf now towers high above me. He raises a hand as if to beat me. I make big, upset eyes and wrap myself in his long leather coat. Comedy can be a weapon.

"Rolf, ah—let him be." Stella's voice is slow and sluggish, thick with alcohol and sleep.

Stella.

Stella, she who betrayed us all, she who lured WLADIMIR, Marushka, Lech, and all our friends to their deaths, she who betrayed me—here is Stella, sitting on the edge of the bed, a thin sheet wrapped around her damp flesh, and, yes, I should strangle her with my bare hands, and yes, they itch, those hands of mine, those hands rubbed raw with the crumbs of Margot's birthday cake and the smooth backs of the cards and the drops of my piss and the skin flakes of the good Herr Doktor and his mistress and my unsavory alliance with Hauptsturmführer Walter—but I also can't take my eyes off her, I can't keep my eyes off the curls that bounce off her shoulders when she feels under the bed for a cigarette—a cigarette, such a precious commodity!—and I can't turn away from the curves that bulge under the sheet, the arch of her hip, the orb of her breast, the dark ring of a nipple pressing against the white fabric, and then her scent hits my nostrils, the slight acerbity of her sweat and the heady sweetness of a perfume called Kantate, all lilacs and vanilla, and underneath that a hint of darker, older memories, a smell of surf and salt and shells, a scent that I recognize, a scent of Satie and slow dissonances on a piano, a scent that transports me back to a night underneath a dark baby grand, a scent that evokes things in me that are not well suited to the moment—and I huddle deeper into the coat and wrap myself deeper in shame. Rolf makes a fist out of his raised hand, then lets that fist fall to his side. I'm not worth the trouble, the bruised knuckles. Thankfully, his erection has subsided.

"You know, Hellll-mut, we just came back from the opera." Stella puts a hand on her breast like an unchaste Madonna, and throws the other one high in the air—she imitates the open mouth and vibrating uvula of the operatic diva.

They are drunk.

"They killed a whole lot of gypsies," says Rolf. "On stage. A whole lot of gypsies."

"An extremely violent opera," adds Stella. "Do you know it, Hellll-mut, *Il Trovatore*, do you know that opera? Violent!"

Smashed. The both of them. Plastered.

"*La Zingarella!*" yells Rolf, and with a mighty jump he lands on top of Stella. She rolls over backwards and laughs her head off; it makes her lose her sheet. They are so very drunk—how does Rolf even manage to get it up?, but get it up he does, and instantly too: His pale impressive cock peeps through the slit of his underpants and pokes at Stella's bellybutton.

"What are you waiting for?" Stella shouts at me. "Come on, get out. Out with you! *Raus! Raus, du Judensau!*"

I quickly gather my little pile of clothes. I also grab the fur coat off the floor—a cloud of Kantate flutters forth—and I rush to the hallway. The blackout curtains are down, the darkness is absolute; my bare toes bump against a man who curses me quite loudly. From all directions people hiss and cry for silence, the hallway must be teeming. I sink down. I feel around me—people and blankets everywhere. The only empty space is here, right at the door, but there isn't enough room for me to stretch out. I lean my back against the wood. The floor is hard and cold, and I can hear everything that's going on inside. I pull Stella's coat over my head to muffle the sound. The perfume that wafts from the collar nauseates me, but somehow also makes me astonishingly sad. Finally, I roll up the coat and put it in my lap. No other place to rest my head than the wood of the door. I don't want to listen, but I can't help it: They are loud, and each ferocious squeak of the bedsprings goes right through my head.

•

Consequently, I am wide-awake when the door opens again, a good hour later—I would have tumbled inside if a soft hand hadn't grabbed my shoulder. It is Stella, and she drags me inside, irresistibly, a finger—I cannot see it, but I feel it—at her lips. The door closes again. It is as dark inside as it is outside, dark as the Gestapo basement, a darkness that feels impenetrable, a darkness to which no eye can adapt.

Who are we kidding with our blackout curtains and our lights-out? As if the English hadn't found us long ago. Evening after evening they return. They don't need maps, they recognize the presence of Berlin by their nightly weariness—it must be about here, yes, here—and then always the same thing: Pull the lever, navigate through the pinpricks of the anti-aircraft artillery, and then that sinking feeling, "Do we now have to fly all the way back too?"

Rolf's snoring makes the bed shake.

We sit against the wall, Stella and I. Now I recognize her again, the other Stella, the Stella I've known the longest, the Stella of the sliding dissonances, the Stella of stillness and tears. Together we lean against the wall, shoulder to shoulder, her hand on my cheek, her fingers feeling for my mouth. She presses a soft tube of paper against my lips. The yellow flame, disturbingly close to my face, illuminates the totality of the known world—for a brief moment the whole universe is pressed inside these four walls, and Stella is a painting by de La Tour, bathing in a glow that looks mystical but in reality is a cheap trick of sulfur and cardboard, a commonplace miracle from a tiny box labeled *Opernpalast*. In the full light of the hungry flame, Stella's face looks bloated; her eyes are red and swollen. Her dress fits strangely; she must have thrown it on in haste. In her lap the cracked teacup she uses for an ashtray gleams. All this I observe in the time it takes her to shake out the flame.

She takes my head between her hands; the heat of her breath brushes against my cheeks. Then she puts the shaft of her cigarette against the glowing end of mine and there is a kiss of fire. (Life's user's manual: How to turn darkness into flesh.) Then she lets go of me. My head bangs against the wall; the hollow echo of oblivion. Stella sucks on the tobacco and I hear her sniffle—is she crying?

Stella whispers.

"At some point, every opera needs a lancer."

This is what Rolf does. He works as an extra in the Staatsoper, that absurd temple of kitsch on Unter den Linden. She's right: No matter whether the opera is German or Italian, there's always a moment amid the katzenjammer when a man with a lance comes onstage—a soldier or a messenger or perhaps a bodyguard. His role is immaterial. He is there simply to advance the plot. He needs not sing. Rolf obviously does not sing. Hear him snore. How could anybody who snores so gruffly be capable of singing? Rolf artfully mouths along with the choir and looks ominous, or messenger-like, or menacing, depending on the context. In the meantime, he peers into the theater from underneath his thick cotton-wool eyebrows like jolly Genovese lancers or messengers or bodyguards are presumably wont to do. The room is never completely dark, and everybody naturally faces the stage—this is a good opportunity to spy on the audience. Rolf especially watches the cheap seats high up in the theater—they are the seats *par excellence* for illegals who come to drown the sorrows of the day in sentimental schmaltz. Rolf's gaze travels past all those rapt, bare faces, and when he sees a familiar one—Rolf never forgets a face, and Rolf knows so many people—he draws complex figures in the air with his spear. These tell the ushers what row and what seat the suspect is seated in; a messenger boy delivers that information to two Gestapo agents positioned at the balcony. During the break, they stroll to their victim. Opera performances are always sold out, the hallways are narrow, and there's only one central staircase from the parquet to the lobby. When two gentlemen grab you by the elbow and whisper that maybe you should follow them, it's too late: There is no escape.

That is what Rolf does. He is a lancer. A piercer of hearts.

And you Stella, what do you do?

The question hums around inside my head, but I don't dare ask it aloud. I can imagine the scene. After the performance Rolf takes his mate Stella to the stucco splendor of the Opernpalast or to café Bollelmüller in the Mittelstraße. The tobacco smoke floats thick and spicy; the jovial opera-goers mingle with newscasters from the local radio station and gutter journalists with freshly shaved baby faces, they brush shoulders with sweaty cellists and blushing girls from the ballet. When Stella and her Rolf enter the café they cause a minor stir, she with her blond locks and her million-reichsmark smile, her head cocked just so above her fox-fur coat, he with his tailor-made suit and his long leather jacket and his felt fedora—he looks like a Gestapo officer, but no, Gestapo officers always operate in pairs and the second of the pair is never a woman. They smile good-naturedly at the bourgeoisie; with nimble fingers Stella strokes the shoulders or upper arms of friends or folks her guts tell her are Jewish. She likes to touch her victims. The unexpected pat causes a brief electrical pulse, a small shock of surprise; it makes their impending death all the more real. The pair of camouflaged officers that follows Rolf and Stella on their *Spaziergang* make a mental note; they wait at the exit and under their raincoats they finger their guns. It's all so easy and so clean, there are no nasty scenes. The regulars and the potential victims are not even aware that anything is happening. The Gestapo pays for Rolf and Stella's *Käsekuchen*—such an abundance of airily whipped lipids on the tongue! Such divinely refined sweetness, sticking so gorgeously to the palate! Rolf and Stella just love this heavenly cheesecake!

They operate the way detectives in the movies operate: They do not speak. There is no need, but, more importantly, there is no desire. Such is their level of mutual contempt.

Yes, Stella despises her Rolf. There is no other way. How can she not feel contempt for her Rolf, that brute who snores every night as if nothing's the matter (he is all three of those smelly monkeys rolled into one—he sees and he does not see, he hears and he does not hear, he speaks and he does not speak: evil, what evil?)? How can you sleep when you just earned two hundred marks by betraying a fellow human being, somebody who leaves a mother, a father, a sister, a brother, a lover behind, sick with sorrow?

For the same reasons Rolf can't help but feel deep contempt for her.

That is the reason—Stella says—why he takes her with so much force, and why he feels the need to do it nightly. Men are like that: A good hard fuck puts a halt to their thought processes. Which is a good thing. Look at Stella: she thinks, and therefore she despises not only Rolf, but also herself. That is why she has her back to the wall, that is why she sucks on her cigarette with such relish, that is why tears roll down her cheek—I can hear it in her voice and in the moist silence that hangs around us like a veil of mist. Her swaggering parade through town is no sign of bluster; it is homeopathic medicine for her self contempt, applied in hysterically inflated doses. And a person who despises herself also despises humanity and all of humanity's aspirations. How does it feel, Stella, to walk home every day to your room in the Pathologie and to know that you have done something completely inexcusable? This is how it feels: Salty wetness drips over my hands.

Stella shakes her head like a wet dog. She shakes my fingers off her cheekbones, and with that movement she liberates herself from my Braille reading of her tears. Is she afraid of what might be revealed?

"It's not the money," Stella says. "Please believe me, it's not the money. It's not the certainty that we will live. It is not the thrill—maybe it is for Rolf, maybe Rolf gets a thrill from it, but I don't. Here's the reason, my only reason: For every man or every woman we get arrested, we're granted an audition before Dobberke. We can suggest a name, and that name will be removed from the list."

That's the explanation? Is it an exchange, a simple, terrible exchange? Betray a distant acquaintance and a friend will be saved? A simple exchange: an eye for an eye, a tooth for a tooth, one insignificant Jew for another? Black marketeering with men in black uniforms, haggling for lives with the masters of death—haggling with the g*ds? Are we ancient Greeks or modern Hindus or Israelites in the desert, are we patriarchs who beg and plead and wallow in the dirt? Are we men who burn sacrificial offerings, if need be with our own son on the altar—all in the name of our People? I think of what I could do if I had become a *Greifer*, of the names I could have gotten off the list: my mother, my father, my friends from the theater. All those people, long dead and gone. I could have simply . . . exchanged them?

A long silence.

I have a question for her.

"Who did you get off the list, Stella?" (I do my best not to emphasize the "you" in that sentence; I don't want to betray my own thoughts.)

"My father and mother, and my sister. They are in Theresienstadt. Theresienstadt is a nice town. Theresienstadt is okay. Theresienstadt is not Auschwitz." (Auschwitz! This is the second time I've heard that place mentioned. What is this Auschwitz?) "Who else?" "I don't know." (She shrugs her shoulders.) "Friends. Rolf."

"What would have happened to me if I'd taken you up on your offer and gone home with you when we met on Ku'damm, six months ago?"

"I would have taken you to the *Sammellager*, the transition camp. You would have been killed, and Rolf and I would have been two hundred marks richer."

"You saved my life? Is that what you're telling me? You saved my life by letting me off the hook?"

"No," says Stella, "that's not what I'm saying. I exchanged your life. By not betraying you some other poor bastard was put on transport, someone I could have gotten off the list."

I have to think about that.

"If I had gone with you, I would have saved somebody's life?"

"No, then *I* would have saved somebody else's life."

"So you saved me? You saved *me*?" I'm confused. My thoughts keep spinning. Stella, poor Stella, wet with tears—tears shed not just for me, but tears, I now know, shed on behalf of all her victims, tears over all the blood that bought freedom for other blood—don't you understand, my Stella, how powerful and rigid the rules of statistics are? How long before there's nobody left to betray? When Berlin will finally be free of Jews, its air pure and all the vermin exterminated, there will be nothing left for the Nazis to do but to kill your loved ones too, your protégés, and when there's nobody left, then Rolf, and then finally you too, Stella, dear Stella, my Stella—then finally you too will go.

And right at the moment when Stella, Stella the betrayer, Stella the guardian angel, Stella the murderess, Stella the heroine, lays her tired head on my trembling shoulder, right at that moment the bang and clatter of china rises from deep in the bowels of the house.

The night is over.

The night is over. Gone are the revelations and deceptions, gone are the truths and the pain, gone are the palpitations of the soul. It is morning. A new day dawns, identical to the old one. There are no further declarations to be made, no further comforts to be gained. Stella disentangles herself from my arms. She opens the blinds. The city is gray as always, but the light that seeps into the room like silent rain, no matter how sad, is still light, after all, the ancient glow of time, both propitious and cursed, shining on saint and sinner alike. Shining, for example, on Rolf, the mightily snoring Rolf, flat on his back, spread-eagled, the blankets thrown to the floor. He looks healthy, Rolf—taut muscles shift underneath a superficial layer of fat. Yet, how grotesque is his nakedness; how repulsive is the sight of his listless morning prick and his lethargic balls. How can the man sleep so soundly? All around us, in the rooms and hallways and basements of the Pathologie, sleep is as brittle as an insect wing. These people fear for their lives, and rightfully so. But although we are safe, neither Stella nor I sleep, and that is also the way it should be: Sleep belongs to the just, and the fact that our deeds and the fate of our fellow Jews keeps us awake, this is proof, living and welcome proof that we have not yet hardened, that a grain of conscience still lives inside us, that a jagged golden lump of compassion lodges inside our hearts and won't let us sleep.

How can Rolf sleep so soundly?

Stella follows my gaze. "Men always fall short," she says. "You could make a motto out of that." She snorts. Every trace of her tears has disappeared; her eyes are hard and small again. Is she only capable of humanity at night, under cover of darkness?

I refuse to accept her premise. "No," I say. "*People* fall short. People." I walk over to her, at the window, at that thin membrane between an outside world that's no longer ours and an inner world that does not bode well. My hand goes to her shoulder. A hand as generous and innocent as the impossibility of sleep, and equally treacherous.

"We are all human," I say. "I am human," I add. "And so are you, Stella, you are human too," I say, and I squeeze her shoulder blade.

Her voice is dreamy.

"Exactly," she says. "Exactly." She puts her hand over mine and squeezes back. "And you too must have done something terribly wrong to earn a spot in this room."

"I play poker," I say. "Or *Skat*. Or hearts. I influence the course of the game. I let whomever I want win, and I share my gains with my employer."

"The magician," she says. "Helmut, forever the cheerful tradesman in illusions!"

Here is a new illusion. My hand slides downwards. I cup a shivering breast. My G*d, I swear it: Every sexual act is a pact. You don't need blood, other bodily fluids are just as good for signing your pact with the devil. Blood is so predictable, so trite, so primitive: I would maintain that the white purity and the ultimate indelibility of semen makes it more suitable to seal the deal.

"I can't, Helmut," says Stella when I press myself against her from behind, when she can't help but feel my urgency. "I can't."

"Because of *him*?" I ask. The words sound hoarse and new in my mouth. We spun a thin web between us last night, and in the meager light of morning it is torn to shreds?

"No."

Stella too has lost her voice. She says "No," but I can feel her body respond; it has a different voice, a different message.

"No. Not because of him. Because of you. Yes—because of you." She breaks away from my embrace, just as she's supposed to do, as is her duty—to break away because the moment of her refusal has to plant its splinters in my soul.

Stella. Stella. Such sweet words, and such harsh words too, in the light of a tired sun trying in vain to wrestle the horizon down.

And Rolf just keeps on snoring.

What, after all, is love, and how much are we willing to pay for it?

•

This is the Pathologie, a renovated doctor's house on Schulstraße, in the back garden of the Jewish hospital. Although it's late in the war there are still a thousand patients in the hospital; a few hundred prisoners are waiting for their transport in the Pathologie. They are everywhere—they sleep on mattresses in the offices, they rest on straw in the dissection rooms, they live under thin blankets on the cold floors of the hallways and the basement.

And this is what evil looks like, untamable evil?

A man, not quite twice as old as I am. A mop of dark-blond hair lies on his head like a wet washcloth. His face is red and empty like that of a butcher. He's fond of gambling and playing cards, and he likes cake.

Hauptsturmführer Dobberke.

At the end of the evening he puts his arm around *Schwester* Elli's waist. The gesture simply indicates that she is his—of course she's Jewish, a nurse in a Jewish hospital must be Jewish; she's the angel of the ghetto of double contamination, racial and hygienic—and he doesn't care that we see his great love; we, the doctor and his mistress and I.

Dobberke is the son of a sergeant major in the police who himself is the son of a sergeant major in the police who in turn—etcetera. He was always destined for mediocrity, promoted by the passage of time only. His membership number of the NSDAP is high: 5,848,662. He's an eleventh-hour Nazi; he became a member for the same reason everyone else joined: By law, all civil servants are required to be a member of the party. Dobberke is reserved and moody. My magician's skills cheer him up. So do the cocktails that he mixes in his office with the ethanol that Elli stocks in her medicine cabinet. Beer no longer works on him. Though sometimes the cocktails have the opposite effect; sometimes the alcohol makes him lonely and restless. When he's in one of those moods he roams the hallways of the Pathologie like a beast of prey, missing the hunt. To anybody willing to listen—and who isn't willing to listen to his executioner?—he'll retell stories of his time in the vice squad. Hunting down whores and their pimps! Those were the days! He drags prisoners out of their bed at two in the morning to play Black Maria with him; he wants them to provide him with any kind of entertainment they can. He shakes me from my sleep and asks me to pluck golden coins out of the air; or he summons me to help him make paper roses at the kitchen table—he got his hands on a ream of pink office paper. He sprays the roses with perfume and carries them sniffling and weeping to his beloved Elli. "Shall we also simulate thorns, Herr Hauptsturm-führer?" "That won't be necessary, Helmut."

Walter Dobberke is a lonely man. "What am I doing here?" he complains. "I'm a wolf in black sheep's clothing, that's what I am!"

Dobberke thinks way too highly of himself. He is no wolf. He's a sheep dog, a small bureaucrat, a blindly compliant traffic cop with no trace of an original mind: just a well-trained puppy. People like him fare very well in Eichmann's system of blind obedience. He's small beer of course: The higher-ups don't even trust him with any real instruments of torture. Dobberke keeps a whip in his desk drawer, but that's all the persuasive machinery he has at his disposal.

What is Dobberke doing here, in what has to be the dark heart of Berlin, the site where we, Berlin Jews, are gathered before being sent to the death camps? What he does is his duty. Dobberke is no idealist, he's no politician. He's no theoretician either. Dobberke does his job. He does what he is told to do. That's all. He has a banal police-officer's brain, servile and stupid. It makes him the ideal person for this job. No sentimental nonsense, but also no excessive zeal, no needless hatred. Duty, duty, duty. It's nice to have a discreet camp commander when the camp is situated in the middle of town.

They assigned him here, to this dull post? Well then, he will make the best of it. Just like us, he did not volunteer to be here. He forgets, however, that he willingly and knowingly became a member of the association he belongs to; we did not. Our club—lest we forget—is the club of those who are fated to die, and die soon. Who would willingly sign up for such a club? Yet Dobberke reasons that our presence in the Pathologie implies that we should play our role as decent citizens and obey the rules, and that we should be good-natured about it too. After all, that's what Dobberke is, that is what Dobberke does. He respects the rules, so why won't we? Every offense, every transgression leads to an explosion. Why don't we simply accept our fate, just like he accepts his? "Do you think I am here because I like it?" he asks when the kitchen help catches one of the prisoners stealing a strip of bacon. Dobberke averts his eyes in sadness. He raises one hand and spreads all five fingers wide, and then he impatiently waves both the prisoner and the guards away: Five strokes with the whip is what his hand signifies. He shakes his head. He is sincerely distressed. Why don't we all just behave?

His superiors have assured him that the Jews under his surveillance are all criminals. And that's the way he treats us; he never stops to ask what exactly our crimes might have been. And his heart isn't in it either. Sure, he calls us Jew-swine whenever others are present, but his inflection lacks the conviction of the true anti-Semite. Criminals, right? He doesn't really treat us any differently than he treated the pickpockets and the smalltime pimps from his vice-squad days, not with the heartfelt disgust that is the moral duty of the well-trained SS-man, or with the notion that an unbridgeable evolutionary gap gapes wide between us and him, like the gap between man and ape: that there's a superficial resemblance, but we ultimately are two different species, with clear advantage on the Aryan side. Dobberke thinks it's all a question of good manners and a decent upbringing. Dobberke doesn't mind playing cards with sleepless Jews at three in the morning; it's not beneath him to offer them a pint of his beer—even if his playmates are the same men he sent outside earlier in the day to get a good thrashing after some dust has been found in a hallway they were supposed to have cleaned.

Therefore, it's not as strange as it might seem that on the first morning of my stay at the Pathologie, Dobberke storms into the room where the three of us are sleeping off our night of murderous thoughts, with the ever-snoring Rolf a massive barrier in the center of the bed. He's simply bored and looking for some entertainment. He grabs me by the arm; he practically drags me out of bed. Rolf mumbles something in his half-sleep, and Stella pretends that she's dreaming sweetly, or perhaps she really is. While Dobberke hops impatiently from one foot on the other at the door—has he already gotten a head start on his daily allotment of ethyl and apple juice cocktails?—I quickly throw some water in my face and put on my clothes. Then I follow him to his office, my stomach grumbling. A fanned-out deck of cards awaits us there, a bleached tarot, ready to be read.

The days in the Pathologie are long; they are waiting rooms for the evenings when I play my subtle games with and against Dobberke, and when Stella and Rolf go out hunting.

I become more ambitious, aesthetically. I put some symbolism into the cards. I deal the doctor's lover the queen of hearts, and I give him the king of hearts—he can throw his card suggestively on top of hers. I counter with the jack of hearts and smile shyly. Or I deal Dobberke nothing but black cards—the clubs that look like swastikas in bloom or the spades with their spiky tips. The king of spades only belongs to him, and whenever Elli joins us, I make sure she gets the queen of spades.

In his office, I spread out the cards for them. I pretend that cartomancy is an old Jewish art—numerology, *mein Herr*, cabbalistic mysticism, you know? But whoever shuffles and deals the cards, the story they tell is always mine, mine and so many others' as well: the story of the ages, a story of deceit and injustice.

●

The days go slowly. The building whispers chaotically in high German or low Yiddish; every prisoner has eyes of hunger and fear. I don't want to know whence the hunger or why the fear. I do not speak to anybody, and nobody speaks to me.

·

After the last card has been put on the table, after all the beer and cocktails have been drunk and all of Elli's cookies eaten, Dobberke pays me with a handful of coins and some cigarettes. I go to my room and I lie down on the bed, fully dressed and with a cigarette and a match ready in the breast pocket of my shirt. I try to catch some sleep before Rolf and Stella invade. I count the number of plastered squares on the ceiling by imagining the position of the beams. I imagine what would happen if I took an axe to those beams. The room would collapse and under the suddenly untenable weight of the roof the rest of the building would cave in too, and we would all be gone in a splendid cloud of dust and flesh. Every time I contemplate this scenario, peaceful waves of sleep surround me; I put my thumb in my mouth like a toddler and smile serenely until I'm carried away into the deep ocean of blissful blackness. When Stella and her lover come crashing into the room, I move to my spot in the hallway. I light a match on the sole of my shoe and smoke my evening cigarette among the cries of protest and jealousy from the anonymous crowd, and I listen, ear to the door, to the nightly ablutions inside. When the last moan has died out and the mattress no longer echoes with the giant's rumblings I crawl back inside. I take off my pants and shirt and fold them up neatly on the chair at the foot of the bed. In my frayed underwear I climb back in, as far removed from the happily snoring monster as possible, and I begin again my comforting count of the invisible white squares on the ceiling.

·

Stella and I stand by the window. She tells me about the old *Sammellager* in the nursing home at the Große Hamburgerstraße in the heart of the Scheuneneviertel— the old Jewish neighborhood in the shadows of the golden dome of the Great Synagogue. She was living there the day I met her in the street. You could see the oldest Jewish cemetery of Berlin from her window. She had a good view of the grave of Moses Mendelssohn, the great scholar and philosopher from the time of Frederick the Great. Mendelssohn was a big proponent of integration of Jews and Germans. As a service to the gentiles, he translated the Pentateuch into German.

The very fist night there Stella stood at the window—"Just like we're standing at the window of the Pathologie now, Helmut, watching city life roll by. On an open space in that venerable cemetery with its picturesquely sunken monuments, there was much laughter and merriment. A few of the guards had taken off their uniform jackets; they were playing soccer. Four jackets marked the goal posts. The ball they were using must be flat, I thought, it refuses to bounce. Then I had a closer look. The object that they hit and kicked back and forth was not a ball. It was a human skull." Stella wipes her eyelids with her thumbs. That window, with its view of her captors toying with death in the scent of fruit trees, all that was long past—way back in the springtime of 1943.

Stella and I, we tell each other stories about our childhoods; it now seems like it was a golden age. We talk about lost loved ones. She folds her hands into a cup and sings forbidden jazz standards in my ear. "I've Got You Under My Skin." She says things like: "You always had a special place in my heart. I saw you watching me, all those years, and didn't appreciate it. Yes, of course I noticed you watching me. You were watching me exactly like you're watching me now." She sings again, "Love For Sale." But when I come closer, she pushes my hands away.

She tells me about the *Sammellager*. "There were way too many of us, in the Große Hamburgerstraße, there wasn't enough food. On the night before each transport, the people who were on the list got a piece of cardboard with the letter T to hang around their neck. Some of them were so hungry that they ate the sign. When the guards came to get you and you only had the piece of string around your neck, you were shot on the spot."

•

Stories, stories and meditations.

Were we lambs led to the slaughter? Sacrifices in Avraham's name? Prodigal sons of the Great Father? Led and misled by our leaders, who were wolves dressed in Christian sheepskin? In Berlin—rumor has it—a farmer is raging through his flock, killing his animals.

Is it that simple? Somebody has to stamp the documents, somebody has to collect and pass along the addresses. It shouldn't have been difficult to create a small fire in the archives, not too hard to arrange a gas leak, and what if we had all raided the Jewish commissariat with torches? That is what amateur historians say after the war. Those who were not there. They blame us for our own deaths." It's your own fault," they say.

The Jew as victim is omnipresent in the history textbooks. The truth is richer than that. What is it we could have done? Would we have been allowed to revolt? Can you imagine what would have happened, what a massacre would have ensued had the *Gemeinde* refused to cooperate? Do you think we really had a choice?

The truth is more confusing.

That famous Dutch Jewish girl Anne Frank would be 66 years old now. She and her family were betrayed by a decent law-abiding Dutch citizen who considered it his civic duty to rat them out. He probably thought long and hard about it; it made him feel good to rid the world of one more Jewish family. He never got caught—I say "he" because I can't imagine a woman doing this. A man who is 85 years old now, shuffling along the Amsterdam canals, convinced that he was right, that there's no reason to stand up and proclaim, "Yes, that was me. I did that. I killed that family with my words." We in Berlin were hunted down by our fellow Jews. That's more comprehensible. What the *Greifer* did was gruesome, but at least the *Greifer* received a reward: some money and, more importantly, the gift of life—their own life and that of their dear ones. The citizen of Amsterdam who denounced Anne and her family gained nothing from it, except the satisfaction that the itching fur of the planet would be rid of one more Jewish flea. Stella too is a betrayer, but her betrayal is a survival strategy, for herself and for others.

This may sound horrible, but I feel admiration for her. At least she was doing something. Wouldn't those illegals haven't been arrested without her anyway? If not her, then somebody else—right?

•

"How does that work, palming a card?"

I laugh. Men at urinals, they have the strangest questions. Well, I explain, you don't. Cards are too large to be hidden in the palm of a hand. But you can slide them into a sleeve or a pocket.

"Can you teach me that, boy?"

And so we are back at school. This time I am the teacher and a dangerous man in black is the student. I touch the Hauptsturmführer's skin, I roll up his sleeves, I spread the cards between his fingers and in my heart the pain of memory boils, the memory of the days that WLADIMIR was my teacher and he poured all his tenderness into gestures just like these, and how I, callous and stupid, failed to notice.

•

Stella at the window. The light is painted by Vermeer. The loneliness in her eyes shoots straight through my heart. She looks as if she has just lost her only friend in the world. But I don't go to her, I don't speak. I rush to the bed and I sit on the edge. I take out my deck of cards and I analyze the trick that I will teach Dobberke tomorrow morning. The tricks are no longer stored inside a handy encyclopedia in my head; they live in my fingers. I chose a trick and I perform it as slowly as possible, carefully observing the shifting of the muscles in my hand. It is so much part of me, the movement and its rhythm and tempo, that I have great trouble slowing down my performance—once started, the flood of eloquence in my fingertips is hard to stop.

"Shush!" I say when Stella tries to start a conversation. "Shush! I need to concentrate!"

•

As far away from Rolf as possible, that's where Stella sleeps.

If this were a novel, the writer could make his choices, and each of these would be correct. In fiction, everything is possible, everything is permitted.

Neither of us had a choice.

I had no choice.

I have no choice.

A man says, "I lead my life," but that's an outright lie. My life leads me. My life leads me.

I am not a saint. I have never been a saint.

None of us is a saint.

If *das Fressen*—the stomach—takes priority over morality, how much farther then must survival stand above every form of ethics.

I slept with Stella.

Whether she loved me, or cared about me, or whether this was an act of vengeance or loneliness, or whether it was merely the kind of love you make when your city lies in ruin—what does it matter? Let the exegetes sort out the deeper motives; they are the dry kind of human for whom such things matter.

What is the alternative, my dear audience, my beloved readers? Do you want a sweet story that is easy to swallow, with amiable characters to effortlessly identify with, a story that fits like a glove around your preconceptions of the events I am about to tell you? May I recommend Anne Frank's diary to you?

This is the truth.

The first lesson in Holocaustology is that nobody understands the survivor.

412

This is not ill will; it is a self-evident fact. They—you, my dear audience—cannot comprehend. Their—your—perspective is always wrong, because your point of view is moral. There is nothing moral about a biography, there is nothing ethical about history: It's all a naked sequence of bare facts. Events happen the way they happen to those they happen to. To say otherwise is to take away human freedom; it denies the existence of stupid bad luck or simple good fortune.

Lesson number two: The information we could give you to make you understand is exactly the kind of information you do not want to hear.

So, I slept with Stella.

Can you share a bed with a woman, a woman you had an adolescent crush on, a woman you—face it!—admire, a woman who is ripe and warm and deeply unhappy, and not have this happen?

Every evening I slid into that bed on Stella's side, and every evening she promptly pushed me away. I landed on the floor and walked over to the other side, to Rolf's side—Rolf, the man who just a few minutes ago was engaged in vigorously fucking this woman; Rolf, the man with the strong, deadly arms; Rolf, the man of violent sleep. G*d be praised for Rolf's massiveness: As soon as I touched him, he would roll away and settle into the deep trough his bulk had made in the center of the bed, leaving me just enough space to lie down without touching him. There I lay, ardently counting the imaginary squares. It was a blessing that through the sound barrier of Rolf's snoring I was not able to hear Stella's shallow breathing.

If a mountain of a man lies between the two of you, the aspiring lover can just as well take the indirect route: he can step out of bed and walk around it. Two lovers don't take up much more space than one person.

I had considered this. Of course. But Stella's rebuttals made it impossible for me to carry out this plan. And then . . . Well. Let's say that one night Dobberke had given me too much beer. Let's say that in my sleep-drunk state I made a small navigational error when I came back from emptying my bladder. Let's say that Stella was too sleepy to shake me off. Let's say she maybe thought I was Rolf. Let that be the game we played. Let's say that she put her arm around me in an automatic reflex.

I can't be blamed, except in that I returned her caress.

Maybe this is a good excuse: that the perfect darkness made it all feel like a dream? The darkness had exactly the right measure of unreality to make our lovemaking possible. In the dark, who can tell the difference between longing and the fulfillment of that longing, and who knows with whom one is fulfilling it with? And of course Stella and I, groping and licking and biting, do know that this ghost is me and that that ghost is her; we're well aware that it's my sex and not Rolf's that is suddenly sucked into hers. But it would be so easy to deny it.

There is longing, yes, and hunger. We make our love slowly, almost breathlessly, in the absolute dark—we don't want Rolf to wake up. This doesn't make it a tender loving experience. It only increases the tension.

One of the great joys of the sensual lover, I have been told, is to examine the beloved's naked body, every square inch of it; to observe how that body changes under one's touch, to watch what swells and wells up, to see the veins widen and the pores open up, to watch the lover's pupils dilate, to see those mirrors of the soul suck the light right out of the room.

I never experience that joy with Stella.

I believe it is tender and loving. I believe I love her.

Such are the illusions of youth.

It was all the body, the body, the body.

We make love in suspension, in almost motionless caresses, in furtive strokes of fingertips and tongues, without giving in to the urgent dictates of arousal—all because of Rolf. We smother our moans in the hollow caves of each others' mouths. This is something WLADIMIR had prepared me for. The true magician has mastery over heart and fingers, the true magician watches himself in an imaginary mirror; the true magician plays his audience with a holy kind of reverence. For Stella, I perform miracles of transformation and multiplication. Under my hands she becomes somebody different, she becomes . . . *more*. In the darkness of seeing and not-seeing Stella becomes all women. Her breath is Eve's original breath, her breasts the cluster of grapes kissed by Solomon's lips. When I retreat to pledge my love offering on the bare skin of her belly, my mouth open wide but without making a single sound, she is my altar of alabaster, my long-lost grail, and not the murderess on high heels who leaves at dusk saluted by the Nazi guards.

None of this makes it love.

One can even argue that it makes it less like love, precisely because she becomes all women.

Can I call her my angel, I who am consumed by her awesome presence? It is good that I can't see her; her embrace is overwhelming enough. To see her might have turned me into stone—that much beauty is unbearable.

If you want to look for a simpler explanation: I spent so much time preparing for my master classes with Dobberke that she must have felt left out and lonely. We started something of a friendship, an exchange of feelings and ideas, and then I retreated. Easy fix: to exchange the terrifying intimacy of the soul for the far less intimate community of the body. What Rolf does with her is screwing, and nothing more: Ultimately, it does not satisfy. All that fast pounding, all that relentless hammering away, or so I tell myself, takes care of her urges; an itch gets more than scratched, a craving erased, but after the orgasm has subsided another hunger lurks—what Stella desires is nothing less than *love*, a prolonged hour-long raga after the raging three-minute tango of lust, an act in which we (precisely she, precisely I) flow into each other, flow, yes, with a fluidity that dissolves all boundaries, not just the boundary between us, man and woman, but, deeper than that, also the cold glass membrane that separates us from the world—every boundary, including that between good and evil. My cock is tidal, it ebbs and flows inside her on the rhythm of Rolf's snoring, with tantalizing tantric slowness, and in the hollow embrace of her cunt I touch the center of her being, a center that—although I did not realize it at the time—is formless and empty. Had I been a Californian sage, I would have said: "It is *atman*"; I would have said: "There in the vacuum of her secret halls, the confluence of Wisdom and Skilful Action erases the duality of being, and there my blind bald heart-shaped cock-head touches Stella's Buddha nature, cavernous and true, the core of all existence."

The Buddha in bed? Stella says she loves to look into a man's eyes when he comes. "The emptiness in that gaze," she says, "that unfathomable emptiness and at the same time that absolute presence in the moment." I should have been alarmed at those words. I failed to notice the rejection—on the contrary, I found her statement deep and sweet. I never saw her face in a state of orgasm; she never saw mine. Instead, at the *moment suprême*, I put my fingers on her cheeks and my wrists at her throat. Then her lips opened and she bit down, sometimes on the fleshy part of my thumb, sometimes into my tongue, and often she drew blood, but I never observed the miracle of her contracting pupils or the butterfly kisses of her eyelids.

She describes her lover's ecstasy to me. The angelic light, she says, the secret blaze of bliss, a glow not unlike that you can detect in the eyes of someone who's just been arrested. What comes to the surface is the demon in every human being—the demon who rejoices in the torture of the body that holds it captive; or maybe what appears is an angel who delights in the just punishment and the impending castigation, an opening of the veins from which it can ascend freely to the heavens?

Stella, Stella feels trapped in her moment of orgasm, dragged in front of a heavenly judge, bound and shackled, beautiful as sin.

Stella, Stella, twisting snake, the color of fire.

Knowledge acquired through description is different than firsthand familiarity.

•

Dobberke is no natural. This whole magic business doesn't come easy to him. His fingers are too fat to be suited for more than the most elementary manipulations. His meager progress makes him happy nonetheless. The first time he deals me an ace of hearts he's proud as a peacock. He can hardly contain his excitement when he pretends he's one card short and then slides the unwanted card back into the deck, into a spot where it will be dealt to the adversary. Elementary, dear reader, but it works: He wins a few reichsmarks. He is very proud of himself, so proud that it would tip off the Herr Doktor and his tart, if only the lovebirds had eyes for something else besides each other. I try to dampen his enthusiasm; I tell him that it's one thing to have a skill and to apply it faultlessly and another to make sure nobody knows you're applying it. When you lie, you have to lie all the way, I say; the fingers have to do their work without any involvement of the mind. That way, when one gets caught (for getting caught is inevitable), one doesn't have to feign innocence: One's innocence will be real and honest—the mind was occupied with something else entirely.

The mind was occupied with something else entirely. A lonesome traveler at the edge of a deep abyss. In the ravine, a gleaming river heads to the sea. Wrestling matches in the night. Wrestling with the mythological river demon, to pay for passage. Reckless, reckless. I beg her, "Let me go, the dawn has dawned." She teaches from the Bible. "I will not let you go unless you bless me." There we go then. I retreat; with a hand slippery from her own juices, she briskly jerks my penis. And while she churns, at the precise moment the spasms take me, a different hand, much larger and much hairier, slides down my sweaty spine and cups my balls from behind. And that hand squeezes.

Picture the revenge of a man who has had the presence of mind to wait in cold blood until you have come on the stomach of his lover. Imagine that man's grip around your balls: it is firm and relentless, he clasps you as though he's squeezing a lemon—a crushing grip, a twist of his wrist, and through the night the scream of an animal in agony sounds—my scream. The noise calls in the guards, many of them—they fill the room and in the light of flashlights dancing over the bed their faces look terribly grim.

The look in Rolf's eyes is the look of triumph. The victory of he who knows how to chose his moment, the coup of he who knows how to wait and bide his time—an Olympic triumph of the will. Rolf was there, awake, all this time, convincingly snoring, and I can read in Dobberke's bewildered eyes that I have done the most dangerous and stupid thing a magician can do: I have underestimated my audience (raucous Rolf) and I have made myself dispensable in the eyes of my patron by teaching him (Doberman Dobberke) the secrets of my art, thus making myself hated (Rolf) and superfluous (Dobberke).

Rolf, that hairy devil. The devil is G*d's instrument: He is G*d's axe, G*d's grappling hook.

•

Go away. I wave him away. Go away, go away. My arm feels so heavy I can hardly lift it, so weak are the muscles, so heavy weighs the bone inside.. Go away! My brain, scarred with the darkness of the bunker, dares to ask, What happened to Stella? And it also dares answer that question: Nothing happened to Stella. Stella is the best of all *Greifers* and in a city that is almost free of Jews the best of all *Greifers* is exactly what Dobberke needs. Stella's tricks are the only thing that keeps him and his increasingly uncertain enterprise afloat. When the source of Jews has dried up, the authorities will terminate the *Sammellager*. Then Dobberke will be sent to the front. Therefore, nothing has happened to Stella.

I am inside the bunker, in the vault underneath the Pathologie. Whenever it rains, a thin layer of slimy water spreads over the floor like a fever. Dogs—Dobberke's ink-black bitch and her ill-tempered mates—bark behind the door. The darkness here is even more black and breathtaking than the darkness in Stella's room—the night cuts deeper than the night in Stella's heart. Stella's heart is dark—I know that now. Stella has the power—she could plead with Dobberke for my life, but she did not do so. The person who gets out of the dungeon after less than a day is Rolf.

This is not surprising. It's her way of being faithful. Dobberke must have forced her to make a choice. She can't let the both of us go free: We would kill each other, and although that isn't exactly against the Nazi principles, it doesn't look good, and it would necessitate a report. Rolf is Stella's prior love, Rolf is Stella's business partner—and who am I? The pale paramour, the meta-lover in the dark, a ghost that can't abide the light of day. I was never more than a dream to her. A character in a romance novel. Somebody she never even looked in the eye.

Why would you trust a lover you've never looked in the eye?

Plus, why would you prefer a lover whose scrotum is stiff from internal bleeding—a lover who most likely will never be able to make love to you again?

•

With our heads to the ground like Karl May's Indians, we, the captives in the basement, feel the thundering of the bombs shudder through our bodies. This is how we distinguish day from night: The rumbling in the earth announces that morning will come soon.

Head to the ground: The first few days I can't even stand up because of the pain. No, I haven't been beaten. That would have been superfluous; Rolf has sufficiently disabled me. And why would they torture me? I have no more information to give to them.

We hear the guards grumble in the hallway. The apocalypse is only starting, they say. They expect that the English will increase their efforts. That's not much of a comfort. How much more rubble can this town produce?

Other sounds, a different clock: the rattling of trucks, come to pick up the prisoners and bring them the station. These are furniture trucks. They never arrive before ten at night and never past six in the morning, and never during an air raid. Dobberke sometimes rides behind the convoy in an ambulance. Sometimes the guards hand out hammers and nails, as if the prisoners are going out for a short night of forced labor. Yes, Jews are sheep; they do not think, they are not dangerous; you can hand them hammers—fine, heavy hammers—and nails—good, sharp nails—and they will meekly climb in the back of a truck, thinking they will be back in the morning, thinking they will spend the night contributing to the rebuilding of the town. I have never seen these transports because the building was blacked-out between ten and six, but we heard the sounds, and we could guess what was happening.

The trucks leave.

They only return the next day, and empty.

Soup and potato stew in wooden bowls. We slurp. We eat with our hands. We are not to be trusted; knives or spoons or forks are kept away from us. We do not know each others' names; we do not even know how many of us there are, it is that dark, and what does it matter? Do we really want to form attachments for the last few nights of our lives? It's better to prepare; better to bury yourself in the small needs of your own mortal soul.

Then, in the middle of the night, a scratching in a corner. Rabbit claws on the sides of a cage: a friendly, civilized sound, and suddenly we are all wide awake. Wood on cement. A spoon, smuggled in by one of the Jewish *Kapos*. We are not to be trusted with cutlery. Hope is not dead, or not completely. The house rests on a foundation of brick, and the seams between the bricks are filled with cement. Those seams are vulnerable: One can scrape away the cement grain by grain. Grain by grain with the back of a wooden spoon that gets thinner with every scratch. We crawl together into the corner and whisper encouragements to our hero. Somebody else takes over, somebody with less patience; we urge him to be quiet and more careful.

Something has happened.

The impossible: We are making an attempt to escape.

What a romantic way to commit suicide, so much in the spirit of Karl May. "If you lay so much as a finger on her, cowboy, I'll bang my head against that wall until I die!"

We share the work. I am a specialist in secrecy; I keep watch at the door. I click with my tongue when I hear the guards approaching and then the scratching stops. The guards slide the bowls of food inside with the tips of their boots and close the door quickly. They are afraid of our stares, and the stench in the room makes them sick. (They have not provided us with buckets. We do our business in a corner close to the door.)

The ridge in the seam deepens. Three or four days of scraping and we can remove one of the bricks. I was afraid that, like the Count of Monte Cristo, we would end up in an adjacent cell, but when we remove that first brick a gulp of chilly evening air gushes into the cell—air that smells like air, oxygen that makes us drunk with happiness.

After this one brick has been removed, it becomes easier to take out others.

We still don't know each others' names, but we get excited at the prospect of freedom. Some of the men wrestle in the dirt for the right to go out first. We have been given an opportunity. The nights with Stella made me forget the bombings, but now the violence outside makes me restless. Here we are, rats in a cage, and rats in a cage have less chance at survival than rats that have the run of the sewers. It's not meekness that characterizes us Jews, I believe, so much as the odd belief that everything will turn out right, that we will get through this. Resilience. With every ounce of *Berliner Luft* wafting cool and generous through our cell we get stronger and tougher. We ration the bread to build a supply for the night of our escape. We will have to run through the garden and climb the wall, and we will have to be quick; we need the energy.

How many bricks did we manage to remove? Seven. I switch jobs; I am fast with my fingers and I can work blind. I sleep next to the little pile, ready to slide the stones back into the hole, each in the correct place, when the watchman wakes me up.

How many more do we need? Thirteen bricks would do the job—our stay in the basement has made us thin.

How much time do we have? All the time in the world.

How much time do we need? At this pace, no more than a week or so.

A week is either an eternity, or it passes before you know it.

One evening Dobberke visits the basement. I know the man well: I recognize his footsteps in the hallway and his smell when he steps into our cell, even though he hides in the darkness behind the flashlight and does not speak. He aims the light at each of our faces; it pauses perhaps a little longer at mine, a small prophetic star. The beam also travels along the walls. When it caresses the loose bricks I can admire my handiwork: The stones are lined up perfectly; if I didn't know where the hole was, even I would have suspected nothing. Finally his flashlight points to the door and he follows the pool of light back to the corridor. It took less than a minute. The door is locked again, and we breathe.

The day of our liberation arrives, or rather the night. We eat our leftover bread. We do not speak. The bread swells in our stomachs; we're not used to eating so much food (what? three ounces?) in one sitting. We huddle down in front of the hole. I remove the bricks and pile them in the correct order on the floor in case we get a last-minute inspection. Then we get in line. I opt for a spot not too close to the front of the row, and not too far back. I am hoping for some safety in the middle of the pack. When we hear the first air raid siren of the night we can hardly contain ourselves, but we wait until the thumping starts.

•

I was right. The winner of the wrestling match, the man who got out first, is shot on the spot. A lot of bullets are fired that night. One hits me in the leg. Yes, I get shot, but I am alive.

"Bite," they order man number one. The first man must be the leader. The barrel of a shotgun is forced between his teeth. One of the soldiers gives the man an uppercut. Blood and teeth splatter on the floor in a beautiful dadaist pattern. Somebody pulls the trigger. I can't go into a museum and see a Pollock without being reminded of that moment: The skull that explodes, brains that splash on the grass, tapeworms of blood and glial matter that drip from the open pan of bone. The man (I never knew his name) falls over backwards; he arches his body as he keels over, as though he's seen too many Babelsberg movies. They leave the body in the garden. Rats rustle in the shadows under the moon.

The rest of us (now I can count: there are eight of us) are led back inside the building. We crowd into Dobberke's office. A quick interrogation in a hail of blows, the barrels of shotguns poking in our stomach: Where did we get the tools from, how far and deep does the conspiracy reach? Then Dobberke himself rushes in, his eyes red and swollen, his medals rattling and his hair on end. He is still buttoning his coat, and his suspenders are askew. Was he already asleep? Or had he been fooling around with *Schwester* Elli? More importantly, is he drunk?

Dobberke gets straight to the point; he waves his pistol for emphasis.

"*Raus, in den Gang stellen, nebeneinander.*"

We are lined up in the hallway. I place my bet. I know Dobberke's unstable temperament and I also know that drunkenness makes him short of breath. I take the next-to-last spot. We get handcuffed.

Dobberke paces in front of us, looking each and every one of us in the eyes. Whoever averts his gaze gets a slap in the face. When he gets to me he bends down quickly and whispers a few words in my ear. At the end of his inspection, he turns on his heels and puts his pistol back in its holster. From his drawer he retrieves that famous instrument of terror, the cat-o'-nine-tails. Tonight the job will not be left to his helots; Dobberke himself will mete out punishment. He is angry, Herr Hauptsturmführer Dobberke, oh yes, angry beyond recognition, fuming mad: His eyes shoot sparks, the whip trembles in his hand.

The guards tear the shirts off our backs. They push us against the wall. Dobberke is not satisfied with simply hitting us, no, he takes a few steps back, as though this is an athletic event and he needs an approach run. He strikes with all his might. The leather hisses, it smacks against bare skin with a wet sizzling sound. After the fourth man, Dobberke takes off his jacket; he briefly retreats into his office, panting and wheezing; he slumps down in his chair and wipes his face with a handkerchief. He blows his nose long and hard. Then he comes back outside.

I am number seven. I was right. When Dobberke gets to me, he is quite worn out. The beating I receive is painful, but less vigorous than what my neighbor got. For the last man, however, the apotheosis, Dobberke gathers all his strength.

Then we are thrown back into the basement, but in a different room, the floor awash in an inch of muddy water. Our handcuffs are linked together with long chains of iron. After the brief dash into the night garden and the wealth of light in the hallway of the Pathologie, the deep darkness is unbearable, and the damp cold air burns the wounds on our bare backs. The basement is empty; there's just a chair in the middle of the cell. We can't lie down in the water, and it's too cold to stand. So we walk. Round and round we go. My leg hurts. Politely, out of respect for each other's stupid bravado, we take turns sitting on the chair. When it's my turn to sit, only my body is at rest. My mind keeps turning, shuffling around the room along with my comrades, and I have to follow their revolutions, otherwise the heavy chain will wind itself around my bleeding torso. When the next person in line courteously pokes me in the ribs I am still as exhausted as before.

In that isolation chamber we can contemplate our great, great sin. Nobody comes to get us, and the absence of punishment, the maddening uncertainty weighs heavier upon us than any sentence could. If Dobberke has to think so hard about this, won't our fate be the worst of the worst, worse than the mythical Hades we have heard whisperings about—worse than Auschwitz? This is what we think, each man to himself, for we dare not speak our sinister thoughts out loud. From the neighboring cells we hear moaning and from time to time sharp screams. Is it nighttime? The trembling of our exhausted legs is no longer distinguishable from the trembling caused by the bombs detonating.

In the third day of our loneliness, in the third day of our sleeplessness, the third day of our hungry circling and our desperate wandering, the cell door opens. A serf throws a tin box on the chair.

"*Da. Für euch. Von Dobberke.*"

A gift from the Hauptsturmführer. The dented box contains cigarettes, Dobberke's favorite brand: Finas Kyriazi Frères. This is how he shows his appreciation, his respect for our gutsiness, for that last manly dangling of our collective balls.

The man has another message for us as well, a one-word message, a word that after all this waiting almost sounds like a relief. That word is "Auschwitz."

If only Dobberke had included matches in the tin box.

•

One word never gets spoken: the word "death." Other words are preferred. The word "evacuation," the word "relocation." We are "put on transport," thereby assisting in "cleansing" a "territory." We are being "resettled." The government is working on a "final solution."

Let's take a step back—shall we talk about Good and Evil? Dobberke is not to blame: He's an underling, a common cop, a man who lives to oblige. The man responsible for providing the Führer and the German People with solutions was a certain Adolf Eichmann, head of the Gestapo's Jewish division, and only thirty-six years old when he signed the protocols for the final decisions—the definitive, ultimate solution to the Jewish Problem. In the pictures he looks like a clerk, the kind of man who files folders for a notary public. "Sanitation." "Removal." This is what death looks like: bureaucratic and administrative—a bit boring, frankly. A small entrepreneur shoulders a spray vat and walks around your kitchen. Gone are the cockroaches. On to the next customer.

Where else have we seen this kind of dull banality? Yes, right, in the carefully hidden family movies from a certain private archive. Did you ever see those, the Hitler family home movies? *Hitler auf dem Berghof*, goofing around with his dog (this scene is shot in color: the Führer wears a beige suit, he has a bright red band around his arm and a feminine blush on his cheeks); Eva happy and naked under a waterfall; her Wolfi nearby with a few of the Goebbels children in his lap—he strokes their blond heads and tells them stories that are apparently funny (no sound on this one, unfortunately). Hitler's biographers hunt for his presumed secrets. There is scholarly dispute concerning the number of his testicles. One or two? Difficult to say given that the proof has been burned with the rest of Hitler's body. From his potential monorchidism psychologists have derived all kinds of psychological trauma. They pore over the suicides of the teenage girls he supposedly loved with relish. All the elements of his biography point, so they say, to an unfathomable darkness in his character. All analysis, however, breaks down in these movies and the utter banality they display. None of these scholars can explain the man's sheer mediocrity, they fail to comprehend the lazy bum who liked to sleep until late in the day, the slob who loathed bathing, the dullard whose table conversation always centered around his past in the Flemish trenches, the hypochondriac with the weak stomach and the rotting teeth, the petit bourgeois with the bad taste in paintings. Hitler likes the German Romantic period; in a last romantic impulse he marries his long-time sweetheart and together with her he goes to his death—it can't get more romantic than that, holding hands while you shoot yourself through the head.

We look for explanations, and we keep looking. Academic discussions galore, and there's no danger that they'll ever end. Our biggest fear is that our efforts will lead us nowhere, that our only conclusion will be that Hitler was nothing special, simply a man like billions of others in the world, a man with middle-class tastes in interior decoration, a man destined to be a greengrocer at best, if fate hadn't hit him so hard. This is our biggest fear, because if this is true, then we need to accept that perhaps there is no overarching Evil, no eternal *Böse* to incarnate itself in a particular type of deranged individual. If there's really nothing to distinguish us from Hitler, then the whole world turns sinister; we can no longer push Evil away into a corner, the corner of the radically different, the corner of the unique, the singular, the corner of pathology. If Evil wasn't extinguished with Hitler's death, it lives on *in each and every one of us*—each of us is exactly like every other, exactly like Hitler. For twelve long years the German people elevated that man to the status of a g*d; his enemies and history made him into a demon. But he is neither. He was a man, a human being. That is all.

The twenty-five year old of today, or the thirty-something, or even the fifty-five year old can easily afford retrospective moral outrage. They can afford to live in the illusion that they are cut from ethical hardwood, that they, had they grown up the 1920s, would have separated themselves from the crowd. These beliefs are so self-evident, they feel, that they do not need an explanation. I disagree. It is easy to claim moral superiority in the absence of empirical data. In the end, the essence of man is cruelty and betrayal. The *condition humaine* is selfish recklessness. See Rolf. See Stella.

It's hard to maintain that certain people, that whole groups of people could be morally superior to others. Doubt, my dear Paul, doubt those statements whenever you hear them. The human being, every human being, is complex. Never judge a person and certainly never judge yourself before you have seen that person in all possible circumstances, before you have seen yourself in all possible circumstances. All possible circumstances.

•

What did Dobberke whisper in my ear, on the night of our foiled attempt? "You should know, Helmut, that I wanted to spare you. That I left you in that basement until I could forget all about you. And then I would have released you. And, *mein G*tt*, I had almost forgotten about you."

•

They don't want to cause any commotion. This is an administrative decision. Dispassionate as erasing an error. How does one deal with cattle that have been infected with foot-and-mouth disease? You transport them in closed trucks to some distant pasture, you drench them in gasoline, and you light a match.

"Come on, lazy-ass Jew, walk. Come on, you stupid fuck!" The old man limps. He has a wound in his leg, a wound from the Great War, an injury sustained while defending the fatherland, a wound sustained in a battle to keep Germany free, in a war fought to protect men like this young soldier screaming at him. The soldier grabs him by the ear and drags him back into the station. I don't want to know what happens to him there.

You can still smell it: These cars have been used recently to transport livestock. Cattle, sheep, pigs. Animals are treated well—they are valuable. Bruised or battered meat loses its texture and taste, and so does meat laced with stress hormones. Although it's perfectly edible, it is impossible to sell. Straw covered the floor and troughs with food and water were put inside each car. Jews, on the other hand, are not a marketable commodity. No need for straw or food or drink for us.

Cars without windows bump through the darkness of the countryside. Cars full of discarded organ meat wrapped in perishable flesh, and cold sweat, and silence.

•

Cattle transports have priority over the transport of Jews. Our train has slowed down and halted so often along the way that nobody reacts to this most recent slowdown. We have been underway for a couple of days now. During one of our stops, the guards threw buckets of food inside the wagons without caring too much if the buckets landed upright or not. Another time, a few cars were added to the train. We get soup bowls, but no soup.

We are packed in tightly. We've been inside for a long time. Our senses get numbed; you have to numb your senses to survive. Bodies press hard against other bodies; we do what we have to do, urine and excrement flow from our soup bowls onto the floor; the stench rolls through the car like thunder. My eyes sting; my mouth tastes sour. Here and there a dead body, covered in vomit and feces—I'm now so far gone that it doesn't affect me: Cruel but helpful calluses have grown over my soul. There's a small crack between the planks of wood at the far end of the car. I don't have to fight to get a spot there: One look into the darkness of my eyes and you know enough to let me through. I sit at the crack then, and inhale in gulps the smoky air that enters the car; I sit on top of a dearly departed fellow prisoner without friends or relatives. If somebody dares to protest my inhumanity, my lack of respect for the dead, I yell at him to shut the fuck up—isn't it better this way? I take up less space, don't I? Now one more of us can sit down, right? So sit down, you moron, and SHUT THE FUCK UP! At first, the body is suspiciously warm—the man must have died of a fever—then it becomes cold and stiff, the way dead bodies do. He makes for an excellent bench. Even as I ride on top of the cadaver, I realize that perhaps the calluses on my soul have grown too thick, but what can I do? Blame it on the couple of few weeks of close confinement, blame it on Dobberke, blame it on Rolf or even Stella.

The people riding with me are all people from the Pathologie. These are the people I never looked in the eye before. All types of people. Factory workers sit next to orthodox shop-owners from the Scheunenviertel who lean against elegant women in silk dresses who hold on to men in gold-rimmed glasses. All of us share the same bleak space, all of us grind against each other—the thighs of the doctor's wife press into the workman's ass, and those two don't even share a language.

I press my eye to the opening. We have passed through many silent villages. No animals outside, no people either. This place is deserted too. The sky is cloudless and a full moon shines drunkenly over the eerie fields. I do smell something strange: a bitter, woody, rotten smell unlike anything I've ever smelled before. Our journey started at the Reich's very center; now we have ended up, I feel it in my bones, at its outer edge. There's nowhere else to go; there is no beyond, this is the terminus, the end of the line, the end of the world. Despite the stench I drink greedily from the night air. Our breathing has slowly filled the inside of the car with carbonic acid; it gathers at the bottom, a deadly invisible cloud. That's another reason for our apathy: lack of oxygen.

The train has halted in front of a big building. A wall stretches out as far as I can see; in the middle there's an edifice with fat square doors, like the gatehouse to a gigantic farm complex or maybe an army compound, crowned with a roof in the shape of a pyramid. There is writing high above the gate, but there's not enough light for me to make out what it says. Two words, with a dash between them? The name of this station?

Then the gates open wide, and the train starts moving again.

We go inside.

Yes. No doubt about it. This is the end of the line.

In the moonlight the windows in the gatehouse gleam dull and mysterious, a shield of lead to keep the radiance of the world outside. A cloud of dust and steam dances around the train; the first careful silver of the breaking dawn is punctured brutally by the probing fingers of the floodlights. Behind those lights smolders a less explicable flickering orange glow.

We inch closer, at a snail's pace, to a big platform of concrete. I hear familiar sounds: dogs barking, officers shouting orders. The smell is stronger now; an inexplicable wave of panic wells up inside me.

The brakes screech; the train halts. The sound of running boots and the grating of metal over metal. A shudder travels through the train: They unbolt the doors, starting at the head of the train. The shouting in German and what might be Hungarian intensifies; finally the door of our car is rolled open. The surge of hot, musty air from inside makes the soldiers recoil. Then they are at the opening again. They yell at the top of their lungs, we should jump off the train, right now, *now*, hop-*hop*HOP!

I and a few others slide down onto the ramp; behind us the soldiers—dressed in black, elite troops of the SS—jump into the car and shove the remaining folks outside, nudging them with their rifle butts. Somebody moans when he hits the ground and collapses—we don't know what happens to him, the soldiers push us ahead. They bark their orders: Form two lines, five abreast—one line for women, one line for men, children with their mother, quick, quick, *quick*! GO! No time to look around and get our bearings, no time to return and help the weak, even if we wanted to. We instinctively understand that this is impossible; the gate we entered marks the border of humanity and compassion—states I have long since transcended—and what counts here and now is brutal strength and quick instinct. I do my best not to limp. That's the only thought I allow into my head: I will not limp. My leg screams with pain, but I keep a straight face, I move with excruciating lightness and piercing grace.

A soldier walks past the lines, shouting out, "*Zwillinge, Zwillinge? Zwillinge!*" A set of identically dressed twins runs to him, he directs them to the head of the line. There, a young officer in a white doctor's coat regulates the traffic. A man ahead of us stumbles and falls. "Don't look! Don't look!" A soldier rushes over, his dog barks at his side. With his boot he pokes the man's side, and when he refuses to get up, the soldier takes out his pistol. There is no hesitation; he shoots the man through the heart. Our eyes are wide with terror, our hair stands on end, but we keep going, we keep up the pace, we look straight ahead, the blood boils in our veins as we get closer and closer to the man in the white coat.

I am thankful for the cold air and the sudden surge of adrenaline; my head is clear and empty at the same time—I am ready for survival. I stumble over a bump in the ground, but I grit my teeth against the pain and continue; in my head I rehearse magic spells.

I turn my gaze to the officer in white.

Like Dobberke, the man does not speak but gestures—he divides the stream to his left and right with a flick of his hand. And although he does not speak, he does whistle. I recognize the melody: It's the opening aria from *Le Nozze di Figaro*—the future bridegroom crawls through his room on hands and knees, measuring whether the wedding bed will fit. The doctor looks sharply at each prisoner. Sometimes he interrupts his whistling to ask a short question; sometimes he briefly touches a body part. After each examination, his hand flutters and his gaze turns momentarily hazy, as if he sinks into an alternative reality that has nothing to do with the drama that is unfolding before him. It *is* a drama, for it becomes clear what left and right mean: The old and frail, the men who limp, the men who are too thin, the men with open sores or wheezing lungs, they are all gestured to the left of the good doctor. Once he is satisfied with his decision, the doctor resumes his whistling. His coat is immaculate, blinding, painfully white. The tips of his boots catch the first rays of the sun; the death's-head on his hat shines like a beacon. There's a short break when he lights a cigarette. He seems to be particularly interested in eyes; behind him a third line forms: twins and people with very bright eyes. (One of his experiments concerns changing the color of the iris, preferably in twins. He or his assistants inject the dye directly in the eyeball and register the effect. The effect is always excruciating pain; often blindness results.)

"What is it you do? What kind of work do you do?" he asks a man a few spots ahead of me in the line. The man thinks for a second; maybe his hesitation is brief enough not to be noted by the doctor. "I work the land," he says, talking very fast to cover up his pause. "Farmer, I am a farmer."

The doctor nods and extends his arm to point the man to his right. Then he reconsiders. Maybe it's the hopelessly Berliner accent of the man.

"Can I see your hands?"

The pretend farmer shows the back of his hands.

"Can you turn them over?"

His palms are smooth, not a trace of calluses. The doctor cocks an eyebrow. A soldier pushes the man to the left.

Two more to go. (Left.)

One more. (Right.)

It's my turn. The doctor opens my jaws and looks inside my mouth. Then he guides me, his hand on my chin, to the line on his right-hand side. It all happens so quickly that I hardly have time to realize that I have been saved; I am already moving again, marching among the blessed. Deep joy and gratitude fill my heart; the eyes of my companions gleam with the same happiness. In the light of morning we march past a grassy field. Simple houses lean against each other like in any other town. It's a soccer field; the smell of frying bacon wafts from the open door of one of the houses . What kind of place is this? Compared with the *Sammellager* behind the hospital this is paradise. The inmates start making jokes, relief spreads through the line.

We do not look back. We are a small group—much smaller than the group on the left side. What will happen to them, to the people on the left-hand side? It is only a fleeting thought.

We arrive at a barrack. There are maybe thirty or forty of us; more people step inside and then the doors close behind us. We are given instructions by a young man with horn-rimmed glasses and a short, carefully clipped beard. His lips are wide and sensual. His accent is high German; he enunciates clearly, he sounds overly polite. He has a little potbelly. A young *Privatdozent* in German literature, put by accident into a blue-white prisoner's outfit. Those who brought suitcases are asked to write their names and addresses on the lid with chalk. The suitcases are small and light; the weight of silence hides in the folds of the leather.

•

What an anticlimax. I go home, the same way as always. It takes me an hour: the U-Bahn to Alex, then the S-Bahn to Potsdam Stadt. The car rattles just the same as always. The cars bathe in the same harsh light. As always, the little heat bomb scorches my calves. The slats of the wooden seats poke at my spine. No surprises in the panorama either: the Reichstag, domeless for sixty-two years; the angel of triumphant gold; the fairy tale castle of the president soaking in its tranquil artificial dusk; the deserted platforms of the Grunewald station from which so many were deported (including De Heer); the long dark trip through the woods past the little weekender huts with their satellite dishes thirsting for the heavens, and the shyly running deer; the gray buildings at the edge of town sprayed with graffiti; and finally the walk from the station to the Neue Brücke—below me flows the Havel, behind me rises the round bombe of the Nikolaikirche backlit against some frivolous feathered clouds. A police car passes by slowly: A stranger alone in the street at this time of night, it raises suspicion. It's cold out—it is always cold in Potsdam. It's late—it is always late in Potsdam. The last bus must have left long ago. I decide to walk home, adding another forty-five minutes to my trip. I take the path along the southern edge of the palace grounds. I feel like I'm trapped inside a Magritte painting—the world is dead, yet the ground is breathing.

•

The end of our conversation.

I thank De Heer for his testimony.

"What? What?" De Heer turns his head from left to right, an old mistrustful cockatoo.

He fumes in silence. Then he explodes. "It is not my obligation, dear sir, to testify. My obligation is to forget. It is a misunderstanding that only living mouths can tell stories and that, just because I am one of the last survivors, it is my duty to get up on stage and speak. That is too much responsibility. That is too much to ask. Besides," says De Heer, "what do I have to say? I do not believe the myth that society has made out of history. I cannot live up to the sainthood requirement. I hardly feel like any of this was real."

•

The Holocaust robbed its victims of something essential, namely the obligation to prepare for one's very own, very personal, very private death. In Auschwitz we did not die, as every human should, in accordance with who and what we were; we died an exemplary death as the definition of a species. We died like wildflowers on a wide field being weeded.

Historians, even the best of them, do exactly the same. On the one hand, they insist on personal authenticity, and nothing short of authenticity will do, meaning authenticity in the narrowest sense of the word. They aren't interested in the historical context of the events you relate to them, in the entire truth of the past; they're only interested in the personal history of the author. Then, at the same time, they deny us that authenticity. There is a sanctified literary genre, a canonical form fixed forever by the early works of writers like Elie Wiesel and Primo Levi, a framework for us to pour our story into, and this, they maintain, is the only acceptable way of speaking of the Holocaust—the monologue of the Noble Jew who speaks in short uncomplicated sentences, a cool, objective, restrained voice delivering a cool, objective, restrained exposé. Why should we, survivors, have to conform to that image, to that requirement? What flows through our arteries is fresh red blood, thickened with hormones and chemicals of our own devising—each of us is different. We are more than lumps of identical ash sprinkled with water; we are not depersonalized golems called to life by the magical fact of our survival.

No, I was not a lump of clay during the war—I was a glistening fish in the stream of time, I swam and dove and splashed. I was who I was; I am who I am. My life is my life—it acquired its shape by what I did and by what others did to me; I became myself by vice and virtue and circumstance. We got gathered. Our lives have a lot in common—all of us who went through the *Anus Mundi* and were shat out again shared that experience, and nobody else shared it with us—but still, my life is my own.

Why should I have to tell my story? Why should I let you publish it, neatly edited, annotated with explanatory footnotes? Every act of editing is an act of falsification. The memoirs of all the survivors are tainted by The Style—*this* is how you write about it, *this* is how you approach the sacrificial offering: this way, and no other. All those orthodox memoirs are by definition fraudulent—they falsify the individual, they subject the subject to the form. Isn't that what you were going to write too, Paul? Isn't it? A predictable book that will arouse feelings of guilt; another stuffy hagiography from which all impurities have been excised? For instance: my affair with Stella, my collaboration with Dobberke, my death ride on the back of a cold old corpse—if you could, you would omit all that, wouldn't you, or you would at least give it some clever twist, no?

What is it that any single human leaves behind? Our footsteps fade in the wind, our bruises crawl back under our skin, and even our scars and tattoos disappear with our bodies into the furrows of the earth.

I repeat. The day will come when even this story seems insignificant. This war will be as distant as the First Crusade, as irrelevant as the Hundred-Years' War, as immaterial as the tribal wars in the prehistoric deltas of the Tigris and the Euphrates. People will say: Nothing exceptional happened. It was a war, you know, just a war. That is what it was, nothing less and nothing more. It might make a nice subject for a novel; it could serve as an interesting background for a blockbuster movie. It was, they will say, a predicable step forward in the technology of mass destruction, a new step on the ladder of a sad but inevitable evolution. The first orchestrated genocide, important only for that. Perhaps worth a line or two in an electronic book. Maybe they will create mythical figures out of our century, half-fictional characters like Richard Lionheart or William Tell. Maybe Hitler will be remembered as the butt of jokes in a big budget musical extravaganza. More likely, he will turn into some kind of tragic hero: a sick man, utterly convinced that his fatally flawed view of the world was correct, a man who died in the arms of his lover in a bunker while the world burned. Somebody like Nero or Caligula, a vague classical reference that makes us shiver for a second. The stuff of legends, just like the legends of that once wandering and now extinct tribe, the Jews—there are even still some jokesters around who claim to be their descendants.

It is done. It is over. Nothing can change that. Nothing will ever heal the wounds. Certainly not some old token Jew wringing his hands in front of a row of wooden benches covered in adolescent love poetry. If we, the survivors, are heroes, then heroes are as ordinary as empty gum wrappers, as common as escaped pets, as trivial as lost car keys.

The German youngsters of today know their history well. They can recite the facts. Himmler: chicken farmer and schoolteacher, owned a signed copy of *Mein Kampf* bound in tanned human skin. Characteristic quote: "We want guns, not butter." It's so easy: The student works her way through the prescribed reading list and she writes her little politically correct essay. Perhaps she can coax a better grade out of the teacher if she smudges the ink of her handwritten treatise, somewhere in the more moving paragraphs—a drop of tap water can do wonders. No, I am not a cynic. This is the ritual that marks the transition to one's adulthood as a historically conscious German, somebody who reads Paul Celan, someone who can quote Primo Levi. The kind of person who has dinner at Oren, the kosher restaurant underneath the dome of the Neue Synagoge, and eyes the waitresses in amazement: gosh, real Jewesses, right in the heart of the old town!

What's wrong with this picture?

What's wrong is the identification with the victim.

Nothing, absolutely *nothing* happened to those sensitive beautiful young Germans. That's the simple truth. They should not shed a tear. If they had been born a few decades earlier, chances are they too would have stood by the side of the road, spitting at us—I guarantee you that. Their parents, their grandparents, were never in danger. Of course there will never be a pogrom in Germany ever again, as they so solemnly swear—we Jews made sure of that. We left.

And let us not forget that shortly after Levi finished his memoirs, he somehow plunged down the central stairwell in his apartment building, crashing to his death on the marble floor. First he survived Auschwitz, then he stepped out. These boys, these girls, they keep on living. And they are the ones who should determine what and how we can write about the genocide of European Jews? They force the survivor into a role, they make him into a literary convention and rob him of his uniqueness—the survivor should be a moral bridgehead like Wiesel, earnest like Levi, precociously innocent like Frank, and preferably as smart and well read as any of these three. They cannot bear to hear anything else. The survivor has a duty: He has to move us to tears, he has to be an idol to admire, a hero to mourn. Behold the old ladies in their fur coats lining up in front of the movie theater. Tears smudge their mascara, but for once that's okay, because this is ritual cleansing—they are receiving the holy sacrament according to Spielberg. When they walk out of the theater, they lean against each other for support and they tear each others' wigs off in grief. Then they go to Café Einstein or maybe to Kempinski and discuss what they just saw, and shall we see each other again on Saturday and shall I make the reservations this time? Can three hours spent watching a Hollywood movie purify the German people of their sins? Truth is not damaged by untruth: Truth is damaged by being kept quiet. They weep for the survivors, they might even remember them in their Christian prayers or beg them for forgiveness, but they do this only on the condition that the survivors keep up their end of the bargain—that they should be saintly, nothing less than saintly is all that is acceptable. This is fiction: The fact of one's survival does not imply that one has been chosen; it does not imply that one is better than the ones who did not make it —having lived through the Holocaust is not a *noblesse* that *obliges*. Holocaust survivors are human like everybody else. Why not allow us to be greedy and boring and bitter and selfish, if that's what we are?

To survive: This is the stuff that myths are made of, and a myth is what these German self-purifiers are looking for—the platonic binaries of love and hate, of good and evil, of beauty and ugliness, of wisdom and recklessness, and it all happened in Technicolor, right in their own backyard. For G*d's sake, if you want myth, read the classics, but leave my terrible biography and me alone. An identifiable group of people murdered another identifiable group of people. I think that this fact alone is terrible enough.

And what about those terms, those definitions, those words—do we need a handy label, something to make these experiences comprehensible, something to tame them? "Holocaust," what does that mean? It is a corruption of the Greek word *holokauston*, itself a translation of the Hebrew *olah*, a technical term used in the Torah. A religious word: an offering consumed by fire, a cremation. Why this word, then, and why this secondhand bastardization? Why the implication that the genocide is a ritual sacrifice by fire, an offering that pleases the Lord? Why suggest it was anything other than blind hatred and wild destruction?

History—and this is the only truth about history—yes, history is the lie people tell to give meaning to their pasts.

"It's not a sin to be alive," I counter. I think of all the lively boys and gals in the bars in Oranienstraβe, of all the young students living it up in the streets around the Immanuelskirche, of the young artists hard at work in the Kulturbrauerei or Tacheles.

"No," says De Heer, "But to live with an unjustified belief in one's moral purity: that is wrong, terribly wrong. We are all sinners. But somehow we, Jewish survivors, have to pretend to be pure. We are not—I am not. I have to live with the idea that I'm guilty of the fact of being alive. Why did I survive, and why not those others? I wasn't better than them. This is the reverse of the guilt the Germans have to deal with, but we, the Jewish survivors, we have taken up our guilt much more readily than the sons and daughters of the executioners."

•

All these things I ponder on my way home: De Heer's story and his whole long, violent diatribe. I consider his arguments; I turn them around in my mind—on the subway, on the train, on my walk and again during my final sprint. I started running when I reached Charlottenhof. It's so damn cold (it's always cold in Potsdam), too cold for a leisurely walk, and I run so fast that my breath is spread behind me in tiny puffs. The rhythm of the wheels seemed crueler than usual tonight, and my running more necessary and desperate than ever. The dark pane of glass in the door of the guesthouse is an empty screen for me to project my dreams onto;

tonight my dreams disgust me.

Another little miracle, or perhaps not: During the last few meters of my sprint Mefista comes running out of the bushes. She joins me with palpable enthusiasm. We both pant in the hallway when the door pulls itself pneumatically shut behind us. We are safe.

What did De Heer say? We were free. Free. Free. They came out of the shower room, they marched into the labor camp, and they were free.

And what he said at the end: "You cannot understand. You cannot understand a man like me. Nobody can understand a man like me."

I take the cat in my arms. She climbs happily onto my shoulder and drapes herself around my neck like a warm scarf.

Even worse—what he wanted to say is: nobody is *allowed* to understand me.

He said it too.

These were his last words: "Go away. I don't ever want to see you again."

He picks up the stack of papers, his story so far. "There," he says. "There!" He is furious. He rips the papers to pieces, he throws the shreds at me and I shake them off, but they get stuck in my hair, they creep inside the neck of my sweater—I'm snowed under with his words, with his life, with his anger. He's gone too far, much too far. I close the laptop and press it against my chest. I grab my coat from the coat rack and run outside. I have no time to wait for the elevator, I run down the stairs. I feel hot, almost electrical surges in the soles of my feet whenever I reach each landing—I do not see them coming, my eyes are wet with tears.

•

I hear her footsteps in the hallway. They come nearer. They stop at my door. What in the world does she want from me?

She knocks softly. I stay where I am, flat on my back, staring at the ceiling.

She knocks again, with more urgency. I don't move. Did I stop breathing? Mefista presses her head against my side. She too keeps silent, except for her soft purring.

What does she want from me, this woman? I hear something brush against the door: her hair? Perhaps she's bending over; perhaps she is looking through the keyhole.

She knocks a third time, louder. She pleads.

"Paul? *Paul*?"

"*Meine Herren.*"

It's hard to believe that this is the man we've been chasing so long. This is the man who, by merely existing, caused us to build the city on the Hill? This is the most dangerous German alive? He looks like a boy who was just chased out of bed, his stiff mop of strawberry-blond hair slicked back with a handful of cold water, all spikes and whorls. He looks much younger than he is, forty-four, much thinner than in his pictures. He's also visibly exhausted. It gives him the air of an Irish bard with a hangover after an night of raucous singing at the pub.

Still. There's something sinister about this man. It lurks in his heavy, expressive eyebrows; it hides in his deep, penetrating eyes—his gaze travels, with devilish intelligence, back and forth over the faces of those who have captured him.

This is him, then—the man of multiple sorceries. The man who just by the power of his intellect exalted man's biggest fear, uncertainty, to the level of theory, religion even. This is the man who personally forced Einstein's *Herrg*tt* to take up the dice and gamble; this is the man who taught us how to live with the ultimate impossibility of knowing. Like a voodoo priest, he pierced the heart of physics with the needle of his mind; he gored the dragon of false certitudes with nothing more than the naked blade of his logic. He hacked open the mystic heart of matter, and it bled a blinding light.

This man who knows it all knows nothing. The great scientist is an ordinary blowhard, a boy with tangled hair and an unhealthy dose of intellectual hubris. I pinch myself to keep from laughing out loud at his pompous professorial speech. He addresses us in German, of course, even though his English is as good as Bohr's or Einstein's. This is his turf, and he marks it for us. He knows all there is to know about the atom, he says, and he will show us the way. Yes, a long howl of scorn would fit the occasion. Listen to what he has to say: "If my American colleagues care to understand the uranium problem, I will happily show and explain to them the results of my investigations."

That is what Heisenberg says. Goudsmit, the leader of our expedition, rubs his forehead with an impatient gesture, and I dare not look the German in the eye, for fear that my irritation, my annoyance, my contempt would shine through. Who is Heisenberg kidding? Us, or primarily himself?

"Would the gentlemen be so kind as to accompany me to my laboratory?"

Yours are purely imaginary sorceries, Mister-*Herr*-*Professor*-*Direktor* of the Kaiser-Wilhelm-Institut; Mister First-Among-Equals of German physicists, Mister Werner-Heisenberg, *the* Werner Heisenberg.

The cream of the crop of German physicists is gathered here, in the little mountain town of Haigerloch, all wearing their nice little suits and tiny ties—von

Weizsäcker, Hahn, von Laue, *e tutti quanti*. They brought a small army of technicians with them, a few masons, a bunch of lab assistants, all very happy that they escaped the draft into the *deutsches Heer*. They promised Hitler the ultimate weapon and they gathered all their brainpower and all their technical skills, and what is it that they achieved? We visited the laboratory yesterday, Goudsmit and I, a hole hidden away in a cave in the rocks, a cave with a church built over it, and in that hollow mountain we found a cauldron of heavy metals suspended over a dry water well. This is all the alchemy Heisenberg and his cronies have been able to muster: a witches' brew of uranium in a bath of heavy water. The most primitive of nuclear reactors, a firecracker, a fizzler. Professor Heisenberg, a damp firework is all that you produced, and now you're going to proudly explain the significance of your fiasco to us? You don't know who we are—WE ARE THE MEN WHO MADE THE BOMB—and you're going to show us your miscreation as though it was the Holy Grail? This is too pathetic for words. It makes me yawn.

The movement of my jaw gets Heisenberg's attention. His gaze moves in my direction, but only for a second; before it can even reach me it returns to Goudsmit. What a characteristic moment of supreme arrogance, what a brief cold stare—out of the corner of his eye he registers my youth and purely on the basis of that superficial trait he decides that I am insignificant. Heisenberg and Goudsmit know each other—their friendship dates from way before the war, they used to pal around together at conferences. I am an unknown, a nobody from a country that produces nobodies by the millions, and therefore Heisenberg despises me at first sight—somebody not even worth making eye contact with. Or does he recognize me as Jewish? Maybe Heisenberg, the principled doubter, is like all those other millions of Germans infected by the disease of prejudice as spread by the regime?

I want to step up to the German; I want to fold my hands into a bullhorn and shout into his petulant little ear that I, and I alone, in my tiny little dorm room in Cambridge, Massachusetts, figured it out, that I derived the formula, the secret equation that has eluded him for all these years, even though he had all the resources of the Third Reich at his disposal. I am somebody, Herr Heisenberg. Even better: I am smarter than you are, much smarter, smarter than your whole fucking elite corps of German scientists. Unlike you, Mister Heisenberg, we, Jews and Americans on the Hill, we got the job done—or almost.

•

That was April. It's July now, and it is that man, that Heisenberg, who should be sweating here in the dustbowl of Alamogordo, not me. I'm still trying to get my aching body together. I am sick with jetlag and the gruesome aftershocks of my turbulent flight back across the ocean in the bomb bay of a junky B-29. I feel so lonely, so terribly lonely among the men I built the gadget with, just a few months ago—lonesome and pale with grief.

•

Love cannot stay hidden long on a plateau surrounded by nothing but the blue, blue dome of heaven in all directions.

Alles will schweben. As soon as they put Goldfarb in uniform and shipped him to Germany, it became impossible for them to write each other things of importance. Each of them was on a top-secret mission—she was building the American bomb and he was hunting for the ghost of the German gadget. Neither of those matters could be freely discussed. Politics were excluded from their conversations, and so was love: It was unthinkable to write endearments to each other when the censors read everything over your shoulder. Censors, it turns out, have no sense of humor. The army takes everything literally. He had sent his Hannah a bottle of excellent Rhine whine, accompanied by a letter on the official stationary of the US Army. In that letter, he asked her jokingly to analyze this sample for radioactivity—a stupid joke and a trick to get the bottle to her quick, through army channels. The bottle got seized before it reached her and indeed, as requested, analyzed in the laboratory, thereby ruining the wine, the joke, and the long-distance seduction. (The sample was negative.)

Goldfarb had started his career as a mathematician, then had become a physicist, and now he was a soldier. Mathematics is the science of the ideal world, the world stripped of its noisiness; physics is the science of the palpable; and military men know all there is to know about death. When she stopped writing, he was neither surprised nor alarmed. Sometimes it's more painful to dance around a topic than to not say anything at all.

Even when her silence persisted, he did not despair. Sometimes it's better to forget about a separation than to be constantly reminded of it. Why should he despair? He had certainty. Certainty about her, certainty about their love. He knew she was his, and he was hers. Theirs was a love for the ages: enduring, grand, and without reservations. Such love needs no words.

When he finally got the letter, signed by Oppenheimer himself, it was like being shot in the chest. A grenade exploded in his heart, A knife plunged into his guts.

Goldfarb had always lived in the spirit of his people; he had always believed that any measure of happiness in a man's life will have to be paid for by an equal amount of unhappiness here or in the afterlife. And, *oy vey*, Goldfarb's good fortune in love had been tremendous.

He himself had been the cause of the tragedy. Oppenheimer's letter made this very clear, no matter how carefully the scientist had weighed his words. The letter was simple and objective. Hannah had suffered a miscarriage. The associated bleeding, unfortunately occurring during a night journey by train, could not be stopped in time. Medical assistance had come too late. She was declared dead on arrival in the hospital.

Mad with self-pity and anger, Goldfarb ripped up the letter, then crumpled up the fragments and he threw them deep into the ruins of one of the many interchangeable chimney towns in the Ruhr. As if his rage and a simple ritual of exorcism could undo what he had done.

He had planted his seed deep inside her. It grew, and then it stopped growing. As though his child, their child, had been a piece of fruit, a delicate apple from a distant paradise that turned out to be incompatible with our world; an apple of love promptly attacked by parasites. Her womb had been eaten from the inside out.

There was no reason to shred the letter; the act of reading it had destroyed it already: The flow of his tears had dissolved the blue ink and what had dripped off the paper got sucked up by the sandy soil. Ink. Oppenheimer had handwritten the letter; he had carefully contemplated each of the words and envisioned their impact and effect. His compassion was evident in the clarity of his style, meant to create distance in the reader.

To hell with sympathy! Fuck compassion!

Goldfarb had brought about Hannah's death all by himself; the Supreme Being of the Hill told him so, had whispered it in his ear. In his mind's eye Goldfarb saw Hannah shriveled up in the dry wind of the plateau—her dear bloodless face whipped by the wind, pale, her nostrils dried out, her priceless skin parched black and brown. Inside her magnificent flesh, other flesh had rotted and withered. The rot had spread; she died. Simple as that.

It was Goldfarb's fault, he and nobody else caused her death. He had sold the secret of the Hill; through this blood pact he had hoped to win her love and through her love eternal youth. But everybody knows that the spilling of blood only leads to more bloodshed.

Their betrayal had not been discovered. Oppenheimer himself had handwritten this letter in royal blue ink, and he had promised to fly Goldfarb to Site Y when the time was right. All these things were signs that their secret was safe. But what a clumsy monument they were erecting for his Hannah on Site Y!

Hannah had kept their betrayal carefully hidden, just as she had kept her pregnancy hidden, even from Goldfarb—up until the moment when her pregnancy killed her.

Hannah had suffered a miscarriage.

The gift of his semen had grown into a rotten useless piece of fruit that had gouged out her stomach, refused by her beautiful, slim, sweet body. His seed, offered in pride and in joy, had turned out to be poison.

•

And now he is back on the roof of the world, high on that table-mountain in New Mexico. It is July 14, 1945.

Goldfarb stares out the window of the guesthouse. He lights his pipe—real Virginia tobacco, impossible to get in Germany. He puts his finger on top of the flame. The evening sun colors the eastern mountains red; they are surrounded by a faint cover of feathery cloud in shades of mandarin and mango. It is a hazy, phosphorescent red, and Goldfarb shudders when he remembers the name of that mountain range: Sangre de Christo.

That he is standing there, breathing in pungent clouds of tobacco instead of lying flat on his back weeping—this observation makes him shudder too.

•

The biggest burden, the heaviest weight—what if a demon slipped inside your deepest loneliness one day to tell you, "This life, as you are living it and as you have lived it—you will repeat it and repeat it again and again and countless times more, and nothing new will happen during these repetitions; every moment of hurt, every cry of joy, every thought and every sigh and everything that seems either infinitesimally small or looms inexorably large in your life will return, and it will all happen in exactly the same order. Even this little spider that's crawled onto your writing desk, and that moonlight between the trees, and this very moment, even my own visit—it will all happen again. The eternal hourglass of existence will be flipped over and the sands will fall, and again, and over again, and you too will fall your selfsame fall—you little fleck of dust!"

•

Hannah walking the planks of the Hill—perfection personified. The mud splattered her ankles, but she had the sun g*d wrapped around her hips.

The woman who had loved him to the point of fainting.

Sex with Hannah had never been a quiet confluence of souls. He sank inside her and he simply dissolved into her foaming world.

Often he had felt obliged to dress with his back turned to her, to hide his mounting excitement—let the morning chill outside tame his hard-on.

The ebb and flow of her sizzling self-expression in bed. (And on the creaking couch.) (And on the cheap kitchen table.) (And on that most dangerous and backbreaking *topos*, the stairwell in the office after closing time.)

Hannah was an erotic chameleon who sculpted him into her favorite positions with tempestuous frivolity; and all the while, she—the self-declared Mata Hari of these foreign steppes—had relentlessly educated him on the finer points of bolshevism. *Oy vey*, how her breasts, like a pair of happy young dogs, had stood in the way of her didactic enterprise. How she had paced through the forest of lit candles, walked among the Molotov cocktails that had set his soul on fire, his semen leaking down her thighs while she ardently discussed the oppression of the proletariat—for a moment it had looked as though she was carrying all the weight of the subjugated masses on her own magnificent shoulders. How she became anxious when she talked about the persecutions in Europe; how she shrunk with suffering and how she finally expressed her hopes for the global victory of scientific socialism and strode across the linoleum in her sovereign nudity like some proud Middle European duchess, her chin held high, her neck taut, and how his cock, overcome by her rhetorical talent, had risen to the occasion too, looking forward to the promised revolution with ardent zeal and equal firmness.

It was painfully clear that compared to their doggedly blissful political couplings, their lively sucking and their quasi-omnipresent screwing, nothing else in life was of much importance. Not even, or so Goldfarb found (and feared), the thrill of scientific discovery. (Or—looked at from the miserable present day—how obvious it now was that nothing is so effective at producing unhappiness as love.) His achingly beautiful, his terribly deadly, his terribly dead *agent-provocatrice*. (He is a whole alphabet of love's bitter aftertaste, from absurdity to zombie.) How dreadful, how delightful to have experienced this, to have looked inside passion's purple jaws and be swallowed whole.

In memoriam (1): The nest scent of their postcoital bed. In the crispy silence of the night, two cigarettes write intertwining equations in the air.

In memoriam (2): The winter sparks of static electricity in her hair. A halo of fireworks sends tiny tantalizing shocks to his prick.

In memoriam (3): The Pueblo ruins on the Pajarito plateau. Hannah and Gold-farb wallow like happy lazy cats in a shallow puddle of brackish water. "Look what you do to me," she had said. He rolls her tiny clit between thumb and index finger as if it were a slick marble in a bowl of oil. On the soft fur of her sun-hot belly he writes his *Sonetti Lussuriosi* in white ink. The path they walked down afterwards had been lined with exuberant wildflowers, and there were butterflies too—he remembers it well.

In memoriam (4): She opens her thighs. She lifts her skirt. She does not wear any underwear. She says: "Read my lips," and she bends over and spreads her alem-bic, the center of his attention, wider. (After a long night of hard work in the lab she had often stepped out of her overalls in the living room. On her knees in the cool star-light she proudly hissed at the moon, her panties halfway down her thighs. Her fingers fumbled with his fly and the meatloaf on the table hardened in its cooling gravy.)

In memoriam (5): She waits for him in the bedroom, the heat turned up high; white like sea foam she lies on a vast expanse of black parachute silk; heavy combat boots is all she wears, their laces undone, open like mouths—open like the chalice of her sex that she spreads for him with two lazy fingers. She wears Goldfarb's outsized service gloves, and the black leather glistens with oil, the same oil she's spread liberally all over her body. Her legs open and close like scissors, she heaves and sighs. Then she turns onto her belly and gets up on her knees. When he slips inside her, effortlessly, breathlessly, she comes instantly, without making a sound, her breath scorching.

Goldfarb knows better than anybody that grace is granted by exceptional priv-ilege only; that everything which is true is also fresh and miraculous; that Hannah had always been clad in the curtain of the Temple.

Goldfarb coughs; he chokes on an unexpectedly rich mouthful of smoke. Oh, all the things he had wanted to say, all the things he should have said, but never did. "I love you." But can you say that? Is that enough? "I am a different person because of you. I cannot go back; you make me whole." Before he left for Europe she had told him, "We are two clocks, set to the same time. We each go our own way, we travel for months, and then we meet again. The clocks still show the same time. For them, time has not passed." Why did he have to be such a smart-ass, why had he quoted Einstein and his general relativity principle: that the clock always ticks faster for he who travels?

You made me whole. And I, I have ripped you apart. Hannah's baby, that mi-nuscule monster, had eaten her alive. Goldfarb's baby. Goldfarb is the bigger mon-ster that killed her. Their child, that was, but will never be. Their child, that was, but never should have been.

•

Jornada del Muerto, Alamogordo. The ride to Ground Zero shakes him up to the point of nausea.

The landscape is sparse. There's nothing for the eye to hold on to, except for the tall-legged spider of concrete and steel. There are, for instance, no century-old cathedrals robbed bare by iconoclasts, no magnificent buttresses and glazy-eyed gargoyles spewing acid rain, no baroque pulpit, no hard benches to beg forgiveness on. (Goldfarb has visited quite a few of the cathedrals of his homeland by now. Some are even still standing.) This tower in the desert looks more like the rooftop water tanks of the American city where he used to live. Except that there's no water here. No moisture at all. Only rustling sand. Even the snakes move sideways and with visible disgust across the blistering expanse.

Those who have held a gold-wrapped test tube with plutonium in their hand know the seductive heat of that metal. It feels like holding a small rodent. In the tower hangs the bomb, safely secured in its hammock of steel cables, and it radiates its invisible glow of alpha and gamma particles into the night. The bomb breathes—the bomb is alive.

The tower in the desert looks like a gallows tree, and in the back of the Jeep, Corporal Goldfarb, flanked by two clean-shaven MPs, fears for one panicky moment that his betrayal has been discovered after all; that for his triple treason—his betrayal of Hannah, of America, and of humankind—he will be crucified on this monstrosity, his own destructive creation.

The sand around the tower is smooth, its grain finer than that of powdered sugar. It seems almost liquid; too liquid to be real. It's like a synthetic dream of sand, the sand of classroom physics problems, sand as it exists in an engineer's mind. It gleamed silvery-white in the midday sun back when they first arrived—as if the sand too had been flown over especially for the occasion. Its whiteness hurts the eye, and the wind etches ever-undulating wave patterns on its surface. Waves in a grainy universe—this is exactly the stuff we and all that exists is made of, according to the hero Dirac, according to the failure Heisenberg.

Now that the bomb has been loaded, the whole world revolves around this assembly of steel, even though only a select few know of its existence. The bomb, in all its terrifying power, in all its sheer recklessness: The bomb is the avatar of a grim and heavy-handed g*d—the bomb is itself a g*d the size of a pineapple.

•

(And all his love evaporates, like a mud pool, rising in a small, pathetic, hardly noticeable cloud, to drift over the cheerless landscape, the dry and barren bone-colored sand of Alamogordo, New Mexico, Jornada del Muerto.)

•

There was a painting wrapped in oilcloth in the basement of their camp in Berlin, at the Grunewald Hunting Lodge. It might have been a Cranach. It depicted the biblical Judith. In her right hand she carries a sword as naked as her body, its point is driven into the ground at her slender toes. Blood glistens on the blade. The fingers of her left hand are entwined with the adder hair of Holofernes's severed head. Around her neck a collar of gold armor, heavy as the chains of a prisoner sentenced to death, cold as the Damascus steel in her hand. The chain mail twists just like the general's body must have contorted in the abyss of love's oblivion at the exact moment when his throat was slashed by the Jewess, who got herself sprayed with both the general's hot semen and his even hotter blood. She could have killed him earlier; she could have murdered the man in his sleep, but Judith opted for the more plausible progression envisioned by the Jewish mystics: First one knows love, then comes death.

Are you truly innocent when you dream? In this, the last night of innocence, Goldfarb dreams of the painting, and in his dream Judith's face changes into Hannah's. In a reflex of self-preservation, Goldfarb's brain yanks him wide awake before he can see whose head it is that Hannah throws on the cobblestones with so much force that it pops open like an overripe melon. He turns on his flashlight. It is two in the morning. Outside, the bomb is swinging sweetly in its bay, ready for ignition.

•

He had spent a night and a day in Berlin, deep inside the Russian Zone. The men of the Alsos mission were the first Western division to enter that hallucinogenic city. They penetrated it on the sly, almost subcutaneously. Any good archeologist can reconstruct the flesh of a city from its skeleton—even when its walls lie crumbled in the street, and iron beams reach out of the rubble like question marks, they can say: This was once a city, this was what it looked like. But Goldfarb is no archeologist. The city remains incomprehensible to him, unrecognizable, and the sounds of non-consensual sex ringing from the ruins only adds to this feeling.

The Red Army has taken over Berlin, and everything the city contains. Its ruins, its gold, its priceless works of art, its fearful women—see them stand with their backs to the wall in their basements.

Standing in the midst of that much rubble makes you dizzy. It's as if you're looking at the world from a great height. Stones and plaster, walls through which one can see the sky, angry clouds raised like clenched fists.

The *Berliner Luft* is saturated with gunpowder. By breathing this fiery air and drinking the bubbly local beer, the spirit of the Germans has taken possession of the Red Army. The Russian captain has hardly had time to check in this party of peculiar and technically forbidden Americans and already a barrel of the bawdy brew is traveling their way, passed along over the heads of the crowd. This is also the way women are passed around—someone yells the name of a recipient ("Hey, Fyodor Ivanovich, the next one is for you!") and the gift is delivered, rarely with the wrapping intact.

It is best, the officer explains, to have a buddy lift her skirts (if she's still wearing those) and fold them neatly over her head—it silences the bitch, and it's helpful not to see her eyes, you know, they reflect everything that's happening at the business end—it's quite distracting. And for the Alsos boys' edification the captain offers a demonstration, right in the middle of the hallway of Elector Joachim II's hunting palace, the oldest surviving royal building in Berlin. Cheered on heartily on by his troops, he fucks the poor woman rather perfunctorily to the rowdy beat of the *Musikalisches* puking of the long row of future victims lined up against the wall. From the stairwell, soldiers throw leftovers at the couple as if they were hecklers in the loges of a theater; they spit with puckered lips, trying to hit the floozy in the eye. They make grotesque animal sounds, hysterical background noises that somehow fit this whole manic-depressive *Krieg*. The cheers pick up pace when a splinter group of the Hitler Jugend is brought in; a migraine-prone lieutenant asks his men to please use the bayonet for their cursory execution—gunshots echo so loudly in the marble of the *Schloß*. "We have peace now," pants the captain when he's done. The moaning of the *Bürgerfrau*, however, suggests that all is not quite so nice and cozy.

Fires everywhere in the city. It's as though the lid of hell has been lifted. Rusty eagles hang askew from sagging nails: the proud banners of Prussia shot out of the sky like ordinary geese, to be roasted with chestnuts. Goldfarb spies a dead body in the street, torn open by panzer tracks; ants march into the open cavities of chest and mouth with all the excited chaos of a fresh discovery. Goldfarb sprinkles the maggots in the man's flesh with Lysol from his flask; they hiss and contort like rice wafers thrown in hot oil. A bomb disposal unit must be at work close by: Every few minutes an explosion stirs the chilly air, dust clouds make the crows take wing, and the fragile postwar leaves are shaken from the trees.

What happens when the terrorist networks and the political reality overlap? What if the violence of the new state is indistinguishable from the violence of the Reich that's been subdued? What if those who liberated the camps—Sachsenhausen, for instance, in Oranienburg, a stone's throw away from the city—fill them again with ideological adversaries?

And then there are the refugees with their hollow eyes and their sunken rib cages that look like two bony fists pressed tightly together—the refugees are everywhere, there's no escaping them. They marched for miles and miles through the cruel cold of cruel April; rags, sometimes even newspapers, are wrapped around their feet in lieu of shoes. Sorry specters, only kept together by their tattered clothes. They tell him (they tell everybody), "There is no homecoming. There is no home." The refugees from the east bring stories of mass graves and of wolves that hunt the steppes anew, hungry for even the most emaciated human flesh; stories of roving gangs of partisans who are battling the last, still faithful SS units; stories of murder and arson and looting and rape. Nameless, they wander through the city as if it were a Berber camp. They wear clothes stolen from scarecrows or lifted from clotheslines or pilfered from the rotting corpses of soldiers hanging half out of the cockpit of their shot-down Stukas. It is the exodus of the century, bloody footprints in the clay and sand and mud overwritten with tire tracks; an endless column of people stuck in an eternal "now" where the horrors of yesterday shrink to incomprehensibility and the idea of a future is unheard-of, nothing more than a socialist-realist dream of a table and a bed. The diaspora of those who are guilty of picking the wrong mother, or of having loved somebody of their own sex, or who committed the foolhardy crime of not keeping their mouth shut. Has the world around them gained any wisdom through experience? Are they headed towards a golden future, with plenty of sweet wine for everybody, and tolerance galore? The refugees: They call them "the liberated." But if we would ask them, they would tell us, "There is no liberation. We will never be free."

What is perhaps most bizarre is the pretense of normality. People dressed in city clothes and city shoes, people with earnest businesslike city faces climbing over the piles of rubble with a determination that suggests a goal in life and a place to go. To Goldfarb they look like wound-up automata, jerky toys that go on forever, disappearing behind this dingy door or that dirty heap of scrap metal, looking for something—although they themselves don't know what. Black ants that labor at something—it's not clear what—with grim resolve. This then is the new German order? Just a few days ago these same people, equally determined and wound-up and oblivious, marched happily behind their Leader, their jaws filled with deadly formic acid; without a second thought, they planted their teeth into any individual who threatened the colony and its sacred brood.

Goldfarb wanders through town. His guide, a POW schoolteacher, shows him the monuments, or rather the spots where they used to be. The Reichstag is a half-burnt postcard of itself; the Brandenburg Gate is pockmarked beyond recognition. A traffic cop cheerfully points the stream of refugees and widows the way to the black market in the bombed-out Tiergarten. "Here," says the guide, and he gestures at the empty sky, "was the balcony where the Füh . . . where Hitler waved at the cheering crowd, back in '33." There is a hint of nostalgia, even regret, in the man's voice.

Goldfarb wanders through the town. A girl, perhaps eight years old, holds out a biscuit tin painted with Prussian motifs: an emperor on horseback, a sugar princess with bright pink cheeks. She opens the lid. The tin contains a hundred cigarette butts. She looks at Goldfarb with big eyes. Would he want one? "She learned to collect those in the camp," a woman says. The woman puts her hand around the girl's shoulder. No, the woman is not the girl's mother. The girl's mother is dead. The camp, you know. Gently, the girl closes the lid again. The woman shrugs. "It is her only treasure."

A box filled with ashes.

Goldfarb wanders through the town. He thinks of those who are no longer here. His father, for instance. He rarely thinks of his father. But today he thinks of him. A box filled with ashes.

Goldfarb wanders through town. He has no sympathy for Berlin.

•

The moon hangs in the sky like some strange, half-eaten fruit, pregnant with otherworldly juices. Around Luna, the stars swarm in the bluish black between the ghostly clouds like a cluster of young snakes disturbed in their nest.

The men are dressed in black and gray suits; it's as if they are already watching the event on the black-and-white newsreel. The whole Hellfire Club is here; with their heads back they stare at the plethora of pinpricks in the black velvet, the rocky vomit of the Big Bang. They have labored in the Mojave Desert just like Israel in the Sinai.

•

And when the world was created, YHVH filled it with sacred light—"There," He said. "Let there be light!" And there it was, in accordance with His wisdom: light. Light—it is G*d's original tallis; it is the Shechinah's radiant garment, brighter than the sun—for the sun was only created on the fourth day. G*d's light is the light that Adam saw shine over his world. G*d locked that light in a Jewel, the Zohar, and the Zohar was handed down from Adam to Seth; Seth gave it to his son, and Seth's son gave it to his son; it was handed to Enoch and to Metushélach, and each of them slept in the Light's glow; and from Metushélach it went to Léme, and from Léme to Noach, and the Light lit his way through the dark storms of the Flood, and with him the Light was stranded on Mount Ararat, and it rolled from the deck into the deep, deep sea. And when the waters receded, the Light was hidden in a cave, the cave in which Avraham the newborn was left for fear of King Nimrod's anger; and the angel Gavri'el descended into the cave and fed the baby Avraham with milk and honey from his thumb; and from the grotto Avraham the youth walked into daylight with the Jewel, dented and dirty, tied around his neck on a rough string of yarn. Avraham gave it to his son Yitzchak, and Yitzchak's son Ya'akov stole it with his father's permission, and Ya'akov wore it on his heart when he dreamt of Ladders to the Heavens, and he gave it to his beloved son Yosef—the Light shone in the well, and it kept the scorpions at bay for three whole days and on the third day the traveling caravan of Midianites passed and from the pit their bucket raised the thirsty Yosef. In Yosef's ear the Stone whispered the correct interpretations of Pharaoh's dreams; Móshe stole it from Yosef's coffin; the Stone was the Light on the Ark. In the Radiance of the Light, the Words of the Law shone, until the Romans extinguished it.

How, then, by what vagaries and detours, did that Light travel from Ur of the Chaldeans over Kná'an to Gizeh to Jerusalem to Rome to Berlin to Chicago—and now to Alamogordo, Jornada del Muerto? How did Oppenheimer, that g*dless communist, steal the Light? Is this G*d's will?

Today, they—Christians and Jews and atheists together—will crack the Jewel as though it were a mere egg. They will trample it and splinter its shell and the Light Liberated will flood the world: the Light, bearer of the Law of Life and Death. Good and Evil will surge and speed from horizon to horizon, and how could that Light be less than blinding, its roar less than deafening; who would be surprised if its heat could tear open a man's skin and expose his deepest fears? If it filled his bones until they burst? If it would rip apart his liver and his guts?

•

When Hannah saw the glow of the Jewel, its blue halo, its dizzying aura, she knew—even before the Geiger counter started rattling like crazy.

She knew. It was too late; this was the end. Frisch had wiped away the subcritical mass as quickly as he could, he swiped Lady G*diva from the table in one fell swoop, and he ordered everyone to leave the room—"*Schnell, Mensch, schnell!*" In the heat of the moment he switched to German—and when everybody had left, he had, in that room still reverberating with radiation, drawn the respective positions of metal and people on the chalkboard. Then he had covered the board with calculations and computed how much energy each of them had absorbed. In the big shower room where they washed the hot poisonous breath of the dragon off their naked and shivering bodies ("*Schnell, schnell!*"), Hannah suppressed a bitter rage at the back of her throat. The nurse looked at her quizzically, and Hannah looked away (was her pregnancy already visible?). She wrapped herself in the fresh hospital linen. In the sick bay, Frisch handed out his prognoses. All of them had received doses close to but under the generally accepted critical threshold. They might become sick, but they would survive.

What does radiation do? Ionizing radiation absorbed by human tissue strips electrons from the atoms that make up the molecules that form the body's tissue. When the electron that binds two atoms together is dislodged by ionizing radiation, the bond is broken and the molecule falls apart.

Your body falls apart.

They would survive. The men would. But what would happen, Herr Doktor, to that growing, secret, vulnerable monster, protected only by the thin fleshy layers of my womb? When the child in my womb dies, I too will perish.

•

When the Divine descends to touch the Earth. When the Earth rises up and storms the Heavens. It is time. The fiery cloud of unknowing surges upward, the magnum opus of the Almighty Chemist, a pillar of hellfire to awaken the heathen: The Blind Idiot G*d is raised from His slumber with a mighty jolt and He roars, and with Him all the g*ds of light—Lucifer, He-Who-Bears-the Light; Apollo, He-of-the-New Dawn. Kali, black, red-eyed, and bloodstained, stumbles under the weight of her necklace of skulls and opens her mouth wide to alleviate the pressure, her blood-dripping tongue rolling over her lips. They, the one G*d and all the others, grab the most terrifying Shofar ever heard and forever away the blow the dust of His, of Their Creation.

•

The men from the Hill are ready for their close-up. But they are not ready for this, for this horrifying swelling, this petrifying thunder—they are not ready for . . . for . . . for this:

Odious.

Radical.

Gigantic.

Awesome.

Scarifying.

Majestic.

•

Oppenheimer, *der Chaos wunderlicher Vater*, shows his face in profile, his impressive nose overshadowed by the sharp brim of his straw Stetson. He speaks his carefully rehearsed message for the history books ("*I am become Death, destroyer of worlds*"), but his hand in his notebook also draws, over and over again, little dancing Shiva figures, black and red on the yellow paper.

The cruel curtain splits. Fermi climbs out of the trench and lets the nuclear storm wash over him. Like a wind-swept angel he floats above the sweating, dancing, thumping ground. He tears pages from his notebook; they are immediately grasped by the magnificent storm. In a minute or so he will calculate the power of the shockwave from the distance traveled by the pages, but right now he measures the power of matter unchained directly by the sensations of his body. Ashen-white rain flogs his skin—he bleeds. His eyes are wide with terror and his dry lips sing, "*Oh, can you see, by the bomb's early light?*"

In their memoirs, soldiers in the frontline often describe the strange joy that rages through them when the bullets whiz past heir ears, the high that comes with the realization that they're still alive. This here is the combat experience of the physicists, and they are intoxicated indeed. The seconds before the flash of otherworldly Light (seen, felt, experienced more through the body than through the retina) are followed by the rolling shockwave that slams the heavy gate shut. Giddy with joy, they clatter like drunk and manic skeletons in an Ensorian waltz of death.

Once there was Nothing. Now there is Everything.

Time splits in two; the world splits in two. There is before and after. There are

no gradations: This is a binary-digital event. The Zero clicks and becomes One.
After this 1, nothing can be 0 the way 0 was 0 before it became 1.
Something has happened.

•

At the moment of explosion, at Time Zero, Goldfarb turns around and stands up
in the trench. With moist eyes he stares into the fire and then he quickly closes
his eyelids and claws at them, but it is already too late: The first nanosecond of the
new birth etches its Sign upon his retina, the inverted sign of the Law, the Law of
Life and Death, the Law of Good and Evil. Then his head is clad in thunder. A long,
deep, cosmic *oooooooMMMMMM* bounces through the dustbowl and soars up
Compania Hills and Oscuro Peak, and Goldfarb's retina is scorched; the Sign,
rotated 180 degrees by its transition through the vitreous lens, the world in
translation, the world explained in its unfolding, its transformation—the world
is a liquid glass vessel blown apart under the mighty breath of the alchemist.
A letter burns on his retina, a Greek letter, a minuscule majuscule in the focal point
of plutonium, the marking of the One G*d, gloriously, glowingly Eternal, His
transcendent Brand: the very last letter of the alphabet, the very last revelation,
the omega: Ω.

•

Herbert Anderson can see clearly through the periscope of his tank while it
cautiously approaches Ground Zero. What he sees amazes him. A jade blossom
blooms in the rusty soil. The desert sand has melted and solidified, the grains
frozen to an expanse of turquoise glass, four hundred yards wide, twenty feet deep.
The tank crushes its crust into millions of emerald pebbles. The stench of death
floats over the brittle disk; the bones and flesh and guts of hundreds of sand
rabbits crunch underneath the wheels, their charred shadows tint the magical lake
of green with black. Scorpions and lizards—they didn't survive after all—have
been cooked inside their shields of scale; they fall apart when the tanks' treads
touch them. The proud Joshua trees are simply gone, evaporated.

•

Goldfarb realizes that he is still alive, that he is sitting on a big boulder, temporar-
ily blinded by the onslaught of photon violence. His ears ring with the echoes of

thunder, both his retinas have been marked, perhaps forever, with an inverted omega, and his teeth are gritty with sand. The darkness that hangs so palpable and still in front of his eyes is the dark of the night after the birth of a new sun—G*d has retreated, his greatcoat of flames wrapped tightly around His freezing body—and Goldfarb realizes that this new darkness is nothing less than the Future.

Alive. But is it the same alive as an hour ago? Existence has acquired a new halo, a haze, a tint, a color unlike anything ever seen before—this is the way the world would look after the Supreme Being knocked you out with a well-placed uppercut.

In no uncertain terms, unalterable by even the vilest of vulgarities, unassailable by even the most base attempts at humor, unyielding under even the most misplaced references to ill-understood Hinduism, the physicists—purest among scientists, merchants in models and equations, dabblers in speculative philosophy, masters of the certainties that are by definition uncertain, relativists and lovers of the quantum, kings of Minkowksi diagrams and Lorentz transformations—during the split second when the atom split, in that scorched landscape of glass and pulverized nature, the physicists had finally (finally!) come to know Sin . . . and what a gruesome sin it is: Here in the desert, where G*d sealed His compacts with His people, they committed the most ghastly of adulteries.

Suddenly they fall silent. They scratch their heads. Their skin feels like parchment, their lips are dry, their arms fall limp at their sides. There is nothing left to say. Only General Groves does a little dance. He throws his cap up in the air for joy; he rides jubilantly into the sunset on the bare back of an imaginary bronco, on his way to Washington to collect his medals.

The most ghastly of adulteries.

This new darkness is nothing less than the Future.

•

"Long time no see, *Paolo mio.*"

"I cherish my solitude," I say.

"Sure," says Donatella. "Of course. Maybe you should enter a monastery or something?"

"Too busy. Too many monks."

"Indeed. And there is that one nasty precondition, of course."

"Celibacy?" I venture.

"Faith."

Is it just a coincidence that she's always in the kitchen whenever I need to grab something, or that she needs something whenever I'm there? I feel like an idiot, a lost and lonely soul, standing in that kitchen with Mefista's bowl in my folded hands.

"If you would excuse me, *Paolino*? I have stuff to do."

"Sure." I walk behind her, feeling miserable.

"Honey?" A deep voice booms from her room.

"Oh, and goodnight!" she says. Did she wink at me? Did she just fucking wink at me?

ד

EXALTED, SANCTIFIED

This is the way it goes.

An army jeep drives to the little mound. A white tarpaulin is stretched over the roof of the vehicle; a squat red cross is painted on the white cloth.

The car parks at the southernmost edge.

An SS-officer and an SDG-*Scharführer* get out.

The *Scharführer* carries four green canisters. Each is about five inches high and four across.

The tins have been delivered by the DEGESH.

DEGESH is short for *Deutsche Gesellschaft für Schädlingsbekampfung*—the German Department for Pest Control.

The two men walk across the lawn.

Their destination: four square blocks of concrete, each covered with a wooden lid, spaced about fifty feet apart.

They arrive at the first block.

The men produce gas masks from the small pouches at their belt. They pull them over their nose and mouth. It doesn't take long; they've done this before.

They open the wooden cover. The block is hollow.

They open the airtight seal of the first canister. They pour the contents inside the opening—bluish-purple pellets, the size of peas, slide down the hole.

The hole is the mouth of a lead pipe; it spirals into the ground like a corkscrew. Hollow columns of concrete surround the pipe. Slits have been made in the columns; these correspond to perforations in the lead pipe. The columns support the crossbeams of an underground hall. The walls and floors of that hall are covered in white tiles. It looks like a gigantic bathroom.

Showerheads hang from the ceiling. Each of the showerheads is connected to the end of a conduit that is connected in turn to a single long pipe that runs across the full length of the ceiling.

Think biblically—you are inside the belly of Leviathan.

Think evangelically—you see a thousand crosses, each arm ending in a gargoyle.

Think like a plumber—you wonder how there could be sufficient water pressure to feed each of the showerheads with more than a trickle.

The answer to the plumber's question is simple. The showerheads are not meant to spew water. The showerheads are dummies; camouflage, so to speak. The hollow columns are what the room is really for: the distribution of the purple pellets. Before they even hit the bottom of the pipe, the pellets evaporate; the gas seeps through the slits in the columns into the shower room.

This is what the room is about.

The gas is hydrocyanic acid.

Also known as prussic acid.

In German: *Blausäure*.

The brand name on the canisters is Zyklon.

Zyklon-*Blausäure*. Zyklon-B.

The canisters read, in German: *Cyclone, to be used against vermin. Attention, poison! To be opened by trained personnel only!*

Cyclone gas.

Whirlwind gas.

It whirls from the holes in the columns.

The underground hall is filled with naked people. Hundreds of naked people stare at the showerheads, expecting cool, cleansing water to rain down.

No water will come.

The showerheads are not connected to a water main.

The showerheads are not connected to anything.

Watch the columns.

They sputter.

A blue mist fills the room.

First the first column, then the second, then the third, then the fourth.

A humming. To the two men on the lawn it feels as if a gigantic anthill springs to live under their feet—time for the new queens and their court to swarm. The ground trembles; a droning rises from the earth, the murmurings of a million insect wings. Angry and furious at first, but soon the sound starts to fade—it gets quieter and quieter and then even more quiet. Then all is still.

The whole process takes approximately ten minutes.

Twenty minutes into the process, an electric suction system is activated and the doors are opened. Mining carts roll inside—there is a rail in the center of the room.

The men who push those carts are we, the men of the *Sonderkommando*—the Special Commando. We wear rubber boots, and gas masks just like the SS-men outside. The powerful fans suck most of the gas out the room, but we do not to take any risks. Deadly bubbles may have formed in the smallest cavities between the dead bodies.

The dead bodies are not spaced out evenly across the room. There's a big pile near the last column. A pyramid of useless flesh, a tower of drowned humans, washed up against the wall. It looks like a nest of gray roaches was smoked out of their burrow; they crawled away into the farthest corner where the gas would reach them last.

As if delaying death by a few seconds changes anything.

As if you can escape death.

The gas attacks from below; all breathable air is pushed to the ceiling. Children are the first victims. They sink to their knees in a coughing fit.

This alarms the adults. Panic ensues. People run away from the whirling gas, they follow the last mouthfuls of oxygen to the back of the room. Then they flee upwards. Not a pretty sight. They fall over each other; they trample each other underfoot. So great is their yearning for that last gasp of breath that they simply fight their way up and climb the pile of the dead and the dying. Sharp toenails dig into eye sockets; panicky fingers look for purchase in gasping, gaping mouths. The last of the living fight a relentless, merciless battle just to live for a single second longer.

The pile of cadavers. At the bottom: the children. Bruises in black and blue cover their bodies, and blood thick as syrup flows from their mouths and noses. Then the adults, the strongest ones on top. In the rare faces that still have eyes you can read the terror. The few lips that have not been ripped apart by clawing hands are frozen in an eternal silent scream.

In the dressing room, the first Sonderkommando group is already busy loading their carts. Shoes, clothing, glasses, rings, handbags, bracelets, necklaces, brooches, handkerchiefs, hats. These objects go to the disinfection chamber. They will be reused, redistributed among the German population.

We are the second group. We approach the pile of bodies hose in hand. Fear and death loosen the sphincters. And there is all the blood. We hose the dead bodies down with powerful, well-aimed blasts.

We pry the bodies loose. Some are entwined in a wrestling hold, others in what must have been a last loving embrace. Lovers. A father with this son. A mother with her daughter. It is terrible work, disentangling those limbs; it is terrible to deny the dead their last support. We attach cotton belts to the bodies' wrists. The bodies are slick with water; the belts provide purchase; this way we can easily slide them over the floor. We drag the dead to the carts; we load them up. Then we push the carts to the elevator.

A carload is about twenty-five dead bodies. More if there are children. We ring a bell. The elevator door opens. We drag the bodies inside. We ascend to the crematorium—three of us living, twenty-five dead.

The floor is made of concrete; a furrow runs along its length. We drag the bodies through that channel to the mouths of fire. The floor is slippery with water and with the blood that seeps out the bodies' noses and mouths and ears. Water and blood flow into the furrow and into a drainpipe. Water and blood mix with the earth's soil.

We turn the bodies on their backs. Other men, the third group, break the jaws open with crowbars. Men with hammers and chisels and rusty pincers hunt for gold inside those broken mouths. These men are certified dentists. We call them the woodpecker commando. Gold teeth go into a vat with hydrochloric acid, to remove the last remnants of bone and flesh.

The cadavers are loaded onto a stretcher made of iron bars; three bodies per stretcher. We push the stretchers to the black iron doors of the ovens. The doors open automatically. A hellish blaze, a sucking sound, a cloud of steam, the hissing of fat. Then it is over.

Outside: flames on top of the chimneys, and thin gray plumes that climb to the skies.

This then is the way things go in Auschwitz-Birkenau.

Dead bodies, cadavers.

All of one kind.

People born from the wrong kind of father, the wrong kind of mother.

A people.

My people.

My people.

My *people*.

This is where my people end up, this is how it goes, and every illusion we might still entertain about humanity, about ethical progress, about openness and tolerance—it all ends, and it all ends here.

This is the way it is. This is the only way it can be. Let me be a camera with its shutter wide open. I will observe and record, just observe and record. I will be passive, I will not think. One day the film will be developed. The images will be printed on glossy paper, the paper will be submerged in fixer solution and the truth will appear, and the truth shall endure and set us free. But a camera with its shutter permanently open records nothing. Each point of light is burned with equal emphasis onto the silver emulsion; each point of light overwrites another glimmering point. What emerges from the stop bath is a blank page, blindingly white—each trace of each particular episode has been erased.

It is, shall we say, finished.

•

Twice De Heer has disowned me, his biographer. Both times had been quite dramatic, rather theatrical. Twice my crime had been to ask a question. What have we learned from these events, from this twofold rejection and from the twofold reconciliation that followed? I for my part learned that it was better to keep my mouth shut. No comments, no personal observations. What did De Heer learn from our separations? I can only guess. We are good Germanic men: We do not talk about such things. I assume that he learned that he couldn't live without me—or rather, that he had grown rather fond of the regular retelling of his story. Humans are, after all, addicted to stories, and the story of our own life is the most captivating of all. Telling a story presupposes an ear. I was that ear.

Telling stories is a frightening experience. But listening can be terrible too. And the act of listening can be equally addictive. I missed De Heer in those days between rejection and reunion. I missed his giddiness, that feeling of let's-get-started. I missed the way his eyes glazed over when he dove into his story. I missed our mutual daze when we returned to reality at the end of each episode. I missed the countdown painted on the walls of the city; it seemed to announce the end of De Heer's story the way the increasing page count of a book indicates that the end is near. That countdown, luckily, was still far from zero. More than De Heer himself, I missed his story. All aspects of it: the anticipation when I made my way to the Mitte, the listening itself, the note-taking, and my silent contemplation on the way back. I loved to sit in the loneliness of the S-Bahn, my tired sleepless head pressed against the dazzlingly cold window of a wobbly train. I loved being carried away at high speed on wheels of sparks.

My childish belief in literature as light entertainment is long gone. We cannot change the course of the world, but what we can do is rework the text until it creates the illusion that the world indeed has changed, or that at least a part of it has become less impenetrable. Even though the words I work on are somebody else's, the text is my text too. It needs to be finished. It is my calling. The writer therefore goes back to work, grateful for his role in society. He is a servant, of course—a servant of the Text; and Text is Truth, at least for the time it takes to read it. What could be nobler than to open up a man to the reader's mind? To slide his life—a chronicle of the interaction between flesh and time—between two covers?

This, after all, is the real stuff. My own work, my fumbling around with the milliseconds of the mind—what does it matter? It has nothing to do with reality. Is a research career in experimental psychology something that elevates a person? Does it lead to words that make the reader shudder, the way Jozef De Heer's story makes me shudder?

In other words, does it still make sense for me to walk those one hundred feet from the guest house to my office? My writing room becomes my office; no longer an *imaginarium*, but a room in which I write down life. I condense events onto paper.

I filled the first few days of my exile with editing. "I have to work, honey," I tell the cat. Honey? Where did I get that? Seven pounds of fur and claws, and I call it honey? And work? Editing De Heer's monologues? That's hardly work, is it?

I pull the stack of paper from underneath Mefista. She jumps off the table and lands on the floor with a soft thud. She walks to the bed on stiff, disgruntled legs. She hoists herself up and drapes her body over my pillow, her tired chin on top of her crossed forelegs. She sigh a nice deep sigh. It sounds like the beginning of a sad conversation, but then she decides to go to sleep instead. These sound effects should be worked into the manuscript, I think, and then I think nothing else for a long while, because I sink into De Heer's world—I see it as clearly as if it were my own.

•

It hadn't been easy to regain his trust. I needed Donatella for that. She was the only person I knew in Potsdam. Therefore, I swallowed my pride and my grief. Her life is her life, I told myself. I have to accept that she doesn't want me to share it.

So I asked Donatella for advice. She got very excited. "A Holocaust survivor? He's telling you his story? And you blew it? Oh boy. Oh-boy-oh-boy. Wowie-zowie!" Her advice is simple. "Don't give up," she says. "But be smart. Visit him around dusk. The human heart is at its most vulnerable when the sun goes down. The heart sinks with it, you know—mimetic desire. The early evening makes a man more open, more pliable."

"Lovers," she adds, "often meet around dusk. It can't be a coincidence."

•

I follow her advice. It makes me restless. I sit in my room and write and rewrite. It goes slowly. I have to cut and paste large blocks of text on my old Toshiba and print out page after page and then edit in pen—and all the while the city beckons me, and the man who lives in that city.

I take the noon train. I'm alone in the car. I get out at the Friedrichstraße station. I love this station. It's my favorite labyrinth—I never manage to locate the first, fastest exit to the street level. Maybe there isn't one. So I wander and I use my long-forgotten wayfarer's instinct until the noise of the street wafts down a hallway and I feel the city's suction ruffle my hair. This time, I emerge next to the *Tränenpalast*.

De Heer's descriptions of the town accompany me on my walk. Or rather, they force me to look at Berlin anew, as if the screeching of the trams, the prattling of the two-stroke engines, the sliding and ticking steps of the pedestrians offer answers to questions I didn't even know I was asking.

I am early; I am way too impatient. I go to Museum Island and buy a day ticket. I see Cranach's painting of the fountain of eternal youth: Old women enter the baths from the left and emerge on the right as pretty young things. Only women take the bath—the men rejuvenate in a different way, as depicted on the far right: They engage in merry congress with the newly minted maidens. I see an impossibly slim, diamond-encrusted evening dress that once belonged to the now forgotten movie star Helena Guna. I see medieval swords. The first manuscript page of *Die Blechtrommel*, Gunter Grass's masterpiece, hangs on the wall. Grass wrote in such neat blue handwriting that it looks like a forgery. I stare at a monumental seascape by Gerhard Richter and lose myself momentarily in its waves.

When the evening falls—evening comes early at the end of winter—I take the U-Bahn.

It's busier now. The sounds of my fellow passengers put me in a pleasant trance—fragments of conversations drift by, sometimes the contours of sentences leave a brief impression on my consciousness—polyphonic music in multiple languages, a nice accompaniment to the resigned purple of the dusk. It's all so different, so trivial compared to the storms inside my heart.

I press the button next to De Heer's name. I hear nothing, but still I plead, my lips against the iron mesh; I beg to be let in. I put my ear to the intercom but I hear nothing, no trace of white noise, nothing that indicates that he's picked up and is listening to my plea. Behind one of the many windows somebody sneezes cheerfully. Then I return to Potsdam.

•

Donatella's recommendation is to make my visits strictly predictable. Every other day, at five o'clock sharp, I ring the bell. The regularity absolves him from picking up the receiver out of sheer curiosity; it also decreases the risk that he will open the door because he thinks I'm somebody else, thereby forcing a meeting he might not be ready for—that would spell disaster for both of us. "You can bet on it," says Donatella, "at a quarter to, he'll be peering out of his window just to see you walk up the street. And you can bet he watches you leave, too."

I stood at that door so often, letting his piercing gaze rest on me from above. It took a tremendous amount of effort not to look up.

"Good," says Donatella. "You showed him you're serious. Now is the time to withdraw. He'll find that interesting, believe me. Put the ball in his court. Wait. Just a little more patience. It won't take long."

She's right. After a week that lasts for ages—I'm so bored that I even go back to my office; nobody seems to have noticed my absence, nobody seems to have missed me—I find a card in the mailbox. It isn't signed, but who else would send me a card? It is covered in letters from an ancient mechanical typewriter, hammered through an equally ancient, ink-deprived ribbon; letters that are written almost exclusively in relief, in impact—as if the card had been written a long time ago, and time itself had done its best to erase the message. Only my name and the address of the *Gästehaus* are clearly legible, written in sharp blue marker with a firm hand. This is what this first card says:

> Swiftly and soon,
> Exalted, extolled,
> Beyond any blessing and song.

The back of the card (or is that the front?) shows the Brandenburg Gate in sepia, as seen from Pariser Platz. A picture from long ago, long before the Gate was bricked in and became the symbol *par excellence* of the divided city, the divided world. The cars look like bonbon boxes in the picture; their spare wheels are attached to the tops of their trunks, like giant life preservers. Under the brand-new stamp, the cardstock shows traces of being repaired, and there are scarcely visible impressions of ink: The card is second-hand. I assume that the original ink has simply faded, or that De Heer has chemically removed it.

"A nice symbol," says Donatella. "The Brandenburg Gate thrown open by a time machine. *Very* encouraging. But let's wait before we do anything, shall we? There's no rush!"

The second card dates back to 1939. Or at least that's the year printed underneath the image. It was stamped yesterday. Express mail from Berlin. This card is in mint condition and bears no message. The card came in an envelope, accompanied by a typed letter; the type font is the same as that of the machine used for the first card. The paper is amber-colored in the center and brown at the edges; it crumbles with age. Cheap writing paper, with lots of acid in it. When I unfold it, it cracks and breaks into two identical halves. On the card an aerial photograph of a building in the shape of a horseshoe. It is the Tempelhof Airport; on the runway an airplane ready to take off, a *Deutsche Lufthansa* plane shaped like a bomb, with sharp delineated swastikas on the horizontal stabilizers.

"Wonderful. The airport in Kreuzberg, built by the Nazis, but later used for the American-British airlift. Another good sign. Just wait a little while longer, will you?"

The piece of paper says:

(1) Red: political prisoner, interned for his own safety. Could also be somebody who let his guard down and told the wrong joke to the wrong audience.

(2) Blue: illegal emigrant. Somebody who tried to leave the country without asking the regime's permission, and got caught in the attempt. Although one would assume the country would prefer to get rid of such a person, he gets detained.

(3) Purple: Jehovah's Witness. Enthusiastically spreading the message of the Bible is an offense punishable with forced labor.

(4) Pink: homosexual.

(5) Black: asocial. Homeless, squatter, parasite, gypsy.

(6) Green: convicted criminal. The soothing color of grass. Don't say Germans have no sense of humor.

(7) Yellow, two equilateral triangles outline in black; the triangles share a center point, one is rotated 60 degrees relative to the other: Jew.

The greatest of these seven is the yellow star. What mark will bear the leftist, emigration-prone, homosexual, criminal, homeless Jew? He shall wear the yellow star.

The third postcard depicts, in dreadfully optimistic Technicolor, the big engineering marvel of the German Democratic Republic: the television tower on Alexanderplatz. It is shown in spotless white against a vibrant blue background—not a cloud in the sky, there in the GDR. This postcard looks mint, a souvenir that might once have been used as a bookmark. Donatella has her interpretation ready, I think I can guess it: Let's open up the lines of communication, and on a grand scale.

The text:

> The continent is full of buried violence, of the bones of antediluvian monsters and of lost races of man, of mysteries which are wrapped in doom . . . The whole continent is a huge volcano whose crater is temporarily concealed by a moving panorama which is partly dream, partly fear, partly despair.

Looks like a quote.

"What if," I say, "What if De Heer is implying something else entirely? A simple description of the historical eras he lived in: the empire, the Nazi regime, the communist era? What if the progression is as follows: an open gate, a building closing in on itself, a sealed globe? And let's not forget how history changed those buildings' meaning. The Brandenburg Gate became a symbol for unity sixty years after the picture was taken; the airport became a symbol for the solidarity of nations ten years after the picture; but what does the television tower stand for? Nothing ever happened there. Is it possible, is it even permitted, to read a moral into these postcards?"

"Whatever," says Donatella. "They're postcards. They contain a message, and a message has been written between the lines as well."

I display the cards in a neat little row on my writing table, using, respectively, a lamp, a tiny flower pot, and an empty water glass as support.

"Three cards is enough," says Donatella. "Tomorrow, you'll go back into town and at five sharp you'll ring his doorbell. I bet he simply opens the door, no questions asked, and picks up his story exactly where he left it, as if nothing happened." Donatella! She knows all there is to know about the game of attraction and seduction. Where does that knowledge come from? She shrugs, "Don't be silly, boy. I'm a woman!"

"Oh, and take a bottle of wine with you or something," she yells after me. "This one, for instance." And from her doorway her slender hand passes me an equally slender bottle of Frascati.

•

How can you switch off thinking? It's impossible not to think. It's impossible to deny who you are. As a consequence, it is impossible to record anything objectively.

Behind one of the gas masks comes a humming sound. When we take them off, the humming becomes a whisper, a low mumbling in a language that I don't understand—it's not German or Dutch or Yiddish and it doesn't sound like Hungarian or Polish or Czech or Hebrew either.

[*Exalted and sanctified*
be His great name . . .]

I clip a meat hook behind the cotton belt. There goes another oblong lump of flesh; it hobbles over the ribbed concrete, it bobs in its own blood.

What language is this?

[*. . . throughout the world,*
which He has created according to His will.]

It sounds familiar.

[*And say, Amen.*]

And around me everybody, everybody but me mutters, "AMEN!"

[*May His great name be blessed*
forever and to all eternity.]

It finally dawns on me. This is Aramaic. Somebody is saying Kaddish.

There are three dead men on the iron grill. Their broken jaws gape at the ceiling. The oven door opens.

[*Blessed and praised,*

glorified and exalted,
extolled and honored.]

The little fat that remains on the bodies hisses and steams. The heat scorches my eyelashes. My eyeballs dry out. The smell of burning flesh. I jump back and the oven door closes. I cough, I retch. I wish I hadn't taken off my mask.

The smell of burning flesh.

Flesh turned into meat.

Burning meat.

[*Blessed be He,*
beyond all the blessings and hymns,
praises and consolations
that are ever spoken in the world.]

It makes me sick and hungry at the same time.

Such a disgusting, blasphemous thought!

[*And say, Amen.*]

I join in, despite myself.

I have never been a man of faith—my story so far has told you that. But this time I am part of the choir.

"AMEN!"

I know the rest of the words.

[*May there be abundant peace from heaven, and life.*]

How can a man sing this song?

How can a man pray, here and now?

Auschwitz-Birkenau. The air we breathe is death itself. The ghosts of the gassed, the spirits of the hanged float through the air. What rains down from heaven, the fine powder that coats our shoulders and crackles under our feet, that dust is a never-ending rain of human remains, the sediment of death—the sediment of those human bodies we just delivered to the oven. Birkenau is the most unclean place on earth. Peace should come abundantly from heaven? *For us and for all Israel*?

[*And say, Amen.*]

Threefold: "AMEN!"—"AMEN!!"—"AMEN!!!"

The next patient.

[*He who creates peace*
in His celestial heights,
may He create peace
for us and for all Israel.]

The celestial heights, where stands His throne. The dead are with G*d?

[*And say, Amen.*]

"AMEN!"—"AMEN!!"—"AMEN!!!"
He—the Lord—calls them?
"AMEN!"—"AMEN!!"—"AMEN!!!"
This is how it will be?
The man reprises his chant, from the beginning.
[*Exalted and sanctified . . .*]
From the beginning, with the same response:
"AMEN!"—"AMEN!!"—"AMEN!!!"

We return to the barracks.

"Who are you? What's your name?"

It's cold, but the heat of the ovens still bathes the skin around our eyes in radiance. I shiver in my thin jacket. My pants flutter around my thighs: they're too big—I wasn't careful enough during the selection procedure.

The name of the beardless rabbi is Katzenellebogen. "But in the new land, I will be called Katz," he says, "and my beard will be full, and my locks will curl like the mane of the Lion of Judah."

"You will go to Israel?"

"No, I will go to America." The dreams people have, in the midst of such destruction!

"Then I will call you Katz," I say. He beams. I use the word *Sie* for "you"; he doesn't offer to switch to the friendlier *du*. Even in Auschwitz-Birkenau there should be *Ordnung*: the vertical distance between a rabbi and his *Gemeinde*.

"Close your eyes, young friend. That darkness, that not-seeing, that's where you come from. Now open your eyes. This, all you can see, is where you are now—this is where you lead your life. This is where life has led you."

I close my eyes. I stumble over a hole in the road. The men giggle.

How strange, in this place, this friendly giggling.

"You know, it is true—peace comes from above. It might be better to keep your eyes open then, no?"

•

A STORY ABOUT RABBI AKIVA

Rabbi Akiva strolled through a graveyard by the side of the road.

There he met a naked man, black as coal. The man carried a huge stack of wood on his head. He labored under his burden. The man looked like a ghost, but he suffered like the living.

"You are laboring so under your burden, man!" the rabbi exclaimed. "If you are a serf and your master forces you to carry such heavy loads, I will buy you and set you free. If you are poor and people shun you, I will give you alms."

The man refused the rabbi's money with a simple gesture of his hand.

"Do not delay me, good sir, or my masters will get mad."

"Who are you," asked Rabbi Akiva, "and what is your crime?"

"The man you speak to is a dead man. It is my sentence to chop wood and to take it back to where I dwell. It will serve to heat Gehenna."

"My son, who were you in the world, and what was your crime?"

"I collected taxes. I favored the rich. The poor people who had no money I condemned. For a man like me, no salvation is possible."

"I will pray for you," said Rabbi Akiva.

"Your prayer will serve no purpose. I have heard the spirits talk. What they want is impossible. They say, 'If that sinner only had a son, and if that son would only appear before the congregation and exalt G*d's name—if he would only say, 'Blessed be the name of the Holy One!' and if the congregation would respond by saying 'Amen!' and he would only add, 'Exalted and sanctified be His great name,' and the congregation would endorse that too, then his torture would end.' But the spirits know I never had a son. I left my wife when she was expecting, and I do not know if she carried the child to term, and I do not know if it was a son or a daughter. And even if I did have a son, would they have instructed the son of a sinner in the Torah? I do not have a single friend on earth!"

"What is your name?"

"My name is Akiva. My wife's name is Shoshnia. I hail from the town of Lodkiya."

The rabbi pondered this for a while. Then he said, "I'll see what I can do."

And when the rabbi finally reached the town of Lodkiya, and asked about the man Akiva and his wife Shoshnia, the people he questioned said, "May his bones be ground to dust! May the memory of Akiva and his wife Shoshnia be banned from this world!"

The rabbi asked about the child of the woman Shoshnia.

"That child is a bastard, the son of a whore, a heathen. We didn't take the trouble to circumcise him."

Rabbi Akiva asked to be led to the boy, and he circumcised him at once. He presented the boy with the book, but the child refused to read the Torah. To soften the child's heart, Rabbi Akiva started a fast that lasted for forty days. At the end of the fast, he heard a heavenly voice.

"Rabbi Akiva, why do you mortify yourself for such a stubborn child?"

"Lord of Lords, it is for You I am preparing him."

And thus the Lord, blessed be His name, opened up the boy's heart and the boy began to read. Rabbi Akiva taught him the "Hear O Israel" and the blessing after the meal and he instructed him in the principles of the Torah.

He introduced the boy to the congregation, and the boy spoke, saying, "Bless the Lord who is blessed!"

And the congregation responded, "Amen!"

And the boy said, "Blessed be His great name!"

And the congregation responded, "Amen!"

At that very moment the man, the boy's father, was released. That same night, he appeared to Rabbi Akiva in a dream. He said, "May it be the wish of the Almighty that your should find joy in the Garden of Eden. You have saved me from the sentence of Gehenna."

And Rabbi Akiva was filled with joy and he declared, "Your name, O Lord, endures forever, and Your memory lives in all generations!"

And for that reason it is customary that the evening prayers are attended by a man who has no father or mother, so that he can say Kaddish: "Bless the Lord who is blessed!"

A story about Rabbi Akiva, told by Rabbi Katz, in KZ Auschwitz II, in a barrack that used to be a horse stable.

There are variations to this story. The burden of wood is sometimes a labor of Sisyphus; sometimes the wood serves for the man's own pyre—every single night of his life as a ghost, he is burned at the stake. In some of these stories, the man is guilty of oppressing the poor; in others his sin is sexual congress with a girl engaged to be married, and the sin took place on the day of Yom Kippur.

"So, we say Kaddish to beg G*d to release the guilty from hell?"

"They are guilty, after all, my boy," says Rabbi Katz. "But we are all guilty of one crime or another."

"No," I say stubbornly. "They are not guilty. All they are is dead."

Katz hums. "*Modeh ani l'fanecha . . .*" What? A psalm of gratitude?

"What does the name Israel mean?" asks Katz. He answers his own question, "The name Israel means: He who wrestles with G*d."

"Woe to the children," says the rabbi, "who have been banned from their father's table. And doubly woe to the children who have banned themselves from their father's table."

I won't let him off the hook.

"What a cruel and inhumane G*d, needing to be praised all the time!"

"No, what a human, insecure G*d—He wants to know if we still love Him. How human: He *cares* whether we love Him."

"G*d is a shivering bride?"

"G*d is in the throes of love. When you come home at night, my dear boy, would you want your lover to stare into your eyes, gauging the unfathomable love you feel for her? Or would you want her to intone a simple 'Hello' while she continues to cook your dinner? Or have you never been in love, my poor child?"

"So all this is . . . a trial? G*d's test to see if we still love Him?"

The rabbi bows his head. "How can you say that, how can you even think that this is G*d's will? Just like the lovers' path often leads through valleys—there is temptation, one may lose one's reputation, there are worries about money—so too the paths of G'd and man may diverge. What does it mean to be human? We are from G*d. We are free, we are bound. Look around you: This is what the National Socialists do with their freedom. It has nothing to do with G*d. And then the question arises, What do we do? Do we look for comfort in the arms of that ever-faithful Beloved? Or do we ascribe our problems to His interference? Isn't it better to face our problems together, like good lovers do? Together, so that it strengthens the bond between us? And isn't it justified then that He wants to know where we stand, Him and I, you and Him?"

I keep silent.

"Come on then," says the rabbi. "What is your answer? And don't tell me. Tell it to the Lord Himself!"

I make a last attempt.

"Why are the souls in hell? Why do we need to pray for them? Didn't they deserve heaven, just for having lived in this terrifying world?"

"Hell is where they lived on earth," answers the rabbi. "It would be too much of a shock for them, I think, for the Lord of the Heavenly Hosts (Holy! Holy! Thrice holy!) to raise them instantly to Eden. Gehenna is a place of purification. Don't you think, young man, that any soul liberated from this camp would be at least a little soiled?"

"The Kaddish doesn't mention death, or grief, even once."

"No, but the Kaddish rails against the dark. Against nothingness. There is the word 'consolation.' Kaddish accompanies the soul to heaven. Kaddish teaches the soul the right language. Prayer is what assists the soul—the soul knows no other friends. Right? Not for nothing the prayer is called *Kaddish Yatom*—the Kaddish of the Orphan."

I stay silent for a long time. Then I say, "I have no father, I have no mother."

"Good," says Katz. "We can use you! Repeat after me: '*Exalted and sanctified . . .*'"

Who is this G*d? I do not find Him. I look around me, I do not see Him.

"If G*d was visible, we would throw away our lives in the contemplation of that miracle. We would lose our lives in the continuous contemplation of the Creator. That is why He has hidden His face. That is why He is only visible to a select society of the dead."

Repetition awakens. Repetition dulls.
"*Exalted and sanctified . . .*"
I say it, day in day out, that prayer, at the mouths of fire.
The rabbi asks me to lead the prayer. I have no father, I have no mother. Kaddish Yatom.

"All has been provided," says Katz. "We have been offered freedom. There is no paradox there."

"What about *our* suffering?"
Rabbi Katz has a story about the dispute between the Talmudic schools of Hillel and of Shamai. Hillel claimed—this was right after the last exile and the destruction of Palestine by the Roman army—that it was better for humans not to be born than to be born. Shamai on the other hand claimed that being born is preferable over nothingness. After long discussions they arrived at this compromise: It is better for a man not to be born, but now that he is here, it is better for him to lead a mindful life.

This is how we bend nihilism until it turns into pessimism. We have to live in the world we live in, and be content, because it's all we have—painful or not.

"The art of living is the art of unhappiness?"
"It is certainly an art."

When we prepare for work and march to our assigned waiting rooms, we sometimes meet a group of people on their way to the gas chambers—the men and women whose lifeless bodies we will drag to the ovens in less than an hour.

We don't speak to them. We empty our eyes. I see a naked blind man stumble into the tiled room on the arm of another naked blind man. He slips. I watch him cry. He, only he, of all the hundreds around him, knows what's in store. He cries, that blind man. It is the only thing his eyes are good for.

"The wood, young friend, remember that, serves to heat up Gehenna. Rescue a wretched soul, and hell gets slightly less hot."

I consider myself lucky. I have no friends in the camp, no family, no acquaintances. None of the people these bodies once belonged to has ever held me at their breast. Unlike some of my commando mates, I don't need to be removed from the room when the cadaver I hold in my hands turns out—once again—to have been a friend.

The eye has to stay dry to see clearly.

Rabbi Katz insists.
"Where do we meet G^xd? Here, where the parallel lines of the railroad meet; where those endless glistening knife-thin mirrors for the sky intersect. That nonexistent crossroads—that's where man meets his Maker."

Hope.
Did I discuss the stages of hope with you?
Hope. This cannot last long. One day the limit of what is permissible will be reached and the good citizens of Germany will awaken and protest. Soon.
Hope. They will get rid of the communists, and then it will all be over.
Hope. They will stop at the *Ostjuden*, the Jews from Poland, Czechoslovakia, Hungary, the Ukraine. They wouldn't kill the German Jews, would they?
Hope. That somebody starts a fire in the cabinet where they keep the files. (A carelessly discarded cigarette, perhaps?)
Hope. They will transport only the old folks and the infirm.
Hope. All they do is move us to a new place. *Umsiedlung*, isn't it?
Hope. Somebody on the platform will forget to count the deported.
Hope. They will forget to lock the lock on the cattle car.
Hope. You will be fit and strong and young enough to make it to the right-hand row.
Hope. That when hard labor has broken the body, death will be painless.
Hope. That your loved ones might escape death.
Hope. That death will be quick.
Hope. That we will be reunited with them *in paradiso*.
Hope. That maybe from this drunken feast of death, this terrible fever glow that infects the snow-pregnant sky, the Lord will hear us. That—incited by our prayers—He will return.

What will happen to us, the pariahs of the Sonderkommando? Rabbi Katz knows: We accompanied our predecessors to the ovens, he says. We laid them to rest, we laid them in ashes. Prepare yourself. As soon as a new Kommando is formed, it will be our turn. In Auschwitz, the dead bury the dead. "Come on! *Exalted and sanctified . . .*"

"All twenty-two letters of the alphabet were carved in the Lord's arm, from *Aleph* to *Tav*, from Ox to Cross. And all of our names are etched in the palm of His hand."

No letters on my arm, no name—just a number. Katz puts our forearms together, his and mine. He makes a few calculations and then he nods enthusiastically. I am happy for him, but I do not ask what the numbers tell him.

Once all of this was strange to me. I was a stranger to my own faith. I considered it a blessing to be a stranger among my own people, a free and independent spirit. Now I know better. In the camp, under the smoke of Birkenau, I become what I never was during the prosecution. I become—like my mother, like my father—a Jew.

From the book of Psalms: "The sacrifices of G*d are a broken spirit; a broken and a contrite heart; these, o G*d, You will not despise."

Slippery bodies, stiffening even as we haul them away.

"*Exalted and sanctified . . .*"

"You know, we rabbis don't say Kaddish in mourning. For us, it is the prayer we say after study. You finish an essay and you pray to G*d to bless the teachers and their students. You pray for the students of their students and for all those who look favorably upon the study of the Torah, here and in foreign lands."

"What are you studying then, Rabbi, in Auschwitz-Birkenau? Where is your Torah here?"

"Our Torah is written with a finger in the dust. In the ashes." Katz sketches a trident in the gravel outside the barrack. The letter Shin, the letter Tooth, the letter that is tied in the burial shroud with a bow after the tahara, the ritual washing, is done.

"They were purified in fire. You can't get purer than that."

The bodies are getting lighter and lighter. What happens to the dead? When they were still alive, their footsteps weighed but little on the earth's surface, but now, liberated from their soul, they weigh nothing at all.

What is a refugee? Somebody who does not die in the town where he was born.

What is a refugee? Somebody who mourns his dead in a town where he wasn't born.

"In the King's palace there are many rooms," says Rabbi Katz. "and each has its own lock. But there is a master key: the broken heart. When a man truly breaks his heart before the Holy One, blessed be His name, then he can enter any gate."

This is no basement somewhere in Schöneberg. Here the rats freeze to death right next to the flesh of the prisoners who died during the night. Even the rats are too weak to plant their teeth into that meat.

It is hard. My G*d , it's hard! On the way back I stop and puke. My brothers stand in a circle around me on the path; they hide me from the guards' view.

"In the whole Torah," says Katz, "There is no prohibition of mourning, and not a single commandment to comfort one another."

Everybody who does not mourn, as prescribed by the wise, is cruel.

*See now that I, even I, am He, and there is no G*d with Me: I kill, and I make alive; I wound, and I heal: neither is there any that can deliver out of My hand.*

Gunshots in the night. A group of men decided to throw themselves against the electrified fence and end their lives. They never get to the fence. Instead, they die in a hail of bullets. Mission aborted; mission accomplished.

"*Exalted and sanctified . . .*"

Rabbi Katz's fever does not diminish. My nausea grows worse.

"Young friend," says Rabbi Katz, "were you not the blasphemous one who rode into this camp seated on top of a dead old man?"

I hang my shaved head in shame.

"Yes, Rabbi, I was that man. But now . . . I am no longer that same person. I am different. Reborn."

"And did we not break bread together? Did you not, when I felt weak, share the last few spoonfuls from your bowl with me, the last slice of turnip at the bottom—did you not feed me from your very own spoon?"

"I did, Rabbi Katz."

"Well then, my young friend, I think that old feverish dead man has taken his revenge."

Indeed. The rabbi and I, we are ill, really ill, terribly ill. The last men and women who die in Auschwitz will be accompanied to the mouths of fire by other men than us. Our comrades lift us on their shoulders and carry us to the sick bay. Scarlet fever, immediate admittance into the *Infektionsabteilung*. That journey on the shoulders of our blood brothers, shivering in the freezing cold, shivering with internal heat. Is it my imagination, or do I hear cannons sound from afar? Is there an army coming our way?

Here we lie, on plank beds.

The room is small, ten feet by fifteen; there are ten bunk beds carved out of raw wood. A bucket for emergencies. Katz and I are number twelve and thirteen in the room. All of us have scarlet fever or typhus or diphtheria. Here we will lie for forty days, a nice Talmudic span of time, if we don't die of fever sooner. After the forty days, we will die because we will be judged too weak to work, and we will be led to the gas chamber. These then—we both know—are our last days on earth.

The hollows below my collarbones gather sweat that leaves salt crusts when it dries quickly and mold when the drying goes slowly. My joints are stiff. My digestive tract shuts down; I am one long cramp from mouth to anus. I no longer know who I am or where I am, where I begin and end. Am I this bony body? Am I the straw of my mattress, so strangely discolored, with its suspiciously crusty spots and odd smells? Am I the earth? Do I encompass the sun? The sun that stubbornly refuses to shine over this town? This Auschwitz?

It is here that the full force of the Kaddish hits me. Rabbi Katz mutters the prayer under his breath. As long as I can hear his voice, as long as the *sanctified*s are strung together with the *exalted*s, etcetera etcetera, Katz is alive, and I am a happy man.

It is here that the full meaning of Kaddish hits me. We do not say Kaddish for the dead. Kaddish is a prayer for the living. But it pleases the living to think it is for the benefit of the dead, and this increases the complications.

I lie on my back. I lie peacefully. Patiently, without questions or sorrows.

"*Exalted and sanctified . . . exalted . . . sanctified . . . Blessings and hymns, praises and consolations . . . in the world . . . abundant peace . . . from heaven . . .*"

Hello sir. You wear an armband. Letters in a nice sans serif font. You are a "O. Artz." Thanks for your visit. How nice of you to lift up my shirt and bring me up to a sitting position. How sweet of you to put your prickly mustache against my back and your cold ear to my lungs. Thank you for making those reassuring throaty sounds. Why do you look so concerned when you visit my friend Katz? My friend Katz, he's so thin! His eyes are so small and red! He smacks his lips when he says Kaddish.

The room is a small Babel. Two Italians share a bed. There a few Hungarians. A couple of Romanians. A Spaniard, a Greek. A small bunch of Frenchmen, just arrived. All prisoners of war. *Ach*, what do we need words for?

A man comes to shave us. He is Spanish. He talks with his compatriot, a long and hushed conversation. One of the Italians translates for us, in broken German.
"*Morgen alle Kamarad weg. Alle, alle.*"
Everybody is leaving? Tomorrow? What can that mean?
"*Weg.*"
Yes, that must be the sound of cannons in the distance.
The Russians are getting closer.
Will we go the way of all flesh? Are they stoking the ovens?

I get up for the first time. I want some water; there's a little saucepan with water in the corner. Is there a cup? Does anybody have a cup? I want to moisten the dry lips of the rabbi. He can hardly speak, you know, and he is saying Kaddish for all of us.

The final mutterings.
"... exalted
... abundant peace ...
... from heaven ..."
The stream that once was inexhaustible dries up. What remains are lips that crack and smack until that terrible dreadful dry sound finally dies out too.
"From heaven."
To heaven, Katz, my friend, Katz my father, *Katzelein-mein*: to heaven. Why would the Lord let you burn in Gehenna? I hope the shock isn't going to be too big for you, coming face to face with the Eternal so suddenly.
I stand up, in the small space between two beds. I recite, loud and clear:
"*EXALTED AND SANCTIFIED BE HIS GREAT NAME*
THROUGHOUT THE WORLD ..."

Then I collapse.

The Italians lift me from the floor—you can't lie down on the floor, not with all the bugs crawling around. They throw me on my bed. I'm so thankful, I rattle off words of gratitude: "*Danke schön, bedankt heren, merci beaucoup, thank you so much, gracias,*" until I hit the right language: "*Grazie, mille grazie.*" The smallest of the two grins. "*Bitte,*" he says, "*bitte schön. Nun aber Ruhe, ja? Schon Ruhe, ja?*" Yes, thank you, yes, I will stay calm. Sorry! Sorry!

"*Exalted and sanctified . . .*"

An old, weak man who did such difficult work: to drag the dead to the fire of the ovens and to save their souls from the fires of hell. I was the one who killed him. I murdered Rabbi Katz with an act of kindness.

What did the rabbi say? We are all guilty of one thing or another.

"*Exalted and sanctified . . .*"

I say my prayer in silence.

Kaddish is not said by a man, Kaddish is said by a son. A son without a father. I am, I *am* a son of my race.

Two nurses come to take the body away. One would have sufficed; the rabbi doesn't weigh much.

•

"*Alle, alle weg.*"

That Herr O. Artz pays me another visit. All the folks who are capable of standing on their legs have to go, away from the camp, away with all the others. They're leaving? Leaving this hell? Madman that I am, I try to get out of bed, but I have to hold on to the top bunk or else I'll fall over. There is no way I can go. I am condemned to stay. The Greek goes. The Italians stay. They pretend to be weak, even though they can walk just fine.

We have a window. We stare outside. There they go, in long, sad, shuffling columns, dancing slowly with death.

The Italians sigh. "They'll never make it. Watch them. If they have to march for even a day, they'll collapse with exhaustion. And then they'll be shot because they slow down the march."

And we? We feel the ground shake with explosions and I wake from my slumber: The Russians are there! The Italian, the smallest of the two, corrects me. It's just the rubber factory burning. The Germans must have blown it up themselves, for fear it would fall into the enemy's hands.

This makes me very afraid. What will happen to us? The Italian laughs it off. As if they would waste valuable explosives on us. Then he turns grim. "As though the Russians will find anyone alive in the camp. They might need a week or so—we'll long be dead by then." I stare at the pan with water, at the last kettle of tepid soup that the guards brought in before everyone left.

"We might freeze to death too." Indeed, the prisoners who worked in the furnace room must have left. It gets colder and colder. I wrap myself up in my blanket. It doesn't help much.

Big news. One of the French poked his head around the corner, so quickly that nobody saw him. The ovens have stopped! Of course they did, but it's big news nevertheless. The eternal flame over Birkenau is extinguished. The floodlights are still on, though, and there are soldiers in the watchtowers.

The next day a SS-Scharführer passes by. He appoints the thin Italian as the barrack elder, and orders him to make a list of all prisoners, in two columns: Jews and non-Jews.

The left-hand column contains a single name: mine.

I know what that means.

I shake so hard that the man who sleeps in the bed above me climbs down to find another bunk.

It is late in the evening when the lights inside the building are switched off. So are the floodlights outside.

I recognize the sounds instantly: Airplanes are circling above us. They must have seen our lights—they must be on a reconnaissance flight.

They turn back.

I slip again into a restless slumber.

Then the unimaginable happens—the whole barrack shudders, glass breaks, and an orange glow invades the room. A direct hit on the camp. The planes returned! Judging from the glow, quite a few barracks must be on fire. If the wind blows from the wrong direction, if the Russians come back to finish the job, we are lost—we will be burned alive. Or did the SS blow up part of the camp? The Italians push one of the beds against the door. Outside a small crowd has gathered, jeering and yelling; the inhabitants from a barrack that caught fire, looking for a place to sleep. "Typhus!" yells one of the Italians. "Dysentery!" screams the other.

To no avail. The refugees bang at the door, they beg for mercy, but we do not let them in. After a while they leave. It's simply too cold to stand outside and plead; they try their luck elsewhere, trudging through the snow on bare feet. Through the window I see their silhouettes outlined against the glow of the fire. I retreat, the cold that comes through the glass is too harsh. It must be ten below zero.

The Italians have pushed the bed back. They open the door and keep watch in the doorway. They have demolished one of the unused bunks; each of the men holds a plank full of nails in his hand as a weapon. They nailed the rest of the planks against the window to provide some insulation. Pale specters shuffle around the barracks; they soil the snow with their uncontrollable shit. The Italians curse. Snow is our only water supply.

Detail: Nobody shoots at the ghosts in the moonlight, the wandering ill. The light in the watchtowers stays off. The towers themselves appear empty.

We push the beds close together to make an open space on one side of the room. We make a pile with the rest of the wood of the unoccupied bed; the straw of Katz's mattress goes underneath. One of the Frenchmen rubs stones together until a spark jumps. The straw catches fire. We close the door.

The Italians go on a raid. The booty they bring back is beyond all expectations: a small potbellied stove and a few buckets filled with potatoes from the kitchen. The potatoes are frozen but that doesn't matter. In the kitchen they also found some herbs; they roll those into cigarettes. They were safe the whole time, they didn't see any SS-men. We sit around the stove and burn the last of the wood. We smoke and make plans. We need more food, we need coal, and we need a fresh supply of unsoiled snow. I feel stronger today. I promise I will join one of the Frenchman on his foraging trip tomorrow.

Gunshots. A soldier shoots at looters. The sound of an explosion, probably a hand grenade. Again a glow over the barracks.

Dead bodies in the courtyard. Whether they were shot by the soldier or died of illness and exhaustion, we do not know. I say Kaddish for them, wordlessly. The others don't go for old Aramaic prayers. "We're no Jews, huh?" says one of the Frenchmen.

That even the crows, connoisseurs of carrion, delay their feasting on the camp's dead bodies for a full two days after the ovens have been extinguished—this says a lot. The crows remind us of the SS—their suit of feathers so black that it sucks the light off things. One of those birds picks at the window, right next to my ear. It has fresh red blood on its beak. Maybe one day we will see and hear other birds?

Birds live in high places, and they see everything. Birds are the favorites of the g*ds. Of course they stay away. There is nothing for them here, in the collective cloaca of humanity. This is good for us too. Birds that sing—the thought is almost unbearable. Birds that fly and flap their wings and soar to the skies—that is an unfathomable mystery. Such beauty does not belong here.

My first trip outside, and I immediately slip on the ice and twist my ankle. I have to be carried back inside. The others look at me with mistrust. Am I feigning my injury? I'm glad when my ankle starts swelling. It hurts, but at least it shows that I am honest, not some freeloader.

More news. A shooting took place in the kitchen of the SS-quarter. The zealous soldier finished the job by blowing up the kitchen with a hand grenade. Who was this man? Why did he come back? Why did he do this to us, motivated by what hatred? Or did he just shoot out of a sense of duty?

Our foraging team has penetrated into the part of the camp where they kept the English prisoners of war. It was a long haul through the snow and ice. In their buckets they carry coal and real cigarettes and books—not to read, but to burn in the stove. They also found canned food and a box with playing cards. They empty the buckets and go back outside to fill them with snow.

Cards! I sit up and reach out with greedy fingers. It requires some persuasion before the French agree to give them to me; they want to play poker. My hands are too cold and the calluses too thick to perform any prestidigitation, but I show my bunkmates a few variations on guess-the-card, as well as a trick of my own design, of which I'm very proud—the cards never leave the hands of the volunteer, and yet the selected card moves through the deck, driven by the random numbers that a second volunteer whispers in the ear of the first. My cellmates scratch their heads. How does he do that? I beam. I am no longer a pariah, a weird little Jew.

Later that evening I win a game of poker, and they accuse me of cheating. I do not deny it. Cheating has become second nature to me now—perhaps I did cheat, without realizing it. I am, however, an outsider again.

Cadavers are strewn across the spaces between barracks. On their bellies and backs the crows triumph. Nobody has the strength to bury them. Anyway, how would we be able to drive a spade even an inch deep into the frozen ground?

Now, next to our barrack, one of our own lies dead.

One of the Romanians died in the night, on the floor, with a long death rattle and horrible screaming. He slept in one of the top bunks and it isn't quite clear whether he died because of his fall or whether death chased him out of his bunk. We dragged him outside. I helped, my ankle is healing. With pages torn from English detective novels I cleaned up the trail of diarrhea and blood, then I burned the paper in the stove.

We have a brief ceremony outside in the cold. Somebody puts a blanket over the man, even though we know the blanket will be stolen as soon as we step back inside. The remaining Romanians sing a song with deep resonant voices, something quintessentially Slavic and somber. After their song, I cannot contain myself: "*Exalted and sanctified . . .*"—but as soon as I open my mouth, one of the Romanians slaps me hard across the face. We don't have the same G*d. I'm sorry, I had forgotten.

•

A child's autobiographical memory starts with the story. Before it can remember anything, the child has to be able to perceive connections between events: It has to know the schemata that govern the world, it needs the skill to organize events chronologically, and it has to learn to leave out superfluous details. Memory is literature. It is condensation, schematization, and imagination. There is the past that one lives, and there is the memory of that past—not much more than a well-meant fable. What is memory? Dendrites stretch out their tentacles, the nerve endings feel their way through the brain and push glial cells out of the way. They establish the absurd near-contact that nerve cells have with each other and ejaculate their neurotransmitters into empty space. All this tickles the neuron. Sodium pumps potassium into the intercellular liquid and a wave of electricity moves through the axon. What is encoded is the connection. The structure of the brain has altered, the information density is increased just a little. Pathways that are stimulated more often remain alert; memories that are retrieved less often fade away; ultimately they will be confused with other, similar events. Because the amount of space inside the skull is limited, memories have to fight to survive. Memory is a meager attempt to hold on to something long since lost, through a wrestling match in a wet, spongy organ.

•

I stand knee-deep in the ashes of insanity. I say Katz's Kaddish as a Kaddish for Katz: "*Exalted . . . Sanctified . . .*"

Kaddish is begging, pleading.

I am saved, I am purified, I am alive.

"Kaddish is for the living," said Katz.

It helped. The fever is gone. The wound in my leg has healed, my ankle is no longer swollen. And my soul, how is my soul doing? Is my soul saved? Or at least healed?

"If you let yourself go," said Katz, "if you denounce your Jewishness, then you have in fact surrendered to the Nazis. Then they are the ones who prescribe the Law—they have become your Torah. And then, my boy, you should be ashamed!"

I look around. Suddenly I can see it. In the haze of the winter morning, in the docile eyes of the roaming cadavers, in the horrified stares of the Russian soldiers. I can see it: *the blinding exaltation.*

Or is that just the photograph in the camera in my head, suddenly getting developed?

•

It took me half a year to get back home. But what kind of home? Berlin has always had that *panta rhei*, that perpetual motion; the city reinvents itself every few years, but the changes wrought by the end of the war seemed deeper, more painful, more radical than even I had anticipated. The British and the Red Army had done a good job.

They have a lovely parable, those Christians, about the return of the lost son. Although he smells of swine and the cheap perfume of a thousand whores, a bed is prepared for the prodigal child; he is offered expensive jewelry and tailored clothing; a fattened calf is killed and grilled.

That wasn't entirely the case for us, the Jews. What happened to the world? The changes seemed so radical. Women haul rubble away in wheelbarrows. The Tiergarten is naked soil: The seeds of carrots and cabbage are waiting in the ground, potato spuds are being planted. With nothing but shovels, people dig building pits for the new colossuses. All this is a sign of renewed trust in the future.

What about the past? There are border crossing posts at the strangest locations, where there was never a border before. Our old street is unrecognizable. Half the

•

I will never see Stella again. I go to the old cemetery. It's no longer there. The gravestones have been destroyed or hauled away. Here and there I can still read a fragment (*Die Stunden unseres Lebens sind eingezeichnet in den Sand der Wüste*). I put a stone on the one grave that's still standing, Moses Mendelssohn's. I find the grassy field where the guards played soccer with a skull. I look up at the window of the Altersheim where Stella must have stood. She isn't there. She is somewhere else. But where? What would I do if I ever saw Stella again? I would throw my arms around her, that much I know, but would I embrace her or would I strangle her?

I will never see Stella again, except in a picture in the newspaper, her head shaved and covered with a shawl. She looks like an old woman. Her eyes are empty. She is a different kind of survivor.

There is no room for me in my own house. I, newly minted son of Israel, get myself registered with the *Gemeinde*, in the eastern sector of Berlin. There are new, impressively large ledgers, the kind of bound volumes used in accounting firms to record credits and debits. The size of the books is impressive, but the pages are mostly blank. Our balance is paltry: So few have returned from the camps. The office of the *Gemeinde* is a gossip mill. I hear the story of a man who made the long journey home only to shoot first his wife and then himself.

No, I do not want to emigrate. How would my name sound in English? What would it be in Hebrew? I grew up here, I want to stay and see how the town raises itself from the rubble. "You hopeless idiot," says the lady of the *Gemeinde*. There is tenderness in her voice when she says it, but she does say it.

I travel to the ruins of the theater. I dig up my books. An American soldier points his gun at me; he orders me to put the books down. Looting is forbidden. I put the books in his hand and start to pray, "*Sh'ma Yisrael Adonai Elohaynu Adonai Echad.*" The man drops his gun. He too is Jewish. I lead us both in prayer: "*Exalted and sanctified . . .*" When we're done, he hands me back the books.

I rent a room in the eastern part of town, in a building pockmarked by grenades. In the east, the antifascist sentiment runs strongest: Revolution is brewing. Marx said that thought makes the man. I can identify with that idea; Marxism was, after all, my father's religion, and wasn't the importance of the historical situation the core of Katz's ideology? Moreover, in the east the spirit of the Jews still roams the streets, even though almost all the Jews are gone. At night, the bars and the streets fill with the quintessence of the Jewish mindset: A whole generation of students and workers double as troubled Jobs, a race of wrestlers-with-angels and dreamers-of-ladders, incurable pessimists who nevertheless still think something can be done. To shrug your shoulders and yet grow wings. They dress in black turtlenecks and wrap long scarves tightly around their faces, to keep the cold out and their emotions in. These youngsters are like the best of my people, hopeless romantics, terminally unlovable, rejected by life if only because they rejected life first. I feel at home in the east. And a man needs to dream, right? And hope? Keep hope alive? Even though we know the dream won't come true? The important thing is the thing itself, the act of faith, and faith is everything.

What else did I expect? I was a prideful Jew; I felt that I was different, that I was chosen. Now the world will know how this feels, and the world will not forget our suffering.

Who am I kidding? It is as if the Holocaust never happened. The world, just a little bit shaken up because of this little bit of war, goes right on—business as usual. As if Hitler and his ilk had done no more damage than a biker riding though a cloud of mosquitoes. The neighbor's wife does laundry, the pigeons coo on the roof. Nobody is waiting for us, nobody let the geraniums wither in their window boxes out of grief, none of these Christians has taken the time to say a prayer for us. It will take a long and arduous judicial struggle to get our property back. In Auschwitz-I, Catholic nuns move into a building at the edge of the camp, the building that used to be a movie theater before the war—it was slated to become an officer's mess for SS-officers. What are they doing there? The pope beatifies Edith Stein—a Jewess who became a Carmelite nun and died in the camp. She is, they say, a martyr. They never mention that she didn't die as a martyr for the Catholic faith, but that Christians killed her because of her race.

The right to even be here, the right to sit on a bench in a park in the city where I live—it is a right that will never again will be self-evident and unproblematic. When the universe ended for all those men, women, and children, the universe also continued. Auschwitz, Belzec, Bergen-Belsen, Buchenwald, Chelmno, Dachau, Dora/Mittelbau, Drancy, Flossenburg, Gross-Rosen, Janowska, Kaiserwald/Riga, Koldichevo, Majdanek, Mauthausen, Natzweiler/Struthof, Neuengamme, Plaszow, Ravensbrück, Sachsenhausen, Sered, Sobibor, Stutthof, Theresienstadt, Treblinka, Vaivara, Westerbork—these were not eschatological times, this was no Armageddon. The world survived, much like the mosquito cloud survives the biker. The people just disappeared. Their houses, their cities are still standing, more or less. It's just that other people have moved in; others who survived the war with much more ease.

Maybe, I wonder, there is a need for synthesis. Shall I write my story? I won't be the first, but there is a genuine need for contemplation, for a new light to be shed—just like lovers separated by fate need a thousand comforting variations on the story of the deep waters keeping two royal children apart; just like seekers need a thousand revisions of the myth of the untraceable Origin. This is the ultimate story—Auschwitz, Treblinka, Theresienstadt. This is the ultimate myth of the end times, the story nobody ever dared to write, except for Hitler, who wrote it in bodies that became cadavers; the final story, the story that closes the story of the universe, not the way a Victorian novel ends, with all plotlines converging nicely in an elegant conclusion, but, on the contrary, a story that unravels: The universe dies in the chilly silence of a cold tiled room, in the chilly mouths of lead pipes from which an indifferently hissing purple whirlwind flows—the chilly screams get muffled; blood cools slowly, slowly, *slowly* in the arteries; and then there is nothing but silence.

No more poetry after Auschwitz? Often I think: Poetry is the only art form still allowable. Every theory, every fiction, every human drama lost its power on that tile floor. The only thing still permissible is to dress our daily, unforgivable delights in the deceit of a dishonestly rarified language.

I am lucky. I cannot be identified on sight. I wasn't long enough in the camp. Many of us never shed certain habits: They eat their food fast with their backs against the wall and lick their spoons feverishly, as if this is the last bit of food they will ever receive. They read the sunset for signs of approaching frost or snow or rain—it might determine whether or not they will make it to the morning. I am lucky, I can't be identified on sight. I will be able to start a new life.

History shrivels. We should have learned from Auschwitz. But even Satan, He who danced in the flames that crowned those chimneys, shrinks over the course of the centuries. From the bright angel of the Talmud he turns into a conniving voyeur and then into a clever thief of hearts. Would He still be able to fulfill His ambition, Hitler's ambition: to stop the stars in their course, to bring down those great balls of fire? *Heute die Welt, morgen das Sonnensystem*?

The years pass. Evil turns into a court jester; the wounds are easily forgotten. Hitler becomes an empty metaphor—"Idi Amin is a second Hitler," "Saddam Hussein is a second Hitler," "Mobutu is a second Hitler." Hitler's memory gets tamed, and the Nazi years become a story. Even in the Staatsoper you can see soldiers on stage in the long gray coats of the Wehrmacht; caps with a death's-head on them can be spied in the wings of the theater. Is the world evil, or is it just idiotically forgetful and basically g*dless?

That evil is the only reality, that happiness and kindness are just a thin veneer over a reality that tortures and terrorizes and inspires nothing but despair: This is the only verifiable truth about the human condition. There is no other. That should have been the lesson learned from the war, the lesson both Jews and Christians could agree on. *Quod non*. What can I do but say Kaddish?

•

The study of the history of Judaism implies travel. De Heer points at his bookshelves. He gets up with a sigh, and fetches a thin book bound in black leather. He opens it to the last page; it must be a Hebrew text. I notice for the first time that the wall of books also separates the living room from the kitchen, and that this wall is made of glass. Every time he takes out a book, he opens up more space. Every time he takes out a book, he makes a path for light to shine through, he makes the apartment larger.

The secondhand bookstores in Berlin are filled with Judaica. Cheap, too: People who move into new homes find these books stacked in boxes in the attic, stuffed in cracks between the floorboards or hidden inside closets. They can't read them; they carry them to the bookstore and make a few pennies.

"I know," says De Heer. "What happened to me is the most terrible thing that can happen to a person, and what do I do? I grab a book! How Jewish! In any case, it's something to do. I read, and sleep invades my eyes. And although every book is a grave, and surely these books here are, each of those books contains plenty of life too. Each of these books testifies: Hitler did not win.

"There was a time when I was afraid that my wall of books would tumble—how strong and secure is an East German *Plattenbau*? Can the foundation hold all this weight? I was afraid I would be buried underneath that pile of books, that I would get crushed and suffocate. I no longer worry. I no longer think books will be the death of me.

"My father was a violinist. I listen to a solo piece by Bach, the most German of all composers, a piece full of order and regularity, played by Heifetz, the most Jewish of all violinists—playing with the fleeting precision of a small blowtorch. That kind of stuff connects our cultures. It isn't much, but there isn't anything else.

"I used to be jealous of the people who walked underneath my window in

DAEDALUS

A man with an axe. A man with an axe should be posted at the door of every man visited by happiness—to remind him how much sorrow there is in this world; to remind him that no matter what abundance of peace and love and understanding may be his, disaster will invariably strike—a sickbed, poverty, or cooling love— and that he will have to face those days of hardship on his own, that nobody will come to his aid, just like he himself shunned his neighbor when his neighbor was visited by a stroke of bad luck; just like he himself didn't lend his ear to those struck by misfortune.

What might that axe be? What form should it take?

An axe in the shape of a story perhaps. A story about Auschwitz. An axe to cut through the smugness; an axe to decapitate any happiness that is too-good-to-be true. An axe, perhaps, in the shape of a hammer—the kind of hammer, for instance, that comes with a sickle.

·

She sleeps.

She is so close—less than a room away.

She sleeps.

Nothing separates us besides a roomful of air, some eiderdown and cotton, and a large measure of perhaps unnecessary self-restraint.

Her name is like a galaxy. She swears it's her real name. She swears she was conceived under the influence of a dark constellation, in a town shrouded in a permanent fog. She swears there is no name that would suit her better; she swears this name reflects her nature perfectly. Her mother gave her this name. "No name suits me better than the name my mother gave me," she says. "My mother made a name for herself. A beautiful name, but not as beautiful as the name she gave me. My mother's mother never gave her a name. My mother's mother gave birth to my mother. Then she let the murderers take my mother away. My mother's mother carried my mother inside her womb, yet she never embraced my mother in her heart."

This is what she tells me.

Heavy stuff.

She speaks of a father she never met, a father whose name even her mother doesn't know, a father who might not even be aware of her existence. Then she speaks of a grandfather, her mother's father; a grandfather whose name she does know, but nothing more—until today, he was nothing but an untraceable trace.

Her grandfather's name is Paul Andermans.

She produces a photocopied document from her wallet—like a man, she wears her wallet in the back pocket of her jeans. It is a contract, an Acknowledgment of Paternity signed by both the mother and the father, as well as by a witness. The father's name is Paul Andermans; I can't make out the mother's name or the name of the witness—the names are censored, perhaps on the original, with broad strokes of black ink. (Who did that?) The document boasts many stamps: the lightning runes of the SS, a proud hammer-and-sickle, a cross that was likely virulently red but has turned gray in the act of photocopying, the hammer-and-compass of communist Germany, and all kinds of variations on *Vertraulich*—Confidential—in a wide variety of fonts. The baby girl was born in 1944. The document declines to provide her with a name.

This is a strange coincidence. The daughter of that baby girl visits Potsdam for some undisclosed reason. She decides to have dinner in the Mensa. She picks up a copy of the university newspaper *Putz*, just something to read while she eats. In that newspaper she reads my name: "*visiting Scholar aus Belgien*." She turns hot and cold at the same time. She's found Andermans. She thinks about it, seated at that table; she sits and ponders until the Mensa closes, until the cashier finally kicks her out. Her mind is made up when she passes the guest house on her way to the bus stop. This then is where he lives, her grandfather, the man who conceived her mother in an SS stud farm. Finally she will meet him. She rings the bell, but she gets no answer. She waits. She goes for a walk. She returns and rings the bell gain. Still no answer. Another walk. Increased anxiety. Then her meltdown. Then I appear. I am indeed Paul Andermans, but alas: I am just a few years older than she is. And then she learns that the visiting scholar has an uncle. That uncle may well be her grandfather. There is no way to verify this statement, because as far as Paul Junior knows his uncle died in the war—he went missing in action sometime in the spring of 1945; he certainly never made it back home. She learns that Andermans' signature on the paternity document might very well be the man's last sign of life.

"The man left for the front? And was killed? He probably never even met his daughter?"

I spread my palms and shrug my shoulders. I know nothing. I can't help her.

"She was deported to Auschwitz, you know. She was less than a year old."

I raise my eyebrows.

"For no reason at all. At least, no reason other than the color of her skin. Just a shade darker than was acceptable for an Aryan baby."

She inspects me, that woman of stardust, her gaze travels all the way from my head to my toes. "She can hardly have inherited that skin tone from her father."

"What happened to her in Auschwitz?"

"She was one of Mengele's little angels. One of the good doctor's experiments."

"How did she . . . ?"

"It was late in the war. They found her in a barrack, all alone, naked, wrapped in a blanket. This document was pinned to the blanket. It ended up in the Stasi archives, as you can see. Why the East German secret service took an interest in her, I don't know. Maybe it's just that every document eventually found its way into the Stasi archives."

"It is a miracle she survived."

"Indeed. Few of Mengele's children escaped the flames."

"Then it's also officially a miracle that you're alive."

"Absolutely," she says. "It's a miracle that I'm alive. My existence is a marvel."

Somehow she doesn't sound very convincing. She has repaired her mascara and repainted her eyes during a brief session at the sink; at her request, I politely averted my eyes while she did this.

She folds up the document and puts it back in her wallet; she slips it behind her ID card.

A night of miracles. The woman yawns and says, "It's time for bed, don't you think?" I nod silently; she kicks off her boots. Then she peels off her jeans and lifts her sweater over her head, and these are earnest and businesslike gestures. When she is done undressing for the night, she wears a Nine Inch Nails T-shirt, a black pair of men's boxer briefs, and a pair of black ankle socks. The-miracle-that-she-is rolls itself into a ball on the spare bed that serves as my makeshift couch. She is a little hedgehog without quills, and that little hedgehog now inquires whether there might perhaps be an extra blanket for her to use.

An extra blanket, sure. I tuck the little hedgehog in.

Then I pull my chair next to the bed. I watch her sleep. Her sleep is like Mefista's—fast and furious dreams experienced with complete surrender. Her neck and throat are white and smooth like Nefertiti's, and beautifully slender: a pedestal of alabaster elegantly supporting all those memories.

Her story sounds extravagant to my ears, but also strangely moving. What a densely knit web of circumstances brought her to my room! She breathes with superb timing; I stand and stare. My eyes trace the outline of her body beneath the blanket. I am looking for something that might remind me of him, my uncle. Something that might remind me of myself—after all, I look like my uncle, or so I've been told. The slender neck is all we share. A foot and a calf peek out from under the blanket, the foot is somehow bare, and I want to kneel down to raise the sole of that foot to my lips, the foot that carried her here. If I had nail polish, I would restore the black of her toenails; if I had a file, I would scrape the calluses off the balls of her feet. That small foot with its pointed toes is so utterly different from the flat duck's paws I inherited from my father. Her nose, narrow and straight, looks Swedish or Norwegian or Danish to me, an interpretation belied by the fire that smolders in the smoky almonds of her eyes. Her irises, I remember, are almost black, with a few golden flecks that lighten up the circles of darkness. She is so completely un-Flemish. Her fingers as well are too slim to be molded in the polders. Her skin shows no trace of freckles, quite unlike my dad's or mine. Her lips are a startling shade of chocolate, in complete harmony with the color of her eyes.

Even more astounding is that my first impression was correct. I do know her; I have always known her. Is this possible? Every night she visits me. This young sleeping woman—I dream of her every single night. Is it possible that this most intimate experience, the fantasy woman that lights up every boy's heart, is a mere foreshadowing, an announcement, a reverse echo bouncing through a Feyman universe? I never believed in love; I never believed that love was more than a coincidence, a random ripple in the living fabric of the cosmos, a gravitational wave pulling two random dots together. My view on the matter is decidedly unspiritual: No matter how holy my love may feel, my lover is not my destiny; no mystic higher power has brought her to my side for all time. I have nothing but contempt for the idea that two people, and exactly *these* two people, are meant for each other—that is nonsense, nothing more than sentimental garbage.

But now: Look at those eyes. Look at those eyes. I have always known these

urban night that is half Jack Daniels, half full moon. This is the light of Caligari, the dusk of the doomed, and oh, how hushed is the room when the very last of the silver sequins spins to the floor in the very last of the meager light, how incredulous when in that dreamlike light the discarded strips of white paper suddenly stir to life, again twisting and turning and arching and lurching—soundlessly they slide up the trunk of the baobab, snakes thirsty for blood and hungry for murder.

A sharp scream from the assistant and SIGNORELLI—who had somehow ended up fast asleep on a corner of the stage—jolts upright. He wipes his eyes with big theatrical gestures. When he finally looks up, he is stunned by the woman's predicament. In mock panic he runs around the stage until he stumbles over the pillow he slept so soundly upon—a heating pillow with an obscenely flapping electric cord. A sudden idea strikes the magician: He brings the cord to his mouth and blows and blows, and under his breath the pillow grows, and the magician quickly climbs on top; he rides the gigantic balloon as it keeps expanding and expanding. He throws away his jacket and tears the shirt off his body—cross-legged and in a gold-stitched vest, De Heer travels to the starry ceiling. Out of thin air he plucks a gold turban and out of the turban comes a plastic pen—when the magician puts it to his mouth, the sound of a snake charmer's flute is heard. Weak spots and bumps now appear on the pillow, latex is stretched to it breaking point, and the inevitable happens: When a violent drum roll bounces off the walls, the balloon bursts—but no harm is done: The magician is seated high and dry on the back of a live elephant, its trunk ending in a gargantuan plug. The animal is visibly shaken by its sudden appearance on the stage.

The crowd applauds furiously, for with the help of the elephant SIGNORELLI is able to rescue his assistant once more and right on time too: One of the snakes was already nibbling at her toes. Back to back, the man and the woman ride the nervous gray colossus. But this is not the end of it: One clap of the magician's hands, another one of those electric pops—and in a tiny cloud of fireworks the animal's tail just vanishes. Another pop, another round of sparks, and gone are the tusks. One more and the trunk falls off. For one brief tantalizing moment, one ridiculously exciting instant, the floodlights shine on a massive oversize pig that blinks its eyelids in wonder, and then, only then—*poof!*—does the whole naked elephant disappear: It dissolves into thin air and the magician and his accomplice land on their puny asses with a firm thud—*boom!*—on the hard floor.

I am amazed. He did it! De Heer realized his lifelong dream, or rather WLAD-IMIR's: An elephant vanishes in front of a few hundred thousand witnesses—never before attempted, never before seen, unique in all of the world! When I turn to De

Heer to congratulate him on his thirty-year-old feat, he puts a finger to his lips and points at the screen. It ain't over until it's over—how true!

From the wings, three gentlemen stumble onto the stage. They wear gray-green uniforms with short pants, and sun helmets. They carry big guns too; the gents must be elephant hunters. Uh-oh! They are angry that their prey has eluded them. They brandish their weapons at the magician and his bride! And uh-oh again: When SIGNORELLI gets up from the floor to cast his spells, he stumbles and staggers and no words come from his mouth. What happened? Is he exhausted after all these magical feats? Did his fall injure some internal organ necessary for performing his tricks? Whatever the case, it's obvious that the magician's powers are fading fast. He still tries, and at first he succeeds. A snap of his fingers and the rifle of the first hunter turns into a monumental hammer. A second snap, and the second man holds a gigantic compass in his hand. But with that trick the magic is utterly exhausted. Whatever SIGNORELLI tries next—increasingly desperate finger snaps, rapid-fire incantations, commanding gestures—nothing happens, nothing helps. This would be a good moment, the television director reckons, to insert a few close-ups of the studio audience. We are treated to images of lips trembling and fingernails being bitten, to pictures of swollen eyelids and snot slowly dripping down silky chins. Then the children burst out laughing: The two disarmed hunters take up toilet paper by the armload—the snakes freed of their spell—and wind it around the magician and his assistant; they tie them to the mighty baobab. The hunters run comically around the tree (a hint of Cleese there), and roll their eyes like cartoon cannibals. With the empty paper rolls they build a wall, knee-high, around the prisoners. What follows is entirely dictated by the logic of storytelling: There is still a gun left, and so the third hunter takes aim and shoots. Twice he pulls the trigger—one ball of lead for SIGNORELLI, the other for SIGNORELLI's lover. Just then, when all seems lost, the magic returns: The paper chains fall to the floor, and magician and assistant alike spit out a silver bullet, and before they know it the hunters and their little wall dissolve in a sudden spiral of whirling white sand and the crackle of fireworks. This brings down the house. The children jump off their chairs and shout; their mothers have tears in their eyes and squirm with delight; their fathers clap and beam with the joy otherwise reserved for dramatic sporting events or political meetings. In short: Feet stomp, hand palms turn bright red, and the dome of the tent ripples with the uproar.

•

"Coffee, perhaps?" I find my glass filled with piping-hot coffee; the tea is gone. A Sonja filter balances gracefully on top of my mug, but the filter paper is dry as a bone. The toothpaste has been transformed into a tube of Swiss condensed milk. Gone are the roll of toilet paper, the pillow, and the pen—no longer needed. The concertina and the razor are still on the table. I return my attention to the television screen.

The applause has finally died out—it took a while. A little clown in bright makeup now climbs onto the stage from the orchestra pit. He is accompanied by a bunch of mock-cheerful midgets disguised as mushrooms. There's no magic here: The costumes are clearly made of papier mâché, the humpbacks are strap-on packs imported from Babelsberg, and the little dance is awkward at best. The midgets recite a bad poem, some rambling randomness about a mushroom:

> *Pilze von nur geringem Werte*
> *Sind die bekannten Ziegenbärte!*
> *Genießbar wohl, doch beim Genuß*
> *Den echten Pilzen ein Verdruß*
> *Und recht:*
> *Ein Pilz der Haltung wahrt*
> *Trägt einen Hut und keinen Bart . . .*

(Allow me to translate: The coral mushroom may look nice, / But it has neither bite nor spice. / Fry it, it still won't taste good / And we all know it never could: / A mushroom that's well-engineered / Wears a hat, and not a beard.)

An angry red head appears in a corner of the screen; it is SIGNORELLI. The loudspeaker crackles and zigzag lines shoot across the screen, then the screen turns black. A hairy technician's hand places a sign in front of the lens: The connection with the studio has been interrupted; the television audience is advised to be patient—the broadcast will resume ASAP. The sign is dated June 16, 1961.

I look at the coffee table: The razorblade has gone.

•

Not every city is built upon rock. Some, like Amsterdam or Brussels, float on top of a swamp; others, like Paris, have a beach hidden underneath the pavement. If not for its buildings, Berlin would be a sandy desert. In the nineteenth century, many an Italian or English mail-carriage tourist would wonder in his travel diary who or what decided to erect a whole g*ddamn city in the middle of the Brandenburg

Heath. (The answer is that the city started as a German bridgehead into the Slavic lands in the thirteenth century.) Sand is a sure sign of a rough climate; of an arid, dry, blustery life.

The sand is Berlin's deepest secret. The city may look grand and solid, but this is no more than a superstructure, a gypsy camp of stones floating above a naked dustbowl. It is hard to imagine that a city like this could be stable. If it isn't constantly revised and reinvented, not continuously rebuilt, it will evaporate. And let us not forget that sand moves on the wings of the wind. Everything that is buried in sand will sooner or later be uncovered. By definition, a city like Berlin cannot conceal its secrets for very long.

Every desert needs its bearded, half-mad prophet, a crazy man who doesn't fully realize what he's saying, but still needs to say it—he is on a mission from G*d. On June 15, 1961, a bearded prophet emerged from the Berlin desert and spoke:

> *I understand your question as follows: There are people in West Germany who want us to mobilize the construction workers of the GDR to build a wall. I am not aware of any such plans . . . No one has any intention of constructing a wall. The construction workers of our capital are mainly busy with house building and their manpower is being fully used for that.*

For prophets there is no middle way. You are for us, they say, or else you are against us. Listen up and convert and believe, or I will spit on the ground (how quickly does the dry dust suck up the dribble!), and then you better run home ASAP.

A prophet of this caliber cannot be ignored: The bearded madman is none other than the First Secretary of the Central Committee of the *Socialistische Einheitspartei Deutschlands*, the head honcho of East Germany. His name is Walter Ulbricht. Ulbricht's madness is not visible from the outside. He does not yell and shout; he does not gesticulate wildly, nor does he roll his eyes. Although his accent betrays his Saxon roots, his individual words are clear and comprehensible. The madness and the impenetrability lurk in the sequencing of the words. Construction workers? Build? Wall? Not aware?

This remarkable statement is an excerpt from a television interview. It is Ulbricht's answer to a question asked by Annamarie Doherr, a journalist working for the *Frankfurter Rundschau*. The question: "In your estimation, does the institution of a Free City of Berlin imply that the Brandenburg Gate becomes a border between states?"

Both the question and the answer are widely broadcast in both Germanies. Instantly, a small cottage industry of textual exegesis emerges. On either side of the border, self-appointed political philosophers plant their elbows on oakwood bar tables or on the Formica leaves of office desks, and set themselves the task of trying to translate Ulbricht's four sentences into simple common German. Even the Americans and the Soviets get in on the game. People talk and talk until they are blue in the face. What the hell did Ulbricht mean?

Ulbricht's is the skillful answer of a crafty politician. It may sound vague and even besides the point, but it is in reality completely clear and leaves nothing to the imagination. There are only two possible interpretations. The first possibility is that Ulbricht speaks the truth. In that case, the Secretary has heard some rumors (through the party council, perhaps, or through Moscow) about an imminent closing of the border. With his statement, he indicates that he does not believe that this will in fact happen. After all, how could it? Ulbricht has not been involved in any decision on the matter, and therefore a border closing is impossible. If Ulbricht speaks the truth, then the corollary is that someone is keeping him out of the loop, probably preparing the downfall of the old fox. Anyway, under this scenario, the border will inevitably be closed. The second possibility is that Ulbricht is lying. The idea of closing the border is indeed very much in his mind. (The "wall" he mentions is of course a rhetorical fiction, a metaphor. All exegetes on all continents agree on that point: It's simply ridiculous to think one could build a solid wall that would enclose the whole German Democratic Republic.) Under this hypothesis, Ulbricht uses the interview to test the waters. How strong is the resistance of the people of the GDR to this idea? What he says is clear: No wall will be built. But of course the workers and farmers in the GDR hear what they are meant to hear: Somewhere in the hierarchy, somebody has suggested building a wall. Bold ideas like these have a tendency to linger in the mind—both the mind of the ruler as well as his subjects. The knowledge that a wall might be built allows the people an opportunity to vote on the issue—namely to vote with their feet. If the statement causes a mass exodus to Marienfelde, the West Berlin refugee center, then Khrushchev will be forced to make a decision. Either he can intervene and thereby save the GDR from obliteration, or he can give up the country. The first of those options leads logically and paradoxically (the longer the GDR resists building the wall, the more certain it is that the wall will be built) to the closing of the borders. A metaphorical wall. Causally speaking, it is then the very discourse surrounding this fictitious wall that will cause its realization, completely independent of the question whether or not somebody actually suggested the idea in a

Politburo meeting. The wall will only remain unbuilt if every GDR citizen happily remains where s/he is, or if—even more unlikely—the Soviets decide to relinquish control over German politics. In the beginning was the word, and the word shall become symbolic barbed wire and imaginary concrete.

Oh, before I forget it—you have to know that über-comrade Ulbricht has a nickname, inspired by his Lenin-beard. That nickname is Goatee—in German: *Ziegenbart*, also the German name for the coral mushroom.

•

What use is dissidence? What do openly dissenting opinions accomplish? What is the so-called courageous writing of the so-called dissidents worth, the poison-pen literature of the self-declared rebels, the verbal diarrhea of those oh-so-dangerous enemies of the government, the ones that think that texts can bring down a regime? What does it amount to? The dissidents themselves are certainly dejected and disgruntled—their writing smells of vinegar, as if their pens were dipped in their own sour piss. Their words blow through the streets like sand (what a fine, all-encompassing metaphor for the GDR-era that is!): It stings the face for a minute, then the wind dies and it's over; their words have gone, dust returned to dust. Of course we, citizens of the new Germany, love to read. We read a lot; we read anytime we get a chance. Look around you on the U-Bahn: Everybody has their nose buried in a book. Literature helps us deal with reality by helping us ignore it, doesn't it? We love to read the classics, especially foreign authors. It makes us forget that we're traveling from Pankow to Lichtenberg or from Marzahn to Prenzlauer Berg. Instead we can dream we're on a train to Paris or London, or on our way to New York City—the swaying subway car is an airplane cabin in the grip of turbulence. What we want, no, what we *need*, is not revolution, but diversion. All the highfalutin clichés of the *samizdat*, all those speculations about nothing—the only thing these embarrassingly self-absorbed essays achieve is causing some ephemeral annoyance to the pundits, a brief itch that ultimately harms nobody except the irritant who caused it. Have you ever seen a bull stung by a hornet? That's the effect I'm talking about. If only the regime weren't so vain; if only it could just ignore all those novels set in Caligula's Rome; if only it didn't get upset about novellas set in the animal kingdom; if only it didn't take all those ridiculously overlong poems about the joys of botany personally—then each of those works would be of no consequence. Now the regime's paranoia sees a heartless assault on the core values of socialism in almost every piece of writing, and somewhere in the hierarchy somebody is bound to be readying the whip. It's a self-perpetuating system, of course. Punishment does not deter the authors, however, because the only way the dissident writer knows that he exists is by the shudder that travels through the bull's body when the hornet plants its tiny sting in its torso; he measures his relative importance by the duration and frequency of the shake-up. But apart from that: Words are words, words, words; no riots are incited and our daily lives don't improve one bit. Dissident writing is a supreme form of arrogance: a flood of words, diarrhea, like I said—it may flood the pasture, but the bull itself stays safely on its hoofs, elevated high above the shit.

I admit that dissident writing is good for one thing: It supports the local economy. It brings money into your favorite café—and a lot of money too. Reading makes you thirsty, and you need someone to discuss what you've read with. It doesn't change anything, but it makes the beer flow.

That's the way *I* think about it, anyway.

Certainly now. Less than twenty-four hours have passed since Ulbricht's mysterious statement and already my colleagues have their jokes about the leader ready. They've built and destroyed a fake wall; they had a stupid nursery rhyme written and performed. What does it have to do with me? Absolutely nothing, and so I do what I always do: I head over to my usual watering hole and I sit alone at the bar.

I shake my head. What were they thinking? They want to use our television show *Mosaik* as counter-exegesis, as a guerilla media outlet for post-Marxist dialectic opposition? Give me a break! It's a television show for toddlers, for Pete's sake. *Mosaik* is a television show for tykes!

Here I am then, on the evening after the broadcast. Look around you, my dear friend; this is where I like to hang out: A medium-sized *café chantant* on Kollwitzplatz with a small stage and live music and dancing-girls, and tonight—like every night after the broadcast of the program that's made me as famous and as rich as a non-apparatchik in the German Democratic Republic could ever hope to be— I have only one goal in life: to get drunk as completely as is humanely possible.

I am close to forty years old.

I don't feel too good. I don't sleep as well as I used to. I have bones that ache in the morning, and I need more and more coffee to face the looming gloom of the day. And when the day is done, I need more and more alcohol to help digest its utter uselessness. My joints crack when I sink into my makeup chair and G*d knows I need the glue-on mustache and the brown pancake make-up and the lipstick and the eyeliner—I need all the disguise I can get, these days, to feel even remotely human. Next to the mirror there's a hook for a straight razor. The hook is bare; I shave at home, and with a safety razor. The naked open *Rasiermesser* of the stylist inspires nothing but anxiety. On the table in front of me, the Moccadur machine spews its vile liquid into a glass canister, and I sniff that cloud of Cuban import coffee as if it were opium vapors. In the fridge a bottle of Goldi brandy is waiting for me, as well as a bottle of vile Vita-Cola to mask the former beverage's taste. All these disguises of the body and the mind, all these dialectics of poison and antidote—and at what price? Do they postpone the rotting of my soul for even a second?

Indeed, there is life after Auschwitz, I think on such evenings. But a happy life it ain't.

We opted for a collective disguise, we, the circus act of *Mosaik*. In the spirit of German romanticism we reinvented ourselves as a troupe of joyous Italians, a big nest of siblings or kissing cousins or something like that. We all live in one big trailer and we all sleep (do we live in a collectivist society or what?) in the same big bed under the same humongous quilt comforter. Mister Weisz—a master of ceremonies for a variety of traveling circuses before the war—calls himself Signor Bianco. Our youngest member, Hasenclever—he wears a curly pink wig and plays deaf-and-dumb—becomes Kluger Hans: Hansie Smarty-Pantsie. His revolutionary bride—I don't think I ever knew her real name—is called Bianca. I thoroughly enjoy throwing knives at her; one day I hope that something will go seriously wrong with the industrial-strength electromagnets in the wooden board behind her back. We wear fake mustaches, we comb gallons of pomade through our hair, we adopt funny accents; the little kids love us. We can hear it when we walk past the city's playgrounds: Just like we do, Young Pioneers wish each other "*Gutem-oRRRRken*" and bid farewell with a "*Ciao bellllisime!*" while they graciously lift their little scout's hats and foppishly wave their little blue neckerchiefs. Hasenclever and Bianca consider themselves the court jesters of the GDR; they fancy that our television work is an opportunity to "playfully examine the rituals and symbols of societal life in the East." Yes, they put quotation marks there too, bending their disgusting little fingers in the air for emphasis.

"Court jesters?" I say. I bring up the fact that we perform our tricks in front of the whole nation, not just the inner circle, and not at some sumptuous royal banquet, but after the bromidic stop-motion adventures of Pittiplatsch, Schnatterinchen, and their lusty dog Moppi. "Playful?" I object, and I accuse the counter-revolutionaries-in-training of a form of protest that is nothing but a fashion statement. To protest is exactly what you are supposed to do if you want to be admired in the hip bars where they sell Western liquor—and that's the only reason they do it: to earn themselves a daily free sip of single-malt Scotch.

Ah, the look in Bianca's eyes when I say things like that. Her pupils glaze over, her fingers arch around an imaginary trigger. When the revolution finally comes, her eyes tell me, when imagination is in power at last, we will banish you from our big quilt. The slut! Sometimes when we're filming one of our sweet bed scenes, she grabs a hold of my smashed-up balls and squeezes so hard that tears spring to my eyes, and I need to avert my face from the camera. Yes, when the revolution comes, on Red Friday or Black Sunday or whatever it will be called, rest assured that they will put me up against the wall and pull down my pants: They'll make me die mooning the new leaders—when the glorious dawn of the revolution comes!

That is why I drink, and why I drink alone. I drink to the inevitability of a bloody future, a future I don't want to face sober. This latest bit of cleverness on the part of my co-workers, the quick insertion of some ridiculous, politically inflammable material—the cardboard wall, the dim-witted poem, the dancing mushrooms—how foolish was that? Does Smarty-Pantsie really think his silly spiel will mobilize the masses? I still hold my old Jewish belief that every man's back is just strong enough to carry the wood for his own pyre, enough wood to burn himself as a sacrificial offering for the g*d of his choosing.

How insulting too, this latest stunt. Insulting to me.

This should have been the evening of my greatest triumph. An elephant, a whole fucking elephant, a complete pachyderm, tail, trunk, tusks and all, a four-ton mammoth, vanishes in front of a live audience. Broadcast nationwide on live television. Not just vanishes—the g*ddamn animal disappears by bits and pieces. No screens, no mirrors (okay, not a *lot* of mirrors), and with the house lights on. It took me years, years of pondering, years of planning, and years of training patient Krishna, the elderly ex-dancing queen of the state circus.

I performed the trick, but I might as well not have bothered. Nobody will talk about it. All they'll talk about in the bar, at the dinner table, and around the coffeepot at the office, will be Hasenclever's foolhardy political stunt, and the interruption of the broadcast.

•

Anybody who works for television knows where they can find me after work. It won't be long then before the Stasi, the secret service, will make its entrance, two clay-colored men in long clay-colored overcoats. The big band—by this time of night slimmed down to a quintet—will keep on playing and work their way through the popular tunes of the day with growing despair, anxious to drown out the ruckus in the barroom. That's what I like about *Zum Kastanienbaum*: It reminds me of my days in Rumpelpeterchen's theater. Though I can't play cards here—the customers all know me from television, they recognize me even without mustache and hair grease; they know I know my way around cards. Never again will I be able to play a game of poker, at least until everybody has forgotten my face—which is unlikely, given how often they rerun our show. I sit and drink and turn down a couple of indecent proposals. I've gotten used to this kind of attention over the years; I do the brushing-off wearily, but politely: I make a few quick jokes in my fake Italian accent and sign my name on the back of the woman's shopping list. The more I drink, the easier the jokes come.

I watch the spectacle on stage: A few Russian whores too old and worn-out to spend their evening hanging around the Fountain of the Friendship Among Peoples gyrate somnolently to the nonexistent beat of some patriotic string piece by Brahms or Mahler. It's cold out, and although you can make more money by sucking off some horny sailor in a back alley by Alex, it's much more comfortable to shake your tits in a shady pub like this. And that also makes me sad. When one of the hookers approaches the table, I slip a ten-mark note inside her garter, and then I wave her off. Leave, okay? Go away, piss off. There's no more schnapps? I drank it all? Give me a glass of that dreadful Rotkäpchen Grand Mousseux then. What shall we drink to? To the collapse of the thought police? To an early heart attack for Ulbricht? To humanity? To—ha! ha!—the future? Let us drink, bartender, my dear friend, let us drink to the past, the glorious past!

Well, there will come a time when I will have to leave this bar.

If not under my own steam, then supported by two plainclothesmen.

•

A man with an heavy accent approaches me. He proposes to tell me a story in return for a cigarette. I promise him a whole pack of F-6s, if he only makes it brief. *Oy vey*, a story from the shtetl. There are Jews again in East Berlin, and they all find me—they have their Jewdar on.

The story is about two Polish towns separated by many miles. One town is rich and has developed quite a taste for sin. The townspeople built themselves an achingly beautiful synagogue with a nicely sculpted Ark. Inside that Ark an antique Torah is kept. Nobody knows exactly how old it is. Old, *ja*? Very old. How old? From Moshe's time, *ja*? And although the sinfulness of the town is kept indoors and out of sight, the Lord G*d looks deep inside a man's heart, and when the Torah is passed around during the Shabbat service, the letters tremble for fear of brushing too closely against those awful sinners.

The inhabitants of the second town are poor as dirt. They have a tiny synagogue and their Ark is empty. The congregation is simply too poor to afford parchment and the services of a scribe. And yet they scrimp and save, because an Ark needs a Torah. They buy a bunch of sheepskins from a traveling salesman and they bring in a cheap scribe from Lodz—not a very good one, one who likes to hit the bottle and so doesn't have a very steady hand. The man sews the pieces of sheepskin together and he has a good stiff drink with the *rebbe*, and after that he gets tired. When he gets to his cottage, he lies down next to the open scroll and starts snoring.

At midnight, the scribe wakes up. A strange glow illuminates the room. The window is suddenly blown open and letters fly inside, a stream of letters, one after the other. The letters dive for the table where the scroll is spread open and they arrange themselves on the parchment, one after the other, each in its proper place. The writer, drunk with wine and sleep and religious awe, falls to his knees and presses his forehead into the dirt and shuts his eyes tight. When he opens them again, the glow has gone and the window is closed and the scroll on the table is black with letters and words, sentences and stories, and the scribe begins to read, and when he establishes that the scroll is complete and that it contains the totality of the Law—from the creation of the world to Moshe's death—he puts on his sandals and runs out, yelling and screaming and waking people up to tell them of the miracle. And the townspeople pile into the cottage to see the scroll, and they too fall to their knees in amazement. And the inhabitants of the first town, they are wide awake, because their rabbi heard noise in their temple and saw a light in their Ark—and they too are staring at a scroll of parchment in amazement, except that their roll is barren and empty.

The inhabitants of the poor town are very proud of their Torah, and when it's carried around the temple, the faithful push each other away to touch it with the fringes of their tallises, for this Torah, or so it is said, has healing powers.

I sip my beer and slip the storyteller the promised pack of cigarettes.

"And what's the moral of this story?" I ask. "That we're better off poor and decent?"

"No, the moral is that G*d retreats from those who need Him most."

"Thank you," I mumble. "Thank you." The man's Talmudic wisdom is completely in agreement with my own experiences on this earth. "And of course the rabbi of the poor town didn't pay the copyist one cent, I presume? G*d Himself did all the work?"

"You got it," says the man.

"Amen," I say, and I give the man an extra ten-mark note. Russian whore or Jewish storyteller, they all work at the same rate.

•

On my own steam then, out of *Zum Kastanienbaum* and into the first inkling of dawn. Not because I want to. Because I have to. The bartender wants to go to bed. I try to reason with him—I come here every week! Keep the place open, man, and I promise I'll order a beer every fifteen minutes! I'll pour it into the potted sansevierias you have lined up so nicely in front of the windows, I'll treat everyone who comes through the door to a glass of Rotkäpchen and I'll pay for each glass of that horsepiss as if it were a bottle of Veuve Cliquot! Anything you want, anything, just you keep the damn bar open. I'll come in every evening next week, dammit, cooled *Sekt* for everyone! No, the bartender doesn't want to keep the bar open. I hear him thinking, Who do you think you are, just because you have your face on television? Or maybe he's smarter than that and realizes I might not be able to keep my promise. Who knows if I'll still be a free man tomorrow?

I stumble into the dawn, feeling weak and filthy, and there they are. Finally. They follow me in the obtrusive nonobtrusive way that characterizes all cops of every era, every country, every denomination. Soon, one of them will put a hand on my shoulder and put it to me that I am quite drunk, and that it might be better for me to take a cab—and lo and behold, what a coincidence, at exactly that moment a big empty car will magically appear at the curb. They will hold the door open for me; one of the men will put his hand on my head and force it down, and I will get in, because what else can I do? One of the plainclothesmen will sit to the right of me, the other to the left. There will be no need for words. The driver knows where we are going. I know it too. We are going to Normannenstraße. The address has changed and the name of the establishment too, and the mores have softened a little—maybe—but, fundamentally, everything is the same as ever.

Everything is the same.

What made me come back to this country? The way history has ground to a halt, here. Yes, here we go: I feel a hand on my shoulder and tires wheeze softly against the curb behind me. Everything has stayed the same. G*d, I'm so glad that I'm drunk, I'm so glad they waited for me outside—I am so nicely smashed, so sheepishly calm tonight . . . so meek, so calm, so sleepy, so dull.

Here I go again, I see. I mumble. I can't help it, it always happens, at the strangest of times. Here I go: "*Exalted and glorified . . .*"

An old sentimental bore, that's what I have become.

•

The heap of ruins they call Berlin.

An airplane from Moscow lands at Tempelhof Airport on May 27, 1945. It has Walter Ulbricht onboard, as well as Wilhelm Pieck, the old veteran of the German Communist Party. Moscow is not too happy with these communist Germans. Where was the resistance against Hitler? Why did the pressure on his government cease completely in 1933? Stalin considers the whole clique a bunch of slimy ass-kissers. With the possible exception of Pieck they are all idiots. But idiots are useful; independent thinkers are the ones that cause trouble. The one he despises most, that fawning moron Ulbricht with his thin goatee and his shrill voice and his lazy accent, Stalin appoints as their leader. Ulbricht may from time to time play the part of a prophet, but Stalin will always remain his Allah.

The plane circles low over the city. Fear and shock fill the heart of the newly-crowned and airsick Ulbricht. This is the country he's supposed to rule? Where's the town? Is this some kind of joke? Did they fly him to North Africa, to the desert between Mecca and Medina? Ulbricht realizes that he may be the head rooster, but no matter how loud and proud the rooster crows on top of his dung heap, the dung heap will always remain a dung heap.

As soon as the new Leader of the People lands, things get worse. The extent of the destruction is painfully obvious. The city, once a maze, has become the map of that maze. Rubble is piled up high in the streets and the piles are taller than the buildings they came from. After all these years of cozy exile it is alienating and disorienting to hear the comrades here speak German, not Russian. That language—the language of Hitler and Göring and Goebbels and Himmler and Bormann and Hess—seems incompatible with the socialist ideal. And everybody in Berlin, even the most fervent communist, complains about what the *frontoviki* of the Red Army have done to the town. There isn't a single Berlin man who still owns a watch, not a single woman who didn't have to run away from a grinning bolshevik—and very few of these ever managed to be quicker than the soldiers. Worse, the Russian troops who rule the streets have nothing in common with the charming salon socialists from the Kremlin. They make campfires in the middle of the boulevards; free-roaming Cossack ponies nibble at the garbage that litters the sidewalks; malodorous camels stroll arrogantly through the smoking remains of the boulevards. The war has been over for almost a month, but still the city is smoldering, you still have to watch your step or your foot might land on a loaded grenade. Is this a joke? Is this a Babelsberg film set?

The citizens call the Soviets Mongols. Almost none of the soldiers actually hail from Central Asia, but the long hard march has etched their faces with the brown and gray of sun and dust; their eyes are fixed in a permanent squint that protects them from the glare of the snow and the biting wind. They do indeed look as though they crossed the Gobi Desert, or descended from the slopes of the Himalayas.

Burnt-out tanks line the side of the road and starving children dive in and out of the turrets. They live inside the tanks, it seems—the stench of urine and feces rises from gashes in the warped bellies of the steel monsters. The Leader of the People and his delegates drench their handkerchiefs in *Kölnisch Wasser* and hold them to their mouths. The reek of the rotting turds mixed with the smoke of the cooking fires makes them nauseous. Ulbricht politely refuses a bowl of cabbage soup. On their walk through the evaporated street grid they have to make way for camel-and-horse caravans, the carts loaded with whatever valuables the soldiers have been able to get their hands on: jewelry, watches, all kinds of household goods, light bulbs, kitschy paintings, and plaster busts of Hitler with the nose punched off and a mustache of real-life shit painted above his lips. The only green spaces in the city are the few remaining Jewish cemeteries, grown over with weeds that nobody dares to pick: barrenwort, thorn apple, dead nettle, hemlock, witch-grass, beggar lice.

This is Time Zero. The eyes that stare at Ulbricht from the ruins, the stares in the street—they all are cold and hungry, hungry and cold. "What are those guys doing here?" is what the stares say. "Those gents in their fine summer suits, with that smell of cologne around their heads and the scent of fine cigars on their clothes? What planet do they come from?"

It brings tears to Ulbricht's eyes. Not tears of compassion with the suffering of his People, mind you—Ulbricht is not capable of such compassion, such empathy. To Ulbricht, the People are an abstraction, a theoretical, abstract, political notion that has nothing to do with the flesh and blood and sweat that are such an onslaught on his senses. Ulbricht's tears are tears of fear and regret—the task that awaits him is overwhelming, nearly impossible to accomplish, and if he botches the job, what will his good friend Stalin say?

•

What's going on here? This car isn't one of the showy Wolga M-24s that the Vopos—the Volkspolizei, the People's police, ha!—usually reserve for jobs like this: They usually ride you to your doom in a car as big and comfortable as a hearse. It also isn't one of those boring mud-colored Trabi P-601s that everybody drives.

It's a brand-new sky-blue Citroën GT 19, an expensive French import. So what's up? Are we going sightseeing, my friends? *Ost-Berlin am frühen Morgen*? I sit pressed between two men who chew gum that smells distinctly capitalistic, and I lean my drunken head against the soft leather of the backseat. This is turning out to be quite an interesting night. As far as I can tell, we are not headed for Normannenstraße. We aren't stopping on Alexanderplatz either—we drive past the hunched cathedral, past the stately yawning columns of the Altes Museum, past the empty lot that used to be the City Palace, and then by the cracked-open dome of the Neue Synagogue. "Hey, comrades, where are we going?" I ask, but all I get for an answer is silence and the expensive aroma of peppermint extract. We leave town and pick up speed—this might be a long trip. We turn north, to the wooded suburbs. The only possibility—this is not the car of some simple policeman, this is the luxury car of a powerful man—is that we are going to the most infamous of all suburbs. To the enclave of power—to what the Berliners have dubbed Bonzograd, the plutocratic ghetto called WaldSiEDlung.

•

The tram service is interrupted. The U-Bahn tunnels are flooded. When a train leaves the station, hundreds—no—thousands of people rush out of the rubble and storm the wagons. They hang out the windows, they climb onto the roof, their hands claw at the doorknobs, their feet seek purchase on the narrow ledges of the stiles. They want to break out of the city, they want to go to the countryside, where there is still food. Every train becomes a *Hamster-Express*. Less than four years ago this was the capital of the most powerful nation on earth. The Reich reached all the way from the Ural to the North Sea; now the city that once ruled the earth is down on its luck, so poor that at dusk, when the few factories that are still working close their doors, the power shuts down. But it doesn't stay dark long: There is the flickering glow of wood fires lit to feed the body and heat the mind, and in that uncertain glow the Berliner can read his future.

Markus Wolf gets stationed at the Masurenallee, behind Bahnhof Zoo, to work for the radio station, the old *Berliner Rundfunk*, now renamed *Großdeutscher Rundfunk*. The program he puts together is pure propaganda. It is titled *A Sixth Part of the Earth*, and Markus, who goes by the alias Michael—"Mischa"—Storm sings the praises of the new superpower, the almighty Soviet Union. The program doesn't touch on the new German reality at all; it remains silent on the subject of ubiquitous rape or the fate of the German POWs held in Sachsenhausen or Buchenwald;

there's no discussion of the new German border at the Oder-Neisse line, alarmingly deep within the prewar boundaries; no topic is broached that could upset the good citizens of the newly divided empire. And although the only voice that can be heard in the German ether is that of propaganda, the populace is still ordered to hand over their radios at the nearest military post. This is a clever move. It turns listening to the radio into a forbidden fruit, and hence a highly desirable thing. Wolf's show is so dull that nobody in their right mind would tune in ordinarily, but now the masses listen.

Propaganda. Propaganda. Words and words and words. The communists plaster genitive after genitive. You are now listening to the President of the Delegation of the Presidium of the Upper Soviet of the Union of Socialist Soviet Republics. Somniferous declarations follow somniferous declarations. The Nazi propaganda was meant to arouse the masses? Well, the communists will do it differently: Their propaganda will lull you to sleep. You'll be done reading the newspaper in five minutes, and all you will have learned is that all is well with the world. You don't even have to *read* the newspaper. The picture on the front page says it all: a happy farmer seated proudly on top of her potato planting machine; an earnest-looking scientist in his white frock, holding a test tube to the light; a worker in open overalls staring intently at his punching machine.

From time to time, I browse through a school textbook. I do it to educate myself about the glorious history of our precious state. I derive joy from this exercise. These are no doubt the most boring books ever written: a near-endless sequence of party meetings, party congresses, party conferences, plenary sittings, proclamations, five-year plans, and jubilees. These books strengthen my belief that this is a land that I can live in, perhaps the only land I can live in. A land where every little peep is of historic significance, which implies that every event is swallowed by an ocean of historicity. The imperialist past—the statues of Prussian kings, the bombed-out palaces—gets carefully destroyed. The commies blow up the statues and monuments without giving them a second thought; they carry away the remains and replace them with the stylized icons of the Soviet g*ds and impersonal neoclassicist Marxist architecture. This delights me and it strengthens me in my belief in the future—namely that there won't be a future, that an eternally tedious now is ours forever. Everything that threatens to enliven the study of history—eyewitness accounts, photographs, colorful maps—is cut out of the official textbooks. Indeed, history itself gets abolished. After the creation of the SED, the Unitary Socialist Party, "a German state has been crafted whose path is determined by the character and laws of the world-historic epoch of the transition from capitalism to socialism." Ah, here is the accompanying sound effect: One after another, the sleepy heads of schoolchildren hit their wooden desks.

"The directive of the Party Meeting for the development of the People's economy was substantially exceeded and the so far most ambitious and most incisive program to enhance the life of the People has been realized." Yes-yes-yes. It is now official: we live in the greatest GDR in the world!

"Closer ties to the Soviet Union. Intensification of the revolutionary vigilance. Battle against the capitalist hold-outs in the economy. Expansion of the secret service. Fencing off of the imperialistic opponent."

Oops. This is what should have woken up those dissident souls. That heaping-up of words, that syntactic churning—it confuses, it numbs, it drowns out thinking. It's not their fault, of course, that the opposition has fallen soundly asleep.

•

"Comrade, please believe me, I am innocent. It wasn't my idea."

He waves my words aside with a flick of his hand—never mind, let it be, it's all right. The gesture is also curt—let's not lose time over this.

"No, I am serious, comrade. I did not know about their plans."

The man clears his throat. It makes me shut my mouth. Their usual tactic is to let you talk until you incriminate yourself. It's a good sign he wants to do some talking of his own. He looks remarkably chipper and lively, given the hour. Is this the time he usually starts his working day? Does he wake up before dawn to watch over town and country, his big shock of hair impeccably slicked back?

For the first time I hear his voice. "Comrade De Heer, we know all that already." A brief pause during which he peers at me intently through his heavy, horn-rimmed glasses. "We . . . took care of that, Comrade De Heer."

He lights a cigarette and stares at the plume of smoke, a bit distractedly, as if he was observing this phenomenon for the very first time: the burning of tobacco. Then he turns his attention back to me.

"You will get new colleagues tomorrow."

"Oh."

"My wife, you know?" It sounds apologetic. "She handles these things."

We are seated in armchairs of Socialist Eastern Design and the wall is decorated with the same floral wallpaper that covers a million other Berlin living-room walls; the curtains are identical to the ones in all those other million living rooms. On the coat rack by the door a pumice-colored raincoat, the kind that mystery writers like to dress their underpaid detectives in. Next to the coat a thin-brimmed felt hat in the same color. The house is nice, but not excessive. This big cheese lives the life his People live. That sky-blue limousine—its color matches the color of his eyes—is his only visible luxury.

But who is he? I recognize his face from the television news. He is a quiet, nondescript character, always a few steps behind Ulbricht, always smiling a hard-to-decode smile, as if Supreme Comrade Ulbricht has just told them all a good joke, and that joke is still running through his head—but nobody has ever accused Comrade Ulbricht of having a sense of humor. Is the man opposite me one of the powers that be, or merely the pumice-colored shadow of those powers?

"*Genosse* SIGNORELLI." The ashes of his cigarette crumble neatly in a plastic ashtray of populist design. He keeps his head cocked. His glasses sit a bit crooked on his nose, I now note. He watches me carefully. I open my eyes and empty my gaze. "*Aber Genosse!* Don't you recognize me?"

I must be radiating fear, for he raises both his hands, palms upward, in a gesture of blessing and reassurance. There is no penalty for not recognizing major establishment figures, the gesture implies. I look more carefully, I subtract the glasses, I abstract away the jacket and tie and the smooth stateliness of his haircut, and I look deep into his eyes. And then I recognize him, in a flash that is fifteen years old.

Oh my G*d!

•

I am inside a store opposite Bahnhof Zoo, at the edge of that pilfered garden of Eden. It's pretty easy to pick up a pack of cigarettes. A quick slight of hand and the cellophane pack slides coolly down my sleeve, the static electricity tugging at the little hairs on my arms.

Shoplifting is the spice in my life. I am twenty years old; I imagine where in the world I could go and what I could do. The continent lies in front of me, free and open. Every breath is a lungful of freedom. Where could I go? How about Amsterdam, the city that seems so neat and prim and proper, yet seethes so magically with inner turmoil? Brussels perhaps, the town known for its stiff and formal architecture of decay and for its rational surrealism? Or maybe I should go to New York, the metropolis at the other side of the ocean, and become a total stranger in the midst of ten million other total strangers, staring up at those colossal buildings all day, those newfangled cathedrals for the only g*d they know there, the g*d of

Money? Should I go to Hollywood? Get a small acting part as a shrewd card-playing Jew, or work as a tamer of elephants, or perhaps play the part of an action hero/ resistance fighter in some television series? Or maybe I should go to Palestine? I'm sure they can make good use of any quick-witted, able-bodied Jew they find. This is my favorite pastime: to daydream of escape. The world is my salty oyster; I am convinced that deep inside its pinkish white flesh a small piece of grit is being wrapped in pearly matter—even as we speak—just for me.

I know my lesson, the lesson learned from WLADIMIR. You always need a cover and you should never raise suspicion. I am careful: I always buy something small, for instance one of those shoddy newspapers that fall apart even as you read them. I never steal more than one pack a day. Today I slip something else inside my sleeve as well: a deck of cards, good strong prewar stock, way too expensive for me to buy. I am uprooted in my own country, my own town. This is the kind of sorrow that turns grown men into poets, but I resist that temptation. Instead, I slip the pack of cards into my sleeve. I don't know it, but with that small theft I am investing in my future.

I stay where I am, exactly because the world is so open, so wide, so ready, so much mine for the taking. The possibilities seem endless, and time stretches out endlessly too. That is what I think, anyway. I don't realize what is happening to me, what is happening inside me. That the very air that I breathe contains the city's essence—literally: bricks ground up underneath the tracks of tanks, beams turned to ashes in the cooking fires, concrete shot to dust by grenades, sandstone crumbled in the diesel fumes. Inside my body, the city rebuilds itself; inside my lungs, in my blood, in my bones, inside my flesh a new city grows, a Berlin reborn. I wander through the piles of rubble—oh, why don't we give the city a new name?—and I watch my footsteps in the dust. Am I plowing through fertile earth, or am I making a futile furrow in a pile of old ashes? I do not realize that inside me the new Berlin mixes with the ashes of Auschwitz, with the dust of the dead: The last remains of an almost extinct race, breathed in at the burning mouth of a gaping oven, finally coming home to the capital of the Reich.

That is the real reason why I stay in this city, why I *have* to stay in this city—a reason based in mysticism. Even though I, the young know-it-all, do not realize it; even though it's only now, after fifty years of grief, that I understand—after fifty years of misunderstood restlessness: I stay to say Kaddish for all those whom nobody remembers—Jews whose loved ones are dead, and now that the wind that carried their ashes has subsided, now that the river that washed away their blood has dried up, now that the genetic code of their existence has been laid bare and blown away, now they need my prayer more than ever. As long as I live in this city,

I am the humble and unknowing avatar of those dead, thereby keeping them alive in a city that was never theirs, and that could never have been theirs—the city of Berlin that is in turn only hospitable to me because the gassed and the cremated live inside me, because I carry their pain. For their sake, I bear the humiliation of still being a Berlin Jew after all that has happened. To have survived is what we call it, as if no further explanation is necessary. But *what* did we survive? We cannot give *it* a name, *it* is so fearful, so threatening, so undefined, so indefinable, so beyond analysis, it must be, *it simply must be* unintelligible—it, it, it, double Dutch, stammering, stuttering nonsense. Words trivialize. Words—every word shrinks reality. Can you compress the whole horrible truth into sound, into a breath?

The word "Holocaust"—good, we talked about this before. Holocaust is not the right word. What about that other word: "Shoah"? Shoah is a whirlwind, a big darkness that challenges the imagination, a disaster of unseen proportions, utter destruction and ruin. But what happened was not so incomprehensible, not so inexplicable. The story is simple. People murder people. When we hide that simple fact behind a veil of awe, when we drape the events with the color of mystery, when we mask the *reality* of Auschwitz, then we make the whole episode unthinkable, impossible to comprehend, an aberration of history—and by so doing we encapsulate the Shoah, we fix it in time, and thereby commit the terrible mistake of making it *repeatable*.

I repeat: It's so simple. At the end of the platform stands a man with a pointer. He points: to the left, to the right, to the right, to the left, left, left, right, left, and the words that accompany this staccato rhythm seal the fate of humanity.

It is that simple. In Auschwitz, fate pointed me to the right. Now, I force myself to take the other route, I force myself to go to the left.

It is early in the morning, early after the Hour H. Around me the city springs to life—there is no better way of putting it: The city springs to life. Berlin in 1945 is a city Frederick the Great would have loved: freshly ruined neoclassicism and skinny sniffing dogs as far as the eye can see. I walk through the streets of the old town and my stomach growls—I need some cash to buy some breakfast. I sit down on a pile of rubble and spread the cards in front of me. I play patience; from time to time I look up to admire the view, or so it seems. The jagged tower of the bombed-out church stabs at the clouds like the broken neck of a brown beer bottle. Behind the ragged silhouette there is a wide gap in the rubble, a boulevard of dust that used to be Tauentzien, the street where I lived as a child. On the corner, where half a façade is still standing with its superfluous windows intact, was the Romanische Café, where Father played the violin and drank with his painter and writer friends.

I blink. It must be a fleck of dust in my eye—these memories mean nothing to me. I wait for American soldiers with money and cigarettes in their pockets and gum in their mouths; American soldiers always have time to spare.

Here comes one. He walks this way. He sees me. Ah, a little kid sitting on top of a pile of stones with a deck of cards. How sweet!

"Shall we play a game of poker, little guy?"

"Uh? Poker? What is poker?"

Poor naïve "Amis." They believe unconditionally in beginner's luck, they truly take me seriously when I pretend that I don't know the game and that I earned those first few bucks by pure luck. It's so easy to rob them that it almost makes me feel guilty. Almost. And they even leave me with a smile—the little guy won, the little guy had some good luck coming to him. G*d, sometimes they even offer me a bar of Hershey's chocolate after I empty out their wallet.

I am "the little guy." What the hell do those stupid fat Americans know about my five-year struggle for survival, about my escape from the genocide—don't they realize that such things cut the soul right out of a young man's body and replace it, forever, with a distrustful spirit as old as the world?

A shadow walks out of the church lobby.

"Friend," says the man. His smile is so solemn that it looks plastered on his face. I know the type: a sheepish, self-possessed asshole, somebody with a message and a mission. I am his friend, sure, yeah, I am his friend.

"*Genosse*," he adds. Ah, one of the commie zealots. He puts his finger on one of the cards.

"We have a lot in common, comrade."

Oh yeah? What? Hunger? Subversion? Are we both magicians? Are you perhaps Jewish, sir?

"A game of poker, mister?" I ask. "Or would you prefer me to follow you to the public restrooms—is that what you want?"

I get a slap in the face for my frankness—unexpected, quick, sharp, refreshing. G*d, that feels good. My ears tingle and fireworks go off behind my eyelids. This is better than coffee, better than tobacco, better than those sweetish cigarettes the Amis give you after a trip to the public toilet. Better. Much more real.

It reminds me of my mother—can you believe it? It reminds me of the time when I was a little kid, sitting at the window, watching the torches dance and the people sing—the time when I first saw those stars dance inside my head.

I give the man my full attention.

•

And now that same man sits in front of me, fifteen years older. What's his function again? I rack my brain; I do not know. A colorless figure in Ulbricht's shadow. Indeed.

•

"Let us climb on stage, my dear companion, for a fine and ideologically correct display of socialist-realist magicianship!"

"Yes, indeed, let us entertain and educate the children of our fine country's farmers and workers, my dearest comrade!"

Hasenclever and Bianca make a vaudeville of our show. They are ironic, even downright sarcastic. "How can you be a socialist-realist magician?" They ridicule our business, right in the hallway between our dressing room and the stage, as if that hallway isn't bugged, as if the electrical wires carrying our voices aren't an integral part of the nerve system of the omnipresent Stasi.

"Think about it," I whisper in Hasenclever's ear. My mouth is dangerously close to his earlobe; I could simply sink my teeth into it and tear his whole ear off his skull and carry it around with me like a bloody trophy, a small victory against the romantic arrogance of the swashbuckling privateer. "Maybe one day, after you have learned the finer points of socialist magic, you might be capable of some valuable subversive-reactionary juggling?" My teeth almost touch his cheek. Ah, the temptation to bite! "And if you don't like it here, *Mensch, jeh doch bloß nach drüben . . .*" The eternal exhortation: If it's so bad here, why don't you just go to the other side?

Hasenclever turns his ear away and he shouts, loud and triumphantly: "Maybe that's exactly what we're doing, you old fart!" And he scurries up the stairs to the stage. For good luck, he grabs a handful of blond Bianca's tiny tush, and she swiftly returns the favor. So this is their escape plan? Being booted out of the country as heroes of the counter-revolution? How ridiculous!

•

I am dead tired. It can't be later than six in the morning. My interviewer of course is wide awake. "Tell me the truth, *Genosse* De Heer. What did you hope to accomplish with that . . . remarkable . . . performance of yours?"

Optimism is the key to socialist realism. And isn't optimism the main ingredient of every magic show? Isn't therefore magic the socialist-realistic art form par excellence?

·

"We need lies, my young friend." The man's arm sweeps over the surrounding catalog of ruins. My ear is still tingling from his slap: a pleasant sensation.

"Lies. To help us deal with this reality. Lies help us survive. Morals, religion, science, they are all lie generators, systematic large-scale contortions of the truth; their goal is to make life worth living, despite the daily despair that holds us in its clutches. Despair is unreal—that is the message. Our only reality is the future—we believe in the future. To cope with the truth, to look truth straight in the eye, you have to be a liar by nature. I might even add: You have to be an artist." He looks at me, his light-blue eyes swim in his face. His gaze is no longer stern, instead it is full of concern and questions. Indeed, just like a mother who has just slapped her son for a very good reason.

"Comrade, can you be a liar? A liar for the truth?"

By way of answer, I dig a pair of dice out of my pocket. Without a word, I throw a double six. The man whistles between his teeth. He is an empirical socialist; he snatches the dice up from the dust and ventures a throw himself: a two and a three. He whistles again.

"Morals, religion, science, all corollaries of our desire to be artists?" I toss the dice high in the air and at the apex of their parabolic path they vanish, just like that, eaten by the void. "What about politics, comrade? Isn't that also just an art form like any other, a kink in the system?"

I spit in the dirt. Where the glob hits the ground, a worm squirms out of the earth, fat, bloated, and sluggish like all other earthworms in the city—these animals feed on the dead, they clean up the corpses—they're overworked and overfed these days. The man observes the wriggling creature, then he steps on it. He examines the sole of his shoe and checks to see if the trail of slime and blood is real. Then he returns his gaze to me.

"Useful," he says. "One day, I am sure you will become tremendously useful to us."

"Good," I say, and I extract another worm from his left ear. "Call me when you need me. I accept cash."

·

I protest. I tell the party official—what am I thinking?—a story about old Rabbi Löw from Prague.

The beautiful Esther appears before the High Rabbi Löw; she complains about her husband. "He tears my hair out, he beats me up, and for no reason at all. Rabbi, I cannot stand it! Would you please talk to him, wise teacher?"

The rabbi tells her she is right, and he calls her husband in. The man complains that his wife is a lazy bitch. All she does is kvetch with the other women in the alley; she neglects the household.

The rabbi tells him he is right, and he sends him back home.

The next day the woman stomps angrily into the rabbi's house and yells, "But we can't both be right! Either the wife speaks the truth, or the husband does!"

The rabbi thinks for a minute, and then he replies, "Well, you're right about that too!"

"At what point," I ask my interlocutor, "does the state's concern for its people turn into a nuisance?"

He imitates Rabbi Löw. He thinks for a minute.

"There is a rumor, my dear and dearly appreciated friend—and the story you just told me substantiates it—that you believe in G*d. People have reported hearing you mumble before and after each broadcast. You have the intense stare of a believer. So you seem to be prepared to surrender your life to a Being that does not exist, Who does nothing for His children. Well then, doesn't it make considerably more sense for you to offer your heart to the glorious future of our socialist state, which does exist, wholly and totally? The state is real, and truly feeds its sons and daughters. You have to understand, comrade, that every human being prefers calm over the torments of free will. Humanity wants to be shepherded. We feel liberated when the anguish of responsibility is lifted from our shoulders. Hence the socialist principle of loving dependence. We will . . . we will herd you. We will give you what you crave: a quiet life. We remind you that the joy of parenthood is sweeter than any other joy on earth—sweeter, certainly, than the joys of liberty. You are fragile and so is your joy, unless we, *we*, ground it in reality. Does one leave a cage of precious parakeets open?"

"Do birds not return to their cage, comrade, if they truly love their masters?"

"But, dear comrade SIGNORELLI, so many cats are on the prowl in the outside world!"

He goes even further.

"May I remind you that fascism has been vanquished by our Soviet friends, and our Soviet friends alone? They conquered Berlin, they liberated the camps where you and yours were held. Doesn't this demonstrate that history inevitably progresses along the lines of a necessarily bloody, but triumphant dialectic logic? Do you remember your return to Berlin, your long trek through the eastern countryside? Were you not confused, bitter, angry—yes—positively embarrassed about your compatriots, who had allowed all this to happen? They didn't care; they consented; they did what they were told to do, and they did not do what was forbidden to them. This is what allowed the Nazis to have their way with people like you."

Then he plays his trump card. "You were part of the resistance, comrade De Heer. We do not forget that historical coincidence. I too was held captive in a camp, as you well know. Moscow appreciates personal courage. Not everybody in this country had that courage. There were those who emigrated."

I get his meaning. Ulbricht, who did emigrate, is an old-fashioned Stalinist. But Stalin is dead; he has fallen into disgrace. The Stalinallee has just recently been renamed Karl-Marx-Allee, and Stalinstadt is now again called Eisenhüttenstadt. Those are sure signs. Ulbricht was Stalin's watchdog. Ulbricht no longer fits the zeitgeist; it's only a matter of time before his successor will be appointed and that successor might very well be sitting opposite me, a cup of coffee in his hand, biscuit crumbs littering his jacket, a boring provincial with not a hint of imagination, a petit-bourgeois wide-eyed mooncalf without any ideas of his own. In short, he is the right man for the job: He personifies the GDR itself.

We get down to business.

"Listen," says the man. "You heard *Genosse* Ulbricht. Nobody has any intention of constructing a wall. Imagine that—a wall that would separate the two million two-hundred-seven-thousand eighty-four West Berliners from the one million seventy-one-thousand seven-hundred seventy-five East Berliners! Straight through a city of three million: bricks, concrete, barbed wire! So many miles of wall! Who could even consider such a tremendous enterprise! And it would have to happen fast, too—in one night, in a single night, so that the wall is up before the British and the Americans can protest. Impossible, don't you think?"

I nod. He's crazy. A wall, a real wall made out of concrete? Crazy! Off his rocker!

"*Genosse* SIGNORELLI, you have such great skill and expertise—you make full-grown women disappear, and full-blown elephants. Would you—you who are such an expert in vanishing techniques, in distraction and secrecy—be able to build such a wall, if you had enough manpower at your disposal?"

"No. You could never have enough manpower at your disposal to pull off such a feat."

"But what if a whole nation took this task upon itself, dear comrade? A whole nation, with its army, its police, its volunteer *Kampfgruppen*—a nation that could draft hundreds of thousands of men and women, a nation guided by an organizational genius, somebody who knew exactly what he was doing and why—somebody like you? Would you still think it were impossible?"

"No," I reply. It's the truth. "That would make it possible. It would still be extremely difficult, but nevertheless possible."

The last of the gin and wine have vanished from my bloodstream. Such a far-reaching, ambitious, audacious, wildly perverted plan! At the risk of my own life, I quote Fontana: "To lock yourself in means to build a wall around yourself; to wall yourself in means death."

The statesman sighs. "Yes, such a wall would be divisive. But it could also save the world. First of all, the wall would save us. It is a necessary act of cosmetic surgery: We remove the sore called West Berlin from our collective body. Second, it will save the whole of Germany. If it goes up fast enough, the Western allies will be completely surprised. If they are unable to intervene in time, they will decline to intervene at all—tanks firing grenades in the streets is not desirable from a public-relations standpoint. By refraining from military action, they will in fact admit that the division of the territory is real—that there are two Germanies. While we from our side retreat behind the wall, thus indicating that we relinquish our claim on West Berlin. Look at it that way, and the act of building the wall becomes an act of peace. Truly! It is a gesture of respect, of mutual recognition! Peace! Peace in our lifetime, comrade."

"But then?" I ask. "What happens after? What happens after the wall's finished?"

"Then we will finally be alone among ourselves, *Genosse* De Heer—and we shall know happiness. May those years last until the end of time."

"No—I mean: what will happen to *me*?"

"You too will be alone among ourselves, *Genosse* De Heer. And you too shall know happiness. We will take good care of you. It will be the nation we wanted, *Genosse* De Heer—the German Democratic Republic will finally become the nation we have always wanted it to be, the nation we deserve. From then on, life will be interesting. Now at last we can start the discussion—everything is in motion, something is happening, and you wouldn't want to miss that, would you? If it's really as bad here as you and yours have dared to insinuate, why did you stay? Why do you think *I* stayed—why do you think writers like Heym and Brecht and Wolf stayed?

Trust me, or trust at least your artist brethren. Why be stubborn? This is the place, this is the nation that you live in, the land we have shaped together, philosophers, writers, musicians, pedagogues, workers and farmers. Come, my dear young friend, come! Come, and throw yourself into the loving arms of socialism!"

What's this? Is he really spreading his arms? Are his eyes moist with tears? No, of course I don't throw myself into his arms. I just ask my question.

"Do I have a choice, Comrade Honecker?"

The future *Obergenosse* parries immediately, and what a beautiful reply it is: a quote from Hegel.

"Freedom, my dear friend, is insight into necessity."

"Thank you, *Genosse*." He shakes my hand and then presents me with a minuscule notebook. "Could I have your autograph? It's for the children . . ."

As I am being led down the garden path, to the winged limousine that waits for me with open doors, he sings to me, in a high loud baritone, each word a slap in the face:

Ist der Weg auch weit
Kleinigkeit!
– jederzeit startbereit!

(The road may be long;
but don't let it scare you, no
—always ready to go, go, go!)

•

Commando of the Border Police
Order # 002/6
Commando Post Pätz

At HOUR X + 30 minutes, vigilance at the western borderline will be increased to prevent border violations from either side and to avert further infringement on the territory of the German Democratic Republic.

Staff officers will be dispatched to brief their divisions.

Border troops will be fully deployed in order to intervene instantly should trouble arise.

The highest density of troops and materials will be maintained at the sites of frequent illegal border crossings and at the flanks of the checkpoints. In sectors where border violations are expected, plainclothesmen of the border police will conduct additional patrols. Motorized brigades will be at their disposal for back-up.

Political-ideological instruction will be given to police personnel of all ranks and to the officers by commanders and political divisions appointed by the Party.

We expect all orders and instructions to be followed to the letter and we insist that the secrecy of the operations be secured at all times.

Reconnaissance units of the border police will be given the task of identifying the enemy and his actions. Events will be evaluated as they unfold.

First report at **HOUR X + 4 hours**, consecutive reports every six hours.

Signed,
Erich Peter, colonel

•

Saturday afternoon, August 12, 1961, Wannsee, Berlin (West). It is summer. The sun is out; it is pleasantly warm. Berlin is basking in the sunshine. It seems like half of all Berliners have descended on the lakes at the edge of town; the other half is no doubt enjoying a good glass of beer at one of the many downtown sidewalk cafés.

A pale man in beige shorts and a white shirt with rolled-up sleeves strolls among the throng of half-naked people, his hands neatly folded behind his back. The beach is sandy, so sandals would have been the smart option, but the man wears his familiar stout black moccasins, agleam with a fresh coat of *Eg-Gü*. White tennis socks fall around his ankles, their elastic having long since given up being elastic. His nose is covered with a thick paste of sunscreen; his black sunglasses slide down with every step. His face carries a polite but detached smile, the kind of smile that communicates that, yes, he is a friendly man, but, no, he does not want to chat with you. His progress is slow and unremarkable; he walks with the measured grace of a farmer inspecting his farm on Sunday morning—the weather is fine, the wheat is growing nicely, all I see from here to the horizon is mine, and all I need to do today is go to church. Some of the folks on the beach have a vague sense of familiarity when he passes by, but they do not recognize him. He is not one of their neighbors, and he doesn't look, well, *special* enough to be on television. Maybe he's one of their kids' teachers? He looks the part. Or maybe he's the new pastor from the Lutheran church around the corner? Well, that's possible too, now that you mention it.

The Party Secretary for Security Matters is one of the few living beings who knows what's going to happen tonight. He's certainly the only person on this beach who's aware that this may be the very last time he takes a stroll here, although many of the beachgoers, like him, live in the Eastern Sector, which will be locked down after 1 A.M. tomorrow morning. Earlier today, when he woke up to this sweet day of radiant sunshine, he had been very tempted to drive all the way to the radio station and tell his fellow citizens to please enjoy the glorious day while it lasted—the sun is out, folks, why don't you take the train to our wonderful lakes, why don't you take a hike in our beautiful woods, you never know, folks, dear fellow comrades—who knows if this will still be possible tomorrow?

The operation hasn't been launched yet. One phone call from the Secretary and the whole thing will be aborted before it's even started, and nobody, nobody but a few trusted members of the Central Committee will even know that such an operation had been planned. Everything depends on one person, and one person only: Erich Honecker. But Honecker has no doubts. He will do what he has to do—for the greater good of his country.

The Secretary shields his eyes from the sun with his hand, like any old cowboy or any old Indian. There are rowboats on the lake and swimmers in the water. American soldiers have soldered the masts of small sailboats to their surfboards and try to catch a nonexistent breeze. At the edges of the lake gigantic portions of cow meat are being seared over charcoal fires—one thing Berliners have learned from the American occupiers: Open-air roasting is fun! Most of the young women are dressed in that newly fashionable Western garment: the two-piece bathing suit. It makes their breasts sway most attractively when playing badminton. The acid smell of potato salad. Young half-naked mothers chat with their children; pairs of young lovers share a reflecting aluminum blanket; the keys of BMWs make titillating bulges in the tiny lycra swimsuits of cocky young men with severe tans. A stand sells hotdogs with sauerkraut, another Ami-German fusion food. A few daring souls have dropped all pretense and parade around naked—let's see if that little wiener can find itself a nice set of buns. Isn't that the head honcho of Siemens down there, being rubbed with coconut oil by two ladies in G-strings, one on her knees at his hairy toes, the other cradling his glistening bald head in her scantily clad lap?

Honecker's sunhat is the same color and model as his felt rain hat. His sunglasses look exactly like his reading and working glasses; they are even tilted at the same angle.

Honecker observes the events on the beach. Yes, people are doing well, here in the West. Once the wall is up, we Easterners will do well too. This is his strong conviction. When we build that wall, the same abundance of liberty will wash over the GDR. With one difference: The GDR will always be aware of its past and its historic role as a bulwark against fascism. People in the West, they forget, sad to say. With a vengeance, it seems. Look around! This is Wannsee, *the* pleasure spot of 1960s Berlin, and yet it is also one of the most terrifying places in the city's history. Less than a mile away lies the villa used by Hitler's accomplices to plot the *Endlösung*. This is the place where the seed for humanity's most terrible and inhumane crime was sown; this is Ground Zero for the most atrocious of genocides, and yet the masses play and work off their guilt with sports and mindless entertainment. Can't you see that we *need* a wall—that we need to keep these corrupting pleasures, this repulsive superficiality out of our field of vision?

The secretary sighs. The secretary is tired, tired of trudging through the sand and tired of the massive historical burden placed upon his shoulders. He looks for a spot to sit. He forgot to bring a towel. Well, why doesn't he just sit down in the sand, it won't hurt. A group of toddlers is hard at work with steel wire and soap suds: Brittle bubbles float through the summer day and pop on the sand, just like the gentle, almost imperceptible surf of the lake bleeds to death at the flood line. The lake swells, and with the swelling of the lake a sadness swells in Comrade Honecker. A disgusting spectacle, to be sure, but at the same time . . . beautiful and . . . warm and . . . touching in its self-evident . . . joyfulness.

Humans think too hard, thinks the party secretary.

Next to Honecker sits Petra Hanke, her lovely derriere planted firmly on a cheerful, bright-red towel. She wears the cutest one-piece bathing suit in the world, fire-engine red as well, and a pretty baseball hat, and the hat too is as red as can be. Petra loves the color red. It is her battle color, her father's color. Petra lives with her mother in one of those modern flats in the Mitte, on Karl-Liebknecht-Straße. The flat is small and although the building is brand new, big cracks appeared in the living room wall last month. Still, when Petra leans out the window at just the right angle, she can see a piece of the cathedral.

Petra was born late in the war, but her daddy wasn't present at the blessed event. Her daddy was a prisoner in Sachsenhausen, a bright red star pinned on his striped costume. Petra never knew her dad; she never met him. Not too many men returned from Sachsenhausen.

This is the first time Petra's been to Wannsee. She doesn't have a good reason to be here, except for the nice weather. But why not, right? The lake is on the map, it's part of town even though far west, and her girlfriends have told her that Sundays at Wannsee are loads of fun. Lots of cute guys and stuff. Good ice cream. Make sure you get invited to one of those barbecues. It's not hard. Just smile at one of the *Amis*; that'll do the trick.

Petra knows very well who the man next to her is. Ten years ago, when she was a little girl, Honecker visited the clubhouse of her group of *Junge Pioniere*. He spoke at length and with passion about peace and progress. While he was speaking, Petra watched him with her mouth wide open. This man had been imprisoned by the Nazis, just like her dad, and he had survived. Maybe he had known her Papi, in the camp? Maybe the words coming from his mouth were Papi's? Papi, she knew, had the same dream this man has: To let peace and progress reign. But evil men decided that waging war and fighting was so much easier than being nice and forgiving your enemies and making up, and so they locked up her Papi. And then he died.

In the hallway of her school there was a poster with a picture and a slogan. The slogan was, "Hard at Work for Peace!" The picture: a pilot in battledress. Emotional kitsch—she understood that now—but when she was eight, she wondered if her Papi had looked like that too, so handsome and resolute, his gaze fixed on the horizon where he could see the red glow of the socialist future approaching. Maybe her daddy had worn a helmet like that too; maybe the helmet had absorbed the worst of the blows he'd taken in Sachsenhausen?

No, some people simply didn't love peace. One day in fourth grade, the teacher asked them to speak about the most important things in their life, the one thing they couldn't live without. One after the other, the students stood up and delivered their answer. "*Meine Mutti.*" (The other students rolled their eyes.) "*Mein Teddybär.*" (giggling.) "*Mein Tagebuch.*" (Her diary—*hee hee*!) It was Petra's turn. She quickly jumped off of her bench—her pigtails jumped up too—and loudly and clearly she announced her happy answer to the world: "*FRIEDEN—UND SOCIALISMUS!*"

Peace and socialism! Half of the class giggled out loud, and the other girls hissed at her like cats: "You brownnoser!" "Teacher's pet!" "Aaaaaaass-licker!" Little Petra turned around, trembling with anger, and with all the strength and dignity she could muster, she hit the girl behind her on the head, and then she screamed off the top of her lungs, "*AND LEAVE ME ALONE FOR A CHANGE, YOU G*DDAMN FUCKING BITCHES!*"

Well then. Not exactly the triumph the little girl had been hoping for. The teacher dragged her out of the classroom by her ponytail. It isn't easy being a pacifist.

Petra stares at the big man. Would it be appropriate to tell him how much she admires him? What he has meant in her life? Should she ask him how things really were in the camps? Even while she considers these options, she already knows perfectly well she won't do it. This man is busy defending our beloved country and its beloved peace, and now he takes a break. It would be unfair to disturb him on his one day off, never mind how much he is with and of the people.

Then a weird thought lights up in Petra's head. *Genosse* Honecker looks a tiny bit glum. Tired. Weary even. What if she did something to cheer the comrade up? Something simple? Wouldn't that be a small contribution to world peace?

Petra looks around. There are many women on the beach who walk around in just their bikini bottoms, and some even wear no clothes at all. When they pass by, the Genosse's gaze invariably hooks onto them. He must like the view. Petra can't blame him: all those fit, healthy, tan bodies—such zest and vivacity in the bounce of those breasts, so joyful and sunny! Everybody embraces summer, and summer hugs everybody right back. Everybody is ready for love—the earth itself, the whole planet bathes in the warm glow of the sun's affection, warming itself up, readying itself for the better times that are bound to arrive, thanks to the workers' and farmers' revolution! What a responsibility rests on the shoulders of this helmsman! And Petra can't help but notice that—brief episodes of nudity aside—comrade Honecker doesn't look very chipper. A deep frown is etched in his forehead, the beginning of a nervous tic plays around his mouth. Why not cheer him up? Why not give the man some joy, a little innocent relief, something to make him forget his troubles? Petra has never been naked in public before, but just for the Secretary she could slide down her shoulder straps and uncup her breasts; maybe she could roll down the suit until it looks like a pair of panties. Wouldn't that bring joy to the beleaguered statesman, a pure and innocent display of young, healthy German beauty?

To camouflage her intentions, Petra grabs a bottle of tanning oil from her red purse. It's easier than she thought, sliding down the shoulder straps and rolling up the fabric. Not the act of courage she thought it would be. Feels good too. She starts rubbing the oil on her skin. A bit weird though, to feel the sun's warmth directly on the white skin of her breasts for the very first time in her life. She must admit that the light makes her skin look beautiful, with all its hues of white and pink and blue. Her nipples are happy too, she notes, they reach up to soak in even more of the rays.

Then, suddenly nervous, she clears her throat and—oh my G*d, what is she doing? she doesn't even dare to look at the man!—she sticks the bottle under the Secretary's nose.

"Would you be so kind as to oil my back, *Genosse*?"

Honecker, lost in his daydream, unaware of Petra's sacrifice for Folk and Country, sees an unknown object enter his field of vision—something dark and oblong and, well, sudden. Instinctively he lashes out. His clenched fist hits Petra's arm hard. With a scream, she lets go of the bottle—it flies up in the air, spinning. Hot, sun-soaked oil gushes from the whirling bottle, big dollops spraying from its one-eyed cap. A spiral of splashes splatters on Petra's bare stomach, but it's the Secretary who gets the full load. The pulsating jet of unholy ointment hits him right in the crotch. *Aaaaah!* As if stung by a bee, the Dawn of Socialism rises, nay, jumps up, and sprints away as fast as he can, no looking back. He hurries to the shelter of the concrete promenade, two dark-suited gentlemen in tow; one of them grabs the Genosse by the arm and pulls him close to his body; the other one runs backward and waves his gun over the heads of the astounded crowd.

Petra's color scheme is now complete: Over her face and her once milky breasts the blood-red blush of humiliation spreads instantaneously. People around her cheer and jeer; they laugh at her and point a collective finger at her chest. Petra pulls up her suit as quick as she can and, grabbing her towel, she runs to the water, crying uncontrollably, pushing her way right through the miracle of the soap bubbles. The toddlers cry and run off in all directions; their fathers start cursing the senseless woman in a multitude of languages.

•

Horst Ewald wipes the sweat from his brow. They've been working for hours, loading rolls and rolls of barbed wire into the trucks, and there's no end to the job in sight. Horst is mad. This is so typical. This would have been their Saturday off, and then they call us back to do some more useless g*ddamn work. How much do you want to bet that we'll drive this stuff around town all night and then unload it tomorrow morning on this self-same spot? Look at the sergeant—he's as mad as we are. Even he doesn't know why we're doing this.

•

Saturday afternoon, August 12, 1961. Lieutenant-General Schneider opens the envelope containing instructions.

19:00 The commanding officers of the police will convene in room 5614 to be briefed about the operation. **20:00** meeting in room 5614. The sealed orders will be opened. The higher ranking officers will be briefed about their tasks. Section Headquarters will meet in room 5614 at **21:00** to receive their instructions. 23:00 Officers of all police stations are to be called in for a meeting in room 5614 at **24:00. HOUR X:** start of the operation.

Lieutenant-General Schneider rubs his fleshy cheeks. What on G*d's beautiful earth is going on here? Are they crazy? A full-scale military drill in the heat of summer?

•

Genosse Honecker sits miserably in his gleaming Citroen, his back propped up against the backseat, his loins girdled with a thin snow-white bathing towel of East German manufacture. The driver and the bodyguard are arguing in the front. What if the girl had come closer? Did she have a knife? Why didn't you just arrest her? But what if this was part of a conspiracy, you saw how quick she was—what if there had been a whole gang of them waiting in the woods, ready to abduct the comrade if we took the bait and engaged the girl? Couldn't the Ministry have sent more men?

Etcetera.

The kind of reproaches that always come too late.

Honecker yawns. He is deeply unhappy. He sits naked underneath the towel. His ass sticks to the leather seat. His bodyguards had taken no chances. The contents of the bottle had looked and felt like suntan oil, but what if a deadly acid had been mixed in? So the two men had stripped their boss in the bushes and they had thrown a few bottles' worth of mineral water over his crotch—the guy at the little lakeside kiosk had refused to hand his water supply over to them, so they had been forced to take it at gunpoint. Then they wrapped the Secretary in the rough cotton towel and carried him to the car.

Honecker doesn't listen to the conversation between his two bodyguards. There is only one thing on his mind. The wall, the wall. More than ever, there is only one solution to our problems, all our problems: Let there be—the Wall!

•

At 18:00, in accordance with instructions, Schneider opens the envelope in his office on Alex. This envelope contains a single sheet of paper, a simple equation, handwritten, scribbled in great haste:

X = 1:00

•

Petra sits in the S-Bahn, going east. Honecker and the unfortunate incident are far from her mind. She sits and thinks about Jörg; Jörg is all she thinks about.

Jörg lives in Dahlem. He studies at the Free University. He was the tanned muscular boy on her right. Jörg had seen the whole thing happening, and unlike Honecker, Jörg had fully appreciated Petra's gesture of cheerful exhibitionism. When she dove into the water, Jörg ran after her. When she swam away, Jörg followed her. In the mild surf of the lake he had put his arm around her shoulder, and on her towel they had kissed with lips that tasted of algae, and then they had rubbed each other dry with said towel, and then they went to get some ice cream, and then they sat down at a sidewalk café, where he treated her to a *Berliner Weiße mit Schuß*, teasing her about her choice of drink—such a girlie beer!—and she had replied that she was a girl, after all, in case he hadn't noticed, and he said he *had* noticed that, oh yes he had, and then she climbed aboard his motorcycle and they drove to his parents' place. She didn't remember too much about the house. A terribly sad stuffed egret stood watch in the hall, and there was a marble pedestal with a bust of a man with his eyes poked out—Oedipus?—and lots of dark wooden bookcases. She would have loved to look around a bit, Petra loved books, but Jörg almost immediately dragged her upstairs to his bedroom. "Am I your first Jew?" he asked, and this made her laugh so hard that sex became momentarily impossible. Afterwards, in the deepening dusk, he accompanied her outside and pointed the way to the Botanischer Garten station. She didn't like it that he wouldn't walk her there, but he told her his parents were on the way, and it would arouse suspicion if he wasn't at home. He was supposed to study hard for his exams, you know. "What do you study?" "Philosophy." "So," she asked, "Marxism-Leninism?" and that made him laugh again. "Was I your first Marxist-Leninist?" she asked and Jörg almost collapsed with laughter.

Petra rides the S-Bahn and thinks of her new boyfriend. She gets off at Friedrichstraße instead of Hackescher Markt; she's in the mood for a stroll. For some reason, the evening inspires her to sing, a song from her childhood as a Young Pioneer. "*Ist der Weg auch weit, Kleinigkeit, jederzeit startbereit.*"

A theater near the station shows the movie *Im Westen nichts Neues*. There are few takers, the movie's been out forever. A bunch of teenagers hangs around in the lobby. When Petra passes by, they imitate gunshots and shout lewd invitations. Petra is used to this. She sticks her cute little button nose into the wind and arches her back, thus showing off her breasts all the better, to renewed catcalls.

Apart from that small gang of street urchins, it's remarkably quiet tonight. Shouldn't there be more trains? It's probably just some new restricted Saturday night schedule. At the corner of Friedrichstraße and Unter den Linden, Petra hesitates. Does she really want to go home already? Maybe she should get a cup of coffee in Café Espresso—Stefan Heym often hangs out there, and he's her favorite writer—but she keeps on walking. It is a night that inspires walking.

The boulevard is quiet too. She turns her head to the right, to the Brandenburg Gate. The last light of evening shines through the columns, and the wind blows the fine sand of Potsdamer Platz low over the boulevard. A few police cars drive down Unter den Linden; a group of men seems to have gathered at the gate.

Then she turns left, to *Mutti* after all. The Staatsoper blushes in the sunset and the cathedral's dome lights up in gold; the façade of the Rotes Rathaus looks like it's on fire. This is her favorite time of day: the horizon ablaze in different hues of red and red and red.

· ·

It is 11 P.M. Adam Kellet-Long, the East Berlin correspondent for the Reuters press agency, gets into his Wartburg and drives to the Ostbahnhof. Every night, the freight trains that carry the official GDR newspaper across the country leave from this station. The paper is only officially available the next morning, but Adam likes to read it as soon as he can; he likes to be informed, wants to scoop the other agencies. He has his contact person in the station; in return for a few westmarks they snatch a copy from the pile for him.

Adam walks through the arches of the entrance gate with a hint of nervousness in his step, just like he does every night. His man Achim walks towards him, likewise a bit anxious. The exchange process occurs quickly and graciously, just like every evening—nothing that would raise suspicion in someone watching: Under the cover of his jacket, Adam hands Achim the folded-up bills, while Achim slides a thick stack of papers underneath Adam's arm, and even before Achim pulls his hand away, Adam has the newspaper pressed tightly between arm and rib cage. Without slowing his pace, Adam walks to the kiosk and he buys his alibi, a pack of cigarettes.

Adam is an impatient man. As soon as he gets back inside his car, he puts the paper on the passenger's seat and opens it up. Only a spy peering through the window of the car would know that something highly illegal is going on, but Adam is vigilant; he watches the street from the corner of his eye and keeps the engine running. The pack of cigarettes gets tossed on the backseat. He'll throw it away when he gets home—Adam doesn't smoke. One of his secret pleasures is this daily destruction of a pack of smokes, the small satisfaction that every night he takes an addict's daily portion of tobacco out of circulation.

His eyes scan the front page—nothing there. Then he leafs through the rest of the paper. All is well: As usual, the paper contains nothing but filler. This or that government official has visited this or that factory, this or that farming collective has managed to pull off another record harvest. Just like every other evening, Adam asks himself why he bothered to leave his apartment on Schönhauser Allee to make the long drive through the dullest of towns to collect a newspaper filled with words as lifeless as this city. And why oh why does it give him such a thrill to do so, night after night?

That good old GDR. Nothing ever happens here.

•

I stand in the shadow underneath one of the arches and I watch Kellet-Long fold up his newspaper. He drives away, tires screeching; people like to get away from their disappointments fast. This, if I may say so, is one of my better ideas: to have a single copy of the newspaper printed, tailor-made for this nosy American correspondent. The man is too stupid and too convinced of his own cleverness to realize that the Stasi has been on to him from day one. Or day two, to be precise. Achim is one of us.

The brick behind me begins to tremble; I feel it in my back. The train is leaving, spreading its news to all corners of the land. The newspaper speaks of the border closing and appeals to the nation's solidarity—it calls for a general mobilization of the *Kampfgruppen* and the police units. The good old GDR—nothing ever happens here. This is to our advantage. People go to bed early, and they get up way before sunrise. They read the paper because there's nothing else to do. Police officers will converge on the capital even before dawn.

I take the last S-Bahn train west. I know that the train will stop in Friedrich-straße, and that this will be its terminus for the day—no further border crossings are allowed tonight. I know that at this late hour, all the taxis will be in their garages. Whoever wants to go to the *Bundesrepublik* will have to walk. I don't care, I wrap my black cape tightly around my body. The Brandenburg Gate is less than ten minutes on foot from the station. Well, first I'd like to spend a few hours in Café Espresso, if it's still open.

•

Midnight. It's now Sunday, August 13. In the Marienfelde refugee center, a secretary calculates the number of GDR refugees that came through today. Two thousand six hundred sixty-two, a record. Could it be the weather? Nice and warm, it drives the people outside and the air outdoors fills their heads with ideas? The secretary neatly copies the number into an account ledger. She makes another quick calculation off the top of her head. At this rate, it'll take less than six years. In 1967, the other Germany will be empty. That's too early for her retirement, but maybe she can get a transfer to a better post, for instance in the peace and quiet of the Black Forest.

•

Honecker sits down at the conference table, bought especially for this occasion. His hair is freshly combed, his face neatly shaven; he has a good dose of aftershave dabbed behind his ears. He wears a brand-new suit in a businesslike gray. His hands caress the mahogany. The tabletop is smooth. A nice cut. The chaos of nature kept tightly in check, its fractal dimensions tamed by the woodworker's saw. One day, Honecker imagines, splinters of this historic table will be sold at renowned auction houses for exorbitant sums of money, with impressively stamped certificates of authenticity attached: At his table, the fateful decision was made; on this table, dear people, Honecker's hands rested during *the* defining moment of European history.

Here we go, indeed. This is where it starts. In less than two hours, the true history of the GDR will begin, the state's very own Zero Hour. The seven people who sit around the table, his closest staff, are the only ones who know what's going on. Between 8 P.M. and midnight they have trickled into the building, one each half hour, so as not to arouse suspicion.

Comrade Honecker spreads his hand on the tabletop, his fingertips on the wood, his wrists slightly lifted: two elegant spiders made of human flesh. His nails are perfectly manicured—Margot had insisted on that. The Secretary pushes back his chair with the back of his thighs. The occasion calls for a leader who stands tall and straight, ready and still, already fixed in history. From his leader's stance he begins his speech, starting with a summary of the planned operations for the night: "*Meine sehr liebe Genossen . . .*"

•

In the central office of the BVG, it is becoming clear that something is amiss tonight. One of the stranger consequences of Berlin's split is that the GDR manages the S-Bahn, while the Federal Republic runs the U-Bahn system. The central office of the BVG closely monitors both. This is also a matter of national security. The politicians far away in the West German capital Bonn worry that the GDR might use the subway system to invade the Federal Republic with large hordes of *Kampfgruppen* or soldiers. Don't laugh. Bonn thinks that this is a plausible scenario.

The remarkable thing is that exactly the opposite is happening tonight. An anti-invasion. Trains that go to the East do not return to the West. It's as if night itself has devoured them. The BVG engineers hold a brief meeting. Nothing of importance, they decide. Did you see the data on the numbers of refugees today? Records are being broken, my friend. Ulbricht is just keeping the trains behind to make it harder for folks to leave the GDR. Nothing to get nervous about. Nothing, for instance, to call the mayor out of bed for.

•

In Strausberg, about twenty miles north of *Hauptstadt Berlin*, a party is winding down. There were plates with salmon spread with butter, there were Kaiser rolls with caviar, there was a chilled salad of thinly sliced calf's meat with capers, and there was vodka and schnapps and champagne from the Crimea. A big sheet hangs stretched between two tennis poles; an Egyptian film about the Suez Crisis had been shown as the main attraction. It's late, the food is all gone now, and so are the drinks. All that could be said has been said, all the small talk is exhausted. Time, then, for digestion and rumination. Seventy officers of the National Popular Army, decked out impressively in dress uniforms, the full collection of their freshly polished medals glittering on their chests, bow their heads and muse and burp.

It was a party, so they had been told, to celebrate the birthday of one of Walter Ulbricht's deputies; which one and what his name is they've forgotten. The party is as dead as can be, but they can't go home just yet. As long as the minister stays, the generals have to stay as well.

Two waiters carry a big grandfather clock into the garden. When the clock strikes midnight, the Minister of Defense climbs onto the stage. In the deadly silence that follows, he strikes his empty wine glass with his dessert spoon. Then he smiles pleasantly and takes a sealed envelope from his inside pocket. After a short, solemn cough he asks the nicely intoxicated generals for their full attention.

•

Yet another order travels through the night: The workers of the national printing shop may now be released. These are the men that a few hours ago printed the extra edition of *Neues Deutschland*, as well as the thousands of posters that will be glued to all the *Litfaß* columns in town. What the paper contains, we've already mentioned. The posters inform the population about the closing of the borders; they offer clear instructions about what is expected of them in the immediate future: mobilization of the workers and soldiers, and calm resolve. The workers of the national printing shop have been locked inside for the whole sunny afternoon. A simple precautionary measure, to make sure none of them leaked information about the great event to the media or the general public. Now that the plan has been set in motion, they can be released.

•

Seventy slightly tipsy officers sober up instantly. The map of Greater Berlin, projected on the sheet, sways ghostlike in front of them. The border—they know it well—is indicated in black. This line, so specifies the minister, indicates the position of the *Kampfgruppen der Arbeitersklasse*, the volunteer corps of army reservists recruited in the factories. They will do the real work. The black line indicates the front, so to speak. An imaginary yellow line behind these troops indicates the position of the professional police, the Vopo, as well as the riot teams. The third, line, red, three hundred yards deeper inside the GDR, is where the *Nationale Volksarmee* will be positioned. The idea to organize the troops in concentric circles was mine. That way, the grim, trigger-happy professional soldiers are last in line; the only troops who deal directly with the population are the much friendlier volunteer soldier-workers.

The standard procedure is explained, and it's made clear that nobody is allowed to deviate from it. Were border security to be violated, one has to shoot in the air; under no circumstance can any soldier shoot to kill without an explicit order from his commanding officer, except when attacked directly, and then only if his life is undeniably threatened. The minister emphasizes again that the operation is top secret; so top secret, in fact, that many of the nations' ministers—and here he snickers—are as yet unaware that they will wake up in a Germany that is newly divided and newly secured.

Lieutenant-General Löffler asks the Minister of Defense what to do when the situation—that's what he calls it, discreetly: "the situation"—"gets out of hand."

Everybody knows what he means: What if the West Germans open fire? What if they invade? The minister evades the question. "There are no procedures in place in case of a potential massive border violation," is all he says. Everybody knows that such an eventuality would mean a world war, but these words are never said.

The generals rush to their service cars. The drivers have been alerted; they have the engines running: Any of the commanding officers who does not reach his position on time will be punished. There is no need to ask what the punishment might be.

General Löffler strides to his vehicle with quick, heavy steps. He worries about his men. He's not afraid they might lack in courage; on the contrary, years of training have instilled in them such a vivid image of what the enemy is capable of that they are, if anything, over motivated. It might prove difficult to keep them at their positions, to keep them from invading the Federal Republic with mounted bayonets. His primary job tonight will be to keep his troops in check, to make sure that neither he nor his subordinates do or say anything that can be interpreted as an order to open fire. An over-excited soldier will look for any excuse to kill.

•

Jörg is in bed with Hannelore, his steady girlfriend, in her apartment in Potsdam. Tanks rattle underneath their window, Russian T-34s and T-54s. The alarm clock reads 00:20. A strange time to start military maneuvers. Those g*ddamn soldiers have no respect for a pair of poor philosophy students who had too much wine and want to sleep!

Hannelore is half-awake now; she moans. Oh well, now that they're both awake, why not make the best of the situation? Jörg turns to his lover and while the tanks make the bed shake, he takes a nipple as sweet and intoxicating as any of Lenin's dictums between his lips, and his hand, as strong and irrefutable as any of Marx's theoretical niceties, slides cunningly between good Hanne's most alluring legs.

•

The truck clatters over the cobblestones of Prenzlauer Allee. The rolls of barbed wire in the back scrape against each other with a thin grating sound; it hurts Horst's ears.

To drown out the sound he turns on the radio. Strange: no news bulletins. Instead, the radio spews nonstop swing and jazz. Horst is too young to see the obvious association, the association with those first happy heady years after the war, the days when black muscular American soldiers roamed the streets with broad smiles on their faces, impressively gleaming saxophones tucked nonchalantly under their arms, secretly feared and admired by Nazis and freethinkers alike—a time when wounds became scars, a time when the first signs of progress became visible, and with progress the possibility of festive entertainment enjoyed without guilt or a feeling of blasphemy. That has to be the only explanation for the choice of music—communists have little taste for improvisation and the individual expression of individual emotion.

Horst has been told that he and his men are on their way to "control the border." That makes the four of them feel rather stupid. What exactly does it mean? How do you "control a border"? So Horst just nods his head in time with Benny Goodman and squeezes his eyes shut against the smoke of his own cigarette, daydreaming that he's on his way to a bar on Broadway, or at least in Paris.

•

2:30 in the morning. The West-Berlin police informs city hall that "twenty-three armored transport vehicles have taken position to the east of, but not under, the columns of the Brandenburg Gate."

•

2:55 in the morning. A Vopo informs headquarters that he and other agents have closed crossroad number 34 to all traffic.

•

Well-fortified by caffeine, I walk through the concentric circles, the cordons that mark the transition from the old heart of town to its new borders. Like a shaman, I hold my talisman in front of me, a document so impressively official, so irredeemably alive with stamps and signatures that it makes the group leaders of each circle—first a Russian, then a German army colonel, then deeper within the circle a Vopo officer, and finally, right at the Gate, a worker-volunteer—literally take a step back. Such awe does the piece of paper provoke that it makes them click their heels and salute. And then I stand in the innermost ring of the circle, the edge of the knowable world. The West has not completely vanished yet—I can still discern its glow at the horizon, a hazy orange halo of streetlamps and neon signs that lends a unearned mystic aura to that g*dforsaken place—but tomorrow this radiance will no longer be our concern; tomorrow, we can put the ephemeral desires provoked by that beacon behind us for good.

The border is now closed. Each half of the town, I can feel it, will soon become *terra incognita* for the other. The thirst of each in turn to know the other will evaporate almost overnight.

Look at me. Tonight I, the television magician, am elevated to the status of a threefold wizard.

One. The exorcist builds a wall.

Two. The sorcerer turns the East into a nation.

Three. In the West, the devil's apprentice sinks a whole city into a hole.

Simsalabim! Not too bad for one night's work, no? This is my masterpiece and nobody will ever know it. I will never get the recognition I deserve.

One man holds a tall iron rod steady in the crack between two cobblestones; another man hammers it into the ground; a third man keeps watch, a semi-automatic under his arm. Repeat every thirty feet, and do this sixteen thousand times, and there you are: The magician takes his bow and bids you farewell in the thundering silence of the United Nations.

I tap my feet to the rhythm of the hammer blows. Don't blame me. It's not my fault. The wall was going to be built with or without me. Its existence is independent of the decision I made in Honecker's living room. I said yes because I consider it better—safer—that a magician leads the operation than a general. Watching the event unfold, and even in the full knowledge of all the tricks behind it, I am amazed at the speed of the construction, at the easy confidence of the workers, at the gestures that build not only a wall, but a lasting monument to the durability of socialism. The certainty in the workers' hands, the faith in their eyes—the conviction, the trust that they are building a better future. It may not be a triumph of architecture, but one has to nevertheless admire their decisiveness. It is the same decisiveness presented by a divorcing couple in a court of law: For the very last time we work together to bring about the peaceful deconstruction of our common life—it is a kind of murder and yet it is invigorating.

The Brandenburg Gate rises high above me. In between the hammer blows I hear the rustling of the wind through the barbed wire; a familiar sound that takes me back fifteen years in time. Which is the sweeter music: the ordered hammer's voice and howl of the wind, or the disorderly silence that prevails in their absence? Either appeals to eternity. I empty my mind, and here I go again: "*Exalted . . . glorified . . .*" No place on earth should be g*dless. My presence at this crossing point— as a victim, as a survivor, as one who says Kaddish—blesses and anoints this newly erected monument to the atheist nation. Every city is inhabited by ghosts whose only job it is to make sure that we do not forget. They call for revenge, for *Wieder-gutmachung*. But forgetting is so necessary. All we want, at heart, my many brothers and sisters and I, is peace and quiet, a silence so absolute that the licking of our wounds becomes audible. Maybe that's what the wall will do: create a land of the pure, a land of innocents; all ex-Nazis exiled on the other side of the border—fascism will never happen here again. A land of penitents. The heart of the matter, the curse of the covenant, is that Job was *blessed* by G*d.

When the rod is driven into the ground, sand spews out of the hole, the old familiar sand that covers the city and muffles her multitudes. The Berlin sand that, praise be G*d, makes it hard for myths to get a hold; the sand that keeps life fickle and practical, dusty and rootless, and people rootless and wandering.

This is what Honecker, that profound mystic, gave us—the living and the dead: peace. Peace and oblivion. The Wall surrounds those he loves, and those that love him surround him. The chirping of crickets can now be heard again.

•

We stand on De Heer's little balcony. It's chilly out; apparently the world is unaware that it is springtime. De Heer points downward and to the east, his finger describing a long snaking trail through the network of streets.

"There!"

It was less than 5 years ago that the Wall fell, and it's astounding how little still reminds us of its location, except for the oblong desert scar where Potsdamer Platz used to be. A little further down south De Heer points out the ruins of the Anhalter Bahnhof—the arches of a half-buried Roman viaduct.

That is where it stood, or lay, or curved, or whatever it is that walls do. A warped ribbon of gangrenous concrete, the sand between its barriers of steel and concrete raked as carefully as the sand in a Zen garden in Kyoto. Each civilization gets the monuments it deserves. In its first few years, the Wall was a symbol of the madness of politics; each violation of the Wall a testimony to sanity, to the silent rapprochement of two artificially separated nations. Now that the wound has almost closed, we might surmise that whatever mindset divided these two populations will soon be unified too. The capitalists of modern Germany have big plans for this narrow desert: office towers, upscale unaffordable housing, and a mega-theater for large-scale entertainment of an innocently superficial variety.

De Heer snorts. "Our nation built one hundred miles of wall. In one night. Imagine how I felt then, on that hot August night, a latter-day Daedalus, designer of the narrowest, longest labyrinth in the world—fully aware that I would be trapped

inside my own creation, knowing full well that the sons and daughters of the country would pine for escape and burn their wings in the process—buried alive
under the collapsing ceilings of improvised tunnels, drowned when their rubber
boats were shot to pieces, their bodies ripped apart by dogs, or simply bleeding to
death in the sand with a bullet in their backs, no more than an arm's length from
those other Germans, distant citizens of a different and forbidden country—and
that nothing could be done about it—nothing but wait.

Am I guilty? Am I guilty of having the same youthful impatience that filled
my fellow citizens, of having the same unbearable itch, of that same lack of adapt-
ability?

We, the East German war generation, we understand something the West has
never quite understood. That the Wall itself was nothing more than a symbol. The
real border, what really divides us, is human behavior: The patrols, the checks
at he border, the dogs—that's what makes a strip of land a border. Without humans watching over it, the Wall would be ridiculously easy to cross; if you were in
good shape, you wouldn't even need a hook and a rope. We also understood, from
the very beginning, what the West assumed was impossible, namely that the Wall
would one day cease to exist as abruptly as it was built. The Wall was nothing but
a cruel emblem of our weakness. It would never withstand a popular riot. G*d!
How absurd the Wall was! It just kept the illusion alive that two planes of concrete
divided the two Germanies, and not their ideologies.

Only Westerners ever called it the Wall. We, inside the zone, used the term "antifascist protection embankment." Later we called it "the border," or even "border
security." The whirling dust made the border policemen look like g*ds descended
from some holy mountain, wrapped in clouds to shield themselves from view. It
pierced right through the heart of fascist Berlin—right through the places that we,
and not the West, had carefully dismantled and removed from public memory.
Do you see that empty space in between two apartment buildings, where that children's playground is? Hitler's bunker is buried there. The Wall's sands have seeped
through the cracks in the concrete, they have scraped the murals off the walls
and the blood of Adolf and Eva off the floor; the Wall cleansed this most unholy
of spaces; it disinfected it, it filled it up, it plugged all its holes. And there, where a
sandpit catches the last rays of sunlight, another infamous spot, the headquarters
of the Gestapo on Prinz-Albrecht-Straße—the place, most likely, where my father
died. We made it a monument against hate. Between the Gestapo HQ and the
bunker stood Hitler's megalomaniacal chancellery, now shaved down to nothingness, and a little further on were the offices of the secret service. The Wall and its
sand liberated us from the ghosts of our fascist past. That was its true function: It

bought us time, it bought us peace, it bought us isolation. A final metaphor for you: The Wall is a tapeworm that gnawed its way through the city, and where it chomps and chews, it cleans out the digestive tract. Shit still happens, but it passes through this city much more quickly now.

De Heer snorts again, or perhaps he smells the evening air. "You know, the air up here by the Wall used to have a hint of the beach to it . . ."

•

When *Mosaik* returns to the airwaves, it becomes a prosaic, escapist spectacle. I've enough of it—I get myself transferred to production. A few times a year I still make an appearance in a small dialectic segment in which I play myself. The name SIGNORELLI remains, but I no longer wear a disguise; I drop the silly accent. I step into the lights in my sailor's sweater and my corduroy pants, just the way I am, and I explain to breathless children how they can become magicians themselves. I explain the secrets of simple card tricks; I haul a little girl into the spotlight and make her squeal with delight when she performs a simple vanishing act in front of millions; I show an impressionable little boy how shredded banknotes can be made whole again. For tricks of the latter variety, we invent our own currency, *Mosaik* money that's only valid in the closed world of the television studio; otherwise, we would have to destroy the image of Karl Marx imprinted on every bill, and that would be blasphemy. Although my beginner's lessons could be interpreted politically-metaphorically—Stefan Wolle wrote an article about that in *Sinn und Form*, right after the *Wende*—I decline to comment and refuse to speculate on the "meaning" of my teachings. When asked, I keep mum and drink my beer; the drunken bystanders interpret my silence as "deep" and "dissident." They can think whatever they want—thoughts are free, interpretations are cheap. These critics share WLADIMIR's opinion, which is also Honecker's opinion (after all, he recruited me as entertainment for the first national congress of the FDJ), namely that magic is more than entertainment, that the magician has a role in society—that he keeps the sense of wonder alive, that he points to the necessity of not-understanding, that he impresses upon the masses the belief that the world is amenable to transformation—a mere act of will will do it. I'm supposed to have infused my people with hope; I am called a tender anarchist. Well, if it helps them to shine a light through the thickening smog of lignite and ideological nonsense that hung over this country in the '70s and '80s, so be it. I myself think I was just enjoying the smile on the face of some freckled munchkin, suddenly six feet tall, who runs to reclaim his seat in the audience after performing a successful feat of magic. Too many people of my generation still get tears in their eyes when they see a child play alone in the streets; too many of us see the skeleton in every kid. "*Exalted . . .*" I mumble behind their backs. "*Glorified . . .* Be happy in this bricked-up land, my child, the future will be better! The future will be bright!"

None of the tricks I teach the children ever goes wrong. In case of mishaps, we reshoot—in the socialist world, nothing ever goes wrong, we all succeed. Every child is an *allseitig gebildete sozialistische Persönlichkeit*—an all-round socialistically educated person.

"See?" I ask a little boy. "Here is a snail, and here is a razor blade. This is not magic, this is biology. The snail crawls over the sharp edge of the razor blade, can you see it? And what happens? Nothing happens! No blood, no cuts. The snail floats on top of a layer of slime, slime it produces itself for just that purpose, and this allows the naked and very vulnerable animal to move over the most terrible terrain, to climb the sharpest of rocks, to swim over the pointiest of thorns." Chew on that, German comrades-*Demokraten*, I think. The little boy is even more politically astute than I am. "What about the jellyfish?" he asks. "Can a jellyfish swim through a field of barbed wire?" "No, it cannot," I respond. "The difference is that for the jellyfish the layer of slime is the jellyfish itself. In the example of the snail, the slime is a production good." (This is a fragment of the show that many commentators will write about. Their analyses amuse me; they also frighten me. In their eyes, the most trivial of things become enormous metaphors. Did the Wall make dissidents of all of us—*law-abiding* dissidents? From the orchestral pit sounds an orchestral version of some *Pionier* song. Deep inside each artist—or so claim those cigar-scented critics in between their coughing fits—there is always the tension between the conventions of genre and the libido of improvisation.)

I work on a new trick. I stand on the stage naked and completely shaved—no sleeves, no underpants, no body hair. Nothing to hide. A member of the audience fires a bullet at me. I fall down, I bleed. Then I climb to my feet, and I extract the bullet from my flesh with my bare hands. Then I run into the wings, a dripping trail of blood in my wake. A gigantic screen above the stage replays images of the event, images shot at a thousand frames per second, and the slow motion clearly shows the bullet leaving the nuzzle of the gun and entering my flesh. You can see the impact knocking me back, and blood gushing from the wound in my stomach. It is a dream. A nightmare that visits me every single night.

From time to time I meet Westerners in the bar. They hunt me down. *Mosaik* is apparently a small cult hit with a certain type of intellectual in the West. To these folks the GDR is one gigantic amusement park. Honecker-Land. The trains puff up hills. The telephones still have real rotary dials. The doorbells ring instead of emitting an electrical chime. You need to get up out of your chair to switch channels on the television. Chimneys have actual plumes of black smoke coming out of them. You hold your late-night discussions in the kitchen because the children sleep in the living room. "How cozy!" these *Wessis* say. "Such a nice, old-fashioned country!" I don't believe their little spiels about the West. All *Ami* lies! A little box without wires that controls your television? Factories that produce no smoke? Who ever heard of such things?

This is the world we live in. We have our very own brand of chaos. Cars made out of pressed cardboard. Rusty cast-iron urinals. Man-sized mechanical scales on the U-Bahn platforms. Shops that don't advertise what they have in stock, but rather what they're out of: "No jeans today"—signs yellowed with age. Restaurants sport similar signs: "No hot lunch today"; "No cake and coffee." An ill-tempered employee stands in the doorway to scare customers away with a few well-aimed insults.

At the same time, the GDR is still an old-fashioned Land of Cockaigne. You can get the thickest and juiciest beefsteaks for pennies, provided you manage to bluff your way past the world's grumpiest waiters. Fifty-six marks per month—thirty dollars—is what I pay for this apartment. Mortgages have a set 1% interest. A loaf of bread costs eighty-five pfennig here, and three-marks-fifty in the West. Fifty pfennig for a pint of beer. Coffee is twice as expensive, but that's not a problem: Every true German prefers intoxication over awareness anyway.

Everything is neatly planned. If you understand the system, you'll breeze through life. Smart people put themselves on the waiting list for a state-sponsored car—a Trabant or a Wartburg—as soon as they can, that is, on their eighteenth birthday. Then three years of military service, five years of study, a wedding financed by an interest-free loan, your first baby, then your second, five years later your very own two-bedroom luxury home, another three years to equip it with the necessary furniture, a little later perhaps a television set and by the time you're watching *Mosaik* from your very own couch, your car is delivered to your very own front door!

My fellow citizens and I, we stand at the edge of a stream. We want to get to the other side, but rather than swim or build a bridge, we wait until the water evaporates.

Did you know that the medieval Mongolian warriors locked up their enemies in airtight iron chests and then held a sumptuous banquet on the lids, their enjoyment of food and drink greatly enhanced by the sound of their enemies thrashing about as they were suffocating? In the GDR, the box was a lot bigger and made of concrete.

•

The anti-architecture might have gone something like this:

Two middle-aged gentlemen—let's call the smaller one Michail and the tall one Helmut—take a stroll around Kreuzberg. The smaller man is Russian and he looks the part. The other is German and he looks the part too. The both of them wear long woolen overcoats. To defy expectations, the German sports a small astrakhan hat and the Russian an elegant pearl-gray fedora. It's chilly, their breath escapes their mouths in clouds. They do not speak. Helmut points to a low wall at the bank of the river Spree. The two men sit down. They look at the water. The concrete is freezing cold. They do not speak. Their buttocks go numb with frost.

Each of the men holds a thermal mug. Helmut bought them at a Starbucks at some airport or other. He gave one of them to Michail as a present. The Russian was gracious enough to pour a generous shot of vodka into both. The cold, therefore, doesn't sting as much as it could.

In the sky, clouds chase each other; their paths reflected in the water below. These two are important people; two bodyguards keep watch at a discreet distance. Closer surveillance seems unnecessary. Who in Kreuzberg would pay attention to two fat men sitting on a low wall overlooking the river Spree? They must be tourists taking in the spectacle: The Wall stretches in front of them on the opposite bank. People go about their business—ethnic Turks schlep their overfilled grocery bags home, drag queens in full regalia try to scare the students, and pickpockets hunt their targets among the drugs dealers and the hustlers. Michail and Helmut are worldly men; they do not look around in amazement like tourists would—Helmut and Michail just sit. Nothing astounds them, except for that bloody Wall. Can you believe it?

"That whole business with those missiles, Helmut," Michail sighs.

"That whole to-do with the Wall, Michail," Helmut responds.

They keep staring straight ahead, their fingers clenched tightly around their mugs. It's cold, did I mention that?

Like everybody else around them, these men belong to the nuclear generation, the frightened generation, the generation of Europeans who have lived most of their lives under the threat of the Bomb. The generation with a clear picture of the enemy. The enemy is the one our missiles are pointed at. The difference is that these two men can do something about it.

Helmut steals a peek at the president. Michail is a restless man, he has a hard time sitting still, his fingers drum on the sides of his mug. He's simply too nervous, energetic; his head darts back and forth, his eyes take in the expanse of madness and ugliness that's spread out in front of them—the Berlin Wall, that cynical eighth wonder of the world. They both grew up with this artifact—an artifact built by an ancient civilization, something that's always been there. What does it have to do with them? Helmut steals another glance and realizes that this impressively fit fifty-something with his elegant Italian felt hat—that this man *is* the enemy. Why? What makes the president a bogeyman, what makes the country he hails from an empire of evil? What evil thoughts is he supposed to be hiding behind that wine stain on his forehead?

Both world leaders raise their mugs to their lips at the same time. Two Adam's apples gulp simultaneously. A harmonious collective sigh escapes from two mighty breasts. The sigh has to do both with their enjoyment of the hot beverage and the sadness of the view. Michail turns his head in Helmut's direction at the exact moment that Helmut turns towards him. The leaders of Europe, steeped in the cold of the Berlin soil, open their mouths simultaneously. "Are you thinking what I'm thinking?" They say it at the same time, in English, and the absurdity of the situation makes them both chuckle. Michail puts his arm around Helmut's broad shoulder at the same moment that Helmut starts to embrace him.

"I think I can convince George to send those missiles to the garbage dump."

"And I think I can persuade Erich to take a sledgehammer to this concrete monster."

The men disentangle themselves from their embrace, and each extends his hand in a manly gesture of deep understanding. They shake on it.

"It's a deal," says Michail.

"It's a deal," says Helmut.

Michail winks at him.

"Well," says Helmut. "That's that. And now, how about a visit to a nice old-fashioned *Kneipe*?"

"I thought you'd never ask," mumbles Michail.

•

I'm startled by a loud noise. A screech of discord, like an accordion in its death throes. Indeed, the concertina has disappeared from the coffee table; in its place a laptop has appeared, *my* laptop, its screen alive with a text in blue characters.

I get closer and I read: "The concertina has disappeared from the coffee table; in its place a laptop has appeared, *my* laptop, its screen alive with a text in blue characters. I get closer and I read: 'The concertina has disappeared from the coffee table; in its place a laptop has appeared, *my* laptop, its screen alive with a text in blue characters. I get closer and I read . . .'"—and so on, probably ad infinitum.

De Heer: "Write it down, Paul. Write it all down. Only memory, my dear friend, delivers the truth. My memory is humming in the guts of your machine."

•

Of course I now wish I had said goodbye to De Heer in a different way—in a better way. But what do I mean by that? Less silence? A hug instead of our usual handshake? I realized it at the time, but it didn't register fully: De Heer's story is done, bled to death in this unspectacular anticlimax—a soul beyond saving flooded with an acute awareness of the ultimate uselessness of its actions. This then is the end of Jozef De Heer's official biography—the half-assed description of the half-assed death of a regime? But how could I have done better, how could I, at that moment, have asked more incisive questions about this last, depressing period of his life? I will meet him again, of course, for the final edit. Or so I think.

I should have been a better listener. In this last section, De Heer himself had handed me the defining metaphor of his life: the old sly maze-builder Daedalus staring into the eyes of the young, impish, would-be lout Theseus.

But of course my mind isn't exactly focused on De Heer. My mind is occupied with Nebula. This explains a lot of my negligence that night. I think of Nebula. The whole long way back home, I think of Nebula.

•

She's still there.

As soon as I arrive at the bus top, I look up to my window (I'm early today, so impatient that I'm coming home while the buses are still running), and there I see her silhouette, blurred in a haze of condensed vapor.

She stands at the window, sighing. The outside world is cold, and inside it's warm. My heart jumps in my chest.

(Is she waiting for *me*?)

Her sighing breath hits the window. The window and the mist close her off from the world. The world knows her not.

(Is she waiting for me?)

Her impatient sleeve wipes the mist away. She sees me. She waves at me, with anticipation, with joy, with eagerness.

(For me!)

She doesn't look up when I enter the room. The radiator is set to high, banging and clanging away. Yet the room seems quiet. She doesn't move. I go to her. I press myself against her, I throw my arms around her, I fold my hands over the bowl of her navel. She is warm and alive. We look out over the former horse stables, over the arch of the Communs, over the dark blue night that creeps into the sky.

I think of Stella at the window of the Altersheim, her gaze roaming over the destruction of the Jewish cemetery. I think of Stella and De Heer, looking over the wasteland of the Pathologie. I think of De Heer standing on his balcony, contemplating the Wall that he helped build. And while Venus ascends over the roof of the Aula Maxima, I think of Donatella and what she knows of the darkness of the night and the age of the universe. How young is humanity, and how young are we, Nebula and I. Without saying a word, Nebula arches her back. She rests her neck on my shoulder. A short sharp cry at our feet: Mefista winding herself around our ankles, tying us together with her velvet tail.

The room is strewn with books, piles and piles of books; books on the table and books on the chairs and books on the makeshift sofa where Nebula spent her makeshift night—they aren't mine, they aren't the books I read for work, nor the novels I brought with me. They must be Nebula's books—tons of them. Some lie facedown with their spines cracked, others have impatient tongues of newspaper that hang luridly from their hungry pages. These books are yearning to speak, eager to testify: words circled in red, blocks of text in fluorescent yellow.

Nebula didn't spend the day here, then. She did something better. She went back to town to get her things. There's a difference between staying and coming back. I say it, just to taste the sound of those words.

"You came back."

"I came back."

We stand cheek to cheek.

"I dreamt of this, Paul. I dreamt of you. For a long time. It seems I've dreamed of you for years and years. Don't laugh. It is true. I dreamt of you."

"You . . . dreamt . . . of me?"

"You took my head in your hands. I dreamed you kissed me."

"It was a dream."

"We kissed each other. Your hands caressed my hair. Your fingers slid over my ears."

"My hands were soft?"

"Your mouth was soft. Soft and warm."

Nebula turns around. She takes my head in her hands. She puts the palms of her hands against my cheeks; her fingertips slide past my ears, into my tangled hair. I close my eyes.

"Like that," she says. "It was like that." And then her mouth closes over mine—her lips are hot and persistent, her tongue presses moist and urgent against mine. We breathe around each others' lips. Slowly, carefully, we drink each other in.

"Like that," she reaffirms when we finally release each other.

"So soft," I sigh. "So gentle."

"Like in a dream."

It's a mad existence, and it's all that we share.

The night and Nebula. Our mirror images in the windowpane, locked in a sweet and firm embrace. Nebula and I, together, for always. Like in a song.

She breaks loose.

"I have to go," she says. "I really have to go."

Nebula, so close to me that our breath merges on the cold plane of glass.

"I'm so late. I'm so terribly late!"

Late for what?

My eyes are wild with panic.

"Will I see you tomorrow? Tell me I'll see you tomorrow!"

"Tomorrow? No, tomorrow I can't. Maybe late? Late at night? Can I do that? Can I come here late? Middle of the night? May I, can I? I'll leave my books here, okay? Is that okay? Okay? I'll see you tomorrow . . . tomorrow night?"

PART THREE

SATTVA

ר

LIES

"Happy birthday, my dear sweet sir!"

"Hey. Hey! Wait a minute!"

"HAPPY BIRTHDAY!"

"But it isn't . . ."

He protests in vain; the woman-whirlwind has already ducked under his arm and slipped inside; with a limber sway of her divine hips she's closed his door and now she's grinding her ass most alluringly against the wood.

Well. She locks her gaze into his, she bats her eyelashes, and then she peels off her long leather gloves.

"Miss? What do you think you're doing? Miss?"

She doesn't reply. Although it may not be clear what she *thinks* she's doing, it's obvious what she *is* doing: She is taking her clothes off, right there, right now. Is this some kind of joke?

"Miss . . ."

Off goes her jacket. She turns around and places her palms against the door, then she sticks her tush out at him and shakes it likes she means it. Yes, it's a gorgeous sight; yes, he likes her tight little skirt; yes, her smile when she turns around is radiant and generous—but this must be some kind of mistake. He didn't . . . Hey, why is she locking the door? Hiding the key in the lace cups of her bra? And why does she come right at him, her head thrown back like some Spanish dancer?

"Miss?"

She's unstoppable, untamable, on fire, and he can't help himself—what's he supposed to do? He watches with mouth open as she comes right at him in a

558

flurry of fancy flamenco footwork, her whole body a superior percussive instrument—his protest sounds meek: "Miss? Uh?"

"Happy birthday, dear sir! A most happy, happy birthday!"

•

The rattling of the key in the lock wakes me up. It's disastrously late. One of the cleaning ladies sticks her head around the door. She observes the chaos—the books and papers—and appraises my sleepy head peeking from under the covers. Then she throws the door shut again, with a deep depreciatory snort—diese Philosophen!

My poor head aches. I contemplate the battlefield. My friend Meneer De Heer is a platonic lover of letters, the kind of man who catalogues his books carefully; they each have their place; he uses long slender strips of acid-free paper as bookmarks. Nebula has a different relationship with literature—cracked spines and dog-ears don't bother her; torn-out pages litter the floor like cards hastily abandoned after an illegal poker–game, the margins filled with words and pencil sketches, and those markings in turn marked by hurried circles and a forest of fierce exclamation points. Nebula clearly has a physical love affair with the word, and for some reason this moves me greatly.

I have to pee; I need some coffee. How can I navigate the room without breaking my neck? Books, books, books—thousands of pages, printed, annotated, dragged to my lion's den by a young woman, her back no doubt bent under the weight of those words.

I too love words.

How can I resist this temptation?

And these are books loved by my . . . beloved.

First let me get a cup of coffee. After that, I'll read.

•

The woman stands in front of the mirror. Her calves sing, her hips swing; she dances a supple waltz to music playing only in her head. Except for the sliding of her feet and the rustling of her clothes, the room is absolutely quiet. She is utterly alone; she hugs herself while dancing; she caresses her shoulders with tender hands. Her feet whirl on the carpet in three-quarter beat; this is a fast waltz, a waltz that, though performed solo, has nothing solitary about it—if you could see her dance, you would know that she doesn't need anybody else, that the only dance partner she wants is her self. Her fingers dig into her own flesh—rougher, more possessive now; she has her eyes fixed on the mirror, she stares at her own reflection, long and hard.

A shoulder strap slides down. The woman hums. The other shoulder strap slides down too. The dress slips gracefully to the floor. A silk slip—or would that be satin?—glows in the candlelight like liquid gold.

She lifts the heavy crystal atomizer from the dresser. She dances her private circles, the bottle in one hand, the rubber pear in the other, and then she squeezes— she waltzes through the cloud of cologne and soaks up the scent signal in the thinness of her undershirt, then suddenly stops spinning—like a stone released from the end of a taut string, she continues her movement in a straight line, headed straight for the mirror, a murderous march towards her terrorized and terrorizing image, with all the aplomb of a model on the runway, with all the sangfroid of a Bengal tiger descending from the mountain. With both hands she raises the heavy bottle high above her head—never halting—and then she lets loose, with a mighty banshee shriek, and hurls the bottle *mit voller Kraft* at the icy plane of frightened glass.

The woman's reflection shatters in a jingling waterfall of silver.

From the dark hollow of the empty mirror frame, exactly at the spot where the woman obliterated her own wide-eyed reflection, two different but equally terrified eyes stare right back at her.

The eyes breathe. They stare, they truly stare, big and wide with the realization that the tables have been turned, that the onlooker—the voyeur—is now on display, and no voyeur likes being exposed.

Curious eyes. One is made of glass and perfectly spherical; we can assume it is innocent. The other eye is presumed guilty—it is human and male and blue as the deep sea in a midnight dream: a shimmering crystal hidden in the purple shadow of a black cap. Crimson droplets drip from a diamond shard in its eyebrow; eyelids bat the blood away.

This woman is a Bengal tiger, oh yes: Her mouth hangs open, her gleaming teeth are ready to bite.

The man is young—he smells of soap and sweat, but he is not a child; there is the scent of inscrutable spices, a heart of darkness. Here he stands, the perpetrator in his mystic vault, and blood drips slowly to his chin; it falls on his jacket and gets soaked into a fabric that is blacker than the night itself, darker than the limitless emptiness of the farthest regions of our vast universe.

There are miracles in this world. For instance, that the woman, less than an inch away, does not sink her teeth into his throat, that she does not extend her tongue and lap up the mixture of sweat and blood, the juice of life itself; that she

560

does not then and there rip off the man's shirt and slash his tender nipples with her canine teeth.

•

"Mira is my name, sir. Admire me!"

•

A spear of glass glistens in his hand. Nervous lines of gold and silver shoot through the room, quivering reflections of the dying mirror in the man's shaking hand. The hand has a will of its own. The hand wants to do just one thing, the thing it is trained to do: to slide the sharp knife of glass over the woman's white throat, to cut the skin, to slash her windpipe. Murder lives in this hand, and the man has to apply the full force of his mind to deflect its automatic motions. He clenches his mind like a fist and then he lets go—his hand too is now dripping with blood; a small cry hangs in the room like a tiny bat.

The soldier and the woman face each other; he in full military regalia, she in silk underwear. Each goes against their nature: The soldier does not kill, the woman does not love. They tremble with the effort of it, strings pulled so tight that they could break the bow. They draw hard, quick breaths—the hurt soldier, the angry woman. They stare deep into each other's eyes, teeth bared, souls exposed.

•

"Mira?"

"Call me Layla, if you'd rather. Or Eris. Or whatever you like. My name is Mira, or Layla, or Eris, or Mira-Layla-Eris. Pick one. It's your choice. Mira, of the escort service *Girls Incorporated*. Here's my card!"

"I don't need to know what your name is. I don't want your card."

"Exactly! All you want is to know is what I look like naked—*right*? Well, yip-pee-ki-yay and cock-a-doodle-dandy, here! We! *GO*!"

•

She licks her lips. She has something to say—she can feel it coming, although she doesn't know what it will be. She is afraid to speak—any exchange of words will be so much more trivial than the skirmish that preceded it. The language of words is so much more trivial than what the body has to say.

She licks her lips. She strokes the soldier's head with a lazy finger; her nails linger over his fresh wound. He flinches.

He grabs for her hand.

She deflects his move, and this helps her find her text: It resides not in language, but in her hands. With confident fingers, she tears a strip of fabric from her slip; she winds the silk around the soldier's bleeding palm. Another piece of fabric goes around his forehead. While nursing him, she ties him up, with fast, assured movements.

The soldier too has found his voice. He stands at attention, his clouded pupils fixed on the banal Bavarian wallpaper. His face has turned to stone; he does not blink when she applies the tourniquet. This pleases her. No more than a few seconds have elapsed since the moment he wanted to . . . take hold of her? Push her away? Press her against him? Just a few seconds, and he's already slipped back into his role, that of the firm, unyielding warrior.

She looks down. What's this? The soldier wears wool scarves wrapped around his boots? So he can move around in the small alcove of his cell without making a sound? She recognizes the symbol embroidered on his armband all too well: A silver dwarf holding a burning wheel of gold, and a man with many arms dancing frantically in this ring of fire. On the right side of the man's collar she notes the familiar lightning runes; on the left three silver flower buds, underscored with a single silver line.

"*Look at me.*"

His eyes meet hers.

"At your service, ma'am."

He is at her service! She likes the timbre of his voice. Measured and self-confident, as to be expected from a man with an impeccable Aryan pedigree, a man trained in the best officer's school in the world. There is a certain roughness around the edges of his vowels that makes her knees weak—a latent informality that could be interpreted as an insult or an invitation. There is also impatience in his voice, and this has nothing to do with getting caught—she has established that the soldier is no voyeur; he is simply doing his duty—it's just that his mission is in jeopardy, and this angers him.

"If Herr Himmler is so hell-bent on seeing me in the buff—he could just ask, you know?"

The soldier does not speak.

"I'd gladly mail him a nice set of nude pictures, and I'll personalize them for him too."

The soldier keeps his peace.

"Tell him, will you?"

The soldier swallows a mouthful of saliva. He had it easy until now: His role in this play was one of immobility and four words of automatic dialogue. Now he has to speak; worse—to improvise.

"I do not know where my orders originate, ma'am."

He licks his lips. He is an amateur actor getting ready for his monologue. His next sentence begins with that most dreaded of all pronouns, "I . . ."

The actress cuts him off.

"Listen," she says curtly. "Listen. I need nothing from you. I don't need to know who you are, and I don't want to either. I don't want to know what it is you're doing, and I do not want to know why you do it. I don't want to know your name. What just transpired here has never happened. We won't talk about this. You get another one-way mirror and you glue it back in place. You understand? We'll do what needs to be done. We'll play the roles we need to play. Yours is prescribed by your superior, mine by life. I act, you record. That's all. We'll keep it simple."

Taking his eyes off her requires effort. She can see him readying himself to spring to attention with a curt "*Jawohl!*" She does not give him the satisfaction. She slaps him in the face. Just like that—because she can. Then, while he's still shocked by the blow, she raises her chemise above her head; for a brief moment she joyfully offers the full weight of her breasts to Earth's gravity and to the onlooker's gaze—naked and glorious she poses by the bed. She hears his sleeves rustle and then, with perfect timing, she slips underneath the covers, secretly smiling at the impotent click of the camera. Time for bed, Helena Guna, time for sweet dreams. Tomorrow is another day.

•

"And you'd like to see my tits too, wouldn't you? Yeah? You'd love to see those, wouldn't you, those pretty little perky tits of mine? Well, here they come!"

•

I'm glad I took the trouble to make coffee. I need the sharp tang of caffeine; I need a clear mind and a will of steel. The books invite me; their presence incites me. They lie on their broken spines, calling to me. Their dog-ears and bookmarks beckon me, as if Nebula herself—where did she go?—is telling me, Take, read. Read, here, look: Read *this*—I marked this passage for you, just for you.

And so I read. The first book I pick up opens up of its own accord; its improvised bookmark, an autumnal twig with oak leaves, drops from the pages.

I read what is written.

And what I read shocks me.

The words hit me as hot and startling as a lover's slap, cold and chilling as a bucket of ice water from a balcony above, searing and burning like a lighting bolt from a clear blue sky. Of course!

The shock, the incredulity, the silence. I feel it build, I can't escape it, it rises from the pages and freezes my spine; it sets my hair on end. A whine rises from my lips, I shake with disbelief, yet I am fully aware of the irreparable harm, the indelible shame, the impossible humiliation of the revelation.

•

"But before I bare it all, dear sir, before I get buck-naked for you, on all fours, for you, sweet mister—before I take off every little last bit of fabric, I do have to request that you sit down, sir, on a chair, yes, that one would do nicely. Surely you understand. It's a simple precaution. We, the girls from *Girls Incorporated*, often get touched inappropriately. It's nothing personal, sir, just company policy. Allow me to shackle you with these wrist cuffs covered in leopard fur. It's fake fur, sir, do not worry—no animal was harmed. They're soft. Very comfy. Yes, like that, thank you, just like so, yes, you hands behind your back, wrists closely together. Just relax, sir. Great! There we go! Thank you very much, sir, much obliged!"

•

I close the book and it slips from my hand—all strength has left my fingers. The book falls flat on its back and opens on that same damn page again, on the same obscene passage, the same string of repulsive sentences. I pick it up again; I return to the poisonous paragraphs like a man who can't help going back over and over again to a gaudy mistress in a cheap motel—she's no good for him, yet he cannot resist her. The toxic fog of the words—the nouns, the verbs, the adjectives, the adverbs—rises up to my aching throat; they make me gag, they cut into my breath, they scrape the inside of my skull: Words I know so well, so well that I could speak them by heart:

The first man in line goes to the tables. He removes his wristwatch; he points at his wedding band with a question mark on his face, and after a brief nod from the soldier he puts that on the table too. We follow his example. Those tables now contain our lives, lives we thought we had saved from the claws of the soldiers in Berlin. Now they are lost after all. Rings given in friendship, rings given in the promise of eternal love, the futile wealth of diamonds, watches whose hands will soon be frozen in an eternal now, wallet-sized pictures that contain the useless memory of a summer day. I have nothing to hand over, and that makes the soldiers suspicious. I am asked to bend over in the middle of the barrack. A soldier pries open my cheeks, a flashlight shines in my asshole. I blush violently.

My hand, my shaking G*dforsaken hand reaches for another book. It too opens all too willingly to a suitable passage; its words resonate painfully in the taut spider web of my memory:

> I stand next to her at the window, at that thin membrane between an outside world that is no longer ours and an inner world that does not bode well. My hand goes to her shoulder. A hand as generous and innocent as the impossibility of sleep, and equally treacherous.
>
> "We are all human," I say. "I am human," I add. "And so are you, Stella, you are human too," I say, and I squeeze her shoulder blade.
>
> Her voice is dreamy.
>
> "Exactly," she says. "Exactly." She puts her hand over mine and squeezes back.
>
> Stella and I stand by the window. She tells me about the old *Sammellager* in the nursing home at the Große Hamburgerstraße in the heart of the Scheunenviertel, the old Jewish neighborhood in the shadows of the golden dome of the Great Synagogue.

I do not need to read more; there is no need to open any of the other books. An icy veil of darkness seeps into my bones; a chill builds around my heart. It's so obvious; I should have realized it so much sooner: De Heer's story is so universal because it *is* universal. His voice was not his own, it was a multitude of voices, countless voices—*none his own*. Voices I didn't recognize—but Nebula did. She discovered echoes in stories that I, naïve fool, did not question.

As I said, there's no need to continue reading. Still, my hand digs mechanically through the pile, opening book after book, and I recognize each of the marked passages—if not the exact words, then at least the basic narrative. Some of the names on the cracked spines are familiar—Levi, Frankl, Semprun, Gay, Durlacher, Spiegelman, Wiesel—others I read for the first time—Beck, Sowalke, Greenberg, Frister, Kielar, Deutschkron, Wyden, Wilkomirski, Skakun, Steinberg, Schwartz-Bart, Krowin, Weinberg, Sutzkever, Cohn, Delbo, Romano, Orbach, Borowski, Eliach, Nomberg-Przytyk, Latour, Glick, Eichengreen, Kraus, Pillin, Gurdus, Yevtushenko, Morgenstern, Gotfryd, Rashke, Fink, Lagnado, Ganzfried, Dekel, Greif, Klemperer. Names drenched in Middle European melancholia, names smelling of old tears and the mold of cardboard suitcases rotting in the attic. The books are dressed in gray and black and other dusky hues; the cover images show barbed wire and striped uniforms and searchlights and shards of glass and train tracks. The blurbs warn the reader not to enter the author's world, for he or she will never be the same—advice confirmed by the deadness in the eyes of the black-and-white author's photographs, eyes burned out from the inside, all light gone. A theater of shadows, a choir mumbling atonal songs, an inexhaustible pool of well-earned tears of unquenchable grief and bottomless remorse.

It took Nebula less than half a day to read De Heer's story in a language she does not understand. It took her less than half a day to recognize his sources and to trace them in her library. Think, Paul Andermans, think. Why would anybody compile an autobiography based on the stories of others? What in G*d's wide world is going on here?

•

"Ha!"

She sits in his lap. A naked woman, amazingly attractive, straddling a completely dressed man chained to a kitchen chair with sexy little manacles. De Heer has entered the world of pulp fiction, a world he did not realize truly existed. He has become a model in a glossy ad for an irresistible, expensive cologne—it's an impossible world, but well, here he is, chained and with this lady in his lap.

She twists and grinds. Her bare buttocks dig into his groin.

"Ha. I just wanted to feel that," she says. "I just wanted to check—does it all still work, down there?"

Check?

"Your story had me worried."

What story?

My story?

Who is she?

Who am I?

"Never mind!" Mira shrieks. She slips off De Heer's thighs and bends over, her legs straight, her back arched while she sways her hips—and thus (this newly discovered world of the romance novel lapses all too quickly into the rawer forms of pornography) De Heer is directly confronted with the silent eye of Mira's vulva, tastefully framed between her thighs. As if to aid him in his meditation, Mira grabs her ass cheeks and splits that fetching fruit. He's just about to thank her for her thoughtfulness, when—G*d almighty!—the little rumpled star of her anus contracts in a spasm and opens up to reveal its deepest secret: Out of Mira's asshole shoots a minute cylinder of silver that lands right in speechless Jozef De Heer's lap.

Mira turns around, all swinging breasts and swagger. She plucks the cylinder from between De Heer's thighs. It looks like a bullet, a bullet made of silver, or perhaps silver-plated lead. Mira bites down on it and the walls of the bullet cave in under the pressure of her teeth. What an astounding act! She spits the twisted metal into the palm of her hand; her quick fingers retrieve a little tube of paper from the wreckage, a miniature scroll which she proceeds to unfold and hold up to De Heer's eyes.

"Did you enjoy my magic act? Would you care to read the message?"

Simultaneously De Heer nods that yes he did enjoy her performance very much, and shakes his head no, he cannot read it, he's an old man, he needs his reading glasses. In the breast pocket of his shirt. Yes, there. Thank you.

Even with his glasses on he has trouble reading the missive. The document is as small as a mezuzah parchment and the letters could just as easily be Hebrew. No, they're not, the note is written in the gothic script that went out of fashion with the Nazi regime. Now that De Heer looks more closely, he notes it's not parchment after all, but old, yellowed paper. Half a century old, something like that. Is the bullet that surrounds it authentic? The piece of paper is dated 1944; the words are written on the minuscule but official-looking letterhead of the *Arbeitsgemeinschaft für Frieden und Aufbau*, the Working Society for Peace and Development, an outfit he's never heard of. An equally official-looking but equally bogus wax seal is attached to its bottom. Whoever has created this artifact loved his work. This fills De Heer—falsifier *extraordinaire*—with nostalgia.

The message itself is not exactly one of peace and love. It's an account of all the crimes the man to whom it has been dispatched—himself, then? Jozef De Heer?— is guilty of. Crimes against humanity, that is. Active participation in genocide. The letter ends with: *Das Urteil wird nach Kriegsende vollstreckt.* The sentence will be carried out after the end of the war. But isn't that language itself decidedly postwar?

Carried out? Presumably with this bullet?

"Why am I reading this? What does this have to do with me?"

Mira-Layla-etcetera sits down, again in his lap, a leg on either side of De Heer's thighs. She wriggles with her bottom until she's sitting comfortably, then she throws her arms around his neck and presses her breasts against his belly. All De Heer can think is, I hope she isn't going to stain my good pants; I hope I won't have to go to the dry cleaners tomorrow to get some female slime trail taken out.

She does her best to sound sweet. "There are rumors. About an ex-SS officer who pretends to be Jewish and hangs out with skinheads."

"So?"

"A real arrogant bastard, you know?" She licks his earlobe; her finger trails the edge of his five o'clock shadow. "A real Nazi. A dominant macho. An *über*-man, *na*? Imagine that! A mass murderer walking the streets of Berlin as if he belongs here! Doesn't that alone call for the death penalty, dear sir—arrogance and mass murder? And what do you think of the man's filthy lies? Isn't it bad enough that a criminal like him doesn't freely confess his sins, that he trivializes his involvement in the Third Reich—isn't he all the more detestable for dreaming up a fictional autobiography, and not an innocent tale, but heroic memoirs at that? Doesn't that aggravate his offenses? No? You don't think it does?" The woman's fingernails wander over his neck; they slide horizontally over De Heer's Adam's apple, from left to right, from right to left. Small scratches, playful enough to be playful, painful enough to be painful. The gesture leaves nothing to the imagination.

"What makes you think I'm that man?"

"Ah! It is not just the lack of anger you're exhibiting now, or the lack of surprise—you've obviously heard this story before! And it's not just your tone of your voice, either—my G*d, it's so clear you must have been a high-ranking Nazi pig! No, it's because there's proof. Pictures. Documents. Mentioning you, dear sweet sir. Showing you in three-quarter profile, and well lit. Official pictures, your full name printed underneath."

"My name?" De Heer scoffs. "Ma'am, you can look it up. Go to the archives. There are always archives. Look me up. I've lived in Berlin most of my life. In 1944, I was arrested by the Gestapo—there must be proof of that. I was transferred to Auschwitz—I must be on one of those long lists they keep there. I was liberated by the Russians—the Red Cross can confirm that. I reestablished myself in Berlin in 1945—that too is well-documented."

"Oh," says the young woman of *Girls Incorporated*. "Of course Jozef De Heer lived in Berlin and so on and so forth. I also bet that he arrived there a few years earlier than the man who calls himself De Heer now. He might even be a few years younger?"

"You doubt De Heer's existence? You doubt that my name is Jozef De Heer? Can you untie my hands? I'll show you my *Ausweis!*"

"No, dear sir, I don't doubt De Heer's existence for a moment! And I firmly believe you carry a passport in his name. But I am not looking for De Heer."

This genre transformation is staggering. Now we've moved away from pornography and have landed inside a Victorian novel: intrigues, name changes, accusations. So be it. As long as nobody faints and needs smelling salts, everything will be all right.

Mira is insisting on a dramatic pause. Then she repeats herself.

"The man I am looking for is not Jozef De Heer."

She puts her hand over his mouth, because she knows what he will reply, "Hallelujah then, and set me free, for I am Jozef De Heer!" She brings her face close to his. It's much more effective, being this close to her victim; besides, she will taste this privilege, the privilege of revelation, only once in her life. She takes a deep breath before she says it. Then she goes on, an actress from a line of actresses, "*Helmut Hinkel* is the man I'm looking for."

She has her cheek against his; she looks straight into his eyes, watching them grow wide as she speaks the name "Hinkel." Her cheekbones register the trembling that travels through his body—the leaps and bounds of profound disgust and fear. It must be fifty years or more since he last heard this name. Mira has hit a bull's-eye. Her theory must be correct, then. Hinkel is De Heer's real name.

De Heer is speechless, completely dumbfounded. He knows that if he doesn't respond quickly, if he doesn't deny the allegation immediately, her certainty will only grow.

"Where did you get this nonsense? I've never heard of this man!"

"Where did I get this?" Intuition, my dear old man. Or call it fate, or mere coincidence: the fluke that sent me to Paul's room and then the listlessness of a lost afternoon in the *Gästehaus*. The listlessness that made me ache for something to read, and the curiosity that made me open a folder labeled 'De Heer.' How nice that the linguistic kinship between Dutch and German made it possible for me to understand the writing. Nicer still my fabulous memory for detail. And now you yourself offer me the ultimate proof: Your own body betrays you.

Mira clears her throat. "Adolphe confessed."

"Adolf?"

"And the Stasi wrote it all down."

"Stasi? Adolf? Who is Adolf? I know no Adolf."

"You do. Not Adolf. Adolphe." With crooked index fingers, Mira-Layla-Kismet-and-so-on indicates a set of quotation marks in the air. For the first time, De Heer is truly afraid. She means it! The whole thing: the bullet, the death sentence! This woman will kill me! Who is she? Look at her, see how she jumps up with excitement, see how she dances through the room, convinced of her gruesome righteousness: what flexibility of limb! What a gorgeous body! Look at those nipples, at the dizzying curves of those magnificent breasts! See how she forces herself on the world—what a sight! How long since I saw a woman's body like that? This Mira is a killer babe!

Yes, how long has it been since I saw a woman like that—a body that looked *exactly* like that?

•

There's also a folder on the table, in the midst of all those books. It contains a modest stack of papers held together by a flimsy cardboard cover, marked and rumpled, faded with age. What is it that guides my hand in that direction, what is it that forces my hand to push aside the rubber bands that keep it closed, why do I let the photocopied pages rustle through my fingers? (There's also a still more mysterious package on the table, about the size of a cigar box, in the thick black plastic foil used to wrap ink cartridges or light-sensitive material. The package rattles softly when I shake it, with the metallic sound of a steel spring. I do not open it—it's so well wrapped that Nebula would notice my transgression.)

I open the folder. Page 1:

T—Operativ-Vorg.

Lieg.-Nr. (stamped: *VIII / 430 / 61*)

There is a *Beginn* to the file (stamped: "13 August 1961"), but it has never been officially *Beendet*.

The paper is rough and gray, the right-hand side of the photocopied page is frayed, possibly the outside edge of a file that's been opened and closed too many times. The upper right-hand corner is a blank white rectangle, maybe the back of a business card, perhaps of the person who copied the file, probably put on the page while it was being copied to cover a name and address.

At the center of the first page somebody has scribbled a single word in big letters, the word *Omega*. The "*Band-Nr.*" is 1.

I turn the page. A photocopied paperclip with a photocopied picture underneath. Although the picture quality is low and the copy much too dark, I recognize the man. This is the elegant magician with the thin mustache, triumphant smile and all. This is Signor SIGNORELLI, also known as Jozef De Heer, fifty years younger, in a uniform I recognize immediately—the same uniform my uncle wore in his war pictures. I turn the pages: more photographs, in chronological order. With every page the man loses more of his swagger and gets more gray hair; deeper wrinkles settle around his eyes and bitter lines play around his mouth; at the same time the light in his eyes grows dimmer and dimmer. That this is so clearly visible in such bad copies is testimony to the incisiveness of the transformation. In less than a minute I see a young man with deadly bluster dull into a nagging bore, the kind of man who sits in his favorite watering hole riding his hobbyhorse all night, a man without illusions forcing his weariness on the world. There are dates next to the pictures, hasty scrawls in many different hands. The most recent picture dates back to 1985. Poor Jozef De Heer: even for the authorities your last years in the GDR are old news, not even worth a picture. What good is a rebel who no longer rebels?

The next few pages contain a questionnaire. First and last name have been censored with black felt pen; the ID number has also been made illegible. The first page contains the official request to open the investigation; the entry is dated 13.08.1961. At the bottom of the page I find the rank and alias of the informant and his contact: *IMK/KW "Adolphe" (koordiniert mit Ultn. Greve).*

Table of contents.

First report at the OPK, page 1. First report of the OPK, page 2/4. Report regarding intercepted communication with negative cell. Findings concerning the correspondence between tape recordings and anonymous verbal-negative comments. Data analysis by the OPK, page 6/9. Handwritten report of the IMB "Harzberg" dated 9.11.1974, page 3/5. Operative information concerning substantive revision of the certified mailing of 31.4.1975. Statement concerning the data presented on 17.8.1982, page 2/2.

Etcetera. And so on. And so forth.

•

"We both know who *Adolphe* is, don't we?"

"*You* seem to know. I have no idea. Enlighten me, dear Madam Mira, explain to me who this mysterious Adolf is."

"Not Adolf. Adolphe. Just like there is only one famous Adolf, there is only one famous Adolphe. Sax. The inventor of the saxophone. Who else could our Adolphe be than the horny player Rolf Isaaksohn?"

Mira-Layla-Eris-Circe. She stands right before him, her fingers on his wrists. She registers the increase in his heart rate. Maybe he didn't know he was being spied on, maybe the name of the informant shocks him; whatever the cause, his heart rate spikes. De Heer manages to look quizzical; he frowns his eyebrows in innocent ignorance—such a lying bastard!

"Rolf. One of your neighbors. Rolf Isaaksohn. You knew him well. Don't pretend you didn't know that 'Clemens Eberhardt' was just an alias."

Of course De Heer knows Rolf. His pupils cloud with anger, but the sweat that collects underneath her fingertips and in the hollow of his collarbones is open to interpretation. It still could be surprise rather than fear, or maybe—better be careful, girl!—it signifies his readiness to spring into action.

Mira jumps up. She produces a file from her briefcase and throws it nonchalantly on the table. Better to show the man something—enough to make him realize she is not bluffing, yet not enough to make the limits of her knowledge obvious.

It works. De Heer cannot keep his eyes off the little stack. It is so close and yet unreachable. He wishes his hands were free; he wishes he could leaf through the folder; he wants to see the extent of his betrayal with his own two eyes. Well, he should have known that one of his men would spy on him. There's always a Judas. But Isaaksohn is dead and gone now, and that's a good thing. What worries De Heer is this: Who came up with that pseudonym on the cover? Who, who, who in the Stasi knows of his connections to the Omega project?

Nebula is enjoying herself immensely. This is the reason she sought out Hugo's troops. She had a mission—she was on a manhunt, tracking the ones who still hadn't been punished by the courts, for whatever reason—laziness, lack of time, or foul play. She wanted the men who were responsible for the almost-murder of her grandmother. Her motive is the most honorable of motives: revenge, pure revenge, revenge in the name of the dead, who cannot claim vengeance themselves. Where better to find traces of the guilty than in a circle of neo-Nazis, with the old men hiding behind the scenes, the old men enjoying their small state pensions in small unlit state-sponsored apartments, the men who pull all the strings but keep themselves carefully hidden from view? Nebula never believed in the spontaneous revival of the extreme right. Such organization on such a grand scale implies conscious design. The wild kids who carry on on television, those bizarre-looking mutants—is she really supposed to believe that they just found each other and started their well-orchestrated terror campaigns all on their own? There had to be a big organizing principle, and she would uncover it. That Hugo and his gang had helped her realize her other dream—filming the script that she's carried with her all her life—that was an accident, a pleasant side-effect.

Oh! The long ride by train and subway, all the way from Potsdam to the heart of Berlin—the excitement making her tremble in her seat with such agitation that her fellow passengers stared suspiciously at her out of the corners of their eyes. Is the girl running a fever? Is she on drugs? Well: Here she is. She has him cornered. Finally she's found her man! SHE'S FOUND HER MAN! Hugo had told her his fairy stories, tall tales about a man named Liebenfels who had lived inside the GDR for forty years as an infiltrator. A well-respected citizen of the swine and vassal state, disguised as Auschwitz-victim, awarded with the *Banner der Arbeit*, member of the *Vaterländische Verdienstorde*, and so on, while in reality he was—hold on to your socks!—a *real SS officer*, and a high-ranking one too! This was the man she wanted to find. It took Nebula months; she moved in with the gang; she cooked for Hugo and his disgusting friends; she did their laundry; she waxed his boots; she slept with him night after night after night, and kept herself busy making her movie. All that time Liebenfels had been nothing but a disembodied voice over the telephone, an occasional cell phone ring that had made Hugo rigid with deference. Hugo did try to track the man down—he revered him, after all, and he was the brain behind their operations—but he had never succeeded. Hugo suspected that Liebenfels lived in one of the apartment buildings on Leipziger Straße. A few months ago Liebenfels had ordered one of Hugo's couriers to deliver a package to him at the *sozio- und multikulturelles Zentrum CHECKPOINT am Spittelmarkt*, something urgent that had made its way from the Potsdam cell to Hugo's lair. Liebenfels had appeared in disguise, the courier said; he looked like any GDR prole: Clean-shaven, his hair slicked back with grease, even to the point of wearing that ubiquitous GDR-type navy blue captain's cap and the oversized set of glasses that went with it. This Liebenfels incarnation had looked quite grandfatherly, with his pipe and grubby sweater and tweed house slippers. That last detail had caught

Hugo's attention: the slippers. Liebenfels had to live close by Spittelmarkt.

And now Nebula is finally here, in the metaphorical den of the metaphorical lion, and she has the lion tied to a kitchen chair. She's so excited—if she wasn't so disciplined she would ride his leg like a horny bitch and come right in his lap.

Once before she believed she had located the Great Leader:

Isaaksohn-Eberhardt is a stupid dolt. When setting up the Potsdam hand-off, he had left his telephone number on Hugo's voicemail. It's easy to trace a phone number. Leipziger Straße indeed, right near Spittelmarkt—it fit the profile. You talk to the cleaning lady, you promise her one of those television-VCR-satellite-dish combinations from Hugo's endless supply if she just gives up her job. ("Not a big deal. The house-cleaning business in Berlin is a seller's market, isn't it, Özlem, sweetheart?") Özlem then introduces you to her ex-employer as an old friend who would be willing to take over the job. You get the job, no questions asked, no references checked. Eberhardt looks you over once and it's decided—it really is a seller's market.

You're disappointed. It doesn't look like he's your man. Herr Eberhardt has nothing grandfatherly about him; he's just a useless old man with no visible sign of intelligence. He has way too many black-and-white photographs on the mantle. You dust them off, and while doing so you memorize the faces. You do not recognize these people, but one day this data might come in handy.

You start to understand why your employer wasn't interested in references. He watches your every move. With *that* kind of stare. Not a useless old man: a dirty old man. You suppress your disgust. You smile. He looks; you open up the top buttons of your blouse. Of course you do. That's the way life is.

During the next round of cleaning the man grabs you from behind and squeezes your breasts. Hungry, greedy hands. No gentleness; just kneading, as if you were a bag of dough. Your breasts hurt, later that evening. You had expected more finesse from a sax player. You're really disgusted now, but you keep on smiling. Next time he approaches you, you wiggle your ass against his dick.

You get a raise. He asks you to come over more frequently. It's springtime. Windows get opened. New buildings are going up all around. More dust in the air, right?

Of course you stop by more frequently. You clean his apartment, and when he takes his prick out of his pants, you take it in your mouth. As soon as it's over and he falls back onto the couch with a long *aaah!*, you spit his semen into a flowerpot. You hope the plant dies. Then you turn to him again, and smile.

You suffer through all this because you have to gather information. You don't need proof of Eberhardt's guilt. He has Hugo's number, he's a middleman, and he's the right age to have been a soldier in the war: He's guilty all right. The information you're after is Liebenfels's identity. Eberhardt knows Liebenfels—and you will too. As soon as your employer shuffles to the toilet and you hear the whining sound of his meager farts, you open up the appointment book he keeps next to the phone. You learn nothing new.

You propose a big spring cleaning—maybe Mister Eberhardt could go for a long walk through town, so you can work undisturbed? You know, really rattle your pails, go flat on your belly and dust under the bed? The man protests. You'd almost forgotten: You're Turkish, not to be trusted. If he leaves you alone, you might steal his stuff. You surprise yourself: You put your hands on your hips and you cock your head and you suggest that maybe after the cleaning you could wait for him, so that he can inspect everything, you know, see if you did everything right? He can inspect every nook and cranny, does he get it? Isaaksohn blushes unexpectedly. He slaps you on your ass and grabs his coat, and before you know it, he's gone.

You hit pay dirt in the very first drawer you open. A photo album, and you recognize a few of the people from the history books. Eberhardt is a fool indeed—he didn't even lock the drawer. Here he is: his younger alter ego Isaaksohn, arms around his young bride, the infamous traitor Stella Sonderlicht. And this: a picture from the war years, a high-ranking Nazi shakes Isaaksohn's hand in the ruins of the city. Isaaksohn looks proud; the officer's expression is one of supreme ennui, like that of every celebrity photographed with a nobody, a frown of impatience flutters around his mouth—his mind is clearly elsewhere. But he did sign the picture.

Underneath the album you find the file you've been looking for. It bears the code name Omega. You glance through it. The file is not about Isaaksohn, but the name Adolphe suggests that Isaaksohn must be the informer mentioned in the text. The name of the subject has been made unreadable with black ink. Not on the copy, but on the original, or on the copy that this copy is a copy of. The subject's real name, however—the name he operated under during the war—that name isn't censured. It doesn't ring a bell and that's what makes you realize you've found *him*. You've read everything there is to read about the war, everything, really everything, and seeing a name you don't recognize, the name of a man who seemingly had an unremarkable war, a run-of-the-mill SS officer who was trying to hide this ultimately trivial fact for no obvious reason—that's a clear sign that something important is going on. The photocopy seems recent. Probably stolen by Hugo's gang during one of their raids on the former Stasi headquarters in the Normannenstraße—a raid ordered by Isaaksohn, perhaps, to get this very file into his hands. Was Eberhardt blackmailing his boss? Did he deposit the original in a vault in the *Deutsche Bank*?

You hear the key turn in the lock. Eberhardt is home earlier than expected, and he carries a bouquet of flowers in his hand. Did he turn sentimental—is he wooing you in his old-fashioned way? The smell of Löwenbrau hangs all around him, and in his eyes you read the same drunken horniness that Hugo displays so often; it makes you feel terminally exhausted.

Let's get this over with, Isaaksohn, let's finish the job! "Herr Eberhardt!" you cry in happy surprise, and you walk to him, your hips swaying, and you unbutton your housecoat as you approach him, starting at the top and going all the way down, and you throw away the coat just at the moment you reach him, showing him the clean beige cotton underwear you bought at the Salvation Army store for this purpose. Eberhardt drops the bunch of flowers on the floor—what a pity!

"Ha!"

With an old man's battle cry the traitor jumps on top of you.

·

"Eberhardt? Isn't that the neighbor who died a few months back from a heart attack?"

"A heart attack. Oh sure. Yeah, right, a heart attack."

Mira smiles; her fingertips rap absentmindedly on the tabletop. There's a naked woman sitting in my lap, muses De Heer, and unthinkingly she's drumming out a rhythm on my table. A most peculiar situation! Oh yes, this woman just read me my death sentence. But that voice of hers, that timbre, that depth, that sultriness—it takes me back fifty years.

"On the day I . . . I went to the hospital."

Mira whistles. She walks over to the credenza and without hesitation she opens the right door to uncover a bottle of Glenfiddich and a clean glass. She pours herself a drink. It takes a while, but then De Heer understands.

"You . . . you know my apartment. You've been here before."

By way of reply, Mira raises her glass in an absurd toast. Now he recognizes her, *he recognizes her*, a memory rises to the surface from a nebulous part of his brain.

She had needed a drink that day. You've done your civic duty—the traitor Isaaksohn, the man who was responsible for the death of so many Jews, lies dead on his bathroom floor, his neck broken, his victims avenged—and when you walk back through the hallway you hear a terrible death rattle. Karma, you think. You take a life, you save a life. So you break in and you call an ambulance. You stay behind; all this life and death business makes you thirsty. You search the place until you find a good bottle, you take a swig, and then you disappear into town. (And if you hadn't been so aroused and so in need of a good drink, maybe you would have had a closer look at the victim, and you might have recognized him from the pictures.)

"What is this? First you save my life and then you come back like a harpy to end it?"

Nebula smiles. "Is that a problem, Herr Hinkel? Something in your eyes tells me that you feel ill-suited to this life—that you'd rather be removed from it. I don't deal in death. My gift is justice. Not just a gift to your victims: Death will liberate you too."

She waltzes the liquid around in the glass; she sticks her nose on the lip of the glass and breathes in the whiskey's complex aroma.

"This what it's all about. A man's life is nothing but a quest for one singular moment, for the edge, for death. You move towards it all your life, a plump, inert little object adrift on the seas of time. And now it's finally happening. This is the maelstrom. This is the moment. You're almost home. The final solution to your life is in sight. Aren't you glad, Herr Hinkel?"

"*Prosit,*" Mira adds, and she raises her glass again.

No, she does not drink the whiskey down in a single gulp, as De Heer had hoped. She sips. She has complete control over her actions, and that much is disturbing. She will remain sober for no other reason than that the circumstances call for soberness, for acting in cold blood. De Heer shivers. She has a plan. She brought a death sentence, and she will carry it out.

"Can I have one too?"

"But of course! Be my guest."

She pours him a drink, as though this is her apartment and he the intruder she's tied to the kitchen chair—she grants him a last drink before the authorities arrive.

She puts the glass to his lips. Her skin is cinnamon gypsy, but her tits are unmistakably Swedish.

A killer babe!

•

The body is an envelope, skin and flesh wrapped around . . . around what? Around more flesh, around spongy guts and mucous membranes, around a skeleton both firm and frail. But inside all of this, a stunning *something* is alive, the something that makes us love all this packaging and makes us forgive its clumsy beauty and the relentless beating of its arrogant heart.

You may see a beautiful woman—a woman like this one, a woman like Helena Guna—and you'll be hit by the usual dose of the usual hormones: no secrets there. But every neurochemical storm abates eventually, and what comes in its place? Chemicals don't explain why you keep looking at her, night after night; why you keep looking even after you've given your semen to an army-issue handkerchief; why you—how shall we put it?—keep worshipping, even after all pituitary prolactin is reabsorbed and you realize you bit down too hard on your hand to muffle your moans. I watch her, night after night; I watch her performing acts that some would consider outrageous and depraved, and I know she is untouchable to me. Yet I keep worshipping. Because of this *something*. This soul. Helena's soul. I worship Helena for her soul. And after what my eyes have seen, I also *pray* for her soul.

"The camera loves her."

Certainly. But every camera is blind. Its caresses are guided by a living, admiring eye that is in turn piloted by bundles of nerves that eat their way down into the brain—a direct line from Lena's soul to the photographer's. The ambient light falls around her most elegantly, there's no doubt about that, but it's the photographer who makes it so. The photographer picks his moment and it is this decision that makes the image, the irreparable precision of light poisoning the layer of silver emulsion.

A breathtakingly beautiful woman in a pleasing light. The incomprehensible curve of a hip, the mysterious softness of a belly. In the end, it's all the photographer's self-portrait.

Forget sleep. Nobody sleeps. The model tosses and turns underneath the sheets; the moonlight seeps in through the open window and takes her in its arms. I become the camera, I get drunk on the midnight air, I swell with the moon. She is a miracle: I swear it, she sucks up the photons, the pale disk in the window becomes a spotlight. What emerges from the developing bath is spectacular in its sharpness and touching in its abstraction.

Thus begins the miracle. The miracle of her feigned nakedness, the miracle of our contrived intimacy, the improbability of her simulated closeness.

Wait. What did I do? I opened the shutter; I made celluloid pregnant with moonlight. That's all I did. This was my job, my duty; I was just following orders. Did my supervisor condemn me to lust, knowing full well what he was doing? Did he purposely arrange for me to meet my blonde fate?

A scar on her belly. The mysterious softness of a belly, etcetera. At the center of that softness: a testimony to transgression, to wonder, to fable. The scar is in my pictures. She makes no attempt to hide it, neither from me nor from her lovers, and I do not keep it out of the frame. A vertical line from pubis to belly button, a serrated gash in her flesh.

Scars are what make a woman beautiful.

My boss agrees. I see it in his eyes. They linger over the elongated mark. It has never before been shown before—not in her publicity shots, not in her movies. I know that my relationship to him is strictly hierarchical and that I should keep silent, but I cannot but speak. I tell him, "A woman is made beautiful by her scars."

He nods. "Her men."

I frown quizzically.

"The true scars of a woman are the men she loves," he clarifies.

Good. I lied to Helena. I do know where my orders come from. They come from this man. A direct line to the top of the regime. He and I are the only ones who know. The only way to keep a secret secret is to cut out the middle man. In that case, if the secret leaks, you know who let it out, you know whose throat to slash.

I am no photographer. I am a spy. My boss is not interested in Lena's nakedness, but in the men with whom she shares this nakedness. I know just enough about photography to be able to develop the pictures in the darkroom built especially for that purpose at Bad Stolz. Again the same principle: My reason for developing the pictures has nothing to do with art but everything to do with the secrecy of my mission. I hand the pictures to my boss whenever he's in town; I never mail them or send them by courier. My boss doesn't care about the artistic composition or the erotic merit of the material. His one criterion is that the faces of the men are clearly identifiable; he wants it abundantly clear what the diva is doing, and with whom.

She lies on her belly on top of the white sheets. She looks me straight in the eyes through the glass of the one-way mirror. The gramophone blasts its forbidden sounds: Cole Porter, Hoagy Carmichael. She sings along softly; perhaps some of the lyrics are meant for me. Does she mean it when she mouths, *In the silence of my lonely room, I think of you?* Or should I hear, *Don't you know little fool, you can never win?*

She supports herself on her elbows; the full swing of her breasts rest lightly on the mattress; the curves of her buttocks, inviting yet untouchable, echo those of her breasts perfectly. I am *Satan in slacks*, the man she's waiting for, the man who will press his full weight down on her, his rippling stomach perched on the small of her back, his well-oiled erection neatly arranged in the crack between her buttocks, and then she will reach around and guide the blunt spear of my sex to the edge of her little winking star, inviting me to sink inside her to the hilt, to possess her in that most private of openings—so that she will be fully possessed, fully taken, fully *mine*.

I have witnessed this scene—Helena Guna's anal congress with a soldier—many times. Worse, my file contains many pictures of such events. As my supervisor requested, I concentrate on the men's faces and leave the locus of penetration out of focus, but, equally conforming to my boss's request, no doubt remains as to which of the diva's body cavities is being violated. Lena, my Lena: It's so crystal clear what causes the expression of pain and lust on your sweet angel face. Lena, my Lena: It's so clear you do not love them. While they do this crude and brutal thing to you, their sweat is dripping down your back, they bruise your hips with the their claws, and yet your gaze is locked into mine—mine are the eyes you stare into: Your one true man is the invisible shadow behind the glass.

If you'd be just so sweet and only meet your fate, dear.

But are you really looking at me? Or are you staring at yourself, entranced by your own image, sweetly in love with this mirage? Sometimes I wonder.

So many men, I assume, jerk off to pictures of the diva in the privacy and comfort of their homes; they bring themselves to climax over what they imagine she could do for them in bed.

I need no imagination. I have knowledge. I know what happens to her during orgasm; she's come so often under my scrutinizing gaze. Her eyes close, her throat gasps for air, she howls at the moon—I've seen it all, I've documented it in countless photographs. It's my conviction that I am part of her climactic ritual: It's not just the fucking that catapults her into seventh heaven—it's my gaze that sends her over the edge.

My gaze, yes, or her own. This much is not completely clear.

And then I develop the photographs, and I am invariably disappointed. The image seems . . . empty. There's no better word for it. Printed on glossy paper, her bliss seems strangely vacant, her elation false, her grimaces lose all connection with the storms that raged through her body; they're nothing like the whirlwind that tormented her when I watched her live.

Damn it. I am in love. My heat must radiate through the glass; how can she not feel my passionate, helpless devotion?

I am in love and she sucks that energy into her body.
I am in love, and she—she toys with me.

Night after night after night.
She toys with me.

I am in love with the Reich's most famous actress. Shall I order champagne, dear reader, or perhaps a cup of hemlock?

Her men are all alike. Blond studs with well-toned bodies, their muscles acquired not on the battlefield, but in the sports hall of the barracks. They resemble each other so much that it's hard to tell them apart, but I have the impression that the faces—the eyes and nostrils—that loom over Helena's blonde little tuft are different each night. She goes through men like she goes through napkins. Though there are exceptions. As far as I can tell, the repeat performances have little to do with the men's skill in bed. Helena Guna is an enthusiastic and eager lover; she seems happy with every man she meets, and why shouldn't she be: Sex with a real-life movie star should inspire every man to glorious feats. Her reprises must be the consequence of a busy schedule more than anything about the men themselves. (I'm so busy! No time for lunch! Let's see whose name we have in our little appointment book . . .) If you ask me, these repeat visits always take the edge off the performance. These men have had time to think about their conquest, and so are no longer overwhelmed by Helena's status as star turned flesh. They are less inclined to be led; they take an active role in the choreography, and their initiative rarely pleases Guna. The woman has her rituals; she likes to have it her way. First she undresses, then she strips her man. She weighs his scrotum in the palm of her hand; she makes sure he's sufficiently erect. (Hygiene, racial and otherwise: She inspects the foreskin.) She likes to go through a few positions, and always in the same order: First missionary, then Helena on top—she rides slowly at first, then she accelerates, grinding her pubic bone against his, moving faster and faster, all shrieks until she finally comes. For a man with extraordinary stamina, she grabs the little bottle of oil.

I do not mention this out of prurient interest. I want to point out that Helena Guna is a woman of ritual. One could see her congress as a form of prayer: The content may change, the form remains immutable. Helena's only steady boyfriend, the only fixed term in the equation, is yours truly, the humble photographer, her acolyte. I am there for her, every single night, the faithful servant of her pleasure, and by succumbing to vicarious lust I too am part of her ritual.

It makes me wonder. Helena Guna is an actress. She can simulate any emotion. The libidinous tornado that rages inside her—is it real, or mere playacting?

I look closer. She walks into the room, wearing *that dress*, the world-famous dress that fits so closely around her body that rumor has it an army of seamstresses is called in every morning to sew it around her waist. (I don't know for certain, I leave the room when Helena takes her morning bath. I walk to the barracks, I eat my breakfast, I go to bed.) She peels it off. She stands naked. She opens the man's buckle, she unbuttons his fly. She throws herself onto the bed. The man dives on top of her, kneading and purring.

Helena.

This is where scar tissue forms.

Helena.

Drunk, vulnerable, inviting, teasing.

But always the same, always the same.

She grabs him by the balls. She reaches for his cock.

Delving, delving, delving.

Scar tissue.

Falling, falling, falling.

A trap, an ambush, counterfeit?

From fresh wound to healing?

Break through the glass!

My mouth.

My mouth is dry as parchment.

I am my camera. Music plays on the gramophone, low and lazy. She is alone, no lover in sight. Through the double boundary of mirror glass and spherical lens she peers into my soul. The shutter clicks. There's no reason to take pictures now. But the shutter clicks, to the rhythm of the needle. The shutter clicks, it's true, but we both know better. *I* click and *she* clicks, and in the act of photography subject and object become one—one with each other and one with the melancholy sounds that come out of the Odeon's horn. We languish, she and I, in a warm bath of humid jazz and white noise and dry clicks. I focus on her navel, then on her eyes or on the pearl necklace of her spine, then on the wet comet tail of her sex or the drops of spit on the tip of her tongue. Think of what part you want to see, and the viewfinder will find it. Think of what part you want to photograph, and light will fall upon it. She and I, we do not belong to this world—we live in the absolute certainty of the cosmos, we sing through a night that knows no end, forever together, forever alone.

Or is this performance merely staged for my boss? Does she think these pictures are meant for Himmler? Or does she maybe have a book in mind. a glossy coffee-table book with glossy pictures, the glory of her body exposed to every man's gaze—in return for a nominal fee—for all eternity?

Bombs over Berlin. The rumbling doesn't keep Munich from its sleep. A transitory phase in the war. Hitler will soon unleash his secret weapon on London and then it will all be over. All: the war, the struggle of humanity, history itself, all collapsed under the mighty arm of the Great Leader.

It's more difficult than I thought, loving Helena Guna.

I observe her night after night. I see what she does. I register her moral turpitude, her artificial abandon, her pale fire.

How can I watch this, every single night, and still love her?

And yet. I do love her. How could I not?

I stand in the dark. I wait in the shadows. I wait.

I photograph her. I watch her most intimate moments, separated from her by no more than a veil of glass.

Her gaze, the eyes turned upwards in ecstasy—I too close my eyes and I too climax. I don't even touch myself.

I am pure.

I do not touch myself.

I do not touch her.

She is pure.

I do not touch her.

She is pure.

Nobody touches her.

She is wholly herself; she is hers alone.

The words we spoke that first night, the night when our odd romance began with blood and screams, those are the only words we've ever shared. The only time she touched me was when she wound a strip of fabric around my wound. I still keep that bandage inside my duffel bag; it's the only tie that binds us now.

•

"Hum? Sorry. I zoned out for a second."

"Isaaksohn."

"Oh? Isaaksohn? Yes, Isaaksohn. We didn't know each other well. We passed one day in the hallway, after I'd just moved in. Even though we'd never met, we recognized each other. From time to time we played a game of chess together."

Denying makes no sense. The question is, How much information can he divulge without harming the cause? Mira stands at the window, nursing her drink.

"We always recognized each other, you know. On the subway, on the street, in restaurants—I recognize them everywhere, my kinsmen, the illegals, and they recognize me. Like gay men recognize each other. We have no need for secret signs. That was the reason the Gestapo needed folks like Rolf and Stella. They had the sixth sense, they recognized their fellow Jews. That you have recognized us . . ."—De Heer clears his throat—". . . implies that you are one of us. An illegal. A guilty undercover agent. A traitor."

Mira spins quickly on her heels. Her voice trembles. "No! That isn't true! It simply . . . No, it isn't true!"

De Heer looks at her blankly. Where did that outburst come from? "You recognized me, didn't you? After you were finished with Isaaksohn, you came here. Instinctively, you recognized me for who or what I was, and you did the cruelest thing you could have done: You gave me back my life and its eternal torment."

Mira clicks her tongue; she seethes with impatience. "No! You were dying. I broke in because you called for help, Herr Hinkel!" She pleads—Mira pleads! "I put one hand on your forehead and the other on your chest. My touch calmed you down, it soothed you, you slipped into a quiet slumber. All I recognized was the struggle of a dying man. That was all I saw, that was what made me force the door. That's my talent, Herr Hinkel, to recognize a life that's running out."

Silence.

"And that's why I'm here now."

"You're serious, then? My life has run its course?"

Silence.

"If you had recognized me back then as a traitor, would you have left me to die?"

Silence again.

Her silence is not born of cruelty, that much he knows. That Mira is confused baffles De Heer. It baffles him more than her apparent desire to kill him. It saddens him too. Very much. If the Angel of Revenge herself is hesitant and uncertain, what then? Who then will grant him rest and forgiveness? De Heer's lips move, he mutters under his breath, incomprehensible words in an incomprehensible language.

•

And then: another evening, another man. I don't mean another man; I mean: another kind of man.

A timid type. Soft. How shall I put it? Reverent. Different indeed. Not a man to throw himself happily on top of her. More the type to approach the altar with veneration.

Why did she pick this specimen? I watch him stagger inside and I think: Ha, Lena will eat him alive! He almost doesn't dare look at her, and when he does, he can't tear his eyes away. The poor kid! I give him five minutes, and then she'll throw him out! The boy looks so nervous I wouldn't be surprised if he came on top of her shoes as soon as he dropped his pants.

But—oh no! I witness a remarkable transformation. The Lena on the bed is no longer the Lena I know, the voracious and vociferous fornicator who likes her men ravenous and rapacious—she now resembles nothing so much as a coquettish yet concerned country maiden. What's going on here? Is she gathering material for a new role? I have no other explanation for this behavior, no other account for the repulsive scene that plays in front of my eyes, so clearly forged and phony: a soft-pornographic Heidi movie.

You think I exaggerate?

Helena wears a dirndl dress, can you believe it? She pours her timid lover a glass of Riesling, as though she's a politician's wife at a dinner party, steadying the nerves of her husband's guests with light drinks and idle chat. They both drink their wine in awkward silence. They sit ten inches apart—a full ten inches! This man made it to the boudoir of one of the world's most desirable women, and he doesn't even try to touch her! Verily, verily I say unto you: A true gentleman he must be! And then they kiss, tenderly (yikes!), and then she undresses him. and (I can't believe my eyes), *she gets down on her knees for him* and washes him with soap and washcloth. Where is the reckless Lena I know so well? The Lena who devours her men like a she-wolf, who chews them up, skin and bones and all, and then spits them out again? This isn't my Lena—this is a sleepy sheep. And this little guy, he's a sheep too, an anxious bleating lamb; if Helena hadn't presented herself on hands and knees he wouldn't even have found her little hole, I swear, the stupid fucker!

That position, the coitus a *tergo* in the usual opening is, as you know, unusual for miss Guna. Like its anal variant, it's an ideal position from which to watch yourself in the mirror. And Helena does—she raises her head from the pillow and looks deep into the vertical pool of shimmering glass. But then! She looks straight through me—I swear: She snubs my burning eye, she rebuffs my aching lens, she aims her gaze directly at her lover, she locks her eyes straight onto his, reflected in the glass, and then—inconceivable!—all hell breaks loose: Lena, my Lena, my sweetly terrifying Lena, disappears, and in her stead a raging fury appears, foaming at the mouth, twisting, turning, pumping, churning, a breathless bitch lost to the world—awash, afloat, adrift in a rolling, demonic tide. I have never seen her like this, spitting and cursing, shouting obscenities, banging her rump against the man's thighs, and then she raises herself, one hand firmly planted on the bed and the other sliding hungrily between her legs and digging deep into the tender flesh around her clit, and in the swelling surge of her orgasm she bares her teeth and throws her head back, her tongue lolling violently, her eyes rolling out of control, until her gaze—again—finds her lover's, and then the wave of her orgasm washes over her; she comes, the million-dollar movie star, and the man redirects his gaze to the million-dollar spectacle before him: his cock pumping away between the wriggling million-dollar cheeks of her wriggling million-dollar ass, and then he locks eyes with her again, he forces her gaze upwards with his, high to the heavens, and then it happens, *Mutti-meine-Mutti*, good Lord!, and together— I feel like I'm going to throw up! Never-before-seen footage! A Helmut Hinkel exclusive!—they climax together, roaring like lions, throats wide open, teeth bare, hoarse and raucous, and the man collapses on top of her—spent, exhausted—and she collapses too, a squirming mass of flesh, and her last gaze, the gaze of abandon and triumph that I feel, that I *know* she owes to me, is denied me and aimed at the boy instead, and then—oh shame!—she raises her eyes to ceiling once again, to the Darkness of her Maker, Helena Guna one with the Oblivion of Heaven (what did that boy *do* to her?), and then she goes for it, the actress, she screams out the most banal, the most trivial, the most terrible cliché: "*Oh, mein G*tt! Mein G*TT! MEIN G*TT!*"—Ah! Ah! AH!—and gagging with pleasure they go limp with bliss, exhausted by the flood that's swept them both away, and tears stream over his face and hers—*What in heaven's name did that boy do to her?* She must be faking it, of course she must be faking it, she's an actress after all, the best there is. This is impossible. This cannot be, *this is impossible,* and I will never forget this, I will never forget this for as long as I live: Not once, not once has she looked at the man behind the mirror!

They are sound asleep, the bastards. I always spend the night in my cubbyhole, I lean against the wall in half-sleep and jolt awake when I slip to the floor. But tonight I'm so angry at the world that I can't even wait until the snoring starts. They are pressed against each other like two spoons in a drawer! The scandal! Mad with rage I click the mirror frame open, and shaking like a leaf I enter the bed chamber. They are too far gone to even notice me. I regret that I didn't bring my knife. They make such awful sounds in their contentment: They smack their lips, they wheeze. I stand and watch his repulsively bony hand resting so possessively on the Helena's snow-white flank, and I bring my ragged teeth to his naked throat. In the middle of the night in a villa near Munich, I consider killing a man with my bare teeth—I consider puncturing his jugular and ripping out his Adam's apple. Then a short happy sigh escapes the mouth of my beloved Lena. A cloud of wine and garlic caresses my cheek, and I run out of the room as fast as I can, on my woolen clogs, my eyes soaked in tears.

Let me repeat it. An actress has no voice. An actress has no mind of her own. Actresses have pawned their lives: Her body is on loan.

It's not her fault. It's the fault of that man. I will kill him. He stole my Lena from me.

That man. What maddens me, what enrages me above all is not that he took her body, but that he stole her soul.

Under the harsh light of the office lamp in Party Headquarters in Munich, the pictures look unsurprisingly obscene. My supervisor assesses them carefully. He is calm and detached: He studies them objectively, he reads the blueprint of the future in those streaks of black and white and gray. He peers through his magnifying glass to hunt for details that might have eluded me: the date on a newspaper on the dresser, the insignia on a uniform jacket, the chronology of fading scratches on a woman's skin.

He straightens his back. He cracks his knuckles. His voice sounds tired, disappointed.

"I had expected better taste from her."

I keep my expression as blank as I can.

"More ambition. High-ranking officers. Prominent politicians." He puts his finger on the photograph, right on top of her latest lover's skinny ass. "Not these . . . these . . . nameless nobodies."

I understand. Herr Himmler's sex between the diva's lips, or three of four of Bormann's fat fingers in her little slit—that's the kind of visual archive that matters. It has political consequences. Emil Bannings in her bed, or a couple of soldiers out past curfew—that stuff might make good fodder for the tabloids, but it's of no real consequence.

"How far along is she, do you think?"

"I beg your pardon, sir?"

"How far along is she? How many months, do you reckon?"

I am flabbergasted. Is Lena pregnant?

My boss looks at me wearily. "I have six children. Do you think I would miss a detail like that?"

I feel stupid. I who stared at the naked body of my untouchable lover for hours on end, I who know all the nuances of her flesh, its many colorings, its manifold dynamics—I have never noticed. To me, the swelling of her belly meant nothing more than that the actress was finally happy, eagerly partaking of the unrationed food in the Lebensborn house. In the growing darkness of her areolae I saw only joy from all the lovemaking—"Yes, a couple of months, I guess," I stutter.

My boss thinks out loud. "Who could be the father? Certainly not this stringy fellow, whatever document they made him sign."

As prescribed by army etiquette, I accompany my supervisor to his car. When he bids me farewell, absentminded and courteous as always, he hands me an envelope, half an inch thick. I know these envelopes by now: They contain a hefty wad of cash as well as new orders. I raise my eyebrows.

"Berlin," he says. "The Berlin-Potsdam area."

"What about Miss Guna?"

I am an idiot. I know I'm not allowed to ask such questions.

"A lost cause."

That's what my boss says. Helena is a lost cause. She disappoints him. He discards her with a casual wave of his hand. Guna? Screws the wrong men. Pregnant. No longer interesting. Nothing to see here; move on, people.

My boss puts his hands deep inside the pockets of his long leather coat—the coat made famous by his official photographs and by the newsreels—and he strides to the car. The driver runs out and opens the door for his boss. The Minister turns around and takes his right hand out of his pocket. He waves at me briefly with that bare hand—it is almost the last farewell between us, although neither of us suspects it.

Miss Guna, a lost cause? I open my envelope. What typical cruelty: My train leaves in an hour. There will be no goodbye. I hope it doesn't break Helena's heart, to be in her room all alone at midnight, to hear nothing but silence from behind the mirror. I know it breaks mine. What exactly does that mean, a lost cause? Am I one too?

I never broke through the mirror. I never laid a finger on her. I willed myself into believing that I loved her too much to ever be able to touch her; that I loved her with a love so pure that it completely transcended the body. My fingertips would have caught fire had they made contact with her skin.

Caught fire.

•

"What are you doing?"

"I'm cutting the clothes off your body."

"I can see that. Why are you doing it?"

"I want you naked."

"Well . . ."

"I want to touch your cock."

"You want *what*?"

"You heard me."

" . . . "

" . . . "

" . . . "

"There. Almost done. Sorry it took so long. Your kitchen scissors are quite dull. I should have brought my own."

"Excuse me for asking, but do you happen to like older men?"

"My interest is purely clinical, Herr Hinkel. I am phallomantic."

"Oh."

"It runs in the family—my mother was very good at it too."

"Phallomancy?"

"Phallomancy."

"You're joking, right? Tell me this is a joke. This has to be a joke."

"Not at all."

"You read the future from . . .?"

"I read dicks, yes. The skin is a blank canvas—all obsessions leave their mark. Sorrows, preoccupations, the ruts of ever-recurring thought patterns—it all nestles in a man's pores, it etches itself into his skin folds. In those of the penis too. I will read you and tell you who you are, Herr Hinkel. But I do not read the future. There is no need. I already foretold your future, didn't I? Didn't you read the parchment?"

No reply.

"The schlong never lies, Mister De Heer."

"You hold the proof of that in your hands."

"Smartass."

"You are an exceptionally beautiful woman."

"Thank you. I've been told that before."

"And what do your hands read, if I might ask?"

"This is not the actual reading. This is the preparatory phase. Every piece of data requires the appropriate measuring device."

"Are you implying what I think you're implying?"

"Uh-uh."

"And why did you use Yiddish slang? Do you think I am an *Ostjude*?"

Mira does not deign to answer. She grabs a small bottle of mineral oil from her purse. A droplet here, a droplet there, a droplet for him, a droplet for her. While she massages it all in, she hums quietly. She loves her job.

"Well, well." Mira readies the measuring device. "I'm anxious to find out what this will reveal."

"Don't expect too much," says De Heer.

Mira closes her eyes and lowers herself.

This then is what the erstwhile executioners look like, and it's not a pretty sight. Extended bellies (Isaaksohn) or emaciated bodies (De Heer), crooked spines, thin tufts of sparse hair on skulls overgrown with dark brown spots. Herr Hinkel yelps when the *magicienne* turns her back to him and sinks into his lap. Time has had its way with him, like it had its way with Isaaksohn. They should be grateful for the aches of old age, Isaaksohn and Hinkel and all the others. Their victims did not have the luxury of suffering from them.

The ritual is slow and silent. A deliberate and careful reading requires concentration and careful calibrations, frequent repositioning of the instrument with the occasional rereading of certain passages. Sometimes a paragraph needs to be studied multiple times to fully grasp its meaning.

If Hinkel could only sit still! The man behaves like a patient who's being auscultated by his doctor. Nebula understands. It is such an intimate assessment, and the silence makes her customers uncomfortable. But there's nothing she can do about that: Small talk will override the weak signal she seeks to decode.

"Uh."

"Sh!"

"Uh . . ."

"Would you please remain silent?"

They labor in silence.

". . ."

"..."

"Sorry. I moved. An involuntary twitch."

"It's okay."

"Would you care to let me in on what exactly my organ is telling you?"

"Shut up!"

"..."

"..."

"I.."

"Mister Hinkel, would you please shut up? And please don't start each and every one of your sentences with the word 'I.' You are unimportant in the greater scheme of things. Soon you will be dead and gone. Or do you think your death sentence is a joke?"

"It's extremely difficult for a naked man to take an equally naked woman seriously, Miss Mira."

"Oh! Well. A nicely absurd statement. Remember that the angels go naked, Herr Hinkel, among them the Angel of Death."

"..."

"..."

"What did you learn from Isaaksohn's reading?"

"..."

"..."

"Isaaksohn's dick mentioned you, among other things."

"..."

"..."

"But what it told you wasn't not clear enough to lead you directly to my flat?"

"..."

"..."

"You know how oracles work, Herr Hinkel. They reveal the deeper aspects of reality. They don't bother much with the details."

"..."

"..."

"Will this take much longer? Just a question."

"Just a minute. I'm still missing part of the message. Yes, here. Quite hard to read. Wait, I need to get just a little bit higher. Could you twist your hip a little? Yes, like that. Wonderful. Thank you."

"..."

"This is a difficult passage—the writing is minuscule, the letters formed in haste. How smart, it's written on the inside of your foreskin—you didn't go all the way in claiming a Jewish identity, then, hm? What does it say? It looks like a quick and intimate diary entry scribbled in pencil between the lines of a real book—and it's like an eraser is sweeping over the words even as I read them. What does this say? . . . Meat? . . . Mega? *Omega!*"

"What?"

"Shit! Shut up! G*d, this is hard! Here—the lines are fading. You're willing them away, aren't you? You're somehow making the inscription disappear? Faster now, Mira girl, read faster, and be careful! No, it is not mega . . . Meta . . . Or is it? Mega . . . Megaton? No, Metatron. That's it! *Metatron!*"

Instantly, De Heer's facial expression collapses, and so does his erection. She must be right. This must be the correct interpretation of the slyly hidden passage. He in turn feels her body shudder, a shudder that travels all the way to the root of his waning hard-on—and this way he knows that she knows.

Metatron! De Heer cannot control himself. He blurts it out.

"O yes! Let it rain, oh Lord, rain down your blessing from the heavens: the blinding beauty of your Angel, the Angel of Your Presence, the Angel of Revenge! The Holiest, the Glorified, the Most Exalted, the Angel METATRON!"

Mira punches De Heer in the face with her elbow, but her gesture somehow lacks conviction. Her mind is elsewhere. As soon as she heard the name of the Angel, the name she has been looking for for so long, a chill strong and bony like a tiny fist of silver clasped her heart.

•

The books open my eyes. I begin to see the lines, the flow of unacknowledged quotations, the intertwined fragments, the paragraphs with words bent out of shape to form a new, fraudulent narrative. Some of De Heer's paragraphs are almost exact quotations; others contain just the gist of the original story. The liberal use of literal quotation amazes me. De Heer—or Helmut Hinkel—recited them so believably, as if they were indeed spontaneous retellings of his personal story. I note with shame and mortification that I managed to mangle them, and more than once I misguidedly edited the words of one or the other great writer into grotesque clichés, all in the name of an unbroken style. I now understand why the orthodox style is so powerful—De Heer's rant in one of his few plausibly authentic passages notwithstanding—its openness allows the reader to inject his or her own suffering into the story.

Well then. De Heer must have practiced hard for this performance; perhaps he practiced for the better part of his life. Maybe to the point where he himself had come to believe his own fake biography.

And even while I am appalled, the uneasy suspicion creeps into my mind that De Heer's work is an admirable triumph—from this mishmash of voices and stories a legend grew that somehow transcends the individual fragments. It makes me uneasy to admit it, but perhaps his hodgepodge biography is after all a service to humanity, a perpetrator's bizarre monument to the victims—*his* victims. Could it be? Is this all a dream, a monstrous and misguided dream—inexcusable yet pure of intent? De Heer's monument may be a fake, but perhaps his intentions were good?

But even if this optimistic interpretation is correct, I can never forgive De Heer for playing with my head, for manipulating my synapses, for deliberately tricking me into such emotional turmoil—the predictable feelings of revulsion faced with the inevitability of history, the expected disgust vis-à-vis the unthinkable indifference of the masses, the usual horror at the coldness of the executioners. Yet, what he did differs from our little, daily lies in scale only: We are all magicians, writers, photographers, lovers, and parents—we all know the merit of fiction, we're all experts at fabricating lies out of echoes of the past and secondhand rumors, we all weave half-truths out of figments of reality, and we get away with it.

Such coolheaded betrayal!

•

"A man gets lynched for his deeds. Not for his intentions, or for who he is."

"I'm going to get lynched?"

"Figure of speech."

"Good. Death by hanging horrifies me. What will you do to me? Didn't you just try to convince me that Death is compassionate? Will you be equally compassionate—quick and fair in the execution of my sentence?"

"You are mistaken. What makes you think I'll be your executioner?"

"You don't have the courage to carry out the sentence yourself? You have underlings? A private *Einsatzgruppe* of assassins at your disposal?"

Mira looks at her fingernails. She admires De Heer's civility. All this time, he has been addressing her—they speak German, of course—with the formal *Sie*. This man refuses to deal with death—his own, personal death—on an informal basis; he treats it with respect: dissident respect, but respect nevertheless.

Then she says something that startles him. "What was all that about, Herr Hinkel—all that nonsense about the birds in Auschwitz being silent?"

How does she know I passed through Auschwitz?

"How do you . . ."

"Your autobiography, Herr Hinkel."

His autobiography—all truth, all fiction—the story he worked on for so long, all in his head. The only human being he ever shared it with was that young man, his scribe, who took dictation in this very room, sitting on the chair Mira has tied him to. The roots of De Heer's hair prick to attention.

"Is this your idea, Frau Mira, is this *his* idea of a practical joke?"

Mira is suddenly fascinated by a hangnail on her left hand. De Heer's brain creates an instant conspiracy theory. That Andermans kid is a schlemiel, but this Mira is a woman with brains and initiative.

"The boy—Andermans. Is he the one who sent you?"

More unresponsiveness on her part, and this increases De Heer's agitation. He twists in his chair—"Ma'am, I am a first-rate magician, I can free myself from this precarious situation whenever I want." Mira doesn't look at him, but she raises one eyebrow, creating a splendid asymmetry. She'd like to see that, is what her expression says.

"Okay. Maybe not right now. But as soon as you've left, my dear lady, I will drag myself, chair and all, to the kitchen, where I will free myself in an instant, using just the smallest strip of metal."

Mira coughs discreetly.

"Good for you! Glad to hear that! I don't have to worry, then, that you might die for lack of food or water."

"I'll call the police. You must be high on their wanted list."

"It doesn't really look as though the police made Rolf's death a high priority, does it? Did they even interrogate you? Do they even know you had such close ties with the Jewish Jew-traitor?"

"Still. Detectives like their crimes solved. They might get a promotion out of it, or a raise."

"Go right ahead. If you have nothing to hide, if you are who you claim to be, go right ahead. But what purpose will it serve? You know nothing about me, and you will never see me again."

A snort. "I know I can reach you through Andermans."

"Maybe. Maybe Andermans also doesn't know who I am. Maybe he doesn't know where I live. Maybe he'll never see me again either."

"How will you kill me, if you leave the building and allow me to liberate myself?"

"You yourself decide your time of death, Mister Hinkel. It's all up to you. As long as you stay inside the building, you're safe. But once you go outside, you will be tracked down and hunted. You remember the Gestapo? You must have seen them in action, I presume, up close and personal? Something like that will happen to you. Resistance will be futile. Don't negotiate with your attackers, it will only incite them more. This will neither hasten or slow your demise—it will only make it more painful. I have read your autobiography. I have been told that you are ready for the sojourn into the night, for your return to nothingness. But I want to see tears before I believe that, tears of remorse, not for the loss of your own life, but for the lives that you took from others, innocent others—you will know the mercy of the death-blow only after your executioners have seen those tears."

Is this the end of the conversation? Apparently so: Mira gathers her belongings, starting by picking her clothes up off the floor. De Heer has almost forgotten that they are both naked. First she straps on her bra, then she looks for her panties. De Heer averts his eyes: For some reason, watching this woman getting dressed is a more intimate act than witnessing her undress, as if her whorish get-up as a strip-o-gram isn't the disguise, but her nudity itself. With every article of clothing she puts on—shirt, fishnet stockings, miniskirt, jacket—she reveals a new, crueler, part of herself. De Heer shivers in his chair. This woman knows no compassion. Why doesn't she throw a coat over his old bony body and grant him some dignity? Here he sits—old and exhausted, thin as a reed, worthless and wordless. Tears, he wants to say, tears are nothing like me.

Then, already in the doorway, her silhouette crowned by the white neon light from the hallway, she turns around for one final, remarkable piece of information.

"I was born in Auschwitz."

Silence.

"Or rather, that's where my mother came from."

More silence.

"I am a child from Auschwitz."

Yet more silence.

"She survived. An orphan, a gypsy child."

"Ow! Excuse me. I bit my tongue."

"See you, Herr Hinkel. See you in hell, where the both of us will burn forever, in the section reserved for ruthless killers."

.

Tears? Look who's fighting tears: She steps out the door, and as soon as Mira-Layla-Eris-Circe-etcetera crosses the threshold to the real world, a different human being emerges from behind the facade of crumbling bravura—a woman more innocent, more apprehensive, more subject to the laws of provenance and inheritance than the "Mira" character could ever be. She left the apartment as she found it: lights out, curtains drawn, because these are the symptoms of his guilt—a man drives out his midday demons by artificial darkness. She recognizes these symptoms; she too is glad that dusk has fallen, that the air has turned cool and liquid. Her breath leaves a hint of cloud on the glass of the front door. As she opens it, a shadow slips inside behind her, quick and stealthy, without so much as looking at her—then she is outside, on the street.

The cobblestones buzz. The subway train comes rolling in, and Nebula walks faster. She runs down the stairs of the Spittelmarkt station just as the train is ready to pull out; she slips between the closing doors just in time. As she catches her breath, she looks around her. Men are either openly staring at her, or they quickly look away when her gaze meets theirs; women press their lips together in contempt. Nebula had almost forgotten what she looked like: a cheap whore on the way to her *Strich* on Alexanderplatz. She is a woman of many roles, the last in a long line of actresses, and now she forces her way into a tiny spot on one of the benches. The performance is over, she needs her rest. The women on either side of her quickly scoot away; they couldn't bear physical contact with this depraved creature of the night. Nebula leans back and lights a cigarette, right underneath the no-smoking sign. She lifts one arm above her head and clicks the window open; the compartment floods with ice-cold evening air. A fat little lady with an equally rotund purse rounds up some courage, but when she starts to lean towards Nebula, the latter growls some coarse vulgarity and the lady retreats. Everybody in the car shrinks and shrivels—crazy woman alert! At the next stop—Märkisches Museum—they all run for the door.

Nebula is finally alone. She has her black jeans in her bag, and a black turtleneck, and black Nike sneakers. She pulls on the jeans underneath her skirt, then she throws the latter out the window. When the train arrives at Alex, she is fully dressed and wrapped in her hip-length leather jacket, every trace of makeup wiped off her face. Her tears are gone too and a bitter sneer nestles around the corners of her mouth.

She did nothing wrong. De Heer deserves to die, and she did him a service with her carefully considered plan. She had gone through a number of alternatives. She could have sent him a copy of his file together with an anonymous letter pasted together from headlines in the *Bildzeitung*—"TONIGHT, OLD NAZI, I'M COMING TO GET YOU!" The next day, she would send him a hastily scribbled postcard: "*I apologize, I couldn't make it last night. I'll be there tonight!*" And then the day after: "Sorry, I had some unexpected company, but rest assured, I'll be there soon!" It's easy to push a man over the brink and into heart attack.

Too late now. The dice have been cast. The first man is standing guard at De

Heer's front door; the troops have their orders. Just thinking about the old man gets her angry. Who does De Heer think he is, what gives him the right to pretend he's somebody other than who he is—a man from the other side, from the unreachable other side of the mirror—what gives him the right to pretend to stand on the side of the victims, on Nebula's side?

•

At this same moment, the moment when Nebula tastes the bitter almond flavor of her fundamental loneliness and the ultimate uselessness of revenge, I experience my very own epiphany. I stand in front of the window when it dawns on me. The cat is perched on my left shoulder and the crows are swarming in chaotic patches over the park when that most terrible and hateful of hypotheses hits me: De Heer's story, the story he dictated to me as if he was none other than the angel Gabriel whispering his sacred intimations into the ear of a sacred scribe, *is* an honest story, a Kaddish from the heart, a well-meant shiva, his own attempt to declare a day of Atonement, his personal Yom Kippur. Maybe he'd been wondering, in his heart, all those decades, What might have happened if things were different? If he had been born a Jew in the times and circumstances he described, might not his life have turned out just the way he told it? In the alternative world he created, parallel to his own, Jozef De Heer is quite real, and Helmut Hinkel is nothing but an unbelievable fiction. There can be no clearer demonstration that circumstances matter more than personality than in the autobiography of this irredeemable trickster—it's a tried and true cliché, of course, that so much of what we become in life depends on grace and fate.

This revelation is intolerable. Time and place and circumstance are no excuse for his crimes. "We did know, we knew it all along, but there's nothing we could have done, not with those people in power." Is this a valid argument? Excuse me, Eternal Judge, we are only human, powerless in our lives, characters on a stage. Viewed from the lofty heights of Your throne it may look as if our lives are quick improvisations, but that is not the case. We suffer through our lives, dear G*d, our personal histories an permanent part of the wider history of the human race—history alone breathes life into the lifeless clay of our existence. We breathe history like a fish breathes water; we float on circumstance like a seagull drifts on the air. History flows through our gills, its thermal energy lifts our wings; without it, we are nothing.

Deliver us, G*d, or g*ds, if You exist: Deliver us from evil, deliver us from ourselves. A knife bites, a scream of pain, and a bloody piece of foreskin tumbles into a silver bowl: Is this child now fundamentally different from the stump-nosed child crying in the next room? Fairness and unfairness, justice and injustice, are these characteristics of the individual, or vulgar names for the ways of the world?

I don't know it yet, but this is De Heer's last day on earth. His final hours on his ultimate day. The death of a poor jaundiced man living in an apartment that smells of dried apricots, sadness wafting from the furniture.

De Heer, a one-man Rosetta stone.

·

De Heer rubs his wrists. He was really scared there for a minute, when the iceberg Mira was pretending to be part of a conspiracy, or rather a counter-conspiracy with manifold arms and multiple roots, an international intrigue. But then there was her naïve comment about the birds in Auschwitz, and the reference to her gypsy background, and that was an instant antidote for his fears. Whoever Mira is, she has no idea who De Heer is, and what ties he has to Auschwitz and the heart of the Third Reich. Yet De Heer (even he has taken to calling himself "De Heer"; after all, he's used that name at least twice as long as he used the name Helmut Hinkel) doesn't know whether this information should bring joy or despair. Given Mira's ignorance, her threat could be totally baseless, a tasteless joke from a deranged mind. But even if she really does have a small army of guerilleros waiting for him outside, it doesn't really matter at this point. Her sudden appearance, whatever the cause, is the axe that rapped against the surface layer of ice that covered his heart for the better half of the century. The warmth of the outer world now seeps through the cracks, its fire, its friction, its upheaval. The ice is melting and the cracks in his heart widen—it falls apart.

Mira is absolutely right. De Heer is tired of life, and maybe life in its turn is tired of him. He's survived two dictatorial regimes; twice he's collaborated opportunistically with an empire generally assumed to be invincible, and twice the empire was vanquished. Twice he lost his country: The Reich is gone without a trace, and the East is hardly recognizable anymore. He was an apprentice-alchemist who buried the newly uncovered secrets of nature; the architect who built impenetrable walls with concrete sheets no more than three inches thick. The mirror that Mira held up to his face on this last day of his life reflected nothing more than the empty image of another mirror, an echo of emptiness through which a single lonely plume of smoke rises to the sky. Empty but not silent: The shrill cry of a Polish finch, amplified a thousand times, pierces his eardrums.

Where did his loyalty lie, all those long years?

With the Plan.

The Plan. Is there anyone alive who still remembers where It originated, who sowed Its seeds, why It matured, and under what circumstances It took on the bizarre shape it has today? De Heer vaguely remembers how the Plan evolved from necessary to risky to superfluous, and then to what It is today: toxic for everyone involved. But there isn't anybody, not even De Heer himself, who can take on the responsibility of killing It. It feeds on Itself, the Plan. It leads Its own life. It is a monster that chews up Its children, small (Isaaksohn) and large (De Heer), a monster that keeps Itself alive through cannibalism. Mira herself is living proof of this. Only a few months ago, De Heer had been ready to sacrifice his life to sabotage the Plan. In February his death would have been useful; in February his death could have stopped the wheels from turning. At that point he was the only link between the Plan and Its implementation. But Mira saved his life and he had hardly returned home when the cell phone started ringing and he got sucked in again, almost unthinkingly taking up his indispensable role in the ever growing bloat of the Plan.

Or is he deceiving himself? The Plan is much older than the legions who will finally carry It to Its fruition. And that's the way it should be: It is these reincarnations in every new generation that make the Plan robust. It is parallel-distributed. It is eternal, and so much more than the sum of Its parts—for none of the parts fully comprehends the full extent of the Plan. The Plan has become the hidden reason for De Heer's existence, the reason for the network of relationships that he has built around himself, the reason that he packed his heart in ice.

No, when he looks at matters more carefully, he sees that the Plan would have survived his demise in February.

Even more certain is that his living or dying today is completely irrelevant to the Plan's execution.

Mira was right. He is done with life, and life is done with him.

What Mira doesn't know is that she is hastening his death by only a few days. He had hoped to stand on the balcony on the Day itself, with just a towel wrapped around his waist, bathing his body in the glow of the new sun, lapping up the hot rays, dying languorously, ecstatically in the delightful searing blaze.

De Heer sits at the dining room table. Once in a while it's good to stop one's daily activities and just sit and think. Who would have dreamed that his death would arrive in this guise—so bold and so articulate, so persuasive, so overwhelmingly obscene, so Freudian in its implications? De Heer can hardly stand the beauty of it all. No need to choose between death or glory—Mira gave him both.

He gets up again. He paces back an forth in front of the shelves. His hand finds a book with Hebrew letters on its spine. He stole it, a long time ago, from the villa in Dahlem in which his Special Unit had been housed. Later he carried this book and the few others he had pilfered from the villa to an antiquarian—only Jews still love old books, only Jews still cherish the illusion that the past can hold some comfort. None of the books had contained a sacred text, as he had secretly hoped. The book in his hand is a collection of Hassidic fairy tales; it speaks of curtains of fire, of voices that echo in attics, of creaking doors that open to the past. He had no use for it; with his knife he hollowed out its pages and from this cavity he now removes his most prized possession: a half-disintegrated folder with the final pictures, the very last photographs he took of Helena Guna.

It doesn't take much to turn a man's mind into a *terrain vague*. A man sets out to describe the world, *his* world. Years pass, and he fills the black slate of his mind with random scribbles (kingdoms lost, leveled Alps, friends gone, enemies vanished into thin air, nebulae whirled out of existence, bridges burned, walls riddled with bullet holes, shattered windowpanes) but then he notices that the repeated scratching of the chalk has left deeper, indelible markings: Hold the slate just so and the light reveals a portrait of his own face. Where does that labyrinth of lines lead to?

This is where it leads to. Secret pictures of a reality that never was. The signature of an ultimate unreachability. The stumbling specter of Helena Guna rises from the past, and it makes De Heer's eyes mist over with a drunken nostalgia.

The teary eyes of the Maker meet his creation. Like YHVH's work, De Heer's has gone so terribly awry. He observes the debacle with all the gentleness his soul still holds, in the improbable light that lengthens a memory from a single second to an eternity and compress a span of hours into a single moment. The ungraspable quality of his love and its decay appear to him both exasperating and comforting, for this is *his* memory, inalienable, and it is its horrifying incommunicability, its final incomprehensibility that makes the events unique and real. And, yes, now that the final moment has arrived, now that the way back is forever blocked and the flight forward abruptly obstructed, he finally realizes that life is not a simple narrative; not a novel in which all of life's trials carry a meaning, no matter how chaotic and random they might seem; not a web of threads converging splendidly in the very last pages—where a Plan is revealed after all, seamlessly executed by its many ignorant protagonists, antagonists, and extras. No, De Heer's biography is different, It didn't sprout from a single brain, but from the irredeemable disorder of life. It is only fitting then that the defining moments of that life be ungraspable, that the memory of it must slip through the mind's fingers, slick and slimy like an eel. For a second—a second that lasted half a century—De Heer had imagined himself to be part of a Plan. Now he finds himself alone.

I did not kill Helena Guna. But I was watching as she destroyed herself with exceptional ardor, and I mistook that ardor for lust, mistook her self-destructive urges for a strong will. I did not shield Helena from the violence that she inflicted upon herself. And even had I been more astute, how could I have stepped out of the mirror? It would have meant my own death. And now it's too late to beg for forgiveness—who could I beg for forgiveness? That young woman who just left, with her overabundant sense of justice? Nobody can grant me forgiveness. My impending death, whether brought about by others or self-imposed, does not erase anything. My death is an empty gesture. Nobody gets anything out of it. Not me, and not anybody else.

A man raves on. A man lies on a burlap bag filled with straw. The doctors say that he speaks in tongues; he pushes his words through a poisoned throat. But I recognize the gargling, sputtering sounds of my mother's language. A man my own age, terminally ill, a man who vaguely looks like me. A Jew. I ask him, "*Wat is uw naam?*" Stranger, what is your name? I am well-acquainted with Jews. My teacher was a Jew—the great unknown master WLADIMIR, who died of a gunshot wound. I shot that bullet, after I infiltrated the insurgency, after I betrayed all of them, after I took his lover in a muddy clearing in the forest.

A long time ago I promised the authorities to write my memoirs. Good, I said to myself. Why don't I write the truth for once? The good in Hinkel. The bad in Hinkel. The ugly in Hinkel. The very ugly in Hinkel. The utmost ugly in Hinkel. Then that idiot showed up in his disposable nightgown, carried in on a wave of violence I myself had helped unleash more than half a century ago. We started talking and before I knew it I told him the official version of my biography, the biography of Jozef De Heer, the version in which I am first a victim of National Socialism and then the unsung hero of the socialist democracy. It wasn't that I lacked the courage to speak the truth. It was simply force of habit. The story I dished out to this hapless stranger had become more familiar to me than my own life. Lies? There were no lies. The truth—Hitler, Auschwitz, the Wall, man eating man—the truth is the truth, independent of who brings it to light. How superficial is authenticity! There is more eloquence, more instruction in the most complicated lie than in a simple truth.

The wood I carry on my back, the wood for the pyre, is my own words. Words on paper—such flammable material!

Here is the picture I was looking for. A portrait from happier days, taken during the next-to-final night. Helena Guna sits in bed, cross-legged and a bit tipsy, and she leans towards the photographer, her hands folded around a playfully slanted champagne glass that is almost empty—one last swig remains. She has a wet finger at the brim, ready to elicit sweet flute tones from the glass; the bowl rests against her swollen lower lip. With her elbows she props a pillow against her chest—her hair is tangled, her eyes smile directly at the camera and an escaped nipple likewise smiles at the lens; her mouth too is almost ready to smile. The picture is wonderfully in-focus; you can count the settled stardust of her freckles on her knees and lower arms. She's so young and beautiful—and so elegantly wasted. Helena Guna, three months pregnant.

This is the photograph I slip into a big cardboard envelope. I address the envelope to Mira, care of Paul Andermans. On the back of the envelope I write,

"Mira—I knew your grandmother."

Of course I recognized Mira. How could I not? She has the same body, the same defiant and childish stare, the same slender fingers, the same willowy neck, the same smile-that-isn't-quite-a-smile, the same nose that hesitates between pride and mischief; even the constellation of her beauty spots is eerily similar to Helena Guna's. Her eyes are different, yes; Nebula's eyes are brown and almond-shaped, and her skin doesn't have the same breathtaking transparency the movie star's did. But even those eyes and the cinnamon skin I recognize.

I look out the window, to the sandy plains that bathe in the yellow city light reflected from the underside of the clouds—the plains from which soon, and without me, the latest version of Berlin shall rise.

I write another sentence: "Mira—I saved your mother's life."

It doesn't matter. It is done. There: From the veils of the past I see another awkward specter loom, in a black uniform.

That hesitant creature is me.

•

Where is she going?

She shakes her hair loose. She freshened up in the restrooms at the Alex station. Dressed in black, she looks like any of the thin-lipped *Kulturgroupies* that prowl around town on a Friday night.

Maybe she'll get wasted and stomp the night into the ground at one of the trendy discotheques around Zoo, her arms raised high, her hands fluttering like doves, yelling along to the staccato beat, "*We're a-li-i-i-i-i-i-ive*," repeated so often that she might even come to believe it. Or maybe she'll wander the streets of Kreuzberg and let the odors soak into the wool of her sweater, the frying oil and falafels and kofta ('the hamburger of the prophets!"), the donuts and french fries, the cheese stench of the "New York style" pizza, the half-nauseating sweetness of baklava and gelato and chocolate chip cookies and *Kaiserschmarren*, the sickeningly earthy smell of quiches and stuffed *Paprikas*, the synthetic bouquet of random deodorants, the tang of pomade, the crispy aroma of Chinese *kroepoek*, the obscene rubber reek of tires, the omnipresent malignancy of the cigarette smoke—and then she will let the dawn's early light guide her into one of those *Kneipe* with tea lights cut from fresh onions and join a vehement discussion of the unknowablility of *das Ding an Sich* and the inappropriateness of the brain-mind dichotomy, drifting in and out of the same old boring "quantum physics equals Eastern philosophy" argument, all those tedious replicas of half-baked *Uni* conversations that are the invariable prelude to dreary sex on an unmade bed in some shabby dorm room.

She doesn't even know what train she's on. The bends of the River Spree look more ominous to her than ever, more foreboding than any other spot in Berlin. In Friedrichstraβe Station she couldn't stand it any longer; she switched trains, without looking. She was headed for Potsdam, but did she really want to go to Potsdam? She let the crowd carry her along, she drifted with the crowd up and down stairwells and through long corridors, and then she took a train, the first one she saw, and made a few random transfers until she completely lost her way. The U-Bahn train rides high above the city and offers Nebula a look inside the windows of once proud nineteenth-century palaces now cut up into small single-family units. Women do the dishes and kiss their children goodnight; they brush their dogs while their husbands read the paper and watch TV. Shirtless bachelors lift weights in front of the windows, facing outwards with dark despair in their eyes.

She could go to Ku'damm and have a quick bite at one of the cheap restaurants for tourists and busy shoppers, the furniture bolted to the floor and the lighting shrill as a tanning salon's, the smiles of the boys and girls behind the counter frozen into chimpanzee grins; after her meal she could go to the corner of Joachimsthaler to listen to the American missionaries cheerleading for the Lord ("*Gimme a why, gimme an aitch, gimme a vee, gimme an aitch—Y-H-V-H—Yehovaaaahh!*") and then maybe roam from *Videoarkade* to *Videoarkade*, numbing her senses in the nervous bath of cheap, indifferent porn until she feels enough loathing for life to find a scruffy hotel and catch up on her dreamless sleep. Or she could go to Tacheles and score a few ounces of broad-spectrum marihuana, and then chat up the person next to her: "Hi, I couldn't help it, I saw you leafing through your copy of *Schöner Wohnen*. I share your passion for floral wallpaper and fake kelims. Want to have a drink with me at *The Green Door* and see what happens?"

She could opt for noble solitude. Go to Café Einstein in the old villa in the

Kurfürstenstraße, where the Viennese waiters get stoned on their own old-fashioned snobbery, and order a café latte and stare at its reflection in a green granite table. Or spy on the upper crust of Berlin cultural life through the silvered glass of the flaking mirrors in their opulent, neo-Knobeldorfian gilded frames—the actors and writers and professors and painters who grieve for the world in their tight black suits and tiny Armani glasses while they eat slices of pear torte as if this was their last night on earth, but that this night would never end. The street outside glistens with a different type of sorrow: the underage heroin whores in fishnet stockings, fishing for Benzes.

A piece of graffiti flashes by.

"*Der Führer lebt!*"—The Führer is alive!

A scribble underneath, in a different hand: "*Im Argentinien.*"

And all those numbers, most of them down to single digits now.

Paul can have her books. She no longer needs them. Her mission is accomplished.

But she has to make a decision, doesn't she? Where should she go, what shape will tonight's numbness take?

•

Head in hands. Light head. Heavy hands. Heavy head. Light hands. I no longer know how I feel. Once I heard a man groan from the depths of his treacherous heart.

The train stops in front of a big building. A wall stretches out as far as I can see; in the middle an edifice with fat square doors, the gatehouse to a gigantic farm complex or perhaps an army compound, crowned with a roof in the shape of a pyramid. There's writing high above the gate, but there isn't enough light for me to make out what it says. Two words, with a dash between them? The name of this station?

Then the gates open wide, and the train starts moving again.

We slip inside.

Yes. No doubt about it. This is the end of the line.

In the moonlight the windows in the gatehouse gleam dull and mysterious, a shield of lead to keep the radiance of the world outside. A cloud of dust and steam dances around the train; the first careful silver of the breaking dawn is punctured brutally by the probing fingers of the floodlights. Behind those lights smolders a less explicable flickering orange glow.

We inch closer, at a snail's pace, to a big platform of concrete. I hear familiar sounds: dogs bark, officers shout orders.

The brakes screech; the train halts. The sound of running boots and the grating of metal over metal. Shudders travel through the train: The soldiers unbolt the doors, starting at the head. The shouting intensifies, German and some unintelligible language, all hard clicks and sharp vowels. I slide the bolt open. The cold air and the sudden surge of adrenaline do me good, my head feels empty and clear at the same time. I step outside. Chaos on the ramp. Soldiers jump into the cars and shove the remaining folks outside, nudging them with their rifle butts. Somebody moans when he hits the ground and collapses; the rest keep on walking, the soldiers push them ahead. The SS-men bark their orders: Form two lines, five abreast—one line for women, one line for men, children with their mother, quick, quick, *quick*! GO! No time for the prisoners to look around and get their bearings, no time to go back and help the weak, even if they wanted to. The soldiers force them to march, five abreast, two lines; if necessary they hit the men and women with their whips or their batons.

A soldier walks past the lines, shouting out, "*Zwillinge, Zwillinge? Zwillinge!*" A set of identically dressed twins runs to him, he directs them to the head of the line. There a young officer in a white doctor's coat regulates the traffic. A man stumbles and falls. "Don't look! Don't look!" A soldier rushes over; a dog barks at his side. With his boot he prods the man's side, and when the man refuses to get up, the soldier takes out his pistol. There is no hesitation: he shoots the man straight through the heart. I shrink back when I hear the shot; the instant sharp stench of shit and blood mixes with the diesel fumes. Underneath all that there is a deeper smell, more ominous, something rotten, a smell that makes the nostrils go wide with fear—the stink of scorching flesh, the fiery stench of a dragon's breath, indescribable, revolting, final.

In a uniform black as ink I stand in the floodlights of the ramp at Auschwitz-Birkenau and I see the breath of the prisoners rise to the heavens and merge with the soldiers'. This is the place around which it all revolves—this is where the true war is fought, the war that never stops, the war that still goes on, even now that the war on the battlefields has long been lost. This is the machine that keeps on churning, even now that the Wehrmacht is powerless, fruitlessly spinning its well-worn wheels in the air. We aren't supposed to mention it, but we all know it, each of the young men with their whips and sticks and pistols and the hypomanic shimmer in their eyes—we all know it: This place, this hellhole, this is Hitler's true priority, and this will be our downfall.

I am young, an architecture student plucked fresh from school and taken under the wings of a great architect and an even greater physicist. I know the laws of physics, even the forbidden ones that were devised by Jews. I know the term "singularity": the point at which all laws break down because a variable has been carried to its very limits. The voyage to the heart of the black hole, the backwards calculations to the beginning of time, forward to the point omega: all divisions by zero, mathematical impossibilities, terms in an equation that extends to infinity. Impossibilities that nevertheless have to exist, because everything has a beginning and everything ends. And here I stand, my boots stuck in the half-frozen mud of Auschwitz: I stepped into a singularity, an unimaginable reality on which logic cracks its teeth. I realize all too well that it is impossible to escape from a black hole once you've crossed its invisible perimeter. Once inside the Schwarzschild radius, you can never get out. Once you've entered the confines of Auschwitz, once you've stood on that ramp and smelled Death rising from its chimneys, there is no way back, no return home. You will carry the curse with you, the slow rot, the gangrene that sooner or later will strangle your soul.

Yes, that fresh breath, the breath that fuses the tortured with their tormentors—my breath joins theirs too, brushing up against Death himself who floats at low altitude over the camp, a dirty cloud of ash.

I walk past the lines, the lines of men, women, and children. Their only crime is being Jewish. Being Jewish in Aryan Germany. I can't look them in the eyes; I simply can't bring myself to do it. I turn away, I bend my head to the ground. I have been taught I am superior to them, they explained it well, genealogical theories galore, but when I see this—the secret murder machine in action, the snorting shorn SS-men who stomp the ground like Arabian thoroughbreds, the mass of people walking to their deaths in complete submission but with wild-eyed panic on their faces—who here is the superior race?

At the end of the line stands the young officer with the white coat over his black uniform. A demon disguised as an angel. The guardian at the Gate.

He does not speak, his hands do the talking. They flutter, quick like banners in the wind. I have to talk to this man. This man is my only connection to Lena Guna. I feel dizzy. This war—I do not understand this war. Things aren't so simple as they used to be. Many things have happened, but they are not true. Other things are true, but they never happened.

The restless, delicate, mute, articulate fluttering of his hands.

To the left.

To the left.

To the right.

Left.

Right.

Right.

Right.

I stand to the side and I look over his white shoulder at the faces of the approaching herd—I can look at them now, because none of them looks back at me: they all have their eyes fixed on the doctor.

There is no hesitation in the doctor's mind. A dragging leg, a festering wound, an emaciated body, an all too anxious look in the eye—these go to the left. Strong, healthy, clear-eyed—to the right. The hand of the doctor is diabolically eloquent: Toscanini directing the premiere of La Bohème with nonchalant elegance. Whenever necessary, the doctor's hand urges a patient to pause—we are all patients of the good doctor, he is our savior, he is our hope, for five minutes he is an absolute, our g*d—and then the hand descends, cold and naked . . . and for a moment the whole world rests in that white, priestly palm. His hand opens mouths with the decisiveness of a horseman; his hand pulls down an eyelid as if this curtain of flesh is a satin veil covering the deepest secrets of creation. For a second, one is touched by Life and Death.

It is six in the morning. It is dark and damp and cold, but further down the path there is that ominous, strange, hellish glow, and the doctor is wide awake, vibrant and merry. The few steps he takes are a dance, his footwork swift and certain. He is well-equipped to do his work. His posture reflects pride: He is proud of his skills, proud of his efficiency, proud of his precision, proud of his youth. This doctor, the man who saves the upright in heart, he too is a cog in the unstoppable machine, a small replaceable part of a much bigger whole, but a necessary part nonetheless. He is the flywheel that eases the operation of the machine.

A restless murmur rises from the waiting crowd, like the buzzing of carrion flies; probably prayers, supplications in a language none of us understands. It puts the soldiers on edge—what is it that these creatures demand of their g*d, and what if that g*d hears them? Ah, those murmurs! Together with our joint breath, together with the smell of scorching flesh, together with the stench of cattle and shrouds, they rise before the Throne.

A child goes to the right, its mother sentenced to go left. She protests. She screams. She screams for her child, she does not want to leave it. The man in white revokes his ordinance—mother and child both to the left.

I have just witnessed a woman murdering her own child.

This camp is situated at the far end of the world, but its existence is no secret. I traveled from town to town; I slept in barracks; I heard the stories. I have known men who were in the Einsatzgruppen. They showed me their photo albums—look, here I am in old Warsaw, isn't it nice? And this is Günther's birthday party, we got totally smashed that night! And here, that's me again, see, we're shooting Jews in the woods by Kazimierz Dolny, if I remember correctly, you can see them falling, see? *Mein G*tt*, such hard work, it was *so* cold that day!

Guns are inefficient. How do you kill a few million people? You need a machine, a machine with well-oiled cogs that revolve around each other with as little friction as possible. A machine made of brick and mortar, a machine that spews death out of all of its mouths; a machine kept in operation by men like doctor Mengele—cool, rational, logical men. Men who know exactly what to do, and why. This camp in a far corner of the world is no secret. Its existence is dictated by logic. "I never had anything to do with the camps." All those innocent SS-men who declared this—what bullshit! "I never knew. My hands are clean! Clean!" *We had everything to do with the camps—we all did.* We all knew this was the end point, even if we didn't know where or how. Extermination was the only possible exclamation point after Hitler's, after Germany's reasoning. *This is the spot*, the true axis around which the war revolves, the only justification for this whole absurd war. As such, it is the core of my existence and that of the Reich. And deep inside I know the truth: That whatever side you land on, left or right, the doctor's finger ultimately points to the chimneys that tower over the camp in the brightening dawn, the source of the hellish stench and demonic glow. Each of the people I see today—they are people, people, *people*—will disappear into the mouth of the oven, each and every one of them—no one will escape.

I read the terror in their faces and I feel a spasm in my own heart.

The line shuffles on, and then the last customer appears before the doctor.

The doctor's work is done. The doctor turns around.

Behind his back a third group has formed, the group of children who came in identical pairs. Without realizing it, I have backed away from the line of death. I have landed in the group of twins, a black giant in a small crowd of pale-faced children.

The doctor turns around to inspect the new arrivals.

I hand him the envelope with my orders. He nods and opens the packet with a quick sweep of his fingers. Nice, slender, long fingers, and I understand that these are the carefully manicured fingers of death.

The doctor examines me; his gaze travels from head to toe as if he has to make a life-or-death decision on my account as well. Then he rereads the message, just to be sure—the doctor is a cautious man. Once more he looks me in the eyes, looking for G*d knows what—the real reason I'm here, no doubt.

He sighs. Then he turns around and starts walking, moving away from us at great speed, and the children quickly assemble in his wake. I stand perplexed. Then the doctor stops unexpectedly. The first pair of twins bumps into his backside, but nobody laughs. He takes out the envelope and reads the message a third time. He turns around and scans my face yet again. I straighten my back. I look back at him with, I hope, the right mixture of self-assurance and humility. The doctor deliberates. Then he makes—how is this possible!—an inviting gesture with his hand. I hear his voice for the first time.

"Come and join us," says Mengele, and he turns on his heels. I run to the end of the line. We walk through the camp, a cluster of ducklings heading to the water behind their mother duck. What speed! This much is clear: when Mengele has made up his mind, when the good doctor at last knows where he's going, there is no stopping him.

The woman I loved bore a child. That child, the child of the woman I loved, the child that made her belly swell—that child is here. In Auschwitz.

"Come and join us," Mengele said, and his words give me hope.

That child, the child I am not the father of—that child is my only tie to Helena Guna.

•

It's a thunderbolt from a clear blue sky, the article in the newspaper. I read it on the train, on my way from the Kaiser-Wilhelm-Institut to the barracks in Potsdam. The paper almost falls out of my hands, the news is so big, the shock so inconceivable. The world-famous movie star has died, completely unexpectedly, without warning, after what they describe as "a brief illness." The nation is advised to mourn.

This can't be true. This is impossible. Helena? The Helena I knew was a ball of compact energy—her lust for life bordered on invincibility. A sudden illness? I don't believe it for a minute—there is no germ, no bug in the world that could get a hold on my Leni.

What happened to her baby? I calculate. If she was three months pregnant when I left, then, well, let's see . . . the child must be six months old or thereabouts.

Another story makes the rounds as well, rumors whispered in the barracks at night. Someone heard it from a trusted somebody who once shared a dorm room with somebody who briefly worked for the *Lebensborn* division in Munich. The story goes that the famous movie star had given birth to a child, and while that part of the story is certainly true, there is also a nagging, upsetting detail: namely that Helena's child *is not white.*

This is unthinkable. Helena's child not purebred? It's perfectly mind-boggling. How could it be? Didn't I witness Helena Guna copulating night after night with only the most convincing prototypes of the Aryan race?

Then I think again. When people make mistakes, don't they tend to make up for them with exemplary behavior, a flight forward into exaggerated purity and self-castigation? What if Helena's addiction to Aryan men, her search for icy-white skin and lake-blue eyes had served the purpose of cleansing her of her one mistake? What if her stormy love life was a self-inflicted punishment, a pointless attempt to rewrite the memory of the flesh, the memory of her womb, some sinful white magic to beg for a bizarre kind of forgiveness?

If the rumor is true, if the child was indeed conceived in racial impurity, then things look very different now. There is no way Helena would have been allowed to keep the baby. It's possible—I know my colleagues, I know how the SS operates—that the infant was killed in the delivery room, right in front of Helena's eyes. I don't believe in this sudden illness. I do, however, believe this: That Helena—passionate Helena, the woman who embraced life with all her might—could have died of remorse, of grief and remorse.

It makes me restless.

I can't sleep anymore. I want to know.

I want to know the truth. I want to know what happened; I want to know what really happened. I want the truth, the whole terrible truth; I want to know what possessed Helena.

I am crazy. As if the truth ever set anybody free! As if I could bring Helena back to life, if only I knew the truth!

As if I could bring *myself* back to life.

The mission took me more than a year. The most obvious source of information would be my boss, but I can't ask him. He may be an absentminded professor, but that kind of question would stir his interest.

My assignment in the Berlin area proves to be long and tedious. I have time on my hands. Slowly I ingratiate myself with one of my superiors, a man who works in the Reich archives. I quit smoking and I hand the man my ration of cigarettes. From time to time I get him a bottle of schnapps from the endless supplies we SS-men have at our disposal. I provide him with Parisian perfume to give to his mistresses; I purchase it at inflated prices on the black market in the barracks.

I lend him my ear; with inexhaustible patience I listen to his interminable moaning about nothing. I pretend to empathize with the superficial sorrows of his ridiculous love affairs and his vindictive bitching about promotions that were so unfairly denied him. I listen and listen—I listen until I almost faint.

You need patience when you want to learn a terrible truth, the patience of a Zen monk: to sit and sit and sit and listen attentively to hours and hours of white noise. And I have this patience—it's one of my best assets. Still, I do admit that towards the end I was tempted to seal my ears with wax—the man was seriously getting on my nerves. I feel deep sympathy with whoever might have crossed his path, with his unfortunate subordinates, and especially with the wrong-headed women who so thought that it would be a good idea to share their bed with this relentless nincompoop.

Patience then, and the answer I ultimately get with my patience shocks and gladdens me. My contact slides a piece of paper towards me with a name, a number, and a place of residence. The child is alive! But the address makes me tremble: The girl was transferred to KZ Auschwitz-Birkenau. I know the name. Auschwitz has long ceased being a rumor; I have heard of it many times. Quite a few of my colleagues have worked there. They were transferred back to the capital because they couldn't bear it any longer. They are easily recognized: the ones who spend most of their times lying on their backs, staring at the ceiling. The war causes many wounds, including wounds in the soul, and those wounds fester long after you've walked off the battlefield. Judging from this evidence alone, Auschwitz must be a most terrifying place.

I try to talk to those ex-Auschwitz boys. They accept my cigarettes but they keep staring at the ceiling, empty-eyed. It gives me the shivers. A place too cruel for words, that's where the child, Helena's child, lives. I shudder because in that year of waiting and listening I've almost begun to consider the child mine.

Even now I need patience. I know where she is, I know her name, I have her ID number, but I can't just walk away from my assignment. I have to wait for an opportunity to travel to Poland. It takes months of waiting. Waiting for a transfer, waiting for a vacation—and neither of those two opportunities seem likely. Yes, I have patience, but this final bout of waiting almost drives me to the brink. I know her name, I have her ID number. I know where she lives: Auschwitz-Birkenau. I have to see her!

If she's still alive. What are the odds? This fabled Auschwitz-Birkenau is a harsh, barbaric place—that much I have gathered.

Waiting.

Waiting. Waiting.

And then the minister—at last!—sends me to the south, to put the final touches on a mission that I started long ago, near the Swiss border. I know that the shortest route from Potsdam to the *Schwabische Alb* does not go through Poland, but I falsify my travel documents—I can take that risk, for *her*. (For whom? Who is the woman I take the risk for? The child? Or her dead mother? Or is it for the benefit of the guardian angel on my shoulder, the angel who keeps whispering in my ear, telling me how bad the war is, how unforgivable, how what almost started as a game—building secret hiding places, disguising ourselves—will end in tears, tears that will never dry?)

•

The children's hospital is a shock. The patients are thin and shy. Are they still children? They don't look me in the eyes, they are distrustful; even their bodies turn away from me reflexively. When I do manage to catch some child's gaze, all I read in those eyes is a disturbing wisdom and an indomitable sadness.

Among the twins she is alone. A child with no brother or sister to lean on, without the comfort of a commonly constructed language to stave off the ugliness of the world—Aria Guna is a silent and lonely child. Sullen. Suspicious. She has long black hair; she wears a wool sweater and leather boots. She is one of Mengele's angels: Her head was never shaved, she was never made to put on the striped uniform. I do not know where she got her clothes, they don't seem like something Helena would have chosen for her. She wears a necklace with an Indian g*d in a circle of flames. Did anybody ever smile at her, in her brief life? I take her in my arms and she shivers. "*Nicht Angst*," I say, and I caress her hair. I call her by her name. Aria. She looks at me briefly and without expression. Is that my name, sir? Do I have a name, sir?

I take her by the hand and the sleeve of her sweater slides upward. I see a number. It's not an ink tattoo like the other prisoners have, but a bubbling burn mark. She's been branded by an iron. When she shakes her head I see blue spots on her neck, swellings around the needle holes from which the doctors extract a few centiliters of her blood each day, G*d knows why.

I don't know what they've done to her exactly. I don't ask questions. Sometimes she whispers in short bursts; the sounds don't resemble any language known on this earth. It's not clear whether she's talking to herself, a child making up an imaginary twin sister, or whether she's talking to me—she so rarely looks up. I know she was naked during the experiments; I know that the doctors drew marks on her body; I know that she was measured and observed. Everything she secretes is collected. Blood, urine, stool, pus from the corner of her eyes, tears, glandular discharges—it all gets sucked into glass tubes and decanted into glass vessels and mixed with chemicals and put underneath the microscope. One of her eyes is blind. They washed her eyeball in a special liquid. The seeing eye is brown. The blind eye is of an improbably clear blue.

What has she seen with that one eye? Was she in the operating theater when Mengele cut pieces of stomach tissue from an unfortunate pair of twins, without anesthesia? Was she there when he retrieved a still beating heart from a child's chest, sawed wide? Has she heard him boast about the difficulty of his research, about how necessary it is, how scientific and beneficial to humanity's progress?

Look out the window of the sick bay: There is the platform, and a new train just rolled in, full of stench and *morituri*. The children watch it with numb indifference. Are the newly arrived still alive, or is the shuddering jolt of the halting train a prophecy of the final stroke of death inside? Was she looking out the window that sunny summer morning when a group of Hungarian rabbis stumbled out of the cars, dressed in long black coats and wool pants and fur hats despite the 85 degree heat? Did she see Mengele's eyes narrow at the sight? Did she hear him order the sweating rabbis to step out of the line and sing for him; did she see them raise their hands and stomp their feet, intoning the *kol nidre* to accompany their bizarre dance? Did she see the impassive doctor observing it all; did she see him getting bored and walking away while indicating to his subordinates to direct the men to the left?

Look out the window on the other side. That empty lot used to be the gypsy camp. Whenever Mengele walked through there on his way from work to home, the men would play their fiddles for him, mazurkas and polonaises and waltzes, and the women would hit their tambourines and dance—they all knew the doctor loved music. "Uncle Mengele!" the children cried. "Uncle Mengele!" And he gently stroked their bald heads and softly squeezed their wasted cheeks, and he put sticky chocolates in their eager little fists. Was she watching, that sweet and timid Aria, on the day the whole gypsy camp was lead to the ovens; the day Mengele took his favorite little boy by the hand and stuffed his mouth with candy and deposited him neatly at the door to the gas chamber?

Even children understand. Even children who are barely a year and a half old understand. What is there to see in Auschwitz-Birkenau that even a child barely a year and a half old *couldn't* understand?

There is a rumor that the doctor forces teen twin pairs to mate with each other. There are rumors that there are children in the hospital with no spine, with their genitals taken out, with an open wound where their kidneys once were. How can I hear these things and see what I see, and keep on believing that this war serves some noble purpose?

From time to time an airplane flies overhead. Aria is too young to think, Please, bomb the camp. Please, release your thunder. It doesn't matter if I die, it doesn't matter if we all die. Release the bombs, let us bury this place—its cruel history, its gruesome present, its atrocious future—under the splattering fireworks of your explosives. I see the planes draw their vapor trails and I hear mortar fire in the distance—the barbaric hordes approaching from the east: the Huns, the Ostrogoths, the Mongolians, the gangs that will bring down the Reich—and I find myself praying. I pray that their advance may be swift, that they may be at the gates soon.

The advancing hordes keep me in the camp. I simply wanted to collect Aria and flee south. This is not possible. "What do you think, sir officer, sir?" asks the man in the administrative office. "Do you think we'd send trains out under a hail of artillery fire? I don't think so, sir! You'll have to be patient."

Ha! Patient! I sleep on a cot next to Aria's little bunk. In the terrible night, when she tosses and turns under the weight of indescribable dreams, I lay my palm on her cheek and I cover her hand with mine. When I can no longer bear it, I take her in my arms and rock her struggling little body. Sometimes she wakes up and looks at me with piercing unblinking eyes, and in the confusion of her half-sleep she allows me to kiss away her tears.

In the mess hall the rumors multiply. The camp commander considers a march, an exodus of all prisoners. I understand what that means. It's just death in another disguise; it's the SS refusing to take responsibility for their actions, a cowardly retreat to destroy all human evidence. The last witnesses will die by the side of the road, buried in haste or dumped into trenches; they will be written off as victims of bombings or infectious diseases. I understand that nobody who leaves will stand a chance. I understand that only staying behind will give me a slim shot at survival. I also understand that the camp commanders will only allow those to stay behind who are already sentenced to death.

One morning, Mengele doesn't show up. He's just disappeared. Some say they saw him load his suitcases into a car and drive off. Nobody is certain that he actually left today. Maybe he went missing a few days ago? The doctor is so omnipresent that he seems to be present even in his absence.

What shall we do? The doctor's assistants look quizzically at each other. They shrug their shoulders. What else is there to do? From the pockets of their lab coats they produce their needles and their syringes, and their catheters and measuring tape and their pens and notepads. Life goes on, doesn't it, and with it their all-important scientific research.

Mengele has disappeared. It's time for Aria and I to work on our escape plan.

We are alone in the room, he and I, in Barrack 12 of the prisoner's hospital. A sign on the door says: Infectious Diseases. He is hallucinating. I speak to him, in my own hesitant, broken Dutch.

"What's wrong with you, man? What ails you?" "Scarlatina, *mein Herr*." "Are you in pain?" "I am in much pain, *mein Herr*." "What is your name, friend, and where do you come from?" "I am Jozef De Heer, Mister Officer, I live in Berlin, but I was born in Amsterdam." "Do you think you will live long, Meneer De Heer?" "The doctor told me that my chances of survival are slim at best, *genädige Herr*." I thank the man. He called me "gracious sir" and I am gracious: I pretend to leave the room and then I assault him from behind and cut his jugular quickly and painlessly, just as I learned in Bad Stolz. Blood sprays from the wound and I quickly roll the man out of the bed: Let him bleed to death on the mud floor, not on the sheets. I need those sheets, those sheets infected with scarlet fever, for my own bed. The sick bay will be my hide-out, a real fever will be my alibi. I have a shot at survival: I am well-nourished, my bodily resistance must be strong enough to pull me through the fever—it is an innocent infection, only deadly for folks like Jozef, weakened by hard labor and a lack of decent food.

I wait patiently. I light a cigarette. When the man—the new me—seems sufficiently bled, I pull up the sleeve of his striped jacket. I commit the number to memory. I have my knife and an ink jar stolen from the doctor's desk. I will spend the next few hours carefully copying his tattoo on my own arm. First I undress his body. Then myself. I wrap myself in De Heer's rags. I scrape the flesh off his lower arms to erase the number. I slide his naked dead body through the window. With a thud it disappears into the mound of snow that has collected there. Maybe somebody will come and take the cadaver away; maybe not. I lie down on the bed and cover myself tightly with the wool blanket. It is full of holes. I shiver with cold, and I keep shivering. I say to myself: You delivered a man from his suffering, quickly. He didn't feel a thing. Be glad. You saved both him and Aria a long and painful death. Be glad. You are a new man. You are free!

I have to go get Aria.

I shiver. I shiver.

I shiver.

I have to go get Aria.

I have to infect her, and keep her by my side.

I keep shaking and shaking.

I feel so tired, all of a sudden. So terribly tired.

Aria?

The ground shakes. Explosions. The Soviets attacking us with mortar fire? The SS blowing up the ovens to destroy proof of the camp's purpose? I lie in bed and shiver and shake. Something small and warm crawls up against me. Is that Aria by my side? Have I done it? Have I found the strength, did I carry her here? Or did she find her way to her foster father all by herself? I have no memory of anything at all, the world just spins and spins. Did she find me all by herself?

I hear noises outside. Am I imagining this? I hear men screaming orders, I hear the rhythmic thumping of boots and wooden shoes. I hear the noises fade in the distance. Am I imagining this?

The hollows below my collarbones gather sweat: it leaves salt crusts when it dries quickly and mold when it dries slowly. My joints are stiff. My digestive tract shuts down from mouth to anus in one long cramp. I no longer know who I am or where I am, where I begin and end. Am I this bony body? Am I the straw of my mattress, so strangely discolored, with its suspicious crusty spots and odd smells? Am I the earth? Do I encompass the sun? The sun that so stubbornly refuses to shine over this town? This Auschwitz?

I'm no longer alone in the room. A man with a death rattle in his throat. Slime oozes from his mouth and words well from his lips, words in an incomprehensible language, words of prayer. Urgent prayer, desperate prayer, resigned prayer—each of these three emotions fight with each other, they drown each other out. A man who believes in something. I do not consider him pathetic or laughable. I envy him. I envy the mind that, in this time, in this place, on the edge between life and death, can still send a prayer to the great beyond, a prayer that runs deeper, much deeper than the need for the salvation of his dying body. I do not understand his language, but I sense the urgency in his voice.

"What is this prayer, rabbi?" I ask. My voice is hoarse, hoarser than I've ever heard it, air exhumed from deep inside me and pushed through a larynx of dried-out leather. "What is it you're praying for?"

The man does not interrupt his prayer.

[. . . *throughout the world*

which He has created according to His will.]

"What is it, rabbi? Who is it you're praying for?"

[*Blessed and praised,*
glorified and exalted,
extolled and honored.]

The barracks are shaking again—it must be mortar fire.

[*May there be abundant peace from heaven*
—and life!]

"It's a prayer for the dead, my friend." A third voice, with a Latin accent. An Italian Jew? A Spanish terrorist?

It is cold in my bed. Am I still alive? Why is it so cold? Where is Aria?

What is a refugee? Somebody who does not die in the town where he was born.

What is a refugee? Somebody who mourns his dead in a town where he wasn't born.

I feel my mattress, even though I know that all I will find is emptiness.

Aria! Where is she? Did she succumb to the sweltering fever? Did she leave with the other children? Did she go quietly, all alone, into that long dark night? Is she dead now, frozen solid on some wintry field?

Where is Aria?

Where is Lena?

Is Aria with Lena?

And where am I, where is the proud Helmut Hinkel, the dapper soldier, the man who was once so convinced of his own worth he didn't feel the need to look life in the eye?

"*Exalted and sanctified . . . exalted . . . sanctified . . . Blessings and hymns, praises and consolations . . . in the world . . . abundant peace . . . from heaven . . .*"

From my bunk, incapable of forming words, I see my barrack-mates drag the rabbi's dead body away. He lies so light in their arms, an insect dried out by the desert winds. No, his G*d didn't help him. So how can I expect his G*d to help somebody like me?

•

I stare at the envelope on the table. It takes me a while to realize what it's doing there and what it contains.

How long did my flashback last? A second? An hour?

I am no longer afraid of death. Death is the instrument by which we measure the scale of life, just like the body is the instrument by which we measure the passing of time. My life. My body. All those layers and layers of noise. Where is the signal? What is the signal? Is there a signal?

I gave away my life—or I sold it, if you prefer business terms. Three times. Once (or twice, or perhaps only once after all) to the maximalism of great ideals. Then, more privately, I gave my heart to Helena and her daughter: the dance of death and then the steamroller of loss. Then, the deeper, grimmer secret: the despair, the incisive cynicism of the Plan, or the few fragments of It that survived the years. The Plan, hollowed out, superfluous, no longer buoyed by the Idea, beached like some hapless whale who suddenly got afraid of the ocean. We watch it belly flop, we watch the sign language of its drowning, and we do not understand.

Mira came storming in, and now I know that Aria lived. Good. And to know that Aria in turn gave birth to a daughter, that is good too. If I were a bit more sentimental, I would say it adds meaning to my life. She is not my child, but she survived the camp because of me. In a certain sense, I did give birth to her. That counts for something. And yet, it fills me with sorrow and regret.

I turn the envelope over in my hands. Over and over. I need to mail it. Now. If I don't mail it now, I might tear it up. Why should all secrets be revealed? See, my resolve is wavering already.

As it is, I'm out of stamps. I've been out of stamps for as long as I can remember. Who, after all, would I write a letter to?

What time is it?

All the post offices will be closed. It's cold out. I can wait until morning and then walk to the post office across the street. Or I can take the subway to Zoo; that post office is open until midnight. It would take half an hour. Express mail. The letter will reach Andermans tomorrow. I turn the envelope over in my hands. No, I need to get this in the mail today. If I sleep on it, if I look at it in the clear light of the morning, I'll have neither the courage nor the generosity to send the picture out. And, honestly, only now do I appreciate that my knowledge of Mira's mother and her grandmother is a valuable bargaining chip, that this is knowledge that can set me free. Mira dear, without me you wouldn't even exist. How's that for an outstanding debt?

I grab my coat from the rack and I rush out the door, envelope firmly in hand. I decide to take Mira's threat about the legions waiting to kill me as metaphorical: the promised tormentors as biblical demons.

Is that a shadow I see, ducking away into the stairwell? Is that a soft voice I hear, talking into empty space, questions and answers at an esoteric border crossing?

Two men start walking ahead of me as soon as I step out of the building, two lung-shaped outlines in the mist. Had Mira told the truth? They go down the steps to the station; I turn into Niederwallstraße.

I see the red tip of a cigarette glowing ahead. Is someone waiting for me?

I turn around and walk into Seydelstraße.

There too a tiny pinpoint of red.

I regain my composure. Why would this have anything to do with me? Is this what paranoia feels like? I repress a shiver and turn around.

Spittelmarkt Station it is then. The two men are waiting on the platform; black jeans, faded and torn at the knees, ride low on their hips. One of them looks one way, the other the other way, as if they aren't sure which train to take. Their wool hats are pulled down deep over their ears and thick scarves cover their mouths and noses—I can't make out their faces. I walk to the platform where the next train to Alexanderplatz is due, the train that comes from Zoo. Four more minutes, according to the electronic information display. The men edge closer. Behind my back I hear the train running in the opposite direction come in, the train for Ruhleben. The train stops. I don't move. The doors open. I keep my eyes fixed on the tunnel from which the Alexanderplatz train will arrive, any minute now. Then, when the metallic voice announces that the train for Ruhleben will depart momentarily, that the doors will close and that boarding is no longer permitted, I quickly turn around and sprint into the nearest compartment. The conductor cusses at me through the loudspeaker but I don't care and the doors close right behind me as the train jolts to life. My two assailants did not expect this—they realized too slowly. My train slides past their impotent gazes. One of them spews angry words into a cell phone.

The train is almost empty. The tourist hordes have long since deserted the east, opting for their budget hotels around Ku'damm; the natives prefer the Kreuzberg-Prenzlauer Berg axis for their partying needs. More than enough room in the car to sit down and wipe the sweat off my forehead. Peace and quiet!

Peace? The face of a young man appears at the door that separates the cars. He entered so silently that it seems he just passed through the glass, a soundless demon materializing in my presence, leaving only the vaguest memory of the creaking of a steel door; a delayed blast of ear-biting cold air follows in his wake. Everybody pretends not to have noticed, yet the familiar reek of warm fear spreads through the compartment—a skinhead has just made his entrance, the herd is paralyzed.

And see: At the other door his doppelganger appears, another silent well-shorn angel, feet firmly planted in the aisle, his gaze—I do not raise my eyes, but I can feel it prickling on my neck—aimed directly at me..

Hausvogteiplatz. I get up, I want out, but a muscular shoulder rams hard into my chest and I fall back into the cushions. The men sit down, one to the left of me, the other to the right, and all the while they maintain firm body contact. Right opposite me a third man takes a seat, obviously the ringleader. Bleached porcupine spikes peek from under his wool ski hat. He holds a book in his hand, a much-thumbed, yellowed paperback.

Of course I recognize him. And of course he does not recognize me. He does not look deeper than his prejudice, he looks no deeper than he thinks. Political fools are all impressionists. The trouble with impressionists is that they are in love with the light, the gleaming surface of things.

These are my creations, okay? I can't help it.

In the beginning, when we first started gathering this muddle of dull muscular hulks, I had my doubts. Will this work? Start a neo-Nazi movement with the kind of violent simpletons that are naturally eager to do the dirty job, I thought, and before you know it, you'll have wiped out the whole extreme-right spectrum of politics; they'll discredit themselves in no time at all, if the infighting doesn't do them in first. But no, they are still around, my rough-and-ready battle machines. These three hold their cigarettes between thumb and middle finger, in true cowboy style; they capture the hot smoke in the hollow of their down-turned palms. The two mute heroes at my side I don't recognize—I know the leaders, I've lost touch with the troops. They are cogs in the wheel of the Plan, why should I care about the cogs in the wheel?

The man on my left is the first one to open his mouth. "What's that smell?" he asks the brute to my right, and the brute to my right—they've played out this scenario a thousand times—grins back at him, broadly and stupidly. "I know that smell—it stinks of Jew! Don't you think it stinks of Jew here? Huh?"

In the upturned brim of his hat the leader wears a calendar leaf. The date on the piece of paper is April 30, 1995, a date that makes me shudder.

My creations. Much like Buddhists maintain that every human being houses an already awakened soul, so I have always claimed that inside each of us lives a bloodthirsty dog, a barbarian soul. And this bloodthirsty soul, I always thought—I've seen it with my own eyes, half a century ago—needs much less coaxing to come out and burst through the surface than the bodhisattva.

"It smells like Jew." I've witnessed countless conversations like this one, more than half a century ago, in those terrible, ignorant days. Amazing what that single word, the word "Jew" can do; remarkable how quickly our few fellow passengers (they who do not see, they who do not hear) move to the edge of their seats, ready to leave the car at the earliest opportunity. The masses always react the same way. They reacted the same way fifty years ago, they react the same way now, they will react the same way fifty years from now. This is what we sowed, I and those who over time became mine—exactly this sort of intimidation tactics. Now the time has come to reap the terrible harvest.

Hugo has watched two of his men hold their victim in a stranglehold so often—some stupid fuck who didn't get out of the way quickly enough, some brave fool who gave them a nasty look, some miserable sap with the wrong skin color—while a third man, appointed by the boss, shoulders the baseball bat and lets it swing with that deeeee-lite-ful swoosh. Swoosh-*crack*-swoosh-*crack*. The power of wood swung with a skill built up through hours of deliberate practice. To hear a fellow human being scream, then moan, then fall mute—it gives you such peace.

The old man opposite them will grant them that privilege tonight; he will provide Hugo and his henchmen with that rare sense of quiet. And this is no semi-random victim: This lecher had dared to violate Nebula, Hugo's bride. Of course Hugo does not recognize him. He hasn't seen Liebenfels that often, and certainly not recently, and then always in disguise. Remember, Hugo is an impressionist. Plus, his judgment is clouded by alcohol and by what Nebula has instructed him to see.

Hugo closes his Karl May paperback—*Menschenjäger*—and gets up from the bench. The movements of the train make him swagger. Very macho. He pulls down his pants and bends over; he presses his ass into the pathetic old satyr's nose. "You can kiss my ass, you dirty Jew. Here, pucker your lips, and kiss that pink little flower with your nice little tongue, won't you?"

The man on De Heer's right puts his mouth against De Heer's ear.

"Fucking Jews—they fucking get on my fucking nerves, man."

De Heer nods in agreement, he doesn't know why.

"No, really man, they fucking make me lose my fucking shit, you know?"

The present and the past flow inexorably into the future. My biography runs to its end, it is no longer negotiable. All idle speculation, all unrealized abstractions collapse. All that could have been and all that was now points to a single decisive destination, an ultimate point omega that has always been inherent in the present.

—Ouch! That was cowardly; he got me right in my face with his fist. Blood flows from my mouth.

My G*d. It is happening. For real. Right now.

One of the men extracts the envelope from my hands. Did I really press it that tightly against my chest; is this then my last valuable possession, the thing I hold on to until the very end, the photograph of the one true love of my life?

They extract the envelope from my hands and I start crying like a baby. The men laugh, loud and with gusto. They exchange high-fives over my bruised shoulder.

May we die when the moment is right. May we face death with clarity. May we not deceive ourselves when the moment has come.

I am only half-conscious when they drag me out of the train into the station deep beneath Potsdamer Platz. Propped up by the two underlings, I am hauled into the maze. We go up and down stairs until I have no idea where we are. Deep underground, that's all I can tell. The leader throws the envelope into a garbage can; he does it with utter nonchalance. We round a corner and then another one; I am dragged into an disused railway tunnel. In the wobbly light of plastic cigarette lighters we go, three dark trolls carrying an awkward load to the forge.

The underground tunnels have a secret energy; the roaring cars of the trains on the neighboring tracks speak to each other in the eerie language of screeching metal, a language as unfathomable as the underwater whistling of whales, a language that only makes sense here, below the surface, in the other city, in the alternative network, in the labyrinth that architects from the distant past sank beneath the town. We walk through man-high tubes of steel and concrete that float uncomfortably on the ocean of shifting sands. Rats scurry away, and half-hidden in the sand a gigantic head looms, bronze and six feet tall, an ancient statue with a wet forelock and the unmistakable mustache, its mouth open, waiting to prophesize. The head has fallen on its cheek; the obscene vertical mouth, with its little tuft of hair, resembles nothing more than a colossal vaginal opening with teeth, ready to give birth to Hell.

There you go, De Heer, into the tunnel. Into the heart of darkness. Into the sun of torture. In the name of the victims. Viva hate, long live contempt, bravo for revolt, hurray for death. May the sand weigh lightly upon you, Jozef De Heer, the sand of your holy land. You see stars behind your eyelids. Tumbling embers. Creation falling apart in the act of creation itself. The dream that one day we will all be brought together, gathered in a no longer unfamiliar homeland, that a Messenger of the Kingdom will arrive at the last possible moment—that dream has always seemed improbable and now it is dead. I tell you, there is no such messenger, for there is no such message; no homecoming is possible. Only the billions of last moments exist, and nothing else matters. You can sweep the shards together—November 1938, a villa in Munich, the gaping wound in the heart of Berlin—but it cannot undo the events themselves. Wounds may heal, but they never heal seamlessly. History will always be this: an incomprehensible collection of last moments, beyond repair.

·

There is the rain. Always the rain. Rain gargles in the gutter pipe; drops tap against the window. My breath has misted the glass. It isn't entirely clear whether a world still exists on the other side of the pane, and even if it does, the incessant beating of the rain makes it doubtful that such a world would be any more hospitable a place than the confines of my small room. The cat fishes a candy wrapper out of the wastebasket; She licks up the remaining sugar happily.

A small stone hits the window,

My heart skips a beat.

Nebula?

I wipe away the condensation, but all I see is my own reflection. I turn off the lights, and then I see her, in the front garden, completely soaked, wet hair clinging in clumps to her skull. She bats her eyelids while looking upwards; she wards off the stinging rain with one hand at her brow. Her eyes light up when she sees me.

I hurry down.

Her body language, the way she won't meet my eyes—for a second she looks vaguely guilty. It's the same kind of stealthy shyness I sometimes see in Mefista when I find her next to a little bird dead in the garden.

Paul, you're a sentimental fool. Listen to yourself speak: "I missed you."

I love her answer.

Her answer is: "Good!"

Suddenly I hold the delightful twin orbs of her buttocks in my hand, tight and graceful as the lowercase letter omega.

"Paul, you're an amazingly familiar kind of stranger."

To watch her take a shower: a glittering cherub riding on a cloud of steam. Her body is the color of Assam tea mixed with milk, of raw cane sugar, of alder honey. To touch her downy cheek with my nose; to stand naked together in the warm spray.

She didn't bring an extra set of clothes. I wrap her in one of my T-shirts; I watch her try on a pair of my boxer briefs.

Back in the room she calmly steps back out of these articles of clothing. She sprays a good amount of my deodorant in the air and walks naked through the scented cloud.

"Okay," she says, suddenly all business, and she puts her hands on her hips. "I'm ready. Take me."

It's that simple.

The roughness of her breath tickles the naked surface of my eyelids, it blows hot over my sore lips, it rains over my temples, it melts inside my ear. She forms words deep inside her throat, words of an irreversible necessity.

"Not like that," she says. "Like this."

She keeps her liquid black eyes open.

A woman who guides me. A woman who guides my hand. A woman who lies in my arms, naked and warm. A woman who guides my touch. A woman who knows what she wants.

What she wants is me.

A woman towering high above me. Sliding slowly and carefully over my yearning cock.

And when she finally closes her eyes they tremble, like tiny flower petals.

•

Around midnight, as is appropriate, a workman will approach, dragging a big, overflowing bag behind him, a bag made out of opaque, waterproof plastic, a bag rustling with all the secrets and rumors entrusted to the moss-green garbage cans of the BVG—old newspapers, apple peels, tissues soiled with all kinds of bodily fluids, the letters of past lovers—and he will turn over the garbage can that contains the very last message that De Heer sent out into the world, and he will put the envelope inside the bag and send it off to the dump, where vegetable juice and ketchup and tears and snot will erase Paul's address, where the picture of Helena Guna will be bleached away by acid and nibbled on by centipedes, and time too will do its cruel job, and De Heer's last meaningful words—his last act of love and its only documented proof, the secret picture of Helena Guna—will finally become just another fragment in the never-ending web of stories of the never-ending city.

•

Nebula closes the door of the guesthouse behind her and steps into the street. It's midnight and she's dressed in the clothes Paul loaned her; his jeans, his sweater, his jacket. She craves the evening chill, she craves a cigarette; she needs some time alone. She can smell his body on his fingers, she can taste him on her tongue, she has the scent of his semen on her breath.

It's stopped raining.

Did she scrub herself clean enough under the shower? Has she been able to rinse De Heer's death off her completely? Or did she infect her lover with her murderous karma?

The onset of migraine scrapes at the underside of her skull. The character she created for herself, an existential angel in black, a minor G*ddess built for sex and ritual slaughter, a wayward artist on the way to self-immolation—all those roles seem flat to her now. No coherent 3-D picture emerges. A second-rate biographer would jump at this opportunity and say that she is fundamentally incomprehensible, that people only project their dreams onto her, or that she instinctively reflects the dreams of others. Maybe such a biographer would connect this to the impossible grotesqueness of being a woman under the patriarchy, but such fragmentation, dear biographer, characterizes each of us, every human being, man or woman, and it is doubly true for those who love and are no longer alone.

About now Paul must wake up and realize that she is no longer in bed beside him.

This is what she saw from the window of the train, this is what made her decide to return to Potsdam after all, to Paul's arms, to his bed: the looming golden angel on her column. The guidebooks tell you she is the G*ddess of Victory, but Nebula knows better—tonight the Angel Metatron shines through the golden apparition. It is April 28. The countdown on the fences and concrete walls, on the abandoned factories and the brick churches is almost done: All the numbers are down to single digits. The lowest number she spots is 2, and this number is written on the base of the Angel's column in fresh wet paint that glistens in the floodlights. Metatron is the Writer in the Sky, the Angel who dutifully notes down all human secrets in G*d's own ledger. He keeps those books safe behind lock and key for all eternity. Metatron is the Wheelbarrow of G*d's Presence, the Shechinah aflame, the Blazing Voice from the Burning Bush, the Throne of Glory, the Glow of the Moon. Metatron carried the Tribes through the wilderness; He carries prayers through the nine hundred layers of Heaven and lays them before the Eyes of G*d. Metatron: the Temple of Heaven is His. He is the prophet Enoch, the seventh patriarch, crowned by G*d, vested with seventy-two wings and countless eyes, his flesh turned to eternal flame, his muscles become pure fire, his bones glowing red, dressed in storm and whirlwind. There are sources that call him the smaller YHVH. Is he the demiurge? The G*d of earthly regions? The ruler of seraphs? The one who keeps Leviathan at bay? The monster who will devour all sinners in the Latter Days? Yes, He is all that, all of this is Metatron, the humble servant, the fiery body of the Shechinah.

What does this have to do with Paul? Nebula doesn't know, but there is a connection, she can feel it in her heart, she can feel it in her gut, it burns in her pussy: In Potsdam, in the guest house, the solution resides. And that is why she returned, that is why she disembarked at the next station and took the first train back to Potsdam, and that is why she walked the long walk, forty-five minutes, through muddled muddy streets, in the pouring rain: the only way home, to Paul. The walk, the strength found in her renewed conviction that what she needs above all, in the recklessness of springtime, in the whistling of the wind through the deserted town, is shelter. A place called home. A solid roof, a warm blanket, and, if possible, the brief shock of an orgasm.

Whatever it is that led her to Paul, whatever twisted and intractable logic brought her back to the guest house, liberation has not yet been achieved. The question, here and now, is as follows: Does she want to penetrate deeper into the mystery? Or will she flee?

She turns her eyes to the sky, black and impenetrable.

The sky answers. It starts to rain again. A clear sign.

And so, for the second time this endless night, Nebula retraces her steps.

A solid roof, a warm blanket, the brief shock of an orgasm.

Nebula smiles. The way he made love to her. Eager and amazed. As if he couldn't begin to fathom his luck. As if she were a G*ddess.

She already knows what she will tell him, after her second orgasm of the night.

"We all die, sugar. That's why we have to love each other so hard."

The happy ending, in life, in literature, in art-house movies—it's severely underrated.

ש

OMEGA

"Why don't you use it as a framing device? That's the classical trick, isn't it? Pestilence reigns, and the last of the sane are holed up in some far-off corner, or else an army captain hides from the worst of the battle in a poor man's hut and finds an illuminated manuscript, or a young woman tells her lover a thousand-and-one stories over a thousand-and-one nights? In your case: An old man steeped in history shares his life story with a young man, and so on? And why don't you mix it with our story, and with what's happening in Berlin in the present day? It all fits together nicely, it would create the illusion that your story is anchored in reality, and you know readers never mind a bit of romance."

Silence.

"Where does it all end?" I ask after a while. "How can I find a suitable ending to this pack of lies?"

"*Here* is where it ends," she says. "Here, in your bed, between the rumpled sheets, with my head against your shoulder and your hand in the hollow beneath my breasts. Exactly here: your hand almost on top of my heart, but not quite." She formulates it so nicely; her words lead me back to a childhood filled with Lewis Carroll and the Brothers Grimm—a simple touch can accomplish the wildest transformation and a seemingly trivial act like walking through a door can change the world forever.

"But this isn't a good ending," I object. "A story that ends with *boy gets girl* and vice versa reeks of schmaltz and cliché. No self-respecting story can end there. That's the moment when life *begins*."

"I mean, you could contrast the demise of an old man with the blossoming of young love."

"Wait a minute! What do we know about the end of De Heer's life?" (And what do we know about the blossoming of young love?)

"I mean: the end of his biography, and the end of the lie of his biography."

"The lie. Here I am, in bed with you, and I worry about all the time I lost typing up De Heer's stories, and whether or not the manuscript can be salvaged for publication. Don't I have anything better to do?"

"You could make me breakfast, for instance. All of this has made me pretty hungry. I'll take a shower while you do that, okay? And can I borrow some dry clothes from you again?"

•

I walk into the kitchen and I switch on the light. The fluorescent tubes come alive with obvious reluctance; their blue flicker makes the place look like a mortuary. How sterile this landscape: the clean Formica of the kitchen table, the gleaming stainless steel of the sink, the unforgiving surface of the oversized fridge. I am surprised I notice this for the fist time today.

The American, Bill or Mike or whatever his name is, sits at the table. He was constructing a breakfast sandwich in the dark, some convoluted contraption that requires numerous jars of complicated condiments, many layers of virulently orange cheese, a bunch of baby gherkins, and pounds of stark white frayed meat. Two impossibly spongy slices of white bread bind the whole thing together. I understand why he likes to do this work in the dark: It's better if you can't look too closely at the ingredients. It seems quite late for breakfast, but then I realize it's Saturday. Since I excluded myself from the circle of office slaves and abandoned myself to this useless book, I've lost all sense of time.

Now Zhu too comes into the kitchen. He winks at me. Why does Zhu wink at me?

Then Donatella makes her entrance—dramatically, of course: She rolls her hips and her long hair balances precariously on top of her head in a topknot held together by a colorful bunch of crayons. As always, she's come prepared to act in what might be a key scene in the ongoing performance of the play *Donatella Against the World*.

"Well," says Mike or Bill or Matt or Dave (when I came in I only got a grunt, but Donatella is worthy of a full monologue). "Donatella. Alone this fine morning?"

He gets a dirty Italian look for his troubles.

"Oooooooooo-weeee!" Dick quickly takes a big bite out of his sandwich, thereby rendering himself effectively incapable of further speech. White lines of mayo leak over his hands. The effect is slightly obscene. Donatella now turns her gaze to me, and her eyes gleam with anger. Am I really seeing what I think I see? Is a little grenade of envy exploding behind her eyes?

"Yes, I'm all alone this morning. But this guy there, he sure wasn't alone last night!" Why does this sound like an indictment? I replace the coffee filter. "Yes, don't you deny it, buster. I heard you all too well, you two lovebirds." I press the start button. With much gargling and sputtering—an old communist protest—the machine springs to life.

Bill licks his white bloodless wounds. "The doors are thin here, huh? *Nein*? *Ja-ja*!" I would love to push his grinning Yank's face deep into his sandwich. Poor Zhu joins him in his mirth, but with some hesitation. A big joke of is unfolding before his eyes, but he doesn't exactly know what it is.

"Why is this girl of yours running around in your clothes, Paul?" Women are like that. They pick up on details and they store them for later use. Donatella knows my wardrobe.

"She can't go back to her place. Boyfriend trouble."

"Ha! Paul! I never thought you had it in you—such a shy, quiet boy. A real hit-and-run, huh? My goodness! The dapper abduction of a Sabine virgin! Whence this sudden surge of *life is a limited time offer—act now*?" Donatella's smile is sugary sweet, but her lipstick is traffic-light red; her mouth looks like it was freshly carved with a butcher's knife; her gaze is deadly. "What were you doing, Paolino? Gathering some extra material for that book of yours, those magnificent memoirs of a long-gone apocalypse? Time for an appendix, a happy final chapter? Life goes on, or something along those lines?"

"Exactly. That's exactly what we were doing," says Nebula. I'm surprised she didn't pick a black outfit, but faded blue jeans, rolled up at the bottom, paired with my precious vintage khaki *Rust Never Sleeps* T-shirt. She hasn't applied her usual black eyeliner or black lipstick. This morning Nebula meets the world with a naked face, her hair pulled back in a young girls' ponytail. "And that's still what we're doing. And, by the way, isn't the weather gorgeous today!"

The two other boys in the room nod happily and gratefully, as though Nebula had dragged the high-pressure zone into the Brandenburg region personally. I hadn't even noticed the change in the weather. Inside me a new sun was burning, and therefore the real sunshine outside hadn't even registered. But it's true, even this tiny windowless kitchen seems flooded by brightness.

Zhu walks over to Nebula and extends his hand.

"Zhu!"

"*Gesundheit.*"

"Ah?" asks Donatella. "A final chapter?"

Nebula sits down. I hand her a mug of coffee and raise an eyebrow. She shakes her head—no, she likes her coffee black. She smiles at Bill and then she gives Donatella a conspiratory look.

"You heard about the book? Well, did Paul ever tell you how the guy's Auschwitz memoirs end?"

What's going on? Donatella is listening!

"Listen up. The main character is in the sick bay. Somebody dies and gets dumped in the snow. The narrator has scarlet fever, but he survives. He and the men melt snow for drinking water; they loot the SS kitchen and the mess hall. They do it just in time, the next looters who enter the kitchen get shot to death."

Donatella whistles between her teeth. She sits down too. No chair left for me. "Primo Levi," she says. "'The Story of Ten Days.' The final chapter of *Se Questo è un Uomo.*" She whistles again. "The guts!"

"Uh-huh." Nebula takes a sip. It perks her up.

"And the rest?"

Matt has finished his sandwich, and this conversation isn't going anywhere he wants it to go. He leaves the kitchen. Zhu walks out after him, unsure if he should stay. The women don't even notice that the two men are gone. I put two plates on the table, with a butter knife for each, and I slide the bread basket over to Nebula, as well as the butter and the jam. Donatella grabs the second plate. So I get a third plate out of the cupboard and a third knife. I sit down on Mike's chair. The seat is still warm. I shudder; I don't like this kind of second-hand butt rub with a guy I can't stand.

"Have you ever heard of Stella Sonderlicht?"

"The infamous Jewish Venus flytrap? Sure!"

"Exactly."

"Oh—woah!"

"Fascinating, isn't it?"

"How exciting!" Donatella hands me the jam. "And what did the old man say when you confronted him with his plagiarism, Paolino?"

"Well . . ."

"We haven't confronted him yet."

We? We're a team now? And what about that "yet"? Where is this going? Nebula puts her hand on my arm. "Paul is very upset, and a bit confused." She shakes her head. The poor, upset, confused boy.

I'm not sure whether I like her tome. I try another sentence: "So I . . ."

". . . too upset, I think, to even go and see the man."

Donatella looks at me with pity in her eyes. "Poor boy. You blew your postdoc for *this*?"

Excuse me? I blew my postdoc?

"Oh well," Nebula sighs, and she nibbles on her jam sandwich.

"We have to go see him," says Donatella. "We have to talk to the man, don't you think?"

"My thoughts exactly," says Nebula.

"Well . . ." But before I get any further, the ladies have already left the kitchen.

"Paul, are you coming or not?" Nebula calls out.

There I go then, by G*d's grace. There I go.

•

I can hardly believe it. The three of us are seated on Bus 695, on our way to the Potsdam station, and then to Leipziger Straße, to the den of the toothless lion. I have no idea what I will tell him, no idea what the two women want to ask him, no idea why Donatella is suddenly included in this, and no idea why I go along, except that it's probably much better if I'm around when they confront De Heer with his plagiarism. But why? To protect him? To find out the truth? To see if we can still save his book (let's face it: *my* book)? Or to witness his reaction and carefully incorporate it in my final, utterly sincere, and brilliantly executed chapter— the coda that also contains the mild pornography of me-in-bed-with-an-autodidact-Holocaust-expert?

Nebula is right. Every last trace of rain has vanished, and it's positively balmy out. After this long winter, the sunlight does us good: it almost feels hot. Is it really possible that we're having a cloudless day? Has the suicide season finally ended?

The bus makes its usual slow way to the north side of the park. The sign warns: 30 km is the maximum speed. The sides of the road are littered with Mercedeses and BMWS, parked haphazardly, abandoned in obvious haste. The rich have descended from the big city to celebrate the beginning of springtime in Sanssouci, and they couldn't get to the park fast enough. The paths and meadows are filled with old folks sporting snow-white, well-groomed manes; they walk hand in hand like actors in a television commercial for life insurance or mild laxatives. The crates have been removed from the statues. The unexpected white of the marble hurts the eyes.

In one of his rare philosophical moods, De Heer once told me that the de facto continuation of the split between the two parts of Germany is what hurt him the most. Berliners from both sides of the fence have no real understanding of the people from the other side. They are all subject to the laws of gravity and friction, but they have no bodily experience of what it means to live with each other, of the hardness of shared kitchen chairs or the mercy of the common bedroom, or of the warm air that floats through the open windows of compassion that the Great German house once must have had. Is tourism a way back to each other—East Germans on Ku'damm, West Germans in Brandenburg—or does the fact that people feel like travelers inside their own country merely demonstrate how bad the situation has become? Are we no longer capable of feeling at home on the other side? The weekend tourists walk around as though they are children of royal blood strolling through their ancestral domain, or else they behave like kittens let out in the grass for the first time; they take long tentative steps because every move tickles the belly. Even the citizens of Potsdam don't make themselves at home in the park. My morning strolls in Sanssouci—I like to walk when weighing difficult editing decisions—were invariably lonely. The imperial domain is no garden for the common folk of the GDR; it is a historical fair for Westerners, something that stands outside reality—and this is no reason for celebration. The concrete Wall may have fallen, but the metaphorical Wall is still standing tall. The West Berliners who enjoy the weather in Potsdam are just slumming on the other side.

The S-train to Berlin-East is one of the old communist models, with slatted benches and heavy, customer-operated doors. No window is left unscratched. It leaves the station with a mighty whistling screech and a hint of hysteria in its wheels.

There had been rumors in the Gästehaus about his time of year, tall tales about how the winter would end along with its muggy mist, its dreary drizzle, and sordid snow, and would make way for a jubilant springtime with silver dandelion seeds sailing against a backdrop of sparkling emerald; that little boys would make their way through the pedestrians on Ku'damm, standing upright on the pedals of their tiny bicycles, one hand held high to pluck cherry blossoms out of the air; that the unassailable turrets of our rain clouds would be replaced by cirri, fluffy and sweet like meringue pastries—a time when you would feel the whole world tickling your skin. And see, this mythical day has come. We ride with all windows down, the balmy breeze ruffles through our hair, and welcoming music wafts from the streets of Charlottenburg. We are hungry and thirsty for warmth, and we laugh at the amazing metamorphosis, at the wonders of a city in bloom.

And yet.

And still.

Somewhere past the Lehrter station, forever closed for renovation, we pass the invisible border between the two former Germanies and the familiar stench of scorched lignite stings our nostrils; the signature GDR smell of acrid ash and cold cinders makes us shiver.

"Let's get out at Friedrichstraße," proposes Donatella, "and walk from there. A stroll across Unter-den-Linden, with the young leaves on the new trees, a short half-hour in the sunshine—it'll do us good."

It only takes a few minutes for the train to get to Friedrichstraße, but taking in the contradictory scents of springtime and totalitarianism, the remainder of our journey seems pregnant with foreboding. We are strangers in this town all over again, even though each of us has lived here for at least a few months. As if we are riding into a mirror map of the GDR—it's no longer West Berlin that's the blank spot, terra incognita for Easterners; the former GDR has transformed itself into an unknown bubble universe that can burst at any moment and flood the world. We are suddenly at the heart of a labyrinth of latent danger and subterranean violence: the city turned into a pagan, prehistoric, living, snorting thing. "Let's not forget," Donatella half-jokes, "that all these old *Genossen* received full military training. Every gal older than eighteen knows how to throw a grenade; every young man knows how to mix a Molotov cocktail; every adult knows how to silence somebody quickly and efficiently with nothing but their bare hands, or, conversely, how to get them to talk."

Did we really just leave a safe island—West Berlin—and are we now wading knee-deep in shark-infested waters? The East has this certain *something*. I pull the doors open before the train has come to a complete stop. The world slides by and then it slows down and halts; finally we get our feet on solid ground.

The shivers pass as soon as we bathe in the stifling light of the neoclassicist buildings along Unter-den-Linden. We can be tourists again; we can slip unnoticed into the crowd. Reassured we walk past facades safely tamed with scaffolding, down to the quietly subdued river. I put my hand around Nebula's waist; she puts hers around mine. And then Donatella does the same: She puts her arm around Nebula and so we make a trio, because we are brand-new friends and because it's so immensely pleasant to walk across the most historic boulevard of Old Europe: a German gal and an Italian woman and a Flemish boy. The eternal flame burns inside the Neue Wache; a woman carved from stone cries for the dead son in her lap of impenetrable granite.

A sputtering in the air: a small turboprop above our heads. We stare at the plume in its wake, its capricious trail of freedom. But why does the airplane's freedom make me restless, as if a deeper incarnation within me is trying to fight its way to the surface of my skin? Nebula squeezes my hand. She knows the truth: The present is a flat trompe l'oeil; it only turns three-dimensional when held up to the alarming shimmer of the past.

·

A sputtering in the air. The airplane, a top-heavy Junker, barely clears the arches of the Brandenburg Gate. It's one o'clock in the morning. The horizon is on fire—long, longing fingers of flame reach for the bucking dragonfly that desperately tries to gain altitude in its sharp turn over the inner city. It staggers under artillery fire; its wingtips waggle in a last dazzling salute to the ruins of the chancellery, and in that final nose-dive it finds the necessary speed to take to the sky: Its time has not yet come. This is a short respite, however: In twenty minutes, the cargo plane will be hit by an anti-aircraft grenade and crash into the peaceful meadows of Börnersdorf by Dresden. The pilot, Grundlfinger, the only man on board, will perish in the explosion and in the cargo hold a few pounds of nitrate film will catch fire and its sparks will set fire to the rest of the load—a few tons of precious paper on their way to Bavaria to be stored inside a secret cave in a secret location. The Soviet soldier who shot down the plane will stomp the ground and pump his fist and hoot, proud of his accomplishment. The wheezing of the dead bird, the heavy thud of its impact on the ground, the flashes of light after the crash: another direct hit. The men of his company will rejoice and dance. There isn't much air traffic anymore, so this one victory warrants the uncorking of their last remaining bottle of vodka.

If they had known what was inside the plane they would have run over and saved what they could. Now the whole cargo is lost in the cleansing bloom of fire, as well as a human life—but who grieves over one more life lost in this damned war?

·

Like in any good old noir potboiler, we meet the protagonist at the point where he has lost nearly everything.

I find him in the inner courtyard of an enormous building. Once—and this was less than a few months ago—it must have been a grandiose edifice, the proud palace of an immensely wealthy king. Now it is a dying carcass, half-burnt, almost leveled to the ground. The last remains of a last repast are still strewn across the black and white marble tiles, between the scorched beams and the big blocks of granite: beer and wine bottles—some still full, most of them half-empty—half-eaten humps of bread, tattered knapsacks, and mysterious pieces of women's underwear.

I roam through what once were hallways and I pretend that I'm still looking for a unit to join. But that's not what I'm looking for. What I desperately need is a reason to keep on fighting. There are so many more reasons to just give up, here and now; to slump down on the ground and dress my wounds, to open up one of the brown bottles that so generously litter the floor; so many reasons to simply fall asleep and, well . . . never wake up. To get some rest. More than anything in the world I want to get some rest. To wait for the end—to wait for the end, filled with calm and warmth, filled with trust, with confidence. To wait for the end of this fucking war, this meshuggeneh *Krieg*, this whole misgiven massacre that's taken away three years of my life, my terribly short life—and much more than that: that killed something in me, killed something during those three years of killing and almost being killed; some vital piece of my soul murdered forever. The temptation to lie down like a dog, to never get up again—that temptation looms, but, oh, misguided pride, oh, miscreant mind—I can't bring myself to do it. "My Honor is True" reads my armband, and that motto keeps haunting my brainwashed head. How can I silence that recurring thought, the thought that—I know this much for certain—will bring me face to face with my own death, and probably sooner rather than later? There's only one way to liberate myself, and that's to embrace my impending doom. It would be nice to get killed on the field of honor, after all, that's what soldiers are suppose to do, isn't it?—even if that field is not in my homeland. Germany will never be my homeland, and the Germans don't give a damn about Flanders, and I had to learn all of this too late—on the battlefield. I will not die for a higher cause; I will not perish in the name of some lofty ideal—after all that I have seen, I have no ideals left. This street battle makes no sense; it won't delay the progress of the Bolshevik hordes by so much as a second. They are here already, the Soviet troops. The only reason to keep on fighting is to have it over and done with. I will die, we will all die, and so we will finally gain the well-deserved rest that cannot be obtained by any other means. I welcome death; I long for it. Oh yes, I've tried to hasten it, many times. Once, I stormed straight at the enemy lines, just a whim, pure daredevil audacity. I got a medal for it, a heavy piece of cast iron on a red ribbon, and I had to pretend to be mightily pleased when one or the other harried general pinned it on my breast pocket. No matter how often I stood in the line of fire, no matter how often I put myself in harm's way, no matter how often I clamored for my death, the bullet with my name on it never came whizzing by. My comrades fell, one after the other. Only ten of us stumbled away from the steppes into this g*dforsaken town. I had become their leader by default: the last officer of our platoon still standing. That leader made a few bad decisions, and now I'm the only one alive.

It's not difficult to make the wrong decisions. Nobody from the original *Lange-marck* division—we have since been renamed the *Flandern* Brigade—knows the terrain, and the defense of Berlin is in the hands of the very incompetent street fighters of the *Volkssturm*. The left-behinds. Men judged either too old or too young to fight the regular war at the front. It's highly unlikely that the end of the war will make great strategists out of them, soldiers who will turn the tide at the eleventh hour. There aren't even enough uniforms for all of them; most of them simply wear an armband over their civilian clothes. These slow fat boys, gasping for breath, these toothless graybeards, these amputees from the Eastern Front are the ridiculous Wagnerian dragons that guard the last gate of the Reich that once stretched all the way from the North Sea to the Ural.

I don't know it yet, but I too will die in a few hours. It is good that a man never knows the time or place of his dying, but let's be honest—it won't be a big surprise to me when it comes. This is a death that's been announced in advance, you see—the Flemish boys in the SS are nothing but cannon fodder, and the same is true for the adolescents and the balding town guardsmen. Now I'm here to witness the last incomprehensible struggle of the Empire. Berlin is a battlefield and a killing ground—the gutters stink of death. Why don't they just give up and surrender and let us all go home? See? Give me five minutes to think and I can still hope for survival and a safe homecoming.

I've learned a few simple truths. Things they don't teach you in school; things I'd rather not have learned. They serve no purpose, these lessons—they only haunt me. For instance, that battlefields don't smell of gunpowder and blood like they tell you in stories, but of shit and rotting flesh. That the echo of your own shot in the vastness of the planes can deafen you. That it can get so cold that your breath freezes as soon as it leaves your mouth; it rustles in the air, then clangs onto the ground. That the icy wind can burn your flesh. That it's helpful, after a day of killing, to drink and drink and drink, to drink until the night becomes unrecognizable.

My first shot in the war. There's shockingly little difference between the real thing and what happens at target practice at the barracks: Smoke rises from the barrel, the recoil hits my shoulder. The smoke hangs motionless in the air, then it dissolves. It is gone. And the Russian too: The Russian is also gone.

I killed my first man while looking him straight in the eye. The bayonet met with some initial resistance, but then it slid smoothly through the layers of his muscles and guts. I never believed I could do it—that I could kill another human being at such proximity, a man whose breath was mingling with mine, whose body heat I could feel, whose eyes were looking into mine—eyes that shone with surprise and such fierce, if short-lived vitality. But it turned out I could do it after all, and that I felt disappointingly little while doing it: No horror and no self-contempt; though later I despised myself for not having felt any of those noble, humane emotions.

It happened after a long reconnaissance trip, outside a lonely hut in the barren steppe, far from any other human habitation—I look the Russian in the face while the steel pierces his belly. He had stepped up to me, amazed and delighted to meet another man in his loneliness, or what he assumed was a man—I am so deeply wrapped in my shawls and hat and facial hair that I might just as well have been a grizzly bear or a specter from some nightmare—and now, now that he is hugging me and the blade is sliding through the many layers of otter fur and wool and cotton, and then through epidermis, dermis, and finally, with excruciating slowness, through the abdominal wall, a different kind of amazement fills his eyes, an incredulity that first changes to panic and then to a strange resignation. I press on and I feel—I feel almost nothing. It's a job, and I'm not even relieved I finished the killing before the man came to his senses and sprayed me with bullets.

Now that I think about it, maybe he wasn't a Russian soldier at all, maybe he was just a harmless farmer or a hermit, the lawful inhabitant of that mud hut. Few soldiers still wore regulation uniforms in the coldest of days of the Russian campaign, and there was little time to think. Maybe he was even German, an exhausted soldier who took shelter in that hut for a few days; or perhaps he was a lost youth from Antwerp or Bruges, hiding from the world burning down around him. I will never know; we didn't exchange any words; I do not know what language the man spoke. It doesn't matter; he is dead and I survived.

A poet on the battlefield. A poet trained in Bad Stolz. A miniature poodle jumping through the hoop of fire called history, scorching his fur.

Here sprout faces without necks, arms unattached to shoulders, and eyes rolling around looking for their sockets.

The first man you kill. Time staggers. Your eyes scan the landscape. The rhythm of your hurried breath. Everything is in order. Your legs still carry you.

The skull that holds your thoughts.

Grenades explode. Shock waves hit your chest. Cold air penetrates you. Hot air leaves you.

Your thoughts cease.

The men in front of you, the men next to you, the men behind you—they are sudden fountains of blood. Your boots sink deep into hills of flesh. Your heels crack through a rib cage.

Always upwards.

When they are shot.

Some curse. Some sing.

But they always raise their arms upwards.

They stand still, they stiffen, they raise their arms. Under the shock of the bullet (in their belly, in their chest, in what once was a face—a charming face, a loveable face, capable of tears).

They spit. Blood. Slime. Gall. Words. (Intelligible—unintelligible.)

High, whistling howls. (Artillery percussion.)

Arms raised. And fingers (if they still have fingers) clawing through the clouds; they burst through the stratosphere and hook their dirty split nails into the Eye of G*d.

The blood that spurts. The drops that freeze in the air—rubies clatter to the ground.

And then time itself gets caught in ice—time gets sticky like molasses.

I'm a good shot.

I have all the time in the world.

I sink onto my knees.

I take aim.

I have him in my sights.

Around me the bodies fall, slow and terrifying like lazy comets. Their arms and legs moving in comic slow motion.

Moist thuds on the ground; bags of loose meat hit the dirt.

I wipe the innards, the slime, the blood from my eyes. I look at him. I have him in my sights.

Time staggers. Time bruises. Time bleeds.

Light pressure applied to the trigger.

The first man.

After the battle the gashes and scratches in my flesh burn and throb in the icy cold. Pain is good. Pain is my friend. Pain means survival.

I roamed the battlefield, that night; I looked for proof of a hereafter, an idea of what life after death would look like. Blood sloshed in my boots—and not just my own blood. I interviewed dying soldiers; I put my ear to their dried-out, bleeding mouths, hoping for a first-hand account of the transition. I wanted to find a man who had made the journey to the other side and brought back some message:

a snippet, anything, no matter what. My only discovery: Every man's death looks exactly the same as every other's.

Somewhere in Poland. A forest.

The men and women are naked. Except that some of the men wear shoes. These are the man who dig the furrows. Their genitals waggle absurdly when they throw sand over the edge. The waiting are blindfolded. If they escape, they won't get far, no matter how well they know the woods. The Unterscharführer bums a cigarette. No blindfolds on the children—they won't survive on their own anyway. They stand next to their naked mothers, their little hands in theirs, their little thumbs in their mouths. The proximity of their mother's familiar scent keeps them calm. The Unterscharführer is glad that the children are quiet. "Have you ever shot a gang of kids rolling around on the ground, screaming hysterically? A fucking mess, that's what it is."

I see a girl, six or seven years old; she clutches a rag doll close to her chest. "Those Jews, always clinging to their possessions." The officer asks for a second cigarette. I give him one. We stumbled across their patrol while we were marching to our night camp; he invited me over to inspect his work.

"Hey, look, there's one taking off." It hardly causes any commotion in the ranks. The soldiers look at each other quizzically. One of them shrugs his shoulders. "My turn? Okay . . ." He takes aim and shoots the man in the leg. Another soldier goes to fetch the bounty; he drags the victim by his good leg to the edge of the pit and then shoots him in the stomach. When he's sure the bleeding is proceeding satisfactorily, he kicks the man in the groin, making him roll down the incline. Good. That's that.

The Unterschar throws the butt of his cigarette after the man.

"Terrible," I say, "to prefer such a long painful death over the short shock of the bullet."

"Yeah. Jews are stupid, aren't they?"

The children go first. They stand next to their mothers at the edge of the ravine. The impact of the bullets push their light bodies right over. Handy! Then the women. The ones who don't spontaneously roll down the slope are pushed in by their men, under the threat of the guns. Then it's the men's turn. The last two survivors cover the bodies with sand. Then they get shot too, at close range, with a bullet to the neck. We leave them there. The wolves know what to do with them.

Our march back to camp is longer than the one coming down; we've lost our local guides.

And the flies, the lazy halos of fat black flies that hover over the bodies of the dead in the pit. The flies get buried too. They dig themselves out; they rise black and buzzing from the forest floor like the souls of the departed.

I lie flat on the ground and my face is wet. The far-off rattling of machine guns, the thud of grenades—I got used to it years ago; it is the environment I am most accustomed to. After all this time, it's as if I've never known anything else. I would miss it if it were gone. My true enemy is my memory, the sediment in my mind of what I did and did not do. The killings in somebody else's name, the atrocities I did nothing to stop—they haunt me, they throb through my consciousness, they trouble my days and sour the few dreams I still have. Another reason not to sleep: those dreams, those dreams.

I hear a plane climbing. It's in trouble; its engine sputters terribly. That must be what woke me up. My body can recognize danger on its own. Is it possible that there will ever be anything else other than this—this life of gunpowder and hunger? That this constant, visceral fear will ever be replaced by the comfortable kind of angst that only grips the mind? Reluctantly I stumble outside, disgusted by my own survival instinct. It's more likely that the Russians will bomb the palace than the wide-open street. I stand in the inner courtyard, amidst the craters. In the light of the three-quarter moon I recognize the airplane's silhouette. It's a Junker. One of ours. False alarm.

Then I see the man. He stands next to a cement mixer by a concrete chimney—undoubtedly the air turret of an underground bunker. He wears a uniform with a civilian winter coat thrown over it; I can't make out the insignia. It's an impeccable dress uniform, totally unlike the patched-up affair I'm wearing. In the unexpected company of this fine, clean shaven, well-dressed gentleman I feel dirty, boorish, and—remarkable: *old*. How old is that man at the chimney? Forty? Twenty years older than I am? Yet, he looks so splendid, and I'm a twenty-something going on sixty; I have a gash in my cheek and bullets in my thighs. I've made a long, long journey and am so unbelievably, so irreparably exhausted.

He must be a high-ranking officer. His back is straight as an arrow, and he stands there with such poise, as if none of the whistling grenades could ever hurt him. His movements are deliberate and slow, full of confidence; they betray a deep contempt for wasteful expenditure of energy. This is the body language of a Wehrmacht general, one of those men who throw away their rough army-issue gloves and insist on wearing their own, fashioned from supple calfskin. The man digs into the inside pocket of his coat and out comes a long gleaming object, a gas grenade with a long stem. Men like me climb on top of tanks with those things between our teeth; we open up the hatch with one hand while sliding out the safety pin with the other; then we drop the thing inside and roll off and away, praying that there's a ditch nearby.

The man steps up to the turret. In the light of an exploding grenade I catch a glimpse of his face. I know that man—I recognize his aristocratic face: This is Albert Speer, Reichsminister of Armament and War Industries. I edge closer, lured in by his mysterious presence—here, in the garden of the chancellery, one of the almighty is making his very own direct contribution to the war effort. I want to support him in his mission; I have some extra ammunition on my belt. I want to stand next to him when he performs his feat, the lost Untersturmführer next to the lonely minister; Germanic brothers shoulder to shoulder in the noble fight—in the bunker beneath us a nest of Russian rats must be hiding.

He's startled when I appear out of nowhere with the inaudible shuffle of the combat veteran, but not too much. Every good soldier has his fear under control, and anyone who dares to approach you without opening fire in these days of artillery and sniper bullets must be a friend. He looks at me, and then his gaze moves down to his own hand, as if he can't believe what he's seeing there: a grenade, brand new, freshly painted in camouflage colors, his fingers at the safety pin. He wears his cap high on his forehead like Wehrmacht officers are wont to do—the SS prefers the brooding, deep-over-the-eyebrows look that the Führer made so popular. The light is sparse, but the skin on Speer's face is gleaming as though floodlights shine out of his eyes. He looks me over, and his gaze stops at the medal on my breast—the medal I got for fighting in the east, the Order of Frozen Meat, the *Gefrierfleischorden*.

I salute him. Amazing how your reflexes stay intact: I salute the minister. The man relaxes and he makes a gesture with that beautiful glove of his—no formalities needed, soldier. There's a nest of Russians hiding inside this bunker, in the heart of town, or else a troupe of traitors, a fifth column, and the Minister of Armament will be seeing to their demise personally. I consider the implications of this—what times we live in, when the politicians—the our leaders themselves—take to the streets to battle: what despair, but also, what heroism!

Speer shakes his head at me. He wants to finish the job all by himself. I understand. But I can't just leave. It feels as though I'm nailed to the ground. I'm strangely fascinated by this scene—the close proximity of the most important man in the Reich after Hitler mesmerizes me. Then Speer's knees buckle. He puts the grenade in the dust, as gently, as though it was a pigeon egg. Then he draws his pistol and aims it at my chest.

"Go," he says, and the barrel of his gun shows me the way. It is an order, and I obey. I understand him all too well. It is wartime, and every man wants to keep the honor of his greatest deed to himself. I understand. I retreat.

This is the way it goes. This is how you die. Had I stayed with Speer, I might still be alive. Perhaps. But I shoulder my rifle and I run around the corner—my leg aches, pockmarked with bullet wounds, but it's been aching for so long that the pain has become background noise, a tinnitus of the muscles: no more or less a vital sign than the beating of my heart—and then from the darkness there's a sudden racket, a bang and a clatter, a snorting and whinnying. A charge on horseback through the streets of what was once the most modern city in the world—riders straight from the Mongolian steppes emit high, piercing shrieks that cut right through my bones; their voices oscillate like exotic butterflies in the night air, their eyes are sinister slits in the caked mud of their faces, and in their hands—how incongruent, how dreamy—they brandish naked glittering swords, sharp and straight, clean and shining. They do not wear uniforms, only colorful rags of wool and silk: yellow, red, green, and—the dust and whirlwinds of their journey notwithstanding—blinding white. I press myself against a crumbling wall and shoulder my gun, but it is too late: My movement betrays me and one of the men storms straight at me on his short-legged horse. The others spur him on: "Obey, Yamatsan!" The animal dances around my spray of bullets and when the MP38 runs out of ammunition, I run for my life, even though I know I don't stand a chance. The hooves rumble, the horse breathes down my neck, and a cry of triumph sounds from the rider's throat. The acrid stench of rancid butter enters my nostrils and then, as if this was a game, the rider hits me with the flat of his sword on my neck. He draws no blood, but the dull pain of the blow forces me to my knees. The world tumbles in front of my eyes and my fingers claw in the dirt—and then I vomit my soul out on the soil. The horse snorts, the air displaced by its muscular frame blows over my back, the dust kicked up by its thumping hooves itches inside my lungs—it makes me cough and retch. I look over my shoulder: The horse has one hoof lifted, the dark rider grins, and then the animal stomps me into the ground. My organs are crushed against each other. I close my eyes; the hoof scrapes against my skull and then hits me full in the stomach again. Something is terribly wrong inside me. When the high whine of artillery grenades fills the street, the riders spur on their horses and disappear through doors and windows, and I remain where I am, in the middle of what once was a street, lonelier than I have ever been, and the projectiles whistle around me, and then the din stops, and in its stead comes the terrible sound of almost-silence: a tearing, hissing sound, the sound you hear before lightning hits, the sound of the small shockwave that travels ahead of a deadly projectile.

The ground is warm and moist. I must have lost a lot of blood. The world goes black and white, all distorted like in an expressionist film. This is how soldiers die (one more example of my useless, horrible knowledge): The brain, screaming for oxygen, shuts down, no longer capable of conjuring up a color image. Soon my field of vision will shrink to a narrow tunnel, and then the tunnel will shrink to a point, a blinding white point. Then it will become dark. Dark forever.

I know all this. Now I see it for myself.

I am a tunnel that turns in on itself.

The field collapses.

Is that a white angel at the end of the tunnel? Is that the voice of—impossible, from what depths of memory does she emerge?—Helena Guna blowing in my ear? Is that Helena Guna's hand gently supporting the weight of my torn intestines? Is that . . . ?

Then comes the point.

The singularity.

Lena?

What?

There.

•

Speer turns his back on the ruins. His ruins. His chancellery, his dream: gone. His creations: lost forever. The city is a moonscape of craters and dunes, pulverized brick and crumbled concrete. The metropolis has been reduced to this: Walls lean precariously into each other, chimneys collapse in meaningless heaps, and tumbleweeds of barbed wire roll through the streets. Will all this rough recombinant material one day become a city again, rebuilt by some extraterrestrial race? Speer is quite certain that one day the Quadriga might once again stand on top of the Brandenburg Gate, and that a new dome will span the Reichstag, but he also knows that his own creations are forever doomed. Whatever their artistic merit might be, they never will be reconstructed: They are tainted by their association with the Nazi regime. The tanks and the artillery explosions and the soldier's boots will trample them further into the ground; the rubble will turn to dust and the dust will be scattered to the four winds.

His vision, his dream, his ambition had been to build a town. Germania. Berlin rebuilt, Berlin reborn, a Rome for our times, risen from the ashes. The giant dome at its center, filled with worldly prayer and G*dless meditation, would speak to the nation's very soul. A dome of light surrounded by a thin membrane of concrete, the largest dome ever built, resounding with silence, humming with stillness, breathless with audacity—a place to heal, a place where the world could be seen as a place that knows no bounds. In the encircling walls the statues of the Proud New G*ds would de displayed in enormous niches, Germania herself in the place of honor, and around her the founders of her empire—Goebbels, Göring, and, of course, Hitler. A crown of flames would surround this threesome enthroned in a firmament of light. The esoteric geometric patter of the tile floor would be a symbol of the order that rules the empire; the timeless sparsity of the design would represent the everlasting, imperishable nature of Germany's greatness. And in front of the dome hall, the towering statue of the Führer—one hundred and twenty feet tall, covered in a ton of pure leaf gold, just like Nero's effigy in ancient Rome— inspiring the masses, thronging down the mile-long corridor that would lead into the temple.

This had been the extent of Speer's dream: an architecture for the People, but at the scale of the g*ds. He had wanted to build a city. Nothing more. Now his dream-city lies in ruins, just like the real Berlin—destroyed by its leaders. Now the dream-city's foundation, like that of the real city, lies drenched in blood.

What is he afraid of? He is afraid that the rubble will not be ground down fine enough to destroy the seed of National Socialism; he's afraid that those little silver bullets, carried by the wind of freedom, will land on the loose earth of the German plains and dig their way deep into the fertile layers of Blood and Soil—that one day soon they will again sprout into a multitude of handsome, trigger-happy warriors manning tanks. Brave, bold murderers. Murderers in cold blood. Speer knows. He saw it happen. They all became murderers. Himself included. And all he ever wanted was to build a city.

The boss was angry, yesterday. (That's what we, the inner circle, call him. The boss.) I wasn't there, but I heard the stories. His rage was so powerful, so explosive, the eruption shook them all to their cores. None of those present could remember his exact words, but *der Chef* had become white as chalk, they all agreed on that part, and then—again, all reports agreed as to this detail—his face had turned a disconcerting shade of blue. He hadn't been himself; he had paced the length of the room, bitter and resentful, until he finally collapsed onto a chair, and then he jumped up again and started to yell, *yell, YELL*, roaring like a caged lion, and then his voice broke into a hysterical whine, as though he were just another operatic prima donna. He was so out of it that Goebbels had feared that the Führer would draw his revolver—the boss was the only person allowed to carry his gun into the bunker—and that he would shoot them all down like rabbits. He was capable of it, *der Chef.*

A panzer division consists of three brigades.

That's what started it.

Three brigades.

"Why doesn't Steiner attack the enemy?" The enemy, you see, had already occupied Köpenick and Spandau. "He has a full SS panzer division at his disposal!"

"*Mein Führer*, Steiner's division has no more than eleven thousand men, and they are all dead tired. There isn't a single one of his soldiers who hasn't been wounded, and Steiner has no more than fifty tanks. He's in no position to attack. It would be a miracle if they aren't all slaughtered in the next few hours."

Hitler raises his hands.

"Fifty tanks? That's impossible!"

The generals keep quiet.

Keitel tries again: "Mein Führer . . ."

Hitler interrupts him and yells, beside himself with rage, "A panzer division consists of three brigades!" He measures his words: "A. Panzer. Division. Consists. Of. Three. Brigades."

"Eleven thousand men, mein Führer."

"But a panzer division consists of three brigades!"

Keitel insists. "Eleven thousand men. Exhausted. Demoralized. They can't hold out for much longer, mein Führer."

"But . . ."

"A few hours, perhaps a few days, if all goes well. If all goes well."

"But a panzer division consists of . . ."

Keitel, Keitel, otherwise such a cautious man, such a devoted ass-kisser, such a sly slime ball that the rest of the entourage calls him *Lakaitel* behind his back— little lackey—Keitel finally loses his patience. He doesn't even wait until the boss is done talking. "In a few hours, mein Führer, the enemy will stand in the heart of Berlin."

Then the unthinkable happens. Hitler listens. Hitler stops in his tracks. He listens to the echo of Keitel's words, the cruel words of his field marshal. These words are a death sentence. A few hours! A day or two! Hitler raises his hands to heaven. The bystanders, his staff, are flabbergasted. Hitler raises his hands to heaven and then he asks, in a voice thick with restrained fury, while eying his generals, dark and irate and more somber than they have ever seen him:

"Is. This. True?"

"It is true," says Keitel.

And then the Führer erupts in a storm of rage.

Again his arms rise up and he paces the room.

"The war is lost! THE WAR IS LOST!"

He turns to the men that surround him.

"And you, *you* have lost it for us!"

He points his finger at them, one after the other.

"You, you, and you! Do you think I'm an idiot? That I don't realize that you betrayed me? All of you? You betrayed me! Treason! Treason! LIES! LIES! LIES!" Hitler buries his face in his hands, despairing. He collapses in front of them, his knees shaking. "The war is lost!" he whimpers, and his voice breaks. He rolls over the floor; his arms and legs twitch uncontrollably. For a second, it seems he might lose consciousness. Then he jumps up and he sways with his hands in fists and yells and yells, in the grip of an impotent fury. The words come so fast, their rhythm is so relentless, that it sounds like the fragmented, indiscriminate cursing of a madman, the wild ranting of a dangerous lunatic. Where is the man with the camera to immortalize this meltdown, Hitler in his moment of tragic doom, the last eruption of the greatest man Germany has ever known, this mega-Bismarck, this . . . this . . . ?

Then, finally, his rage exhausted, he slumps down on a chair, and he waves his generals off. "Go, go, go! I have no further orders for you. Go. Go! Go! You band of nitwits!" And abruptly he leaves, goes to his room: a pale shadow, gray as the concrete of the bunker, a pale poltergeist lusting for revenge and murder. The shocked crowd quickly disperses to let the madman through. He bangs the steel door shut behind him. The room is silent. Nobody says anything; nobody dares look anybody else in the eye. The generals leave quietly, one after the other, in that silence that has no name. One after the other they return to their positions— on their way to certain death.

In the aftermath of the Führer's mad outburst I walk into the bunker. I smell alcohol and tobacco and unwashed bodies, and I do my best to look calm, collected, and innocent. I am a newborn lamb, fragrant and clean.

"And you!" the Führer barks at me. He's mad as hell, but still he uses the polite form "*Sie*." Nobody ever came close to him, nobody had a place in that chilly heart of his, not even I, the disciple he loved. "You ignored my orders. Ignored, yes, Speer. Ignored! Did you think I wouldn't find out? Bormann told me what you told the Gauleiters in the Ruhr. You told them that the war was lost and you ordered them . . . Ordered! You, you Speer, have *ordered* them to . . . ignore . . . *my order*

. . . my order, my explicit order to blow up the factories, to scorch the earth . . . you ordered them to ignore that order. That is what you did, Speer! You! You told them that my order was senseless. You told them that such an order should not be carried out. Speer! Speer! Do you realize what this disobedience means? If you were not my architect, I would immediately institute proceedings to try you for high treason!"

"Please do so, mein Führer," I say calmly. "Do what you deem necessary. Please, do so without regard for who I am."

The Führer eyes me angrily. Calm, dignified, and self-assured I stare him down. He knows I'm right. He too must know, deep in his soul, that I am right. It makes no sense to impose a scorched-earth policy on our own people. That would be suicide, for the people, for the nation, for the future. He must realize that this is not just senseless, but criminal. He has to realize this is not how he should go down in history—as the man who put his own country, his own subjects, to the torch in a final act of desperation: the man who catapulted us all back into the Middle Ages.

I try to say all this with my eyes. Hitler is a smart man, and sly; he has an infallible insight. He will understand the wider, the greater, the transcendent perspective. He looks at me, and I see that the Führer understands the reason for my reckless deed, and that deep inside he is grateful for it.

He seems to calm down a bit. "Come on, Speer. Face it. You're overworked. You're ill. You have to take a vacation, right now. There must be an assistant who can run the ministry for a while, while you're gone."

He looks feverish. His face is swollen, as if the stamp of death is already on it; an unnatural red blush adorns his cheeks, and his eyes look yellow. I do not beg; my voice is flat. This is about saving face: saving his, saving mine. "I feel quite well, mein Führer. I am not taking a sick leave. If you consider me unfit to be your minister . . . well, please, fire me."

"You have no choice, Speer. It's impossible for me, do you hear, *impossible* to fire you."

This is going well. This is going very well. I have traction. How far can I go? If I desert my post, if somebody else takes over, then the absurd order will be carried out. It's on the table, and Hitler never retracts an order. He hasn't fired me, nor did he have me killed, and these are clear signs that he wants me to stay, that he doesn't really want his order obeyed. I raise the stakes. "And it is impossible for me to take a leave. As long as I am fit, it is my duty to see to the affairs of the ministry. I am not ill."

A long silence fills the room, and this time it feels like a pause of reflection, not the silence before the storm. Hitler sits down on the edge of his iron bed, and without waiting for permission I take a chair. "Speer. If you . . . if you could convince yourself, if you could be convinced that the war is not lost, then . . . then you can continue your job."

"You know I can't be convinced of that, mein Führer. We have to face the truth. The war is . . . is . . . lost."

A new, longer silence. The man opposite me, the commander in chief, the leader, the boss, hangs his head. An oily forelock tumbles across his forehead. With an exhausted hand he sweeps his hair back. Hitler in all the nakedness of his feelings of despair—a spectacle never before seen. "If you could at least *hope* it wasn't over yet, that the war is not lost. Can you at least have a little hope, Speer?" His shoulders slump. He begs. The Leader of the Nation, he begs me to believe. "Speer. That . . . that would suffice. Hope. That would satisfy me, Speer. Hope. A glimmer of hope."

I do not respond. I avert my gaze. I don't want to see him like this.

It is no use, Herr Hitler. It's over. We all know that; everybody who lives in the bunker knows that—you, Herr Führer, your adjuncts, Fräulein Braun, the cooks, your secretary, your driver, your bodyguards. They all know. It's over. You know it too. It's all over now.

Without saying a word, I slide my chair back. I get up and walk to the door. I leave the man alone on his iron bunk in that smelly underground cave, alone underneath the stolen state portrait of Frederick the Great, the man he looks up to as his hero, the emperor whose power he could never surpass.

I know how it will end. It's not hard to predict. We go back many years, the Führer and I. Not so long ago, I loved him above all. He will find his final strength and pace and pace and then he will yell and shout until he is blue in the face and that ridiculous forelock of his will dance in front of his eyes, and then THE END will come, the real, the ultimate end. He will draw his revolver, and the bunker guards will come running and in his bedroom they'll find his bloody cadaver and Eva's next to his, and one door down Magda Goebbels will put the little capsules with cyanide in her children's mouths with utmost tenderness. "Bite down, Heide, and swallow. Helga, here is some medicine. All will be well. Hilde, Hellmuth, *Liebling*, please, Holde, chew it well. Very good, Hedda." I know him. I know him all too well—his temperament, his spirit, the peaks and valleys of his psychosis, and can foresee the ultimate grand gesture of his final goodbye.

I can foresee it all—the clumsy suicide and the grim comedy of the cremation in the inner garden. The Russians will find his ashes and his skull, only partially consumed by the flames; they will shovel these into a cigar box and ship the box to

Moscow. Once he was the most powerful man on earth, now he fits into a box of *Capitol Stumpen—Rein deutsches Unternehmen.*

Hitler does not need to survive. The Reich is his autobiography. The collapse of that Reich marks the end of his existence. The collapse of the Reich is the end of his memoirs, the memoirs of a man who ran himself into the ground by never diverging from his principles. A story of lies and denial, and a death that comes without the comfort of an afterlife in bronze or stone, without a triumphant portrait in oil in the National Gallery, without breathlessly heroic descriptions in literature. He will forever balance on the edge between grandeur and monstrous disintegration. *Ecce homo!* History will judge him, and undoubtedly it will condemn him, but history will never be able to comprehend the man. I once was his friend, and even I do not comprehend him.

And yet I tried. I went back to the miserable hole in which he had buried himself. I tried to convince him to leave the bunker and to climb aboard one of the ten airplanes that would leave from the Tiergarten that night to Bavaria, to Berchtesgaden, and—well, what? Capitulate? Negotiate for his life? To at least deliver Germany as intact as possible to the Allied forces and thus, ultimately, give the gift of a healthy fatherland to the German people?

I pleaded with him because I knew that if he didn't leave, his entire entourage would die with him. "That is their decision," he said, and an immense emptiness echoed in his voice. This numbness, this exhaustion with life frightened me. "I do not force anybody to stand by me," he added. I continued my plea: Did he not realize that they would all perish, that by his behavior he was sentencing them all to death, since nobody could ever leave him, nobody could ever give up on him? "Oh no," he said "Oh no. People do give up on me. They do it all the time. You did, Herr Speer, you abandoned all hope, and you abandoned me. You will leave, and you will never come back to me."

I pleaded with him for the city's sake. As long as he stayed in Berlin, the battle for the town would continue, the close combat, the endless shelling of every corner of every street, until all that remained would be rubble and smoldering ashes. I begged him for the nation's sake, for the sake of our people's future. It was all in vain. I came to realize, much to my horror and distress, that the nation no longer mattered to him, and neither did the people nor the city of Berlin. Let the Ruhr survive, that was the industrial heart of the country, but the city of Berlin had abandoned him, and as far as he was concerned, it could get destroyed with him. The rubble would be his monument.

Just like anybody else, I had to surrender my gun to the guards before entering his quarters. I regret that I did not insist on keeping my pistol. I should have shot him then and there, before he brought the whole country down with him, before he murdered all those guilty and innocent citizens, before he returned this once proud and beautiful city to the desert.

"I am going," I said. "I am going, mein Führer."

"You go, Speer," he says. "*Gehe. Auf Wiedersehen.*"

He did not look at me when he said that. The Great Leader could not bear to look me in the eyes.

I turn my back on the ruins.

I can't do it.

It is impossible for me to kill that man.

What a defeat. I turn away from the place of disaster, away from the above ground entrance to hell. I drop the gas grenade to the ground. Maybe somebody else will have the courage to do this. Maybe that soldier will return, that man with his face caked in dirt and sweat, that battle-honed hero with his medal; maybe he can throw the grenade down the shaft.

There are tears in my eyes as I start the engine. Tears for the ruins, tears for all that is lost, and—indeed—tears for Hitler. I am no cynic. My tears are honest. He was, I think—I told you so already—in his own remarkable, confused, and twisted way, my friend. But fortunately the plane, the Junker that has all our secrets on-board, the diagrams and formulas that only a physicist can read—fortunately that plane has left the city safe and sound.

•

"Once I had a bit of a crush on you, Paul. That's over now."

"Good," I say.

"What's good? That I had a crush on you, or that it's over?"

"Both," I say.

"I had a crush on you too," I add. "It's over too."

"Good," says Donatella, and her answer sounds every bit as stiff as mine.

"Good," I say again.

"Good," she reaffirms.

Then we keep silent and look up. It's difficult not to see the universe as a metaphor for our existence—emptiness filled with an inexplicable, gravitationally repulsive energy. Donatella, physicist to the core. When she talks about the sun, she speaks of explosions. She grabs my hand. Softly—not forceful, not possessive. Warm. For once, it feels honest.

"You know, we think that so many things matter in life, but none of those things really do matter in the end." But I did think about love, Donatella, all that time—it was love I had in mind. She adds, "Are you sure you'll be happy with her?"

"Of course not," I say. "Who can predict something like that? I know she makes me happy right now. That much is good. It's all I need to know." Why is there this silence between us again? One of those silences that should have been there much earlier, weeks ago? Then she surprises me: "I know what's good for you, Paul. It isn't me."

"Huh?"

"Maybe she is. Don't let that chance slip away."

And right at that moment, the subject of our conversation walks onto the balcony. Donatella does not retract her hand, and I do not retract mine—that would be ridiculous.

What else could we do? He wasn't home.

"Wait," said Donatella. "We'll wait for the man." And with a few turns of a hair pin she let us into the apartment. Every physicist loves Richard Feynman and his silly exploits; Feynman's past as a lock breaker in Los Alamos fascinates them. It's become a fad among physicists to try to match the master's skills. Donatella has gotten pretty good, it seems. And the little chisel that Nebula has in her purse helps too. I frown when I see her bring out the tiny tool. "No lady should leave the house without her chisel," Donatella jokes.

What an idiotic plan. What will we do when he comes back? Will we overpower the old man and deliver him to the police for the heinous crime of plagiarism? Nebula reads my mind. "What else is there to do? What do you propose?" I have no plan. This is a violation of privacy, I know. It is breaking and entering. It is unforgivable.

Yet here we are, underneath the starry sky, waiting for the man. We talked for hours, about the state of the heavens and Donatella's research and about Nebula's movie, almost finished. That's what was inside that impenetrable layer of black plastic, the package on my writing desk—a video cassette with the first rough edit of Nebula's movie, based on a found, anonymous script—and finally we talk about the book.

It seems as if all these subjects—science, art, and memory—have acquired a particular urgency at this hour and on this spot, even though we don't quite know why. This apartment is the point upon which the narrative threads of our lives converge. And so we talk. We go get a pizza in the Nikolaiviertel. We buy a bottle of wine. We return to the apartment. Then night falls. We sit in the dark. We don't dare turn on the lights—we might scare off De Heer in case of his return. Then it gets late. Then it gets very late. Too late to return to Potsdam. Then the bars close. I'm worried. Where is De Heer? The women do their best to reassure me. Maybe he's out of town, visiting family? But he has no family. Maybe he's on a trip, a short vacation after telling his long story? Maybe he fled, Donatella proposes. But what else does De Heer have to hide? Why would he run away?

We lie down on the balcony, flat on our backs, and stare at the stars. None of us feels comfortable spending the night in De Heer's bed. It's a balmy night. Nebula rolls a joint. We smoke. We don't say much. The stars turn. Nebula goes to the bathroom. Donatella and I have our brief moment of evaporating intimacy, our little indiscretion. Nebula returns. She smiles at the hand-in-hand. "Look," she says, "this is the way to see your story. You offer your love. The gift is refused. You move on." Then she lies down next to me and grabs my other hand and kisses me on the cheek. I blush. Then she sits up and rolls us another joint.

"Didn't you see I was using Goldfarb?" asks Donatella. "That he was nothing more to me than a perhaps pleasant but above all useful pastime? Didn't you ever pick up on my contempt for him? For people like him? Did you really think I fell for him? Couldn't you see that I was playing a trick on him, the oldest trick in the book, that I was busy securing money for my research? That I was just . . . just . . . trying to make you jealous, and force you to act?"

No, Donatella, I want to say, I didn't see it. And are you really sure that those were your true motives? I don't say this, of course—you don't mention such things, certainly not when your one-time crush is emerging from the metaphysical fog and finally taking on human form. My hand is in Nebula's. Life is what separates us, Donatella. Too bad.

Below us the red taillights of the cars flash their urgent, indecipherable codes. Above us the stars burn: small, vital, dying explosions in the sky. Our generation got so used to the peaceful world that we created in our image, so used to the idea that things work—that loose cogs fit into each other faultlessly, that the world is an efficient place—that we forgot the workings of the extraterrestrial: that everything by definition and by necessity falls apart and vanishes, and that everything that happens in the world leaves no more than a vague imprint on the cosmic background radiation. Certainly, gravity sometimes gets a clumsy grip on some small part of the universe and clusters some matter together, and then those clumps light up for a few brief moments, but sooner or later they tumble back into the deepest black and disappear from our view forever. We pretend that there's an order to this madness, but physicists like the one Nebula and I have now have beside us are obsessed by the cruel reality of it all—the whirlwinds of chaos, the splendid entropy of fire, the silent, violent eruptions in the darkest parts of the heavens. There are so many chains of cause and effect. The universe is thirteen billion years old, and in all that time nothing has happened that was without meaning, nothing that didn't shape our world and leave its mark. Everything is important; everything matters. And nothing does.

Hence this second joint—to let us take the edge off reality. Hence our staring at the sky and our melancholy mood. Hence the holding of hands, three people joined in love and trepidation. We pass the cigarette and laugh at the cosmic joke we've become. And then we fall silent again. We recognize our own image in the fiery tip of the rapidly vanishing joint. Tonight, on the primitive observation deck of Jozef De Heer's apartment, we learn how empty the world truly is. Nebula playfully shows me the tip of her tongue stained purple with wine, then she intoxicates me with its taste. Donatella rolls her eyes, but in a friendly way. Tonight we are happy, all three of us, beatific, in a weird kind of fearful peace. Tomorrow it will all be different; tomorrow it will all be over.

•

I wake up. It's chilly. A strange red glow glimmers through the street: The sun struggles up in the desert of concrete and stones. An arm around my chest. Nebula's. Her warm breath caresses my neck, her breasts nestle against my back. Have we become sisters overnight? There's a groaning below, a nervous hum, and a certain hard-to-define crispness burns in the air—the new day presenting itself to all humanity, quivering with anticipation. My head aches a little, but not too badly. I turn my head and look around. Behind Nebula, his arm around her, lies Paul, his eyes closed, a big old grin on his face. The truth hits me. He could have been mine, and I could have been his. Now we've lost each other forever. It would be nice if you could review your life the way you review a movie with friends—what did you think of it, what struck you, was it everything you expected? What went wrong between us? What purpose did that unfair passion of mine serve? When did he first notice? Etcetera. And so on. Questions. It doesn't matter anymore—but people like answers, don't they?

I gently disentangle myself from Nebula's embrace and go to the edge of the balcony. Deep below a bald guy sprays a big blob of white paint over a giant "1," and with black he draws a giant circle over that wide white field. Here then is the end of the countdown—here comes the zero. But he leaves the underside of the circle open, and he adds a stalk to the nothingness, two firm vertical lines, and each of those lines get a curly tail—the Greek letter omega, in all its glory: Ω. A little further down the street another anarchist is doing the same—Ω.

I shake my head. Omega? Why omega? Why the parameter that describes the future of the universe? What exactly is this countdown counting down to?

•

"Hey, sweetheart." Nebula kisses me good morning on my forehead

"Hmm." A wake-up groan and a humming with joy.

Donatella is at the railing. She looks pensive. Her hair flows gently on the breeze. She is a sailor from antiquity, on the lookout for bad weather. I gently kiss Nebula back, and together we go stand next to Donatella. There is a whole brigade of painters down there: Each number gets adjusted, they don't miss a single one. What are they counting down to? What does omega stand for?

We slide the balcony doors shut. It's strangely quiet and stuffy inside—as if the air, no, as if time itself has stopped circulating. Or maybe it's the smell of mold-infected books? Even books of the highest moral and religious caliber can lead to hallucinations and psychosis when inhaled. Whatever the reason for our sluggishness, we move slowly through the flat, and we keep quiet. What's this? The morning is blossoming and De Heer's house feels like a house of the dead?

Nebula goes to the kitchen, she says. To check if there's any coffee.

I switch on the light. A layer of dust covers the floor. A thin layer, and all that can be seen in it are our footsteps.

Our mood is dour. As if De Heer is dead, and we are his next of kin, distant relatives come by train from a faraway town. We don't know him all that well, that old uncle, we don't see him too often. We know almost nothing about him, but here we are, making preparations for his funeral. Maybe it's just the aftereffect of the dope; maybe it's the effect of waking up in a strange apartment without a good reason for being there.

And where is De Heer?

I feel lost in this space. There is an almost tangible absence—the vibrations that run through the building tell me that something has gone terribly wrong. But what is it? The apartment looks exactly like it always has; exactly like I left it on Thursday—just more dusty.

Though there's a postcard on the mantle. A postcard with a stamp affixed to it, its backside turned to the room. The address on the card is mine—this must be the fourth of the postcards, never mailed because it was no longer necessary.

The card offers a panoramic view of Berlin, taken from the television tower, facing west. The Dom and the Palast der Republic are sharply in focus, and the Karl-Liebknecht-Straße too, and its confluence with Unter-den-Linden and the Straße des 17. Juni that runs like a slash through the Tiergarten, to the elusive green horizon.

In the center of the card, over a bright spot that's hardly one pixel wide, a red circle is drawn in ink and around it, in gold-colored marker, a spiral of words in De Heer's careful, pointed lettering:

The Sign of Gold Shall be the Sign of Victory—and Shiva Dances!

Donatella rummages through a drawer that she's forced open with the help of Nebula's chisel. She takes out a stack of photographs yellowed with age. A church on top of a cliff. Something that looks like an artful mobile—a cluster of sugar lumps that hangs from a clutter of strings in a regular, three-dimensional network. An aerial picture of the park of Sanssouci; a truck is parked in front of the Chinese teahouse, its trunk loaded with sand.

Then she frowns. A picture of a long, curving hallway with a thin metal tube in the middle—harsh fluorescent lighting overhead. The hallway curves, the snake of white metal disappears behind the bend. Donatella speaks out loud, without thinking.

"Why does this man have a picture of the Metatron?"

Then three things happen simultaneously.

One. Nebula startles when she hears the word Metatron. Her mug slips from her hand, the coffee splatters on the floor making esoteric runes, the porcelain shatters, and one of the shards lands on my naked foot. It draws blood.

Two. Donatella hits herself on the head—she suddenly understands the story that the pictures tell. The one she's holding up now shows a wooden crate filled with straw; on top of the straw lies a sphere of dull metal, or rather two half-spheres joined with bolts. The device looks like a comic-strip sea mine, the ghostly creation of an otherworldly mind.

Three. The power goes off. It's the second power outage in the last twelve hours, but the first we are aware of. The apartment goes dark, the coffeemaker emits a tortured gulp, and the background noises in the building—the near-inaudible stereos, the beeping alarm clocks, the humming cell phone batteries being recharged—all die down. Somewhere deep inside the building somebody pounds on the elevator door from the inside and a doorbell dies in the middle of its ring.

In the sudden absence of sound Nebula asks—and this is event number four— "What's that Metatron thing?"

I remember the words written on one of De Heer's earlier cards: "The continent is full of buried violence, of the bones of antediluvian monsters and of lost races of man, of mysteries which are wrapped in doom . . ." And I also remember: "The whole continent is a huge volcano."

"The Sign of Gold," I repeat, "Shall be the Sign of Victory." The circle on the postcard around the tiny point in the Tiergarten: It must be the angel on the column, the angel Metatron. The angel! "Goldfarb!" cries Donatella. "Goldfarb—he installed a detector on the column." "Tiergarten!," cries Nebula. "To Tiergarten! That's the station closest to the column!"

•

I often asked myself why the Russian invasion was so swift, and why so violent. I always suspected they were looking for something *inside* the city, something they needed to get their hands on, urgently and at any price. As if the looting and raping really served to distract attention from their true goal. This is what they were looking for, I think—or rather, who they were looking for: The man sitting opposite me for the second time, Herr Professor Werner Heisenberg. I get down to business. "Professor, do you remember how you wanted to instruct us about the uranium problem?"

The man hangs his head.

"I humbly confess that I was wrong, Doctor Goldfarb—we Germans know nothing about the atom. You on the other hand—well, yesterday's . . . events clearly demonstrate that you were much further along. You created a bomb, a fully functional bomb."

"That is precisely what I wanted to talk to you about."

"Oh?"

"Professor, allow me to be direct. You've stayed with us for a few weeks now, on this estate outside Cambridge, and quite a few of your colleagues have joined us. Yesterday evening you were all listening to the radio news. You know what happened in Hiroshima. You discussed it with your colleagues."

"Correct."

"And we were listening in. I hope this doesn't come as a surprise. There's a lot to be learned when a group of eminent physicists is gathered in the same room. Here is a transcript, Professor. Tell me, is this an accurate record of your conversation?"

Heisenberg frowns but accepts the folder. Like a true scientist he opens it up at random and leafs through it, to get a feel for the length and style of the manuscript. Then he starts reading from the beginning.

HAHN: They could have only pulled this off if they knew how to separate uranium isotopes.

WIRTZ: Indeed!

HAHN: I remember the work done by Segré, Dunning, and my own assistant. They purified a fraction of a milligram, right before the war, in 1939.

LAUE: 235?

HAHN: Yes, 235.

HEISENBERG: Did they use the word uranium with regard to this so-called atom bomb?

ALLEN: No.

HEISENBERG: Maybe it has nothing to do with atoms. But the equivalent of twenty-thousand tons of TNT—that is unbelievable!

WEIZSÄCKER: That corresponds exactly to the factor 104.

GERLACH: Is it possible that they had a machine good enough to separate 93 from the ore?

HAHN: I don't believe that!

HEISENBERG: The only suggestion I have is that one or the other ignorant amateur has bluffed the press and . . . that it doesn't work at all, in reality.

HAHN: Whatever the case may be, Heisenberg, you are all just second-rate, ordinary bunglers. You might as well pack your bags now.

HEISENBERG: I agree.

HAHN: They are fifty years ahead of us.

HEISENBERG: That I don't believe. It cost them two billion dollars? If you spend two billion on separating the isotopes, then it is entirely possible.

WEIZSÄCKER: If it's that easy, and the Allied forces know it's that easy, then they know that we too know how to do it, when we get back to work.

HAHN: It must have been a relatively small atom bomb—something mobile, something portable.

HEISENBERG: I am ready to believe it was a high-pressure device, but I cannot accept it had anything to do with uranium. They must have used some chemical to speed up the reaction.

GERLACH: They have 93, and they had two years to work on it.

DIEBNER: If they really have it, they were damn good at keeping it a secret.

WIRTZ: I am glad we did not have this thing.

WEIZSÄCKER: I think it is terrible that the Americans did this. It is madness!

HEISENBERG: You cannot say that. You could just as well say this was the fastest way to end the war.

HAHN: That is my only comfort.

HEISENBERG: I still do not believe a word about that bomb, but maybe I am wrong. I think it is perfectly possible that they have ten tons of enriched uranium, but not that they have ten tons of pure U-235.

HAHN: I thought you only needed a tiny bit of 235.

HEISENBERG: If they enriched it a little, then they could build a reactor, but not a bomb that . . .

HAHN: But if they had, let's say, thirty kilograms of pure 235, couldn't they build a bomb with that?

HEISENBERG: But it still wouldn't explode—the average free path of the neutrons is still too long.

HAHN: But tell me then why you always told us that we only needed fifty kilograms of 235 to do whatever we wanted? And now you're saying we need two tons?

HEISENBERG: If it is a uranium bomb, with 235, then . . . well, we can calculate. It doesn't matter whether they did it with fifty, with five hundred, or five thousand kilograms. We can suppose they had a method to separate the isotopes that we know nothing about.

WIRTZ: We had one man working on this. They had ten thousand.

WEIZSÄCKER: Do you think that it is impossible that they used one or more reactors to make 93 or 94?

WIRTZ: Highly improbable.

HEISENBERG: There's a big difference between invention and discovery. With discoveries you can always be skeptical; there are so many surprises. In the case of an invention only those who are not involved can be surprised. It's a bit strange, after we've spent five years working on this. That's all.

WEIZSÄCKER: I think the reason why we did not succeed is that the German physicists did not want to do it, out of principle. If we had all wanted Germany to win the war, we could have done it too.

HAHN: I do not believe that, but I am grateful we did not succeed.

HEISENBERG: Quite possibly the war will be over tomorrow.

HARTECK: And we can all go home the day after tomorrow.

KORSCHING: They will never let us go home.

HEISENBERG: The point is that the whole structure of the relation between the scientists and the state in Germany was such that although we weren't one hundred percent certain we could pull it off, the state did not trust us, and as such if we really did want to do it, it would not have been easy to accomplish.

DIEBNER: Because the bureaucrats are only interested in immediate results.

HEISENBERG: That is not entirely correct. I would say I was absolutely convinced that it was possible to construct a uranium reactor, but I never thought we could make a bomb, and deep in my heart I was convinced that this is what we were working on, and not a bomb. I have to admit that.

WEIZSÄCKER: I don't think we should make apologies because we didn't succeed in making a bomb. We have to admit we did not want this to work. If we had put the same amount of energy into it as the Americans did, and wanted it as much as they wanted it… Well, certainly, you can say it would have been a greater tragedy if Germany had possessed a uranium bomb. Imagine if we had destroyed London with uranium bombs—it would not have ended the war, and when the war was over, it would still be doubtful if it had been a good thing.

WIRTZ: It's so typical that it was the Germans who made the discovery and the Americans who managed to use it.

HAHN: Are you upset that we didn't succeed in making the uranium bomb? I thank G*d on my bare knees that we didn't make the uranium bomb. I have to honestly admit that I would have sabotaged the war if I had been in a position to do so.

HARTECK: We had twenty-seven grams of radium. If we had used, say, five grams of radium as a neutron bomb, then we could have made some measurements.

HAHN: You can't make a bomb like that in a week. In 1939 they had only a fraction of a milligram.

HEISENBERG: Well, a correct procedure would have yielded about thirty kilograms a year.

HAHN: Do you think they'd need that much?

HEISENBERG: Yes, I believe so. But to be honest, I never calculated it, because I never believed one could make pure 235. I have always known that one could do it with 235—fast neutrons. That's the reason you can only use 235 as explosive material. You can't make explosive material with slow neutrons, not even with the heavy water engine, because the neutrons only move with thermal velocities, and then the reaction will make the thing explode before it is even complete. It evaporates at five thousand Kelvin, and then the reaction is already . . .

HAHN: How do you detonate the bomb?

HEISENBERG: In the case of a bomb, it can only be done with the fastest neutrons. The fast neutrons in 235 immediately produce new neutrons, so that the fastest neutrons which have a speed of, say, one thirtieth of the speed of light, will set the reaction in motion. And then the reaction will obviously occur much faster, so that it becomes in practice possible to free those large quantities of energy. In natural uranium, a fast neutron will almost always be absorbed by 238, preventing fission.

HAHN: And what happens when an atom bomb explodes? The fission occurs at . . . What? One percent efficiency? Ten percent? One hundred percent?

HEISENBERG: If it is 235, then it is practically one hundred percent, because the reaction will occur much faster than the evaporation process. Practically speaking, it all occurs at the speed of light. To cause fission in 1025 atoms, you need eighty steps in the reaction, and the whole chain will be completed in 10-8 seconds. Every neutron that emerges from the atom makes two new neutrons when it collides with another uranium-235. So I need 1025 neutrons, and that makes 280 neutrons. I need eighty steps in the chain, and then I end up with 280 neutrons. Each step in the chain needs the same amount of time as one neutron needs to travel 5 centimeters, that is 10-9 seconds, and so I need 10-8 seconds, and the whole reaction will be over in 10-8 seconds. The whole thing probably explodes within that time frame.

HAHN: How heavy would that thing be?

HEISENBERG: Let's calculate. If the effective diameter of 235 is indeed as large as we think it is, a few hundred, and the multiplication factor is around 2.5, well, then . . . about 30 kilograms?

HAHN: How large would that bomb be?

HEISENBERG: About the size of a pineapple, I think.

Heisenberg puts the folder down. "Yes. This is correct. You edited it—there are omissions, and there is the stiffness of the translation. But, generally speaking, yes, the tenor of the document appears to be correct. *So what*?, as they say in your country."

"It appears from the transcript that your colleagues know nothing. Innocent as newborn lambs. And you, you seem to be the most skeptical of all, at least in the beginning. But then, less than half an hour later, you have calculated, seemingly off the top of your head, what the critical mass is supposed to be."

"Doctor Goldfarb, once you know something is possible, it is easy to perform the calculations. You know that as well as I do. I had my doubts about my original equations, but knowing that the bomb exists . . . Well, it simplifies matters: It narrows down the parameter space and then . . ."

I stop him—enough talk already!—and I lean forward. I force Heisenberg to look into my eyes. "Why is it that I do not believe you, Herr Professor? Why do I have the feeling that this news—except for the shock of our having exploded a device like this in the middle of a busy town without any warning—that the news of the *possibility* of the bomb did not astound you all that much?"

Heisenberg rocks back and forth in his chair.

"Will you have me tortured?"

"No, Professor, I will not have you tortured. I will negotiate with you. I firmly believe that you, like Hahn, are very glad that Herr Hitler never had this kind of weapon. You would have never handed it over to him—I believe that. But this doesn't necessarily imply you never succeeded in making your own bomb. And after all, your immediate superior was not Herr Hitler. So why don't we start by discussing your real boss, Herr Speer? What do you think of that?"

•

The omega symbols grin at us everywhere—Ω—grinning mouths without teeth—Ω, Ω—feverish eyes without pupils staring at us menacingly—Ω, Ω, Ω, cumulonimbi rising straight up from the earth, roaring and deafening.

There are a lot of people in the street, young men in leather jackets carrying spray cans and buckets of paint, petit bourgeois in a panic, women who hug their children in despair. The throng of people carries us to Spittelmarkt. We take the steps down to the U-Bahn, but the gates are shut. We rattle at the fence, but it's locked. "Don't you know?" says a man with his ear glued to a pocket radio. "The U2 trains aren't running. Service on S1 has been interrupted. They closed S2: an explosion on Potsdamer Platz, all the trains are stuck down there."

There's no need to discuss our plans—we run through Niederwallstraße, northwards, to the Mitte; we hurry to the Friedrichstraße station. The Bebelplatz is crowded like I've never seen it before. In the center of the square a plume of smoke rises from the monument for the book burning. A pyre is erected on top of the glass—we smell burning wood, the stink of gasoline flames, the stench of burning paper. A smoldering fragment floats in our direction and Donatella plucks it out of the air. It contains a marginally burnt meta-comment: "*Das zicht und quirlt, das zieht und plappert! Das leuchtet, sprüht und stinkt und brennt!*" A screeching fire truck races into the square; the crowd parts. People get trampled underfoot, they scream as they get flattened, and just when the truck arrives at the column of fire, the plate of glass that lies on top of the monument collapses, and in less than a second the empty bookcases of the *Denkmal* go up in flames.

The more seasoned antifascist veterans know which way the wind is blowing. They come running out of their houses, tying their Palestinian shawls in front of their mouths and noses with one hand. There are hastily assembled amateur protesters, well-meaning young women who hold up earnest placards with well-intentioned slogans hurriedly but carefully inked in black marker—slogans still matter to these folks: Slogans need to be legible and held up high. The veterans have other plans; they grab the signs out of the hands of the would-be hippie chicks and utilize them quite unrhetorically as literal weapons in the battle. They hack and chop and hit and slash. The sandpit of the playground in Voßstraße turns into a Roman arena; the screaming martyrs lift their long skirts and run for their lives, suddenly caught between two bands of wild roaring lions.

There is a teeming of black armbands, and skin swells under tight sleeves like the supple muscles of a sneaking anaconda. "Do not think," Hugo had told his men, "that this will be an easy job. Remember our heroes, remember the brave knights of the SS. Think of what it must have meant to them to steel themselves every day, to soil their soles with the repulsive blood of those filthy insects—do not forget that, men, the Jewish pigs are insects! The survival of the Thousand-Year Reich depended on each of these acts of SS courage—it was their duty, to G*d and Fatherland! And here the new Jews are assembled, the yellow race and the Turkish rabble and the weaklings and cowards who collaborate with them. Let's go! Let's kill them!" Every act of violence needs a personal motive, otherwise it is just one more act of perversion.

The antifascists don't stand a chance. Hugo's men are hardened. Their city is the city that whirls, the city that never sleeps, the city that spins and spirals and circles and seethes, the city of bare concrete floors and sleeping bags of cheap synthetic down, the city that shudders and shakes like a wild boar. Life underground was no hell for them: It was limbo—preparation for the cuts and bruises of the coming street fight. It is noble to see oneself as a humble tool in the hands of higher powers, powers that one cannot control and that slither through the world with hissing tongues and greedy fangs, stirring up trouble. Hugo and his men do not believe in guns. Like all technology, guns kill feeling. Hugo and his men are

Barbarians, Ostrogoths, Huns; they want the feeling of strange flesh itching at the end of their knuckles, the crisp scratch of a fingernail sliding into an eye socket, the sharp pop of skulls bumping into skulls—a literal eye-to-eye.

The ground troops hit and slice and kick and pull and push, and right behind the first line of offense Hugo and his aide-de-camp Bøk and a few other fortunates keep watch and shout encouragement, and each time one of the men in the front line manages to isolate one of the red rats they drag him to the sidelines and two of the strategists hold the victim down and a third, often Hugo himself, performs the *Bordsteintreten* ritual—while the two assistants force the victim to bite the edge of the sidewalk with his teeth, the third man stomps him hard and merciless on the back of the skull. Crack! There goes another one! Crack!

•

We fight for a spot on the train. The Mitte is being evacuated, everybody is on their way west. A ghetto blaster buzzes with the latest news—explosions in town, riots all around, all police forces converging on Voßstraße. A massive gathering of neo-Nazis is apparently rioting through the city center. A complete power outage in the heart of East Berlin complicates matters. The eyes of the travelers shoot back and forth in a panic, and one question occupies them all—what's going on here?

Nebula whispers in my ear. Voßstraße is where Hitler's chancellery stood; it's the spot where the bunker lies buried. Voßstraße is where Hitler shot himself in the head on April 30, 1945, exactly fifty years ago. This is the half-century anniversary of Hitler's death, and it is Black Sabbath—*Walpurgisnacht*—to boot. It all seems so logical that it must be a trap. The violence in the Mitte must be a diversion tactic; it keeps the police occupied and far away from the place where it will really happen: the Column. Hitler died at three in the afternoon. It appears that the black hordes have started their festivities early.

The train finally starts moving. It goes slowly, the emergency generators of the S-Bahn net must have a hard time keeping up with the demand. We ride at a snail's pace, hardly faster than a man on foot, and the train shakes violently. Even though the windows are wide open, the naked stench of fear wafts through the compartments. The madness grows. People sink to their knees and start sobbing. A few long-haired young men in black leather jackets stand around a young woman who bleeds from a long gash in her eyebrow. They beg for water. Does anybody have any water to wash her wound? Does anybody have any water? Water, please? A young man has a guitar and tries out a "We Shall Overcome," but somebody grabs him by the shoulder and throws the instrument out the window. The extent of the mass panic becomes clear when we get closer to Bellevue: A gigantic mass of people is inching their way up the Straße des 17. Juni, a procession of pale worms fleeing to the West, to the evening land. They move slowly—there are too many people for even the widest boulevard of Berlin to accommodate.

The train is overloaded with people either sobbing and screaming or silent; their bodies packed so close that they soak up each other's sweat; their arms and legs pressed so tightly together that their limbs loose all sensitivity; there's hardly room to take a breath. The train moves in jolts—as though it too is fearful of what might happen next. When the doors finally open at the Bellevue station—still closed, its exits closed off with steel fences—quite a few of the passengers fall out of the train. They fight to get back on, but the fortunate ones who are still in the car kick at them to keep them out. When the train starts moving again, Donatella, Nebula, and I fight our way to the door. The next stop—if it ever arrives—is ours.

•

The Hansa neighborhood is deserted; the luxury apartment buildings are mute and dead, or maybe it's just the Sunday slumber of a well-to-do neighborhood on the first day of summer: The citizens are all at the lakes or parks or forests far away from the city center, or else enjoying a good glass of beer somewhere at a Schöneberg sidewalk café. We run through the little paths that wind their way through the woods; the big boulevard is filled with people going in the opposite direction. It makes for easy progress: The mob takes the shortest way to Ernst-Reuter-Platz; they look for safety in numbers and keep their target in view at all times—they stay on the boulevard.

There we are at the Große Stern, the end of our journey. The Angel, *Victoria Borussia*, towers high above us, her wings spread wide, ready to fly. She raises her spear in triumph, its shaft festooned with ribbons. The crown of laurels in her right hand seems to flutter in the breeze. Her earnest head, crowned with the Imperial Eagle, watches out over the green.

The Angel of Pure Light.

The Angel Metatron.

The Angel of Death, Gold and Black at the same time.

What time is it? Struggling through the teeming masses, the slow pace of the train—it took us hours to get here. The Angel faces westward—she is caught in striking light, her left leg glistens, her spear blinds us with its reflection, and Donatella points, with open mouth and unconcealed panic, to the flickering wreath of laurels. There are tongues of blinding sunlight coming off the gilded leaves—and there, inside Shiva's ring, the detector is located.

All hail to German efficiency! The crowd throngs around the column—the world is coming to an end, but the monument is still open. We dive into the mouth of the tunnel that leads from the edge of the street to the center of the square—we emerge at the base of the column and run past the mosaics that represent the unity of German Peoples, past the golden barrels of the guns seized from the French armies, through the main gate, and we huff and puff as we—*Ordnung muß sein*— buy our tickets, quick-quick-quick, we have no time to wait for change, and then we run, Donatella leading the way, breathless and with buckling knees we race up the spiral staircase, three steps at a time, all 285 steps to the feet of the G*ddess.

•

Heisenberg's architect lives in Berlin. Goldfarb never meets him—they communicate via telephone and courier—but he values the man's genius. Digging a perfectly circular tunnel underneath a public square in the middle of the war without anybody catching on—that's quite an achievement. It's an invisible structure of high precision and a stark, breathtaking beauty. This is where they installed the cyclotron—or the *Metatron*, as the German team baptized it. They used a two-phase process to extract the fissionable material. First they centrifuged the natural uranium (procured from the Congo, through occupied Belgium) to separate the useful and rare isotope 235 from the quantities of useless U238. They placed the U235 at the end of the circle and bombarded it with fast neutrons until it formed plutonium, microgram by microgram, the harvest of each run too small to be visible to the naked eye; too small to register on their 1944 scales. This cyclotron was larger, more powerful than any of the American machines, and it was powered by the most potent magnets ever made—a true triumph of German engineering. By the end of the year Heisenberg and his team of physicists were brought over to Potsdam in the greatest secrecy. They vanished into the entrance of the tunnel inside Frederick the Great's Chinese Tea House and in its basement they put the puzzle pieces of the bomb together—the bomb Omega. Speer's genius kept the whole endeavor secret. He made certain that nobody knew any more about the project than was absolutely necessary. There was no team, nobody who could betray the full extent of the plan. Only Speer and Heisenberg and a handful of hand-picked loyals knew about the eventual success. The project remained hidden from American spies and hidden from the German public, including Hitler. Speer could have won the war with this contraption, but he elected not to do so—it was abundantly clear that Hitler, the ruthless murderer, would be a lousy candidate to lead the New World Order. Instead Speer and his men concocted a lame cover story—a half-baked reactor somewhere in the deep south of the country, hidden in a well under a cliff that was crowned by a medieval church. The Americans swallowed the tall tale, partly because they were blinded by their own success, partly because the only one in the Alsos mission who had seen through the masquerade had kept his mouth shut. Because *I* kept my mouth shut. Why didn't I tell them? Because the world was better off with a bomb on both sides—Potsdam became Russian territory. But even the Russians accepted Heisenberg's explanation. Why shouldn't they? They had their own bomb, after all, thanks to Hannah and me, and they were satisfied with that, even though they never showed me the least bit of gratitude. I waited for it, I did, I waited for some sign of Russian appreciation. At first I thought it was too dangerous for them to approach me directly, then I forgot about it for a while, then I was grateful that I had stayed in America, and not moved to the East. The GDR never really got built, and Soviet politics became as much of a hornet's nest as those of any Western democracy. It was much better to keep that new knowledge, the secret of Potsdam, under wraps. That didn't prove to be difficult. Speer and I, and Heisenberg, and the architect, we were the only ones who knew enough about the secret to keep it alive, and we kept our mouths shut, and we waited. We waited for twenty years. As long as they have a goal in sight, scientists can be very patient. In those twenty years Speer started a garden in his prison in Spandau, and in that garden he walked his daily rounds, a hazy echo of the circling of the atoms underneath the gardens in Potsdam, thirty rounds a day, five miles a day. When Speer was released on September 29, 1966, he had walked exactly 19,845 miles; he had almost spanned the earth's circumference. "Come and pick me up twenty miles south of Guadalajara," he said to a friend who came to wait for him at the prison gate.

But when Speer was released, the world had changed. The world and I. At some point during that time I had become a man. The boy with his stern inward look was gone. I had become a man; my feet firmly planted on the ground, a man who knows no shame. Twenty years in California, and my world was filled with people who knew me and feared me, with tamed animals that went out to lunch with me and I with them. I spoke to them at conferences from the safety of high podiums, the backdrop of red velvet swaying gently in the mesmerizing breeze of my words. I talked to journalists in pleasant tones and with a slight condescension—just enough arrogance to claim superiority, but not enough to cause serious friction. I became a man from whom so much as a hint of disapproval could shrivel the best proposals submitted to the National Science Foundation or the *Deutsche Forschungsgemeinschaft*. In the scientific journals I regurgitated the same old theories—the editors either admired me or feared me, or they were angling for some favor; I larded them with quotations from a past that was not my own—Kant, Hegel, Nietzsche, Shakespeare, even though I had read nothing more from the works of those great minds than the two-line aphorisms I'd had my students cull from the library. My fame grew with my image, with the imposing, contagious grace of my appearance, my well-tailored suit, my extravagant, fashionable glasses. Three thousand dollars worth of cloth, gold, leather, and artificial ivory around my artificially preserved body—two thousand dollars of gym dues per year. After my death my reputation will vanish with my rotting body—except for that one paper, the paper that established my reputation, none of my writings are important enough to survive their creator's demise. I know all too well that I am no Bohr, no Planck, no Einstein. There is no place for me besides that trinity. So be it. Life is good now: I float through the city, driven by the twelve humming cylinders of my silver BMW, and in the small refrigerator of my lavishly luxurious office—black leather chairs, a mahogany conference table, a few Chagalls on the walls—there is always a bottle or two of Veuve Cliquot waiting for me, ice cold and ready to be popped open, left by some high-rolling admirer impressed by my mere existence.

I am a real man, the way a real man should be: important and contemptible. I am aware of both attributes; I cultivate them carefully. In those years in the States, I thoroughly enjoyed the intrigues that were spun around my person, the many ways in which my young students vied to bathe for a minute or two into the chilly glare of my spotlight, the naïve attempts of up-and-comers trying to win my fickle favor, the barely contained excitement of assistant professors at conferences—Did you see him? Do you know who that is? Nobel Prize!

The most desirable and the most terrible thing happened to me. I saw the annihilation of matter and I knew true love and that love was taken away from me. The things you lose forever—those are the things that stay with you. What we know of death, its taste, its smell (the suddenly useless, rotting, limp lump of tongue in our mouth, the dry palate, those teeth no longer capable of chewing food), we know from the end of love. The blow, the panic, the fall from on high, the clinging in thin air to your beloved, a last futile attempt to bring her flesh close one last time, and then the plunge into the icy lake, the waters closing above our heads, and the sinking feeling that we lack the will to struggle to the surface again.

I loved her, and she left. It hurts. It strangles me.

In order to forget, I allowed myself to wallow in the orgasms I got for free at every conference I made an appearance. For a while, I think, some might have considered it charming. I was *le prix Nobel qui amait les femmes*. The man who looked for his lost lover in every woman he met. Charming and exciting. Then I became pitiable and pathetic. Maybe my addiction to women was noble in origin; maybe the real reason for my compulsion was the rare spectacle that unfolds when a man guides a woman to her climax, a display unique in all of the universe: a human being forgetting herself, delivering herself totally to the moment, to the brief magic of life. Maybe it was noble in the beginning. I very much doubt it.

Goldfarb, the young researcher. Once a keen observer of reality, once a clever experimenter. What happened to him? Where did he go?

Somehow, my mind got disconnected from the wild world that demands an explanation, and I entered the tame realm of what is already known. When I climbed out of my platonic cave I found myself in the blinding sunlight of a mountaintop where boastful former scientists jovially hit each other on the shoulders like football players, where wine and honey and women flowed freely. My evening strolls offered breathtaking views of the labyrinths below where laboratory assistants labored and professors professed their ignorance—when I walked off my sumptuous evening meal burping like a happy baby, and every burp was greeted with tremendous enthusiasm, I felt as though I must be a g*d. I discovered the cheerful, domesticated world of the social networks at the top, and I gladly exchanged my dirty work in the trenches of physics for a taste of the lofty heights of fame.

I didn't make this decision consciously—it wasn't the result of any careful weighing of the facts. There was no defining moment. The expensive ergonomic chair in my office felt more and more uncomfortable; I found myself more and more often in front of the window, reassuring myself that the world outside was larger than the small rectangle I could see from behind my desk. I stood in front of the bookcases and wondered what purpose those cardboard-covered stacks of paper served, what urgent and important information I used to hunt for in these tomes that thereafter I kept collecting out of sheer habit, but left unopened and unread. My hand reached out to the shelves of wisdom, but I did not dare touch them. It was as though a wall of glass had appeared between me and the world of curiosity I used to visit so often. Yes, I never was more than a visitor; I never inhabited science. A scientist who's no longer satisfied with the world in his head is a scientist who no longer bothers to storm the barricades.

There was a moment when this new but not improved Goldfarb rose from his seat to deliver his umpteenth invited presentation and realized that he had nothing to say. After that, my talks became nothing but rhetorical fireworks: I sparkled, but my message slipped away before I was done talking.

I left the field that I grew up in. I started to attend conferences outside my area of research—neural networks, nanotechnology, parallel information processing, chaos theory, evolutionary microbiology, artificial intelligence, virtual reality, cold fusion, computational models of consciousness—and I spewed out my meager opinions on demand. Folks listened in awe, because I'm a Nobel Prize winner and a physicist, and therefore a certified genius. I started giving exorbitantly expensive, invitation-only management seminars for the CEOs of big car-manufacturing companies and Wall Street analysts. I possessed no relevant knowledge and I had no experience in these matters, but people showed up, and the influx of money was gratifying. I distanced myself more and more from the field of astronomy, except for the wide panoramic overviews I wrote for the popular scientific press, my gloriously beaming face printed on glossy paper next to columns filled with nonsense; I looked pensive and somehow inspired trust. It was no conscious decision, but a slow slide—slipping away from the world of thought into the sphere of public relations, easing myself into the comfortable bed of easy success made by ghost-written popular science books and reading tours and book signings. My European earnestness was replaced by quintessential American pursuits: pussy and cars.

I was good at it too.

It is possible, I found out, to talk without believing in what you say, to think without hope, to write without having anything to say.

The call of fame, certainly. But what happened to me was not unlike what happened to Einstein once he lost the energy of his youth. I lost touch with the new theories—they appeared senseless to me, esoteric, more and more alchemical, drifting farther and farther away from what must be the truth. The universe condensed into no less than nine dimensions of quantum gravity, and matter constructed from harmonically vibrating strings? None of this informs us about the workings of the world, but it does inform us about the workings of the physicist's mind, always begging for attention—or so I thought. I did try. I worked through the spaghetti clusters of those impudent differential equations; it made me feel like a graduate student who finishes his work late at night in his little office, only to find that while he was asleep on the couch an overly eager janitor has helpfully erased his breathtaking proof of the Riemann hypothesis from the blackboard. The problem is not that I can't reconstruct my train of thought; the problem is that I can't for the life of me imagine why I thought this riddle was so damn important yesterday. I lag farther and farther behind. Because, unlike the youngsters, I can't start from scratch. Because I got used to relying on my memory more than on my reasoning ability; because my mind got stuck in a comfortable routine. When I work my way through one of these new revolutionary papers, I find myself reconstructing my old thought processes; the new and original can no longer excite me. Look at my latest work, also my last: magnetism, particle interaction. It's merely a faint reflection of what I did in my first seminars under Van Vleck at Harvard. "Fuck," I say, "fuck the wisdom that comes with the years! Fuck the triumph of humanism over nihilism!"

My doubts reach deep. Had I ever been worth anything as a scientist? Did I deserve my fame? There are rumors that I shouldn't have received the Prize, but the student who actually made the discovery.

"Kara, dear."

Dear.

He sits down, on the chair by the wall. He rests the back of his head against the cool wall. He looks tired and exhausted, her mentor. Her boss. Her collaborator.

Her lover.

He holds her manuscript in his hands. She worked on it all through the night, until the crack of dawn—she wanted it finished before he showed up, she wanted him to give it his full attention, in those early, crisp hours of the morning. An explanatory model for the periodic radio scream emitted from the heart of the universe, those regular flickerings in the low frequencies. The palpitations that so many—Goldfarb included—have rejected as mere noise in their data. Kara wrestled with the findings, she let the whole machinery of advanced mathematics loose on the numbers. And last night she managed to inflict order on the chaos; she disentangled the signal from the noise, and she read it and interpreted it, that message from the other end of the universe, that memorandum from the beginning of time.

Goldfarb looks terribly exhausted. Dog-tired.

He only has a few comments.

He licks his lips.

"Not bad," he says. "Not bad at all."

"Look here, Kara," he says. "This sentence . . . Couldn't we reformulate that?"

Goldfarb is a difficult man; it's hard to satisfy him. Her lover is tormented by recurring headaches and frequent stomach cramps. She has managed in the past to make him forget his ailments for a moment, with her mouth on his lips and his hands on her breasts. Now she wants to dazzle him with the brilliance of her work.

Her work. Which he will send off to *Physics Letters*, with his name on it, in front of hers. He is after all her mentor.

Her work. His Nobel Prize.

He will mention her in his speech, he will express his gratitude—without Kara

Nebenzahl's work, etcetera—and in the festive Stockholm city hall he will wonder out loud where she is now, knowing full well that after his publication of the paper she left the academic world and is now breeding horses in Montana, or something like that.

Did I ever amount to anything, as a scientist? As a human being? I stole the foundation of my career from the brain of a child.

When the Uni-Potsdam reopened, two years ago, I dropped a hint that I was interested. I had gotten back to working; the cancer that raged inside me had made me restless. My illness reminded me of the ailment that killed Hannah, the combination of radiation and my growing seed. I needed a secure and secluded spot, far from everything, a place where I could find peace. And once I arrived here I looked for comfort in old, familiar ideas—dark matter, that ever growing and deepening mystery at the heart of the universe. It wasn't my idea, just like the discovery of the pulsar hadn't been my idea, it was something that some clever mind had dreamed up in the 1950s, and then—the ways of the world—everybody had forgotten about it. That is one of the advantages of old age: You remember the good old ideas that lie buried deep inside the library stacks, unreachable to the new young Turks. And there's that other prerogative of age: You have reached a position on the ladder that implies that you never have to do anything of importance again. It makes it possible to pursue an idea that seems senseless, that has no reasonable chance of succeeding. The offer from Potsdam was a gift from heaven.

And then I fell in love. I, the man who had sworn off his frivolous lifestyle in the light of his illness—I fell in love. With one of my students, another thing I thought I had cured myself of. I fell in love with her quick, versatile mind, with her dreams and her authenticity, with her tangled mop of hair and the endearing blush on her cheeks, with the way she twisted her buttocks in bed. Donatella always reminded me of a child coming home after a long day of playing in the woods, her mind ablaze and hungry as hell.

An old man who falls in love—it's a farce. An old man can't afford to fall in love, to truly fall in love, with all that it amounts to—sleepless nights, loss of appetite, the storms of libido. It ate me up, even as those tiny flecks spread through my body and gobbled up my flesh.

She looked like my Hannah—the only woman I ever met that didn't make me think of Hannah, because she *was* Hannah, skin and bones and heart and soul. Or had a tumor already nestled inside my brain? Did Donatella's inexhaustible lust for life overwrite the connections of my memory?

My reputation—the womanizer, the Don Juan of the laboratories, the macho stud of the scientific meetings—got me in the end. She thought she was simply one in a row of countless others, another prop for me to lean on, and that after her another woman would take her place. The truth is that she looked so much like Hannah that I divested myself of my cynicism, that I almost started to hope again, that I—what an unexpected side effect! —actually started working again, for the first time in decades.

Hannah was the first emotional gamble of my life. Donatella was the last. There was nothing and nobody between those two; all the other women merely served to pass the time. That Donatella left me, that she left me because she thought that she meant nothing to me, was just another passion that would wane as soon as she left for her first tenure-track job—that she left me because she couldn't handle my cancer, because she didn't understand that I really wanted her and nobody else at my deathbed—that is unbearable.

And G*d, I miss my mother. The truth of her art. I carried the manuscript of *PanzerFaust* with me for so many years, day after day, until I lost it fooling around with a phallomantic soothsayer in Bath. I miss that book, written with all the enraged passion of a writer confronted with the real possibility of a new Dark Age.

I think—finally—that this is what life has taught me, and it's the old lesson from Heisenberg: What counts is not the truth, what counts is our perception of the truth.

Physics is the summary of all the banalities humankind can see; it is the end sum of all the worthless stuff that enters our eyes and nose and mouth and ears and all that touches our skin. Hence my belated fascination with the unseeable, with that which should not be because it does not fit with our theories. But oh, still—the opportunity I had to gather all these worthless kernels of knowledge! The possibility to have known everything that can fit inside a human brain!

·

Shiva the Destroyer is the symbol of the urge of every human being to transform, to die, to take leave of its current state, of its current shape, of who or what it is: to change, to become new. Shiva is Mahakala, Time Itself, Time that drags the universe to its unavoidable doom, and—transcending Time—to its equally unavoidable rebirth, the return to the source of a new Golden Age, and then again, steadily and gradually, to the soft implosion of death, in an endless sequence.

Shiva is not just the Destroyer. He is also the Creator of it All: Every act of creation depends on the obliteration of what was. He, Shiva, is the essence of destructive transformation, the essence of Time—his gaze is turned to the future. The Lord Shiva is the Great Yogi, his face serene like the blue skies while his feet dance the mad rhythms of Tandava in the midst of the flames and smoke of a crumbling world.

Shiva dances. All things are born, all things fade away.

·

Goldfarb takes his glasses off his nose and rubs his face with his palm. He kneads his forehead and presses his thumb and ring finger against his closed eyelids. He presses hard, so hard he sees explosions in the inside of his skull.

He looks at his watch.

Stunde Null will soon be here.

The mechanism is infallible—he designed and built it himself.

Once an instrument maker, always an instrument maker.

Heisenberg's design was good, but a bit on the heavy side. With the knowledge and experience gathered in Los Alamos, Goldfarb had made a better, lighter, handier gadget. You don't need an army to do this. With the right knowledge and the help of a Chinese postdoc it takes no more than a few years. The core of the bomb is still the near-critical sphere of plutonium that Heisenberg extracted from the Metatron—excellent material, and the matter density was optimal. Heisenberg knew what he was doing. And the bomb is hidden where nobody expects it, far from the riots that serve to distract the masses. The little bald rioters even think that the demonstrations are their own idea.

Naturally I have nothing but contempt for myself. Naked, bald contempt. Contempt for the fact that I am still alive. My one moment of scientific luster I stole from a student; my one deed of moral rectitude I borrowed from my first lover—and the thought that she might perhaps have only used me for that purpose is too terrible to even be allowed into my consciousness. And yes, that this act happened in a vacuum—that the Russians never showed any gratitude, that the Americans never discovered our little plot—this too nags at me. I have contempt for my fickleness, for drifting away from what truly mattered, for drifting into a life of easy undeserved fame that washed away my soul: a life of empty promises. I was nothing but empty promise: a promise of brilliance that was never fulfilled; a man gifted with a reckless love that should never have been. I had talent, but it got lost because I took such care to nip it in the bud.

If I have a message for the world, something to say to my nonexistent children, it would be this: Don't let it happen to you. Don't fence yourself in. I never amounted to much, and what I amounted to is too terrible for words. Hannah's death shook me more than the death of the thousands in Hiroshima and Nagasaki, and my own death will bring no relief, but only tragedy—it's all so human, so terrifyingly human, so contemptible. And this new, final act, this too is ultimately meaningless, except in a cosmic, esoteric sense that only a few will grasp.

There is Shiva. There is Heraclitus. This universe is the same for all of us; it wasn't made by any g*d or man; it has always been. It is here now, and it will always be: An eternal living fire that caught flame all by itself and will extinguish all by itself too. Fire lives in the death of earth; air lives in the death of fire; water lives in the death of air; earth lives in the death of water. The lightning bolt guides all that exists. Fire is the Gateless Gate—the direct, immediate transformation of matter into energy.

The old *Mittel-Europa* lies shot to pieces; the new sun rises over the desert of New Mexico. We are all in diaspora. We are all rubble. We are specks of dust, dizzy from the shockwave that left us in this dry vale of time-space. We are orphans, washed-up stardust. Exiles. The homeland has gone missing.

Here comes the miracle. The Wonder. That we know this much. That we are aware of our position. That a machine has evolved—a cluttered mess of cells—that understands this. That we fight. Fight to transcend our uselessness. That we survive.

(Once I had a dream. I was carried through the night on the wings of the Shechinah. Below me I saw the world shrink and shrink. I felt the hot breath of the stars. The Shechinah carried me to a glowing star, the House of the World, where the souls are created before they descend to earth. In that House I saw the souls being clad with the elements—water, wind, and fire. In that dream the Spirit carried me over Ground Zero, the place where the earth once lit up, and I saw the plain of green jade and a shape carved out of that plain of glass, as if something had torn itself with great force from out of the forge. As if *someone* has torn himself from the deep, for the shape was unmistakably . . . human.)

My escape is not cowardly. Primo Levi's escape, Durlacher's escape, Borowski's escape—they were no cowards. I know how small the a priori chance is that something like the human race could ever have evolved. If the parameter omega had been greater than one, there would not have been enough world-time to generate something as complicated as a self-consciousness-with-language; if omega had been smaller, the stardust would have been scattered long before it could have clustered to form inhabitable planets. The act of suicide, the real act or its manifestation in the world of symbols—the escape into chemical substances, the leap into religion, the lapse into the expressionist art of darkness or the impressionist jumble of light—these are nothing but odes to the complexity of mind vis-à-vis the mute gamble of existence.

Despair is not pathology. Despair is the foundation of all existence. We are all exiles. Allow me to take my place on the front row, allow me to go out on the terrace, a glass of champagne in hand—from here I will have a most excellent view of the event.

It is three o'clock.

Ladies and gentlemen . . . I give you fire. I give you . . . the universe!

•

There is no police officer to stop us, no lowly civil servant of the *Staatliche Museen zu Berlin—Preußischer Kulturbesitz* to prevent us from climbing over the fence around the platform and to jump from there onto the slippery toes of the G*ddess.

This is madness.

Donatella is a Venetian, she spent all her winter vacations in the Dolomite Alps. And Nebula is up for anything. But I, I am a natural coward—I sit down on the toes of the statue, paralyzed by vertigo, and I rub the scrape on my foot while the two women brazenly ascend. The layer of bronze under the gold is rougher than it seems when viewed from below, it allows them ample purchase, but I hardly dare look up and follow their progress on the Angel's apron. And I certainly do not dare look down.

The detector—attached there a few weeks ago with the help of two professional climbers: two loops of steel wire and a cube that contains the transmitter—maybe the detector isn't a detector. It could be the detonator mechanism of a bomb, or it could even be the bomb itself, a small box resting on the G*ddess's palm. Here is our hypothesis. When on April 30th the sun falls on the gleaming wire, the time calculated exactly from the astronomical tables—exactly at three in the afternoon—the critical mass will implode and the gadget will go off—an expert like Goldfarb, with fifty years of study following his blistering sojourn on the Hill, would surely be capable of such miniaturization.

I look at my watch.

It is close to three o'clock.

The sun traces its arc; it creeps to the inner circle of the wreath in the proud, triumphant G*ddess's hand.

Nebula and Donatella climb, grim and stubborn.

The sun traces its arc.

The seconds tick away.

Donatella hoists herself onto the angel's shoulder.

The sun spins, the laurels are now almost cast in shadow, the steel loop is ready to ignite.

Donatella grips the statue's arm. She staggers, then her fingers hook into the golden folds of the angel's robe.

The sun traces its arc.

It is too late.

Too late.

Too late.

THE FLASH OF LIGHT HITS US WITH ASTOUNDING FORCE.

But the FLASH does not rain down from above, as we expected. The seething blindness does not descend from the angel's hands, no, the lighting flash blooms from behind us—it rolls at us from the Mitte, from high above town, so high that nothing blocks the trajectory between bomb and angel. Unobstructed, the photons crash into us—and wherever they come from, the world turns *white* in a hail of blinding torture, the light slaps at our eyes in a blizzard of the purest pain, and the world turns *hot*, and my reflex is to let go, to dive down to the cool and murderous pavement, and I scream and scream and scream and high above me I hear Nebula scream too, and Donatella screams, a high piercing falsetto, and the mass of people below us, washed away in the white, white, *white* flood, screams with fear, and that is the only sound, the only sound in a silence that lasts a lifetime—birds rain down from the sky, down on our heads, and I have to apply all my strength, all my will, to keep holding on to the toes of the G*ddess. And then—an eternity later—the SOUND comes rolling in, a swelling thunder that is suddenly *there*, and it whips at my ear drums, it lifts my skull with a thumping, maddening blow, it roars and screeches and it scrambles my brain and simultaneously there is the SHOCK, a hard OOMPF! in the back, and a massive shudder travels through the metal, and the statue, the colossal angel of bronze and gold, the angel anchored in solid concrete, the angel that had been chained for a century to her column of granite, fixed for a hundred years to her foundation of rock and cement—that

G*ddess shudders in the shockwave, she trembles in the onslaught of the hurricane winds that whip her back, and in the storm she seems to rise from her pedestal, no, *really*, SHE SPREADS HER WINGS in the raging tempest of light and with a mighty groan THE ANGEL BREAKS FREE, liberated from her shackles, and below us the column crumbles, the pillar of granite collapses to the ground and the G*ddess TAKES TO THE AIR. Free and loose she floats in the storm, a slow revolving dive carried by the nuclear gale, and in her wake the winds howl and the air boils around the squealing metal body that dances in the whirlwind, and we— three midgets, three lice on her dripping fleece of gold—hold on for dear life and we scream and scream while we are carried away on the current, floating on the wings of a primal force, bobbing precariously on the flow of gamma particles, the river of seething radioactivity, the scourge of the naked, unbearable heat of matter blown wide open—we zoom over the train tracks, we barely clear the roof of the Technische Universität, and then we descend, we scrape against the facades in Bismarckstraße, and finally a wingtip hits the asphalt and the angel, out of balance, turns on her back and hits the ground with an awful bang, sliding through the street, trailing sparks and blood and ripped flesh, death and destruction following in her wake, and then the blackened angel finally grinds to a halt in a scintillating fountain of breaking glass, in a screeching orgy of twisted steel, in a rain of electrical fire and snapping cables—with her mottled grin of naked bronze she slides into Wagner's Walhalla, into the concrete temple of the new, fallen Reich—with a deafening roar the Angel Metatron digs into the dark and muggy entrance hall of the Deutsche Oper, and three terrified little people, their hands burnt, their hair singed, their spines torn out of place, live, and live, and *live*, and they scream, in the fresh new dawn of Berloshima, they scream at the top of their scorched lungs.

And, a few seconds earlier, another terrible, gruesome, blasphemous event:
   right before the shockwave hits,
   right before the circle of golden laurels caves in,
   right before the detector wire melts,
   right before the transmitter dies,
   right before the G*ddess takes to the air,
   right before she spreads her wings and freely FLIES,
   a new particle,
   created in the heat of the nuclear fission

– **shoots**

through the hoop of golden flames

and
with
divine
precision
it
travels
through
the
narrow
gate

a piercing, lonely scream
the final secret
the universe-closing
the eternal
the exalted
the glorified
MAGNETIC MONOPOLE.

PART FOUR

OM

ת

EPI-TAV

The world, as physics teaches us, is mostly darkness. Out of and into this darkness the universe was born. It is the secrecy of this darkness that binds the world together, in uncertain balance with the equally dark and fundamental forces that tear everything apart—nature has decreed in its laws that it will slowly self-destruct; matter is contractually obligated to commit suicide. From this darkness too, from this symbiosis of the force that separates us and the force that draws us all together, the human being and the human being's being was born. This darkness likewise is the source of art, of the silent and heroic struggle that results when healing and destruction converge. The canvas of life drips with Pollock's night-black paint and the dawn of the modal chords of *Kind of Blue*.

Indeed, you have read these words before. The world repeats itself; it has always been what it always was, and it is always new. The earth on which we live, that gleaming, spinning sphere of azure and indigo, is a limbo that never ends, and no escape is possible.

Donatella dove into this darkness and the bounty she brought back was enormous. She found the element that binds us all, she traced the origin of the gravitational violence that ties the star systems together. She discovered the particle that could not exist—that forever lonesome, improbably heavy magnetic monopole. Nebula and I too dove into that darkness—and not just the darkness of the coma, nor of the blindness that hung like a black velvet cloth over our eyes for weeks.

Where does the darkness originate?

No, Mister Goethe, you were dead wrong. It is not *der Finsternis, die sich das Licht gebar.* It's the other way round. The origin of darkness is light: That flash is the true origin of time—the indescribable violence and heat of the original photons, a wall of fire so impenetrable that it formed a shield against time, a shield against our thinking. That point is forever shrouded in mystery, all our equations break down when they approach it, and it is from that point that one day we will be reborn. The absoluteness of darkness is only measurable by the burning point that preceded it, the fire that lit the universe into being, that scorched us all, that unified us all. That light is the light of creation, the seething, all-consuming point of origin; the darkness is merely its effect, its obedient handmaiden, light's trailing bridal train of shadow.

There was the Big Bang, ladies and gentlemen, and then there was the flash of Berloshima. Berloshima too is an origin.

We sailed through the air, Donatella, Nebula, and I, carried on the melting wings of a burning G*ddess, floating on the scorching thermal lift of destruction, and in that bath of radiant heat we screamed our lungs out like newborn babies. Our bodies were pummeled by subatomic particles newly liberated and furious. They pierced our skin, they buried themselves deep into our pores. For one terrible second, we became one with the violence that created the universe.

We too are now survivors.

But not for long.

We were fortunate, they say. We were fortunate that the bronze skin of the G*ddess acted as a heat shield; we were lucky that we ended up buried deep in the concrete basement of the opera house; we were blessed that we passed out in that deep vault of solid matter. The G*ddess of victory herself protected us. She carried us away, far from the exploding television tower. The angel of gold, Nike, Victoria, became our Metatron, the Angel of Pure Light—she became the Mother of us all.

Others, so they tell us, were less fortunate. The whole Mitte evaporated in an instant. The people who fought their way up de Straße des 17. Juni were killed immediately or else sunk to their knees, vomiting and shaken, and are now dying a gruesome death in the hospitals of Dresden, Leipzig, Halle, Magdeburg, and Bonn.

This is what the elementary particles did to us. They bombarded all the cells that they could reach; they broke open our DNA and cracked the code; they forced the cells to multiply in an uncontrollable surge of growth. We shouldn't blame our bodies—this is our cells' way of surviving; it is their revenge for the dishonorable death of so many of their companions. We became unstable viruses, preying on ourselves, our bodies filled with deadly snipers running amok in the very life form that produced them. A cancer blooms in all three of us, and it is a total cancer, an ultimate war of cell against cell, of life against life. The outcome is simple. Either our cells win, or we survive.

Donatella told us that Goldfarb pretended to have cancer, that he told her the tumors had spread in minute pinpricks all over his body, that malicious growths had lodged themselves in his liver and intestines, that his heart and brain were affected. I didn't believe him, she said, he looked too healthy to me; I suspected a ruse. But he claimed he would die, if not soon, then shortly.

If that much is true, then Goldfarb's bomb has visited his cancer upon all of us. And what a bomb it was! What a precision instrument!

The physicists agree. They write passionate articles in the journals; when interviewed on television, those bearded, bespectacled gents and those short, thin-lipped women can hardly contain their enthusiasm. There was one—I watched him on PBS yesterday—who performed some kind of dance for Charlie Rose, imitating the movement of the electrons inside the core of the bomb, and then he used his whole body to demonstrate how the monopole—the word that's on everybody's lips these days—shot through the collapsing hoop of flaming laurels—*just in time*! The scientists can't stop talking about Goldfarb's calculations, the precision with which he predicted the trajectory from bomb to detector; how carefully he had taken the melting point of the different metals into consideration—the bronze of the G*ddess, the steel of the detector, the lead surrounding the transmitter. The ring inside the wreath had survived just long enough to let that one monopole through; the transmitter had been given just enough time to transmit the signal to Potsdam; the measuring device had been calibrated just right, ready to record this new revolution in physics.

Donatella switches off the television. "Enough," she says. "Plus, the detector design, the calibration of the instrument—all of that was my work!"

Nebula and I nod.

"Good for you," I say.

Yes, all the lady and gentlemen physicists—Donatella included—see a magnificent beauty in the nuclear explosion. But we three have to live with its no less intoxicating real-life consequences. We carry the seeds of the bomb in our bodies—they lodged in our organs, they swarm through our brains. Aggressive chemotherapy and—oh irony!—the wonders of radiation, that's all the doctors can do for us. The prognosis is unclear—this is the first nuclear explosion on such a devastating scale. The medical community has no experience with this kind of emergency. But we're still alive, and it is possible—quite possible, the doctors say—that we will be able to eliminate those foreign particles from our bodies. We hear the hesitation in their voices, and we translate: possible, sure, but hardly likely.

That concludes the news bulletin on our bodies. Our minds, then—what about our minds? Even in the unlikely event that our bodies still have a few years left in them, will we ever be able to expel the contamination that races through our minds?

Donatella frets. Should she thank Goldfarb posthumously, in her Stockholm lecture? Wouldn't that be inappropriate—to thank the man who caused the death of thousands? But she can't ignore his contribution, not after all the to-do about how exact and precise and careful and scientific his calculations were.

The monopole, she says, was her idea. Goldfarb simply had too much grant money lying around, and he was willing to take a gamble. "As he did so often in his career," Donatella says, "he gambled on the brilliance of his students. It worked before. Sure, I couldn't have done it without him. Who else would have been crazy enough to hand a few million deutschmarks to a postdoc for a project that had little chance of succeeding? But I conceived it. Without me, Goldfarb couldn't have done a thing.

"It was my work," repeats Donatella.

And then Goldfarb lent fate a hand, of course. He had elevated the local energy level just enough to give birth to the monopole, and by doing so he handed humanity the ultimate proof of the violent nature of matter, and an indisputable foretaste of the end of everything—we now know for certain that everything in the universe will eventually drift apart, that space-time will not contract, but that it will expand forever, and in the process smother, suffocate, and extinguish. The universe that started with a Wagnerian bang, with blaring brass and thumping timpani, will end with a whisper of *saudade*.

Donatella got her Nobel Prize. That they're awarding it in the same year of her discovery is unprecedented. It's not just a sign of the overwhelming importance of the work—it's practicality. The Nobel committee needs to honor Donatella now, before the radiation kills their laureate.

The hotel room—a much too humble word for a suite with two bedrooms and a balcony with a view of Central Park—is paid for by Nebula's agent. The premiere of *PanzerFaust* was a runaway success at Sundance. The New York Film Festival coughed up some big bucks to get the director and her companions to the Big Apple. They flew us in from the wet depths of the Rhineland where we were being treated in what insiders tell us is the best hospital in the whole of Germany. I love our room. I enjoy sitting on the balcony with my laptop on my knees, the portable catheter by the side of the lounge chair. Finally a warm breeze in my hair again, a balmy, harmless wind—even though it reeks of exhaust fumes, the fresh air does me good. Inside, Nebula takes her pills and talks to the media.

Donatella is touring the United States. She presents her findings in the largest auditoriums the Ivy League universities have at their disposal, and she delivers small invitation-only seminars to colleagues who stare at her with open mouths. She appears on the morning shows and signs autographs in the street.

We are real celebrities. Thanks to all those unknown tourists who roamed Berlin with camcorders in their hands, we were immortalized in full motion and vivid color: the light in the east and the flaming angel with her trail of death and fire—three little people holding on to her fleece.

Real celebrities. A television movie is in the works. A book too—and I'm the one who's writing it, and you'll read it too, if I have enough time to finish it. All those paparazzi that follow us down the street, all the interviews with newspapers and magazines and network television . . . Nebula doesn't mind, Donatella secretly enjoys it, and I hide out on the balcony. When I go walking down Fifth Avenue during my drip-less periods, I put on sunglasses and lower a baseball cap over my eyes.

I love Nebula's movie. It's not for the faint of heart. To let the film truly touch you, you have to be capable of seeing the beauty in even the most terrifying ugliness, shivering when that beauty gets betrayed; and you have to be willing to admit to yourself what this brutal rape might mean for humanity's inner life. I love the slap in the face that her movie is, and I also love the grainy texture of Nebula's images, and her cool, blue palette. It reminds me of the instability of the molecules of our so-called reality.

Yes, I love her film.

Nebula's camera is completely passive for minutes on end, moments when no theory, not a single thought stands in the way of the image: moments of pure sodomognosis. The camera whirrs and registers, more passive than any human eye, and I love those moments—life simply revealed in it most appalling truths. All we need to do is watch the rawness of existence exposed in all its unprocessed grotesqueness.

Nebula's next movie will be different, she says—more humanistic, more symbolic, more tender, and less intelligible—more Wenders than Buñuel, more Tarkovsky than Pasolini. Pasolini and Tarkovsky are the great directors the reviewers compare her to, and I can see why. Von Trier is another easy reference. *Panzer-*

Faust fits in beautifully with the new vogue in cinematography—not just the nervous trembling of the images and their graininess, but like all the Dogmeticis' work, Nebula's movie is also situated on the fading border between the inherent gruesomeness of reality and the all-consuming recklessness of art. Viewed from the lofty heights of our post-Berloshima consciousness, the overarching theme of *PanzerFaust*—the cruelty of man against man, the ultimate ungraspability of humanity's motives—makes a powerful statement.

Of course, a certain segment of the press tries to bring her down. She's nothing but a terrorist bent on satisfying the public's primal urges; her work is an assault not just on the senses but on good taste. Nebula's response to these folks is simple: After Berloshima, who can still maintain that the world is any different from what's in my movie—a dog-eat-dog world, a reality in which no one can be trusted, in which intellect is a dangerous commodity and ideology a fast-working poison?

Her movie, she says, is in no way more obscene than reality; it's certainly no more obscene than Berloshima, where the ground was strewn with human flesh, white and pink and purple and splattered with mud, death frozen in crimson rotting rags, all covered in the white powder of the bomb's ashes. The city crumbled over its dead.

"People swirled down from the air like burning powder," says Nebula, "and you get upset over a movie?"

Of course, nobody believes her when she says that she found the scenario in her mother's things. That's just one of those classic topoi in art, one of those dreadful clichés.

Nebula has fanatic followers. Imitators galore, and the critics dub it "expressionist *verité*," and the practitioners of the genre label themselves the "avant-hard" movement. Nebula resists and resents such labels. "I am myself," she maintains, "I am unique. My work is not derivative. I am myself." This makes her groupies mad; they want Nebula's blessing, her recognition, her hand on their heads. "No guru, no method, no teacher," says Nebula. "But please, if you must: Be mad. An angry filmmaker is a good filmmaker."

"Your new movie," I ask her, "Is it going to be our story?"

Film, book. Art.

We have a choice.

We humans have a choice. We can take up our roles in the drama of life. In doing so, we stand a good chance of discovering ourselves—we only really find our identities in the looks we exchange and in our reactions to the dialogue cues; we learn who we are when we observe ourselves dealing with life's prescribed fears and its expected unexpected denouements. In the obviousness of our costumes, we touch the nakedness underneath. The alternative is to refuse to play our parts and so remain unknown, strangers to ourselves and to each other. Many chose the latter path. We don't have that choice, Donatella, Nebula, and I. After Berloshima we must embrace the fate that life has dealt us.

The downfall of the planet, the downfall of the universe—the coming downfall of all that is or will be has become so painfully apparent to us. Artists—or so they say—take the pain of that knowledge upon themselves. They crucify themselves—powerless, angry, and hurt. The pain of consciousness grows with the expansion of that awareness. The more we know about what touches us, the more we abhor what we do to one another. The more we learn about our rape of the planet and about the insignificance of our horrific deeds in the grand scheme of the universe, the more we suffer.

What can a man who is no artist, and yet dares to look that cruel reality in the face, do? Large-scale destruction is one possible response—large-scale destruction is the only deed that can still make some impact in the consciousness of the masses. Philosophers try to develop ways of interpreting existence, but that is not enough. Our obligation is to change the world. And again there's the myth of Shiva, the tiny g*d whose image is carved on Nebula's loins, the g*d whose image in bronze stood hidden in a niche in Goldfarb's office. "Goldfarb is an avatar of this g*d, a completely realized avatar," Nebula says. "We artists don't even reach to the ankles of his kind of insight."

I love Nebula's movie, I can't say it enough. And she, she likes the way I write about her.

"You're a poet," she says. "You are a poet at heart, and now you're writing a novel with a poet's voice. I'm jealous of you, do you know that?"

"I guess some people got it, and some people don't?" I say.

She grabs one of the heavy cushions from the sofa and throws it at my head. I duck and the cushion hits the floor. Mefista jumps on top of it with an enthusiastic battle cry—she molests the cotton happily with her sharp and eager claws.

I am an Orpheus in reverse. I entered the underworld as a lonely penitent; I emerged as a singer.

•

We cannot forget. Nobody can forget. We made a quantum leap into a parallel universe, in one fell swoop, in a flash that lasted for less than a millisecond. In the gaping wound that Berlin has become, the ghosts can now roam free. The ghosts of dissent and false brotherhood rise from the rift; the ghost of the unforgivable murder of six million Jews, the ghosts of blind nationalism and imperialistic isolationism. They thicken the air, they make it hard to breathe—the explosion let them loose, and now they're roaming the far corners of the earth, looking for fresh prey, for new incarnations. The reconstructed Ishtar Gate at the Pergamon Museum lies pulverized—all language, all meaning, all understanding has been destroyed: The city, once bustling, has returned to its original state: a desert.

We don't make the mistake of believing that life will be better in what is quickly becoming our new fatherland. We have no illusions about personal freedom in this country that so proudly calls itself "America"—as if, enormous though it is, it spans the whole continent. No nation in the world lives in a more splendid isolation, no behemoth more self-indulgent, more indolent and slothful, more nationalistic. People here aren't interested in lessons from the past, nor are they capable of learning from the present. See how they reported on the whole Berloshima drama. The networks repeat the same footage over and over again, until the numbness of familiarity sets in. You know the images. The naked people running in the streets, screaming—television editors have neatly pixilated their genitals and nipples. The helicopter flying over the smoldering ruins, the pilot flying into the noxious plume and losing consciousness—the crash. The interview with the group of American backpackers in the hospital who have nothing more insightful to say than that it was all terrible and that they feel blessed, that they thank G*d for his personal intervention in saving their lives (and His lack of concern, by extension, for the thousands who perished). There are the few seconds of a video tape that show the flash—a tower with a spherical growth in it and then the image is washed out in white and the tourist holding the camera utters a tame expletive before expiring. These are the images they show, these and then the flying angel and us.

It is equally important to point out what the networks do not show. The rotting intestines plastered against the crumbling facades. The gutter rats gnawing on severed limbs. The heaps and heaps of dead bodies on the Straße des 17. Juni. The looters from the hinterland who drag everything they can out of the ruins, who pick the money out of the pockets and purses of the dead. You can't show that on prime-time television—it ruins the appetite. And that's what television is for: to sharpen the appetite, to perpetuate the lust to consume.

One of those carefully censored clips always makes me shiver, because of its connection with De Heer. It's the shot of the birds. They are everywhere, dead, strewn across the squares and parks, littering the streets, their wings spread wide, their eyes and beaks open, motionless like moldy pieces of fruit fallen off their trees. The soundtrack that accompanies those images is nothing but the silence of the city. The gruesome moment in springtime when the birds were silenced— simply murdered.

The three of us, we can't help but think of the dead. Of the actors in Nebula's movie, buried under a rain of stone and concrete. Of Hugo, once Nebula's lover. Of the thousands upon thousands of anonymous faces, all those women and men and children who fled into the streets in the storm of panic caused by the riots. And what happened to De Heer? Did he survive the blaze? Was he hiding, far from it all? Will we ever hear from him again?

And how to deal with Berlin, with that pillaged city, that infected smoldering heap of ashes and stones? Will men in white astronaut suits level the town with bulldozers and build a protective dome over the ashes? Or will they give the city some time and allow the old phoenix Berlin to rise from the hot sand once more? No—the latter is not an option. There's hardly enough time to bury all the dead bodies—the wind and the sand and the rats and the crows and the creepy crawly bugs will have to take care of that. The authorities have erected a cordon of barbed wire around the city's perimeter, to keep looters and desperate family members at bay—they don't want any more victims of radiation sickness on their hands.

"Maybe all those wall-peckers from 1989 and 1990 can hand in the fragments they collected?" Donatella proposes. "Maybe we can glue all the pieces together to construct a new wall to protect us?"

Donatella is a tough cookie.

•

Once I asked Nebula, "Where should the book end?"

And she answered, "*Here* is where it should end. Here in bed, in the rumpled sheets, with my head against your shoulder and your hand on my heart."

Here then is where it ends, as envisioned by Nebula: in bed, an expensive bed in the heart of Manhattan. We lie on our backs, hand in hand. We think of Hugo, blown apart, shattered in the nuclear wind. We think of De Heer. We think of Goldfarb, eaten by a cancer not unlike our own. I think of the unstoppable series of multiplications that are shuddering through every cell of our bodies, and how the minute mistakes in those multiplications are accumulating, and how the sum total of those tiny mutations will kill us: a storm caused by the bomb made by Oppenheimer and Fermi and Meitner and Goldfarb, a chain of responsibility reaching back to man's earliest attempts to control nature. A knife carved out of bone, a bronze axe, an iron hammer—those were humanity's first tools, tools first intended to kill. The human appetite for violence—from axe to fission—is what will kill us, Nebula and I. The speed of our demolition will be determined by many parameters. By the distance between victim and explosion, for instance, and by the duration of the exposure, and finally also by body mass. Nebula is smaller than I am; hence, she will die first.

I clear my throat. I turn towards her. I speak words of love and I look deep into her eyes. These are my words of love: "I want you to die in my arms."

She doesn't need to think about an answer. "Yes," she says. "Yes. I want to die in your arms, Paul." She adds, "There's no place on earth I'd rather die. I want," she says, and she climbs on top of me, caressing my chest, my mouth, my eyes with her hair, "I want your hands in my hair when it starts falling out; I want your mouth to drink my last breath." And she embraces me, with her arms and with those thighs of once immortal magnificence, now stained with the indelible marks of melanoma.

She will be there when I wake up, glowing like an angel with a skin of gold and silver—glowing like the Buddha.

Hello there you little life form, in your nest of stars.

•

Once we pointed the camera at ourselves:

She drapes my body with fruits and nuts, with raw pheasant meat, the feathers still attached, with sheaves of wheat and small pumpkins, with winter squash and chestnuts, with sweet corn and morels, and she glues it all together with honey and then she licks and eats her way through the ripe mush to the coarser growth beneath. It is no bacchanal, it is a tender moment, even when she brings forth my throbbing member from underneath that *tableau mort* and holds it in her hand and kisses it lingeringly. That picture, rife with autumnal splendor, is her testament. Correction: It is *our* testament. This is who we are, Nebula and I. This is how deep the sadness of our love goes; this is how high its joy reaches.

It is a testament.

•

She is asleep. She takes up so little space, and yet she means so much to me. The prognosis may be uncertain, but the progress of our disease isn't hard to predict. Her sleep will become more and more restless. Her breath will grow shallower, little by little. There will be halitosis, and it will get worse and worse—the bacteria in her lungs and throat and mouth will meet with less and less resistance. Finally, the germs will take over and nibble at her flesh. Then her lungs will cave in, and one of those light gasps of breaths will be her last. Heaven has begun to forget her. The earth opens its arms.

I look at her; she lies there so peacefully.

Then she opens her eyes and looks at me—she smiles.

I open my mouth.

"Shush, my darling," she says, and she smothers my words with a kiss.

I enter her, I enter a womb that is warm and wet like springtime. My hips merge with hers and together we make the age-old movements, those strange undulations prescribed to all humanity by the g*ds, purely for the g*ds' amusement. We make love, with a delightful tenderness and the utmost gravity at the same time. For we make *love*. Real, honest, earnest love; forever-and-a-day love; love like a fugue with an ever-increasing number of voices.

We love each other, Nebula and I, with a measure of care and solemnity that is born from insight. We know it now—it's official: The world will go on forever. There is no end.

There will never be an end to the world. Never an end.

SELECTED DALKEY ARCHIVE PAPERBACKS

FOR A FULL LIST OF PUBLICATIONS, VISIT:
www.dalkeyarchive.com